WHEN they had gone, Joseph said, "My he's a nice man!"

"Yes," Grandpa said, "he's one of the finest, steadiest lads I ever knew."

After a pause Joseph spoke again. "Didn't he look sad when he talked about his son? Did the little boy die?"

There was a silence. Then Grandma Kershaw said, "Joseph, there was something dark and cruel. They don't like to talk about it. The police say he was found *murdered*."

Joseph shuddered and said no more.

The Hidden Hand

J. SIDLOW BAXTER

LIVING BOOKS
Tyndale House Publishers, Inc.
Wheaton, Illinois

With memories and warm regard to my esteemed friend, Doug, who knows from experience how true to fact is the nucleus of this story.

First printing, Living Books edition, July 1985

Library of Congress Catalog Card Number 85-50281
ISBN 0-8423-1397-4
Copyright 1979 by J. Sidlow Baxter
All rights reserved
Printed in the United States of America

CONTENTS

FOREWORD

This book, I suppose, would be classified as a novel. Yet it is a novel with a difference. In the commonly accepted sense, a novel is fictional and not factual, whereas the story which unwinds in these pages does so from a factual nucleus. Sometimes actual life takes freakishly "novel" turns. That is what we have in this saga of tangled lives; and because that is so it can be not only entertaining, but something more.

Another point of difference between this story and too many current novels is that these pages are not filled with grimy sexuality and dirty permissiveness. The authors of those smutty effusions of vice and violence claim that they are being realistic; that they are presenting human life as it actually is. Equally so, drains and sewers are real, but must we live in them? What about the fresh air of the mountains? Is not that real too? Ugliness, alas, is real, but must we be all the time looking only at that? How much *beauty* there is in the world today—both moral and physical! Is there not far more real thrill in the beautiful than in the ugly?—and far more satisfaction of mind? Some of the most exciting novels ever written are clean throughout; or, if evil characters and doings are incidental to the story, they are presented in suchwise as to make plain that the underlying morality of the author and his story sides with the good and condemns the evil—which is a criterion of all worthy literature.

There is nothing goody-goody about this book. Some of the actors in its dramatic narrative are corrupt and miscreant. Neither they nor the principal figures who move before us are overdrawn. The portrayals are true to the evidence. The earlier phase of the story takes us back to the days when, in general, faith was simpler and life godlier. In those days, despite the absence of many present-day inventions, and despite many wrongs both social and industrial, life as a whole was not only cleaner, but happier. As one compares the raucous vulgarity, moral rot, and seething unrest of our modern Babel with that quieter, steadier yesterday, one may well wonder whether during the last eighty years or so we have "made progress" backwards.

One further word. As I write about the love and emotions of persons in my story, let none of my personal friends who may chance on these pages think that I am sentimentally infusing amorous imaginations of my own! No; what I try to describe with fullest fidelity is that which I learned directly, in confidential talks with the principal characters themselves. So, now, away to our story!

J.S.B.

ONE
Joash and Agnes

Let me welcome you, dear reader, to accompany me along the highways and byways of my strange story. If ever truth was stranger than fiction, this interweave of tangled lives is. To begin with, if you live outside the British Isles, I must ask you to cross the miles of land and ocean, at least in thought, to the English counties of Cheshire, Lancashire, and that strip of Yorkshire which overlaps the Pennine Hills; for that is where our narrative begins.

I must persuade you, also, to travel back with me into the closing years of the eighteen hundreds, since it is there, in 1890, that we uncover the first authentic link in the chain of strange happenings with which we are concerned. When I came across that first link it seemed to be still shining with a gentle luster which no harshness of intervening years had dimmed. To be more explicit: we are watching a pretty wedding at the picturesque old Anglican church in the quiet little village of Rostherne, Cheshire, England, away back in 1890.

Rostherne is still there, hardly less or larger than at the time our story begins. It seems to have made up its mind not to be disturbed by the whirling wheels and whizzing machinery of our twentieth century, nor to have any part in the clattering hurry of our noisy modern "progress." There it is, sequestered in rural quietude between main highroads but too far from them to hear the hum of their restless traffic. It has never allowed itself either the convenience or the annoyance of a railway substation, being quite content to use the one at Ashley three miles across the fields. Until now, it has demurely forbidden any such blemish on its face as a petrol station or a repair garage. It prefers the quieter habitudes and slower heart-beat of yesterday. I, for one, thoroughly agree with it; for such homey, old-world places (all too rare now) are a soothing balm to mind and nerves. Why *should* it be disturbed, clustering there around its solemn old Anglican church, and on the lapping edge of its deep, brooding lake, Rostherne "Mere"?

More precisely, Rostherne, with its two hundred inhabitants, is in the English county of Cheshire, in the "Rural District of Bucklow." The nearest town of any size is Knutsford, some four miles south, with a present population of perhaps fourteen thousand, and a charm which attracts visitors from all over "England's green and pleasant land." It is steeped in history. Knutsford must have been there away back in A.D. 1000, for tradition deciphers its name as "Knut" (the wise and able king K'nut or Canute) and "ford" as referring to Canute's fording the lily stream between the upper and nether parts of the little community, somewhere between A.D. 1017 and 1035.

The only other near neighbours of Rostherne which maybe we should mention are Ashley and Mobberley. Both are incidental to our story. I doubt whether even today there are more than four hundred persons living at Ashley, girt all around with grain fields and grassy meadows, a few miles northeast of Rostherne; but it still has its little railway station on the Altrincham and Manchester route—known in the early railroad days of eighty years ago as "Cheshire Lines." And what history enwraps its Ashley Hall, once the ancestral home of the Breretons, the last of whom to indwell it was a distinguished commander under Oliver Cromwell! What is more, tradition identifies it as one of wicked King John's hunting lodges in the thirteenth century. Nor is that all; for not only were there secret rooms and underground tunneling, but it was long haunted by a ghost—the "White Lady" with a blood-stained handkerchief.

As for that other near neighbour, Mobberley, it lies some seven miles southeast of Rostherne, and is different. It used to be a village about as small as Rostherne, but more recently it impulsively decided to grow into a junior town with some two thousand six hundred people comfortably domiciled in it. However, the old humpback bridge is still there over Mobberley Brook, roughly dividing the newer "town" on the westward side from the older part eastward—which latter still retains half-timbered thatched dwellings, the "Old Hall," the gray-stone parish church, and Knoll Green.

But now back to Rostherne, the seed-plot of our story. I doubt whether it covers more than sixteen hundred acres. It has no skyline to announce it. Its prettiness is of the close-up kind. But, oh, its seductively beautiful lake— Rostherne "Mere"! One hundred and fifteen acres of limpid charm; Cheshire's largest lake and bird sanctuary, encircled by richly wooded, green-carpeted curves and slopes and grazing fields! Angels pausing there amid some sunset-glow must have doubted whether Eden's paradise of long ago had a demurer loveliness!

And there, right against that scintillating liquid jewel in its emerald-green setting, is old Rostherne Church— "St. Mary's Church of England," with its square, stone tower and age-darkened walls. If walls could speak, those would be among the most eloquent, for they date back to A.D. 1188! The lychgate, notable for an ingenious closing device, was fixed there away back in 1640. The six bells behind the black-and-gold face of the tower clock have clanged out the hours across the "mere" and fields since the seventeenth century. Almost as old as the lychgate are two of the snug village cottages in Cicely Mill Lane. They have nestled there since 1650.

Quiet little Rostherne has never learned the loud language of today; but what voices of long-gone yesterdays whisper through it, especially as evening deepens into dusk, and the low winds, like phantom presences from the past, swish across the "mere" and scurry talkatively round the solemn old clock-tower, or disturb the drowsy boughs and set the aged trees confidentially gossiping among themselves.

Well, there it still is, in the unchanged heart of rural Cheshire. There are no high mountains, deep valleys, craggy escarpments, startling vistas. It is as though Nature wanted to make a restful sitting-room somewhere, flat, pleasant, homey. Oh, those spreading carpets of Spring green and Summer gold and Autumn brown!—those tapestries of wild flowers, hedge blossoms, waving grains, and blushing orchards!—the strong, elegant furniture of oaks and yews and ash and limes and chestnuts and copper beeches and silver birches and cypress and cedars, with a gingko or maiden-hair tree here and there!—the lazy lanes and plenteous verdure, luxuriating cattle, planted fields, market gardens, dairy farms, and profuse rose-gardens!—the hawthorn and holly hedgerows, the primroses, white and purple foxgloves, crimson rose-campion and pinkish cowbells, marigold, pansies, asters, violets, bluebells, cow-parsley, daisies, buttercups, clover, cornflowers, dandelions! The untrammeled naturalness smiles at you everywhere. Clinging all around it there is the shy modesty of being simply beautiful without knowing it; and one may be forgiven for praying that the grimy fingers of modern industry may never wipe themselves on it.

So much, then, about Rostherne and its monumental old church and appealing environ. But what of the wedding we mention? I cannot speak as an eyewitness, 1890 was well before my own advent. But some years ago, when my curiosity had been roused to the point of active investigation, I gleaned from a couple of communicative octogenarians in Rostherne that it was "an awfully pretty wedding." Both those Rostherne grandmothers were in their mid-twenties at the time of the wedding. They remembered it more prominently, so they said, because it was an "all white" wedding. There were not many "all white" weddings then, except "among the haristocracy" and people with "a pile o'money in the Bank of England."

Some years ago it was my pleasure to meet a former

vicar of Rostherne: the Reverend Doctor Thomas Fish. On learning the nature of my enquiry he was genially cooperative. What I wanted was to verify, if possible, the marriage record of that young bridal pair. There was doubt at first whether the Marriage Registers still in the church safe went so far back. Only a couple of years before my calling on the vicar most of those dusty old books of "Marriage Certificates" had been removed to the county town of Chester, to be either buried in obscure archives or disappear forever as being no longer qualified to occupy space in our cluttered-up world of today.

However, in the evening the vicar and I went into the church. The old safe still yielded up its rows of pen-and-ink monuments to nuptial vows; and the vicar turned over page after page near the period I had indicated. We had almost decided that my information had been defective when I recalled the comment of the two old parishioners, that the wedding was in the Springtime. So we decided to try the early records of just one more year. Suddenly the vicar stopped. There it was, before our eyes: the "Certificate of Marriage" which I had set myself to find, with the full names of the contracting pair, their ages, the full names of their parents, their signatures, and the endorsing signature of the minister at that time, the Reverend Thomas Foster Clarke. Incidentally, the signatures of that bridegroom and bride were both in a firm, clear calligraphy which might well shame the indistinct scrawl of many a college student today. It was the names of the bridal couple which riveted my attention:

Joseph Ashley Adair, age 24 years.
Agnes Lillian Robson, age 23 years.

Later on I found myself wondering how that name, "Adair," came to be around there at that time. I could easily account for the names, "Joseph" and "Ashley," but there does not seem to have been any other "Adair." From the maiden name of the bridegroom's mother (Elspeth McNeill) I suspect that there were earlier connections up north with the land of the heather and the thistle. That, however, is of no special point here.

From the two old dames already mentioned, and from a silvery-haired old uncle of Agnes, I was assured that young Joseph Adair was "the brightest lad in the village," and "awful quick" at school, and with "gentlemanly manners, as though he might a 'bin a son o' the gentry." The one black mark against him seems to have been that he had fights—all, so it seemed, with the same antagonist, a boy older than Joseph by about two years; the son of a well-to-do merchant who lived in an expensive Tudor-style house in its own grounds on the outskirts of Knutsford. One of those fights so badly hurt the rich man's boy that the proud merchant himself horse-backed over to reprimand Joseph's father, and was so rude that the two fathers almost came to blows as well! None the less, I was assured with solemn emphasis by the ninety-year-old uncle that everybody in the village "knowed very well it was not young Joseph who started the fights, but the other lad, because he wanted to be 'cock o' the farmyard.'"

From one and another I gathered that young Joseph was a lad any father might be proud of; that he grew up to live "a godly and sober life"; that he completed his apprenticeship in both bricklaying and plastering; and that already, at the time of his marriage to Agnes, he was a foreman in the new building project on the Lord Egerton estate. It appears, too, that right from his infancy his two names, "Joseph" and "Ashley," were slid into each other, to make of the twain the one name, "*Joash.*" Everybody remembered him as "young *Joash.*"

As for the Robsons, parents of Agnes the bride, they had only two children: the daughter (Agnes) and a son (Ronald) two or three years younger. They were not Rostherners by birth. They came from Macclesfield and lived near Rostherne for about eight years—Agnes's school-girl years. After that they moved north over the county line into Lancashire, drawn there by the booming cotton and engineering industry. Whether things did not turn out as expected there I cannot be sure; but after some years they moved back into Cheshire and finally settled in pleasant Knutsford.

From the beginning I had a furtive suspicion that Joash's

fights had to do with his boyhood's idol, Agnes, though some things remained obscure until transpirings years later explained them. Anyway, one romantic secret leaked out, namely, that by the time the Robsons left Rostherne for Rochdale an innocent but heart-deep attachment had developed between young Joash Adair and Agnes Robson. I am sure that even then it was deeper than mere fondness. It was that incipient, simple love which has not yet learned its own identity; nervous, tremulous, but true and trusting. Before the Robson family left Rostherne, Joash had said he would never have any other girl than Agnes; and Agnes had said that Joash was her one favorite till life's end. How they hoped ever to meet again only they themselves could know; for in those slow-moving, pre-automobile days the distance between little Rostherne and Rochdale, Lancashire, must have seemed half the world away to a rustic laddie and lassie.

But how do we know about that touching little love-pact? It leaked out through secret letters. At least they were *meant* to be secret, but owing to a clumsy mistake by a mailman, a letter from Agnes to Joash was handed to Joash's father; and, alas, thenceforth "the lid was off." It is a classic of innocent girlish affection, mirroring the typical young-mind outlook of that time.

> *Dear Joash,*
> *It feels a bit naughty to be sending you this third secret letter. I have never done anything before without mother and father knowing. As I now write this up in the attic I feel like one of those persons in those secret love affairs we read about in the books. Do you think I ought to tell mother? I think Ronnie has guessed we are writing on the sly, because last time I wrote you, before I could get a postage stamp and go to the post-office nearly three miles from here, the envelope with the letter in it fell from my apron while I was helping Ronnie to lift a box of potatoes into the kitchen, and he saw your name and address. He just stared at it and then at me, and did not say one word. He had just been saying that in*

*the last fight you had with Jacques you were a clean
fighter but Jacques was not, and that he tried to
scratch your eyes again.*

*We do like each other very much, Joash. Do you
think it is love? I know you don't want us to be like
those people God punishes for having been deceitful,
and turns everything against them. Do you think we
ought to stop these secret letters after this, and just
wait? But I sometimes think we shall never see each
other again.*

*There are many boys around here. Most of them
work in the cotton mills. On Sundays, with their
Sunday clothes on, they wear big, white collars made
of (if I can spell it) celluloid. It can be wiped clean
instead of washed and ironed. I don't think I like
these town boys. Some of them are bad mannered
even in Sunday school. They don't touch the nebs of
their caps in respect to ladies when they see them in
the streets. Some of them at Sunday school want me
to be their girl and let them walk with me. One of
them called Sydney Adams says he is the best fighter
in his school class. He is the office boy now in a
cotton mill. He says he will fight any boy who tries to
stop him from having me as his girl. But, Joash, I
have told him he cannot ever have me because I have
a boy already. He looked so fierce at that. He said,
"Where does he live?" I almost forgot myself and said
Rostherne, but I stopped myself just in time.*

*What a long letter this is, Joash! I hope you like
reading it. I am still your girl. In my prayers at
nights I keep asking God to let us meet again, but I
do not see how He can arrange it just yet. I pray
each night for you. Now I will finish. I wish my
writing were better, but the ink in the ink-pot here
has got thick. May God please bless you, and help you
in that new brick-laying job you told me about.*

> *With my very, very fondest thoughts,*
> *Agnes.*

What other guileless rascality passed by mail between
Joash and Agnes I did not ferret out. Even when I came to

know them well in their later years, I hardly liked touching on a matter of such tender confidence between them. One thing, though, which I learned, and over which I chuckled years later with Joash and Agnes, was the happy fact that Joash's parents were not in the least degree angry, but were covertly pleased that their dear lad should have set his young heart on such an upright, church-going girl as Agnes. Moreover, Pa Adair wrote to Pa Robson about it, and was relieved to find that the Robsons were just as pleased (with pretended caution) that their Agnes had shown such good judgment and "taken up" with a lad who was such a credit to his father. Nevertheless, since parents are parents (or used to be!) it was agreed between the Adairs and the Robsons that it would not be good parenthood just to wink at the clandestine correspondence between the two offsprings. So, in accord with the custom of parents at that time, they gave Joash and Agnes a resounding verbal spanking, professing to be no little shocked at such subterfuge, and administered the good, old-fashioned injunction: "Never do it again."

But now, back to the wedding. As the handsome, twenty-four-year-old Joash and his beaming Agnes now walk out, arm in arm, from the church vestibule beneath the gray old tower of Rostherne Church, what a scene and what a setting! Spring is full in. All the hedgerows smile in their freshest green. Nature's magnetic wand has decked the trees in their new sheeny robes. The birds are busy mating and nesting, darting, chirping, chattering. The gaunt yet motherly old church stands sharply silhouetted against a fleckless ambient expanse, while in the immediate background Rostherne Mere shimmers with fulgid reflections of sun and cerulean sky. The flagged path over the grass from the tower door to the lychgate is lined on both sides with villagers and friends and well-wishers, including not a few of Joash's workmates on the Egerton estate.

The organ is playing in the church. Joash and Agnes emerge from the doorway. The bridegroom, fair-haired, straight, manly; the bride, demure, flushed, a sheen on her auburn hair, and a shy smile lighting up her oval face. By general consent she is the daintiest bride ever wedded in Rostherne Church. As they slowly step along the pathway the radiant couple are showered with confetti. The two pretty bridesmaids follow closely; and after them the quietly proud parents and relatives, two at a time, to enjoy their own meed of confetti and congratulations.

Mainly, of course, interest focuses on the bridal pair. "What a couple!" "Aye, God bless 'em!" "They looks a perfect match, to my way o' thinkin'." Yes, there are the usual tears. Weddings are strangely inconsistent in the way they play on one's emotions. They have a way of suddenly spraying the bouquets with impromptu tears. We always apologize for such unanticipated liquidity. "How silly of me!" "Just fancy—crying at a wedding!" "Oh, do forgive me!"—and we try to run it off with another merry little laugh which comes out as another little sob! Perhaps weddings will always be this emotional contradiction. Usually the tear-blurred eyes are those of the maturer spectators.

Well, all these had their proper place in that picturesque wedding at Rostherne. The charming wedding-group, the dear old church, the scintillating lake, the flooding sunshine and azure heaven, the bright new tapestries of the Spring, the hearty felicitations, the moist eyes, even the loud, guttural voice of Dave Dillon the blacksmith, with his, "Well, awm blest! Whoever wud a'thowt it!"—all mingled in happy propriety and golden prophecy. The one and only entity which seemed strangely out of keeping was a small, celluloid disc over the bridegroom's left eye. Everybody tacitly concurred that the polite thing was not to mention it: but when the wedding-day sun had set, how could tongues help wagging a bit? "Why on earth did Joash have to wear that eye bandage?" Had they known it, under the cotton-wool pad was a scar which would remain for life—put there by the claws of a human tiger.

TWO
Mike and Millie

Some months slipped away after the nuptial knot tied Joash and Agnes together in their happy union. Then, from the gray old tower, the bells pealed out again across Rostherne's lake and lanes for another wedding. There was the same formal ceremony with its simple, reverent ritual; the same sacred transacting of heart with heart in the presence of God; the same plighting of troth by giving and receiving of a ring; the same solemn avowal, "Till death us do part"; and the same authentic decree according to both the law of the Lord and the law of the land, "I now pronounce them husband and wife." Yet in its peculiar incidentals how different was this later marriage from that of Joash and Agnes! On the marriage certificate, in the black ink and almost copperplate penmanship of the registry clerk, the names of the contracting parties were given as:

Michael Andrew Kennard, age 27 years.
Rachel Amelia Kershaw, age 30 years.

The bridegroom was bound to be eyed quizzically, for he was decidedly unusual, though not in any way actually abnormal. He was rather more than medium height, with a remarkably large head, long, swarthy body and shortish legs. The hair atop his head was already thinning, but his bushy, beetling eyebrows were almost like two sprigs of heather under the brush of which two bright, restless eyes looked out. He had such large ears that as he walked down the aisle a naughty imagination might have been reminded of a hansom cab coming down the road with both its doors open. Rivaling them was a fulsome moustache, not unduly larger than was fashionable at that time, but the two sides of it were firmly curled and waxed to a long point, giving the impression of two bayonets, or two cannons pointing in opposite directions, such as one sees outside the entrance to civil buildings. Everything about him suggested that he was a born actor, except his stumpy legs and weak walk.

But that which evoked the most comment was the bridegroom's voice. Deep, rich, sonorous, seldom if ever had a voice like that been heard in Rostherne Church. Many a preacher, politician, dramatist, would have given nine tenths of his kingdom to have a voice like that. When the minister reached that part of the service in which the bridegroom had to repeat audibly the paragraph beginning, "I, Michael Andrew Kennard, do take thee, Rachel Amelia Kershaw, to be my lawful wedded wife, to have and to hold from this day forward, for better, for worse . . ." the booming of that voice gave the little congregation of rustics a sudden start. Not that Michael Kennard was showing off: no, for with apparent effortlessness the tones rumbled out and rolled round. Later, at the wedding party in the Kershaws' home, when the merry toasts and witticisms were spoken, his laugh was a sort of guttural gurgle which made all the other laughs sound like tinny cackle. It was unanimously conceded, either jovially or uneasily, that he certainly was "unusual."

Mike Kennard had been brought up at Tyldesley, where also he had received twelve years of elementary school followed by two years at a secondary school—a "good start in life" at that time for a "working-class lad." Afterward he was a clerk at some local coal depot, concurrently with which he took a course in "Commercial Training." After that he went to work in Manchester for an insurance company under which he became an "agent" with a "round" of his own on a commission basis. So, by the time he married Rachel Amelia Kershaw he really "knew a thing or two" in a worldly-wise way.

As to his moral character, however, he certainly did not wear "the white flower of a blameless life." The marriage certificate described him as a "widower," but it was only by freak chance that he was not a divorcee. He had been married before and was the father of two children, both daughters. His first wife entered divorce proceedings against him for adultery and unbearable cruelty through drunkenness. In those days divorce was an unspeakably shaming disgrace for the guilty partner. Mike's wife was a sensitive, somewhat fragile little woman; and such was her intensity of grief that one morning, before the court action had been put through, she suffered a nervous paroxysm, fell over a balustrade on to a pavement, and died a few hours later, still unconscious from concussion. Fortunately for Mike, the Rostherne and Mobberley villagers did not know this; yet even so they were all a bit jolted that after waiting so long "Millie" should be taking such a risk with that "unusual sort o' chap" and his two young daughters.

What, then, about the bride, Miss Rachel Amelia Kershaw?—and why did she marry Mike Kennard? For good reasons we ought to take an appreciative look at her. She was born at Mobberley, where she lived until her teens. From her babyhood onwards she was known as "Millie." Little Millie, too, was unusual, though she never meant to be. For one thing, she liked playing with boys better than with girls. She could play the boys' games as well as any of the boys; and those swift little fists of hers could fight as well as theirs, too—which made her a bossy little commander among the girls. She was a quick-witted young rascal, possessing, among other mischievous endowments, the knack of being so irresistibly funny when the dayschool teacher was not looking, that the other girls would giggle and get reprimanded, while Millie's little cherub face showed nothing but innocent placidity when the teacher looked round. As a young girl she was very thin. Her legs were so lean and straight that the other children called her "spindle-shanks." She had a genius for getting into scrapes—and flourished in them. Just two of them may be usefully recalled here, for they indicate qualities which were to mean much in the story of the after years.

A half-mile or so from the row of cottages where the Kershaws lived, the lane humped its back up to cross the railway line. In fact, it was called the railway hump. Over that bridge Millie had to go each day on her way to and from school. Near that bridge was another block of cottages in one of which there lived an older boy, an ungainly lad whom the others impolitely called "fat Bob." He was a scare to younger and smaller children. He used to waylay Millie, and would stand like a gorilla blocking the way over the bridge. "You shan't go over the bridge," he would growl. "I'll get you!" Sometimes she would have to wait in hiding for over half an hour to dart out and get home over that bridge. Two or three times it was a hairbreadth escape past him, achieved only because those two little spindle shanks of hers were a degree too fast for fat Bob. Then Millie made up her mind to do something about it. Her father was working on some new houses being built about a mile away, and he too used to come home over that hump. Millie hid in some bushes and watched. When her father was drawing near enough to the bridge she came boldly out into the open and walked toward the bridge. There stood fat Bob, waiting and menacing. To his surprise Millie slowly walked up near to him, then suddenly ran at him, ducked down and pulled his legs from under him. Down went humpty-dumpty, and like greased lightning Millie jumped so that her knees landed thump on his solar plexus, synchronizing with which out shot those two little fists like a sudden gust of hail on a stormy day. Pa Kershaw came running up and pulled her off, whereupon fat Bob darted clumsily away squealing like a trodden-on piglet. That was the last time fat Bob ever bothered her. Pa Kershaw never tired of telling it to his pals. "I had to run and pull the young daredevil away from him!" he would say with pretended concern—and subterranean relish.

Albeit, not all Millie's escapades won such chuckling parental approval. Now and then nothing but a stroke of superb, split-second strategy on her part averted disaster.

Twice in one week she came home from school with her plentiful golden thatch all tousled, hair-ribbon lost, face begrimed, dress torn, shoe-toes rubbed, and a hole in her stocking knee. Her horrified mother warned her: "See, yer little imp, if yer comes 'ome again like that, I'll have yer sit thar like that till yer fayther comes 'ome; and then yer'll get what for!" Well, a few days later it happened again, and the maternal threat was implemented. Millie sat there in disgrace and waited in self-commiseration for the dread moment, a rash of rueful regrets now stinging her conscience. To tell the truth, she deserved sympathy as much as censure. It was not she who started the rough-and-tumble belligerencies, but the other girls, who either tantalized Millie or pretended to be provoked by something which Millie had done. Furthermore, it was never a tussle of Millie against some other girl, but invariably Millie versus two or three of them. Not a girl anywhere around Mobberley would have stood up single-handedly against Millie Kershaw.

Presently Pa Kershaw loomed in the cottage doorway. "Millie, go into the other room." Millie did so. Pa followed, with thunder on his brow. "Now come and bend over my knee." Millie complied. "Now, then, this'll teach yer to stop that feightin'. I'm goin' t' smack ye reet 'ard on yer backside." He lifted up his hand, but just as it was poised to administer the first whack, he thought to ask, "Tell me the truth, now; what was yer feightin' for?" Millie's reply was devastating. She diplomatically whimpered, "Cause Polly Hislop said her father was better than mine." In that instant a strange paralysis immobilized the parental arm, and the poised hand of vengeance was turned to putty. Rather huskily Pa Kershaw muttered, "See, then, I'll let yer off just this once; but dunna let it 'appen again." So saying, he strode back into the kitchen; and as Millie was putting on her knickers she heard a couple of suppressed chuckles—one masculine, one feminine! Millie had a little chuckle, too, but it was not heard in the kitchen!

When Millie was in her 'teens the Kershaw family lived for a time in Minshull Street, Knutsford. Spirited as ever, Millie had developed into a slim, intriguingly attractive young woman. Knutsford seemed big after Mobberley, and there were courtable youths in abundance. On one occasion Millie arranged to meet four different young men all on the same day at the same time at the same place—the corner of a lane near the old Gorse Common. Hidden behind gorse bushes she watched them all arrive. First one turned up, then another, and another, and another. It was comical to watch the four young hopefuls all strolling to and fro in a restricted area, getting in each other's way. Each kept looking up the lane or along the heath, expecting his fair female. Each repeatedly pulled out his watch and eyed it with puzzled look. Then one of them said, "How d'ye do?" to one of the others, and on being reciprocally "How d'ye doed" fell into casual chatting which developed into a humiliating confabulation. Soon there were four grim-faced Saint Georges all peering round to slay the same pretty dragon! It was days after that before Millie dared let herself be seen in the Knutsford strolling place where the youths and maidens used to give each other the "glad eye."

It was during those Knutsford years that something happened to Millie which changed the whole course of her life. Some would describe it by saying she suddenly became "very religious." If you had asked Millie herself she would have replied, "I have received the Lord Jesus as my Saviour. He has saved me and changed my whole life." Let it be borne in mind that our strange tale which starts unwinding from those two Rostherne weddings is not a so-called "religious novel." References to Christian faith and experience are included solely because they belong inextricably to the tangled skein of mystery and pathos in our story.

Like everything else pertaining to young Millie, her "conversion" had to have a dash of singularity about it. At that time the Methodists, Baptists, Congregationalists, had not invaded such villages as Mobberley and Rostherne. The Church of England mothered those rural areas without rival, and the proper thing for all self-respecting individuals was to go to church on Sundays. But in Knutsford not only were the Non-Conformist denominations operating—there were a couple of "mission halls," one of which was so zealous, after the new "Salvation Army" pattern, that it used to hold open-air Gospel meetings! The very novelty of it always attracted listeners, as also did the dithery cacophonies which often squeaked or groaned from the wheezy harmonium. It was after listening a while to one such open-air Gospel group that Millie acceded to their invitation and followed them to an indoor meeting; and there, for the first time in her life she heard a rapid-fire "soul-winning" address clearly setting forth the need and the way of salvation. Just as the meeting was ending, the horse-drawn fire-engine went rushing by the building, its bell clanging loudly to clear everybody out of the way. At that very moment a kindly woman (one of the mission "workers") tiptoed to Millie and asked her, "Are you saved?" Millie gave a startled look. "Ooh, is the building on fire!" she gasped, and made for the door! Yet that question kept haunting Millie. She wondered why she now kept thinking about God, about sin, and getting "saved." Then something clinched the matter.

An out-of-the-ordinary clergyman from Torquay came to hold meetings. He was the Reverend William Haslam. Among other things he wrote a lively little book called *From Death Unto Life,* which at that time had a wide sale. It includes the account of his own conversion, the peculiarity of which made him a cynosure among his brethren of the cloth. That reverend gentleman was a scholarly, high-principled cleric of the Anglican Church, which he believed to be preeminently *the* church. He not only faithfully preached its doctrines and most veneratingly administered the sacraments, but he was a model of religious properness, while his zeal knew no bounds to make all other persons religious in the Church of England sense.

It would have been comic if not so pathetic, the way he was nonplussed by persons who had this "conversion" inanity, thinking of them as brain-fevered fanatics. He was always finding himself tantalizingly at cross-purposes with them, exasperated at their cocksureness, and exhausting himself in vain endeavors to "regularize" them. When some of them even dared to say that they were "praying for *his* conversion" it either struck him dumb with amazement or sparked him into sanctimonious tantrums that this "conversion disease" should beget such self-confident rudeness.

In that way he went on for years; and no words could tell his sense of frustration that despite all his exhortings and exemplariness his parishioners seemed to have so little stomach for his starchy churchianity. Yet somehow, deep down, he was aching with an unsatisfied longing for something he did not know how to describe—as though he was tenaciously hugging a vacuum. However, his ministerial ups and downs and pious pains were leading somewhere. Believe it or not, the rigid anti-conversionist himself got converted, and in the unlikeliest of ways. He became stricken with a torturing sense of innate sinfulness which no outward religious exercises or ecclesiastical dogmas could change. It flamed up within him that he needed an inward *regeneration*, not merely ceremonial sacraments. This provoked a fearful turmoil, and he became mentally prostrated by the thought of all the souls he had let slip out of this world into the next, resting on the delusion of salvation by church ordinances. Then came a never-to-be-forgotten Sunday morning.

Those were days long before radio, television, cinema, automobile. Life was simpler, slower, quieter. Especially in rural areas like that in Cornwall, Sunday was dutifully observed as "the Lord's Day." People wore "Sunday clothes." Nearly everybody went to church; and the Christian ministry was the most venerated of vocations. What happened to that Anglican "parson" on that momentous Sabbath morn he can tell us in his own words:

> "As I went on to explain the Scripture passage (Matthew 22:2) I saw that the Pharisees and scribes (to whom our Lord spoke) did not know that the promised Christ was the *Son of God,* or that He had come in order to *save* them. They were looking only for a king, the son of David, to reign over them as they were. Something was telling me, all the time I preached, 'You are no better than the Pharisees yourself. You do not believe that he has come to save *you,* any more than *they* did.' I do not remember all I said, but I felt a wonderful light and joy coming into my soul, and I was beginning to *see* what the Phari-

sees had *not* seen. Whether it was something in my words, or in my manner or look, I know not, but all of a sudden a local preacher who happened to be in the congregation stood up and, throwing up his arms, shouted out in Cornish manner, 'Hey! The parson is converted! The parson is converted! Hallelujah!'—and in another moment his voice was lost in the shouts and praises of three or four hundred in the congregation! Instead of rebuking this extraordinary 'brawling,' as I would have done in a former time, I joined in the outburst of praise; and to make it more orderly I gave out that we would all sing the Doxology—which the people sang with heart and voice over and over again! My formal churchmen were dismayed, and many of them fled precipitously from the place. Still the voice of praise went on and was swelled by numbers of passers-by who came into the church greatly surprised to hear and see what was going on!"

For many years afterward that enlightened cleric had a dynamic ministry. No longer was he preaching sacerdotal platitudes, but salvation through the atoning death of a divine Saviour who rose from the dead and now lives in the hearts of all who receive Him. Thousands were brought into what is often called a "saving experience of Christ" through the grip and lucidity of Haslam's preaching. He never made high-pressure appeals, but at the end of each meeting those who wished to enquire further were invited to the vestry. One evening, when the invitation was given, there seemed no likely response, but after some moments of quietness during which all were bowed in prayer or reflection, a low sobbing was heard; then a golden-haired girl walked hurriedly down the center aisle. That night changed everything for Millie.

She became an earnest young disciple. Hitherto she would no more have thought of going into a Methodist chapel or a Gospel mission hall than setting out for the North Pole; but now she kept meeting other rejoicing believers with whom she felt a warm kinship, all of them either from the Methodists or other Non-Conformist bodies. Not that she turned her back on the Church of England. Nay, through the Reverend William Haslam she felt a new debt to it. Yet somehow it now seemed to her that the rural Anglicanism of her girlhood days had taught her religion rather than salvation.

Alas, Millie also ran into trouble with her former Church of England friends, who now exhibited either hostile snubbery or disdainful pity because of her association with Methodists and Mission-Hall people. She was dubbed a "silly young enthusiast." Bigotry was fashionable in those days, especially among clergy and members of the national church who looked down unsympathetic noses at Dissenters, regarding them as recalcitrants and inferiorities. One ardent Episcopalian clergyman preached a sermon about the ship on which our Lord crossed the Sea of Galilee, ingeniously deducing therefrom the unassailable superiority of the Anglican Church. Mark 4:36 was his text—"They took Him even as He was in the ship; and there were also with Him *other little ships.*" With agile originality the preacher explained that the ship in which our Lord sailed was the Church of England, while the "other little ships" were the other denominations!

Notwithstanding everything, Millie tried bravely to remain with the Church in which she had been christened, catechised and confirmed. Once, when she was faithfully attending, there came to her a new ray of light on the "Salvation Army" which, with its brass bands and big drums and unorthodox invasion of slums, was a latter-day marvel, and a wonderful new scapegoat for smug pietists who castigated William Booth and his "army" for doing in *that* way what they themselves would never attempt in *any* way. It was the first influence which turned Millie's thoughts to the dwellers in slumdon. It happened in a half-comical way.

No less a dignitary than a bishop visited Millie's church. His lordship preached on the Sunday; then, on the Monday, there were afternoon and evening gatherings, with a tea-table interval between them. Not as many turned up for that intervening tea-time as had been expected; so the fewer who came sat nearer to the ecclesiastical celebrity.

The bishop chatted affably until, at one point, he was most awkwardly "put on the spot" by an elderly spinster who sat almost opposite him at the long table. There she was, in trim but quaint attire, with her lorgnette and ear-trumpet, her whimsical look and squeaky voice: Miss Patricia Tuttle, if you please, with the well-established reputation of never once having been talked down. In a way, she was good fun, for she had a frisky jocoseness and never took offense; but in social affairs she was the church's *enfant terrible,* an exasperating expert in saying the wrong thing.

"Dear bishop," interposed the squeaky voice, "it is such a privilege to have a spiritual father like you near us for once. Could you help us with something that troubles us these days? What do you think about this fiery new movement called the Salvation Army?" In an instant all ears within range were agog. The kindly bishop fidgeted, then dodged the question behind some verbal shrubbery. Miss Tuttle squeaked back, "Now, now, dear bishop, you haven't really answered, have you?—and we do need guidance from our spiritual shepherds." The bishop glanced at other faces, to see if there was any sympathy lurking there. He did not want to say anything unfavorable about the Army lest his comment should afterwards be bandied about. Again, therefore, he sought refuge in circumlocution. But it was useless. The squeaky voice spoke again. "Bishop, you surely must know what you think; and we ordinary mortals do need your higher wisdom. *Do* you like the Salvation Army?"

Wih a sigh of surrender the bishop replied, "Madam, if you really must know, then I'll tell you. No, I do *not* like the Salvation Army. My problem is that apparently *God does!*" That reply meant far more to Millie Kershaw than to Patricia Tuttle.

From then on, Millie found herself more and more among Methodists and Salvationists, for there she found the teaching and fellowship which at that juncture she seemed to need. Then came the big, life-determining decision. The stirring story of how the Salvation Army began was still new; so were the early "war tidings" of its campaigns to free the devil's slaves in the slums. To many thousands of formal religionists General Booth was an unorthodox crackpot. Even his notable book, *In Darkest England and the Way Out,* was largely ignored in the higher strata of English society. But when the governments of Germany and Austria sent delegates to interview him about his ideas on crime law and prison reform, a sluggish British parliament began to muse that maybe, after all, the doughty general was a genius.

Under its banner of "Blood and Fire," with its band and drum, and the Bible as its conquering weapon, the Army officers and cadets mounted wave after wave of compassionate attack on the down-and-outers in their wretched slums. Thousands were lifted, as the saying went, "from the guttermost to the uttermost."

Later, the Methodists were sponsoring similar offensives on slum and crime and social evils. An appeal for volunteers was sounded in a meeting at which Millie was present. She eventually offered herself for full-time service in slum work. Her parents did not object, though they shed tears in secret. Her one sister and one brother (the former older, the latter younger) were dumbfounded. Millie had always been the heroic scapegrace of the Kershaw family—and they both loved her proudly; she brought such comedy into everything. About that time Pa Kershaw was given a job on the Lord Egerton estate, so the Kershaw family removed to Rostherne, after tearfully seeing Millie off to Manchester where she was to spend two years in a training college.

As for Millie in Manchester, she found herself the youngest trainee there, and soon her sunny disposition and effervescent playfulness made her the most companionable student of the whole bunch. Her frank naturalness and utter absence of "putting on airs" safeguarded her from jealousy on the part of others, most of whom, with that nimble brain of hers, she surpassed in the studies. But above all, it was in the practical aspects that she excelled, as soon became evident in her first post-college assignment as a junior city-missionary in the slummy Ancoats district of Manchester.

It was after some years in the Ancoats work, among the heart-rending flotsam and jetsam of human tragedy, that Millie met a young insurance agent named Mike Kennard.

Several times they happened to be visiting the same house at the same time—he to collect an insurance premium, she with a moral and spiritual ministry to the wife or mother. At first she thought him a jack-a-dandy type, but after several of their chance meetings he was less bizarre in style and more manly in mien. Even so, Millie was not a little disturbed when he started showing up at the mission hall on Sundays and at weeknight meetings. One awkward problem was that he was so gifted. He could lead well and speak fluently with remarkable impromptu aptness and a deep, resonant voice rather like musical thunder. Some years earlier, so Millie discovered, he had been on the Methodist "Local Preachers" plan, at which time he was considered a paragon of preaching excellence and a candidate for extraordinary prominence. Later, for reasons obscure to Millie, he had been quietly "dropped." He had an inborn atmosphere of familiarity. Such was his ingratiating flow of easy conversation that after only a few minutes with people whom he had never met before they would feel as though they had been close friends for years. But the biggest problem was that now, quite undisguisedly, he wanted to win as his wife that golden-haired deaconess underneath that smart blue bonnet.

Millie was now well on in her twenties. In the end she accepted Mike Kennard. Whether it was for real love that she later married him she could never be sure. It was an affection born of compassion for him and his two motherless young daughters. Thus, after nearly ten years of devoted mission work, she became married to Mike. As the Kershaw home was now at Rostherne, that is where the marriage took place. Millie knew Mike was a widower, but did not learn until after wedlock that there had been shameful unfaithfulness on his part, followed by divorce proceedings.

So, we are back again now in the old church at Rostherne, on that sixth day of July 1890. What strange incongruity of background hid behind that bridegroom and his charming bride as they stood before the minister on that fateful day! There were not as many people in the church or lining the path to the lychgate as when Joash Adair and

Agnes Robson were wedded there, three months earlier. As the two newlyweds now walked down the aisle and out through the churchyard there was not the same feeling of assurance in the well-meant congratulations. Martha Tadlock confided to her neighbor, Lizzie Lowden, " 'Tween you and me, awm no' feelin' too comfortable. They're tellin' that this is the thirteenth weddin' this year. An' this day is the sixth day o' the seventh month—that's another thirteen!" Lizzie Lowden was duly impressed by that astute arithmetic, and replied in solemn undertone, "Yea, an' did y'notice that just when the couple walked out o' the church the clock was ten minutes past three?—an' that's another thirteen!" Martha Tadlock's eyebrows rose a full half inch, then in subdued further comment she came back with, "Aye, an' its a bit disturbin' that both their names begins wi' the letter 'K'—Kennard and Kershaw. Y'know the old sayin': 'Change the name an' not the letter, yer marry for worse an' not for better.' " At this, Lizzie Lowden went ashen white. "Ooh, Martha," she gasped, "ye shouldna 'ave said that. It's just a' reminded me: it's not just their last names as begins wi' the same letter; it's their first names an' all—Michael an' Millie!" Martha Tadlock thereupon added her own "Ooh!" and the two faithful souls made a devout compact that they would say "nothin' to nobody" about it.

The wedding tea-party in the humble Kershaw homestead a couple of hours later was a merry time indeed. There was just as much kissing and laughing of relatives and friends as at other weddings, with just as many wisecracks: but one thing which became a rueful memory years afterward was a wedding telegram from an uncle of the bridegroom. In those days telegrams were a comparatively new wonder. Especially were they so to country folk. But then Mr. Mike Kennard was a city businessman, and no less than three telegrams came from the Manchester area. When uncle Josiah's was read out, there was boisterous laugher. "How witty!" "The old rascal!" "That's a new one!" Then there was an uneasy silence for a few minutes. The telegram said: "Just married . . . just perfect . . . just *wait*."

THREE
One Decade Later

As we now get into the warp and woof of our strange-woven drama, the names of persons and places are disguised where necessary. For although none of those who appear in the earlier phases of our story can yet be on earth, their children are, and we would fain avoid hurting anyone's susceptibilities.

The curtain rises on a panorama of industrial sites and bustling activity. We are in the English county of Lancashire, amid that agglomeration of towns which comprise the great cotton-manufacturing and heavy engineering region of England. Its dominating center is the city of Manchester; and its big outlet from which Lancashire's industrial products are shipped to all parts of the globe is the port of Liverpool. Like some higgledy-piggledy lacework the larger and lesser towns or boroughs unevenly sprawl out, bounded roughly by Preston and Burnley to the north; Rochdale, Oldham, and Ashton-under-Lyne to the east; with Bolton, Bury, Wigan, and Salford in the middle; dipping down as far as Warrington to the south, and enringing Stockport, just across the Cheshire county-line.

Never has there been another area like it. In other parts of England there are relieving expanses of green countryside between the towns. But at the beginning of our century, in the more congested parts of Lancashire's industrial belt, mills, foundries, depots, boroughs, sub-towns, "urban districts," all mushroomed amid the fantastic "cotton boom" without the faintest thought of any planned spacing. Towns and towns and more towns; rows and rows and more rows of small, four-room cottages; streets and streets and more streets of cobbled or stone-paved cartways and flagged footpaths; and in between all those towns were long, paved connecting-roads, with mills and clustering brick cottages at intervals all the way along, the total impression being, not so much a plurality of towns, as one never-ending domain of monotonous brick and mortar.

Many changes for the better have taken place latterly, especially since the Second World War. For one thing (a major financial reverse) much cotton manufacture has now run away for ever from Lancashire to the Bombay area of India, also to Japan, not to mention other places where there is an equally suitable dampness. Many of the Lancashire mills are now the gaunt, bony skeletons of one-time hefty giants. Whole groups have disappeared as completely as extinct empires. Still others have been converted to different uses. Slum quarters and dilapidated properties have been eliminated, and in some cases whole districts have been torn down to make way for planned communities. Much is being done to resurrect the native beauty which money-mad industry of eighty years ago trampled into an untimely grave. But during the early years of our story, who among the cotton lords ever thought of letting natural beauty or ecological considerations obstruct the ugly feet of mammon-worshiping "progress?"

Well, we are looking at it all just as the tired old nineteenth century has bowed out and the glamorous-looking twentieth century has stepped in with doffed hat and ingratiating promises of a brave new era. Charles Darwin's two epochal books, the *Origin of Species* and (a few years later) the *Descent of Man,* have had an immense circulation and, along with the writings of Herbert Spencer and professor Huxley, have widely popularized the theory of organic evolution, disturbing the faith of millions in the hitherto uncontradictable Biblical account of creation. The apostles of evolution are blandly assuring the public that although the biologists have been obliged to expose the erroneousness of Genesis they are giving mankind something really scientific and far better than the Genesis myth that man was directly created but has fallen through sin. Man has evolved and is still evolving. Master of his own fate, he has reached a point now, in his upward struggle, from which his development will stride forward with final acceleration to a millennium fulfilling every gallant hope.

This is not just a slipping out of one year into another. It is a new *century!*—a new century with new accents, new guarantees. Evolving man is shaking himself free from the last lingering remains of the brute. The liberalist theologians are running after the evolutionists like yappy little poodles. The new psychology is explaining that "sin" is not really sin at all, but merely an interim impediment in the "upward march of the race." The German schools of the so-called "higher criticism" have spread the "New Theology" throughout Christendom. Scientific scholarship has at last shorn the Bible of its supposedly infallible divine inspiration. The ostensibly supernatural elements in it can all now be explained away as extravaganzas of primitive credulity. Oddly enough, this has "liberated" the Bible (so they say) and made it "acceptable to human reason"! Synchronizing with this there is a new emphasis in the pulpits. They call it the "Social Gospel." Slums must be abolished. Working conditions must be improved. Bigger wages and better housing must be achieved for the masses. What is the good of preaching the Gospel to empty stomachs? Why spend all the time getting men ready for heaven when so many wrongs need righting on earth? Old-fashioned evangelizing must give way to "Christianizing *society.*" This is the new "practical Christianity"—the Church with its sleeves rolled up.

In particular, the new century comes in with beneficent beams on the British Isles. There is a sense of consolidated oneness never felt so definitely before. In the first decade of the twentieth century the British empire is at its zenith, with a population of four hundred and ten million, embracing twelve and a half million square miles (ninety-one times the size of the British Isles and three times the size of all Europe), comprising one fifth of the earth's surface and more than one fifth of its inhabitants, including nearly ten thousand islands and two thousand rivers, the widest-spreading empire ever known in history. Britain's incomparable Queen Victoria has now celebrated both her "royal" and her "diamond" jubilee with spectacular celebrations around the empire. As the twentieth century rides in she has been on the throne no less than sixty-three years! Britons are prouder than ever of the Union Jack and the imperial throne.

Thus, indeed, did the twentieth century make its debut with bright-eyed plausibility, floridly bedecked with humanistic idealisms and glittering promises of a man-made utopia. Little did the crowds who gaily waved it in as an angel of light guess that ere long it would romp the earth like a frenzied demon, soaking the race in the blood of two ghastly world wars. Little did they foresee that the Darwinian theory of evolution, besides being largely disproved as a somber, pseudo-scientific delusion, would drag human morals to the gutter in Fascism, Nazism, Communism, and Freudian permissiveness. Little did they divine that the German-invented "New Theology" with its desupernaturalized Bible would strip the Protestant pulpit of its power and empty the sanctuary pews, leaving the denominations like so many Samsons with shorn locks and blinded eyes. No, amid the merry clanging of the bells on January 1st, 1900, hopes soared high and people were sanguine.

The cotton manufacturing area of Lancashire was just one little spot in the total scenery, yet among its thousands upon thousands of mill-workers the first sunrise of the new century stirred even deeper feelings than in most other places. Amid that sprawling forest of factories and smoke-pothering chimneys life was as bleak and gray for many as a November sky. Those were the days which made owners rich and kept workers poor. For "mill hands" (as the workers were called) life was a hard grind. They had to be at the mills each morning by five minutes to six, so as to be at their looms or spinning jennies or other machines when the great engine started at six o'clock and the whole mill with its several huge storeys and hundreds of workers reverberated under the mighty impact and almost deafening noise of the swift-moving machinery.

Work hours were from 6:00 a.m. to 6:00 p.m. (sometimes 8:00 p.m.) which meant that for six months or more each year the workers had to start in the mornings before the first glimmer of dawn, and, after the day's weary grind, come home again still in darkness. Only at weekends did they see sky and sun—that is, when the cloud-draperies of Lancashire's uncooperative weather permitted king Sol to peep through. Shareholders' profits were skyscraper high. Mill-workers' wages were wickedly low. It was an inhuman disgrace. How some of those undernourished toilers stuck it out, year in year out, is a marvel. The thriving vocation of the undertaker was no marvel at all. Often those mill-workers tumbled into bed at night so worn out that they would never have wakened in time next morning but for the knocker-up.

Incidentally, the "knocker-up" (there were many of them in each town) was an important man in those days. For a small weekly charge he would come round in the early morning, carrying a long pole with which he tapped at the upstairs window, thereby wakening you at the required time. Like most of the mill-workers whom he had to waken, he usually wore clogs, that is, cheap footwear with stiff leather uppers, wooden soles and heels, and thin iron strips underneath, round the rims, to prevent the wood from wearing. The clatter of those clogs as hundreds of workers walked to and from the mills was a sound which one could never forget. But it was in the lonely dark of the pre-dawn that the knocker-up's solitary pair of clogs went clanking down one street and up another, pausing at this or that house while he lifted up his long pole and tapped on the upstairs window until one of the sleepy-heads tapped back on the window-pane with a bleary-eyed "That'll do."

In the Lancashire of that day there were four social strata: the majority poor; the middle class; the upper or "nicely off"; the rich or "well to do." It was a social pyramid with the usual big base, and narrowing as it reached its millionaire apex. One of the most remarkable phenomena was the good-natured "help one another" disposition of the working class. They could grumble loudly when they chose, in a Lancashire lingo which no outsider could understand, and sometimes with verbal decorations too inelegant for reproduction here. Yet on the whole they were so warm-hearted, hospitable, cheery, that it was the trait for which they were most widely known.

Ten years have slipped away since Joash and Agnes (now known as Mr. and Mrs. Joash Adair) were married at Rostherne. They now appear amid those opening months of the new century, and as part of the Lancashire ensemble just described. After they left Rostherne as husband and wife Joash occupied himself for a few years in the building trade, and did well. There was strong pull, however, to a Lancashire town in which Joash's only uncle lived. This uncle was now in his early sixties. He had never married. Twice he had been jilted; and inasmuch as he had little faith in the old maxim that "the third time does it," he thereupon decided in favour of bachelordom. Later, many a woman would have grabbed him, for the older he grew, the kindlier and more attractive he became, as well as financially afflu-ent. The time he would have spent with wife and children he had given to his business, with the result that he had built up the biggest furniture center in town, with its own large renovation adjunct; besides which he operated a con-siderable furniture removal business and a spacious storage warehouse—the Adair Repository.

Uncle Ben had always had a soft spot in his heart for nephew Joash. Soon after the Rostherne wedding he had invited Joash to join him. The invitation was affectionately declined, Joash being a young man of character and drive, wanting to strike out on his own. Later, uncle Ben found an ally in Agnes. The generous but artful suggestion was, that since he, uncle Ben, had far more money than he needed, he would set Joash up in the building line, and Joash should devote only a part of his time to uncle Ben's furniture kingdom. Actually, dear uncle Ben wanted Joash as his partner and successor. The first step was to get him to

Elmerton. During the year 1894, Joash and Agnes settled there—in *Elmerton*.

Bachelor Ben was generous. Nephew Joash was clean-living, hard-working, with brains and initiative. Providence was kind. Everything went well. New districts were springing up. New houses needed to be built. Furniture kept selling. Uncle Ben and nephew Joash loved each other. Soon Joash's building firm grew so large that a crisis developed. He simply could not run his own "Builder & Contractor" outfit and along with it give part-time collaboration in uncle Ben's go-ahead enterprise. Such, however, was exactly what uncle Ben had slyly presupposed would happen, so he was ready with appropriate suggestions. He knew that Joash could now sell his building and contracting business for a large sum which would make him pretty "well off" financially. Furthermore, he had convinced Agnes by diplomatic seed-sowing that the change-over would be beneficial.

One evening nephew Joash came home in an unusually pensive mood. He knew that a moment of major decision was upon him. As he lifted the latch of his front garden gate he paused to reflect on the years of unbroken prosperity. He looked at the handsome house where he and Agnes lived, pondering even more gratefully.

Elmerton was not the most imposing of towns, nor was it one of the uglier. Although it had its quota of those "dark, Satanic mills" they were not so thick as in some other areas. Elmerton had a rather imposing main street, and a considerably impressive town center. It boasted several attractive shopping blocks. It also had its beauty spots: two small parks in its built-up area, and a larger, well-kept park on its southeastern fringe, where, among its variegated trees and leafy arbors, its artistic flowerbeds and excellent bowling-greens, its inviting shrubberies and picnic reserve, one could dodge the sight of mill chimneys for a spell, with a make-believe feeling of "over the hills and far away."

Northeast of the town was the better-class locality, becoming more select as it moved outwards. Branching away from the town was Clifton Road which, about a mile out, began to have upper-class houses and interspersed trees on both sides, thus becoming from there onwards Clifton *Boulevard*—a swanky name there in those days. On Sunday afternoon, that was the mile or so where courting couples strolled arm-in-arm wearing their Sunday clothes, looking tenderly at each other and secretly envying the "upper crusts" who could live in such homes with gardens in front.

Several select cul-de-sacs crossed Clifton Boulevard, the furthest of them being Woodland Bypath; and it was there, sequestered in just about the choicest milieu Mother Nature provided in those parts, that Joash and Agnes lived. Their home was the last of five superior residences, where Woodland Bypath reached the crest of a shapely rise and ended at Kenyon's Meadows which stretched away beyond it. At the rear of the house was a spacious sweep of undulating, intermittently wooded grassland, with the Pennine Hills picturesquely fringing the skyline. Until the slow but insistent invasion by home builders, that stretch of knolls and dells had been an up-and-down wood of oaks and Scots pines, only remnants of which now lingered. The taller, thinner pines had claimed the brow of the incline where Joash had set his dwelling, lifting their bundles of needles above the mighty arms of the oaks lower down. So the delightful home where Joash and Agnes lived and loved was appropriately called "Pinecrest."

All this was in Joash's mind as, at the end of that working day, he paused at his garden gate. He looked at the freshly mown lawn, herbaceous borders, graceful young ash trees and silver birches, the solid but elegant brick house, double-fronted, built to his own design by his own construction team; the pillared porch with its clinging Virginia creeper and its balustrade with lace-like iron traceries of vines, flowers and leaves; the latticed front windows enhanced by Agnes's pretty curtaining. It all seemed too wonderful as he now recalled how he had left Rostherne with his dear Agnes and not more than forty pounds sterling to risk starting in business.

Years came crowding back as Agnes now hastened across the lawn to greet him. "Hello, darling; you seem to have been away so long. I thought the hours would never through. Isn't it a lovely evening? After we've eaten, if you're not too tired, let's go for a stroll by the creek in the twilight. There's a full moon peeping up in readiness, but the sun won't go to bed for a while yet." After an unhurried embrace and kiss they slowly walked indoors, arm in arm.

"Hmm, what an appetizing odor from the kitchen!" Joash remarked as they stood in the ample, oak-paneled hall. "Where are the children?"

Agnes glanced at the handsomest, old-style grandfather's clock which ever came out of uncle Ben's furniture store, and replied, "They should be back in exactly ten minutes from now. You can guess where they are. Uncle Ben wouldn't tell me what it was; but he said he had a little surprise for them. He promised to land them back here right on the minute."

Joash had just time for a quick wash and brush-up. So, after giving his dear Agnes one more worshipful kiss, he slipped away to get ready.

Coinciding to a split second as he reappeared, the two children came bounding in—right into daddy's arms for the usual hug. Was it strange that sometimes he almost hurt inwardly with proud gratitude? Besides all the other privileges on which he had been musing were these—surely the dearest little girlie and laddie on earth, who (as Joash well knew) thought that he was easily the best daddy God ever made.

Evelyn was eight years old. To say the least, she was a super-normally beautiful child. It was not only the light, wavy hair, the pink complexion, the soft yet beaming blue eyes, and the finely chiseled features; there was something about that face which exceeded unusual prettiness. It was so strikingly pure; almost as though some young, heavenly cherub was shining through it. Nor was there any contradiction between that facial charm and Evelyn's behavior. There was the quick agility and vivacity which belongs to all healthy children, but there was no boisterousness or childish unruliness. There was all the busy chatter and laughter of childhood, but with Evelyn it was the continuous bubbling up of loving words and ways from a disposition utterly unconscious of its own goodness. This is no exaggeration. Evelyn was in every trait a young *queen*. She had the royalty of an inborn refinement and outgoing kindliness. The way she mothered her young brother, Rickie, and at times imperiously bossed him for his well-being, was as comical to behold as it was unrelenting. Like any other child, she could cry when hurt, or rebel when there was frustration. She could go suddenly tired and sleepy, as children do, after romping round with seemingly endless energy. She could make her mistakes and do the wrong thing. She had a mind and will of her own. But Joash and Agnes could not recall ever seeing peevishness, selfishness, or the slightest contumacy. She was such a lovable little human angel that never a day slipped away without their thanking Heaven for her sunny presence in the home.

As for young Rickie (short for Richard), two-and-a-half-years younger than Evelyn, he was all boy; perpetual motion, ingenious inventiveness in innocent rascality; fond of his toys and games; secretly glorying in causing Evelyn to scold him; darkish hair like his mother's; frank, open face, healthy looking, and the normal height for his five-and-a-half years.

That was the Adair family of four as they took their places at the dining table on that Springtime evening. "Heads bowed, eyes closed, please," says Joash. "Rickie will say grace." There is a tiny pause: Rickie whispers, "Daddy, it's Evelyn's turn." Joash nods to Evelyn. She voices the simple "Thank you" to heaven. Then they all start—with the children's eating and talking trying to outrun each other like a couple of racehorses. There is no need to ask what uncle Ben's surprise was for Evelyn and Rickie. They are itching to tell. "What d'you think, daddy," says Rickie, "uncle Ben's got a magic lantern!" "A magic lantern!" echoes daddy, with obliging astonishment. "Yes, daddy, he took us down into the cellar and put us in the dark, so that his magic lantern could shine pictures on to a big white sheet." "Rickie," interjects Evelyn, "what did uncle Ben call that white sheet?" She spells it out: "S . . . c . . . r . . . e . . . e. . . ." "Screen," ejaculates Rickie. "When we were all in the dark, except for the light from the nose [Evelyn laughs and says, "lens"] of the magic lantern, uncle Ben put some. . . ."

(Evelyn comes to the rescue; "S . . . l . . . i . . . d. . . .")
"Slides!" says Rickie. "He put some little slides inside the
magic lantern, and such big pictures came on the wall." "On
the screen," Evelyn corrects him.

"Well, well!" exclaims daddy; and Agnes eagerly asks,
"What were the pictures all about?"

Evelyn and Rickie give a lively report. There were pictures of Rostherne Church, and the mere, and the village,
and the row of cottages where uncle Ben and grandpa
Adair lived when they were little brothers. Uncle Ben had
gone to Rostherne specially to take photographs with a
clever new camera.

And which was the picture they liked best? As Evelyn
replied, Joash and Agnes suddenly glanced uneasily at each
other. "I liked the picture of you, daddy dear and mummie
dear, with that nice gentleman and the nice little lady who
was holding me in her arms when I was a baby." "And what
did uncle Ben tell you about it?" "He smiled, mummie, and
said it was a lovely picnic soon after we came to live in
Elmerton. The tall man with the kind, smiling face, and the
pretty little lady were Mr. and Mrs. Harwood. Mrs. Harwood asked if you would let her hold me in her arms when
the picture was taken." "Was that *all* he told you?" asked
Agnes; and Evelyn recalled a bit more. "He said that Mr.
Harwood was from America, and that his family were ever
so rich, and that Mr. and Mrs. Harwood do not live in
England anymore."

Joash and Agnes looked relieved. Then Agnes rejoined,
"Well, isn't that exciting! One of these days we must tell
you all about uncle and auntie Harwood in America. They
would like us all to go one day, away over the Atlantic
Ocean, in a great big ship, and have a lovely holiday with
them. Wouldn't that be something!"

By now dusk was draping the outdoors. Perhaps (Agnes
mused aloud) it was too late now for the suggested stroll.
Besides, after his busy day, Joash might prefer to relax in
the sitting-room. Joash needs no coaxing. It is not yet the
children's bedtime so the two of them help Brenda, the
maid, clear the table, then play at one thing or another
while daddy and mummie sit together as the deepening

shadows finally curtain off the Pennine hills. Then the children are with them half an hour or so. Evelyn wants daddy to listen as she fingers out her simple new exercise on the piano. Then the grandfather clock breaks in with its Westminster chimes and mellow clanging. It is young folks' bedtime. Mummie leads the march upstairs. Daddy, as usual, obstinately sits still. Evelyn seizes his right hand, Rickie his left. What a struggle to pull him out of that chair! Upstairs, prayers are said. There are "Good-night" kisses. The light is turned out in Rickie's room. Evelyn is allowed twenty minutes to read in her favourite "Tuck Me Up" book. With a knowing look, Agnes gives Brenda the usual order to put out the light in Evelyn's room in exactly twenty minutes. Then Joash and Agnes are downstairs for the close-of-day sit together which has been one of the most cherished habits of their home-life.

"What is it that is weighing on you, dear?" Agnes asks. "Is it anything with which un-commercial little 'I' can help you?" They are sitting, hands clasped on the sofa in front of a slowly smoldering fire. "Anything you lack in commercial experience, lovey, is more than made up for by your natural intuition. In any case, after your handling of ledgers and customers at uncle Ben's place from time to time you know a thing or two commercially." Agnes glows back with fond appreciation; then Joash unburdens his heart.

A point has now come, he explains, at which he must make a far-reaching choice between staying solely with his own building business or somehow pulling out and yielding to uncle Ben's pressure to partner him in the Adair furniture center. (Agnes secretly knows it all before Joash says it, but listens with keen sympathy.) Joash marvels again at uncle Ben's unexampled generosity. The dear old uncle asks not a penny from Joash, yet offers him a partnership on a fifty-fifty basis with Joash as the sole inheritor if uncle Ben predeceases him. Uncle Ben is a gem of an uncle, and as congenial to work with as any nephew could wish.

But what about that building-and-contracting firm which bears the name, Joseph A. Adair? It gives a wonderfully good income. Joash does not want to take his own name and signboard down. Yet it was dear old uncle Ben who enabled him to put it up. What should he do? (Agnes knows very decidedly what he should do, but this is not the minute to say it. She listens with evidently tender concern.)

And now Joash says he has been getting what seems to be guidance. The best all-round builder and joiner he ever knew is Ted Matthews who has been Joash's foreman right from the beginning. If ever there was a man who combined practical skills with handling men well it was Ted. The men respected him. Always on the spot, honest, energetic, a man of commonsense: "He's a champion!" Joash really owes his success to Ted. He is a fine Christian man. Joash is thinking that since uncle Ben is being so generous with his nephew, he himself should be generous toward Ted Matthews; and instead of closing the building business, should make Ted Matthews his partner, if things can be satisfactorily worked out. (Agnes is now so intensely attentive, her look is eloquent.)

Joash continues. He will not ask Ted for any down-payment; he will suggest some mutually profitable arrangement and have it all set down legally. Ted will take over full practical administration, thus almost entirely relieving Joash. The two of them will have an equal share in assets (which Ted, of course, will think unbelievably generous), but in the profits there will be an ascending percentage of income for Ted, until, if the business is still growing, Ted will be able to buy the business in part or in whole, if he wishes. During all the years until then, it means greatly increased income for Ted, a good percentage income for Joash, and thus a great benefit to both of them.

This has all been said slowly, with reflective pauses. Joash now wants to know what his patient Agnes thinks. She "knows very well" what she thinks. For several months, now, in the harsher weather, she has kept hoping that her dear man would somehow find a way to close in with uncle Ben's magnanimous offer. But this about Ted Matthews is new. She wants to know what the liabilities would be if the business did not happen to do so well under Ted Matthews—and so on. By and by, Joash yawns. Agnes yawns. It is ten-thirty. Together they kneel at the sofa to ask for a higher wisdom than their own. Then, in fond embrace, they close the day, lips to lips and heart to heart.

Upstairs, Joash says, "I'm pretty sure we should talk it over with Ted Matthews." Agnes rejoins, "Yes, Joash; but wasn't it strange—Evelyn's interest in that magic lantern picture. Did it disturb you, Joash? Did you watch her face? I wonder just when we ought to tell her about that uncle and auntie in America, and the awful, *awful* truth behind that picture?"

FOUR

The Watch Committee

Besides being a prosperous, middle-sized town, with its cotton mills feathering the nests of the rich few and providing stinted livelihood for the numerous poor, Elmerton was a progressive community. Not all its men of means were mean men. Some of its leading citizens were conspicuous for their high ideals and open-handed philanthropy.

Like other such towns, Elmerton had its ugly slum area, round Canal Street and Potter's Row and Paradise Square, where most of the poverty and squalor were of the self-inflicted sort which besets lazy louts and boozers. It was vulgarly known as the "frying pan" because most of those who fell out of it fell into the fire—of trouble with the law. Even in that area, however, two rescue missions carried on a work which had good results, though they were inadequate to the size of the need.

Among Elmerton's forward-looking groups there was the "Free Church Council." All the local ministers were *ex officio* members, and each church was represented in it by several appointees. It was the collective voice of the area churches in matters religious, moral, social.

An arm of that Council was the *Elmerton Watch Committee,* which, according to its name, was a watch-dog on the town's morals. Away back in 1900 it could bite as well as bark. Many a time it had only to growl, and some intending offender against decency was warned off. For instance, inside a threepence and sixpence store (a primitive predecessor of the Woolworth type) a Watch Committee member noticed that the cover picture on some writing pads which were for sale was a scantily clad female in a suggestive posture. She called for the manager. "Sir, that picture is morally offensive. I must ask you to remove those writing pads." The manager answered with a chuckle of amusement. "So we all have to fit in with what *you* like, Mrs. Puritan? You're living yesterday instead of today. Those writing pads will stay there." "Very well, sir, if you won't do it for me, perhaps you will for the police, and come before a local magistrate. I'm from the Elmerton Watch Committee." Livid but beaten, the manager ordered the pads removed. The same thing had happened in connection with posters outside Elmerton's two cinemas and one theater.

The Watch Committee gave decent people a means of preserving decency, instead of feeling helplessly voiceless against encroachments of the vulgar. Cruelty to children or to animals; unclean features in magazines or books or cinema films; the tricking of young people into drinking or gambling; all these could be reported to the Watch Committee, with good results. Yet those Watch Committee members were not "vigilantes" in the American sense, trying to impose summary measures of their own. They worked in respected accord with the local officers of the law, and were much valued by them. There were Watch Committees in other towns, too, and they all did a worthwhile job; but eventually, like the one at Elmerton, alas, they all got "bombed out" by two World Wars, or snubbed to their graves later, by a superior modern "enlightenment" which now allows us to look at every grinning vileness without being shocked.

On a Wednesday afternoon in that first year of the new century, the bi-monthly meeting of the Elmerton Watch Committee was in session. The very fact that they served on such a committee meant that its members were persons of iron convictions and vivid reactions. Some of them had other distinctives, too. There was Miss Whimby, straight as a mast, with pince-nez which tightly pinched the bridge of her nose but wiggled all the time she spoke, as though struggling to get free. She was most valuable in that she always "called attention to the point at issue." In all the speeches she had made in committee, the other members could never remember one in which she had not "called attention to the point at issue."

There was Mrs. Dingwell, stocky and sturdy, whose proclivity for "putting two and two together" was definitely supernatural. During a discussion she would sit in silence inscrutable as that of the Sphinx, her head aslant, first this way and then that way, toward whoever was speaking, as though by putting her ear an inch nearer she might catch a syllable of evidence which others missed. Then, when others had done the thinking, she would rise and, with severe logic glinting in her cold, gray gaze, she would observe that "putting two and two together" the only conclusion they could come to was the one now reached. During her time on the Watch Committee she had put so many twos and twos together, the other members began to fear that there might not be enough fours to go round. However, their apprehensiveness subsided as they began to find that Mrs. Dingwell's putting twos and twos together often left them all at sixes and sevens.

Then, of course, there was Mrs. Tuttle, the talker. Her loquacity was such that she had neither rival nor terminus. It was both famous and dreaded. She was usually assigned tasks which needed little or no reporting on, though even that did not always prevent the sluice gate bursting open and the waters gushing out. Only recently she had been put in charge of the tea and the ham sandwiches at a fundraising "Social" for the Watch Committee, and at the next bi-monthly committee meeting her report on those ham sandwiches had been of such zealous elongation that Mr. Pomeroy, the chairman, quietly rising while Mrs. Tuttle's ham statistics were still elongating, had interrupted with masterly diplomacy: "So grateful are we to dear Mrs. Tuttle, we cannot postpone our vote of thanks another minute.

All of us will agree that in her report we have had both ham and *tongue.*"

One of the less obtrusive members was widow Musgrave, who always wore a brown felt hat with a stiff brim, and brought her straight, black hair to a tight bun at the back, to hold the rear brim up. Although rather slow of speech, she took a grave interest in every topic. Her reading of the Bible convinced her that they were "living in the last days," and that all committee decisions should be made in view of the "approaching end."

Perhaps, also, reference should be made to the diminutive but thrush-throated Mr. Llewellyn Lewis, the Welshman, who at every opportunity brought in some patriotically wangled reference to that new Welsh wonder, Mr. David Lloyd-George. At that time David Lloyd-George (later Britain's prime minister during the First World War) was thirty-seven years old, and was already the morning star of Welsh politics. He was the new dynamo of the Liberal Party, voicing big reforms, and astounding the nation with his scheme for "old-age pensions." The name of David Lloyd-George danced round like magic music in every coal mine and barber's shop from one end of Wales to the other. In the Elmerton Watch Committee, at every ingenious mention of the hallucinating name, our lusty little Welshman would break into rhapsodic panegyrics which oratorically climbed the clouds, and from which the helpless chairman could no more fetch him down that he could lasso a soaring lark or a darting swallow. On one occasion an exasperated committee member had hurled at Llewellyn, "Mr. Lewis, you Welshmen talk about Lloyd-George as though he were God!"—to which Llewellyn had retorted with swelling pride, "And why not? He's only young yet!"

A recurrent feature which often put nerves on edge was the verbal dueling between Hugh Bingham and Bella Tinkler. The former's invariable contention was: "This thing demands prompt action"; whereas Bella Tinkler always tinkled back that "in view of present circumstances" and to avoid "precipitous decision," the members should inwardly "digest" it, and then "bring it up" at the next meeting. In one such tilt between Hugh and Bella the former had gone so far as to label the latter, "Elmerton's most reliable source of misinformation." But what would have been a fearful sword-slash to a self-proud person was no more than a pin-prick to imperturbable Bella. With her ample nose poised Binghamwards and her tricky eyes looking down it, she had pleasantly tintinnabulated back that some of Hugh's ideas were like a drunken man walking a tightrope—"the farther he walks, the sooner he falls off!" Sometimes, after the meetings were over, Hugh and Bella could be seen going down the street together, still fiercely dueling. Yet their jousts were never fatal, for the two of them always turned up with happily healed wounds at the next meeting—ready for a new encounter.

Let no one think, however, that the Elmerton Watch Committee was a coterie of negligible oddities. On the contrary, its personnel, eighteen in all, included some of the sanest, ablest people in the area; and its chairman, Mr. Alexander Pomeroy, was a much-respected Justice of the Peace. As for those members of pronounced peculiarities such as we have spotlighted, they are a perfect pest on any committee, yet we would not be without them for the world. They add spice and sauce to the otherwise dull diet of routine committee work. They provide as many chuckles as pangs; and they are unspeakably invaluable in showing all the other members what not to do. Some people seem born with their hereditary mental pockets full of nothing but "amendments." Their big problem is to live long enough and get on enough committees to use them all up. Others are the generation of the dash-at-its: *their* one hope of avoiding fatal crash is to get caught in enough thickets of amendments! It takes "all sorts and conditions" of us to make up the overall picture of human blunder and success. As the limpid lakes of Haute Savoy perfectly mirror the changeful skies and snow-capped Alps, so did the Elmerton Watch Committee truly reflect the face of Elmerton's well-intending majority.

On the aforementioned Wednesday afternoon there were two main items on the agenda. One was the choosing of a suitable name for a quarterly magazine which the Watch Committee hoped to start issuing. The need was for some name closely in keeping with the idea of *Watch* Committee. One suggested name was *Focus;* but it was rejected because the magazine was meant to supply statistics and comments for public quotation; and a strange impression might be created if public speakers had to say, "These facts and figures are out of *Focus.*" Other suggestions were forthcoming, but each was disqualified for one reason or another, until a point was reached at which Miss Whimby simply had to rise and once again "call attention to the point at issue" which was, "Have we, or have we not, found a suitable name?" Then, as all looks answered "No," she added, "I therefore move that the choice of a name be postponed." Whereupon Mrs. Dingwell, "putting two and two together," seconded the motion, while widow Musgrave gravely reflected that this not knowing what to do or where to turn was another sign that they were "living in the last days."

That unresolved problem having thereby been shunted off the main line, the chairman thus addressed the members. "Friends, as you all know, this could well prove to be the most far-reaching session this committee has ever held. It marks the launching by us of the Elmerton *Police Court Mission.* For some years the Church of England in this area has employed a missionary to work among *men* who get into trouble with the law; but there has never been any such attempt to reach the *women.* We were all deeply disturbed when the latest police court statistics showed an increase of over twenty-eight percent in *female* offenders during the last two years. After earnest thought, we of the Watch Committee felt urged to start a work among the *women* who get into immoral ways and often become criminal characters. What I now report is, that we have been able to appoint the suggested 'committee of twelve,' and we seem to have been providentially guided to the right woman for our missionary."

A moment's pause; and then, "As you know, the new committee, while cooperating with us, will be independent, with its own chairman, officers, rules, and *modus operandi.* One of the happiest auguries is, that Mr. Reginald Bardsley, one of the borough's most highly regarded aldermen, has accepted the chairmanship. And how gratified we are that one of our own members, *Mrs. Joseph Adair,* is to be secretary-treasurer! That name, "Adair," has become a household name in Elmerton—having been built into the very brick and mortar of so many new houses round here, and having entered many a home in the form of "Adair" furniture. All the members of the new committee are here with us today, and we express our warm, good wishes. . . ." The rest of the sentence disintegrated in the spontaneous hand-clapping.

As the clapping subsided, the chairman added: "But now, friends, I have a final surprise for you which, in old-fashioned phrase, 'puts the cream on the milk.' When alderman Bardsley and I last interviewed our prospective new missionary we prevailed on her to visit Elmerton this afternoon, to meet the new committee. She was one of the eleven who responded to our advertisement. Six seemed suitable, but in the ensuing contacts we all came to the same conclusion. There was one who, besides writing with distinctive efficiency and evident insight, had just the qualifications we were after. She is middle-age, married, has three children, was specially trained for this kind of work, has good health, had an excellent record as a student and slum-worker, prior to her marriage, and has recently taken up part-time mission work again as her children became old enough for her to do so. In addition we learned that she is an exceptionally gifted speaker, with such a taking way of presenting the Gospel and advocating our 'Total Abstinence' cause that her coming among us will be a timely acquisition to various groups in the town. According to my watch she is due in exactly five minutes."

However, Miss Whimby craned toward him, imparting in a loud whisper that "the point at issue" was: the lady is already on the premises. Whereupon, Mrs. Dingwell, "putting two and two together," apprised him that the waiting place was the next room. So, as widow Musgrove saw no adverse omen in it that we were "living in the last days," and since Hugh Bingham and Bella Tinkler saw no occasion to duel about it, the missionary-elect was asked in.

There was a welcoming handshake, accompanied by a

musical murmur round the room which unmistakably said, "Glad to see you," and, "We like the look of you." With dexterous courtesies the chairman presented her, concluding, "And now, friends, I know that all of you are eager that she herself shall speak to you. We hope she will feel no nervousness. She is among sincere comrades in the good fight of truth and honor against evil. She need not speak for more than a few minutes, or she may go on for an hour. She can ask questions, or tell us anything relevant which may be on her heart. Every syllable will be of keen interest to us. Ladies and gentlemen, it is my pleasure to introduce to you *Mrs. Amelia Kennard.*"

Yes, it was Mrs. Millie Kennard, nee Rachel Amelia Kershaw of Mobberley, Cheshire; the beloved little scapegrace of the family; impresario of many a harebrained escapade; pummeler of fat Bob; coveted belladonna of the lads at Knutsford; the earnest young Christian; college trainee; city missionary; and later Mrs. Mike Kennard. There she stood, of medium feminine height, erect but not stiff; a little flushed, though calmly poised, and just about as neatly dressed as the most prim and proper female committee-member could have wished—in a dark blue costume, matched on that light golden hair by a dark blue bonnet fronted with a pretty velvet bow. If those committee members had only known it, that little dark blue bonnet was going to be known not only in the slums and in the police court, but all over Elmerton and beyond; so much so that years later the local weekly newspaper would headline her as "the best-loved public woman in the borough."

"Mr. Chairman and friends," she began, "first let me thank you for your generously kind welcome. It does much to allay the nervousness which one feels on such occasions as this. When one is removing to another town, and coming to a new work for a new group of people, especially to such a challenging new enterprise as that to which you have risked calling me, there is much to make one feel diffidence or even trepidation. Inevitably, questions beset one's mind. 'Will my personality be congenial to them? Will my way of doing things prove acceptable? Will my work for them have true success?' Your warmhearted welcome today is at once reassuring.

"The chairman most graciously embarrasses me by saying that I need not speak more than a few moments, or that I can go on for an hour. Like most members of my sex, I must admit that to speak 'not more than a few minutes' is a feminine impossibility [laughter]; but to be given an hour is a gallant liberality of which I certainly shall not take advantage. Recently, I came across a remark of the famous Joseph Parker, that it took him twenty years to learn how to preach a sermon in twenty minutes. Just now I shall not trespass on your patience even twenty minutes. What I have to say can easily be compressed into about a quarter of an hour."

To put it mildly, all present were taken by surprise. The speaker's voice was soft yet sonorous and pleasing. Her articulation was clear, her diction choice, her vocabulary varied, her style relaxed and flowing. They all knew that there had come among them an exceptionally gifted speaker. It was quite evident, too, that expressing itself through those well-chosen words was a perceptively logical mind.

Faithful to her self-imposed limit of fifteen minutes, Millie told them why she had accepted their invitation. She was coming to Elmerton in answer, not just to a much-appreciated call from a committee, but in answer to what she believed was a leading of God. She was coming to Elmerton not just to do philanthropic work, but trusting again in the power of the Christian Gospel to save souls and transform character. She agreed that the accentuated emphasis on "social reform" was only too evidently needed; but social reform without the saving and remaking of the human individual only puts *things* right, not people themselves. It was no use making the house fit to live in for people who were not fit to live in it. Social reform apart from the Gospel of Christ operated on the doddery assumption that better environment necessarily made better people. Her own persuasion was, that underneath all the communal problems was a moral and spiritual problem with which only the Gospel of Christ could adequately deal. In the long run it is not environment which makes the man, but the man who makes the environment. Fundamentally, what human beings most need is not more money and more comfort, but inwrought renewal of their moral nature; not merely social amelioration, but inward regeneration.

Millie concluded by saying that her weapons would be the Bible, prayer, and practical contacts. She intended to start a weekly meeting specially for the type of women they all wanted to reach. She would arrange visitation, use suitable Gospel literature, seek to enlist the sympathetic cooperation of the police and Town Council and justices of the peace. She asked the committee to beware against expecting quick results in a statistical sense. This kind of work was not like running a three-weeks evangelistic campaign in which results were often reckoned by the number of tabulated "decisions." In police court mission-work one was dealing with badly broken earthenware which often took much patience to mend.

The effect of Millie's address was such as to make any kind of outward applause utterly alien. There was a deep, responsive silence which, after an unhurried pause, the chairman hesitantly broke, saying, "Friends, we are all thinking the same thing. We have indeed been rightly guided. Nothing could be more fitting than that we should all bow in prayer, thanking God, and earnestly committing Mrs. Kennard to His enabling power. I shall ask Miss Whimby to lead us." Miss Whimby did so; and what a prayer! As the early Methodists used to say, she was "on pleading terms with God." She knew that she never needed to "call attention to the point at issue" when talking to the Almighty.

In Lancashire, of course, no self-respecting committee would ever dream of holding an augmented session without including that time-honoured institution, a cup of tea and cake or cookies. There was nothing like it for cementing good-natured hob-nobbers in chatty friendship. In the informal conversazione which accompanied it, Millie received a score or so of welcomes expressed with that hale and hearty warmth which is endemic among Lancashire folk, and the same number of handshakes—from the most limply genteel to the most savagely bone-crushing.

Afterward, as they all walked to the street in talkative twos and threes, a quiet-spoken lady drew alongside Millie. "I am Mrs. Joash Adair," she said. "As I am secretary-treasurer of this new police court mission, you and I will be seeing each other fairly often. Perhaps, after the upheaval of your removal from Manchester, you could come round to my home for a meal together and a chat."

Millie gratefully accepted the invitation. They looked into each other's face and preliminarily liked each other. It was the beginning of an unquenchable friendship; but had they suspected what a strange, utterly unforeseeable sequel it was to have, involving murder, intrigue, mystery, and entanglement of their two families, they would have scanned each other far more intently as they stood there after that session of the Watch Committee.

FIVE
Five Steps Downward

What lay behind Millie's offering herself for the new work at Elmerton? The answer is wrapped in shadows. Those two Rostherne weddings in 1890—Joash and Agnes in the Spring; Mike Kennard and Millie in the Summer—were not only different from each other in personages and incidentals; they issued in widely different after-days.

When Agnes walked out of Rostherne Church she was linked to a man of solid worth. He had made few promises, but behind each one was the firm resolve of a true man. He worked sedulously, chose wisely, saved steadily. Agnes was his queen, and she made their first home his palace. He coveted no other man's possessions. He had eyes for no other woman besides his incomparable Agnes. Their marriage vows were silken bands, not iron bonds. Their union was a love-lock of hearts, not merely a pull of physical attraction. In the second year of their life together they sustained a grievous sorrow in the losing of their first child when barely a year old. It happened in such a heart-rending way that ever afterward they kept the memory of it wrapped in a silence which they never broke even to their closest friends. Yet that baffling permission of Providence had drawn them still closer to each other. Somehow, the dews of sorrow distilled even richer fragrance into their reciprocal affection. True it is: husbands and wives seldom know the depth of their love for each other until they have wept together in some abyss of sorrow. Joash and Agnes loved more maturely and tenderly after theirs.

Very different was it when Mike Kennard and Millie left Rostherne Church. Their linked arms scarcely symbolized linked hearts. Before the nuptial knot was tied, Mike had made gaudy promises and gilded prophecies about the superior house and circumstances in which they would soon be living because of the way he was making money "hand over fist" in the insurance business. He was going to be the model husband and father, of whom Millie and the children would be proud.

He was the big "I," but his promises were pie-crust. From the beginning he defaulted. It was a shock to Millie to find that not only did he have no money; he was in debt. He had borrowed even to buy the wedding ring. However, he managed to rake money in from somewhere, and they rented a cottage at the end of a row in Everey Street, Manchester (which long street is still there, only its rows of small brick houses have now given place to other premises).

It was a monstrous incongruity that such a gem of a wife should be handcuffed to such a braggart ne'er-do-well. When it suited he could talk like a saint; but his mind was a cage of unclean birds. He could preach a sermon with flamboyant pietism and unctuous volubility, but his heart was a pestilential swamp of voluptuous carnality. He could sanctimoniously say, like hireling Balaam, "Let me die the death of the righteous," but in actual life he could stoop to behaviour low enough to make a demon blush. He had such a rich, rolling voice and such slick facility of public utterance as could have made him a second Spurgeon; such inborn political grasp and quality of leadership as could have made him a second Gladstone. He had a spacious, windy personal atmosphere which could bowl you over. He was prepossessingly big, yet pygmy-little.

He was a consummate deceiver cursed with all the natural cleverness for it, including a flexible physiognomy which could look as blandly innocent as, at other times, it could look evil, especially when those bushy eyebrows drew down over that long, straight nose with its nostrils distended and the thickish lips parted under that fulsome moustache, extruding square teeth in a revolting grin. Among those who knew him well his arts and wiles cut no ice. None of his consorts would have trusted him with a penny, nor did they pay any heed to his know-all profundity. But with new contacts his atmospheric pressure was irresistible. He could "borrow big." Many were the dupes he verbally mugged.

Moreover, besides deceiving others he was fool enough to be always deceiving *himself*. With juvenile gullibility he whined that he was an ill-treated pawn of fate. He believed that his grandiose schemes, which never came to anything, were thwarted by a jinx of the nether world who had a spite against him. His superstitious imagination saw every frustration as a nemesis. He hugged an even stranger aberration, namely, that Providence now owed him a debt which would surely be paid to him as compensation for the wrongs he had endured! So, like Mr. Micawber of Dickens fame, he was always counting on something to turn up which would change insolvency to amplitude.

Such men baffle analysis. We might well doubt that so many contrary opposites could all coexist as basic components of one personality if history had not given us a Nero, a Herod, a Louis XI, and an Adolf Hitler. In his less conspicuous way Mike Kennard was such. Somewhere in that complex nature, always in a state of civil war, there was *good* which every now and then had a temporary resurrection; but on the whole he was an imposture. At times he could be truculent to the point of violence. He was vain. In those days, working people put a sharp difference between their workday clothes and their "Sunday best." Mike Kennard, even on workdays, always wanted to be the well-dressed gentleman: it meant so much when collecting insurance premiums! He was gaseous and showy, but as trashy inwardly as flashy outwardly. He was just about the most self-contradictory "variety show" ever staged. A bit of success would go to his head, so that he acted like a conceited nabob, and viewed all hard-working others as mere pariahs. Adversity could reduce him to lugubrious tears of contrition for his sins, and he would crawl round with a fawning obsequiousness of the Uriah Heap brand.

Such was the man Millie had married, though most was dexterously camouflaged prior to their Rostherne wedding. Also, there was something about Mike which was likeable. One felt that he was all the while having an heroic battle with himself, and that if only he got reinforcements from another personality he could rout the bad guys who were messing up his territory. It was that likeable something about him, and that need of help, which generated in Millie a fond compassion which she mistakenly thought was love. She was not deceived by his versatility, volubility, volatility: she saw right through to a deep-down Mike inside whom she wanted to rescue, if possible.

All too soon after their wedlock Millie realized how direly she had underestimated the problem. She did not believe in divorce, except for adultery; but several times she considered obtaining a legal separation. Then she would think of the two girls, who now loved her as if she were their own mother. Also, the shame of the separation would reflect on her own Christian profession. What was more, a fixed separation would probably cause Mike to take the fatal plunge which would land him in the gutter—or worse. So Millie kept sticking with her dilemma.

However, after the first three years or so, there were other developments. They had been long enough married by then for Millie to know her man's set behavior-patterns. He would go off in the morning all spruced up for the day's round of collecting the weekly insurance payments and for hunting out new customers. Then he would come home under the influence of drink, and struggle to consciousness next morning with a "hangover"—a sickly malaise which he would self-diagnose as a backlash from over intensity in his work. This would be followed by sporadic visits to a nearby tavern, and several days of plethoric slumber during which his insurance job was a garden running to weeds. An unhappy by-product of this was, that at year's end, despite his dandy apparel and airy chinwag, he was below all the other agents in the amount of business transacted. There was no real fellowship between Millie and Mike, either marital or Christian. Millie gradually reached the verdict that he was not capable either of real love or real hate. However, she kept trying to do the best with what was there. She knew now that only his true conversion—his acceptance of the living Saviour into his heart, would make a "new man" of him; and for that she daily prayed.

Another problem was: he did not know the difference between anger and temper. A good man may have righteous anger against evil, but he will not indulge temper, which is an eruption of distorted passion, never an outcome of calm reason. Mike Kennard was too shallow for intellectual anger, but he had fits of raving temper. At such times he would become dangerous; yet he was too pusillanimous to dare do what he threatened. Millie knew him through and through. His bluff was a bulging balloon. He was afraid to strike her. Besides, in his own pathetic way he knew there was nobody like her in all the world. Now and then, when he furtively prayed, he thanked God for sending her. And sometimes he laid his weary head on the bed and wept alone.

The sixth and seventh years brought things to a crisis. To begin with, Mike lost his job. His agency was now so shrunken, the directors had decided to "farm it out" among three new agents. They had estimated the worth of Mike's round and had generously paid him off with more than the appropriate moiety.

This staggering blow to Mike's pride sharply accentuated a downgrade in him which Millie had observed from time to time. Again and again she had wondered where he used to go on Wednesday evenings and on Saturdays from noon until midnight. She hated to admit what she suspected, nor could she bring herself to act the spy. The answer came in an unexpected way. Two lads—regular young slum ruffians who often went to the mission hall—halted Millie in the street. "Hi, aint you Mrs. Mike Kennard, the woman preacher?" "Yes." "Well, why does *he* go with bad men?" Sick at heart, Millie responded, "Perhaps you had better tell me what you mean." Out it came. "We've seed'im goin' wi'

Andy Bacchus an' Al Sharkey an't'others to them there cock fights at Droylesden; an' we've seed 'im goin' ont' train on a Sat'dy mixin' up wi' them as guz to yon dog-racin' at Falla'field." Millie went limp. A cold sweat covered her forehead. Maybe one of her quick-eyed informers noticed it as he soothingly said, "Sorry, Miss's Kennird, if it's upset yer, but we thowt y'owt t'know."

On reaching home Millie sat and wept. Pouring out her heart to God she pleaded again for Mike, at the same time asking guidance for what she should do.

In any case, as she knew, a major crisis had been pending now for some weeks on financial grounds. Mike was no longer giving her enough money to pay the rent and provide for the children. Over a third of the modicum with which the insurance society paid him off had gone in a drenching booze, and the remainder would likely enough have been similarly swilled away if Millie had not extricated it from him during one of his lethargic dozes through inebriacy. His new plunge into the gambling racket which was connected with the cock fights and the Fallowfield races, so Millie surmised, was a fevered attempt to win by betting what he was no longer earning. Sickeningly enough, as she began to ascertain more reliably what he was up to, she found still worse evidences of moral collapse, until it seemed as though, instead of getting guidance from God, she was being mocked and broken by the worst discoveries any pure and faithful wife can make.

From the beginning of their married life she had found herself up against the most excruciating torture for a pure woman: a husband with inordinate sex passion. Her man's physical appetites corresponded with his swarthy body. At times he seemed all animal. Millie was frightened, but desperately determined Mike should not know it. She realized that her one and only position of command was to preserve his respect for her. If that should crack, it would mean final break-up. She stood her ground. "Do you want a pure, loving wife?—or an animal, Mike? Do you want to be an honorable husband?—or a beast? The honorable husband finds pure joy: the beast, only coarse gratification." Several times, too, those lightning fists had shot into action, and made more impact on him at the moment than words! Sometimes the brute in him would seem as though about to leap out and tear all decencies to shreds; but always that calm, pure, dear face and firm stance tamed him and shamed him. Also, he knew that Millie would actually thrash him, without caring how many neighbours heard, if he ever behaved wrongly while the children were in the house, whether by night or day, and that had great weight with Mike's pride.

Oh, the agony of that prolonged suspense! Millie began to fear that she could not remain master of the situation indefinitely. Her nerves seemed beginning to fray. Then, inexplicably, like a halcyon calm after a shrieking tempest, there came a relieving lull. Mike subsided into seeming normality. He was pleasant, respectful, and outspokenly grateful for the way his dear Millie made the little house such a comfortable home.

But Millie was now to make the most dismaying discovery of all. She had been given enough reason already to believe that when he was away from her he had a philandering mind and lecherous eye. At times she had noticed his roving gaze at female face and figure. Now she learned of his visiting unchaste women. One night, after addressing a mission meeting, she returned home a bit earlier than expected. The children were in bed. Mike was at the kitchen sink, having a swill down—for cottages at that time had no such luxury as a bathroom. In working-class dwellings one had to use an oval zinc tub, and heat water for it on the gas ring. Several kettlefuls were required to give the needed depth of hot water. Either that, or one had to stand at the kitchen sink, with papers or an old sheet spread over the floor to catch the splashes. Mike seemed awkwardly taken by surprise and was plainly agitated as he hurriedly desisted from his ablutions and furtively re-dressed.

It was not until a couple of days later that the incident hit Millie's mind. A strange fear stabbed her heart. Mike was sitting by the fire (every Lancashire cottage in those days had an open fire-grate in the little living room, with an oven on one side of it for cooking and baking). "Mike," she said, "I have an errand or two down the street. I shan't be out long. Put some more coal on the fire and keep warm. I'll be back in good time to get tea ready." So saying, she slipped out.

There were four doctors in that district. Two of them were interested in the local mission at which Millie was a worker. She called on one of them. "Has Mike been to you for treatment this last day or two?" "No." The second of them said, "I somehow thought you would find out, Mrs. Kennard. Yes, he's been to me, in a bit of a panic. Mrs. Kennard, why do you stay with such a man?"

Millie went sick inside. "Please tell me, doctor. I need to know, for more reasons than you suspect."

"Very well, Mrs. Kennard; he's been going to houses no decent man would visit. Then, in pretty alarm, he consulted me a few days ago. I examined him. He has not contracted any disease; but to frighten him back to chastity I thought it good to let him think he *had*. I decided on that for *your* sake. The fact is, he has a fairly severe dose of genital inflammation, nothing more, and I prescribed a treatment. I recommend that you do not say anything—not yet—to disillusion him. Let him feel some of the mental distress he deserves."

It was with a heart heavy as a tombstone that poor Millie dragged back to their dull brick cottage. Her mind seemed to be in a long, dark tunnel the further end of which she could not see. Her spirit quailed. She was in one of those desolating ordeals of inward recoil after which no one is ever the same again. Her faith in prayer, in divine guidance, in the love of God, was suddenly assailed. She was not far from forty. There was no turning back; no undoing what was done. The awful inexorableness of life chilled her. Her marriage bands were iron chains fettering her to a man who now seemed more like a hog than a human. Why had God cruelly allowed her to blunder into an inferno where there might have been a paradise? She doubted Providence. The mystery of permitted evil and savagery, of suffering and tragedy, seemed mocking and crushing. Were evil and anguish, after all, an intrinsic constituent of total reality? Was Christianity, despite all seeming proofs, untrue? Was human history one long travail to bring forth never-ending frustrations? Was God hearing her cry for help and direction?—or was He deaf and impotent, like Baal of long ago? Millie felt that some gigantic dark hand was about to crush out her now feebly flickering candle of faith.

But once again, besides deep plunge there was brave struggle. Millie remembered the buffeted patriarch, Job, and his, "Though He slay me, yet will I trust Him," and "He knoweth the way that I take. When He hath tried me I shall come forth as gold." She mused that the only way God could tutor Job into such final enrichment was to keep Job in the dark awhile. If God had at once told Job why his calamities had been allowed, and how grandly all would eventuate, the whole purpose of blessing through suffering would have been destroyed. There would have been no test of Job's faith, nor could Job have made his transfiguring discovery of God.

Millie further reasoned that it was scarcely rational to let something which we do *not* know cancel out all those things which by solid proof we *do* know. Mysteries never nullify proven realities. The basic facts of the Christian faith and the Biblical revelation are provenly true. It is really true that the Lord Jesus came, lived, taught, wrought, died, rose from the dead, and visibly ascended to heaven. According to the well-tested documents of Holy Writ, He really claimed and proved Himself to be "God manifest in the flesh." He taught that the love of God is both infinite and yet individualizing, and that the Cross of Calvary was the supreme expression of it, in which God effected atonement for the sin of the human race. But was the Bible true? Millie knew her "Christian Evidences" well enough to know how sound are the apologetics for the divine inspiration of the Bible. She began to feel her feet on firm ground again. Yes, the Bible is true. Permitted evil is a mystery, but the darkness has not quenched the light even though now existing along with it. God really cares and loves to the uttermost. "Still trust Him, Millie," an inner voice said. "The God who bled for you on that Cross can never mock you. That Cross means not only that God suffered *for* us, but that He suffers *with* us. Sometimes His most gracious purposes wind to their fulfillment through strange-seeming processes. Everything that God permits, He foreknows, and overrules for our ultimate good, if we will let Him." Millie began to see a light at the end of the frightening tunnel, and to feel again around her the "everlasting arms" of that Love which never lets us go.

And now, what was to be her plan of action? She reviewed the facts. All his promises prior to wedlock Mike had broken. His marriage vows he had violated. He had maintained her and the children at little more than poverty level. His behaviour before the children had all too often been coarse. His anger at times had been brutish. Now he was jobless through his own stupid default. What other remunerative employ for him was there? The answer seemed bleak. Money was needed. Whether Millie and the children stayed with him or not, shelter, food, clothing were now urgently needed. So, resolution number one: Millie herself must get employment.

That much being resolved, she resumed her cogitations. Her years of mission work among other victimized wives had familiarized her with the standard downward sequence. First the man forfeits his job. Then he soaks his misery in drink. Then, needing money all the more, he starts gambling, under the silly delusion that he is going to be fate's favourite—the lucky bloke who hits the jackpot. Then, being in with the hell-bent set, he finds himself in the arms of lewd temptresses. Then, morally wrecked and desperate, he starts thieving or burglaring. Finally, he lands in prison: home gone, wife heartbroken, children destitute. Oh, Millie had wept with those wives and tried to speak words of sympathetic advice. Little did she then think that one day she would find herself in the same pitiful quandary.

She had now seen in Mike the first four of the five downward strides: his livelihood lost; his baptism in beer; his gambling and involvement with the vicious; and now, apparently, his moral and physical defilement with unclean women, perhaps prostitutes. She recalled having advised several wives to leave such husbands in self-defense against risk of communicated venereal disease, and for the sake of the children. Now, she herself was faced with the same danger. One thing was clear: she herself was now forbidden territory to her betrayer, unless and until. . . . She did not know at the moment how to complete that thought. But she now had all the grounds for honourable divorce, both legally and Scripturally. For the sake of the children and herself, should she go right ahead and divorce Mike? What that would mean to him she shuddered to think. Yet strictly that was neither her fault nor her responsibility. Was the answer a legal separation, not outright divorce? If so, she might as well face up at once to the fact that bankrupt Mike would not provide one penny of alimony, even if the court laid that customary obligation on him.

One of the worries which pressed most poignantly on Millie was the effect on the children, whichever step she took. The safer decision seemed to be divorce. She was sure that she could earn enough to provide for them and herself until the two girls were old enough to be earning as well. Dorothy, who was five years old when Mike and Millie were married in 1890, was now eleven, almost twelve (free schooling at that time in England covered up to a child's thirteenth birthday). Mona, whose full name was Monica, was now nine. But there was also now young Joseph. Toward the end of their second year together a baby boy had come to Mike and Millie. That little son was now of acute concern in Millie's troubled thinking, and well he might be; for although she little dreamed it, he was soon to become the dominant figure in one of the strangest tapestries of inter-threaded human destiny. Joseph was now five years old.

Mike's attitude toward the children was a tantalizing conundrum. He was choosy, showy, inconsistent. Dorothy he usually treated with apathy. Millie suspected that she reminded him too much of his former wife, for she was like her in feature and disposition. Mona was full-faced, with deep, roving eyes, yet peculiarly pretty, with rather aquiline features; full of playfulness and sentimental affection. She was one hundred percent daddy's girl. Mike made no disguise of his favouritism. His attitude to little Joseph was beyond analysis. At first he had said, with a look that gleamed with some far-reaching idea, "This little fellow is going to be worth his weight in gold to us, Millie." Later, the nocturnal crying, along with other inconveniences of a baby at close quarters in a small cottage, had exacerbated him to fiendish temper. "Why the blazes did the Almighty ever send us such a squealing little brat!" For reasons of which Millie knew nothing until years later, little Joseph was a continual eyesore to Mike. Yet if ever Joseph became ill, Mike was as snarlingly protective of him as a female Alsatian over her puppies.

Nobody knew Mike as Millie did, but she had now given up hope of ever understanding him. About that time the Austrian neurologist, Sigmund Freud, was captivating many in the medical profession and among the educational intelligentsia with his fascinating "psychoanalysis," or new method of psychotherapeutic analysis based on the proposition that abnormal mental reactions are due to repression of desires, i.e. desires consciously rejected but still having an undercover persistence in the "subconscious." Millie did not know too much about that, though she made good use of the branch library in their district, and was surprisingly in touch with such things for a woman of her station in life. She knew enough about the Freudian "id" to conclude that inside Mike Kennard there was the most enigmatical "idioplasm" from which a human character had ever developed. She longed that God would give her, as only He could, some intuitive perception into that ugly urge which had driven Mike into that libidinous animalism with polluted women.

There was one other development which finalized Millie's now firm purpose to get everything dragged into the open and decisively dealt with. For some time, usually toward the end of the month, Mike had been like a restless tiger pacing to and fro behind cage bars. Alternate month-ends he had gone away for three or four days; and always, when he returned, there was money in his pockets—which he willingly shared with Millie. Where and how was he getting that money? Had Mike taken, not only four, but already the fifth of those five steps downward to ruin—stealing, burglaring? By the time she reached home, Millie's mind had sorted its thinking into clearcut decision and purpose.

Her soliloquy had taken longer than she had noticed. The three children were home from school. Dorothy had set the table ready for the usual Lancashire type of evening meal—known as "teatime," with a bright, clean table-cloth, cups and saucers, plates, spoons, knives. She and Mike were in the kitchen, slicing and buttering the bread. The tea was already in the teapot, ready to be brewed as soon as mother came in. Mike was in good humor; and anyone seeing him for the first time would have said, "What a congenial father he looks!" Mona, as usual, was outside just round the corner, playing "bobbers and jacks" with girl playmates on the flagged footpath. Joseph was out there, too, but came indoors on seeing his mother return. Millie apologized for her lateness, suggested scrambled egg and chips (French fries); and soon the five Kennards were a hungry, happy talkative family at the table.

True to form, Mona was chief chatterbox. Dorothy was the one who got up and buttered more slices of bread as the plate emptied; mother the one who had to say, "Mona, chew your food properly," Joseph, always next to his mother, palish but bright-eyed and questioning; Mike, steadily eating, and between sips of tea asking the girls about school.

Again, according to pattern, Dorothy is the first up from the table, clearing the utensils away, sleeves rolled up, and washing the dishes. Mona postpones, then resignedly grabs the tea-towel to dry the cups, saucers, plates. Little Joseph, not quite knowing yet whether it is work or play, is trying to reach high enough to put the dried crockery and cutlery away. Millie is brushing the crumbs from the table on to a small tray and then into the fire. Mike goes out to the coal shed in the back yard—dusk has now become darkness—to fill the scuttle with coal for the evening.

Afterward all five are in the living-room. The fire for a while is rather black on top with fresh coal, but is glowing underneath and sending out warmth through the lower bars of the firegrate. Father is in the easy chair at one side of the room, head hidden in the newspaper. Dorothy is sitting on a fireside stool, reading Robert Louis Stevenson's

Treasure Island. Mona is peeping underneath the linen window-blind to see if the rain has stopped and if some of the girls are out to play under the light of the street-lamp. Joseph is squatting on the hearth-rug, thumbing through a picture book or deploying his tin soldiers. Millie is knitting or sewing or darning stockings, and at the same time inter-mittently glancing at the pencil notes of an address-in-the-making for a women's meeting. All five of them, at intervals, are interrupting each other with gossipy chatter.

During the evening Millie teaches Mona how to mend stockings; plays awhile with Joseph; interchanges off-and-on remarks with Mike: all the time musing what a happy family they could be if only Mike were different.

Many evenings Mike was out the whole time. Other evenings it was scaring to be in the house with him. His big body seemed to fill one side of the room. If he angrily raised his voice it seemed like a bull roaring. One whack from that big, flabby hand was enough to make any of the children chink with terror. When he was in his better moods home was like heaven to the children. They really tried to love Mike as their daddy, but it was always an unsure love, nervous lest it should wake the beast inside the man. Their basic feeling was dread. On those nights when he came home tipsy, or worse, they would scamper upstairs and huddle together in the cold back-bedroom.

Naturally, all this strengthened the bond of true love between the children and Millie. Over against every vice in their father they saw the opposite virtue in their brave, consistent mother. She was their sure line of defense against the unpredictable monster in the shadow. Young children do not crystalize their thoughts into words as adults do, but they see and sense things vividly enough. Without putting it into words to each other, Dorothy and Mona and little Joseph had the situation "sized up." They did not hate their father even though he cowed them; but they loved Millie with a clinging, affectionate, admiring love which the whole neighbourhood knew. She was so always-the-same; so firm yet so fond; so pranky and teasing. She did not clutter-up the home with suffocating "don'ts," like the well-known type, "Alice, where's Sally? Find out what she's doing, and tell her to stop it at once!" There were certain things forbidden. Trespass meant penalty. The children knew, and conformed. They knew as certainly as if the angel Gabriel had shouted it from heaven that Millie's will, even when severe, was for their good. She was a genius at being mother and playmate.

Next day Mike was away afternoon and evening. Millie knew he was with the Droylesden cock-fight crowd. That afternoon she took opportunity to get advice from a local lawyer who was on the city mission board of managers. Thursday, Mike was home; and in the evening the children were at the "Band of Hope"—a big favourite in those days, for it provided not only helpful talks geared to juniors, and magic-lantern lectures, but songs, recitations, drill, games. So Millie and Mike were alone awhile.

This was the time for the showdown. Millie felt nervous but gripped herself. She was not sure how he would take it; whether he would express lugubrious apologies or spring back with the fury of a panther. Never yet had his thunder and lightning been able to break Millie's pavidity. She knew that in this encounter, especially, it was a necessity that he should not see her waver or quail. She prayed for calmness.

"Mike, while the children are away I want to talk to you. It's serious. I think you'd better put your newspaper down and listen."

"What is it, Millie?"

"It's about our marriage, and the children, and our whole future."

"Yes, Millie." Mike was still scouring the paper, but glanced over it at her, as though momentarily curious.

"Do you remember, Mike, I once told you the usual five steps downward to the break-up of home and the ruination of character?—first, loss of employment, then resort to liquor, then the gambling mania, then immoral women, then thieving or burglaring, ending up in the prison cell, or worse. Even if they let a man out of prison, what is there left for him? Who wants to employ a 'ticket of leave' man? His prison sentence daubs him for the rest of his life. Little did I dream, Mike, when I stood with you in the church at Rostherne that I would see my own fine-looking man taking those five awful, downward steps—"

"Millie, Millie, what in the name of creation are you talking about?"

"Mike, you know that what I am saying is true. All your florid promises are withered leaves. Even your vow to love and to cherish is badly smirched. You are not even supporting us. Part of the pay-off money from the insurance society you threw away in liquid dope at the saloon, and the remainder is now used up. By the time we were married I had secretly saved sixty pounds—a big sum for a country girl, and that, too, is now nearly all gone. . . ."

"Oh, steady on, Millie, you're painting things a bit too black. Think of when I was working, and what bad luck I've had since then. I'm certain something is going to turn up again, soon."

"If you're so certain, Mike, what is it going to be?"

"Oh, well, Millie, I can't just say at the minute; but something is sure to be just round the corner." By this time Mike was fidgety. With a dark look on his face he fingered the newspaper again.

"You'd better leave the paper, Mike, and listen to me. Tonight may be a big crisis in your life. You've taken step number one. What about step number two? You've now taken that, as well, for you are now known as a drunkard. What about step number three? What about the Wednesday night cock-fights at Droylesden? What about the racing and gambling at Fallowfield and Old Trafford?"

Suddenly the newspaper dropped to the floor. Mike turned pale, then red, then livid. Then, with a mighty rally, he bellowed, "What the blazes!"—and banged his fist on the chair arm. "Have you—"

"Mike, you know well enough that your bluster doesn't scare me. What's more, if that hand should ever strike me, you'd regret it for the rest of your days. Besides, you know that what I am going to say is for your good, in one last effort to save you from final disaster. You wonder how I know about your gambling? No, I have not played the sleuth. In fact, although I had my strong suspicions, I determined not to spy on you. My information was given to me unasked by those who have seen you going."

Mike was listening now in glum silence.

"What about step number four, Mike? Why those secret ablutions and the ointment? Dreading the shock of finding out what I didn't want to know, I asked the doctor—the one you went to—and he told me the awful truth. You have gone to the gutter, to the foulest thing a man can do—to prostitutes. You have begrimed your most sacred marriage vow. You have dragged it through a slimy pigsty. You have betrayed a pure and loyal wife in the ugliest of ways. God will judge you. Your physical condition is now a danger to me and the children. You are contaminated—a disease carrier. You have left me only one thing to do if I am to safeguard myself and the children. Yesterday I interviewed a lawyer. Mike, I am divorcing you."

She got no further. Mike gave a deep groan, then made a choking sound. Millie saw beads of perspiration ooze from his forehead and drip down his large face. He seemed to have difficulty in swallowing, as through a sudden attack of dysphagia. Then, with a weary moan, he dragged his heavy hulk from the chair, slumped to the hearth floor in front of Millie, and buried his head in her lap.

For a full two or three minutes he was silent. Then the sobs came, and his big frame shook. Millie thought it best not to speak further—not yet. Her heart-break at his infidelity, and her righteous anger at his low-down betrayal of the children were somehow softened into pity as she now saw him there, limp at her feet. For a moment she had seen the defiant gleam of the tiger, but the next minute that better and so-likeable other something in him had struggled with it till the sweat poured down his face. It is not easy for any man, least of all for Mike's type, even though knowingly reprobate, to sink down in such open self-humiliation as Mike now showed Millie. She looked at him again—so gifted, so dominating, so big with lofty possibilities, yet so weak, so foolish, so self-betrayed. She wanted to give way a bit; but no, not for the world dare she do so. Any maudlin commiseration at that point would have immediately martyred all wise advantage. She must remain inflexible as well as sorry for him.

But now he was able to speak. "Oh, Millie," he said hoarsely, "even your hardest word is too kind. Everything you have said is true. I deserve to be divorced. God knows I do. While you were shaming me with my guilt, Millie, it was as though the angel of doom was sounding the trumpet of divine wrath on me. But, if you can believe me any more, Millie, after I have so deeply wronged you, I swear before God to you that even if you had not dragged it all out tonight, I had vowed that I would kill myself before I would ever be tricked again into such vileness. I really meant it, and still mean it, Millie. Whether you divorce me or not, I will never do that again. If you break up the marriage it will break me up, too. But I'll never be tricked by those damned Delilahs again; and I'll wear my knuckles to the bone to get at least *some* support to you and the children. But please, Millie, *don't* divorce me, if you can possibly give me one more chance. Oh, God! What have I done?"

He turned his face up to Millie. How quickly it had changed! His eyes were red. His look was haggard.

"Mike, it's almost impossible, now, for us to stay together. There can be no affectionate relationship between us. Did you never think what risk a woman takes in getting married?—yielding her very body· to her husband. Only deep love can cause any pure, thinking woman to do that. Mike, you have fouled that sacred trust. I am now forbidden territory to you."

Mike interrupted, "But, Millie, if it doesn't sound ridiculous for a brute like me to say it, deep down I respect and admire you too much to think of you just in that way. You can't say I've bullied you, can you? By Heaven! I'll never touch you, if you forbid me. I'll burn to death first! I could easily sleep down here on the couch at nights, if that'll please you."

"Tell me, Mike, where do you get that money when you go away for two or three days every few weeks? Are you involved in some kind of thieving?"

Mike stiffened a bit, and now, kneeling, looked Millie in the face. "I might have known you would ask that." Then, slowly standing up, "Millie, I swear to you: I'm not stealing. If I'm lying, may God strike me dead this minute! I'm getting it from a cad who owes it to me—every blessed penny of it; and by Heaven I'll make him pay it, too! Millie, I just can't explain it now, but I swear it's *honest*, at least on my side of it. And as soon as I've found out something that I ought to know, I'll make a clean breast of the whole thing."

As a matter of fact, Mike was indeed telling the truth according to his own somewhat warped concept of it; and he honestly did mean to tell Millie all about the mystery money some time later. What he did not foresee was, that as things transpired, she would never know until she had seen him in his coffin.

"I'll take your word for it," said Millie, "but I'm afraid the divorce will have to go through."

Mike turned ashen again. He seemed liable to fall, but managed to stand silently there. Then he staggered into the kitchen, and made for the sink. He got there just in time, and bent over it, vomiting. Millie knew now that this was no theatrical repentance on Mike's part. He was badly hurt. That better something in the man was in such desperate grapple with the cursed "legion of demons" in him that the intensity of it had upset him physically. He was really distraught. Millie could not sit there in callous unconcern. Hurrying to him, she helped him tenderly with face-cloth and towel, then quickly prepared an herbal drink to help soothe his stomach.

"Mike," she said later, "I'm sorry we've had to have this talk, but it could not wait longer. Anyway, so far as divorce is concerned, if it will relieve you a bit, we'll let that lie in abeyance for a few days. Meanwhile, we must say nothing to the children. Try to get a good night's sleep. Or, later, if you should feel ready, I'll make a soothing drink for you— just whenever you say."

Mike put his big arms round her, gently, and kissed her golden hair. "Millie, did you ever read that book, *An Angel*

Guest in Human Guise? I don't remember who the author is, but if ever there was a human angel in a man's life, it's you."

He looked so weary. Tears spilled down his face. How could Millie help feeling fondly sorry for him? She kissed him. "Millie, my love," he responded with a quivering voice, "Why did the Almighty join the best little woman on earth to the damndest, rottenest husband?"

SIX
Midnight and Morning

As things turned out, the matter of divorce not only had to "lie in abeyance" for a while, it became indefinitely postponed because of a new emergency. Millie watched Mike closely. The beast in him was by no means dead, but it had been unexpectedly mauled and was now sullenly licking its wounds. His whole bearing and type of comment convinced her that he had set his face like a flint against unchastity. He was slower, milder, particularly toward the girls; yet for a reason which Millie would not understand until years later, he could not conquer his rasping antipathy toward little Joseph, who quite plainly was growing up with a sickly fear-complex. His pale young face began to have a haunted look. He was furtive and jittery in his father's presence, sensing that his father was irritated by him—which made him chronically nervous. He began to be known among the other boys as "mother's pet," because he always wanted to be with Millie. He was becoming shy and tongue-tied. Then something happened which every mother dreads.

At that time, in England, free schooling was provided from the age of four or five upwards. Monday to Friday, boys and girls had to be at school from 9 a.m. till noon, then again from 1:30 p.m. till 4:00. Joseph was now five.

The month was December. The weather was cold. Millie did her best on very little money to keep her three bairns amply fed and warmly clad, but it was a struggle. In all working folks' cottages heating was limited to the one fire in the open grate of the living room downstairs. Coal was dear.

Dorothy and Mona kept warm and well, but little Joseph, who seemed to have developed an incurable inward trembling through fear of his gorilla-like father, became the helpless little victim of almost continuous shivering. Dorothy, ever his guardian angel, would take her own scarf off and wrap it over his cap and round his chin, then run with him, holding his hand in hers, as fast as his legs could go, down this street and up the next and round the corner and back again, until he gasped and puffed and laughed and glowed. But soon again his trembles would return.

One afternoon Dorothy came home from school an hour before closing time, bringing a pale-faced little Joseph with her. The headmistress of the Infant Department had sent to the main school for Dorothy. "I think you had better take Joseph home. He seems too weak to concentrate. He has a runny nose and he keeps trembling. Perhaps you had better get him home and into a warm bed." Millie gathered her delicate wee mite to her bosom, and sat with him near the fire until he was really warm. Meanwhile Dorothy filled two stone hot-water bottles—the sort used then—and put them into Joseph's bed. Millie made a bowl of "pobs" (Lancashire name for a bowl of bread and milk with a nob of butter in it and a good spoonful of honey to make it extra nice for a young palate) as hot as Joseph could take it. Then away to bed they carried him. Dorothy had been warming the eiderdown at the living-room fire, and now laid it over the bed. Joseph at last was "as warm as toast." In fact, he looked flushed in a way which was not too reassuring to Millie. "There, now, little man! Isn't that lovely and comfy! Off you go to sleep, and wake up a big, strong man in the morning!"

Unfortunately, that was not how he woke up in the morning. He did not wake until the girls had gone to school, but soon afterward he was sneezing, his nose was runny, his eyes were watery; he complained of sore eyes and sore throat, and had a croupy cough. Millie was alarmed. Those were the symptoms of measles. She conferred with Mike. He was not helpful. "Measles, Millie? What's that going to mean?"

"Oh, Mike, it can be quite serious. Surely you know that measles is about the most contagious of all childhood diseases. There's been a good bit of it around lately. It's always more serious in a child five years or under. My *Medical Book for Mothers* says it's the after-effects which make measles and whooping cough so dangerous—pneumonia, bronchitis, tuberculosis. However, Mike, we won't be pessimistic. There doesn't seem to be any sign of the usual rash. We'll keep him warm, and check again a bit later."

As soon as Millie had finished the first household chores of the day she consulted her medical book, with which she had familiarized herself during years of city mission slum visitation. It said that even before the rash appears around ears and face, the eruption can usually be detected on the roof of the mouth. Accordingly, later that day, Millie looked carefully into Joseph's mouth; and there, sure enough, not only were the tonsils swollen, but two little tell-tale papules confirmed her fears.

"Mike, I'm pretty sure now: it's measles. One of us had better go and get Dr. Teesdale. Perhaps it would be better for me to stay with Joseph. I'd be so grateful, Mike, if you would go."

Mike did not want to go. In his opinion there was no need to incur the expense of a doctor. In a few days the lad would be right enough. He was a pest, anyhow. Sulkily, however, Mike was prepared, "as a fatherly sacrifice," to walk round to the doctor's. There were few telephones in those days. Mike had a mile and a half to walk. He missed the doctor, but left a message. It was almost evening before the doctor reached the Kennards' home.

Dr. Teesdale was a mountain of a man, and noticeably disproportionate. He had a long torso of remarkably large circumference, but a very small and rather flat head—as though nature had almost forgotten that such a big trunk needed a head, and had hurriedly clapped one on in the nick of time, but three sizes too small. He reminded Joseph of the big railway engines in Central Station, Manchester, with their huge round boilers and little squat funnels on top, which could not be any bigger because of the low railway tunnels they had to go through. But what Dr. Teesdale lacked in structural elegance he more than made up for in broad charity and excellent qualities as doctor. He was an officebearer at the local Congregational Church, and a keen helper of evangelistic work among the poor. Occasionally he had been in at the Sunday night lodging house meetings where Millie was a frequent speaker. He greatly admired Millie.

From such a big man one might have expected a strong voice, but it was low, smooth and pleasant. By the time he examined Joseph, the latter's face was flushed, the eyes were red, and the usual crop of pimples had become visible. Dr. Teesdale was a genius at buttering up a young boy's ego. He told young Joseph how glad he was to meet him. He knew two or three of Joseph's schoolmates, and had helped *them* throw off the naughty measles. Joseph was responsive to him.

Downstairs, Dr. Teesdale was more serious. "Mrs. Kennard, it's the measles right enough. Joseph's a dear little fellow, but he's not in good shape to be battling measles just now. His resistance is low. Don't misunderstand; I'm not overly worried at the moment; I'm only being frank. You should bring his bed downstairs into the warm room. He's feverish. The disease always runs its course, whatever one may do; but during that time be sure to keep him warm. Let his diet be milk, bread, and light soups. Later, after the peeling period, he can go back to his usual diet. At nights, when you have a light on, put a shade round his bed. Does there happen to be anywhere that the two girls could stay meanwhile—with an auntie and uncle, maybe?"

Millie accompanied the doctor to the street, where his horse and trap were waiting. Before he drove off he said, "Millie, you and I understand each other. We both love the same Saviour, and have the same Christian hope. Get everything you need for that lad of yours. He's not at all well. I'll be round regularly until he's better. Don't worry about the bill. There won't be a penny to pay, dear girl." Then, *sub voce,* "We know what a tough time you have with. . . ." He left Mike unnamed. "Please accept this with our Christian love"—and as he shook Millie's hand, he left in it what seemed to be a tightly folded bit of paper. A crack of the whip; "Gee up!"—and he was away. When Millie opened the folded paper she saw, to her surprise, a five-pound Bank of England note. In those days, to a working-class mother, a five-pound note seemed almost a fortune.

Millie told Mike of the doctor's magnanimous gift, and urged that the very next morning he should take the girls to stay with grandma Kershaw at Rostherne. There was a railway line to Ashley, only a three-miles stretch over the fields from Rostherne. What a break for Dorothy and Mona!

Young Joseph was in for tempestuous weather. After a week the measles eruption began to fade, and the "desquamation" process began. He was so weak, however, that it was another fortnight before he could be reckoned cured. The bluish look over his body continued unduly. He did not go back to school, for the Christmas holiday was then due. It was decided to let the girls linger at Rostherne over Christmas—an expedient which proved providential, for Joseph fell sick again. The measles bout was followed by a more dangerous invader: whooping cough!

In his frail condition he was an easy prey. He took it badly. First there were the usual hoarseness and loose coughing, followed some days later, by the spasmodic retching; then the crowing sound with intake of air, and soon the terrifying "whooping." Scared little Joseph could neither keep his food down nor sleep by day or night. He became a living skeleton. His cadaverous, ghastly-pale face seemed stamped with the prophecy of death. The whooping and coughing spasms continued for weeks. Joseph would go blue with panic, clinging in stark terror to Millie. Then came the culminating ordeal. Like a ravenous beast which had been hiding and waiting, down swooped that dread killer of the weakened, lobar pneumonia, "captain of the men of death."

They were awful days. The girls were kept at Rostherne, and linked up there for schooling. Mike was either glum or raspy. Joseph was edging to the grave. Millie was overwrought through sleepless vigil. Dr. Teesdale was hardly ever away from the doorstep. The fever and coughing and chest pains tore away at the pallid little sufferer. One night a tired Dr. Teesdale put his hand on Millie's shoulder: "Millie, try to face it bravely; he's on the way out. Unless I'm much mistaken, he'll be gone before morning."

Dazed and silent, Millie heard. Mike broke the silence. With a startled look, as though he had seen an apparition, he began expostulating, "Oh, no . . . no! Oh, God, please spare him!"

Languid and heartbroken though she was, Millie could not help feeling a dull sort of wonder that Mike, after such taciturn nonchalance, should at the last minute break out in such volcanic protestation; but it was one of those esoteric contrarieties in Mike's hieroglyphic mentality which only the strange evolution of later events would interpret. His face betokened an alarm too intense for tears. His mouth sagged. His lips quivered. He sank back in his chair and sat with an empty stare.

"Doctor," said Millie, "words could never express our gratitude. You have been doctor, friend, and a hundredfold more. And now, so tenderly, you have prepared us for what seems likely. God will give us grace to bear it, if that is His will. But, doctor, I am going to spend all night in prayer that Joseph may get completely well again."

Slowly, sadly, Dr. Teesdale responded. "Mrs. Kennard, try not to think me hard. After many years in medical practice I can usually tell when a patient has passed the point of no return. My recommendation is: accept the fact. Besides, even if Joseph were to come through, he would most likely be tubercular, or, even worse, semi-imbecile, for the brain may be affected. I didn't tell you before: there's been meningitis as well as the other! No little fellow can take all this without permanent injury."

Nevertheless, through the torturous hours of that night, from that Gethsemane in Everey Street, a godly mother's pleadings broke through to the throne of Heaven with arguments more poignant than any ever heard in earthly law courts, punctuated with "Nevertheless, not my will, but Thine be done." Although it spoke soft and low down here it rang loud around the Father Heart of the universe. "Dear Lord, I vowed that if Thou shouldst send me a son, I would give him back to Thee for the ministry of the Gospel; that he might bring a multitude to know Thee. I entreat Thee now to heal Joseph either by supernatural intervention or by sovereignly controlling natural means. But, O Lord, let it not be mere survival to a life of incurably broken health. Let Joseph grow to strong manhood, as a living monument to answered prayer."

Mike dragged himself heavily upstairs, and without undressing slumped down—was it on the bed or *beside* it? Millie could not be sure. But she *was* sure of this: again and again there were weary groans as though Mike too, in his own way, was talking to the Almighty.

About ten o'clock next morning, Dr. Teesdale's horse and carriage pulled up at the Kennards'. That observant man at once noticed that the window-blind was not drawn down (the usual way of indicating death in a home). He gave three soft raps at the front door, quietly pressed down the brass latch, pushed the door slightly ajar, at the same time asking, "May I come in?"

It was Mike's deep voice which boomed, "Yes, doctor, come right in. We have a surprise for you." Both Mike and Millie looked a unique mixture of utter weariness and hectic relief. And no wonder! There was young Joseph, successfully through the crisis of that awful night, resting peacefully, the glassy look gone from his eyes, and on his face a smile for the doctor!

"A miracle!" exclaimed Dr. Teesdale. "I tell you, this is a miracle! Never before in all my twenty-five years of medical experience have I seen anything more astonishing!" His careful examination of Joseph only increased his surprise. At once he began giving careful instructions to Millie and Mike as to what to do, and what food to give Joseph. "Millie," he added, "I'd like to know what sort of prayer brought such an answer."

Overjoyed Millie had a tongue loosed by sheer gratitude. She explained: "Doctor, on the ground of Scripture passages like Matthew 18, I believe that all who die in infancy are saved; that they are the special treasure of our Lord, purchased by the atonement made for us all through His precious blood. No infant is a Christ-rejector. All such are His, as He said. Also, dear doctor, I believe that all who pass from here to yonder as babes or children *grow* there. They do not remain static. Just as they would have grown to maturity here on earth, so do they grow to lovely maturity up there. I believe there is a wonderful nursery and kindergarten there, with angel guardians and teachers.

"I told God last night that if He preferred to take Joseph and educate him up yonder for some beautiful ministry there, away from this troubled earth, I would acquiesce and praise Him. But then I reminded God that I had already covenanted with Him to set Joseph apart for the ministry of the Gospel here on earth, and that the greatest of all ministries was winning souls for Christ. So I pleaded that for the sake of the many whom Joseph might bring to the Savior, here on earth, God would spare him. But I said that I did not want him spared unless he was going to have thoroughly healed lungs; no brain damage; and restoration to robust health. Then I pleaded hard that God would give me a pledge from His written Word, and He did. It was Psalm 30, verse 5.

> "Weeping may endure in the evening,
> But singing cometh with the morning."

"Oh, doctor, my prayer is answered; and I have a God-given pledge in my heart. This is only the beginning. Big things are wrapped up in our dear little Joseph."

Later that day a large parcel came, addressed to "Master Joseph Kennard." Its contents were enough to bring a flush of exhilaration even into the cheeks of the emaciated patient. Talk about a cornucopia!—it seemed like an advance installment of the Millennium! Never before had such a parcel come to that little dwelling. There were apples and oranges, large black grapes, four large bottles of "Cod Liver Oil and Malt," four big jars of "Benger's Food for Invalids," two king-sized bottles of "Scot's Emulsion," two large bottles of "tonic" mixtures, four squat jars of beef extract, packets of nuts, raisins, and dried fruits. Fastened to the parcel was a note to Millie, giving her instruction as to how to flush the cottage with fresh air regularly without risk of chill to Joseph, and what to watch for in her daily caring for the patient. Pinned to the letter was another five-pound note.

It was mid-February before the girls came back from Rostherne. It had been wonderful, staying with grandpa and grandma Kershaw, but once the January cold and snow had hit the flat farmlands round there, the charms of Rostherne had paled. The biting winds and pitch-dark nights began to induce thoughts of mother and Joseph; of a bright incandescent gas-mantle giving lots of light in which to read or play—instead of the low-burning oil-lamp at grandpa's; of a kitchen tap which poured water out at the turn of a hand day or night—instead of grandpa's squeaking old pump across the shivering cobblestones outside; of paved streets with flagged footpaths lit by big iron street-lamps, where lads and lassies all muffled up in their winter clothes played games which kept them running and laughing and warm.

Yes, let it be admitted, there are times just now and then when even those lamp-lit town streets with their rows and rows of brick cottages all cuddling together in urban closeness as though to keep each other warm, can seem more inviting than the dark, bleak, country lane. Dorothy and Mona did not exactly say it, but they felt it. So, although they were genuinely sorry to leave grandpa and grandma Kershaw, they fairly bounced into Millie's embrace when she met them at the Manchester station.

It was a touching yet almost hilarious reunion. Millie's heart beat with quickened thankfulness as she saw how unfeignedly the three children loved each other. Dorothy hugged Joseph, and cried. Mona hugged him, and giggled. Joseph just did not know how to get the right words. His feelings were running backwards and forwards somewhere in between those of Dorothy and Mona, like a glee-car shuttling between Crytown and Gigglestown.

Nor was it a merely transient display. During the ensuing

weeks it expressed itself in unforgettable ways. Joseph's convalescence after his critical encounter with death was better than normal, but the doctor would not let him go back to school. Dorothy was like a fairy godmother to Joseph. It was she who jumped up in the mornings to make a nice hot drink for him. It was she who asked Miss Wardie, the headmistress, if the school books could be loaned for Joseph to read at home. It was she who asked Miss Thwaite, his class teacher, if she would set lessons each week for him. It was she who sat with him night after night, teaching him reading, writing, spelling, figures and simple arithmetic. She just loved it—and her pupil. She was a young genius, just as kind as she was brisk, and knew how to boss Joseph with the lightness of a feather. Truth to tell, Joseph's quick mind "caught on" to far more through his communicative sister than he would have learned at school, where the class had to slow its pace to suit its less brainy members. It was Dorothy, too, who used to grumble him into being "a tidy boy"; to leave his boots clean and shiny for the next morning; to hang or fold his clothes; to brush his teeth and comb his hair with a straight "parting" on the left side. There was many a tussle to get her protege's compliance, but she knew where Joseph was ticklish, and how to trick a stern impasse into tickle-produced laughter. She had those mothering qualities which often develop most noticeably in the eldest child of a family: so perhaps it was not surprising that by the time she was a young teenager her ambition was to be a trained nurse—"in the dark blue uniform."

Mona also made her contribution, though in characteristically different style. She had an inborn aptitude for killing two birds with one stone. She showed Joseph how to play games—she so loved them herself. It was she who taught him checkers, dominoes, ludo, tiddly-winks, snakes and ladders. Happy were those evening hours, now and then, when all five of the Kennard household together sat round the table for dominoes or "snap cards." Mona was full of girlish sentiment. What she did not give in practical help she made up for in sisterly hugs. Joseph could do nothing wrong, or, if he did, Mona would gladly take the rap in his place. On his sixth birthday, in the February, her present to him was a penny "Spanish juice stick" (a penny was no little wealth to a young girl in those days among poorer people) and a "Spanish juice stick" was enough to set any little boy's saliva glands slavering anticipatively. However, with that diplomacy which was pleasantly peculiar to her, she explained to Joseph that as the Spanish juice stick was seven inches long, she thought it unwise he should have so much after such an illness, and she had therefore cut two-and-a-half inches of it off, which she herself would imbibe for *his* sake!

There had been early snow that winter, but none later. The weather was wet rather than normally cold. After a blustery March, Spring smiled in earlier than usual. Doctor Teesdale had continued calling each week or two. "Millie," he remarked one morning, "this is our chance to put the finishing touches on Joseph's recovery. He's won a grand battle, but the enemy has left the Joseph kingdom badly knocked about. Besides, if he doesn't build strong ramparts now, who knows whether the enemy may attack again later? I think you should bundle him off to Rostherne as soon as May gets well in. This crowded, smoky area is not the ideal place for Joseph just now. The fresh air of the open country would do more for him at this stage than anything else."

Millie discussed it with Mike. The latter was at once in favor, though, unhappily, not from the motive Millie had hoped to find. Up from mysterious deeps in Mike's unpredictable disposition there had erupted a new peevishness toward Joseph. The same Mike who had shown palpitating agitation when Joseph tottered on the brink of the Beyond was irritable, even malicious, toward him now that he had taken a new hold on life. Furthermore, Millie knew that a major hindrance to Joseph's full recovery was his ingrained dread of his father.

Anyway, in the "merry month of May," away we go— Millie, Dorothy, Mona, Joseph, on the "puffer" (railway train) to Knutsford and the sub-station at Ashley, right in the heart of Cheshire's fertile plain, where grandpa Kershaw meets us, carries the straw valise containing Joseph's clothes, and escorts us along thin footpaths through the fields to Rostherne.

Grandpa, now in his sixties, looks hearty but older. He beams on the three children, and oh, what a caress for his own dear daughter, his favorite Millie! There is so much to talk about. Words trip each other up, and clauses tumble into each other as thoughts hurry into speech.

Three more fields, and there it is—the old row of five cottages smothered in late Spring loveliness. The first of the five is grandpa's; and at the door waits a smiling grandma with kisses of welcome. It is Saturday. Millie and the girls are there only until Monday, but Joseph is there (as it transpires) for five months.

What a weekend! How glad the Rostherne folk are to see Millie again!—and the two girls, and Millie's own little son! How sorry they are about his illness! They'll "see to it" that Rostherne makes a "strapping young gent" of him! How moving it is to Millie, being back in the dear old church on the Sunday morning! What memories dance round the mind! Why do they truantly refuse to behave even while the minister is preaching? Why do those silly tears persist in trickling down her face just when she wants to look sedate amid those oblique glances of former chums and neighbors! The three children, after whispery perplexity about when to stand, sit, kneel, and where to find the psalms, litanies, and other parts of the Anglican liturgy, now sit with wondering attentiveness during the sermon. The preacher is not the Rostherne incumbent, but a visiting clergyman. Millie is impressed by the simplicity and practicalness of his homily. To the children he seems to float up into the sky like a kite flying very high on a windy day, but to their relief he knows how to haul himself down again in the nick of time for the final hymn.

Later that Sabbath, while her parents and the three children linger at the teatable, Millie slips out and makes her way down the lane back to the church. Three quarters of an hour yet before vespers, but the church door, as often, is left unlocked. The sun is westering amid an orange and crimson embroidery. A playful breeze wafts gauzy

cloudlets across the sky like trailing veils of muslin. To the
east the sky is royal blue. The countryside has robed itself
again in vernal green and floral beauty. All these, reflected
in the water, are turning Rostherne Mere into a liquid
loveliness almost like those limpid, rich-hued lakes which lie
placid as mirrors amid the Alps. Through the lychgate
Millie diverts her steps round by the side of the church,
picking her way among the well-known gravestones, then
through tangling grass, reeds, and straggling groundsel to
the edge of the mere.

How quiet it is after Manchester! How deliciously lonely
after the endless clatter of clogs! How irenic after the
thudding traffic and clangor of tramcars! How soothing, this
peaceful scene, the hum of insects, the evenfall warbling of
the birds from their leafy coverts! Was this a lovely world
handed down from yesterday which the smoky industry of
tomorrow would choke till it died? Oh, those Satanic cities,
with their foul breeding-swamps of temptation, their ven-
omous slums, their grinding poverty, their moral grime,
their broken hearts! Who could endure those cities after
this?

Millie strolled along the water's edge. The breeze was
fretting the water into slantwise wavelets across the lake.
The reflected colors of sky and lakeside greenery gave
them a scintillating iridescence seen only in early morning
or at evening while the sun is low in the heavens. To Millie
it was enchanting as never before. Now she paused. This
was the spot where Mike had held her in his arms and
smothered her with kisses and made fulsome promises. She
sat down and relived it all. She had thought that the feeling
in her heart must be what people called love. Yet even
then, as she now ruefully reflected, Mike's glamorous as-
surances had seemed suspiciously like "sounding brass" and
"tinkling cymbal." Poor Mike! What a catastrophe of natural
gift without moral grit! Tomorrow she must go back to him.
What about that bigger tomorrow of all the years ahead?

How swiftly, all in a few vivid moments, memory can
panoram the years! And how startling, how convincing are
those seconds when, as by a lightning flash, we "see" with

extraordinary lucidity the hidden meanings of things, and sense a sovereign control leading to a final harmony! Something of that happened as Millie sat there.

And now she glances up at the old square tower. The clock looks down at her so understandingly. It has watched so many and could say so much. At the moment it tells her that there is still over half an hour before evensong. She treads quietly from the fringe of the lake to the tower door. Now she is inside the church. She has gone there to pray—alone. Yes, alone, yet never in her life was she less so. The Presence which means everything to Millie is suddenly luminous. It seems as though the light of the heavenly Shekinah is shimmering through the sanctuary.

She tiptoes to the chancel and halts momentarily where she stood and gave her "I will" on the wedding day. Now she pauses behind the lectern, noticing that the large Bible happens to be open at the thirty-first chapter of Jeremiah. After this she finds the usual Kershaw pew toward the rear of the nave, and amid the mystic stillness pours out her heart in prayer.

"O God, the God of all compassion, who long ago didst hear Hannah's prayers at Shiloh for little Samuel, and make Samuel so great a spiritual leader, I pray for my own little Joseph. Please enwrap him likewise in Thy warm care, and make him a true man of God. As Thou didst answer my prayer when he was at death's door, may it now please Thee to bring him through healthy boyhood to buoyant youth and manhood. Guard him and guide him. Keep him pure in mind. Open his heart early to receive the Saviour. Tutor him in spiritual truths, and make him a true prophet of Thy Word who shall win a multitude to a knowledge of salvation. Hear my many prayers, also, for our two precious daughters, that they too may early know and love the Saviour. Gracious God, hear my sorrowing pleadings again for my husband. Strike deeply, somehow, into his conscience. Startle him into a realization of his lost condition. . . ."

At this point Millie's tears began to flow. Underneath her sturdy nature there had lurked of late a disturbing fear that her strength could not hold out indefinitely to cope with such a dreary, wearing problem as Mike. She now prayed that God would open up for her some local work which, besides providing some further income, would bring blessing to those women in the Ancoats slums. Nay, why should she limit God's answer to Ancoats? (she reasoned). Should she not pray God to open up some suitable and remunerating occupation *away* from the big city, in some town near the hills, which would do so much for Joseph's health, and get Mike away from evil companions? But was there mission work in any of the smaller towns away from Manchester? She hardly thought so.

Millie was not of the imaginative sort, but at that instant the Presence which enveloped her *spoke*—with that voice which is as clear to the mind as a human voice is to the natural ear. "Millie, read the open page on the lectern again." She hasted up the aisle. Yes, the lectern Bible was open at Jeremiah 31. Through one of the church windows at that moment a long, thin shaft of light from the westering sun pointed like a shining finger to verse 16. *"Thus saith the Lord; Refrain thy voice from weeping, and thine eyes from tears; for thy work shall be rewarded."*

As royal David once danced before the ark of the covenant, so Millie could have danced with holy mirth down the aisle in Rostherne Church; but at that climactic moment she heard the loud click of the large door-latch. The verger had come, accompanied by the first three arrivals for the hour of worship. He and Millie knew each other. "Good evening, Millie! You're here well afore time, I see."

With eyes still moist but glistening Millie responded, "Yes, I came early to linger with my memories for a little while—where I was married in July 1890." And after that honest verisimilitude she returned to the Kershaw pew, quietly to await the service.

Some of the world's famous diamonds have had turbulent histories. The Sanci diamond, so named after a French nobleman, was sent by him to King Henry IV of France; but the messenger was intercepted and assassinated. Later, however, the corpse was located and opened, whereupon the diamond was discovered in the stomach, having been swallowed by the faithful servant to prevent its being stolen. It was a feeling of "I'm carrying a hidden diamond" that Millie took the girls (and Jeremiah 31:16) back to Manchester. Her plucky, playful spirit was revived by what she believed to be a heaven-sent reassurance. Mike was no different except that morally he had permanently learned a lesson, and kept scrupulously true to his vow of sexual cleanliness. Never again would that fuddle-minded Samson be in the arms of double-crossing Delilahs.

It would be unfair to call Mike a lazy lout, for he could work like a Trojan at anything he liked. Yet he could lounge about in obviously enjoyable idleness. In one mood he would be as agile as a young orangutan, in another as lazy as Neptune taking a hundred and sixty-four years to dawdle round the sun. His moods strangely affected his face. In one mood his moustache and beard would be as stiff as a witch's broom; at other times as limp as damp hay, and his look that of a weary homing pigeon. In his spruce humors he could look commanding as the Ymer of Norse myth; at other times as ugly as a wart hog. Twice, now, he had got himself into the "jim-jams" (delirium tremens). He had known the "vapours" (fits of depression) and the "blues" (hypochondria). Yet, on the other hand, he had amazing recuperative powers, both mental and physical. He was an avid reader of literature both good and otherwise—political, technological, social, antequarian, *ad lib*, which gave him an engaging even though superficial virtuosity.

True, he had gone the round, seeking fresh employment; but the mill, the engineering plant, the warehouse, any kind of manual labor, was beneath his level. His must be a white-collar job. But if that cut down the range of possible employment, much more did the fact that he had been dismissed from his former job. Yet in going round after jobs he would strut in and out like a generalissimo; then in the evening sit down in jobless misery feeling like a planet lost from its orbit and in outer darkness. Poor Mike! all in one, an insatiate braggadocio with spread-eagle gait, and yet inwardly as lonely as a lost partridge in the mountains; often wandering up and down like a stranger in his own mind.

The fact remained: Mike was still out of work. In those

days there was no out-of-work pay. The only Kershaw income was that mysterious month-end jingle of gold sovereigns in Mike's pocket. Millie had by this time reasoned that inasmuch as Dorothy was now twelve and Mona eleven in a few months, they could safely be left for an hour or two on weekdays, and she herself could seek part-time occupation in mission work. She offered herself at the Manchester headquarters. Seven or eight weeks later one of the women missionaries was transferred from the Ancoats area to Bolton, making a gap which Millie's part-time service filled admirably. Millie had her mornings free, and the whole of Saturday. Thus she was able to attend to the house and make the nourishing main meal each midday. In the afternoons she gave herself to the activities of the district mission center. Precocious Dorothy was Millie's unfailing domestic lieutenant. Always when Millie returned at early evening the house was tidied, the table set for teatime, and preparations made ready for the finalizing takeover by mother. The plan worked with little discomfort to anyone, especially during the lighter months between Spring and Autumn.

As for Joseph, Rostherne was as nearly Paradise as his imagination could conceive. He revelled in it. The pallid little invalid who had been indoors for weeks on end was now outdoors from early morning until twilight lost itself in the deeper dusk. The only "fly in the ointment" was that his "dearest mother in all the world" and the two girls were not there. Even that, however, was happily offset inasmuch as every third Friday Millie came over for the weekend and brought either Dorothy or Mona with her.

What wonders those months of Summer sun and country air and outdoor life worked in Millie's wee laddie! The match-stick legs became well-fleshed and sturdy. The lean face and pasty skin became oval and ruddy. The sunken eyes with their haunted look began to sparkle with zest and joy of living. On her fourth visit, at the end of three months, Millie could scarcely credit that he was the same Joseph; that such a bonny, handsome boy had been embryonic in her fragile, skin-and-bone little invalid. But he was still the same Joseph in gentle disposition, and more than ever a mother's boy. Millie was his idol; the most perfect mother God ever made. From the minute of her arrival he was all hers. It was touching to see. Millie's heart danced. Still ringing in her mind was that verse in Psalm 30 which God had given her during that agonizing night of prayer when Joseph seemed to be dying: "Weeping may endure in the evening, but singing cometh with the morning." There was new music in that stanza now; and there was still more singing to come, had Millie known it; singing even though there were more tears to weep; singing which would go on and on when tragedy and mystery and the last of the tears had been wiped away.

SEVEN
Time Brings Changes

Oh, that Summer at Rostherne! Joseph, now six and a half, became a most devoted assistant to grandpa Kershaw, who had a large allotment at the rear of his cottage—a miniature farmyard except that there were no sheep, cows or horses. At the far end there was a piggery wherein were two parent pigs and several piglings. Nearer the house was a hen-run housing a coop, a loud-crowing rooster and a seraglio of plump hens. Between that and the red-brick backyard where the pump stood were well-kept plots of vegetables, lettuce, celery, rhubarb, and even a strawberry bed. Down each side were gooseberry bushes and blackberry brambles; and in a row down the middle were two apple trees, a pear tree and two plum trees. All that, and such a riot of flowers as Joseph had never seen before. Singing birds nested round there such as never entertained city dwellers; and as a bass antiphony to the soprano trillers and warblers there was the undertone cawing of the crows from their rookeries in the old oaks.

It was all a Garden of Eden to Joseph. Never was he happier than when helping in it. Now that grandpa was retired his sole occupation was his puttering round there. He loved to dawdle round with young Joseph, holding many a drawling causerie on domestic gardening. Never did he work in better soil than the fertile mind of his inquisitive little grandson.

Thus did that Elysian Summer go smiling by, holding its magic wand of healing over the wee laddie from Manchester. The weather clerk was in his most propitious mood, sending week after week of prodigal sunshine from fleckless skies, and balmy breezes cooling the gracious hours and diffusing the scent of a myriad blooms. No wrinkled hand of drought touched the fair scene, for gentle but ample rains refreshed it at just the right intervals. Indeed, most of the kindly showers came after nightfall, as though the admiring sky, too shy to kiss the lovely face of Summer during the daytime, came with secret kisses while the sun was away. Rostherners said there had never been a better Summer.

When Joseph arrived there, tulip and daffodil time still lingered. After that he was able to watch the sweet peas decorate the trellis, and the roses blush into full bloom, and the calendulas reach their brightest flame among the petunias and blue lobelia and laughing carnations—which grandpa called "roses gone wild with joy." He saw May and June transform the rhododendron bushes into gorgeous tapestries and turn the lilac and laburnum trees into delicately attired brides. He gambolled at will among the daisies and buttercups and dandelions which made the meadow in front of the cottage a brightly-patterned green carpet. Nor least was the wonder of the cornfields, in which he watched the grain grow from infant stalk to tall yellow and Autumn gold. For the first time in his life the city laddie saw the fruit "come on," especially the apples and pears, right from the blossom-shedding, through weeks when they were little hard knobs, then shapely green balls, and finally plumped-out, red-cheeked, delicious fruit. Fairyland had become real.

Dotted around Rostherne were the homes of the rich, the "landed gentry." They too were an eye-opener to our little town-boy. They seemed like gods from Olympus. Out they came in their phaetons or four-wheeled landaus, the folding tops turned back so that their occupants might enjoy the sunshine; shafts and wheels and lamps burnished and shiny; their well-groomed horses wearing natty little caps over forelock and ears to keep the naughty flies out, and colorful quilts from withers to croup, to cover them if the sun was over-attentive. In the driver's seat up front the family groom would be donned in smart Summer livery. In the carriage would be the ladies—the matrons sitting in Victorian aplomb with their close-fitting, fancy bodices and plumaged hats, and white-gloved hands holding pretty parasols; and the prim, young daughters, charming in daintiest dresses and sashes, wearing petite bonnets with silk chin-strings, or maybe bright hair-ribbons with a rose or two among the side-tresses.

The upper-class homes had a surround of fenced-in acres. If the house was near the road there would be a high wall covered with green climbers. Now and again when Joseph and grandpa were out walking grandpa would lift his curious young pal shoulder-high to glimpse over. Such "country seats" with their terraced paths and croquette lawns were marvels to Joseph. In one garden he actually saw a game of croquette in progress. The click of the mallets and the scooting of the blue, red, yellow, and black balls through the hoops or in collision with each other so had his eyes popping that grandpa could scarce carry him away. In another garden Joseph's hungry eyes almost stared themselves away at a little boy and his sister riding round on pet ponies. How wonderful to belong to the "gentry"!

Persons brought up in modern America, where the usual social superiority is the quasi aristocracy of "What are you in dollars?"—or people bred in Britain's present "Welfare State," can hardly imagine rural England of the late eighteen hundreds, when the gulf between hereditary upper-rank and commonalty was as subtle as the dusk but as rigid as caste. Aristocracy was not so much a matter of money as of inherited breeding. Owing to misfortunes there were poorer families here and there among the upper class, yet they were still "gentry." Their brogue and manners, their education at exclusively high-breed schools and colleges, and their cultured superiority complex, gave them an invisible but unmistakable badge.

We may well be relieved that those days are gone; yet we have reason to bemoan that in ousting things which were wrong we have martyred decencies which kept life sweet and desirable. Besides the pseudo-dignity of those times with its starch and swagger, there were the genuine gentlemen and gentlewomen whose benevolence, refined manners and exemplary integrity gave a healthy lead to the common folk. There was a general respect for upright moral standards, a public reverence for things sacred, and a keen sense of shock at the vulgar—attitudes which are sadly lacking nowadays. We are so "advanced" today that virtue is derided and vulgarity paraded.

When young Joseph grew robust again at Rostherne life was not the feverish scramble it is today. No smog dragged its poisonous curtains of carbon monoxide and chemical irritants between men and the skies. The automobile had not sent the black dragon of death rampaging on congested highways. The streams and lakes were unsullied. Jets and supersonic aircraft had not drowned out the songbirds or violated the silence of starry night. Lovely world of yesterday!—removed from us by only a stone's throw, yet as inexorably irrecoverable as the years before the Flood! Men had time to listen and learn the mystic language of Nature.

Our precocious young Joseph got a kindergarten initiation into it during the Summer at Rostherne, and a love of Nature which lasted a lifetime. By mid-September the sun drooped west sooner in his shortening circuit, and twilight more quickly shaded into dusk. With rapt gaze Joseph would watch those late-season sunset pageantries through fretwork patterns of silhouetted trees. Though so young, he had a pensive responsiveness to the languid quietude of the countryside twilight and dusk. He would lie awake in bed with the fragrance of garden and orchard wafted through the half-open sash of the gable window. It would seem as though time were pleasantly loitering to the slow tick-tock of the aged grandfather clock down in the lobby. He would hear the whisperings of the old oaks and chestnuts, sharing secrets amid the creeping shadows, as the evening breeze rustled their drowsy boughs. Soon the moon would peep in through the window—but never once found our little man awake.

Tears were shed when the day came to leave his enchanted haven. The one consolation was that he would be back with the mother whom he idolized and his dear sisters. Millie and the two girls came over to fetch him. Dorothy said he was taller. Mona said he was fatter. Millie saw that in every way he looked fitter. There were frolics over the meadow. Joseph showed the girls some of his handiwork among plant plots and flower beds. The girls wanted to know whether he was strong enough to pull water from the obstinate old pump. It took Dorothy and Mona, struggling together till their faces were red, to pull the wiggly iron arm down forcefully enough to get a gush—and then they both got their legs drenched!

Grandpa and grandma Kershaw accompanied them to Ashley station. Dorothy and Mona carried bags of fruit from the garden, both having trouble with their saliva glands. While they waited for "puffing Billy" grandpa said he would sadly miss his young pal who had helped with the hoeing and raking and weeding and pruning—and a glistening tear showed he keenly meant it. Grandma just "didn't know what she'd do" without her kitchen assistant to scrape the potatoes or mash the carrots or chop the cabbage, cut the rhubarb, trim the gooseberries, help bottle the pears, and dry the dinner dishes. When the train slowly glided out of the station the dear old couple looked very lonely as they wept and waved their fond good-bye.

Undeniably, Everey Street, Manchester, was drab after Rostherne; instead of a green-carpeted meadow in front of the cottage, a row of smoke-darkened houses; and instead of a red-tiled patio and old pump and fruit trees and flowery trellis and herbaceous borders to look at through the rear window, a cramped, stone-flagged bit of a yard with a rickety coalshed in it; and instead of the slow, restful tick-tock, of the grandfather pendulum, the impatient ticka-ticka-ticka of the little alarm-clock on the mantelpiece; and instead of the early morning cock-crowing, the blaring "buzzers" (steam sirens) of the factories! Yet that little cottage with its two rooms downstairs and two upstairs had something

Rostherne did *not* have. It was *home,* where the "most wonderful mother in all the world" lived.

Had Joseph only known it, he was to spend all the next two Summers and most of four others at Rostherne, with results beyond surmise. That he should go there again was decided for three reasons. Dr. Teesdale advised it. Grandpa and grandma wanted it. Joseph loved it. At the beginning of each Summer the magnanimous doctor increased his share-hold in Joseph's future by another five-pound note. If we may anticipate for a moment: during his third Summer at Rostherne (then in his ninth year) Joseph found a bosom pal in a wealthy farmer's son. Besides running his sizeable farm, Wilfred's father bred and trained horses. Joseph and Wilfred became inseparable. As a by-product Joseph had his first lessons in milking cows, riding horses, and much more, every long Summer holiday until he was thirteen years old. However, while Joseph was only nine, something happened which changed the whole course of things both for himself and the Kennard family. So, for the moment, back we go to watch the incipient drama at Everey Street, Manchester.

Millie had now taken part-time employ with the City Mission. The next year Dorothy reached her thirteenth birthday, so finished at school. As she was not going to secondary school (few did then) the natural thing was to get work, but that posed a problem. If Dorothy went out to work, Millie could hardly keep her own part-time mission work, for Dorothy would not be able to help in the home as hitherto; nor could Dorothy, while so young, earn as much as Millie. Since income was a prior concern, the decision was reached that for the time being Dorothy should stay home and look after the house, thus enabling Millie to retain her staff work with the mission.

Golden-haired Dorothy was such a capable, conscientious young soul, the arrangement proved efficacious. She was a more enterprising cook than her mother. With few exceptions she put on excellent meals most economically. She had gusto along with quick intelligence, and worked like a young Spartan to keep the house spick-and-span. She so revelled in being domestic manageress it left her with surplus energy which, with characteristic initiative, she put to other good use. She signed on at the Technical College for "Evening School," taking courses in commercial book-keeping, shorthand, and typing. As for Mike, he was still the touchy problem. Micawber-like, he was still "expecting something to turn up," still flying big ideas like fancy balloons which somehow always got deflated in mid air by an invisible pin. In all fairness, maybe he merited sympathy. Trying to find a commensurate job for a man of such impressive dimensions had been a march of misery. With the voice and bearing of a company director he nowhere found a clerk's bench able to carry his weight of dignity. He would scan the newspaper for "possibles" and go off next morning with a dozen "good hopes," only to have them all knocked down like a row of skittles. At last, fortune smiled. He was given a job as accounting clerk with a wholesale grocery firm. For over a year and a half he stayed with it, during which time he regained the feeling of being "the man of the house," bringing a decent wage home every weekend. Then bad luck scowled again. The firm amalgamated with another company. Several newer employees were laid off— Mike being one of them.

It nearly knocked him out. He barely struggled to his feet trying to hit back at hard luck; but that invisible assailant always dodged him and struck again. In other words, Mike now encountered a trade depression which begot new depression in *him.* He "hung his harp on the willows" and slumped into self-commiseration. He became saturnine, grouchy; one day taciturn and melancholy, the next day glowering with choleric temper. Millie's most perturbing perplexity was that his spleen was again peculiarly against unoffending young Joseph, as though by recondite deduction he blamed their own boy for such ill fortune. The haunted look began to creep back into Joseph's eyes; and sometimes, after Mike's thunder-claps, Joseph had a cadaverous paleness which reminded Millie of that awful night when he had almost faded away. The only one who seemed to have any irenic influence over Mike was Mona, who was very much "bone of his bone and flesh of his flesh." Millie was relieved when the time came for Joseph's third Summer at Rostherne.

Then Millie came to a far-reaching decision. She found

herself musing: "Why did we settle here after our marriage? Simply because Mike's job was here. Since he no longer has employment, why need we stay longer? Are there not good reasons for moving? Mike would probably find it easier to get employ in a less congested area, and where he was not known. Maybe they could live in a town near the Pennine Hills where the air was fresher and they could go for outings during warmer weather. How good that would be for the children—especially Joseph! But where could the new place be?

Then, like a sudden shaft of light through a cloud-break, an idea shot into Millie's mind which she felt was heaven-sent. After cogitating several days her mind was made up. At the headquarters of the City Mission she interviewed the superintendent, and explained that as Dorothy had now finished school and Mona was in her last year there, she herself was free again for the work she loved. Did he know of any town in Lancashire, Cheshire, Yorkshire, where there might be an opening? Naturally, his first suggestion was that she rejoin the Manchester staff, though he sympathetically concurred with her reasons for preferring elsewhere.

There was one other reason for Millie's decision. After Mike's dismissal from the grocery firm not only had there been sulks and fulminations against fate, but a lapse into drinking and bad company. Once again he was off to the Droylesden cock-fights and the Fallowfield races. Even more ill-boding was the jingle of money in his pockets afterwards. From a woman at the mission Millie gleaned that he had become a bookie earning commission on other men's bets. She was anxious to tear him away from those demoralizing associations.

When a strategic moment presented itself she challenged him. His reaction was in characteristic phases: first sullen, then vehement, then verbosely defensive. "Millie, I swear to God, I'll never break my vow about those slimy women. I've seen 'em for what they really are—demons in female flesh, the devil's filthy poison-vipers. They'll never get their grinning fangs into this man's flesh again! I could strangle all the damned lot of 'em. And, Millie, God strike me dead on the spot if I'm lying, but I've never put one penny of my

own on any of those gambling tickets. I only act as a go-
between, being sharp at figures, and make a bit of commission. There's nothing dishonest in that. How would *you*
feel, Millie, if you couldn't get a job, and lived off your wife's
earnings? If I could get a job worthy of my exceptional
qualities, do you think I'd come down to . . . to this?"

"Mike," replied Millie, "you know just as well as I do that
the end never justifies the means. I sympathize with your
motive, but I'm heartsick to think that my gifted husband is
back at the swine swill. You may try to justify it to me,
Mike, but can you justify it to God? You have asked me how
I would feel in *your* place. Let me ask how *you* would feel in
my place. My slum work takes me into house after house
where drink and gambling have brought wretchedness—
broken homes, broken hearts, broken health; furniture
gone to the pawn-shop; children starved and in rags. Mike,
drinking and gambling are the fiends that turn husbands
into villains and happy homes into hell on earth. And must
my husband, of all men, become the devil's office-boy? Oh,
Mike, Mike!—what about our own three children? It seems
to me that God is giving you a last chance to break off
before *they* get to know and shudder."

Mike now sat there in morose silence.

Millie sat and watched.

Eventually Mike spoke, "Millie, what on earth can I do?"

That was the chance for which she had been waiting.
She told him of her thoughts about leaving that drab locality for a more salubrious area, perhaps one of the smaller
towns nearer the open country, where Mike would probably have a better chance of getting a job more in keeping
with his abilities, and where the fresher air would be beneficial to all of them. She also reported her interview at City
Mission headquarters. "Mike," she asked, "would you be
agreeable to going, if an opening comes for me?"

Mike's reaction reminded Millie of a watery-eyed sun
trying to smile through sopping clouds. With comical self-
commendation, as though Millie's suggestion were merely
an echo of his own mind, he replied, "D'you know, Millie,
I've kept saying something like this would turn up, haven't
I?"

From that point onwards Mike was the chief enthusiast

for the proposed relocation. In fact, Millie had to quell his effervescent eagerness, reminding him that there might not be any opening for mission work outside Manchester for a considerable while.

However, just when Millie was most resignedly schooling herself in patient waiting, there came the "bolt from the blue." The postman delivered a letter to her from the City Mission superintendent saying that the Watch Committee in the town of *Elmerton* had written him concerning a new project. They were forming the Elmerton "Police Court Mission," to work primarily among erring women, and had been urged to write him, asking if he, out of his comprehensive knowledge of mission work, had any suggestion he might care to make. He had now replied, recommending Millie.

Out came the map book. To be sure, Elmerton was among the mills, but it was a smaller town and skirted the Pennines. Could this be the answer? She was tempted to share the letter with Mike but decided against doing so, lest it should shoot him sky high and then let him down in deep dudgeon. In any case, it might be months before she heard from Elmerton. Committees usually act slowly.

As it turned out, she had not long to wait. Two weeks later a courteous letter came from a Mr. Alexander Pomeroy, chairman of the Elmerton Watch Committee, inviting Millie's application, telling her the required qualifications and the kind of work envisaged. Millie lost no time in complying, though she was careful not to appear as if she were throwing herself at them.

Ten days later Mr. Pomeroy wrote again requesting that she come for a chat with himself and two others at the City Mission headquarters in Manchester. The interview proved most congenial. Mr. Pomeroy promised to report back to his colleagues and then apprise Millie of the result.

It took all Millie's power of self-restraint not to share the exciting likelihood with Mike, but she deemed it diplomatic to keep her secret until there came some definite invitation from Elmerton. It came immediately after the next meeting of the Elmerton Watch Committee; but although phrased with unmistakable cordiality it contained a proviso which left it even yet unfinalized. The ratifying of the invitation was left contingent on Millie's going for an informal meeting with the Watch Committee in Elmerton. The letter begged Millie not to feel reluctance; the venture was new; they were anxious equally for Millie's sake as their own not to make a mistake. The proposed meeting would be of a social kind. They would all be so glad to meet her, and value any advice she could give them. Also, in the event of her coming to live in Elmerton, this would be a useful introduction to friends who were to be loyal supporters of the police court mission work.

Millie went on the day appointed (as we have related), and was "officially invited."

It was near the end of the month. Mike had gone away on another of those strange month-end absences. For the first time Millie had risked leaving the children overnight on their own. Therefore it was a relief to find, on her return, that lieutenant Dorothy had everything well in hand. Mona and Joseph were at school. The house was clean and tidy. An appetizing odor came from the kitchen, where the meat and vegetables were cooking. Dorothy showed Millie a secret knock on the wall which the three children had arranged to give the Bennetts, next door, in case of emergency.

That evening Millie told them they would soon be leaving there, and going to live in Elmerton. As she described that town and its two lovely parks, pleasant shopping center, its lake for boating and the Pennine Range in the distance, and the good-natured people of the Watch Committee, their eyes fairly goggled. Into their young world a new wonder had shone. When bedtime came it was not easy to lull them to sleep. Mona could not stop talking. Joseph could not stop listening. Dorothy could not stop asking. Eventually they dropped off quietly into dreamland with a gleaming new fairyland to fill it.

Mike drifted back the next day in jaunty mood. From somewhere he had replenished his exchequer again and handed to Millie three gold sovereigns. Millie, too, was feeling sprightly, anticipating his pleasure at the good news about Elmerton. That pleasure had to be postponed until

Dorothy went to do the shopping at the local "Cooperative Society" store. Then Millie told him.

Lancashire is famous for its changeable weather, but no Lancashire sky ever changed as quickly as Mike's face when Millie mentioned *Elmerton*. She gasped at the frightening effect. The bland dispenser of gold sovereigns suddenly blazed into raging temper. His large face took on a glowering ugliness. He raised his big, flabby fist as though to strike Millie, but even as he swung it, in that fraction of a second, he decided to let it bang on the table instead; for even in such a blinding fury he respected—or even in his strange way loved—Millie too much to harm her.

"What the blazes have you said you'll go *there* for? Of all places on this cursed earth that's the one I didn't even want to see! Dang it! we're not going!"

For the moment Millie was flabbergasted. Was this just sheer cussedness on Mike's part? Or was there in reality some deep-buried reason for his not wanting to go to *Elmerton?*

"Mike," she said, "we haven't gone yet; and you know that if there actually were some valid reason why *you* should not go, we would alter our plans. But, Mike, you must not fool me. This is too big a matter. In any case, temper never put anything right; it only makes things worse. Simmer down and get control of yourself before Dorothy comes back with the groceries."

With the gloom of Erebus still darkening his visage, Mike peevishly sat down, though like a dragon ready to snort fire again from distended nostrils. Then, slowly, the snorting tendency subsided into heavy breathing, then broody silence.

Millie resumed. "Let's get one thing straight, Mike, while we're alone. Is this outburst of yours just pretense?— or is there some real reason why, strangely enough, you don't want to go to Elmerton?"

Mike remained mute and somber.

So Millie continued. "A moment ago, Mike, you brought me right to the edge of a decision which I nearly made once before. I suddenly went so heart-sick again at your cruel behaviour, I was deciding, after all, on a legal separation. I'm getting older, Mike, and I'm tired of your tantrums. I

can't take much more. I told you with such pleasure about
Elmerton and what it could mean for us. The children are
thrilled. Until now, you yourself have been as pleased as a
bee in clover about leaving here; but now, like a cruel
breath of frost, you have turned lovely flowers into withered leaves." By this time Mike had slumped down with his
head in his hands. He gave a weary sigh but did not reply.

"Maybe, after all, the best thing would be just that—a
separation order. I could get it without difficulty. The children and I can keep ourselves now quite comfortably; and
you seem to have a private income from somewhere. I'm
not just holding a pistol at your head, Mike. I'm not saying:
either you come with us, or. . . . No, I think you can
manage without us; so unless there is some serious reason
why you cannot go to Elmerton, you had better plan on
remaining here without us. I really mean it, Mike."

Plainly, Mike was upset. "Millie, my longsuffering wife,
you can't leave me. I'm not pretending. There *is* a reason
for not going to Elmerton. A man lives there who played a
dastardly trick on a pal of mine. He poses as a big guy, but
he's a knave; and if my pal ever got his hands on him he'd
wring his neck."

"Have you ever met that man, Mike?"

"No."

"Does he know you, Mike?"

"No."

"Do you know him by sight, Mike?"

"No."

"Has he ever done *you* harm, Mike?"

"No."

"Then there's no need for you ever to meet him or to
make yourself known to him. And if *he* doesn't know *you*,
there can't be much problem."

"Millie, you don't understand. There's more to it than
that."

"Then why don't you tell me, and get it out of your
system? See, Mike, I have always said that deep down in
my Mike there's a true man; but somehow that 'legion of
demons' comes surging in and tramples it down till it can't
be seen. Tell me about that man."

"Millie, I wish I could. Damn it! Oh, God, why did I get all messed up in this thing! No, you couldn't understand—not yet, Millie. You'll just have to trust me. But I'll try to tell you before long—I will. I've got to get a few things straightened out first."

"All right, Mike, I suppose I'll have to wait and trust you. Meanwhile, from what you have just admitted I cannot see any solid reason for our not going to Elmerton; and since I believe the invitation from there is part of God's leading, we're going—that is, the children and I are going. If you come with us, well and good. If you decide not to come, then I'm afraid, Mike, this is the parting of the ways."

It was too late for Mike to reply further just then. Dorothy was back with the groceries. "Is daddy ill?" she asked. "Would he like a cup of tea?"

Believe it or not, as the days slipped away and the departure for Elmerton drew near, Mike became almost boyishly enthused at the prospect. How he had solved the problem of the bad guy there was an obscurity tucked away in the pigeon-holes of his own interior curiosity shop.

It was thought good to pack young Joseph off to Rostherne before the removal and until the settling in at Elmerton was completed. He could continue the term's schooling near Rostherne, and then more advantageously start at some Elmerton school right at the beginning of the new term after the Summer holidays.

Removal day came at last: so did the pantechnicon van. The "flitting" (as they call such removals there) was a huge upheaval; but it all went off without even a broken saucer! Leaving Everey Street and the mission work there and the many warmhearted friends was a sore wrench in some ways: but Elmerton gleamed ahead, like the old-time "promised land." Farewell, Manchester: Hail, Elmerton!— and undreamed drama!

EIGHT
Drama in the Making

Click-clack, click-clack, click-clack. It seemed an uncanny noise at twenty to six in the morning. The metallic sound click-clacked through the upstairs window from the murky street below.

"What in creation is that?" asked Mike Kennard as he jerked himself up in bed.

"I'm blest if I know," yawned Millie. Mike slid the lower windowsash up, and peered down. "My goodness!" he exclaimed, "there's hundreds of 'em, all on their way to the cotton mills!"

It was the morning tramp, tramp, tramp of the factory workers on their way to the day's toil. The click-clack was the sound of their clogs on the flagged footpath and cobbled roadway. In those days nearly all mill employees wore clogs—not of the Dutch, all-wooden type, but having stiff leather uppers and hard wooden soles with thin iron strips underneath to give longer wearing.

On they came and passed, those dark figures, slowly emerging into human shape from the gloom at one end of the street, then fading away again in the obscurity at the other end. On they came, males and females, with their clickety-clackety clogs; the men wearing odd jackets and trousers, and with scarves round their necks; the women wearing plain blouses and long skirts, black woollen stockings, and large shawls which completely covered their heads, wrapping warmly round their shoulders.

Still they came, those daily marchers in the hard-pushed army of the rich cotton kings; some of them singly, others in twos or threes, with clatter of clogs and chatter of voices. Some of them were lads and lasses scarcely into their 'teens. Wragley Street, Elmerton, where the Kennards now lived, lay in the direction of five or six large mills.

The clogs now clinked faster. Some of those dark figures were breaking into a trot, lest they should be late and incur a fine. In a few minutes the 5:55 A.M. "buzzers" (prolonged blatant blasts) would set many pairs of clogs scurrying to be at work by six o'clock. Then, at exactly the hour, inside the giant engine room the great levers would be pulled; the huge wheels and straps and pulleys would start rolling on each floor of the several storeys; the loud roar of the machinery would reverberate through the whole building; and the sallow-faced soldiers in the cotton-and-calico-army would move to the attack in another day's battle for bread.

By 7:30 the Kennard family (except Joseph, still at Rostherne) were at breakfast, commencing their first full day in Elmerton. To get settled in their new surroundings took several weeks. Mike worked vivaciously, laying linoleum and carpet, hanging pictures and mirrors, fixing curtains and blinds. He was no greenhorn in the use of tools. He went "all out" to make their new abode look its best—taking full credit for having brought them there!

Wragley Street was barely a furlong, well paved, quite wide, clean and pleasant. All the houses along one side had small front gardens enclosed by a low brick wall with a space for a gate, but gateless. The little enclosure was just enough to hold a hedge of privets and maybe a rhododendron bush under the window. Yet those tiny gardens gave a touch of pleasant green besides keeping passers-by from walking too close to one's window and peeking in. The houses on the other side of the street did not have gardens. With sly naughtiness the gardened side was called the "shilling" side, the other the "sixpenny"! Number 12, where the Kennards now lived, was on the superior "shilling" side!— the end house in a row of six.

The house had been recommended by an *ad hoc* trio of the Watch Committee. Thanks again to that tactical group, the whole house had been newly painted and papered and scrubbed clean. They had munificently forbidden Millie to start on her duties for two weeks after the removal. Even then she was to choose her own hours of work after ascertaining the local court days and police procedures, and mapping out her own plan of action.

Only at one point did there seem to be a streak of niggardliness. The new committee could offer Millie only "one pound two shillings" per week. Apologetically they explained that they were starting from scratch and did not yet have even one pledged subscriber. However, they "hoped to do better" as the work became known. They also undertook to reimburse Millie for every penny of expense incurred in her ministrations.

One pound two shillings per week certainly was no golden goose at which to grab, but the hope of likely increase was comforting. Also, both Dorothy and Mona were now at employment age, Dorothy being now fifteen and Mona thirteen; and if only Mike too could get a suitable job, so as to bring a man's wage home, the Kennard family would be better off than ever before.

The town of Elmerton was too small to publish its own daily newspaper, but in ambitious compensation it issued two weeklies: the *Observer* and the *Herald*. Politically, the former had the Tory outlook; the other spoke for the Liberals.

One morning during the Kennards' second week in Elmerton, goldilocks Dorothy came bouncing in, her cheeks flushed by some exciting secret. While they were at the noon meal she said, "I've got a whacking surprise for you. I can scarcely eat for thinking about it"—which evoked a chorus of "Well, out with it."

"I'll whisper it in mummie's ear and if she's pleased with it, she can tell you." Whereupon Dorothy came round the table, cupped her hand over Millie's ear, and in a giggly whisper communicated the big news. Millie looked surprised, then pleased, and then said, "What do you think! Dorothy called at the Herald office this morning, and she's got a job there!" The very next Monday she "clocked in" through the door of the "folding and dispatch department."

It was decided to keep Mona at home until her fourteenth birthday, as she could now be more useful in the home. Her style was sharply different from Dorothy's. She had a romantic mind, also a singing voice of rare quality. The housework and cooking were done to the tune and rhythm of "By Killarney's Lakes and Dells" or "Way Down Upon the Swanee River," or one of the new Sankey's hymns such as "There Were Ninety and Nine." Her fortissimo mezzo-soprano exploits could sometimes be heard at the end of the street; and, alas, at the same time the kettle might be boiling over or the vegetables overcooking. She was a merry, sentimental young soul, self-willed, hot-tempered, impulsively selfish, yet at heart well-meaning. She soon made friends, was possessive and magnetically jolly, and always got on best if left to her own tempo and methods.

However, that young fledgling, too, was soon to be sent fluttering out of the nest. Dorothy came home from the *Herald* one evening with two other "whacking surprises." She announced that the manager had been so pleased with her neat, quick handwriting, she had been asked to do some copying in the office; then, when they found she could do commercial bookkeeping and shorthand, they had permanently transferred her from the machine sheds to the office, at a salary twice as much as she had been earning!

The other secret was, that Dorothy had mentioned her younger sister to the manager; and when he knew that Mona was nearly fourteen, he had asked, "Would Mona like to work in a millinery shop? My sister has one of the busiest in town and wants an honest girl to help her. If Mona gave her mind to it, my sister would go an extra mile to help her on, for she has no children of her own."

Mona could scarcely believe. She jumped up and impishly whizzed Dorothy round in an impromtu rigadoon, knocking two chairs over. Three weeks later she made her debut in *le beau monde,* the bewitching world of millinery, hosiery, lingerie. Both temperamentally and physically it suited her from head to toe.

It was characteristic of the two girls that some months after their settling in Elmerton Dorothy linked up with the St. John's Ambulance evening classes, for their course in "First Aid"—thinking it would be useful preparation for her becoming a nurse; while Mona joined up with the junior choir of the Elmerton Choral Society, later becoming a leading soloist in its senior concert party.

As for Mike, it was not as easy to swing that piece of heavy artillery into remunerative operation. Despite rebuffs he had not outgrown his adolescent egomania. He was "above" the cotton mill and colliery "hands." As he periodically reminded Millie, he was "not afraid of hard work" (which was true) but naturally he must have an occupation worthy of his supernormal dimensions. Consequently his likely fields of action were considerably lessened.

After firing impressive salvos at various Elmerton business houses, but without achieving ingress, he had to eat at least one spoonful of "humble pie." At the head post office they were wanting extra men for the sorting department during an experimental reorganization. Mike had no testimonial, of course, from the insurance society which had cut him adrift, but he had a quite complimentary note from the wholesale grocery firm. The post office assignment was purely temporary. Mike explained to Millie that there were times when a top-level man had thus to condescend for the sake of wife and family. Also, out of self-respect, he amply advertised to his fellow "sorters" that he had accepted the job only because it was temporary, until he was given a position befitting his superior qualifications.

Millie, on her part, did not let the grass grow under her feet. As soon as the new home was in order she sought introductions to the leading aldermen and justices of the peace who officiated on the local "magistrates' bench," to whom she explained the kind of moral salvage work which she would be attempting as "police court missionary." They evinced keen interest and promised sympathetic hearing of all mitigating factors in connection with female indictees.

Millie was encouraged by the Elmerton police chief—
whose title in those days was "Chief Constable." He and the
"chief inspector" were both of the same mind. "It's more
than time something of this sort was tried. Many of those
women who get nabbed for a first infraction would never
come before the magistrate a second time if only somebody
could intercept 'em and turn 'em round afore they become
regulars. This police office will give you all the help it can,
Mrs. Kennard."

Millie's next project took weeks to get going, and even
then it had a doubtful incubation period. She knew how
urgent it was to have some suitable rendezvous where
"birds of a feather" could "flock together"; a women's meeting not on church premises—for that would label it "out of
bounds" for the type of women Millie was after. It was to be
a real haven of help for women who had been in trouble
with the law or had slumped into smeared pariahs through
drunkenness or unchastity. There would be the magic "cup
ot tea and a bun," an interval for convivial chatting, a sing
of the novel Sankey hymns which had now "caught on" all
over Britain; a Gospel address adapted to such women, and
counseling on their problems; also a register on the basis of
which the women would be visited in their homes or
haunts. The meeting would be run by its own little triumvi-
rate, with an "Annual Social" in the winter and an "Annual
Outing" in the summer; and it should contrive to cover all
its own expenses.

Being unfamiliar with Elmerton, Millie wondered how
she could discover the right kind of room. She consulted
Mrs. Joash Adair (yes, Agnes, the pretty Rostherne bride
of years earlier). Agnes in turn asked Joash; and Joash in
turn asked dear old uncle Ben; and uncle Ben in turn
contacted the janitor of the Mechanics' Institute; and that
janitor in turn reported to the committee; and the committee in turn said "Yes" to Millie.

The Mechanics' Institute was the very place—near the
center of the town, but in a side street and inconspicuous.
Its main hall had a seating capacity of over four hundred.
On the platform was a piano which, although now a semi-
invalid through merciless thumpings by keyboard pugilists,

was still able to cough out a few plaintive chords when Millie's gentler fingers coaxed a hymn from it. On the other side of the platform was an harmonium, but unfortunately its trembly bellows and yellowed keys gave out such hoarse wheezes and sickly moans, it was evidently in its last stages of earthly usefulness. The hall was warm in winter because the whole building (of which the assembly hall was only one part) was centrally heated—a big thing in those days. Also, across a corridor, was a large kitchen with water, sinks, gas-jets, and urns for tea-making. But the biggest surprise was, that the use of the hall was granted free because of the purpose for which the new "Police Court Mission" requested it; provided that the persons in charge of the new meeting undertook always to leave the hall clean and tidy, with all kitchen utensils put away washed in readiness for further use.

The first Wednesday afternoon there were only eighteen women present. At the close each one took a sheaf of printed leaflets explaining the purpose of the meeting, and a batch of invitation cards to hand round among neighbours. Each woman, also, gave the names and addresses of two others whom she would like Mrs. Kennard (our Millie) to visit. Millie was a born artist in such work. Her genial disposition, her unique blend of the serious and the humorous, her golden hair and fresh complexion, her coy smile and womanly sympathy, her smart blue uniform, bonnet and bow, her useful ability at the piano, her pleasant, well-thrown voice, and predominantly her original way of putting the truth over in just the way to arouse and attract that type of women—all those qualities in that one sunny-natured, indomitable little woman spelled victory. In one year's time there was a regular attendance of about one hundred and twenty. After three years the hall was about full most Wednesday afternoons.

Through it all, Millie's faithful adjutant and unfailing friend was Agnes. Millie's nature and hers fit each other like hand and glove; so much so that at times it was difficult to know which was the hand and which the glove. It was a more-than-ordinary affection which drew them closer and closer to each other.

But now, back to young Joseph and his friendship with Wilfred. Not too long after the Kennard "flitting" to Elmerton he came home from his prolonged spell at Rostherne— now well on in his eleventh year. Pronounced changes had registered in him since that first stay in Rostherne when he was only six. In mental development he was ahead of his years. Physically it was difficult to identify him with the skin-and-bone little valetudinarian who had been taken to Rostherne in 1897. He was now sturdy and well-favoured, with evident indications of growing tall. This had been his fourth Summer at Rostherne, and when he arrived at the new Kennard home in Elmerton he was bronzed by the Summer sun, with a healthful glow which testified to nutritious farm food and bucolic outdoor life amid pure country air. It was as though Nature had kissed his frank, young face with the September blush of the orchards.

He was markedly different in other ways, too. There had always been a clinging shyness about him, which Millie liked to interpret as an inborn gentlemanliness; but there was now a cultivatedness of manners too obvious for the other Kennards not to notice. They might have been either amused or annoyed at it but for the fact that Joseph himself was innocently oblivious of it. The explanation was, that during his third and fourth Summers at Rostherne Joseph spent nearly all his play-times among the "gentry."

Joseph's friendship with Wilfred had become a David-and-Jonathan attachment. It mattered nothing to Wilfred that Joseph was from a lower class. He was just as jovially at ease in grandpa Kershaw's humble cottage as Joseph was awkward and hesitating at first in the elegant country mansion where Wilfred lived, with its upper-class household luxuries; its bowers, arbors, lily ponds; its horses, stables, playing park; its menage of gardeners, equerry, groomsman, butler and maidservants.

Grandpa Kershaw was "tickled pink" that Millie's lad had "got in" with such "top nobs." At the other end of the line, Wilfred's parents were gratified that their son had found such a congenial chum while back home for Summertime from boarding school. So Joseph was really "in" with the highborn; and two summers of it left a legibly embossed effect in his manners. Two more summers added their quota, so that by the time Joseph was thirteen the impress was such as to have life-long influence.

There was not a dark line in young Wilf. His unselfishness was a continual surprise to Joseph, a puzzling contrast to what he was used to in the rougher schoolmates at Manchester. Wilf seemed as if he could be happy only if someone were sharing with him. If he were the loser in a game it would never cross his mind to do other than ripple with laughter on behalf of the winner. There seemed to be simply no rivalry in him. With transparently honest relish he exuberated in the fun of others as if it were his own by proxy. He would share anything and give anything away—which at times rather worried his father.

Yet in other respects he was "all boy." His play, whether with a soccer ball or a cricket bat, was brilliant. By the time he was twelve he had trained his own pony in hurdle-jumping. He could go cavorting and curvetting on his father's high-gaited hackneys, and was allowed occasionally even on the sleekest thoroughbreds, which were a high-quality crossbreed from Arabian stallions and European racers. Although older than Joseph he was no taller. He gave Joseph boyish lessons in croquette, boating, cycling, horse-riding; and in the gymnasium taught him dumbbells and prankish tricks in boxing. They were at it from early morning to dusk, weeks on end.

To Joseph it was a world of sheer wonder, and Wilf was his wizard hero. Wilf had not the mental depth of Joseph, nor had he been tempered by illness or poverty, but he was a true-blue sport—the toughest, trustiest young pal Joseph ever knew. He had all the accessions money could buy, but no "edge," and he shared it all like a young Count of Monte Cristo who had more than he could manage.

By no means least, Joseph absorbed something of social *etiquette* without knowing that such was the name for it. He was silently impressed, day after day, by the courtesy of Wilfred's phraseology; his "If you don't mind" and "I beg your pardon" and "May I help you?" and "Oh, don't mention it"—all with such a genteel polish of sincere deference. It was the same at mealtimes with Wilfred's mother and father and two sisters: the courtesy habit of not sitting until mother did; their attentiveness in handing things round, putting others first and self last, not to mention other kindred efflorescences of cultivated mannerliness. To Joseph there was a charm about it all which he would never forget.

Though he was but a boy he could see that their respect and attentiveness toward each other at the table and in the lounge was no mere artificiality while the butler or maids were hovering round. They shared a genuine politeness to each other; and although the conversation was often as chattery and round-about as a mountain stream talkatively dodging round ferns and pebbles, there was a reciprocity in which no one out-talked anyone else. Even amid playful badinage it was the same. Joseph listened and learned. The pleasantness of such etiquette was like sparkling embroidery on those enchanting days.

Such was the mutual admiration between Joseph and Wilf that each Summer until Joseph was thirteen there was only one place in the world Joseph could ever dream of spending the long summer holiday. To be at the resplendent "Fernley Towers" with Wilf was almost Elysian bliss; and all unrealizedly it was doing something in him with far-reaching effects.

For one thing, by the time Joseph was twelve, Oliver, the equerry at Fernley Towers had taken a keen liking for him. That equerry was a professional horseman who not only bred studs and trained horses for competition racing or stunting, but curried and groomed them for horse-show championships. Did he have a sly thought that perhaps young Joseph might become apprenticed as assistant equerry? He certainly treated Joseph like a pupil. Joseph had to learn all about the three main kinds of horses: saddle horses, harness horses, draft horses.

There were some of each in the Fernley stables. Among the saddle horses, used mainly for racing or for polo among the aristocracy, Joseph liked the "American," the quarter horses, and the sleek thoroughbreds. Spellbound he watched Oliver teaching the "American" breed their three-gaited and four-gaited performances.

How could he help being fascinated by the *harness*

horses—the "standardbred," the "Cleveland bays," and the
hackneys with their pompous high-stepping and jumping
ability? Some of the harness horses were being trained as
standardbred pacers, others as show mares.

At first, Joseph was scared of the huge *draft* horses—
which Wilfred's father hired out for heavy farm duty or
industrial hauling contracts. But fear gave place to fondness. The largest and strongest of all, the "Belgian," was
the gentlest. He found that Clydesdales love human company. Even the lazy old "shires" and "Suffolks" soon knew
him, and responded like gentlemen to his handfuls of "feed."
His favourite was a Samsonian "Percheron" which liked him
to be on its back and gently kick its flanks and pull its mane.
He learned a life-long love of horses, and by the time he
was thirteen he was a safe young rider.

A very different contribution which Wilfred and Fernley
Towers made to Joseph's development was to teach him
rowing (on Tatton Mere) and fencing in the Fernley armory,
and even boxing in Wilf's own gymnasium. Andy Willard,
one of the gardeners, was an erstwhile boxing "champ" as a
sergeant with the Scottish fusiliers in the old flint-lock
musketry days. Later he became northern counties' cruiser-
weight champion. He was just as soft-hearted as he was
savage-fisted. Wilfred's father might not have been too
pleased if he had known the extent to which Andy was
teaching boxing to the young Fernley heir.

But Wilf needed a sparring partner his own age, and
Joseph filled the bill admirably. At first Joseph had no stomach for boxing. It was only because it gave such giggles to
Wilf that he donned the gloves and pranced round like a
figurant. However, as Joseph was not an angel, he had a
"dander"; and a few bumps on nose or chin galvanized him
into swift reprisal. Also, as Andy initiated the pair of them
into the "fine arts of fistics," Joseph's zest for boxing grew
naughtily. Andy was impressed. Young Wilf was delightfully
absurd as a punching opponent. He had a flair for perpetual
attack but was too impatient to learn skill in parrying.
Joseph had all the practice one could wish in developing
quick self-defense! Wilf was a nonstop clobberer rather
than a quick calculator like Joseph.

The junior gloves were so baggy that even a big whack

or quick jab landed as little more than a loud slap or shove, but if Wilf ever landed one he at once apologized in finest Oxford accent, "Awfully sorry, old chap!" Every slug provoked a hug! Actually he was hardly a match for watchful, nimble Joseph who found Wilf's face like a full moon inviting a visit from England's famous "Mr. Punch." But although Joseph learned the skill and tricks more quickly and could out-box his game young pal, he never let young Wilf think so. The only two real casualty hits were a black eye for Wilf—from Joseph's elbow!—and one slight nosebleed on Joseph, at the sight of which Wilf almost fainted and required salvolatile.

Yet the deepest of all impacts on Joseph during his summers at Rostherne were those which came through that humble cottage where grandpa and grandma Kershaw lived, and through the tuning of his sensitive susceptibilities to the mystic voices of rural Nature. His bedroom was built into the roof and had two dormer windows opposite each other. So, from his cosy bed or from the old wicker chair, he could look out at heaven and earth in both directions. He surely learned, without knowing then how to say it, that the sky, the sun, the moon, the stars, the clouds, the winds, the breeze, the rains, the stilly night, the dawnbreak, the rainbow, the trees, the flowers, the birds, the insects, the silent loveliness, all have voices—heard inwardly by those who are "tuned in."

Oh, those early mornings, especially after summer night-showers! The herbiferous perfume of rain-washed bowers and drenched flowerbeds! The radiant smile of the glistening earth and uplooking blooms waking with the morn! The slanting sunrays giving the flowers rainbow frills! The hilarious competition of "wake up" cock-adoodle-do's from local farmyard crowers, and the plaintive morning mooing of the cows! The first dartings of the birds past the dormer windows, the busy daybreak chirpings, the shrill song of the robin and the full-throated warble of the mavis; the first flutterings of florid butterflies along the borders and bushes!

To our laddie from the city it was all magic. So many buds and plants; so many gay blooms and fruits; so many birds and bees; so many silvery pearls of dew and rain; so many sounds of singing breeze and sighing zephyr, of rustling boughs and hustling songsters and buzzing insects and croaking frogs; so many voices all saying something without need of words! So many hues and shades in Nature's summer adornments, and so many strings on her wondrous harp! By sheer contrast to the cacophonous din and the dull, hard pavements of the city, it was all the more vivid to our thoughtful young urbanite; nor could he help thinking how clever God must be to manage it all.

Perhaps because of distinctive traits in Joseph's contemplative type of mind, it was the countryside eventide which most enchanted him. After climbing into his high, old-fashioned bed he would linger, half-sitting half-lying, almost looking his young eyes away through the blindless window as he wondered at the darkening cerulean canopy everywhere above, often flecked by powder-puff cloudlets silvered in moonlight. The moon itself fascinated him; sometimes a silver scythe ready for reaping those countless stars which twinkled everywhere like scattered beads; later like a crescent cup similar to the bowl in which grandma served the breakfast porridge; still later a full, round, shining ball slowly, slowly rolling upwards past the window frame. Along the dormer sill the low wind of eventide would heave gentle sighs as though wearied with blowing all day; and to that sighing lullaby Joseph would slowly drowse into slumberland.

Grandpa Kershaw's homey cottage "belonged" as naturally to its surroundings as swans to a lake. From the creaky boards of the two upstairs bedrooms down to the solemn face and lazy pendulum of the old grandfather clock in the lobby, and from the big iron latch on the heavy front door to the wheezy old pump outside the kitchen door at the rear, it was a typical village cottage. Joseph loved the ungainly, squeaky rocking chair at grandpa's side of the fireplace, and the high-backed spindle-chair at the other side where grandma used to sit and sometimes smoke her long churchwarden's pipe.

The dear old Darby and Joan never seemed to hurry, yet they were never behind with anything. They appeared to keep step steadily with the four seasons as part of the general rhythm, doing the next thing next with a contentedness which no millionaire's gold could buy.

Grandma had her own homespun philosophy which continually expressed itself in proverbs and aphorisms. She had a sententious saying to fit every turn of circumstance. The villagers seemed to seek her sage counsel on everything unusual. Many a time Joseph would see her sitting there on that spindle throne of hers like a queen of Sheba dispensing the wisdom of Solomon. By the time he was twelve he had so often heard her stock of pithy adages that they stuck in his memory ever afterwards.

Time would fail to tell all her sagacious interweavings of "Too many cooks spoil the broth" and "Faint heart never won fair lady" and "A stitch in time saves nine" and "It's an ill wind which blows nobody any good" and "Many hands make light work" and "The pitcher goes to the well once too often" and "Pride goes before a fall" and "Don't count your chickens before they're hatched" and "Cast ne'er a clout till May is well out." As she watched Joseph growing, summer by summer, little did she guess the mystery wrapped up in him, or that years later her pithy sayings would come trotting out again in many a public utterance to big crowds by her favourite grandson.

When Joseph once told her that some of his schoolmates had laughed at him for saying grace she promptly told him of a young Cheshire farmboy who had recently visited the great city of London. When a godless Londoner asked him, "What on earth are you doing with your head bent over your plate?" he replied, "I'm saying grace, sir." Whereupon the Londoner sneered, "What a greenhorn you are! You'll grow out of that nonsense here. We Londoners gets hungry, we gets food, and gets full, and gets going, and that's all there is to it." "Oh, really," the Cheshire youth came back; "where I come from, that's what the pigs do!"

On another occasion, when Joseph told grandma Kershaw that some of his city playmates had laughed at him for going to church she looked gravely into his innocent eyes, then replied, "My dear grandson, never forget this: It's better to go weeping to heaven than laughing to hell."

Time never tarries. History never halts. Nature's clock never stops. It is all mystery. Where does tomorrow come from? Where has yesterday gone? Why is today? If the past century now lies behind, why do we say it has gone before? Where does the wind begin? Where does it go? We hear it starting a new rush from over the hill or down the lane. Scarcely do we hear it before it is on us like a swirling but invisible ocean; and no sooner has it whelmed us than it noisily scampers away round the next corner or whizzes itself over the next hill into silent non-existence.

Where is that world in which young Joseph grew up? Gone with the wind? Was it the parent of today? We peer back to catch its silhouette, but we can never recapture its atmosphere. What was once tangible, pulsating, alive, experienced, can now only be imperfectly imagined, never really *felt*. We may paint its roses on canvas, but not their fragrance. There are those moderns who pooh-pooh that simpler yesterday; but all those older folk who can still remember the closing hours of its vanished life-pattern before the black smoke of the First World War came and stifled it will tell you wistfully which they prefer. Modern wiseacres may ridicule the disciplines which conditioned young people in the nineteenth century, but as Stonewall Jackson said, "Self-denial is the root of all manliness." Freudianism and the psychology of permissiveness have surely messed things up for youth today!

But back to our story! Toward the end of the Summer at Rostherne, when Joseph was twelve, two men called to see grandpa and grandma Kershaw. Joseph found them there when he came in for the midday meal. He heard one of them called "uncle Ben" and the other "Joash." As soon as Joseph entered they showed how pleased they were to see him; and Joseph thought it was pretty decent of them, the way they chatted with him as though he was just as grown-up as they themselves were.

They talked with grandpa and grandma Kershaw about people and doings in Rostherne years earlier. Then the tall, younger man said to Joseph, "Well, it's a big pleasure to meet you, Joseph. I have special interest in you because my own first name is Joseph, and when I was a boy your age I lived in this very house. Then, when I grew up, I got married and had a little son of my own called Joseph. For some mysterious reason which only God understands he was taken away from us, but if he were still with us he would be somewhere about your own age."

As he spoke Joseph eyed him intently and liked the kindly yet manly way in which he said it. He was taller than genial, round-faced uncle Ben. Putting his hand on Joseph's shoulder, he added, "I know you'll be having a happy time here, Joseph, and I hope we'll meet again sometime. Look after grandpa and grandma. Make them behave, and teach them their manners! And look after this dear old place which I love so much."

When they had gone Joseph said, "My! he's a nice man, that!"

"Yes," nodded grandpa, "he's one of the finest, steadiest lads I ever knew."

After a pause Joseph spoke again. "Didn't he look sad when he talked about his son? Did the little boy die?"

There was a silence. Then grandma Kershaw said, "Joseph, there was something dark and cruel. They don't like to talk about it. The police said he was found *murdered.*"

Joseph shuddered, and asked no more.

Any family removal from one town to another is a domestic earthquake. Never was that truer than it was of the Kennard transplantation to Elmerton. It had fateful and far-reaching reverberations such as they could scarcely have believed possible. For Dorothy it meant, right away, her first encounter with the business world. For Mona it meant the end of school days, and soon afterward her first experiments as a wage earner. For Millie it meant a new kind of mission work—the first time on her own, and with a brand new enterprise. It was going to bring such surprises, she would never be the same again. For Mike it was going to mean revolution and stark tragedy. For Joseph it was going to mean sudden crash and crisis which would alter his whole life—and that of thousands more.

NINE

Conquest and Exploits

About a mile and a quarter from Wragley Street was St. Aiden's Day School. It was a parochial Church of England School, but like all other such at that time it was part of the national free elementary education. All the denominational schools had to measure up to required standards, but they retained the right to include their own form of "religious instruction."

Usually each such school was near the church from which it took its name. So was it with St. Aiden's, Elmerton. It was in the same two-and-a-half-acre plot as St. Aiden's Church. Joseph became a scholar at St. Aiden's about three weeks after the Autumn quarter had started.

On Sundays the Kennards were Methodists. The main Methodist church of Elmerton had built a mission hall in a new and growing locality. The venture had been planned with wise foresight; a main hall seating about three hundred and fifty, with four small rooms along each side for Sunday school classes and committees, also a secondary hall for a "Primary Department." A vigorous evangelical work was carried on there. The problem was to find enough room for all the boys and girls who crowded in. Because of its nearness to Wragley Street, the Kennard family linked up there—Jennifer Street Mission.

Those were the days in England when nearly all boys and girls went to Sunday school, and when the Sunday schools really taught the Scriptural way of salvation. The German-originated new Biblical scholarship known as the "higher criticism," or later as "modernism," had not yet mauled British faith in the Bible as it did afterward— though the dragon already had its claws in the Protestant intelligentsia. Nor at that time had Sunday schools developed the "modern techniques" based upon "child psychology." None the less, they had a way of handling without over-coddling which really got through.

It was from those schools that most leaders in the early British Labour Party came; for the Labour Movement was Christian in its first impulses and ideals. Men like Ramsay Macdonald and Arthur Henderson and Lord Snowdon were all Sunday school products, and, in their maturer years, "local preachers." What they would think about the godless socialism of their party today may be inferred.

Sunday school was twice a Sunday: 9:15 to 10:15 a.m. and then 2:30 to 3:30 p.m. The morning school finished promptly, to give time for getting to the *church* service at 10:30 (for Jennifer Street did not have its own morning service). From the first the governing idea was that Jennifer Street Mission should operate mainly as a fishing-net to bring in those who later would become members of the central church; so it did not hold a Sunday morning service. In other respects it was a subsidiary "church." It had its own Sunday evening service, besides its large morning and afternoon school. It had its own weeknight meetings, its own "Christian Endeavor" group, its own "Band of Hope," and its own Boys' Brigade.

Sunday, of course, was the big day each week. No factory buzzer blew. The mills were silent, and their skyscraper chimneys abated their sooty-black potherings. People wore their Sunday clothes and tried to look their best. Most people went to church. Many went to Sunday school. Some went to both, making four times in all. In between, both younger and older folk went for walks when the weather was congenial, or they visited each other's homes for cups of tea and gossipy "chinwags."

About that time there was a startling innovation in Elmerton's main park. On bright summer Sundays hundreds of people used to take their walks up and down its interlacing paths, amid its artistic shrubberies, along its well-kept flower plots or herbaceous-bordered greens. On its higher level was a large grassy area where people could sit either on the grass or on one of the wooden seats all round it. About the middle of that grassy oval was a brightly painted, octagonal bandstand; and (what next!) the Elmerton Town Council, with a dash of daring, decided that brass and silver bands should play there on Sunday afternoons for the pleasure of the people!—after Sunday school hours, of course!

Many considered this a worldly encroachment on the sanctity of the Lord's Day. Nevertheless the experiment proceeded, and was a loudly trumpeted novelty. Albeit, when a photographer for the Elmerton *Herald* fixed his tripod there one Sabbath and took pictures of the band for publication, there were those who opined that divine judgment would fall on the nation for such sacriligious ungodliness.

Apart from that, the hallowed first day of the week was guarded by stout fences of custom and propriety: no traffic on the streets, except an early milk van or two and a very restricted tramway service along the main thoroughfares. All offices and stores were closed. Boys and girls did not play weekday games. Oh, those long-gone, lazy, quiet Sabbaths! those walks up the lanes, in the park, round the fields! those tantalizing but secretly enjoyed restrictions! those disguised little games which could be played without grown-ups knowing! that well-behaved, innocent rascality, so sadly missing from these flaccid present days of "just do as you like."

Sunday was a real break. For the many it was a boon by way of physical rest from the grind of the six working days. For others it was a relieving change to the mind. Even apart from the uplift of Sabbath worship and Scriptural edification, the contrastive halt of that one day in seven was psychologically healthful. It was good for both older and younger; both for overworked humans and overworked horses. The simple, Christian disciplines were good for boys and girls. One gets sick of hearing anti-religious psychologists of today talking about those erstwhile disciplines as though they used to be clanking fetters on much-to-be-pitied children. Those who grew up through those days (ask them) never once got a sore wrist or ankle through such "chains." Many a time since, they have thanked Heaven for them. Those Sabbatarian proscriptions engendered a reverence for the sacred, along with a healthy tutoring in self-control. There is far more reason to be sorry for the pampered young folk of today, so many of them bored stiff by having all their own way and not knowing what to do with it!—all too many of them a nuisance to themselves as well as to others, through lack of discipline.

The three Kennard children were soon head-over-heels in the Jennifer Street Mission activities. Dorothy and Mona acquired new plumes; for whereas in Manchester they had been classified as "children" they were now in the "Young Women's Class." Joseph readily integrated himself in a boys' class of his own age-group.

As for Millie, through no seeking of her own she was given a most responsible ministry there. By the time she had been in Elmerton nine or ten months she had become well-known as the bonneted "police-court missionary" through her messages at women's meetings and other church groups where she explained the new police-court missionary work. Her remarkable gifts as a public speaker could no more be hid than "a city set on a hill"; so she was increasingly sought after. The Sunday School Mothers' Class at Jennifer Street needed a new teacher. The practice was to have two teachers, each addressing the class on alternate Sundays. The other teacher was a Mrs. Hodgeson—upper class, elderly and slowspoken. Millie made a balancing contrast. So warm was the invitation, Millie could scarcely decline. Millie accepted; and that grateful group surrounded her with a bodyguard of love and loyalty such as only a circle of broad-spoken Lancashire housewives could give.

There were sunny hours in the Kennard home during the first three years in Elmerton. Millie was in court on behalf of some culprit about twice each week. Most of her work belonged to afternoons: contacts in homes, prison visitation, safeguarding women or girls on their exodus after a term in "dry dock" (as jail was called because there was no "booze" there) and, of course, the vital Wednesday afternoon meeting.

To be thus in the front of the fight against crime and grime brought out all the finest in Millie. The more she saw the domestic havoc and moral squalor caused by the drink traffic, the more she hated the damnable campaign of the brewers to get the nation's women drinking. "No nation ever rises above the level of its womanhood and motherhood," she used to say. "Nothing flings open the door to female demoralization more than the wretched drink." "The brewers make millionaires at one end, but prostitutes and destitutes at the other end." "Anybody who turns a girl, a woman, a wife, a mother, into a drunkard commits the worst treachery against the nation's well-being, and should be *drowned* in beer."

Never did the rampaging monster have a doughtier little challenger in Elmerton than Millie. She started a branch of the British Women's Total Abstinence Association. Each of the members wore a little white metal bow with a gilt edge. In conjunction with Millie's Wednesday meeting and other activities the branch rapidly grew; and everywhere, on ladies' costume lapels, the little white bows moved in and out among Elmerton streets and people, bearing their silent testimony on behalf of teetotalism.

There were two breweries in Elmerton, another on the outskirts, still another halfway to the next town. Their barrels of tap beer and boxes of bottled liquors were always delivered to the various local "pubs," especially in summertime, on brightly painted drays pulled by the handsomest draft horses you ever saw—shire stallions or Clydesdales, with the gayest bonnets, harness bells, and other trappings of the horse milliner, as though beer was the way to bonny health and happiness.

At one point the brewery managements decided to organize a great beer-advertising procession down the main street of Elmerton on a Saturday afternoon. The day came. Their assembly point was Milton Square at the top end of the main street. The assemblage included three brass bands, a score of gaily flagged drays and their hefty horses, with a union Jack waving from every vehicle, as though beer-drinking was a most patriotic duty. There were banners and balloons, also flamboyant advertisements for the products of the proud distillers.

Millie had got wind of this before the announcement appeared in the local press. Just before the whistle was due to blow and set the procession in motion the brewery barons got the biggest surprise of their lives. Who should come marching from Hartley Street into Milton Square but Millie and five well-known magistrates leading a procession of about three hundred men and women, boys and girls, many of them in ragged clothing, some barefooted, all victims of drink. They were in orderly groups, walking four or five abreast. Every group had its own banners; sheets of plain white, rough calico (odd pieces from the mills) and all the wording on them was in thick black. First came the children's block, then the husbands and wives' block, then the parents' block. In the children's block some of the banners read:

> DRINK HAS PUT MY FATHER IN STRANGEWAYS PRISON.
>
> DRINK MADE MY DADDY LEAVE HOME
> AND WE DON'T KNOW WHERE HE IS.
>
> OUR FATHER GETS DRUNK AT THE PUB
> AND THEN BEATS OUR MOTHER BLACK AND BLUE.
>
> DRINK HAS SEPARATED OUR PARENTS AND LEFT US IN RAGS.
>
> DRINK HAS EMPTIED OUR HOME OF FOOD AND FURNITURE.
>
> DRINK CAUSED OUR MOTHER TO NEGLECT US
> AND GO OFF WITH ANOTHER MAN.

In the husbands and wives and parents' blocks there were such banners as:

> MY HUSBAND AND I WERE HAPPILY MARRIED
> UNTIL DRINK CAME AND RUINED OUR HOME.

I MARRIED A PURE GIRL. DRINK TURNED HER INTO A HARLOT.

MY HUSBAND AND I CAME FROM GOOD HOMES,
BUT DRINK BROUGHT US TO THE SLUMS.

THROUGH DRINK MY DAUGHTER BECAME
AN UNMARRIED MOTHER AND SANK TO THE GUTTER.

WHILE DRUNK OUR SON COMMITTED MURDER
AND WAS HANGED ONE YEAR AGO.

DRINK MAKES THE BREWERS RICH AND THE DRINKERS PAUPERS.

There never was a procession like it: ragged, barefooted
children; women wearing common shawls and frayed clothing; misery inflicted by the wretched drink apparent in
many faces. Millie marched her strange army to a halt right
in front of the brewers' assemblage, ready to precede them
down the main street when the whistle blew. At the head of
the brewers' procession was a large, bizzare wagonette
drawn by three pairs of Cleveland bays. Inside the wagonette were the leading directors of the brewery companies,
all spruced up, ready to give bland smiles and benevolent
hand-waves to the people lining the footpaths. When they
saw Millie's conglomerate counter-procession their eyes
nearly leapt from their sockets. Could it be possible! But
astonishment soon became rage. Down they climbed from
their red-white-blue-striped wagonette and strode with
pompous indignation to Millie.

"Woman, what on earth does this mean? Get this riff-raff
out of the way at once!"

But they had reached a Waterloo. They might as well
have tried to dislodge Gibraltar with pea-shooters as dis-
compose indomitable Millie. She replied, "Sirs, if these people are riff-raff, that is what *you* have made them. Why
shouldn't they precede your procession? They are your
best-paying customers! Let people see what you have done
for them!"

"See here, madam, you are breaking the law, and can go
to prison for it: and by Gad, if you don't move these scum
away we'll see that you *do* go! If you knew the law, you

would know that you cannot hold a procession of any kind without legal permit."

Millie opened her satchel and produced her permit, signed by both the chief constable and the town clerk, also a copy of her application for it signed by herself and eight leading aldermen of the borough.

The distillery magnates audibly gasped and visibly writhed. They were furious beyond words, the more so now because a crowd was gathering. Onlookers grasped at once the significance of Millie's crowd. Somebody started a booing and a hissing against the brewers. "Yez, them's the divils that puts the likes of us in the workhouse or the blinkin' jail! Boo. . . . To hell with 'em. They gets rich sellin' liquid damnation!"

But Millie's invisible truncheon struck again. "Sirs, I have shown you my permit. I also took legal advice whether I could march in front of your procession, and there is not a law of the land against it so long as my own procession occasions no breach of the peace. But, sirs, look further down Hartley Street. Will you call *those* people riff-raff?"

The brewers looked. Two blocks down was a batch of about one hundred well-dressed persons. They were all wearing the little white total-abstinence bows, and they waved banners telling what happens when people quit the booze and become Christian citizens. They were Millie's "rearguard," to walk *behind* the brewers' procession!

The brewers bit their lips and gritted their teeth. They were flummoxed. Again Millie jabbed, "Gentlemen, may I see *your* permit?" "No, damn you! You can't. We don't have it with us; but we got one alright." "Yes, you did," retorted Millie; "you got it by verbal request and were asked by the police chief to implement it in writing—which you never did. So you do *not* have a written permit."

The liquor magnates, livid with temper, stomped away stiffly to the rear of their wagonette, where they held a rapid debate and made a quick decision. Their procession was called off (and they never planned another). But Millie's "riff-raff" volunteers thought it unfair to the several thousands now lining the long main street not to give them any procession at all, so *they* marched down it with their grim, testimonial banners, much to the surprise of all the onlookers; and then the well-dressed "rearguard" of one hundred followed, all wearing their teetotalist bows, waving their banners, as they sang, "Stand up, stand up for Jesus, ye soldiers of the Cross!"

It was a stunning exploit. The crowds cheered the "Millie Militants" (as Joash called them) and jeered their contempt of the brewers. It was an object-lesson too telling ever to be forgotten. The whole episode was given a big write-up in both the Elmerton weeklies. It gave wonderful publicity to the Police Court Mission and its courageous little emissary in the smart blue uniform and bonnet. If Millie's name had been blazoned from the Town Hall tower it could not have done more to give her work the boost it needed. She was rather fearful that the brewers would somehow retaliate; but they had far more sense. They knew that the safer course was to let the incident die as quietly as possible.

During that period the evenings at 12 Wragley Street were delightfully harmonious—partly, it must be conceded, because Mike's shift at the G.P.O. was from 2:00 p.m. until ten o'clock. Often did Millie lift her heart to God in thanksgiving that she had such children. They had their faults. They could fratch and collide, for they were full-blooded young humans; they could argue like Philadelphia lawyers, for they had sharp wits and minds of their own; but underneath all they loved each other dearly. To Dorothy and Mona, Millie was "dearest loving mother" just as if they had been her own flesh. No mother could have given them more. She was strong and firm. She tolerated no hanky-panky insubordination. Yet she was so warm and understanding, so reasonable and willing to listen, so fond of fun and playful tricks yet so ready to sympathize and advise; she was their truly loved refuge.

She never fussed or coddled them, but now and then she would give them such a hug and kiss, it would say something which lasted months. When she had to correct them, never did she raise her voice. Nor did she ever make issues over peccadillos; but there were certain basic standards which were inviolate and which they knew simply must be honored. She taught them to practice being emotionally steady rather than impulsive or demonstrative. Home, to those three children, was not merely 12 Wragley Street; it was where that wonderful mother was. Their rippling laughter, their tears too, they brought to *her*. Besides that, as Millie became so well known and respected in the community, they were mighty proud of such a mother.

As the three grew up they could never forget those evenings around the teatable and (in the colder months) around the living-room fire, all the happier (let it be said with a tear) because their swarthy father was not there, filling the room like a spreading bay tree. In later years Joseph loved recalling Millie's anecdotes at those teatable and fireside sittings.

Sometimes she would tell them comical things said at the court sessions. There was the man applying for a license of some kind. The town clerk said, "Sir, you must get a 'recommend' from some civic official." The man replied, "The police chief can speak for me." But chief Snelling stood and denied ever having seen him before. Whereupon the applicant turned to the town clerk and said, "Sir, I have lived in Elmerton twenty-three years and the police chief does not know me. Is not that a recommend?"

There was the man in the dock on a burglary charge. The magistrate asked him, "What is your trade?" to which the man replied, "Locksmith, sir." "What were you doing when the constable surprised you?" "Making a *bolt* for the door, sir." Even the magistrate had to laugh, but he added, "I think, to save you from making more *bolts* we'll put you behind *bars*."

One of the factors which made mother Millie a priceless raconteur was her own roguish look and irrepressible laughter at what she was relating. They used to wonder how she could have such relish of the comical when she had to mix so often with the criminal. Does it sound strange that they connected it with her times of praying? Often they would tip-toe quietly as they heard her praying in the front bedroom, and they would notice as she came out what a happy light was on her face.

There were evenings, too, at that fireside when with

tears Millie would tell them of the heart-rending things. "This morning, Joseph, there were two young lads in court. They were up for gambling and burglaring. The magistrate ordered each of them eight strokes of the birch rod. I stood up on their behalf. Their drunken parents had separated and gone away leaving the boys to anybody or nobody. However, the magistrate said, 'I'm sorry, Mrs. Kennard, but this is the third time these boys have been convicted. At first they were just a couple of juvenile rapscallions up to all sorts of hocus-pocus, but now they are seriously break- ing the law. I hope the birch rod will teach them a lesson.'"

Millie added, "Joseph, my dear boy, that magistrate was right. I chatted with him afterward and he said, 'Mrs. Kennard, it hurt *me* to decide on birching them; but our experience is that too much leniency fosters further crime. Also, there is a time in our life—while we are young— when *corporal* punishment is the most effective deterrent.' Joseph, that's not popular today, but it's true. Strictly speak- ing, law courts were never meant to be halls of clemency to wrongdoers. When they become so, the life of a nation is endangered. Statistics show that severer penalties usually result in fewer crimes.

"That may have sounded hard to you, Joseph, but it is only being true to the facts. Our courts should never be blamed for doing their work when they truly and fairly administer penal justice; for they are thereby safeguarding the community. Administering painful penalty cannot change a criminal's nature, but it can and does deter him from giving way to it. The real fault, Joseph, is not in the courts, but in our homes and schools, and our social system with its industrial inequities, its corrupting theatres and new cinemas which dress crime up as exciting adventure; its sexy dance halls, and the wretched 'pubs.'"

"As you grow into manhood, Joseph, don't be deceived into thinking that the only kind people on earth are those who want to do away with all punishment and let children have all their own way. And beware of that catchword, 'self- expression,' Joseph. In nine cases out of ten, what they mean by 'self-expression' is the expression of only one *part* of the self—the animal part which most needs disciplining."

How far-seeing Millie's prognostications on the effects of Freudianism were, Joseph would live long enough to see. But in those days, before radio and television, it was impossible to forepicture a day in the nineteen-sixties when a foreign diplomat visiting U.S.A. would say that the most impressive thing he had seen in American communal life was the remarkable *obedience* in American homes—"of parents to children"!

Millie had much coming and going with the central police office. The chief and deputies and most of the constables came to know her well. Most of the men were married and were fathers. Again and again, rather than "run in" some female first-offender, they would tell Millie about the incident and get her to call on the girl or woman. Sometimes she would sit with policemen on call, between appointments at court-cases, and learn something of their problems. They, too, had their fund of humorous reminiscences which slapped dabs of comedy on the seamy side of things. Some of these Millie would share with her young trinity at the evening meal-table or afterward.

Whether it was apocryphal or not, Joseph always remembered the one about a policeman who had to take a prisoner to Strangeways Prison. The two of them went by tram from Elmerton to Manchester and got out at the Piccadilly terminus. They set off walking down Market Street. As they were passing a tobacconist's shop the prisoner said, "Pal, I'se simply droopin' for a smoke. Will yer let me just pop into this tobacco shop for a packet o' fags?" The policeman replied, "I'm darned if I will! If you once get in there, how do I know you won't run out through the back door and escape? No, I certainly won't let you go in. You just wait on the path out here while *I* go in and get 'em!"

As far as she felt it wise, Millie also shared with the three children some of the joys and sorrows, rewards and rebuffs, of her work among the down-and-outs. She avoided pinning on their sensitive young memories things which more properly belong to a maturer comprehension. Yet there were aspects which were safely communicable and which she judged might have a warning or guiding influence on them. They all developed a repulsive hatred for the "drink," though tempered by sympathy for the many young persons who are tricked victims rather than deliberate indulgers or lazy sots.

Millie's trio grew up with a detestation of impurity and marital dishonor. Most markedly was this so in young Joseph's absorbent mind. What he saw in his incomparable mother and in his two vivacious but virtuous sisters was such as to implant in him an ineradicable reverence for motherhood and girlhood.

Some of Millie's "case histories" in Elmerton were classics in human salvage. One was a woman who, in her mid-thirties, had sixty-eight convictions against her name—four or five a year from age eighteen. It all started with a glass of beer when she was seventeen. As in millions of instances, that first glass, "just to be social" was the liquid gateway to dirty sex; for even then the sons of Sodom in English society had learned the devil's slogan, "Get a girl tipsy, you can do anything with her." There was an illegitimate baby. From that point her downgrade was steep, until, as the worst of female prodigals, she wallowed in the pig-swill. Again and again she was in prison or punished by fines; sleeping in alleys at night; repeatedly arraigned for "breach of the peace" or "drunken brawl" or "indecent behaviour while intoxicated" or "assault to inflict bodily harm while drunk." At Strangeways Prison they dubbed her the "bad shilling" because she was always turning up there and they were sick at the sight of her. But something almost unbelievable happened to Carol—for such was her melodious name.

Six times Millie had travelled to Strangeways for talks with her. It seemed useless. Apparently all sense of human decency had been drowned in alcohol. Through her bleary eyes she would gape at Millie, and with raucous voice laugh in hoydenish sarcasm.

"Hey, missis, yer needna' cum tawkin' religion to me. Religion's only like slaps o' paint over a muck 'eap. Rich folk wear fancy frills and others dirty clouts, but inside they're a' as mucky as each other. Aha, when I was a kidlet they called me 'little primrose,' but now a'm a piece o' dirty banana skin for folk to slip on. Aha! Serve 'em reet!"

She simply could not believe anyone was really clean—such was her experience of men. Human beings were nice when they were kids, but they all grew up to be beasts. It was no use trying to read from Scripture to her; and the very suggestion of praying with her evoked derisive guffaws which rang along the prison corridor like a ribald mockery of Beelzebub.

Millie did manage, however, to leave her a sixpenny booklet, *The Traveller's Guide*. On its being handed to her Carol threw it up to the ceiling, and when it was coming down she met it with her foot. Then, like a soccer player, she dribbled it round the cell, finally kicking it into a corner where she gave it a savage look.

Yet that ill-treated booklet struck back. Millie could tell so on her next visit. One of the stories in it—about a fallen woman who came to know Jesus as her Saviour and was transformed—had somehow got a foothold in Carol's mind. "Was she a real woman, or is it only a story?" she asked.

"She was a real woman, Carol, though I myself never knew her."

"It's blinkin' 'ard to think so."

"Yes, I agree, Carol, but I know two other women just like her, and one of them lives in Elmerton."

"Tell me 'er name."

"Her name is Polly Henshaw."

If a thunderbolt had dropped into the cell its effect on Carol could not have been greater. "Polly 'Enshaw!" she echoed. "Polly 'Enshaw . . . Polly 'Enshaw. . . ."

"Did you know Polly?" There was no reply. Carol sat there dumbfounded.

Presently she asked soberly, "Where's Polly now?"

"She's still in Elmerton. She's back with her two children, and they're living in Ogden Street. She has a half-time job at Jenner's mill. The older of her boys is doing very well as a grocery assistant and brings a wage home, so they get on quite comfortably.

"Is she reely goin' clean—reel clean?"

"Yes, she certainly is."

"Is she back with 'er 'usband?"

"No, he's in the Territorials yet, but his army service

ends early next year, and they're looking forward then to being always together. She's been to see him at his barracks. They've stayed together and talked things over. He's a decent chap, you know. Everything's forgiven. They really are happy again, Carol; and Polly is a changed woman."

"Well, I'll be. . . ! How did it 'appen?"

"The answer to that, Carol, is: Polly came to know that wonderful Saviour the booklet talks about. It's all true, Carol, if only you could believe it. Why do I keep coming to see you? It doesn't put a single penny into my pocket. It costs me time and fare. If you can believe me, I come because the Saviour puts love for you in my heart."

Carol still looked dazed. "A'm still no sure about yer, Missis what-d'they-call-yer; but a'll tell yer wot: a'll let yer pray wi' me. An' listen: a'm comin' out o' this tin middin next Tuesday. Can yer tek me to see Polly 'Enshaw?"

"I think we may do better than that," responded Millie. "If we can arrange it, Polly and I will be at the gates to meet you next Tuesday."

Before leaving, Millie prayed with her. As she did so, at one point she could not keep back a tear—and Carol saw; for although she knelt with Millie her eyes were watching in befuddled curiosity. At the cell door Millie paused, turned back, and kissed Carol.

"Well . . . blinkin' 'eck! . . ." Carol sputtered; "that's first time in over ten years another woman kissed me!"

The following Tuesday Millie and Polly were there. So was one of Carol's men friends. He was an unsavoury-looking specimen with bushy eyebrows and heavy moustache, bullet-headed and stocky. Millie was not surprised. All too often, when women like Carol came out, there, at the very gates, their seducers would be waiting like hovering hawks. He came at once to Carol. " 'Ello, darlin', I thought I'd come an' meet you."

"So you did, did you?" It was Millie's voice with a ring of authority in it. "It may surprise you to know that *we've* come to meet *you;* and we want your full name and address." Millie beckoned the superintendent's clerk, who had been foreapprized. "This is the man. Get his name and address."

Young bushy-brow's beady eyes contracted to a cat-like stare. "What the. . . !" He got no further. The clerk said, "See, mister, this lady in uniform is an official of the law: and if she has any interference from you, then *you'll* be coming inside these gates." That was enough.

Millie and Polly escorted Carol to the nearest tram stop, and got her to Victoria Station, where they had a cup of tea. Then they boarded the train and duly arrived at Elmerton. Carol could not keep her eyes off Polly. Was this clean, neatly dressed woman with a restful look the former roistering, meretricious Polly Henshaw? Or was it somebody impersonating her?

Polly must have realized that the unspoken question was there. In the railway compartment she looked straight into Carol's eyes and said, "Carol, my old pal, I'll answer your question. It's me alright, but I'm saved, and I want to tell you all about it when we get home."

"Home?" Carol spoke a bit huskily. "But where's home? I've nowhere to go." "You're coming home with me," said Polly. "We've got a nice, clean bed ready for you; and you're welcome to stay with us till Mrs. Kennard can find somewhere suitable for you."

Next day Carol was at the Wednesday afternoon meeting. Millie's Gospel address put the finishing touches to Polly's glowing testimony the night before. Carol required nobody to tell her how deeply she *needed* the Saviour: her problem now was: had she sunk too deeply to be pulled from the mire?

Millie's address seemed to clinch the matter. Carol heard her quote a text about Jesus saving "to the uttermost," and Millie's comment was, "Yes, He can save to the uttermost from the *guttermost*." Polly seemed to be a living proof of it. Yet Carol hung back. It was all too new, too stunning. What about when the mad drink-thirst came on her again? Could Jesus deal with *that?*

The next Sunday evening she was at Jennifer Street Mission; still sober, much clearer in her thinking (thanks to Polly) and again impressed.

Then came the lovely miracle. Early next morning, well before rising time, Carol knocked quietly at Polly's bedroom door. Polly was still asleep. Carol went in and gently sat on the bedside. This wakened Polly, who at once sat up, a big question-mark in her expression.

"Sorry for wakin' you, Polly, but I had to do it. You'll be off to work just after breakfast, so there'll be no time to tell you then. Oh, Polly, I'm not used to this 'eer way of sayin' these things yet, but I think . . . I think . . . yes, I'm converted, Polly. Yes, I . . . I *am*. Polly, please help me to say it: Polly, I'm SAVED!"—and that word, "saved," came out with one great gush of tears, as though the soul's sluice gate had burst open and the pent-up sin and bitterness of years was suddenly flooding itself away for ever—which in very truth it was! The two women, former partners in filth and crime but now born-again sisters in Christ, wept in each other's embrace.

"Get up, now, Polly," said Carol. "I'll tell you more later. Just this one bit in advance, I had a dream last night and in it I got the meaning of what you and Mrs. Kennard have been trying to tell me. In that dream Jesus came to me. It was so strange but so real and startling, it woke me up; and then as I sat up in bed I knew that the shining Figure was still standing near, though I couldn't see it after I woke. I knew He was standing there, offering me forgiveness and cleansing through His death as my Saviour. Oh, it was all so clear: and, Polly, I just opened my weeping heart to Him as I sat up and prayed in the dark. It seemed to me the biggest wonder I'd ever known, that the shining Saviour would come into such a hovel, but I remembered the preacher's text last night: 'The blood of Jesus Christ, God's Son, cleanseth us from all sin'; and somehow Jesus said inside me, 'Carol, that text is yours; I've come into your heart.' Polly, I'm not imagining it; He's come; and my mind feels cleaner already."

As when a stone is thrown into a pond the liquid circles roll out ever larger, so were the effects of that conversion. The slum area in which Carol had been known as "queen of dare-devils" was staggered. Some said she had just gone barmy through the booze. Others said she'd gone plain daft. Others said it was a lot of baloney. But, when, two or three months later, they met her going from house to house with

Gospel tracts—clean, nicely dressed, walking steadily and speaking an altogether new vocabulary—their astonishment knew no bounds. But it was the women she was after. She could talk and weep with them as nobody else could. She had known the sordid depths, and now she knew the one precious, vital secret of dynamic transformation. She became Millie's most successful recruiting sergeant for the Wednesday afternoon meeting.

Millie tried hard to get her a job, but the many years of drink and debauchery had weakened Carol's constitution. Factory work would not do. The area of likelihood was limited. Eventually she was given a job (of all places) at the central police station, where she was so well known! The police chief and the constables could hardly believe it was the same woman, she looked so much younger and comported herself so circumspectly. Her work was limited entirely to the police division, with no responsibility to any other part of the Town Hall. She was made supervisor over the office cleaners, and looked after the tea-and-light-refreshments provided for the men at certain times each day. It was Millie's influence, of course, which put her there, and Carol knew it. The hours were not exacting. She was beyond reach of former companions. Her health gradually returned, and she became most attractive.

Several months after her conversion she gave her testimony at the Wednesday afternoon meeting. Millie announced one week ahead that Carol would do so, with the result that there was the biggest attendance so far. The newcomers included some of the queerest birds from the slum jungle. Carol was nervous, standing for the first time before a large company. That was good. She found, as many others have, that nervousness is often a blessing in disguise. It compels fuller dependence on the Saviour. Also it let all the women know that it was costing Carol something.

Millie called on Carol. All the women clapped; nobody knew why. It upset Carol: she wanted them to see Jesus, not herself. She stuttered, stopped, started again, bungled her words, and stopped again. Her hands went limp. Her face paled. Her head drooped, and she stood in silence for about three elongated seconds, during which the women, struck with surprise by the utterly unexpected, stared tensely. Then Carol looked up, big tears rolling down her face, and in a clear voice without a quiver of nervousness in it addressed her invisibly present Saviour. With eyes wide open and all the women watching, she said, "My dear Saviour, I thank You for humbling me before all my sisters here today. I cannot see You, but I know You are with me. Please help me to be calm and tell them what You've done for me."

That prayer was answered. She spoke slowly but easily, telling her pathetic story of sin and wretchedness. But as she came to the relating of her conversion there was quicker tempo and animation. Her face flushed. She was reliving it as she related it. Then she told the dream. "I can never forget it," she said. "It was no ordinary dream. What I saw in that dream was 'alive' in a way that other dreams never are. Sisters, I know you can't build on dreams: the important thing is how you live when you are awake; but God has to use unusual means with some of us. I know that the risen Saviour came to me in that dream. I knew it was the Lord Jesus; but the strange thing was, He seemed to have someone else's face! Yes, and when I looked . . . when I looked . . . I could make out in my dream whose that face was. . . . It was Mrs. Millie Kennard's! Please forgive me for telling this, Mrs. Kennard [turning to Millie] but it *was* your face."

Among the women there was rapt concentration.

Carol continued. "It was such a strange surprise; and then it didn't seem a surprise at all. It was as though Jesus said to me, 'Carol, there are many people who only learn to recognize Me when they see Me in somebody else.' Then I understood, sisters; and then I woke up. I sat up in the dark; and now it wasn't a dream. I knew the Saviour had come to me; and in my awake mind I could see Him there, the shining, holy Son of God, the Saviour who made atonement for all our sin by His death on the Cross, because God loves us. Oh, sisters, it was wonderful, wonderful, *wonderful*. My heart's door swung wide open. He came in—my living Saviour! Yes, He came into this poor hovel of a heart! With His pierced hands He brought me a blood-bought pardon. He brought me peace with God, and cleansing from all the ugly, ugly stains of those awful years!"

By now her face was radiant. She shone as she spoke. There was a certain almost bewitching elegance about her manner. There seemed to be an aura of womanly refinement round her.

Suddenly, a large woman near the rear of the room jumped up and shouted, "Hallelujah! Sisters, she's a *MIRACLE!*"—and right round the room the muttered echo travelled, "Aye, she's a miracle!"

It was an unforgettable meeting. There were few dry eyes. Here and there choked sobbing could be heard. It was the beginning of gracious salvage in others.

To watch Carol grow in grace was to witness a *developing* miracle. Her yieldedness to Christ and her rapid spiritual education through much browsing in the Bible brought out latent gifts which marked her as one of God's "specials." It was a sorrowful day at the police office, about three years later, when Carol left them. When the men learned *why* she was leaving they could hardly credit that she was the very woman who, in former years, they had often found dead drunk in a slum gutter on a dark, wet night. She was now removing to the Lancashire town of Oldham, to start a home for fallen girls and women.

Believe it or not, that indeed is what Carol did! She became the matron of her own rescue mission in Oldham, and persevered in a noble work of salvaging bodies and souls from the demoralizing grip of drink and the slime-pits of sensuality. Her departure from Elmerton was a keenly felt loss to Millie, for a strong attachment had developed; but all such personal regret was eclipsed by the overall triumph of Carol's transformation.

About that time Alderman Charles Whiting became the Right Worshipful Mayor of Elmerton. In his mayoral peroration to the civic dignitaries he observed, "One gratifying feature is the marked diminution of female criminal convictions in our township. Over a period of four years there has been a drop of 38 percent. My fellow J.Ps. and I are of one accord in attributing this to the efforts of the Elmerton

Police Court Mission through its much-respected representative, Mrs. Millie Kennard."

Yes, there was hard-won success beyond what the Watch Committee had envisaged. But do the powers of evil let a work of that sort go without reprisal? Look out, Millie! The rumble of the devil's chariots is now growing much louder!

TEN

Spotlight on Joseph

Wragley Street had both the advantages and the annoyances of short streets. By artful means everybody in it knew what everybody else in it was doing. One well-worn expedient on lighter evenings or Saturday afternoons was to loll on the front doorstep as though relishing the refreshing urban air but in reality watching, with hawk's eye, other doors and doings.

Another skillful practice was the "I spy with my little eye" technique—the drawing back of the lace curtain just the tiniest bit from the bottom corner of the window, and peeping. It was a sort of good-neighbourly Scotland Yard in which one was always under surveillance, though without ever being arrested.

One afternoon the curtains in Wragley Street simultaneously moved that tiny bit for a peek at number 12. A horse and lorry had halted at the Kennards'. Two men struggled to lift down a large, bulky object concealed by a heavy dust-sheet. Peepers and lollers almost squinted in straining to focus on it. Their vigilence was rewarded. A providential gust of wind blew the covering off. Lo, of all things, a piano!

That evening, at every Wragley teatable the new intelligence was passed round. Eyebrows went up, and no wonder, for in Lancashire those days it was only the better class dwellings which boasted a piano. Working-class cottages had to manage with a gramophone or a wheezy little harmonium which emitted chords like the melancholy baying of hounds at the tolling of a death-knell. If one of the poorer homes *did* have a piano, it was probably a superannuated veteran telling you in trembly tones, "Old soldiers never die"—but making you wish they did.

Millie had bought the piano for a mere song, from an aged maiden lady who had begun to feel that westerly wind in her rigging which bears earth's mariners to the Beyond. It was an old *Cramer* piano with very shiny woodwork and outdated elegance, and inwardly a malfunctioning invalid. But at moderate cost a piano doctor had given it almost a new inside, making its performance at least tolerable.

Even so, its highest and lowest octaves were better for not being heard. If one's fingers made a run from middle C to top A, the last dozen notes sounded like sputtering rain on the thin glass of a greenhouse. If the lowest notes of the bass clef were depressed, the pianist became almost as depressed as the notes. A neighbor thought it looked a "sound investment," but after hearing it he seemed unsure which was worse—the "sound" or the "investment."

Still, the middle area of the keyboard was in tune, with repaired hammers and strings; which was ample, since Millie wanted it mainly for playing hymns and to teach her three children elementary pianoforte. The latter followed the usual pattern: Dorothy went at it "twelve to the dozen," soon being able to play the simpler common and long meter tunes. Mona got as far as "Won't You Buy My Pretty Flowers?" in Smallwood's book for beginners, then languished as though unable to leave the little orphan with her pretty flowers unsold.

As for Joseph, now eleven years old, Dorothy was his tyrant teacher. She seemed determined to make him play that piano if it were the last thing she did on earth. To her must be attributed the discovery of Joseph's musical gift. He excelled. Before he was twelve Millie had him going for lessons to a Mr. Harley a few streets away. Mr. Harley, the son of a nearby grocer, had his Manchester L.R.A.M., and used to charge tenpence per lesson. He averred that Joseph was the slickest-fingered laddie who ever "tickled the ivories." By the time Joseph was nearing thirteen he had mastered Clementi's first book of sonatinas, also those drawing-room brilliants, Sydney Smith's *La Harpe Eolienne,* and *Le Jet D'eau,* and *Gaiete' de Coeur,* and *Arlequin et Columbine,* and *Morning Dewdrips,* and *Tarantelle Brilliant in E Minor,* and others, and could rollick through them with the nimbleness and sparkle of a budding young Rubinstein.

For the first time, while Joseph was eleven, the Kennard family circle was broken by a sad "good-bye." Dorothy had kept up with her "First Aid" classes to the point where she became assistant teacher, and latterly had persuaded Joseph to accompany her. This proved a great help to him later in the Boys' Brigade, when he not only earned his "First Aid" badge and neckerchief, but went on to become a junior instructor.

But about Dorothy: at last her ambition to become a nurse was flowering. A nurse at the First Aid class gave her the application papers for intending nurses. Shortly afterward she became a "pro" at the Rochdale Infirmary. Eager as she had been to go, it was a tearful ordeal when the parting came. In Joseph's fond esteem she was the world's best sister, and when she was leaving home he knew how endearingly their hearts were knit together.

Because of work hours, neither Mike nor Mona could go to the railway station to see her off, but Joseph got a short leave from school to wave her good-bye; and Millie went all the way with her by train to Rochdale. The first year's training was half way through before it was found that Dorothy should never have been accepted. She was only seventeen, whereas the required age was nineteen or over. Innocently enough, in applying, Dorothy had given her correct age, but it had somehow escaped notice. Her tallness, too, gave her the nineteen look. But she saw things in the hospital which too badly shocked "sweet seventeen"; and several times when she came home on her "monthly day off" she would weep in Millie's lap. More than ever she was Joseph's golden-haired heroine.

Henceforth, however, it is Joseph who holds the spotlight. From the first day he started his schooling at St. Aiden's he did well. This was not due solely to mental smartness (nor always to saintly conscientiousness!). He combined with it a facility of focus and a photographic memory. Each year, in every subject but one, he was head of his class; and even in his poor subject—arithmetic, he was either top, along with a very clever girl, or next to it.

Yet there was a darker side. When about twelve years old he had enemies who conspired to humiliate him. Perhaps some such antipathy was almost inevitable. Behind it was jealousy; and there were four factors which generated it. There was Joseph's cleverness. He was tall, athletic, attractive. The girls, in their sentimental little hearts, fell for him as their "Prince Charming." Also, he had a politeness of bearing and speech which from the first had given him an unsought and rather irritating difference from the rougher lads who said he was priggish and swanky.

His principal enemy and rival was Louis Corwood, another smart scholar and nearly as tall as Joseph. He was heavy and strong and of a belligerent cast. He claimed to be "cock of the class"; that is, the best fighter. The other boys tacitly accepted this, taking care not to cross him. Unfortunately for Joseph, the girl whom Louis coveted could not see him for looking at Joseph. So Louis resolved to knock her idol from its pedestal.

He started a whisper campaign. A "fancy bloke" like Kennard hadn't the guts to put his fists up to anybody. Somebody ought to show the girls what a "softie" he was. Then Corwood hit on an idea. In the class there was a gawkish, backward boy named Ned Dimble, with a doltish grin and a brain as self-important as it was diminutive. Corwood and two or three others began to work on Dimble, persuading him that Kennard was trying to make a fool of him and had lied to the girls about him so as to make him seem a daftie.

Eventually, all bristled up, Dimble came to Joseph and

said, "You've got t'fight me." For a moment Joseph was amused. "Don't be silly, Ned. You and I have nothing to quarrel about." But when Dimble thumped him in the chest Joseph's amusement was over. "Look, Ned, you and I have always been friends. I'm not going to fight you." This was just what Corwood and his puppets wanted, for they had said to Dimble, "If you stand up to him, Ned, he'll back out; he's too chicken to fight." They gathered round and egged him on.

So Joseph found himself being shoved along to a piece of ground where the boys—about fourteen of them—made a ring for the fight. Dimble took his cap and jacket off. Joseph left his own on. Dimble waved his fists and then darted at Joseph like a stag with loose antlers. Joseph simply poked out his clenched left hand as a buffer and followed it up with a right-hand jab just to push Dimble away, for he still had no heart to fight. To his surprise, Dimble's squinting face threw itself straight at the left-hand buffer, and his neck got such a jolt from the right-hand jab that he staggered backwards and fell, banging the back of his ginger head on the rough cinders.

Immediately Joseph bent over him and started helping him up. "I'm sorry, Ned, but why must we fight? I don't want to hurt you. Let's quit." But Corwood's voice rang out, "Whoo, Ned, are you goin' a let a barmy swank like that knock you down? He's frightened of you! Let him have it, Ned!"

And Ned did, while the Corwood chorus spurred him on. Joseph just stood there and took it, except that as far as possible he covered himself from Dimble's pounding knuckles. After several minutes he flung both his arms round Dimble, pinning Dimble's arms down, and shouting, "Stop it, Ned! Who's put you up to this? If you want to say you've won, that's alright for me." So it ended with victory for Ned, amid cheers from the Corwood group.

Curiously, it had the very opposite effect to what scheming Corwood intended. Two of the girls had watched the ridiculous encounter, one of whom was Ruby Atkins, the girl Corwood was sweet on. She and a boy named Wally walked home with Joseph over Bowerfield. Wally said, "I'm sorry for you Joe. Why didn't you wallop him? You easily could have."

Ruby Atkins added, with a sympathetic look at her favourite boy's facial bruises, "Yes, you could, Joseph: but it's Loui Corwood who got Dimble to do it. He wanted to make you look like a coward. I hate him."

Joseph reached the door of 12 Wragley Street at the very moment his mother did, by which time his face was puffy and sore. Millie noticed it at once. She wanted to know about it. Joseph told her.

"Is that the real truth, Joseph?"

"Yes, mother."

"Could you really have beaten Dimble?"

"Yes, mother."

"And you honestly let him beat you in order to spare him?"

"Yes, mother."

"Well, son, your mother is proud of you. Even though you lost the fight to Dimble you won a battle over yourself."

Later that evening, Mike being out and Mona at the Choral Society, Millie reopened the matter. "Joseph, I'm proud to have such a son, willing to be humbled through no fault of his own. I want you always to be a man of peace, willing to take blows without retaliating.

"However, Joseph, there are exceptions to the rule. Sometimes not hitting back harms innocent people who are dependent on your defending them. There are times when to cower before evil instead of smiting it betrays Christian principle. Some say that a Christian should never strike back, but I think they are wrong. They confuse the personal with the collective. If as an individual person I am struck on the one cheek, I am to turn the other also, which is the opposite of taking revenge. But if a *community* is outraged by evil-doers the community collectively must *not* 'turn the other cheek.' It must strike back because it is responsible for the safety of its citizens. In that, Joseph, we see the difference between 'revenge' and 'vengeance.' Revenge is a *personal* retaliation and is wrong. Vengeance is a *judicial* responsibility of the community and is right."

Millie paused, looked compassionately at Joseph, then

broke into a hearty laugh. "Poor Joseph! I deserve a good spanking. I'm sure you haven't got the hang of it—or have you?"

"Mebbe I have, mother."

"Sometimes, when I 'let off steam' like this, Joseph, it's because I want to say some things to my only son which may be useful later. There's a lot of fuddled thinking nowadays. The Christian attitude, supposedly, is never to hit back. Treat crime as weakness; coddle the criminal back to good manners. That's the idea of a sentimental psychology which confuses the personal with the communal. Those of us who have to work among criminals concede that many incipient criminals need counsel as well as penalty; but that is very different from being soft toward crime itself. To treat crime and barface criminals with soft gloves is not progress, but foggy gullibility.

"About Ned Dimble. I suspect he was put up to it. What Ruby Atkins said lets the cat out of the bag. I don't mind your losing when you could have won, only I have a hunch that the other boys may now take advantage of you. I never want you to strike the first blow, but neither do I want to paralyze your courage. Try to be friendly with Ned, and find out for certain if Corwood is behind it. If he is, warn him. Warn him while some of the other boys are listening if he won't listen alone. Don't start a fight; but if *he* starts it, then for the honor of your principles, Joseph, stand up to him.

"I would not have recommended you to do so, Joseph, only there is just one more exception to that rule about not hitting back. To cringe before a bully who is bullying others as well as yourself is not Christian charity, but a form of cowardice which betrays others as well as yourself. The only kind of language a bully understands is the kind he uses on others. Bullies are usually humpty-dumpties who have a great fall when somebody really hits them. I shall pray that God may save you from any further fight, but that if you are taken advantage of, you may be given discretion, courage, and victory."

Millie's surmizings turned out to be prophetic. Next morning Joseph went to Ned Dimble in the playground.

"Ned, I hope we can be friends again." Ned seemed pleased, but two or three other boys tittered, and a few minutes later Joseph noticed Corwood talking in undertones to several as though planning something.

Joseph thought he ought somehow to be feeling a bit afraid, but he felt as self-possessed as if his mother Millie were walking at his side. Anyway, nothing more happened that day except that Ruby Atkins sneered at Loui through the railings which separated the girls' playground from the boys' and said, "I'll never be a sneak's girl. Joseph Kennard is a gentleman; and I told him it was you who put Ned Dimble up to fighting him."

Tuesday, Wednesday, Thursday, then something *did* happen. Joseph had noticed that some of the boys who hitherto would not have dared take liberties with him because he was tall and athletic were now almost cheeky. In particular this was true of a boy named Sydney Denton, a young warhorse, fast on the ball, a quick fighter, and a perfect pest because he was forever running up to fellows and clouting them or tripping them up and then running away before he could be caught.

Joseph and other boys were going home after school, as usual—playing soccer, or at least kicking the ball about from one to another as they went over Bowerfield. At one point Sydney Denton was whispering with Loui Corwood; then, while Loui held the ball, Sydney came over to Joseph and asked in a voice all the other boys could hear, "Joe which is the best-known lake in the English Lake District?" Before Joseph could say a word Denton struck him hard in the stomach and darted away shouting, "Aha, it's Lake Windermere—wind 'em 'eer, in yer poor old tummy!"

It is wonderful what split-second thinking the brain can do. The instant Denton's hand whirled out, Joseph saw it and held himself in. Still, the heavy slap hurt, and for a moment or so Joseph was a bit winded. Several of the boys cackled, Corwood the most loudly.

In that moment all Millie's counsel flashed back to Joseph's mind; so did all the boxing lessons with his beloved Wilfred in Rostherne. Again he wondered why he felt so calm, and why just then he should remember his mother's promise to pray. All this flashed through his mind in one supercharged second.

Sydney Denton had darted away beyond Loui Corwood. Joseph began walking slowly over to him, and Denton got ready to dart away again. The other boys watched. "Denton," said Joseph, "I'm going to call you something which should make any boy's cheeks go red. You are a coward if you can hit me like that and run away. I dare you to do it again."

The darter made no reply. Joseph got to within a few paces of him. Quick as an electric spring young Denton darted at Joseph to give him a swift swipe in the face and then whizz away again. But Joseph's brain was as agile as Denton's, and as Denton shot forward Joseph nimbly sidestepped but stuck his foot out and tripped Denton up. The speed of Denton's lunge was such that his fall was the severer. Down he went, face, stomach, hands, and bare knees on the cindery earth. It really hurt. But this time there was no gentleman Joseph bending down and helping the fallen to rise. Like a hound Joseph was down on him, seizing him by the scruff of the neck and rubbing his face in the dirt.

Then Joseph sprang away and said, "Get up, Denton. I won't strike you while you're down. Turn round!"

Denton did so. His face was a sight; dirty, scratched, bleeding.

"Now get up while I knock you down again."

Denton did not move.

"Get up, I tell you."

"I can't"—there were tears of pain as well as scratches.

"Either you get up or I rub your face on the ground again."

"No, don't Joe . . . please!"

"I'll let you off on one condition. Tell me: did Corwood put you up to what you did?"

"Yes."

"Did Corwood put Ned Dimble up to fighting me?"

"Yes."

"Did Corwood tell Ned I had made lies up about him to the girls?"

"Yes."

Joseph helped him up and began to wipe his bleeding knees.

All this happened in a few terrific minutes. The other boys had watched with bated breath. They now noticed that Corwood was beginning quietly to walk away.

"Hey Corwood!" Joseph's voice rang after him. "Are you deserting your pals now that they're getting hurt doing your dirty work for you? You say you're cock of the class. Why have you suddenly stopped crowing? Come and stick up for Syd Denton. Are you afraid?"

Corwood did not turn. He had an extra reason for not wanting to fight just then. He had seen his fair lady, Ruby Atkins, and another girl coming over Bowerfield, and he least of all wanted a shindy just then.

Joseph turned to the other boys. "I say, lads, you know who put Dimble and Denton up to fighting me. He's tried the same with you, Wilson, and you, Farmer, and you, Higgs. When I let Dimble beat me, Corwood got you all booing me, and yet I've always tried to be a good sport. Why don't you boo Corwood for a change? Are you cowards, knuckling under to a bully? Why don't you fetch him back?"

Sydney Denton gave a limping dart after Corwood, followed by Freddie Higgs. "You've got to come back, Corwood, or you're a dirty coward, and the lot of us will bash you."

Corwood was cornered. He turned but stayed where he was. Joseph strode up to him. "Loui, my mother taught me never to fight unless there was no other way, and never to strike the first blow. You've been pretty mean to me, but I'll call it quits if you'll apologize."

"I'll think it over and see you in the morning."

"No, that won't do, Loui. It must be here, with our pals listening."

By this time her pretty majesty, Ruby, was standing by with her friend, eyes goggling and ears all agog. Corwood was in a jam. He had to think swiftly. To apologize would give him a red face for ever. Kennard would accept it as "gentlemanly" but the other kids would take it as a coward's collapse. They would despise him. Ruby's royal slippers would tread him with disdain to the dust. Could he beat Kennard? He had never seen him fight. Maybe this bold front would crumple if he got a few hard wingers in his lungs—and, oh, what a never-to-be-forgotten boost *that* would be for himself!

On the spur, rather white and tense, he hoarsely exclaimed, "I'm danged if I'll apologize to a fancy-gob like you, Kennard," and fitting the act to the word, he plucked off his cap and jacket and rolled his shirt sleeves up above his elbows. "I'll knock all them blinkin' white skittles out of yer mouth, fancy guy."

Joseph watched and waited. At that very moment he felt again a surprising inward steadiness. He knew now that there was no escape from a real fight. He quickly eyed Corwood over again—a fraction less in height than Joseph, but thicker-set and heavier. As he now looked Corwood in the face two other faces swung before his mental vision— his mother's and young Wilf's. The one seemed to be saying, "You're in the right; hit hard." The other seemed to say, "For heaven's sake, old boy, don't forget those boxing lessons!"

The boys made a ring. The fight began. Corwood was going to make a big show of it. He struck the first blow, aimed full at Joseph's face—only by the time it reached its arm's length Joseph's face was not there; he had quickly dodged. Corwood's swing was such that when it struck nothing he overbalanced and fell. Tense as the onlookers were, two or three gave a giggle.

"Get up, Corwood," said Joseph. "I never hit a man when he's down."

Corwood sprang up and tried another swing, equally unsuccessful, but he held himself up this time.

For a few minutes Joseph jerked from side to side, bounced to and fro, bobbed up and down, to confuse Corwood and give him a chance to size up his man. Corwood was a heavy-footed, right-hand slugger, and that was about all. His left hand neither jabbed nor covered his face. He was pretty wide open and apparently knew nothing about boxing. He relied on his bodily weight and right-hand clout.

He reckoned that if only he could just land one of those smashers . . . but he just could not land it fast enough on that dodging target. The other lads had never seen anybody act in a fight as Joseph was doing, and wondered for a minute or two if this was what he would call "gentlemanly" fighting.

"Come on, Corwood," said Joseph. "My mother said I mustn't strike first, but I'll have to if you don't get one in soon"—at which the other boys laughed.

Corwood blazed. Suddenly he changed his tactics—if such they could be called. He lurched the whole weight of his body against Joseph, and at the same time, instead of a wild swing, he thrust his right arm straight forward to Joseph's face. But again Joseph's mind was faster than Corwood's body. The straight arm-thrust went harmlessly over Joseph's shoulder, and Corwood's face met the unexpected buffer of both Joseph's fists.

As Corwood was jolted back, Joseph judged it was the moment to take the initiative. He came in with a sudden combination of left-hand jab on the nose and swift right-hander under the chin. It was done with lightning speed. Corwood reeled, fell, and sat on the ground. He was hurt; but now he was wild. He had been made such a fool, nothing mattered now; and from that moment it was a case of brute force against skill.

He got up and dashed screaming at Joseph, trying to thump him with both fists; but again he left his face wide open, and Joseph remembered something Wilfred had shown him, which was to lean forward with your head a bit down and your arms close so as to guard your head, and get between the other fellow's arms for a rapid pummeling of his face. That is what Joseph did. Corwood staggered back, back, back, back, under the relentless pounding until down he sank, first to his knees, then on to his stomach—not because the blows were as heavy as Joseph could have given, but because he just could not see or breathe or hit back any more. His nose and mouth were bleeding. He was in a mess.

Joseph waited, but Corwood did not rise. "Say you're sorry, Corwood, or I'll give you some more!"

Corwood was silent. The other boys just gaped. They had never seen a fight like this before. Corwood had not had the ghost of a chance against the superb fighting-skill of Kennard.

Joseph stood over Corwood. "Say you're sorry, or I'll rub your face in the ground."

"I'm sorry," Corwood bleated.

The fight was over. Joseph was unmarked. The whole encounter had lasted no more than about fifteen minutes. It was the only fight Joseph had during his school days. He hated the memory of it. Never once afterward was he known to refer to it.

Somebody else referred to it, however, the next morning in St. Aiden's. The headmaster's desk was on a small platform against the inner wall of the main hall, about halfway up the room in which the three senior classes operated in their separate locations. Each of the three teachers had his (or her) small table, cupboard, blackboard-and-easel in front of the class. It was very seldom that the headmaster had any reason to address all three classes together, but if ever such a rare necessity occurred he used to hit a triple ding, ding, ding, on his desk bell.

About half way through that morning after the fight, to everyone's surprise the ding, ding, ding sounded. The three teachers stopped teaching and faced the headmaster's desk. All the scholars turned and faced it, too. Then the headmaster rose and said, "Joseph Kennard, come to the desk."

Turning rather pale, Joseph stepped out from the front row of his class and walked to that dreaded desk, where he stood and faced the headmaster. He knew instinctively it had to do with the fight.

The headmaster held a letter in his hand. It was from Mrs. Corwood.

> *Dear Mr. Burton,*
>
> *I am sorry my boy cannot come to school today. I can only hope he may be fit to come in a day or two. He got home after school yesterday afternoon with his nose swollen and bleeding, a black eye, and his face all bruised and scraped. He seems to be hurt in his*

*right knee as well; and this morning he is quite
sickly. I dragged it out of him that the cause of it all
is that young fiend, Kennard. I think it is a crying
shame when quieter boys like my son Louis, who is
too gentle to hurt anyone, get mauled like this by
young roughs of the Kennard type. I think, also, it
gives your school a very bad name, and reflects dis-
creditably on yourself. I hope you will punish that
young Kennard as he deserves, and make sure such
vicious horse-play does not hurt my poor Louis
again—or I must remove him to some other school.*

Yours,
Harriet Corwood

The headmaster did not read the letter publicly, but he
addressed the school. "I have received complaint about a
fight between two St. Aiden's senior boys after school yesterday afternoon. One of them was hurt badly enough to
keep him from school today. Now I want to make this clear,
once for all: I will not allow such fights by St. Aiden's boys:
they bring disgrace on the school; and I shall punish accordingly."

Addressing Joseph individually, he asked, "Kennard, did
you have a fight with Louis Corwood yesterday?"

"Yes, sir."

"Are you, then, the cause of the harm which keeps him
away from school today?"

"Yes, sir."

"Well, Kennard, you greatly surprise me. I thought you
were the very opposite kind of boy. Evidently I was mistak-
en. I am going to make you an example to the whole
school, while other scholars watch. I shall give you eight
hard strokes of the cane; four on your right hand, and four
on your left. Also, your teacher will set you one half hour's
penalty work after school this afternoon and every day next
week. Step forward, now, and hold out your right hand."

Joseph stepped forward, but before he could hold out his
hand everybody's attention was taken by a stir of quick
movement in Joseph's class; and, to the astonishment of all,
Ruby Atkins ran across the room and stood between Joseph

and the cane. "Sir," she cried to the headmaster, "you can't, you mustn't!" Then, with tears welling up in her eyes, she gulped out, "Please sir . . . it's not Joseph's fault. He's the kindest . . . boy . . . in . . . the school. It was all Corwood's fault sir."

Scarcely had Ruby reached the desk before Sydney Denton darted there and said the same. Madge Kelly plucked up her delicate courage and tripped out to say the same. So did young Wilson and Farmer and Higgs, and four or five others! Never in the history of St. Aiden's had such a daring thing been known before!

For a few seconds every teacher and scholar wondered what on earth the headmaster would do. But he seemed unruffled. With a twinkling glance at the three teachers, and a whimsical expression on his face, and in a tone of affected severity, he said, "Ruby, wipe those tears away at once, and stop blubbering. All of you, listen to me. I ought to give each one of you a swish of the cane, but I'll excuse you this once because I think you're telling me the truth. Never do this again. I will not cane Joseph until I have further information. All of you go back at once to your class—all except Joseph."

As they were going he said to Joseph, "Follow me," whereupon he walked to the big, heavy door which opened on the corridor leading to the boys' playground. Joseph followed. On the way out he thought there was a low chuckle just ahead of him.

The headmaster was rather tall, rather broad, rather portly, rather bald; in deportment rather grave, though sometimes rather bland, and in manner rather severe though sometimes rather humorous. In total he was about the most "rather" gentleman you could meet. Rather cleverly he was always just "rather" enough in one way or another to prevent anyone from presuming upon him. When he and Joseph reached outdoors he seemed "rather" amused, at which Joseph felt "rather" relieved.

"Well, Joseph my boy," he said, putting his hand on Joseph's shoulder, "that was a bonny how-d'ye-do, wasn't it? What those young Philistines did was quite *malapropos*, you know; but at any rate it let me in on the truth, and in a way it was rather plucky. So *fiat justitia ruat caelum*—which means, Joseph, as I hope you know, 'Let justice be done though the heavens fall.' I couldn't think that *you* would start a fight, Joseph, so I read Mrs. Corwood's letter *cum grano salis*. You've been such a well-behaved boy, and you are doing so well with the lessons. What caused the fight?"

"Sir, I don't want to talk behind Loui's back. I hate fighting, sir. My mother has taught me to keep out of it, and never to strike the first blow. I didn't cause the fight sir, nor did I hurt Loui as much as I could have."

"Alright, Joseph. Try to keep out of fisticuffs in future. I see a lot from my desk, and I have my own ideas about Louis Corwood. Maybe it will have done him good; but *(sub voce)* that's strictly between you and me, Joseph. Understand?"

"Yes, sir. Thank you, sir."

Apart from that one unhappy squall Joseph's years at St. Aiden's were smooth sailing. Ruby Atkins and several other young daughters of Eve doted on him. His teachers had reason to be proud of him. Two special honors came to him. One was that he and five others were chosen as the school's best six scholars, with an option to sit an exam which gave successful entrants a scholarship for three years at the Elmerton Secondary School. There were three girls and three boys. One of the girls passed. Two of the boys did. One was Joseph.

Almost on an equal level was, that one evening headmaster Burton called round to see Millie, who by this time was well-known. "Mrs. Kennard, there are two boys at St. Aiden's who are quite outstanding in art—in drawing, that is. They leave others far behind. The two are about equal in drawing and painting, but Joseph has it in *originality*. Mrs. Kennard, if you will let me, I will be happy to pay out of my own pocket for Joseph to have two full sessions under professor Crenshaw at the Technical College. Will you think about it and let me know?"

Much to Joseph's liking was the boys' sport activity at St. Aiden's. In those days there were not the sports facilities in parochial schools that there are today. St. Aiden's was one of the only three schools in that area which had a football team (soccer) of its own. Each school played the other two twice in a season, making four games in all, October to April. In between those St. Aiden's used to make up its own opposing elevens; and some historic (not to say hysterical) exhibitions of freak soccer there certainly were. But the team which represented St. Aiden's against the other schools comprised the pick of the boys.

In that team Joseph was center forward for a time; and what exploits he would relate to mother Millie now and then! There was one that had them laughing for weeks. The forwards were dashing down the field. Joseph had the ball. When he was tackled he slipped the ball to the inside-right, who in turn on being tackled passed it out to the right wing. The wing sped with the ball along the line, tricked the opposing half-back and then drove the ball back across the field slantwise to center. Joseph and the opposing full-back ran for it. Joseph got there first, but the full-back was so close that Joseph had no time to steady the ball before shooting; so he took it right on the slant and shot with all his might at the goal. It went wide of the goal by several yards, and whizzed full speed at a stubby-looking man among the spectators. It was travelling so fast, it was almost at the man before he realized it. Quick as thought he turned his back on it and bent down, hoping it would whizz over him. Instead, it caught him smack on that part of the human anatomy where dutiful fathers apply the hand of wisdom to the seat of learning! Instantaneously there was a sound like the letters "f" and "sh" explosively fused together: "fsh—!" followed by a puff of smoke and spurt of flame! The man had a box of matches in his back trouser-pocket. They had become warm; and the sudden concussion ignited them! He gave a jump and a shout of pain as the flame scorched him; then he hurried off the field with his hand trying to hide the bare part!

When Joseph reported it to his mother, what laughter! Little did he foresee that a few days later he would hear that playful mother relate it to the crowd of women at her Wednesday meeting. Often after school, on Wednesday, he would go round by the Mechanics' Institute and then walk home with his mother after the women's meeting. That particular Wednesday, as he tiptoed in at the back of the room, Millie was nearing the end of her address, and to his comic horror was using the soccer incident as an illustration. "Sisters," she said, "we can often learn a serious lesson from a humorous incident. I know the discouragement and opposition some of you are up against because of your Christian testimony. Face it all bravely. When you see trouble coming, don't turn your back on it like that man on the football field. If you do, you never know what might happen behind your back!"

Besides St. Aiden's there were other factors which blended powerfully in shaping Joseph's future. Transcending all others was the influence of his mother, for whom his admiring love grew deeper as he grew older; though there was one thing which gave her sad concern.

Although very much a boy, mischievous, frolicsome, rollicking, these were in best form. He was truthful, basically steady, and (for a boy) cooperative at home; fairly sedulous in his studies, popular at the Boys' Brigade, keen on music, persevering with the First Aid classes. He was very attractive to girls. By the time he was thirteen and fourteen his masculine puberty was as normally assertive as in any other boy. He could be drawn by a pretty feminine face, but there was no permitted sexual impurity in his thinking; nor did he start flirting about with girls. The influence of Millie and the home had been strong enough to build up resistance against the immoral. He would have no part in the way many boys talked about girls. This might have run him into persecution if they had not been so afraid of his fists.

He certainly was not the goody-goody sort. He made no real Christian profession. He went to Sunday school only because it was "the done thing," and had no scruples about evading church when he could. Those who knew him were the more surprised, therefore, that when he was twelve he won the solitary prize in a competition open to several hundred scholars aged twelve to sixteen—a prize awarded for the best essay on The First Christmas Day.

Nevertheless there was that "one thing" which was a continuing disappointment to Millie. Joseph showed no sense of needing the Saviour; nor desire for spiritual things. Much as he would have shrunk from knowingly grieving his mother, he definitely evinced an antipathy toward what he called "religion." He did not want any religious clamping down on his rightful pleasures. Thanks to what he had learned through Millie he had no allure for coarser things. He wanted to be a man of honor. Yet he also wanted "a good time" in all reasonable forms of pleasure. He wanted his own way, but he wanted it politely. Religion was alright for older folk. He would think about it after he had tasted the world's pleasures a bit.

That had been the set of the sails since he was five. Millie knew the very minute from which it began. When they lived in Manchester, Millie and family often attended the local Methodist church. One Autumn, a week's evangelistic mission was held there. The weeknight meetings were in the lecture hall. After each evening's Gospel address the missioner invited those who were seeking salvation to make their way to one of the small classrooms where Christian workers waited to help them. Millie and little Joseph attended one evening. Although he was only five he was evidently stirred. After several others had gone out and across the corridor to the classrooms he too quietly rose, edged himself to the end of the row, and slipped out to the nearest classroom.

He was greeted here by a Mrs. Meldrum who happened to be a near neighbour of the Kennards. She knew little Joseph well, and with consummate tact said, "Oh, Joseph, how glad we are to see *you* coming! We've been praying this would happen." At once Jospeh felt that he meant something to God. Fancy! people had been praying for *him!* Mrs. Meldrum had no difficulty explaining the way of salvation. Joseph knew it. She pointed him to the Saviour's words in Revelation 3:20, "Behold, I stand at the door and knock. If any man hear my voice and open the door, I will come in." They knelt together; and with the simplicity belonging to a boy five years old, Joseph asked the living Saviour to come in.

When he returned to the lecture hall the meeting "proper" was over, but, as was the practice, there was an addendum "testimony" time when those who had come into new blessing or had come to know the Saviour stood and said so in a few fervent words. Joseph rejoined his mother and sat listening. Much to her surprise, in a temporary lull, up stood her little man, and his voice piped out, "Friends, I'm so glad. Tonight I've taken Jesus into my heart as my Saviour. Such a load has been taken away from me. My sins have been forgiven because Jesus. . . ."

He got no further. Sitting on the seat next in front were two maiden ladies, twin sisters, and one of them said in an audible voice, "How ridiculous! A mere child talking like that!" Joseph faltered, stammered confusedly, and sat down, inwardly crushed. In that one second of brutal hurt it was as though an invisible hand had torn away the drapery of a religious hypocrisy. With shattering vividness it now seemed that this conversion business was a hoax of grown-ups.

The next Sabbath day, as that twin sister sang piously in the sanctuary, if she had known what damage her sarcasm had done to the soul of a boy, her singing would have drowned itself in weeping. The wounded little man wanted no more of talkative "religion." It was all a grown-ups' make-believe. He never spoke of it afterward, but Millie knew all about it and wept many a tear. Sometimes, as she scanned that dear face, so open, innocent, kind, but occasionally so lonely looking, she could see beyond the outer to the inner—a dead flower on a little grave. By the time Joseph left school he was becoming a thorough young worldling.

However, although the enemy of souls often does his meanest work through professing Christians, he does not have it all his own way. A Burmese teacher, Maung Schway-gnong, once said to Adoniram Judson, "My prayers have wrapped you like the perfumes of jessamine and helio-trope." Much less poetically but perhaps more persevering-ly Millie's prayers had enwrapped her growing boy. They had surrounded him with a wall of invisible fire against the grosser sins, and had kept his mind accessible to higher influences.

While Joseph was eleven, twelve, thirteen there were

two young men who made a lasting impact on him. One was Frank Goodall. At the Mechanics' Institute where Millie held her weekly meeting there were handicraft departments. One of these was the "woodwork room." Frank Goodall was in charge of it. He was a middle-height, sturdy man, in his early thirties. The first impression he always gave was that of being a *clean* man. He was clean-shaven, with a clean complexion, lightish, thinning, clean-looking hair; and even amid the sawdust and wood-shavings he always seemed to wear a clean-looking shirt and overalls. His clean look, happily enough, was symbolic. He was a man of clean mind, clean mouth, clean habit and clean work. He was a man's man, and very much a *boy's* man.

One afternoon per month the St. Aiden's senior boys went to the Mechanics' Institute for "woodwork" while the senior girls went for "housewifery." Frank took the more interest in Joseph because he was Millie's boy. Joseph took an immediate liking to Frank because of what he *was*. A friendship sprang up between them. Millie observed again how Joseph seemed to fall in with the right type of person. She liked to think it was a blend of intuition, discretion, and providence.

Often when school was over Joseph would trot round to Frank; more so during winter months when the weather was unfavorable to outdoor sport. He was respectful but inquisitive. Woodwork intrigued him. It was creative and constructive, especially the kind of small carpentry and cabinet-making which Frank did. Your own brain designed it. Your own hands fashioned it. When the article was finished there was something to *see*, of which you could say, "I made you."

Frank made chairs, small platforms, cupboards, and other requisites for the area schools, as well as doing all sorts of repairs. Joseph's company was pleasant to him. He was one of those methodical people who neither hurry nor lag, and who always seem to have time for you but without letting it interfere with what has to be done. He would chat away with Joseph, showing him how to do this and that while steadily keeping on. A keen boy like Joseph learned more that way than being *told* how.

Bit by bit Frank showed him, then let him try. It was a thrill. Joseph learned the different kinds and sizes of hand-saws, rip-saws, cross-grain saws, fine-tooth and rough-tooth saws, back-saws and dovetail saws, compass saws and coping saws. He learned the care and use of planes on different woods; the steel-jack plane, routing plane, tongue-and-grooving plane, block plane, wooden-jack plane, and the large wooden-trying plane. He got his first lessons with the brace-and-bits, the adze, the awl, the mallet and wood chisel; how to use the lathe and "turn" a spindle. He picked up the know-how of disc-sanding, buffing, wire-brushing, how to use the small grinding-wheel, twist drills, and spade bits. He learned the careful craftsman's first rule: "Measure twice before cutting once"; and to know with a cabinet-maker's precision the meaning of those three terms, "square," "plumb," and "level." Fairly soon he became Frank's useful protege, using the different tools as a very intelligent apprentice. Several of the small chairs which went to the Infant Department of a local school were made by him.

Frank Goodall was not "religious," yet he was a living embodiment of manly integrity and reverence for the high-er things. He would be considered circumscribed by the run of people today, but where could you find a happier, better-organized man? He neither drank nor smoked. He never swore or used unseemly language. Yes, he was a "clean" man, but he was *all* "man"; hale and hearty, fond of sports; a great walker all over the nearby Pennines, interested in all the politicial issues of the day and in all the "personalities" of Elmerton. One day he slapped Joseph on the shoulder and said, "D'you know, Joe, my lad, I've always wished I could have a son like you." He had no idea what he would mean in Joseph's life a bit later.

The other man who made a salutary, almost dramatic impact on Joseph was a Sunday school teacher at Jennifer Street. His name was Ben Revell. He was a short, wiry, bowlegged man with black hair and eyebrows, and dark, bright eyes to match. He had a thin face, high cheek bones, deep eye chambers, and a long, firm chin; but a smile like an unclouded moon transfiguring a dark lake into sparkling silver.

For the opening hymn and prayer at Sunday school the whole crowd used to meet in the main hall. After that the different classes went into their separate classrooms or to allocated bays in the main hall. When Joseph was twelve or thirteen he was in number 5 each Sunday with Ben Revell's boys. As in the old proverb, "iron sharpeneth iron," so boys in a group sharpen each other—especially in mischief! Joseph was a frank, likeable boy, but he was no angel. He had a razoredge wit and a naughty proclivity to pranks. Sometimes in class there would be undercover goings-on while Ben was giving the "lesson," until someone (not infrequently due to Joseph) simply could not help a snigger which Ben would hear. Now and then he would catch a boy at the very point of doing something on the sly to make another boy titter, but he was tolerant.

After the "lesson" one Sunday Ben said to Joseph, "I'd be glad, Joey, if you'd step back into the classroom for a moment."

Joseph felt a pang, for to him Ben Revell was a true Christian. To have hurt him by disrespect created a feeling of shame. He prepared himself for rebuke.

When the two were alone Ben said, "Joey, there's something I'll have to tell you. I hope you'll take it in the right way. You know, I love all of you lads. Every day you are in my prayers. I'd give both my arms if I could bring you to know the Lord Jesus as your Saviour. But, Joey, for weeks now, every time I pray, the Lord brings *you* before my mind. He seems to be saying, 'I want Joseph to be a preacher of the Gospel, to bring hundreds of others to know Me; but he's still unsaved; he wants his own way; his heart is bolted against me.' Oh, Joey, I wake up in the middle of the night worrying about you, lest the Lord should turn away from you. Oh, Joey, what can I say to bring you to know Jesus as your very own Saviour?"

All this had been said slowly in Ben's deepish, guttural way of speaking; but at that point he fairly broke down and sobbed, holding his head in his hands. "Joey," he added through his tears, "I'll never stop crying to heaven for you until you know Jesus."

Young Joseph was transfixed. His face went crimson. He felt his cheeks burning. He tried to speak, but the intended words stuck in his throat. In that instant his mind was swept back to that Manchester meeting when he was only five. He heard again, in a distant way, the ridiculing words of that woman. Like the sudden shooting of a bright beam down a dark corridor, it occurred to him that God was washing away that woman's sneers by this man's tears!

Ben apologized for his tears, but he certainly need not have done so. Although he did not realize it, that ardent outgush ended an era in young Joseph's thinking. Well enough did Joseph grasp that Ben Revell's cloudburst of concern for him was no make-believe. He could not get over it: Ben Revell thinking of him *like that!*—and praying for him *like that!*—and weeping about him *like that!* Even if it got no further at the moment, it flooded away the skepticism which had hitherto estranged Joseph's thinking since he was five years old. Later, Ben Revell's tears were turned to songs; but it took a tornado to do it.

ELEVEN
Queen of Hearts

From a hilltop in the suburbs of Geneva one can look down and see the uniting of the two rivers, the Rhone and the Arve. The former, as it emerges from the lake, is clear and smooth. The latter, hurrying down from Alpine glaciers, is roiled and turbid. For a way after they join one can discern the two, still distinct though now together, until eventually the confluence is complete.

Similarly from now onward the story of Joash and Agnes (the Adair family) and that of Mike and Millie (the Kennard family) become inseparably one, moving more quickly into stormbreak, mystery, tragedy, romance.

In the year 1900 we found Joash and Agnes with their two children, Evelyn and Rickie, prosperous and contented in an upper-class home on the outer fringe of Elmerton. Early the next year Mike and Millie with their growing young family came to live at 12 Wragley Street, Elmerton.

We are back in the autumn of 1901, a sombre dusk after a blustery day during which a truculent wind has rampaged among the trees, twisting and tearing the leaves from the boughs, and dashing about in noisy mischief through the suburban gardens, ripping the petals from the last blooms of the expired summer.

But inside Pinecrest, the Adair home on Woodland By-path, there is a genial contrast. The Turkey-red Axminster covering the ample hall looks warm and welcoming in the cheery light of the coloured-glass hanging lamp. In the large sitting-room the four incandescent gas-mantles of the quadriform chandelier are not yet turned on, but the red glow of a well-fuelled fire in the large grate lights up the whole room, creating a cosy indoor gloaming. In the oak-panelled dining room the square table has become oblong by the insertion of an adjustable leaf so that the table can now take three persons along each side and one person at each end. This is because six guests are expected for the evening meal.

In those days central heating was unknown even in better-class dwellings, but people knew how to build fire-places and stoke cottage fires! Each room in a house except the kitchen used to have its fireplace. Coal was plentiful in Lancashire, and nearby collieries kept towns like Elmerton well supplied.

For some years Joash had been Sunday school superin-tendent at Brandon Street Congregational Church. Soon after his appointment he was co-opted to the church dia-conate. There were nine deacons. They met statutorily once a month, and every third month their coming together was at Pinecrest under the genial hospitality of Joash and Agnes. Those quarterly rendezvous at Pinecrest took on a more convivial nature. Items of official business were expe-dited the more felicitously amid pleasant social interchange. The conversations at the meal table and after often devel-oped into confabulations of profound gossip, discussion, and pleasant cross-fire of repartee compared with which the House of Commons was dull.

On this autumn evening of 1901 two of the nine deacons could not come, but Joash and the other six were more than a quorum. Coincidentally the six arrived in three pairs. They all looked blown about, for the erratic wind was still playing pitch and toss outside. First came Mr. Clarence Lochart, the church secretary, and Mr. William Short, the treasurer. The former was a local solicitor in his mid-forties, and looked "every inch" a businessman—though actually there were not many "inches" of him, for he was a little man, after the order of Zacchaeus. Slick hair parted down the middle, spiky moustache—or, rather, two neat sprouts, one on each side the upper lip; black vicuna jacket and striped trousers; he was as obviously born to the ecclesiastical secretariat as a man is born a poet.

By contrast, and in contradiction of his name, Mr. Short was long: fully six feet tall. To some it had seemed risky electing a treasurer with such a name. Maybe it was; for too often, after his finance figures were submitted, the brethren dolefully murmured, "Short again!" Yet he had the true treasurer instincts. Receipts were nectar and payments pangs. Try to get money from him! He had the never-let-go of the bulldog, the "I-simply-won't-move" of the mule, the listen-without-speaking of the wise old owl, and a good-natured smile which completely hid the bulldog, the mule, the owl, in the person of a most gracious gentleman about forty-eight years old.

The other four expected members of the diaconal conclave were a blend of older and younger. There was dear old Mr. Nathan Broadbent, now nudging up to seventy. Everybody liked him—genial, stoutish, florid complexion, shiny and pinky bald head; the happy farmer type. He loved to be first with newsy tid-bits, revelled in playful banter, and kept a lively eye on everybody.

Next was Mr. Edgar Wagstaff, to some degree a facsimile of old Nathan Broadbent in mental traits, though ten years younger and of less portly proportions. He was the owner of a downtown drapery store; a man much respected. He had a remarkable interest in *personalities*—political, social, commercial, religious, national, local, good, bad. Human nature, in its endlessly varied manifestations, fascinated him. He absorbed all he ever learned about people of any significance. He was a walking edition of *Who's Who?* Mind you, his talk about people was never mere tittle-tattle. It used to be noticed that if anybody's darker features were gossiped, he was always disposed to turn the comments to kindlier aspects.

Finally, two younger men were Vivian Kirby ("Viv") and Herbert Holland ("Herb"). They were both in their early thirties. Kirby was head of the "estate agency" department in a large local firm. Holland was assistant postmaster at Elmerton G.P.O. Both were good-looking, keen-minded Christian men. They and all the older deacons had a loyalty to their church minister like that of the legendary knights to King Arthur.

On that autumn evening, the eight persons at the Adair table made a most congenial octad. The meal was such as to overjoy the taste buds of any Britisher—roast beef and Yorkshire pudding with vegetables and condiments to match. As the hearty demolition got well under way conversation accelerated. "Well, this month it's two years since this Boer War began," observed old Nathan Broadbent. "It's a wretched business. I read a couple of days ago that up to date we've lost over five thousand men to about three thousand Boers, and already it's cost us over a hundred and fifty million pounds sterling!"

"That's a fearful lot of money," reflected treasurer Short, with a further nibble at his Yorkshire pudding.

"But what's money, Willie, compared with eight thousand lives?" asked Edgar Wagstaff.

"It must have been a heartbreak to dear old Queen Victoria just before she died last January," commented Clarence Lochart.

"Yes, and a gloomy cloud over the Prince of Wales as he succeeds her," added Edgar Wagstaff.

"Who *are* these Boers, Clarence?" asked Nathan Broadbent, turning to secretary Lochart. "Sometimes they're called Afrikaans, and sometimes Afrikaners. Are they a mix of Dutch and Huguenots? That article I read the other day seemed to imply a mixture of Dutch, Portuguese, French, and German."

"No, Mr. Broadbent, the Boers are not a mixture; they're the South African Dutch, though some others may be mingling with them in this present strife."

"But how come there are so many more Boers than British?"

"Well, I suppose that's because they were there long before we were. If I remember rightly, as far back as the middle 1600s the Dutch made the Cape of Good Hope a calling station for ships going to the East. The Dutch settlers started opening up Cape Colony. It was only about eighty years ago that the Cape became a British possession."

"It's pretty mean of 'em to turn round on us, in my judgment," interposed Herbert Holland, "especially after the considerate treatment they've had from both the Disraeli and Gladstone governments."

"I feel the same way, Herb," said Lochart, "but you have to see what led up to it over a stretch of years. It's been building up ever since 1833 when slavery was abolished throughout the British dominions. That, and the giving of political rights to natives equally with Europeans was more than the Dutch could stomach, because to them the blacks are an inferior race. It was that which started the *Great Trek* soon after. Over ten thousand Boers left British territory to settle in the Orange Free State and the Transvaal. Britain honoured its treaties with them and would never have interfered if the Boers hadn't made a mess of government and bullied the natives and stirred up the Zulus to threaten invasion of the Transvaal with fifty thousand picked warriors."

The meal was about over, but a couple of the brethren nodded, "Go on," to secretary Lochart, who seemed to have the war well in hand. So they lingered at the table while Lochart expatiated.

Eventually Nathan Broadbent piped in, "What a historian you are, Clarence! But why have we British lost so many more than the Boers?"

"Well, at first the Boers had all the initiative, and forty-eight thousand men under arms against only twenty-seven thousand British. They had been secretly preparing for some time, whereas we were unready; and, remember the Boers are born fighters campaigning in a terrain familiar to them, and on hardy ponies which for some time made them bafflingly mobile. They are clever guerilla fighters; and this new kind of trench warfare which the Germans have taught them took us by surprise and cost us heavy casualties. The Germans are jealous of our empire, and I'll bet they'll have a head-on go at us one of these days."

Thereafter other topics of the times evoked lively confabulation: the meteoric popularity of those new Sherlock Holmes novels by Arthur Conan Doyle, and the whisper that he might be knighted "next year"; the latest exploit of David Lloyd-George, the upstart Welsh politician; the rise of the new Labour Movement under the lead of Ramsay MacDonald and Arthur Henderson; the capture by the Boers of that brilliant young British journalist, Winston Churchill, and his clever escape soon after, and his now having become Member of Parliament for Oldham; the wonderful new discovery of "electric light," and the petitioning of Parliament by London occultists to pass laws against electric light as being injurious to eyesight.

By this time they had moved away from the table and got down to church business. Eventually the seven wise men brought their deliberations to a liquid conclusion in a "good night" cup of tea served by Agnes from a capacious Victorian teapot. For those quarterly conclaves to end without that cup of tea and a slice of Agnes's fruit cake would have been, as portly old Nathan Broadbent put it, "like a church steeple without a weather cock on top."

During the tea-sipping and cake-nibbling, Edgar Wagstaff remarked, "What a vital new personality in Elmerton that Mrs. Millie Kennard is!—and what strides this new Police Court Mission is making under her initiative!" It took only one Wagstaff to mention it, and six other tongues wagged while Agnes listened eagerly.

"Yes, she's remarkable," observed Viv Kirby, "when you think what she's done in such a short time. There's scarcely a church now in which she hasn't roused interest in her work among women—women never touched by ordinary church activities."

"I'll tell you another thing," said solicitor Lochart. "She has a rare gift of utterance. I'm in court several times a week; and sometimes when I've heard her pleading on behalf of an indicted woman I've simply had to admire her tact and lucidity and skill. She could easily annoy some of the magistrates, but so far she never has. About six times, now, I've heard her manage to save a woman from becoming a first-timer in prison."

"I can well believe it," beamed Nathan Broadbent, "for I've been chairman twice now at meetings she's addressed. Never in my life have I heard a woman preacher to equal her. She's a genius! To my dying day I'll never forget how she made the words of Revelation 3:20 come alive—'Behold, I stand at the door and knock: if any man hear my voice and open the door, I will come in. . . .' For forty minutes you could have heard a pin drop! Aye, and when she asked if any of the folks now realized more clearly their need to receive Him as Saviour, ten or eleven—most of 'em young 'uns—stayed behind."

Seeing how the others were relishing his role as raconteur, Nathan resumed, "For sure, she's the most remarkable mixture of seriousness and humor I ever met. You sense, all the time, that she's in dead earnest about your soul, and that without any apology she's saying pretty straight things to you; but she's a past-master with striking illustrations which capture your imagination, and she has a knack of disarming resentment by witty humor. And, oh, man! that twinkle in her eyes, as though she's far more tickled by it than the audience!"

Old Nathan was fairly carried away by his adulations of Millie; so, seeing approving glances by the tea-sippers and cake-nibblers, he again launched out. "She seems to have an endless fund of real-life anecdotes from slum work; one minute comedy, next minute tragedy; but whether it's one or the other you always know what she's driving at. I'll never forget a couple of funny happenings she related at the rally of the Elmerton Band of Hope groups. She gave a temperance lecture at Preston, in a hall not far from the river Ribble. Her closing word was that it would be a good thing if every barrel of beer in Preston was rolled into the river. Then the chairman announced the closing hymn, 'Shall we gather at the river?'!"

There was such mirth, Agnes was afraid the children would be wakened upstairs. But all wanted to hear the other anecdote. So, subduing their chuckles, he continued. "She was giving another of those teetotalist lectures—a lantern lecture at St. Ignatius' Church in some town or other, and the notice board facing the main road announced it, *'The Slippery Road to Ruin,* illustrated by numerous *slides'!"*

This evoked further suppressed laughter, until finally Nathan said, "Mind you, don't get a wrong impression: she never tells a story, either humorous or serious, for its own sake. It's all part of her strategy to 'get you' for the vital thing."

Just as they were on the point of separating, secretary Lochart asked, "What about that man of hers? From what I hear, she has a problem."

There was an uneasy silence. Then Herbert Holland of the Post Office agreed, "Yes, she has a problem there. Mike Kennard works for us on a semi-permanent basis. He's an unusual chap; a sort of oversized bee who needs a hive all to himself. You feel him buzzing toward you half a mile away. He's bursting with abilities; so much so, it's a job to control them. However, he's doing his work well enough, and that's all we ask. I have a notion, though, that he's too fond of the beer . . . but I'd better not say more. Let's hope. . . ." Then the six deacons were gone.

During Millie's first three years in Elmerton a choice friendship had developed between herself and Mrs. Agnes Adair. Inasmuch as Agnes was secretary-treasurer of the Police Court Mission she and Millie often consulted together. Millie's vivacious company was always stimulating to Agnes, and Agnes's sympathetic comradeship was a relaxing comfort to brave Millie. Contrary to custom, they soon dropped calling each other "Mrs."—it fell away like a leaf in Autumn. They were two women of solid worth. They learned complete trust in each other, which in turn became true love. It had been a pleasant surprise for them to find that they both came from Rostherne and Mobberley; were both married in Rostherne Church in the same year; that Millie's parents now lived in the cottage where Joash had grown up; and that Millie had a son named Joseph, about the same age as Agnes' little Joseph would have been if they had not lost him in childhood.

During those three years Millie had several times taken Dorothy and Mona to the Adairs', but not young Joseph—

partly owing to his absences away at Rostherne and partly because of Mike's fierce objection. The reason for Mike's bitter antipathy toward the Adairs Millie could not divine. She decided it was simply another psychological twist; at the same time she deemed it wise not to irritate him into worse nastiness.

However, in the late Spring of 1904, when Joseph was thirteen, Millie and he were directly invited to Pinecrest one Saturday afternoon. Joseph had never before seen that sequestered spot on the outer fringe of Elmerton's suburbia. When he sighted the knoll and the handsome house, the trees and well-kept garden, the herbaceous borders and Spring blooms, the spreading fields and the folding Pennine slopes beyond, he was thrilled. In thought he was back again at Rostherne. And now he felt too shy to follow Millie through the gate, though he tried not to let her know. Inwardly he stiffened, and in a boyish way prepared himself to be most polite in such a swell place.

Already he liked Mrs. Adair, having met her several times after the Wednesday meeting, but he wondered if on her own splendid territory she would be majestic like Queen Victoria. However, any such thought was dispelled the moment she met them. "Hello, dearest Millie!" she exclaimed as she sped across the lawn to kiss her. "How good to see you! And what a pleasure to have your handsome son here at last!"

Joseph thought, "What a kind, motherly face!" Taking off his cap most respectfully, he held out his hand to give her a genteel handshake.

Agnes thought, "What a good-looking, well-mannered young gentleman you always are!" From their first meeting she had been pleasantly surprised that Millie should have such an obviously refined son—of such a father.

After Agnes came Joash. One look at Joseph, and he exclaimed, "Well, bless my heart, it's *you* again, my dear friend, Joseph!" Then, noticing Millie and Agnes's raised eyebrows, he explained, "This is the fine young man I met at the Kershaws' in Rostherne. You recall my telling you of him? My! how well he looks!"

Joseph could scarcely believe his eyes. So the man who

had called at grandma Kershaw's with "uncle Ben" was this Mr. Adair of Elmerton! As he held out his hand Joseph said, "I'm so pleased to meet you again," and, just in the nick of time, remembered to add, "How is uncle Ben these days?"—at which Millie and Agnes were again wide eyed.

It was a sunny moment. Joash was the manly but pally sort of father Joseph liked; and Joseph was the clean-looking, alert kind of son Joash liked. Millie sang inwardly, that her Joseph had made such a desirable impression. The fact was, for his years Joseph was an exceptionally prepossessing youngster.

But the moment of moments came when Joash called out, "Evelyn and Rickie, where are you?" First came young Rickie, almost tripping over the decorative stones along the herbaceous border in his curiosity to see the boy of whom his mother had spoken. It was Rickie's turn now to go shy. He had expected a small boy. When he saw tall Joseph with carefully parted hair, smart white collar and bow, stockings with fancy turn-down just below the knee, neat suit and shiny boots, he was taken off guard.

Agnes had to help him. "Rickie, dear, this is Mrs. Kennard's son. He's a bit taller than you expected, isn't he?"

"Yes, mother," agreed Rickie, looking admiringly at Joseph. "Hello, Joseph: my proper name is Richard, but they call me Rickie. You're older than I am, aren't you?"

Joseph held out his hand, and Rickie knew what to do. As they shook hands in best grown-up form, Joseph said, "*You* are a bigger boy than *I* expected. Perhaps we can play a game together"—at which Rickie beamed.

"Where's Evelyn?" Joash asked.

"She's coming, daddy. I pulled her hair-ribbon off and she's fastening it on again."

Rickie's apology was scarcely needed, for at that instant Evelyn came into view, hastening toward them, her beautiful face flushed from the game they had been playing. Surely there never was in any race or clime a more radiantly lovely girl of twelve years old. She captured attention anywhere; tall for her years; light, wavy, pretty hair—just now with a pink ribbon not tied on properly; limpid, rich blue eyes as pure as brightest morning, a facial expression of pure, girlish goodness, and a smile like a gentle sunrise.

Poor Joseph! He forgot his resolution to be the immaculate exemplification of gentlemanly manners—even forgot to hold out his hand as she came smilingly toward him. He just looked at her, from head to toe, as though suddenly seeing a vision of some heavenly seraph. Never had he seen such pure, queenly, feminine beauty before. He was momentarily dumbstruck and just stared at her. As for Evelyn, she stood smiling, unconfused, for she had seen other boys look in the same way: yet there was nothing but transparent modesty in that cherub face.

With a jolt Joseph realized that Millie, Joash, Agnes, and Rickie were all watching him; also that Millie and Agnes were exchanging an amused look. He blushed with embarrassment, and, in a voice which seemed too weak to make itself heard, he said to Evelyn, "I'm so pleased to meet you. I'm sorry I forgot . . . to . . . hold out my hand. You are so different from what . . . from what I expected." Then, in some confusion, he retired inside himself and seemed grateful to find safety in keeping closer than ever to his mother.

Unbelievable though it may seem, Joseph, aged thirteen but decidedly older in mind, had read something in Evelyn's face which went beyond that superb girlish charm. There was something in that shining face which said, "I'm pure in heart; I'm beautiful in mind; and I'm for you, one day." Joseph could not have expressed it in that way, but that is what had happened. All unexpectedly he had seen the ideal in that beautiful, beautiful Evelyn; and his young heart leaped out to it. Although all the girls at St. Aiden's were crazy over him he had never had eyes for any of them, but Evelyn, all in a few innocent minutes, had waved an invisible wand and made something "come alive" in him. Evelyn! Evelyn! Heart-melting Evelyn! What have you done? Joseph will never be the same again!

The remainder of that historic visit was a tantalizing experience for poor Joseph; an unmanageable mix-up of sensory transport and the torture of self-rebuke that he could not better conceal his absorption with Evelyn. As became evident, he felt that his only safety was to cling closely to his mother, and keep his eyes from veering in Evelyn's direction. That nymph, as amiable in disposition as in physical grace, was just as oblivious of Joseph's dilemma as of her own excessive attractiveness. Meanwhile, Millie and Agnes could not help exchanging amused glances as they observed Joseph's heroic but losing battle.

Later, as they all sat round the gate-legged table on the rear lawn for English style "afternoon tea," even Joash and Rickie could see his problem. His eyes simply would keep straying to that rose-pink face and that goddess of girl beauty; and each time he found them slanting there he would wrench them back, looking humiliatingly guilty, and pretend to be engrossed in what the others were saying.

But Joseph's most dazzling moments came later, when the older folk suggested that Evelyn and Rickie should show Joseph round the outgarth while the grown-ups chatted on the lawn. The "outgarth" was much more than its name suggested. It certainly was an extension outside the garth or garden, but it extended some three acres out toward the Pennines. Joash had bought it along with the ground for their new home to ensure that no building should break their eastward view. Besides that, this spacious area was where Brandon Street Sunday School held its annual "Picnic," and where the Elmerton Interdenominational Fellowship held its "Deeper Life Convention."

Between themselves the Adairs called it "Little Eden." It was reached through a rustic archway ornamented at that season by flowering creepers. In it were natural mounds and hollows which Joash's workmen had developed into pretty hillocks and dells, with crazy-paved paths dodging between the shrubby copses, while the grassy surrounds just then were profusely tapestried with clover and dandelion and daisies and buttercups and bluebells and maidenhair.

What a place for playing cowboys and Indians! What a sentimental trysting place for youthful lovers! What an inviting cloister for meditation! Joash had possessed both the men and the means to turn it into a miniature Shangri-La, though in truth Nature had needed little help of picks and spades beyond the scooping out of those secluded little coverts now furnished with rustic seats. Amid the ins-and-outs of that pleasant labyrinth there were five or six of those shady nooks, to which Agnes had given imaginative names such as, "Sleepy Hollow" and "Enchanted Arbor."

If that had been all, it was enough to evoke Joseph's wide-eyed delight, but there was more. An acre to the right there was a vegetable plot and kitchen garden: potatoes, carrots, turnips, cauliflower, onions, parsnips, French beans, peas; and beyond these, lettuce, celery, radish, parsley, cucumber; yes, even a strawberry bed, gooseberry and currant bushes, and a couple of young plum trees! To Joseph it seemed like a part of Rostherne transplanted to Elmerton. Nearby there was an anthracite-heated glasshouse for tomatoes, grapes, and some bulbous plants. Soon Evelyn and Rickie were marvelling that Joseph knew so much about the cultivation of all those various plants.

Would the surprises of that "Eden" never end?—for there, on the open ground toward the Pennine hills were a horse and a pony and several sheep grazing. Rickie explained that the sheep were farmer Walkden's and were sent into daddy Adair's ground now and then to nibble the grass down. The horse was Evelyn's, the pony Rickie's. The horse, being dapple-bay, was called Dapple. The pony was a black beauty named Shortie. They were new there, and the two Adair children were still a bit chary of them even after two or three riding lessons.

Although the horse and pony were feeding without halters Joseph found that they did not resent his approach; they wanted human company. Their sniffs were friendly. He felt them over and declared them fine animals. By this time Evelyn and Rickie were admiring Joseph because of all he knew. Their top surprise came when Joseph quietly sat astride Dapple and went for a merry little canter bareback round the ground. They watched with awe.

That part of the grounds was where the Sunday school picnics were held. There were swings. Never would Joseph forget his euphoric sensations that day as he got the swing going with that heavenly girl on it. As he lifted the chains and seat high to give her a good start, he could not avoid touching her—which he was almost afraid to do. She seemed like a being from another world. Each time she swung toward him she looked right into his face. Oh, that lovely smile! that seraphic face! those sparkling eyes! those rose-pink cheeks! And as she swung right up to his shoulders her soft yet shining blue eyes looked right into his— each time causing a near swoon! This was surely heaven begun below!

It ended too soon. The voices of Joash and Agnes and Millie could be heard, drawing nearer. Evelyn and Rickie pretended to run away, but soon came back. Millie noticed a flush in Joseph's face and a far-away look in his eyes. There was an expression she had not seen before.

"Well, Joseph, how do you like all this?" Joash asked.

From his zenith of happiness Joseph replied, with mature politeness, "Mr. Adair, I had no idea anything could be so beautiful yet so near to Elmerton."

"I'm glad you like it," Joash returned, "and I want you to know you'll always be welcome here. Evelyn and Rickie want you back often."

Joseph could scarce credit that over two hours had sped since Evelyn and Rickie and he had left the older folk chatting on the lawn. The sun was now westering, and from the Pennines an evening breeze was darting about with chilly fingers. They all went indoors. Although the invitation to Millie and Joseph had included evening dinner Millie had appreciatively declined owing to obligations at home. Agnes insisted, however, that before they left, Joseph must try the new piano—just while the maid was preparing a parting cup of tea. Joseph apologized that he was a mere beginner, and evaded. But Agnes had heard a thing or two, so she gently persisted.

After the poor old Kennard piano, this Bechstein seemed almost too rich. Those ringing bass notes and the resonant, pure-pitch top notes made his playing sound excitingly different even to himself. Also, Evelyn's presence afflicted him anew with shyness. He glanced for guidance at Millie. Her look said, "Yes . . . and do your best." Even Agnes, who was something of a musical Aristarch, was captivated as Joseph got going. The way he handled Sydney Smith's *La Harpe Eolienne,* with its chromatic scales and decorative runs;

and then, with sympathetic contrast, Tchaikovsky's plaintive *Chanson Triste*, was almost more than Agnes could have believed possible.

The total impression which Joseph made on the Adair family that day was more than he knew. Millie was humbly proud, and inwardly thanked God for such an upright, gifted son. There were six hearty good-byes at the front gate. Also, while Millie and Agnes were having the usual last-minute "Oh, I forgot to mention," Evelyn stole up close to Joseph and said, in a soft voice which made him tingle from head to feet, "Joseph, when you were introduced to me this afternoon, I hope you did not think me bad-mannered if I seemed to look at you too hard. You see, I could scarcely believe that I was seeing *you* again. I saw you once before, but I thought you might not like my mentioning it with daddy and mummie listening. You go to St. Aiden's School, don't you? I go to Stimson High. Your football team played ours; and I watched the game. I did not want your team to win, but I did like *you,* and the way you dashed down the field. I was standing at one side of the Stimson goalposts when you gave that big kick, when the ball missed the goal and hit that little, stout man on his . . . his box of matches in his back pocket! Ooooh, wasn't it funny, Joseph? I was so surprised when it was *you* who turned up today."

She said it all so confidentially, as though she liked to be near him. It was an almost unbearable thrill for Joseph. He coloured a little and managed to reply rather secretively, "I'm so glad you told me, Evelyn. Yes, wasn't it comical?" He risked one further, devouring look at her—Evelyn, queen of hearts. Those kind, glistening blue eyes were looking so frankly right into his. In those upturned eyes he caught his first sight of heaven.

Millie and Joseph walked down Woodland Bypath (people walked in those days). They had to walk fully a mile to where they could get a tramcar for the Wragley Street locality. As they turned into Clifton Boulevard, Joseph turned round for a parting look at the handsome Adair home. Back there, standing in the narrow road, was one solitary figure, caught in the last rays of the sun as they glinted through the trees. It was Evelyn. Instantaneously

Joseph grasped that she had stayed there hoping *he* would look round. How thankful he was that he had not gone round the corner without looking back! He would never have known she had waited! He plucked his cap off and gave it one nervous wave. Evelyn waved back, then ran inside the gate.

As Millie and Joseph were walking to the tramcar stop, Joseph said, "Mother, hasn't it been wonderful? . . . I don't know why, but I've gone so tired."

"Yes, Joseph," said Millie, "I think perhaps I understand."

As they rumbled along in the tram he sat close to her, and a side glance told her there were two tears trickling down his face. "Mother," he said a bit shakily, "I don't think I want to go there again. . . . I'm glad I'm back with you. I shall never love anybody better than my dear little mother." Reaction was full on.

"Perhaps I understand more than you think, Joseph. You made me proud of you today." She knew the workings of his mind. He had a refined sensitiveness as to the rightness and wrongness of things. She guessed what was quivering within him. He was years ahead of his birthdays. He had loved his friend, Wilf, at Rostherne; yet always he had sensed the "class" distinction. They were not on the same level. The point of parting must come, and he must accept it. He was realizing the same now about Evelyn. He was too young to love as a grown man, but he could love as an unusually mature teenager. He had seen something unspeakably lovely, and his heart had gone out to it. It was no mere "love at first sight" excited by prepossing facial allurements. In the case of Evelyn, that dear face was unmistakably the window through which a singularly pure, kind, loving mind looked out. Young though he was, Joseph had seen it. It corresponded with something in himself which had lain dormant until then. Now it was suddenly awakened by a magic wand. He could have looked his young eyes away. . . but now, the painful aftermath was the realization of that "class" disparity again. He was advanced enough to realize that being with Evelyn could only prove tantalizing in the end.

Millie understood, and drew him closer to herself. She knew others who had seen some object of supreme desire but had realized it could never be theirs, and that through all their earthly years they must carry a grave deep hidden within.

Oh, Evelyn, Evelyn, most innocent of all time's fair enchantresses, can you not see what you have done? All unintendingly you have pulled the string on Cupid's bow, and shot an arrow dipped in love's poison nectar (the only poison arrow which hurts but never kills!) right into Joseph's honest young heart. Poor Joseph is wounded sore. Even now it is badly hurting, for he knows that although he wants you forever he can have you never. He wants to be with you, to play in the outgarth with you—even the girlish game of skipping ropes if only to be with you, to hear your musical voice, to see you looking at him, to be able to touch your hand; but he knows that he ought not to come round to Pinecrest any more. Evelyn, what can he do? Joseph has precociously felt what he ought not to have felt for another six or seven or eight years. He will never be quite the same again. In that, however, he is by no means alone; for no man of quality is ever quite the same again when once he has met his one-and-only queen of hearts.

Alas, there was another reason why Joseph would never be the same again. That night number 12 Wragley Street was in trouble. That trouble had been brewing for days. Mike wanted to know where they had been. Millie would not prevaricate. She said, "Mike, you know that Agnes invited us round. She and I had things to discuss; and besides that, I was feeling ashamed that never once had we ever introduced Joseph to them. I only wish you would have come, too."

That was enough. Mike was slightly inebriated. The bull of Bashan roared its loudest. "Damn you both! Haven't I told you I detest those people? Hypocrites, and dirty-minded thieves of other people's money. I knows 'em."

Turning with savage hatred on Joseph he bawled, "You young pest, if I catch you going yonder again, I'll bash your nose in!"—and swiftly suiting the act to the word, he slapped Joseph so heavily on the face that Joseph's nose bled.

Joseph was so taken unawares, he could not have avoided it. He stiffened, clenched his fists, went white and tense. Millie was startled. She knew how well Joseph could use those swift fists. "O God, no!" she prayed inwardly. "Let me never see Joseph and his father fighting!"

But the prayer was hardly needed. Joseph relaxed. Then, with amazing calmness, he looked steadily into his father's face and said, "Father, if you ever do that again without my giving you cause, I'll fight you in the street and beat you, or else I'll leave home."

Mike listened, still livid with rage, but stunned with surprise. Joseph's words had somewhat sobered him. In sardonic amusement he began audibly soliloquizing, "So the grasshopper lifts itself up against the lion, eh? Poor little grasshopper when it gets crushed under the lion's paw! Listen to me, young fool, I know something about that Adair chap which you don't; and I'm tellin' you: Keep away from there. One of these days, by heaven! you'll know why." Having so said, he lapsed into moody silence.

Joseph kissed his mother good night, bathed his nose at the kitchen sink, then went upstairs to bed. For him it had been a Saturday of exhausting emotional collisions. Earlier he had seen an unworldly purity smiling at him through a human face of shadowless innocence. Scarcely had he left that than he saw Diabolos himself glaring at him with ugly hate through the eyes of his own father! No, Joseph would never be the same again. All in a few hours he had known emotional rapture—and rupture.

TWELVE
The Bicycle Outing

As already mentioned Joseph had struck up a friendship with Frank Goodall, the woodwork man at the Mechanics' Institute. By the time he was thirteen he had become a trustable young apprentice. Frank had grown fond of him, and helped him to put a bicycle together.

In those days not only did most mill-workers wear clogs; many rode "bikes" to and from work, weather permitting, and for outings at weekends. The motor car was then in infancy—little more than a big toy. Many had considered it gravely wrong for the newly crowned King Edward to risk being taken for a ride in one. Edgar Cundy had been "summoned" for furiously driving one along Brighton Road, South Croydon, at sixteen miles an hour!

Most bikes then were fitted with solid rubber tires; though some higher-priced ones now had the newly invented inflatable kind with inner tube and outer tire. The better-off could afford brand new bicycles. The poorer managed with secondhand survivors or with mongrel machines made up of parts from preexisting bikes which had now "departed this life" through fatal dismemberment.

Every lad coveted a bike. Joseph had one. It was a mixture of secondhand and mongrel, with parts incorporated from several disintegrated predecessors. But eventually, when Joseph and Frank had worked on it, and Joseph had fixed celluloid mudguards on it and black-lacquered all the iron parts, it looked smart enough to be enviously admired by the neighbourhood boys. Soon, now, Joseph would pedal that bike into a memorably dramatic episode.

Conscientiously he resolved not to visit Pinecrest again, but the matter was taken out of his hands in such a way as to make him a frequent figure there. Each visit made Evelyn more devastatingly alluring, without her realizing it. As for that ethereal damsel herself, the more she saw of Joseph, the more she was drawn to him.

On the second Friday evening after that memorable Saturday, Joseph was mending a puncture. For the sake of more space he had set his bike, wheels upward, outside the wall of the tiny front garden at 12 Wragley Street. As he was bent down affixing the tacky patch to the inner tube, a soft voice with merry music in it said, "Hello, Joseph." He looked up. Oh, no! surely it could not be!—the Evelyn of his dreams! Yes, she was actually standing there, by her own bicycle, looking down at him, and turning Wragley Street into a shining corridor of heaven! Oh, that tender, happy face! The unexpected sight of it sent Joseph almost sick with delight. His saliva glands reacted awkwardly so that he had to swallow hard before managing to say, "Forgive me, Evelyn. This is such . . . such a surprise. It . . . well, I can scarcely believe it's you. But, Evelyn, why ever have you come—all alone on your bicycle, all this way from your splendid house to . . . ours? I'm afraid it must look. . . ."

She interrupted. "I think anywhere must be nice where *you* are, Joseph. And besides, my mother thinks there's nobody on earth to equal *your* mother."

He had quickly risen to his feet; and, since he did not have his cap on, he had touched his forehead and slightly bowed in the customary expression of respect to a young lady.

"I came to bring this note for your mother, Joseph."

"Oh, thank you. It is kind of you."

Then Joseph's face changed. Evelyn was quick to observe. Apologetically he explained, "Mother's out just now. I'll give her the letter as soon as she returns. It must seem ungentlemanly, but I cannot ask you into the house because . . . my father is in, and. . . ."

Evelyn came to his rescue: "Joseph, my mother said I must not stay, but only hand in the letter and return home while it is still light."

He accompanied her along Wragley Street, subconsciously aware that the lace curtains of all the lower windows had moved a tiny wee bit at the lower corners, in true, Wragley form, so that the "I spy with my little eye" look-outs might not be charged later with sleeping at their posts of duty!

It was a joyful relief as they reached the end of the street to meet Millie coming round the corner. Her face lit up with pleasure to see Evelyn. Joseph handed over the letter. Millie read it, and said, "Thank you, Evelyn. Tell your mother the answer is 'Yes.' "

Evelyn's lovesome face beamed. "Oooh, that's wonderful." Then with a sly smile at Joseph she added, "You see, Joseph, I knew what was in that letter! Bye!"—and away she sped as fast as her legs could pedal. Joseph's face was a study.

"Did Evelyn go into the house, Joseph?"

"No, mother."

"Did your father see her with you?"

"No, mother; I think not."

"Let's hope he didn't. I haven't fathomed yet his dislike of the Adairs. It could be jealousy. We daren't give in to it; yet nor do we want needlessly to aggravate him. You can read Mrs. Adair's letter."

> *My dear Millie,*
>
> *I hope you are not too tired after Wednesday and then yesterday at Minley. You have such an inimitable gift of communicating, I fear we all take advantage of you. But I know the women; and hundreds of us wish you had come to Elmerton years earlier.*
>
> *Evelyn and Rickie insisted I write this note. Since you and Joseph were here they have never stopped talking about it. I know you have to be at Flossie*

*Freeman's wedding tomorrow afternoon, but could
Joseph come round early afternoon and you yourself
later, for the evening meal? If you have to say No, we
shall thoroughly understand, but if you can say Yes,
it will put a big extra smile into Saturday's sky for
us. Don't bother to write a reply. Just tell Evelyn.*

Ever yours affectionately,
Agnes

So Joseph was back again at Pinecrest, one part of him
sighing, "You ought not," the other part singing, "But this is
heaven." That second visit led to a third and a fourth; and
when the schools broke up for the long summer holiday he
was there repeatedly. He was so refined in manners, so
amiable in disposition, so thoughtful-looking at times, and
had such evident good influence on Rickie and Evelyn, that
Agnes increasingly delighted to have him round. As a working-class boy he was plainly dressed, but his celluloid collar
was always a good white, and his dinky bow always
straight; his jacket and trousers were neat (he wore a
complete suit only on Sundays), his bare knees always
clean, and his boots well polished. Even his bike was as
much like "a new pin" as an "old war-horse" could be.

Oh, those golden days! As a boy of thirteen, older than
his years, Joseph had to condescend a bit in games with
Rickie, though Rickie was never allowed to suspect so.
Swings, skipping, ball games, hiding-and-hunting, all had
their turn. Joseph taught Evelyn and Rickie how to saddle
and ride Dapple and Shortie; how to test a horse's condition; how to let it know what you want it to do; how to
groom it, wipe it down, "bed" it for the night. He showed
them how to play croquette—Rickie and Evelyn using junior mallets. They were always ready to pause from play,
however, and get Joseph talking about plants. In short, he
was transmitting with sporty politeness what he had gar-
nered in his mind at Rostherne.

Agnes began to notice a curious feature. Hitherto Evelyn
and Rickie had wanted several children together to be with
them. Now, it was just Joseph they wanted. They followed
him like a double shadow. But it was not only they who

doted on Joseph. Something was happening in Agnes. She saw clearly that his gentlemanliness was no artificial courtliness; it was inbred. She was not blind to human limits and defects; but for a boy he was extraordinarily considerate of others. He could laugh until his sides ached at anything really comical; yet plainly he was more at home in thoughtful periods. He reminded her of Joash when *he* was a boy in Rostherne. Inevitably, too, he reminded her of their own little Joseph, taken from them as a child.

Several times when the three were on the croquette lawn she had watched through a window beside the dining-room fireplace. How patiently Joseph had taught jumpy young Rickie the art of angularly roqueting a ball so as to place it near a hoop for the next shot! How almost reveringly he had held his hands round Evelyn's on the mallet handle when teaching her how to swing a hit! Once or twice, with motherly impulse, she could have hugged him. Indeed, on one occasion she did so.

The three had been into the kitchen for lemonade. Rickie and Evelyn ran out again, and Joseph who, with his usual restraint, had drunk more slowly, was handing the glass back to Agnes with a smiling "Thank you" when she put an arm round him and kissed his forehead saying, "Joseph, we just love you to be round here. Come as often as you like." Scarcely had she said it than she felt her arm wet. Joseph had not been able quickly enough to brush away impromptu tears—and was ashamed.

"Joseph, dear boy, why those tears?"

"I don't know, Mrs. Adair. I'm always happy here, only I keep thinking it doesn't seem right. I'm only a . . . working-class boy, and I can't expect to have Evelyn and Rickie long. And my father doesn't like me to come here. He's unkind to mother and me, but I don't like to deceive him. I'm always afraid he might. . . ."

Handsome young Joseph was already nearly as tall as Agnes. She looked closely now into that face, and, for the first time, behind the frank, boyish alertness she saw suffering—bravely camouflaged but not completely hidden. Agnes wept a bit, too. Inwardly she said, "Millie, what a dear, dear son God has given you!"

Then, with a mothering smile like a sunshaft through rainy skies she said, "I'm glad we've had this little weep together, Joseph. I think we understand each other a bit better now. But if you ever talk again here about being a working-class boy, I'll give you the best spanking of your life. We don't make any distinctions here like that. We love you for what you *are*, and we're mighty proud you come. We know about your father. Perhaps the less we say the better. But you have the most wonderful mother any boy ever had, and your two sisters are real 'young ladies.' You can be proud of them Joseph, as they are of you."

"Mrs. Adair," he replied ruefully, "I'm sorry I mentioned my father. . . ."

"Don't chide yourself, Joseph. Maybe I understand more than you suspect. Your mother and I have no secrets from each other. Let me tell you, once for all, there's nobody more welcome here than you. As for your father's not knowing, leave me to chat with your mother about that. Mr. Adair says that when you are a bit older he would like to have you in the business with him—if you cared."

Joseph could scarce find voice to say "Thank you." He looked right into Agnes's sympathetic eyes, and his trustful look said far more than words.

In that moment Agnes saw, not the talented, debonair young man, but a lonely-hearted boy dragging a big, sad question-mark as heavy as a leaden weight. Inwardly she said, "If it can compensate you for that no-good father of yours, from today you have two mothers."

So Joseph kept going, but conquered himself sufficiently not to go *too* often. It needed all his will-power, for by now, if ever a boy of thirteen loved, Joseph loved Evelyn. The more he was with her, the more he knew that she answered the supreme aspiration of his heart—though at that time he could not have put it in just those words. He knew she was superbly beautiful in face and form and elegant movement, as did every other boy who ever saw her. She herself could not help knowing that she was supernormally attractive; yet Joseph never once saw the faintest fleck of conceit. She was as natural as a thoroughly girlish girl could be, and as modest as a plain Jane.

No, these tributes to that "fair maid" of Pinecrest are not exaggerations. They are the truth without varnish. She was a glad young soul, yet often given to deep thought, for her age. She was brimming with healthful energy—good at games, fleet of foot, quick to react, eager to win, yet never petulantly assertive or competitive or boisterous; willing to lose and laugh, to learn and like; companionable and free from moods. We are not presenting a flawless statue like Galatea, the ivory maiden which king Pygmalion of Cyprus made and then fell in love with. Evelyn Adair was human. Somewhere the imperfections inhering in our hereditary humanhood clung round her; yet they certainly were singularly unobtrusive.

Young Joseph loved her so hard, it sometimes tired him nervously! When he was away from her he would wonder just what it was about her that he so loved. He loved her face—the most exquisite he had ever seen, and it seemed the more adorable the oftener he looked at it. Yet he knew it was not just her face he loved; for if that face had belonged to someone other than Evelyn it could not have had the same meaning. It was the pure heart which looked out at him through those shining yet tender, blue eyes; the warm, kind nature which spoke through that velvet-soft voice; the inner someone who smiled at him with those thrilling lips. Yes, it was that inner Evelyn he really loved, but Evelyn incarnate with that dear face, those dear eyes, those dear lips, that dear voice, that uniquely "Evelyn" way of saying and doing things. He knew now that she not only liked him; she was *fond* of him; for she had shown it and shone it. Once or twice, after a vigorous game, when they had sat in one of the shady nooks of the outgarth, she had leaned her head, with its wavy, almost flaxen hair, upon his shoulder and had put her arm round his neck, so trustfully, innocently, naturally—while Joseph had almost fainted with the exhaustion of suppressed ecstasy!

As for Evelyn: she thought now that there was no other boy anywhere as nice as Joseph. Not only was he such a good-looking boy, he was the gentlemanly, clever son of her mother's best friend. She knew that her mother had taken a peculiar liking to him and that he was Rickie's "hero." It all added up to this: Joseph Kennard was special. She enjoyed having him with her, but sometimes wondered why he was so kind in coming so often! The fact was, she did not *love* Joseph in the maturer way he loved *her*. How could she? She was girl-conscious, knowing that girls and boys are different in body and mental traits. There was gender-awareness but as yet no distinct sex-consciousness; so neither was there that response which accompanies maturer feminine development. Joseph certainly was her "Prince Charming," though in scarcely more than the girl-boy way. Then, all unanticipatedly, not very long after her next birthday, she looked at Joseph in a different way.

Evelyn's thirteenth birthday had been worthy of a young queen. School chums came by invitation; but her majesty's guest of honor was Joseph. There was a sumptious feast with tempting delicacies young folk like; but the main item was chicken, and the wish-bone was given to Evelyn. She had to write her dearest "wish" and hand it folded to her daddy and mummie, who were not to look at it "until the moon came up."

By the time the party was over the moon rode high. When Joash and Agnes released the wish-bone secret they had to laugh, yet with a rather peculiar look at each other. It said: "I wish, I wish, I wish, for a bicycle picnic with Rickie and Joseph to Lake Netherford next Saturday."

Agnes said to Joash, "It's remarkable the way Evelyn has taken to Joseph. It's nothing but a happy boy-girl attraction . . . but I wonder whether more could be developing. Of course they're much, much too young. . . ."

"I thoroughly agree," Joash replied. "Evelyn could not like a better lad than Joseph. But speaking from the male side, Agnes, after observing Joseph carefully, my own feeling is, that he is much maturer than fourteen, and really loves Evelyn—in a boyish way, but real love, all the same."

"What should we do about it?"

"At the moment, Agnes, I suggest we do nothing. On

Evelyn's part it's no more than a frank, innocent liking for a nice boy. As she gets older she is bound to view things differently. If need be, a bit later you and I can have a talk with Evelyn; and Millie can advise Joseph. I think they're both the kind who will listen to reason."

"But, Joash, does love ever listen to cold reason?"

"Yes, Agnes, I think that where love is a light in the mind and not just a fire in the bones it can see wisdom. But let's wait for the present."

"Meanwhile, Joash, what about the wished-for picnic?"

"Well, my dear, if your feminine instinct says 'Yes,' my male logic says 'Amen.'"

Unfortunately the weather-man was uncooperative, for "next Saturday" was gray and drizzly; so was the Saturday after that; and as the summer holidays were now over, Saturday was the only day of the week they could go. Also, alas, besides the unsympathetic weather-man, the minister of nasal affairs decided that Rickie should have an attack of febrile sneezes and wheezes on the Friday before that "first fine Saturday"; so the unlucky laddie had to be appropriately dosed and packed off to bed. Poor Rickie!—because that Saturday turned out to be the one predestined for the picnic!

It appeared at first to be one of those occasional days which seem naughtily designed to tantalize human beings. It just could not make up its mind which kind of day to be—whether to be wet or fine, dull or bright. The sky could not make up its mind whether to be blue or gray. The sun could not make up its mind whether to shine or to sulk behind trailing vapour. The clouds could not make up their mind whether to disperse or to congregate in a gloomy downpour. The wind could not make up its mind which way to blow. It dodged and scampered round in every direction. No sooner had people grabbed their hats against a sudden puff on one side than a giggling swish caught them off guard on the other side, plucking off the men's trilbies and disrespectfully ballooning the ladies' skirts. The watchful weather-cock could not make up its mind which way to point; and the pony could not make up its mind whether to shelter by the wall or frisk in a frenzy round the field; and the smoke from the factories could not make up its mind whether to go up or down or whisk in spirals round the upper neck of the tall chimneys. In keeping with it all, it was not surprising that Joseph and Evelyn could not make up their minds whether to *go* on the picnic or *not* to go.

However, quick-witted Joseph biked round to the head police office to ask if they had the Manchester forecast. Yes, they had. The prophecy was for a quickly clearing sky and a sunny day later. That was enough for Joseph. His arrangement with the Adairs was to be round at Pinecrest by 9:30 or 10:00 a.m. if the weather was favourable. Before ten o'clock our eager young Evelyn-worshiper was at the garden gate, haversack strapped behind his shoulders, and the saddlebag behind his bike bulging with only-he-knew-what.

Naturally he was disappointed to learn that on account of Rickie's indisposition they would not be going (as it seemed), but he did his best to disguise it. One look at Evelyn's face told him how sorry *she* was; but he could not help thinking, "How lovely her face is, even with a shadow on it!" He knew it would be presumptuous to show any sign of lingering there, so he said as cheerily as he could manage, "Never mind; the important thing is to get Rickie well again; and there are several more Saturdays before the days get too short and chilly. I'll get on my way; and I think that since my mother put up this lunch for me I'll go for the outing, and I'll *imagine* that Evelyn and Rickie are with me."

"Oh, Joseph. . . ." It was Evelyn who spoke. "I'm *so* sorry not to be coming with you. It seems as though my birthday wishbone hasn't worked, doesn't it? And I'm not even allowed to read for poor Rickie in case I catch what he has."

Evelyn's remark seemed to click something in Agnes's mind. "Joseph, don't run away for a minute. Wait here. I'll soon be back." And soon back she was, with an exciting twinkle in her eyes. "I've had a word with daddy through the telephone [Joseph thought: My! how wonderful to talk through a telephone!] and he says that in view of the likely good weather it's cruel not to let you go. Evelyn, would you really like to go with Joseph?"

Evelyn's face flushed and her eyes shone.

"Very well dear. We mustn't keep master Joseph waiting. Let's get you suitably dressed, and quickly make some sandwiches."

To describe Joseph's feelings would be difficult. They were a turmoil of manly pride at being so trusted, of strange nervousness, and of amorous transports. "Dear God," he whispered, "I'm sure You've had a hand in turning things round like this. Please do take notice that I'm not forgetting to say 'Thank You.' "

He sauntered through the rustic portal into the garden behind Pinecrest. The morning was becoming resplendent. All nature seemed alive with awaking loveliness. It was the kind of scene in which Joseph's sensitive mind was most at home. Around him was a prodigality of floral glory: marigolds, dahlias, asters, nemesia, petunias, sweet-scented stock, fuchsias, sweet peas, full-bloomed roses. The air up here was translucent enough for every detail on the Pennine skyline to stand out sharply. From the Yorkshire moors a hilarious breeze was dancing over the wide summits and down on the Lancashire side flinging handfuls of redolent incense from peaty turf and odoriferous plants and aromatic gardens.

And into all that there now stepped the demurest, blithesomest girl of thirteen that mortal eyes ever saw! There she stood: the incomparable Evelyn! Ready for the picnic—just the two of them! Oh, day of days! Joseph's entranced eyes took all of her in at one glance, especially those rose-pink cheeks, glowing eyes, and rubicund lips. She wore a primrose cotton dress with a floral pattern, and a dinky sunbonnet to match. Her soft, wavy, light hair was gently tied back with a silk ribbon. White stockings below the knees, and brown shoes fastened with small glass buttons, according to the style of the times, completed the fair picture.

"My!" gasped Joseph. "You look . . . well, I'm lost for words! . . . Do you think such a high-class girl on such a fine new bicycle should be seen out with a drab boy like me?"

"Joseph!" interjected Agnes, "hold out your hand."

He did so, whereupon she gave it a pretendedly hard slapping. "Didn't I warn you that if ever you spoke about yourself again like that, I'd spank you? Evelyn is not going out just with a boy, but with our own dear Joseph to look after her. And in any case, Joseph," she added, with a burst of unusual fluency, "we don't want Evelyn out just with a sartorial dandy or a tonsorial fop! We like you just because you are what you are. Let that suffice!"

She kissed them both, watched them set off, and stood outside the front garden gate with a final wave of her hand as they turned from Woodland Bypath into Clifton Boulevard and headed eastward.

Across the outer edge of Elmerton they made their way to the old Haystack Inn, then jaunted along Old Oak Road, laughing as the bumpy surface jolted them up and down in their saddles. Then they swung round the long, slow bend to the right, where they crossed Moorlands Road which skirted the lower hills.

Now they were slowly rising, but as the path was tolerably smooth they continued pedaling until their leg muscles protested. Soon there was a roughish descent between higher ground on each side, so they rode again, having fun dodging the dents and lumps. Now they dismounted again, pushing their bikes up a steepish incline, then round a sharp curve on to a long, straight stretch. There they paused, puffing and panting, but exhilarated by the view which now opened before them.

It was a captivating scene, basking now in victorious sunshine and fanned by that refreshing breeze which wafted the soft-scented breath of wild flowers, ferns and mosses, and pines and cherrywoods. Away beyond were the higher Pennine summits, with Cragston Pike tower standing on the nearest like an armored giant from times long gone. To the left was a picturesque gorge through which a stream went tumbling talkatively over the stones and boulders. Everywhere around, at intervals, were gorse and holly and rhododendron and blackberry bushes. On both sides of the ravine were groves of poplars, elms, silver birch, ash, and occasional oaks.

The Bicycle Outing

Joseph and Evelyn cycled on a bit further. At one time there had been some attempt at paving for the carts which used to ply to and from the now-deserted Shaggy Hill quarry. But many winter freezings and thawings, besides beating rains, had left the paving badly uneven, with moss and mold in every crevice. Still, it was ridable; so on our two young explorers went until they crossed a stone bridge over a sharp bend in the stream, from which point the stream was on their right, flowing in and out among gurgling gullies and grassy banks ideal for picnicking.

Soon Joseph jumped from his bike and looked down from the rough roadway at a flat, green projection where the stream gave one of its many impulsive turns. Evelyn quickly joined him. They looked together at the pleasant little platform, then at each other, and knew this was "it." Joseph lifted the bicycles down, and would have helped his fair lady too, only she had decided on an unconventional jump, which she accomplished successfully even if slightly inelegantly for such a young gentlewoman. The place was even better than they had seen from the road. There was a shadowy little covert from possible passers-by. The grass was clean and dry, with fern and dock-leaf and pretty red-shank weed all mixed in, and bosky little gorse clumps near by. The gentle perfume of clover and briar and Queen Anne's lace still clung around, and, from a nearby clump of trees Joseph was sure he sniffed a cherrywood aroma which brought a nostalgic whiff of Rostherne.

What a day! What a picnic spot! And (thought Joseph) what an almost unbelievable foretaste of Paradise: the two of them there alone! Heaven's kindliest sky beamed on them. The little hills and vales were laughing and singing. The trees seemed to be gently waving their leafy arms to them. The birds which now and again darted over the stream seemed to chirp a cheery "Hello there!" Even gray old Cragston Pike tower seemed to have forgotten for once to be sombre; the sun now west of its zenith was gilding the turret atop the tower, so that even the stone had to glisten a bit, and the two high-up windows seemed like two eyes winking a sunny "How d'you do?" down to where Joseph and Evelyn were.

Joseph unclasped his saddlebag and produced a tightly wrapped parcel, from which he unrolled a newspaper, two sheets of brown paper, and a square of oilcloth. These he spread on the ground for Evelyn and himself to sit on. "How thoughtful of you, Joseph!" said Evelyn. "You never forget anything, do you?"

They had taken not much more than an hour to come. It was not time to eat the picnic lunch. So they sat for a few minutes—suddenly a bit shy of each other. Then Evelyn said, "Joseph, wouldn't it be fun to paddle?"

"Yes, wouldn't it?" Joseph echoed, but then hesitated, scared lest anything should happen to her while she was in his charge. "But perhaps you would hurt your feet on the stones; some of them might be sharp. Let me find out." Off came his boots and stockings. He dangled his legs over the bank. "Ugh! it's cold!" he exclaimed, with Evelyn kneeling and laughing just behind him.

Then Joseph slowly waded in. Yes, it was rough underfoot. "No place for my dear Evelyn's angel feet!" he thought. Once or twice he almost tripped or slipped and Evelyn called, "Oooh, do be careful, Joseph!"

"Would you mind taking my jacket, Evelyn?" Wading slowly back to the edge he took it off and handed it to her. "I've got an idea," he said. Then, rolling up his shirt sleeves, and using the fallen branch of a tree, he began to move the sharper and more awkward stones, which was not difficult. Each one he moved he put in the same place across the stream until there was a little dam—not too successful, but enough to make the water a little deeper and the bed smoother.

Then he turned round to say, "Evelyn, I think it's not too bad now." But it was too late: Evelyn was already in! "You can't expect me to leave you to do all that by yourself!" she laughed.

Oh, how wonderful it was to put his hand on her, to steady her! And what a time they had!—both of them picking out stones and packing the water-wall higher, and laughing as the water kept escaping! Evelyn's skirt was getting a bit wet. Joseph was worried. Evelyn was not. Joseph persuaded her to lift it a little, then inwardly flogged himself that he should have seen above her knees.

Perhaps the cold water and their exertions had made them a bit hungry. They decided it was now time to eat. Joseph had brought *some* eatables, but Agnes had put up a light snack for both of them, so they tackled that first. Evelyn explained that it was only a "snack" because they were both expected back at Pinecrest for evening dinner. There were dainty sandwiches, two bananas, two rosy apples, two medicine-bottles filled with milk, and one with lemonade. As they were about to eat, Evelyn said, "Joseph, do we say grace when we eat on a picnic?" Joseph felt sure they should.

"Will you say it, then, Joseph?"

"I'd rather you said it, Evelyn."

"Well, I'll tell you what: I'll put a pebble in one of my hands. If you guess which one it's in, *I* say the grace. If you guess wrong, then *you* say it."

Joseph agreed; guessed the wrong hand; and said the grace he usually said at home.

Were ever two young hearts happier? The shady cove hid them from the roadway but not from the sun, which was now well to the west. What with the cycling, the walking, the paddling, the dam-building, the sunshine, Evelyn's face was glowing. She looked utterly beautiful. Joseph looked, and looked, and looked. He was so happy, it hurt again. Once or twice when they were eating she leaned her head on his shoulder and looked up into his face with such a fond, fond smile. He was as full of thanksgiving as a hymnbook, and wondered if he might risk putting one arm just round her shoulder, but decided it would be wrong.

However, there was an electrifying moment coming which Joseph had never dreamed possible. They had finished—all but the last of the lemonade. With a playful twinkle in her eyes Evelyn said, "Joseph, isn't it funny?—I like drinking out of the same bottle as you! You drink part of this, and I'll have what you leave."

"Oh, no, Evelyn, you must drink first; and you can have it all. Yes, drink it all."

Evelyn took a little drink. "There, I've left that for you"—handing the bottle to him.

He noticed her watching him drink, and chuckling at the suction problem in the neck of the bottle. Then Joseph said, "I think perhaps we ought to be going now if we are to have time to see Netherford Lake. We can burn the newspaper and brown sheets, but I'll keep the oilcloth; it belongs to our kitchen."

Evelyn was still watching him and agreeing with what he said, but he was sure, from a certain look in her eyes which he had seen before, that she was thinking up some nice little caper. Then he changed his mind: she was looking too intently. "Joseph," she said, "you are so kind to me. I sometimes wonder why you like to be with me. There are other girls, much nicer than I, who would give all their hair-ribbons away if *they* could have you with them. I do thank you, though. I would sooner be with you than anyone else—except, of course, mummie and daddy and Rickie. Am I naughty, Joseph?—but would you let me kiss you?"

She did not wait for reply. Putting her arms round Joseph's neck she gently kissed his cheek—not just a quick kiss, but a real, affectionate kiss. Joseph could scarce help holding her while she did so, and she liked it. Then, jumping up and away like a sprite, leaving Joseph for the moment in a panicky daze, she said, "There, now; I think we'd better be going."

It certainly was a struggle to get those bikes up the steep and stony rise leading to the higher level where Netherford Lake was, but eventually they contrived it—Joseph zigzagging up with his own machine first, then going down to fetch Evelyn's. Netherford was a fair-sized sheet of water, partly natural—fed from the hills eastward, and partly artificial by way of a dam at the western end. It supplied drinking water to about a third of the Elmerton area. It was pear-shaped, the narrow part being east toward the higher Pennines.

As Joseph and Evelyn came through the big iron gate in the ravelstone dyke at the western end of the lake they read a notice forbidding cycling along the lakeside pathway, so they leaned their bicycles against the inside wall. Then, after pausing to admire the view of the shimmering water, the variegated shrubs, flowers, trees, both wild and cultivated, all around it, and those beckoning Pennines rising high beyond it eastward, they began slowly walking along the path by the water's edge, thinking how peaceful it seemed.

At a bend where the lake narrowed there was a wooden bench capable of seating six or seven persons, and set back a few feet from the lakeside path, in a little recess overhung by a weeping willow. It had been put there as a memorial to some local lady, now in the better land, who had found the water-lapped pathway and its tree-lined solitudes very dear.

It is not easy to describe Joseph's rush of proud, manly, blissful sensation as Evelyn put her hand in his and they slowly walked the furlong or so to the bend where that memorial seat was. There they sat, still hand-in-hand, thinking all those elevated thoughts which are usually excited in us by such uplifting scenes in such balmy weather and on such emotionally happy occasions. Above all, for love-pining Joseph, it was the bliss of propinquity: he was close to his dear queen.

There was no chill in the air even at that altitude, but Joseph thought that as the sun would soon now begin to drop down beyond Elmerton they should be making tracks for home. Evelyn seemed reluctant to leave, but with a trustful look at him she brushed away her reluctancy and began walking back, keeping very close to his side.

Then the unexpected happened. Sudden disaster! Sorry predicament! It came all in a moment. As Evelyn pulled her bicycle from the wall she slipped on some damp moss; the bicycle fell towards her; her foot twisted between the front wheel and the down-bar; then over she fell with the bicycle on top of her! It all happened so quickly: Joseph could not act fast enough. Letting his own bike slide down beside the wall, he leaped to where Evelyn lay—her foot still fast. "Oh, Evelyn! You're hurt! Please don't move; I can see what's happened. Let *me* get your foot out."

Gently, with one hand he lifted and held the bicycle slantwise, while with his other hand he straightened the wheel and dislodged her foot. "Please, don't move your foot yet, Evelyn. Let me feel it first." Quickly leaning her bicycle against the wall, he kneeled down and very tenderly felt round the ankle. Evelyn gave a gasp and a smile in quick succession. The pain was severe. She could not get up.

Joseph was casting about in his mind, wondering what to do. They were some miles from home, a difficult pathway intervening, and evening not far away now. "Evelyn, I think you've not only pulled the ligaments; you've really sprained your ankle; and it's going to hurt badly."

She was half-sitting, half-lying, on the ground. She had gone very pale. With Joseph's help she struggled to get up, but the pain was intense.

"Evelyn, there is only one thing we can do, if you don't mind. Put both your arms round my neck, and clasp them firmly so as not to let go. That will take the weight off the ankle. Then you must sit sideways on my right hand and arm while I put my left arm round you and clasp my right hand with it to make a chair." (Joseph knew from his First Aid classes that this was the easiest way to carry a body under such circumstances.) In that way he slowly carried Evelyn back to the memorial bench and gently laid her on it. Even amid the intense anxiety he could not help thinking, "How wonderful, to have carried a wounded angel!"

"Evelyn, please stay still until I come back." So saying, he ran away as fast as his legs could carry him; jumped on his own bike, and rode back to the bench. His saddlebag was the larger kind which first-aiders liked to carry. Out came bandages. Evenly sat sideways with her legs along the bench. Joseph felt round the injured ankle again. "Evelyn, I'm afraid it's a real luxation," he said.

"Yes," she moaned as agreeably as keen pain would allow, though she had not heard that big word before. "What a lot Joseph knows!" she thought amid her distress.

"These bandages are too narrow and too few," Joseph lamented. Pulling his coat off, then his shirt, he quickly cut out one of the shirt-sleeves to use as a bandage. Next, running along the path to where a few pieces of wood were lying, he picked the straightest, wiped it, washed it in the lake, shook it, wiped it again, wrapped it in his handkerchief, and used it to make a splint. Soon it was fixed to Evelyn's ankle, to keep it rigid; then the thinner bandages were used to tie it securely, and finally the shirt sleeve wrapped the whole ankle and splint.

"Oh, Joseph!" Evelyn's voice had never sounded so tender.

"Just rest a minute, Evelyn. I'll be back in a jiffy." He sprang on to his bike, rode it back to the big, iron gate, turned sharply to the right, and disappeared with his bike among the bushes. He ran back without his bike, picked up Evelyn's, and raced back with it to her.

"You could not have lifted your leg over the upper bar of a boy's bike, Evelyn, but I want you to sit on the saddle of your own. Take hold of me; lift yourself up on your good leg; then put the bandaged foot through to the other side of the bike, and I'll help you into the saddle." This proved none too difficult. The only snag, momentarily, was that when Evelyn was safely perched in the saddle she forgot to cease clinging to Joseph!

Much relieved, Joseph wheeled her on her bicycle back to the iron gate, which he had fixed wide open. Now they were through, but then came the biggest problem of all. How were they to get down that steep, stony descent to the pathway below?

Evelyn blanched again. "What can we do, Joseph?"

"I think there's a way," he said reassuringly. "First of all, let's get you to the wall. Lean hard on me. Put your good foot on the ground, then pull the other slowly over. There! That's it. Now, just lean on the wall."

Inwardly he was scared. He could get the bike down, but how Evelyn? As he maneuvered it down he marvelled at his own foolishness that he should ever have struggled to get the bikes *up*.

But now, the toughest problem of all. He clambered up again to Evelyn. When he had got his breath he said, "Evelyn, I wonder if you would mind. . . ." (She saw his face flush as he hesitated.) "There's only one way we can get you down there. After that we should manage alright. You cannot climb down, and I cannot lift you down. I'm going to put that piece of kitchen oilcloth down, folded double, and my jacket on it, for you to sit on. I'll sit in front of it, and we'll move slowly down while you keep that bandaged leg

THE HIDDEN HAND

and ankle stiff. Keep both hands on the ground, to prevent any slipping; but *if* you slip, I'm in front, so don't worry. I'll gently pull you; try to avoid the projecting stones."

In that way they slowly accomplished their descent—not without some giggles from the patient, for it was indeed a comical sight.

Thank heaven! They were down! Joseph scraped the soil from his trousers and boots. Then he reached for the bike. No, that would not do; he must get Evelyn up first. "Give me both hands, Evelyn. I'll pull, and you will let yourself come up on your good foot."

This accomplished, Joseph pulled up the bike, and again she was prized into the saddle.

"You can't pedal, Evelyn. Just sit firmly, and I'll wheel you along. I've left my own bike up there, hidden in the bushes. It'll be alright until I can come back for it."

So they struggled along on the bumpy road which now seemed bumpier and ten times as long. He could not help thinking of another Joseph, long ago, who took his wife, Mary, somewhat like this, but on a donkey, to Egypt; and at that moment he would have given anything to change that bike for that donkey!

Would Moorlands Road *never* be reached? Ah, there it is, at last, down that decline! Careful! careful! Don't go and have a spill just at the end! "Evelyn, are you thinking what I'm thinking?"

"You mean the gathering darkness?"

"Yes, the sun has gone. They'll be anxious for you at home. It will take at least an hour and a half to walk back to the Haystack Inn, even if we cut off half way along Old Oak Road and go by Redhills Lane; and there's not a lamp the whole way. Even then, there's not much light between there and Pinecrest."

"Do you think we could really manage it, Joseph?"

"What do you mean, Evelyn?"

"I mean what I think *you* mean. You will ride the bicycle, and I will cling to your back."

"My! you are a plucky girl, Evelyn. One spill, you know, and we'd be in awful trouble!"

"I'd take any risk with you, Joseph. I shall never, never

forget today; especially that bench where you tore your shirt sleeve off to bandage my ankle. It's all going to work out alright; and my foot is feeling easier."

"I think we might just about get home in the light, Evelyn, if all goes well. You needn't get off the saddle at all. Haven't you seen how boys often pedal bikes standing on the pedals? Or perhaps, if you can sit to the back of the saddle, I can sit just a tiny bit on the front of it, to take some weight off the pedals, lest either of them should break."

Neither Old Oak Road nor Redhills Lane was paved, but they were utopian after the lumpy, up-and-down paths among the hills. Evelyn kept her arms loosely round Joseph's shoulders, and leaned closely on his back, as he pedaled away. At first, being unused to a girl's bicycle and to the weight of two persons instead of one, he made several hair-raising swerves; but gradually he got the "feel" of it, and there was little danger of further mishap.

When at last they turned into Woodland Bypath and came in sight of Pinecrest there was such a relief from tension that both of them laughed together and exclaimed, "What a story we'll have to tell them! Whatever will they say?"

They reached the gate. "Stay in the saddle, Evelyn. I'll steady the bike. . . . Now put your good foot on the ground. Now let go of the bike and lean on me. Stay a moment while I stretch to open the gate. There, that's it. Now, let's do that chair trick again: your arms round my neck; my right hand under your knees, and my left hand clasping it to make a chair." Evelyn seemed to like it; and in that way he carried her over the front lawn to the door of the house.

But there were two eyes which they had not escaped. As the sun had gone down, Agnes had begun to feel some concern. She knew Evelyn was a careful, thoughtful girl, and that she could not be with a more trustable boy than Joseph. But Netherford was a long way even on bicycles. They should have been home by now. Had anything happened? From time to time she had gone to the window to see if there was any sign of them. One of those glances developed into an astonished stare. There was young Evelyn, clinging affectionately round Joseph's neck, while he was Quixotically carrying her across the lawn!

The ring of the doorbell had not half died away before Agnes was at the door. Joseph, still carrying Evelyn, and a bit out of breath with the hard ride, saw the questioning look on Agnes's face. "Mrs. Adair, Evelyn has had a fall and sprained her ankle. I'm afraid it's a definite luxation [he had always liked that word, learned in the First Aid Class!] and I think the doctor should come and see to it."

"Come in, come in, Joseph!" exclaimed Agnes, her words colliding with Evelyn's simultaneous "Oh, mother, Joseph has been so good to me!"—which Agnes gratefully heard even though not answering.

"Mrs. Adair, I feel so much to blame. This would never have happened if I had not taken Evelyn to Netherford."

"No, no, mummie; it's not Joseph's fault at all. He couldn't help my falling; and if I'd been with anybody else I might still have been up there when the darkness came!"

"Well, well; let's hear quickly all about it, and we'll see about getting Dr. Cairns."

"Mrs. Adair, will you mind if I just slip out to bring Evelyn's bicycle in from the road? And would I be rude if I left Evelyn to tell you what happened? Before it gets darker I've somewhere I must go."

There was no distrusting that honest, earnest face. Agnes's concern had subsided, except for Evelyn's ankle. "Very well, Joseph. Do what you know is right."

He tip-toed apologetically to the door—feeling somehow that respect required his treading lightly with such clay-dirtied boots. As he put his hand on the handle of the inner door Evelyn asked, "Joseph, were you angry with me when I kissed you?"

Agnes was as taken aback by that question as by the sprained ankle. She gave a quick glance at Joseph. He had gone crimson.

"Oh, no . . . no, Evelyn," he stammered. "It was so kind of you. I knew I was unworthy of it."

"You are the worthiest boy in the world—you and Rickie. Isn't he, mummie?"

"Yes, I think he is," agreed Agnes. Then, with a teasing look at Joseph, she said, "What *I* would like to know is: Did

Prince Charming kiss her royal highness, too?"

Joseph strove to smile, but not even a forced smile would come. Instead, there came that other look which Agnes had seen once before; a look which seemed to make his eyes like windows of an inner loneliness. "Oh, no, Mrs. Adair; I would not dare. . . ." He did not finish the sentence. Two tears slowly dripped down his face. He slipped out, and was gone; though not without their noticing, as he turned to go, a sizeable hole in the seat of his trousers!

It was not until later that they learned why Joseph was anxious to get away. Amid the night-time darkness he made his way wearily back over the miles to Netherford Lake for his bicycle. Fortunately the half-moon managed to give him its best help. His bike had plenty oil in its lamp, and he was able to ride safely back. He knew he dare not go home without his bicycle, or his father would ask why, and begin probing; then there would be ructions.

It was a worn-out young Joseph who came home that night. However, as a kindly providence had so ordered it, his father had gone out, and remained out long enough for Joseph to tell his "dearest little mother" the whole adventure—even including the kiss. Millie hid his torn shirt and gave him another. She also cleaned his soiled clothes, gave him a good, warm supper, and packed him off to bed with such a kiss as even Evelyn could never have given him.

THIRTEEN
The Storm Breaks

For some time affairs at 12 Wragley Street had been going awry, at least as regards that bulky personage, Mike. The job which he had been given at the main post office lasted longer than had been envisaged, albeit the time came when the reorganization contract was completed and the temporary employees were paid off.

Mike thereafter found himself on another round of job hunting, and, alas, the prey seemed elusive. At times it seemed like the proverbial searching for a needle in a haystack. He did indeed capture two occupations, both of a clerical kind, which, with a break of three months between them, covered about two years. Then he was on the unemployment list again.

His biggest problem, as always, was himself. His preponderous presence and swelling voice and nabob-like swagger were too impressive for the obtaining of modest employ. The difficulty was that of fitting a whale into a sardine can. Mike himself considered it a mystery of uncooperative providence that in view of his personal superiorities the invisible "Powers that be" had not seen to it that he was made a financial magnate or at least a company director.

When he found himself out of work yet again, and saw

diminutive people compared with himself getting jobs while he himself was left like a pelican in the wilderness, he became angrily protestive, then peevish, then discouraged, and eventually sour. He still continued his mysterious month-end disappearances, and came back with money jingling in his pockets; but he also needed wage-earning employment; and the dreary drag of frustration wore him down.

Several times Millie caught the smell of beer. Gradually disguise was flung away. Yes, he was drinking again, and "why the devil shouldn't he?" This dragged on for weary months—a sore problem to Millie, preaching, as she did, "total abstinence." How could neighbors and others help talking when they saw the "police court missionary's" own husband with the unsteady gait of a tipsy man?

It brought an equally sore trial to Joseph; for with the return of sullenness and drunkenness Mike's inexplicable acerbity toward Joseph flared into new evidence.

On one occasion when Joseph came home from school his father was sitting there worse for drink. The sight of Joseph seemed to irritate his insensate spite into fury. In a garbled way he began to acuse Joseph of having been sneaking round to the Adairs—those "blasted parvenues and skulking hypocrites!" Then, with a savage lunge, he swiped his heavy hand across poor Joseph's face before any dodging out of the way was possible, causing a discolored eye and a swollen lip.

In fact, that occurred twice, and in each instance, as it happened, the next day Joseph was with his vibrant pal, Frank Goodall, the woodwork man. "What in the name of creation! . . . Have y'been fightin', Joe?"

Awkward silence.

"Joe, is it that blitherin' father of yours?"

Tell-tale sadness in Joseph's face.

Frank's usually jolly face clouded. Joseph was his favourite lad. Frank was more than fond of him. He also knew Mike Kennard by one or two casual contacts as well as by plentiful hearsay. He was angry. "Ugh, Joe, what a strange man that is!—and with a dear lad like you for his son! By jabbers, Joe, I wish you were my own son. If that father o' yours lays his big, fat hand on you again, I'll say something that'll surprise you, and startle him as well!"

Well, that "big, fat hand" did smite Joseph again, giving him a slit lip and a facial bruise. Frank saw it. Thunder darkened his brow. His sturdy frame stiffened and his fists momentarily clenched. Then he relaxed and put his strong arm tenderly round Joseph.

"My dear lad," he said, "maybe I shouldn' say what I'm goin' to say, but it's time somethin' shook your father up. God forgive me if I'm bein' a blabbermouth."

Putting his hands gently on Joseph's shoulders, and looking intently into his eyes, he began: "Joe, lad, d'you know, I don't think that father o' yours is your *real* father. I've wondered more than once or twice how such a bad father could have such a good son. Yes, an' I've wondered why you are so different in face and feature and complexion and figure."

Joseph listened, wordless.

Frank continued. "One day, a few weeks ago, when I was coming up Simmonds Street, your father was coming out of the Nelson Tavern. He was a bad bit drunk and sort o' wobbly. He nearly got run into by a horse and cart in trying to cross the road and get to me. He sidled up and started talking in a maudlin' way. "Oh, yez, mizter Frank Goodall, I knows yer. It's you who gaffers that woodwork shop at the Mechanigs' Inzitute, where mi wife haz her Wedney meetin'. Fine guy, aint you, Mizter Goodyall? Yes, I . . . I knowz yer. Yer thinkz Joseph's a fine laddie, don't yer? Well, now, who'd a'thought it? I'll tell yer . . . I'll . . . I'll tell yer . . . a bonny liddle secret. Yes, I will, an' all. Let me . . . let me . . . whizper it in yer ear. Aha, Joseph's no' my son at all . . . real name isn't Kennard . . . it's . . . it's . . . Ash . . . Ash . . . Ash . . . addy."

Frank paused. Joseph was astounded.

Frank resumed. "Joe, I did my level best to get him to say the word more clearly but he was too fuddled. All I could make out was 'Ash' and 'addy'—a bit like 'daddy,' don't you think?"

Joseph went sickly. His mind was dazed. Strangely, Frank was echoing what Joseph himself had latterly wondered.

But now that Frank had said it, it came like a hammer blow. Could it be?—could it *possibly* be that his father was *not* his real father? That certainly would explain a lot. But was it true? Attempting a smile, Joseph feebly said, "Thank you, Mr. Goodall. It makes me wonder [two tears slowly trickling down his swollen face] who I really am. If I'm not *his* son, whose am I?"

He looked so lonely and so limp that Frank (usually undemonstrative) put his arms round Joseph and said, "Look here, Joe, maybe I shouldn't have told you what he said. Let's forget it, if we can. P'raps he was just dribblin' nonsense in his tipsy mix-up. But I'll add just one thing: if he keeps treating you cruelly and you want to leave home, there's shelter and welcome waitin' for you any time under *my* roof, and we'll be proud to have you."

Joseph held out his hand, which Frank gripped warmly while the tears dripped silently down Joseph's paled cheeks.

Mike's bouts of bad temper increased in frequency and velocity. Joseph, who had now left St. Aiden's and started at the Elmerton Secondary School, made a practice of not returning home each day until he knew his mother, Millie, would be there. However, one day, even with Millie present, Mike flared into another tantrum, venting his spleen upon inoffensive Joseph. Once or twice it looked as though he would cuff Joseph, so, at one such point, Joseph looked steadily at him and said, "Father, you know I don't speak back to you when you keep going at me; but I'm fourteen now, and I want to ask you something. Why do you hate me? Why are you so angry at me all the time? Is it because you are not my real father?"

If a ghost had suddenly stood in the room the effect could not have been more petrifying. Mike seemed instantaneously strengthless—as though a puff of wind would have blown him over. Millie, too, was unconcealably startled. She looked anxiously at Mike, then at Joseph, and was about to say something, but bit her lip and remained silent. Mike sank back into his chair.

Joseph, still calm and collected, now asked Mike directly: "Are you my real father?"

But the beast in Mike had recovered from shock. He glared at Joseph, eyes blazing with temper. "By heaven!" he bellowed, "if you ever ask that again I'll knock your darned head off your blinkin' shoulders! If I'm not your father, who the devil is? Whose been putting ideas into your stupid noddle?—is it that Frank Goodall pal o' yours? Tell 'im if I ever get my hands on 'im I'll knock his nose in with one of his own mallets!" Bang came his sledge-hammer fist on the table with such force, even that oft-thumped piece of furniture jumped as though caught off guard. Having thus thundered and thumped, he stamped out of the house snorting to Millie, "You can expect me when you see me."

Millie and Joseph stood for some minutes in uneasy silence. Then Millie said, "Joseph, my own dear.boy, I was proud that you kept so calm just now. I hope you will always handle yourself that way. Maybe these stormy days won't last much longer. It's a funny thing, I know, but underneath all these outbursts I really believe your father loves you, but he's not at the point where he will admit it. I think you are winning, though, Joseph, if only you can hold out a bit longer. The balloon of his pride is so full of gas, it's almost at bursting point. One of these days he'll say he's sorry; and what a day that will be! I myself have had more to put up with from him than you know; but day and night I keep on praying for him, and I believe that God will yet change him."

There were tears glistening in Millie's bright eyes. She brushed them away and said, "Let's get the tea ready, laddie. Faith in God and a good cup of tea go well together."

"Yes, mother, but tell me: Is my father my *real* father?"

Millie replied, "You want a frank answer, and you shall have it. I'm sorry if someone has put that question into your mind. I know your father is very different from you; and I'm thankful tó heaven that *you* are so different from *him*. But, if you can believe it, Joseph, deep down in your father there's a heap of good too. I've seen it. But he's had such a lot of frustrations, it's got him really down these last few months. He can't get work, and it cuts his pride to the quick that he has to live on what others earn. He's not sleeping well. He's nervous and irrascible, and he's back to the drink—as you've seen. Try to bear with him a bit longer. I have one or two influential friends trying to find him a good job. He's your father alright—the only one *I've* ever seen you have, anyway! But one day soon now, when it seems wisest, I'll tell you some things about your father and you which I think will explain things that puzzle you. Until then, Joseph, trust me. I won't deceive you."

But Mike kept drinking and was becoming more dangerous. Millie grew nervous about it. She had a word with the next-door neighbors, Mr. and Mrs. Tom Hibbert. Tom was a plump, strong man who worked at a printing office in the town; and wife Tilda was a most congenial hob-nobber. Millie asked that if ever she knocked on the wall, Tom would come and see what was going on. She also asked Eddie Stoddart, one of the younger policemen on the force, who lived in the next street beyond Wragley, to have a word with Mike. She might even have felt a twinge of pity for Mike if she had heard Eddie's choicely worded warning to him as to what he could expect if he ever laid a hand on her! Yet when Mike was afire with the booze such warnings were about as deterring as a red light to a blind man or a big drum to a man stone deaf.

Late one afternoon, all in a few fateful minutes, the dreaded yet unexpected happened. Joseph came home from school, as usual, about the time he felt sure his mother would be back home. Unfortunately, she had been delayed, seeking information about a woman prisoner. It was not Joseph's fault that he arrived before Millie, for he had waited until after 5:30 p.m., and Tom Hibbert next door was already home from work.

Mike, after a fruitless afternoon of job-hunting, and a few drams too much, was sitting in his chair cursing fate, and angry at Millie's delay. The fire in the grate was almost out, and no meal was ready. It was just then that Joseph came in.

When Joseph realized that Millie was not yet home his heart sank, but he said as cheerily as he could, "Hello, father."

As a tiger stalking its prey stiffens up before the final spring, so was it with Mike. Joseph was the prey. Without replying to Joseph's "Hello," he surveyed him archly. Then, with a cruel glint in his eyes, he said snidely, "So you think you can deceive me, lad, eh?"

"No, father, I never try to deceive you."

"You young liar! Didn't I tell you not to go round to those Adairs again? Who was it went biking with young missie Evelyn a few days since? You thought nobody saw you, didn't you? Aha, my boy, I've had you watched, I have! So she's your little lady, is she? Let me tell you: that pretty wee doll has a no-good father who plays about with women!"

Joseph was about to protest, but his father saw it. Springing from his chair, he landed a resounding thwack which burst Joseph's lip and knocked a tooth loose and made his nose bleed. Joseph reeled against the table enough to topple it over, so that a plant-pot and two glass vases went crashing to the floor. And above the noise Mike's voice roared, "I'll show you whether you can defy me, you young devil!" As he so roared his look was such that Joseph seemed to see the very face of Satan leering at him. Next door, Tom and Tilda Hibbert jumped. "Tom!" cried Tilda, "he'll murder him!"

Tom Hibbert rushed out through the front door, strode over the low garden wall between the two front doors and burst in to number 12. But he was not alone. At that very moment Millie arrived, having walked up from the police headquarters with p.c. Eddie Stoddart on his way home. So Tom and Eddie and Millie all came in together.

Just as they came in Joseph was darting out—Mike reaching after him. Joseph quickly brushed by them, but Mike, in that instant, found two strong men in his way. With a wild look in his eye, like a thwarted beast, he gave a deafening roar. Swift as lightning he shot out a mighty blow right to Eddie Stoddart's jaw, which felled him; and before the astonished Tom Hibbert could act, Mike let out a wicked left and a murderous right full in the face. The heavy blow itself might not have knocked Tom out, but it flung him back with such a bang of his head on the wall that he sank down unconscious.

Eddie Stoddart still lay there. He was hurt. It all happened with bewildering rapidity: Before Millie could gasp out a word Mike shoved her out of his way as easily as knocking a candle over. With a mighty feat of strength which would have ruptured most other men, he lifted Eddie Stoddart up, dragged him through the vestibule, out through the garden gate, and dumped him in the gutter. Then he ran back into the house, grabbed Tom Hibbert, who was still dazed, dragged him likewise out to the foot-path and rolled him into the road next to Eddie Stoddart.

By this time every curtain in Wragley Street had Saint Vitus's dance; folk had hurried to their doors; scared children had gathered round with awe-struck faces. And now, also, Mike went running down the street, shouting, "Joseph! Joseph! Come back, come back, Joseph; my poor boy! My poor boy! Don't run away! You don't know all I've suffered for you! I didn't really mean to hurt you! Joseph! Joseph! Don't run away! Forgive me! Forgive me!"

It was getting dark before Mike came home, after scouring all the area. He was white, but not with anger. He was trembling, but not with rage. He was sweating, but not with heat. He was sick, but not with eating. He was utterly limp, but not with hunger. With a ghastly face he sank into his chair. For a while he stared blankly into space. Then, dropping his large head like a leaden weight into his hands, he sobbed and sobbed and sobbed, until no more would come.

"Millie, Millie," he groaned, "I've done it this time. Joseph won't come back. I know it. I know it. Oh, Millie, Millie, he's gone. He's *gone!* And he's gone before I could tell him!"

"What do you mean, Mike?—gone before you could tell him?—tell him what?"

"Oh, God! what have I done! What has the devil done through me? Joseph's gone before I could tell him!"

"Mike, what do you mean? Tell me, and don't keep me in suspense, especially after all the havoc you've made, and the disgrace you've brought on this house. You're probably right in thinking he won't come back. If I were in his shoes, *I* wouldn't. Mike, what have you done to my dear, dear boy? Will you break *my* heart as well as his? If Joseph doesn't come back, I'll be half in the grave myself. What is it you should have told him?"

"Oh, Millie, Millie [sobbing again], he's fourteen now. There was only one thing keeping me back from telling him."

"Telling him what, Mike?"

"Telling him *who he really is!*"

FOURTEEN
No Roof But the Sky

Astonishing is the swiftness with which a human mind can think in an acute crisis. In a split second, as his father's hand struck him, Joseph realized that a fateful divide had come and that he must run away. Besides peril from his father's demoniacal malevolence the tension now was unendurable. Grabbing his cap he darted from the house just as the persons already mentioned arrived, but too quickly to recognize any of them except Millie. As he dashed down Wragley Street wondering where to go, his brain outran his legs with its quick answer. He must get to the hills where nobody would think of following; then make his way over to some main road for Manchester. By so doing he could sneak undetected to somebody or other whom he had known there.

Evelyn flashed into his mind. He must say good-bye. Pinecrest was not much out of his intended direction. Alternately running and walking as breath and strength would allow, he hasted up Granville Road and along winding Goshen Lane out to Clifton Boulevard and Woodland Bypath. Fate was kind. He did not need to go right to the house. Evelyn was in Woodland Bypath with two other girls and Rickie and a couple of other boys from Stimson High

School. Not only Evelyn but all the others were quelled by the sight of Joseph, his face still bleeding, running up to Evelyn. "Oh, Evelyn, I'm . . . so sorry. . . to interrupt . . . but I'm . . . I'm running away from home. I daren't stay longer. . . . My father . . . Evelyn, you know. I don't know just where I'm going: it must be where no one can find me. I may never see you again. I want to give you this locket. It's real gold. Will you wear it sometimes and think of me? I must run now"—and he was gone. As he regained the corner he gave one quick glance back, but Evelyn was not to be seen; she had sped into the house crying, "Mother, mother, Joseph Kennard is running away from home!"

On Joseph hurried, out beyond the last few straggling cottages, along Redhills Lane, by the now disused and supposedly haunted shale pits, and across lonely Moorlands Road, into the first reaches of the Pennines. He had been this way before with the Boys' Brigade, lugging tents and picnic victuals—most of which latter were gormandised before ever the camp site was reached! This was the way he had come with the queen of his heart on that romantic outing when she had sprained her ankle.

Now he was into the hills, amid the ups and downs and twists to that higher, straight stretch along by the stream where Evelyn and he had picnicked. Dazed with grief and apprehensiveness though he was, he could not help glimpsing the evening beauty of the scene: the slanting rays of the westering sun causing vivid contrasts of golden fingers and hieroglyphic shadows between the trees up and down the slopes. All the while the idea was strengthening in his mind that he should make his way to Manchester, climbing over Cragston Pike and going down on the Yorkshire side, perhaps in the direction of Marple, Stockport or Hyde. If only he could reach Cragston Pike and its high, octagonal stone tower before daylight faded! Could he? Just now, with the sinking sun catching the turret, the tower looked for all the world like a masked Ku Klux Klan man, with the two windows as two eyes peering through slits at Joseph as he struggled toward it.

Momentarily breathless, he paused where Evelyn and he had sat and eaten together, and she had kissed him. "Oh,

Evelyn, what is happening? Shall I ever see you again? I don't know what lies ahead, but leaving you is leaving heaven behind—you and my brave, precious little mother!—and Dorothy and Mona!" But he dare not go back. Nor dare he linger. He must run as well as walk if he is to reach Cragston Pike before nightfall. What a mercy it is not raining! Now for the struggle up the shaggy steep of the old quarry to the higher level of Netherford Lake.

In his emotional upset, and with eyes repeatedly blurred by tears, he slipped backwards several times, at one point cutting his knee and bruising his shin. With a gulp of grief now and then, at last he was at the top, near the iron gate in the ravelstone wall. Now he was hasting along the gravel path to the wooden bench at the bend of the lake where he had doctored Evelyn's ankle. By the time he reached there he was staggering rather than running, exhausted partly by exertion, even more by suppressed panic. That bench in its willow arbor was a welcome refuge for the moment. He slumped down on it; his hands dropped limply; his head sagged down, and he sobbed his sore heart out.

After a while the fountain seemed to dry up, and his sobs ceased, though his heart was still unconsolably forlorn. It began to seem a weary impossibility to gain Cragston Pike before dark. Yet he could not wander up and down those never-ending hills all night. A sense of destitution gripped him. Sinking down on his knees at that bench, for the first time in his life he really prayed. Often had he "said his prayers," but there is a big difference between that and really praying. For the first time in his life Joseph "cried to God."

"O God, please help me! If I've done wrong in running away, please show me what to do. O God, I don't want to run away from my dear mother, but I can't go back to my cruel father. O God, I've no one else now to trust but You. Please, God, help me to trust You; and do please guide me."

It was difficult to control the nervous trembling which had come upon him, yet he now felt steadied, and had a comforting hunch that God would look after him. He stood up and exercised, including some "running on the spot" to overcome his trembles. Then the first big test came. Dusk was beginning to creep over the hills. The breeze over the water was chilly. He knew now that he would have to find some shelter out-of-doors. What about the quarry? No; if he stumbled there in the darkness it would mean death or being crippled. He simply must get to Cragston Pike away up yonder, hoping that perchance its heavy door might be unfastened.

Off he set, at first running, then trudging or stumbling as the ground rose fairly steeply and the only path grew either stony or uneven. Sometimes the gaunt tower would seem near, then become lost to view by a turn or dip, and now again it would move away as a hillock came between it and Joseph's view. The light was fading. Joseph began to fear he would not reach the tower. Worse still, he felt raindrops on his face.

At last he gained the only high hump before the actual summit where the old landmark stood, looking more than ever like a stern sentinel challenging all who would cross the county border into Yorkshire. He paused, winded through the stiff climb, till his pounding heart subsided. On glancing round, what a surprise! There, seeming now so distant, in the bosom of the sunset afterglow, were the mills and chimneys of Elmerton, visible because of the elevation to which Joseph had now climbed. The tall chimneys, mottled in the fading glow, looked like so many giraffes with their long necks all craning toward him with a "Good-bye, dear boy; we're going to miss you; for even the longest of us cannot peep over to the Yorkshire side of the Pennines." It was visible only for a couple of minutes; then, like the last flicker of a dim-burning oil-lamp, it disappeared in gloom. Elmerton was gone!

The dark cloak of night was falling upon him. Joseph made a last gallant spurt. One further short dip, followed by a circuitous ascent, and he was actually at the tower. He and night arrived together, though it was still possible to make out the shape of the tower as it lifted its shoulders and helmet high into the dark sky. But now, hand-in-hand with night came fear. The tower which had been Joseph's hoped-for shelter now scared him.

He was hungry. His inner clothes were damp from perspiration; and his outer clothes were wet from the several short showers which had caught him. The tower looked eerie. He almost hoped its door would be locked. He lifted the heavy latch and pushed. With a creaking, grating noise, much too loud for darkness and aloneness, it opened. He was afraid to go in. Did poltergeists or bugaboos or escaped criminals lurk there? He peered inside several minutes, and as his eyes became adjusted to the darkness he discerned that the flagged floor was quite bare. To relieve his nervous tautness he called, "Anybody there?" and was startled to hear, "body there" in reply—the echo from high up in the turret.

A minute or two later he had a kindly ally. The moon had climbed high enough to smile over the hilltops whenever the scudding clouds allowed. Thereby Joseph could see the stone steps and iron side-rail of the spiral stairway winding round and round inside the tower to the top. Soon there came a further factor which peremptorily decided he must go in. The spasmodic showers now gave place to squalls flinging heavy rain down. Either he must go inside or get soaked. So, groping warily, he shoved the door half-way open, where it stuck, and in he stole, expecting some heavy hand to grab him by the shoulder.

Between the rainy gusts the moon broke through, showing a clear, starry sky above the fitful cloud-drifts. It enabled him to pick out plainly the stairway, so he braved the idea of going right up to the turret windows, to make sure there was no one else in the tower. Up and round he went, his footfalls waking weird acoustical answers. At the top was an iron platform. Joseph looked out through the two windows. The moonlit hills, and Netherford Lake looking like a silvered lagoon, were a sight such as Joseph had never seen before. For a moment he forgot his fear; but a shadow moved stealthily over the lake as a cloud brushed past the moon's face, and the moon seemed to say, "Get ready, laddie. There is worse weather coming. Up here I see big clouds tumbling across from Norway and Sweden over the North Sea and across the Yorkshire moors. They always get angry when they reach this Pennine Chain which blocks their way. They are too heavy to clamber over these high summits without disgorging a lot of their liquid weight. Sometimes you can hear them rumbling and grumbling before they get here. They mass together for a combined struggle to get over, and then there's a real big storm. You'd be better lower down the tower, Joseph; and stay there till morning." Joseph was sure he heard the moon say so. Anyway, holding the iron rail carefully, he slowly descended to the ground again.

All was still now. Not a night-owl screeched, not an insect buzzed, not a moth flitted by. Joseph left the door open enough to let moonlight and fresh air in. He decided to sit and doze on the third stair up, out of drafts, and behind the door. He exercised again to warm himself. Then he put his cap and handkerchief underneath himself and sat leaning against the rail.

However, wearied though he was, he could not doze, for he heard an ominous rumble in the distance. It came again and again, each time louder, which told him how quickly it was nearing. Half an hour later the attack was full on. It was as though all the cannonry and soldiery of the sky were embattled in one concerted assault on those Pennine ramparts. To Joseph it sounded like a mighty cavalry charge supported by heavy artillery. First came the lurid flashes and thunder crashes. Through the partly open door Joseph could see the awful forks of fire actually strike the high ground; and in one terrifying flash which lit the whole heaven he saw a tree struck, two or three furlongs away.

Then came the heavier rain. It fairly lashed down, and at times, when flung along by howling blasts, it came in sheets. Even inside the tower's thick walls the noise of frenzied wind and pelting rain and banging thunder was almost deafening, and Joseph shut the door even though then he was in deep darkness. He was no coward, but up there, amid that ear-splitting fury, he was pretty shaken. He had seen thunderstorms before and had felt the kind of alarm that most young folks do; but that was down there in Elmerton *beneath* the storm, whereas now he was high up *amid* it.

The battle raged for over an hour. Then the storm-clouds went rumbling and grumbling away out west to disturb the slumbers of those Lancashire towns down there, and then exhaust themselves over the Atlantic.

Joseph opened the door again. There were filterings of watery moonlight at intervals now. Soon he was sorry he had not kept the door shut. Two small somethings slipped in by his feet. Then he saw two pairs of red eyes darting about. He had unpleasant company—rats! Joseph grabbed his jacket and whisked it at them. He never knew before how quickly rats can mount a steep stair. He groped up after them right to the iron platform. Then they made a dash down again to escape his swishing jacket; but they were not so successful in descent. One found its back legs too long and went rolling down, banging on every turn of the iron rail until it fell through to the ground below. In the darkness Joseph trod on the other, and the pitiful squeals were enough to wake every hidden goblin in the tower.

Nor was that all. Joseph was never to forget that first night as a fugitive. Scarcely had he got without the rats than a huge, dark object, darker than the darkness pushed in. Something soft and slimy slobbered his face. Then there was an ear-splitting roar which made his hair stand on end. It was a huge, black bull. Joseph sprang back and fumbled up the stairway while the bull struggled at the door, first to get in, then to get out. Struggle as it would, the beast could not get that door more than half open. Eventually it got its wedged hulk free and trotted off.

Soon afterwards the moon was shining clear again. Joseph peeped out and was surprised to see, not just one bull, but several, which suggested that there must be a farm somewhere near.

Up yonder, the moon was now reigning like a queen after a victorious battle. She seemed to say, "Didn't I tell you, laddie: the storms may come and go, but the hills remain, and I keep shining. I am the same moon that young boy, Abram, looked at, in Ur of the Chaldees, as far back B.C. as you are now A.D., when he was about as old as you are. Joseph, dear laddie, lean your head on the rail, and sleep."

Did the moon actually speak?—or was Joseph dreaming? All he knew was, that about nine o'clock next morning he wakened, still on the same step and leaning against the iron rail. He felt rather stiff, but not cold. The morning was sunny, and the tower held the warmth. What had seemed scaring in the dark now seemed pleasant. But as consciousness returned so did the dismaying realization that he had run away from home and was a fugitive. He must get away quickly.

Leaving the tower and looking eastward he was surprised to see a farmhouse not more than three quarters of a mile down the slope, and a road beyond it, running north to south. He knew now why that particular hill had been chosen on which to light the beacon in earlier times, and to have the tower erected on it later. It had what is known as "crag-and-tail" structure—deep declivity on one side but an easy slope on the other.

He made for the road, to call at the farmhouse and ask would they give him a cup of milk or tell him the best road for Manchester. Along the roadside was the usual unmortared stone wall, and further along was the clumsy wooden gate into the farmyard, so were the usual couple of dogs. There were also three boys, one large, with a prognathous physiognomy, and two small, whom Joseph rightly took to be the bigger boy's brothers. They had watched Joseph reach the road, and as he now approached the open gate the big boy accosted him: "Yo canna' go in thar' unless yo' feight me."

Joseph's heart sank. He was hungry and dispirited. After such a night, why this? Was God punishing him for running away? "I don't want to fight you," he said. "I'm too hungry to fight anybody. Besides, I don't know you, and I haven't done you any harm. If you won't let me ask your mother for a cup of milk, I'll go further along the road."

But the fat swaggerer strode into the middle of the road, and with a truculent grin said, "Yo canna' go that way either unless yo feight me." The other two boys chuckled. "Ha, ha, ha, nobody ever gets by 'im without a beatin': an' if they run past 'im we sets the dogs on 'em! Ha, ha, ha."

Joseph was cornered. For a second or two he went limp with frustration. Then he stiffened. Although a good lad, he had a naughty dander. Hunger can feed anger. Fury woke within him. It was all he could do to respect Millie's sententious word, "Joseph, anger may be right at times, but temper never. Anger may be reasonable, but temper is temporary insanity." Joseph was not sure in that instant whether he measured up to Millie's standard, but he sure wanted to measure up to that prognathous mug and knock the grin off it.

"Alright, you big-bellied bully," he said tensely. "Come on. You strike the first blow. My mother told me never to strike the first blow."

The flabby farm lad waddled up and gave Joseph a thump on the chest. During the next few minutes he must have thought the heavens were falling in, for he certainly "saw stars." Joseph feigned to be aiming a left jab (which the fat lad tried to stop) but suddenly altered and shot in a hard right (a trick learned at Rostherne). Then, before the big lad recovered from the jerk-back of his head, there came a pelting of left, right, left, right. The bully's hands went waving wide. Joseph swung both fists under the chin— about the only way to lift such a young hulk of fat. Partly through the double biff and partly through tripping backwards over the curb, the swarthy Goliath fell as only one hundred and sixty pounds of blubber could.

His nose and lip were bleeding. Joseph pulled out his handkerchief and bent over him. "I'm sorry, you idiot. Why did you make me do it? I hate fighting; and you don't know the first thing about boxing. You think it's hard to knock a fat boy down, don't you? But it's a lot harder to get him up once he's down. Come on. I'll help you. . . ."

He got no further. While the two smaller boys stood gasping, their eyes nearly popping out, somebody else had appeared. It was their mother. One glance at her persuaded Joseph not to expect much sympathy from that quarter; but he was mistaken.

She was femininely bulky and saggy, with a face as round as a frying pan, a large mouth with thick lips, but a row of perfect, white teeth, and a jolly smile far too nice for the vocal blast which accompanied it.

"There, now, yer daft mutton-head! Haven't I towld yer, one o' these days ye'd lift yer blitherin' fists up once too often? I see'd it a' from the winder. Yuv got what yer blinkin' well asked for! And then, just think on it—this 'eer young gent offers yer 'is 'ankie, an' offers ter 'elp yer up! Get up, yer big fat lout. Go an' wash yer mug at th'pump. An' you two little devils 'oo egged 'im on: if yer darst do it agin, I'll knock yer little blockheads reet off—I will an' all!"

After this spontaneous maternal *copia verborum* she turned, all courtesy, to Joseph, and said, in a voice like the bleat of a lamb after the blare of a bull, "Yes, young man, I see'd it from that winder. Wot was yer wantin' to com 'eer for, luv? Come an' tell mi 'usband an' me wot we can do fer you."

Inside the farmhouse was so different from what Joseph had expected, he could scarcely credit it. The house was slantwise to the road. On one side of the door was the kitchen with its window looking across to the gate. On the other side was a living room where sat a man. Both kitchen and living-room were as clean and orderly as her culinary majesty looked the opposite.

"Sit down, an' make yersel' at 'ome," she said. "Nay, wait a minit, yer rascal: come out to the yard again while I brush all that loam off yer clothes. It's better in th'yard than on mi cushins.

"There, now, that's better. Sit down an'—nay, wait a minit agin. Jist cum 'eer to this sink, and wash yer 'ands an' face wi' this carbolic soap. Then you'll feel better an' look better too. Cum on, lad: dinna mind mi watchin' yer. Go reet round th'back o'yer neck an' up t'yer elbows.

"Didna I tell yer, yer'd feel better? Now, sit down an' tell me all about yer trouble."

Joseph was about to speak, but again she interrupted in her roughish, kind way, to make it easier for him. "Yer see, I knows a lot about puttin' two an' two together. When I sees yer 'eer this early in a mornin', wearin' clothes different from what farm lads wear, an' all dusty; an' when I 'ears yer say yer's 'ungry, I says: two an' two makes four alright. An' I'll tell yer what them four is. One: yer a town lad. Two: yer must a' slep all night i' yon tower. Three: yer brought no food wi' yer. Four: yer must 'ave left in a 'urry. So, yer runnin' away, an' yer 'ungry. Is that it?"

"Yes."

" 'Ave yer dun somethin' wrong, an' yer runnin' from the police?"

"No."

"Very well, then, yer runnin' away from a drunken muther. No, not a drunk muther, or yer wouldna' be dressed like that. Yer runnin' from a bad father, eh?"

"Yes. But Mrs.—may I have the pleasure of your name?"

"Barton—Mr. an' Mrs. Freddie Barton."

"Mrs. Barton, you are so clever at putting two and two together, you remind me of Sherlock Holmes."

"Sherlock who?"

"Sherlock Holmes."

"Who in creation is 'ee—or 'er?"

"Oh, Mrs. Barton, you should read some of the stories about Sherlock Holmes, the London detective. They're written by a medical man: Conan Doyle."

Voice from living-room: "A' knows about him. A've got one of his books here; but Tizzie doesna' read much."

Mrs. Barton (Tizzie) spoke again. "So I'm Mrs. Sherlocks, am I? What's yer name, young mister?"

"Joseph."

"Well Joseph, I dunna know what Sherlocks would a'done under the circumstances, but it seems to me it's a gud breakfast yer needin' just now, not a detective. Go an' sit wi' Freddie while I gets it ready. Freddie, come 'eer an' meet Joseph."

Seeing the two of them standing together, Joseph hardly knew which they reminded him of the more—George and the dragon or Beauty and the beast, though he was now sure that no knight would have killed such a rough but motherly dragon.

Joseph was so famished, he twice apologized for eating so much—which she ignored. "You see," she reflected audibly, while Joseph was eating, "you're no' the only one who's cum to us in a mornin' from that tower. It's had a few strange customers, an' it sort o' makes us a bit wary. Twice we've 'ad a dangerous criminal hidin' there. Not long since we 'ad a boy who'd sneaked out o' the Borstal. An' we've 'ad slum lads who'd dun some'at wrong an' were runnin' from th' police. Aye, an' ther were that nice little woman huddled up there all night last November—runnin' from 'er gamblin' maniac 'usband. She were starved an' tremblin' when she cum in 'eer. An' about two weeks after, they found 'er corpse at th'bottom o' Stagshaw Steep!"

"Son," she resumed, "puttin' two an' two together, I thinks yer a good lad; but 'ave yer told me the real truth?"

"Yes, Mrs. Barton. My father is now cruel. . . ."

"A'm askin' no curious questions: but tell mi just one thing. Where's yer makin' for?"

"Manchester."

"Manchester! Heavens, lad, yer canna' walk all that way. 'Ave yer got friends there?"

"Yes."

"Well, see, Joseph. If yer waits till about eleven o'clock, Freddie's goin' a few miles partly-wot i' that direction, an' 'ee'll take yer in th'buggy."

So, by about eleven, Freddie had Bess harnessed and in the shafts of the old two-wheeler, and away they jogged— but not before those wide, jolly lips had given Joseph a resounding smack of a kiss. "If things dinna go as yer expects, luv, dinna 'esitate to cum back. We can find a job 'eer, temporary like, yer know."

The final surprise came when Joseph left Mr. Barton, having ridden about four miles. Mr. Barton pointed a way over the hills which, he said, would save Joseph some miles if he did not get lost by taking a wrong turn. "And," he added, "if you ever get lost at night when the moon's not full, always remember the light side of the moon faces west where the sun's gone down."

There was a rustle of paper. Pulling two compact packages out from somewhere, he handed them to Joseph. "God bless and guide yer, Joseph. Tizzie says there's enough 'eer for two meals, if you can just get a cup o' tea somewhere. Gee up, Bess."

Joseph's gratitude was equaled only by the dismal feeling of being a pursued fugitive which clung round him. However, his physical hunger had been graciously answered, and his spirit revived by "the milk of human kindness." The lure of the open spaces gripped him. Not a chimney in sight. Not a village. How different from the smokiness of the crowded mill towns! The silence of the hills was itself their speech. They needed no other voice, but only people able to listen. The day was bright, the air balmy. So the new young Abram set off for some hoped-for "promised land," though he knew well enough that Manchester was no earthly paradise, luscious with "grapes of Eshcol."

Freddie Barton had told him to make for a white farmhouse about three layers of hills away. The Manchester road was there. Toward that object, therefore, Joseph "set his face like a flint." But those three layers proved much wider on top than appeared at a distance, and the glens between them were both deeper and wider than Freddie Barton had surmised. Somewhere in the second, with the white farmhouse lost to sight, Joseph went astray.

It was not due to carelessness. No longer was there a path. Every time he went lower, in order to cross, he was in puddles. Soggy quagmire and sloppy morass were everywhere in the lower parts. In fact, the whole elongated basin was a marsh. Twice Joseph was almost up to his knees. His stockings were wet through, and his boots inside were slimy. Nor was his courage helped by a sheep's carcass lying midway across. He simply had to keep on the higher, firmer ground winding round with the seemingly endless valley. Eventually, on reaching a place where the depression was not as deep and the ground was firm again, he found at least one explanation of the extensive bog. A pleasant stream, fed from the hillsides, went purling down, little anticipating how soon it would lose itself in such an oozy mess.

As the stream went rippling over the stones, slowing down here and there in curling eddies or deepish pools, Joseph saw his chance for a rest and cleanup. He swilled the mire out of his boots and wrung it from his stockings which he then laid over a boulder to dry in the late-afternoon sun. He filled in the waiting time by washing his feet and face and body in successive ablutions. Then, refreshed but very hungry, he devoured a good part of the ham sandwiches, fruit and buns given him by Mrs. Tizzie Barton.

Was it wise, or foolish?—he allowed himself to doze. The

struggle uphill and down, again and again, the miles along the slope contiguous with the marshland, the strong oxygen of the uplands, the breeze, and now the warm sunshine after a cold shower and a satisfying meal, all blended in a soporific influence which drew Joseph's eyelids down in a gentle coma—a short oblivion which he repented of soon after waking.

He must have slept for some forty minutes. The sun was westering too quickly. He was "miles from anywhere." His boots and stockings were not only dry, they were warm. He quickly put them on and set off to the top of the next rise, which would reveal (so he judged) the white farmhouse now fairly near. Alas, when he struggled to the high viewpoint, not only was there no sign of that farmhouse, the whole contour of the overlapping hills was different.

Except that his knees were getting rather stiff and his feet a bit sore, he was feeling refreshed; and although he knew he was in a predicament he was not stricken with fear, for there was indication of a dry, clear night. Actually he was in more danger than he guessed. Only those who have experienced it know the hazards of being lost amid mountains stretching in every direction, with unseeable valleys, treacherous bogs, craggy drops, no recognizable landmark, and night coming on. The only guide is the sun in early morning or late evening, or the moon in its quarter phases on a clear enough night, and some knowledge of what lies to the four points of the compass.

Joseph had only the dipping sun as his guide. Knowing where the west was, he felt sure he must go northward for Manchester. Cuping his hands over his eyes he peered in that direction. There seemed to be only hills; but as he slowly scanned from left to right he thought he saw a road. Yes, it was!—for he could descry a vehicle of some kind moving along it.

A song of relief leapt to his lips, but it died at its birth as he realized that he could never reach that road before dark. What should he do? He fixed his eye on a rough cairn on the next hump in line between himself and that road. If he could reach that cairn, he could easily reach that road early next morning. So thither he pressed, down through the stones, ferns, gorse, heather and thistles of the intervening valley, and up the long, slippery slope to that next hilltop. What had seemed like a cairn was a shepherd's halt with a rough wooden roof atop its two stone sides. Further on, Joseph could just make out drystone dividing walls, which told him he was near farms again. Twilight had now gone, however, and in the gathering shadows he could no longer see that distant road.

So his second night, also, must be spent amid the lonely outback of the hills! But the weather was kind. The shepherd's shelter gave useful cover. There was a flat stone intended for a seat. Joseph had kept the paper bags and string of Tizzie's two food parcels. Amid the dusk he was just able to gather soft grass and fern to fill the bags and fasten them for a pillow which, with his handkerchief over, was not too uncomfortable. He strewed layers of fern and weed-leaves over the slab on which to sit. Then he put two square stones on which to rest his feet while he sat. Altogether, it was not too bad. Indeed the night felt slightly warm. As he sat there he thanked God for safekeeping thus far. It seemed as though he could at least doze without shivering until morning came. All unexpectedly, during that second night as a wandering escapee, Joseph underwent a mental experience which affected all his later years.

"As iron sharpeneth iron," solitude and stillness stir deep reflection. One of the savage penalties inflicted by our mechanized modernity is its never-abating din which murders silence (that healing balm for nerve and brain) and incapacitates the soul for undistracted meditation. High among those moonlit hills, that night, Joseph thought more deeply than he had ever done before.

Breaking upon his mind like an inrolling tide came years of Millie's teaching. Amid that nocturnal hush, the moon and the stars lit it all up with solemn grandeur. Overpoweringly it struck his mind that this immense universe of solar and stellar marvels, of colossal and intricate orderliness, of rational man and God-aware conscience, could no more have evolved from blank nothing than a gnat could mother an elephant. In the native instinct of his humanhood he *knew* it. Without God the universe is the absurdest conundrum. He needed no scientific demonstration to tell him that "evolution" as an ultimate explanation is grotesquely irrational. In that sense, at least, sitting there alone in that shepherd's halt, he found God.

With growing clearness, too, his keen young mind sorted the difference between "opinions" and "convictions." As a result of widespread teaching, he himself had been drawn to the opinion that everything had evolved—though he had never let Millie know this. Now, amid that nocturnal solitude he found himself listening for the first time to the voice of his own soul; and in it he heard the voice of God-implanted truth. Joseph suddenly saw that opinions are products of the head: convictions are dictates of the soul. A man *changes* his opinions according to self-preference; but his real convictions change *him*. A man will *argue* for his opinions. He will *die* for his convictions. A man will hold "opinions" on dubious evidence; but his "convictions" are a part of his very life. Joseph was face to face with his convictions, and one of them was that the Bible account of man's creation, and that alone, is worthy either of man or of God.

But if God made everything, who made God? If someone made *Him*, then He cannot be God. Yet if He was not created He could not have come from nothing, which means that He must have existed for *ever!*—stunning, tantalizing to the mind: a Being without a beginning! Could one possibly accept that? One of Millie's sayings came swinging back: "Mysteries never disprove realities." Another came back: "We cannot explain God; but God is the only satisfying explanation of everything else." And yet another: "The biggest mystery about God is not that He is triune, but that He never had a beginning—which baffles us at present because everything else we can think of has both a beginning and an end. But if everything else has a beginning, there must be Someone somewhere who *never* had a beginning." At that point Joseph began to get lost in abstruse profundities: yet there and then he found the stepping-stones to a deep, unshakable belief in God—the God of his mother's Bible.

That set him thinking about the Bible; and with a lucidity

he had never dreamed of he "saw the point" of his wonderful little mother's emphasis on the Bible. He had heard her say, both in public and in private, "The Bible is the most basic of all issues, for it claims, as no other literature, to be the directly inspired Word of God. If it is indeed inerrantly inspired, then we have certainty about God, about origins, about man, about morals, about the race's future, and about human destiny on the other side of the grave. But if the Bible is anything less, then on those basically vital matters we do *not* have certainty; we are only groping, like the non-biblical religions."

What a mother she was! How logically she put things! How well she had drilled him! Like an artillery charge it swept over him on that moon-silvered mountain brow. Yes, it was the Bible and certainty versus mere human speculation and *uncertainty*. Joseph "saw" it, and would never unsee it.

A strange classroom it was, that lonely laddie, in the middle of the night, among those Pennine summits, beneath heaven's vast chandelier of moon and stars, listening to that imperious voice from within himself, to a mother's voice floating over the miles, and to another Voice from somewhere deep in that mysterious space!

It is a psychological marvel how luminously the human mind can grapple with a problem and grasp the shining solution when under subtle influences such as those which invaded Joseph during that lonely soliloquy. Even mysteries shrouded in a deep gloom seemed to gleam with hitherto unsuspected meaning, as though shone upon by some starry flashlight. As he thought of his mother and the little home in Wragley Street he found himself staring again at the ugly face of evil scowling at him through his father's malicious eyes. Why should hatred, cruelty, drunkenness, and other evils be? Surely God did not predetermine them and all the agonies they inflict. Or (awful thought!) did He? Is God cruel? Does He mock mankind? Or did evil originate against God's will?—if so, how can God be sovereign? Or, if God knowingly permitted it, *why?* Mystery!

It is said that Gautama Buddha did some of his deepest thinking when he was only fourteen. Others in time's gallery of fame have left on record thought-crises in their early 'teens. But never did a boy of fourteen think more penetratingly than Joseph Kennard during that night. What a harvest from years of patient seed-sowing Millie was beginning to reap in the mind of her runaway son!

Joseph recalled hearing twice a sermon of Millie's on "Why Pain?" He could recapture three out of her five propositions. She had said that if the Bible is truly divine revelation, then (1) evil and pain have *not* always existed. The Bible tells how they began. (2) Evil and pain will not always continue. The Bible says they will end in a "new heaven and a new earth," with every tear wiped away. (3) If the Lord Jesus Christ is really God incarnated in our human flesh, then when He died on the Cross God Himself not only suffered *for* man, to make atonement, but He suffered *with* man amid the present curse of evil and pain. Only vaguely could Joseph re-think the other two points, but they were to the effect that in Christian believers the Holy Spirit makes all this comfortingly real; also that God overrules the sufferings of Christians so that "all things work together" for their eternal good.

Like a flash, Joseph saw the force of those two "ifs." *If* the Bible is the Word of God, we have true light on the mystery of evil and pain. And *if* Christ is indeed God the Son born into our humanity to be our Saviour, then God suffers *with* us; and on that awful Cross we see the unmistakable demonstration that God *loves* us.

It was all so swift yet so vividly clear; Joseph's mind almost reeled. With overpowering definiteness he saw that if the Lord Jesus Christ is *not* absolutely God, we have no real proof that God loves us. If God gave only a *creature* to die on that Cross, it cost Him no more than a millionaire tossing a coin to a beggar. Also, if Christ is not absolutely God the Son, then, like all other created beings, He is merely finite—in only one place at any given instant. He is not simultaneously everywhere, and therefore cannot indwell the hearts of His people everywhere.

Young Joseph could not have so expressed all this at the time, but he "got" it. He also saw that only an absolutely divine Christ could make an infinite atonement for the sins of the human race. Not that Joseph then and there accepted Christ as his Saviour. He was stubborn. He had ideas and plans of his own with which he did not want even God to interfere! None the less, he "saw" those great truths with such perspicuity as he would not have thought possible a few hours earlier.

He could not help thinking about the Old Testament story of Jacob who fled from home to escape the revenge of his brother whom he had tricked. Jacob fled over the moors and had to sleep there through the night, with a stone for his pillow. Joseph became occupied comparing himself with that troubled fugitive. He remembered how Jacob had dreamed of the shining ladder up to heaven, and had awakened exclaiming, "Surely, the LORD is in this place!" How long after midnight Joseph did not know, but with that Jacob-episode in his mind he gradually succumbed to somnolent influences and slid into slumber, thanking the moon and the stars that the night was just as amiable as the preceding night had been turbulent.

Slowly he came back to consciousness as the dawn was trying to wipe from its sleepy eyes the early mists. Encircling him was a view he would never forget. Everywhere for miles around, like the helmeted heads of old-time warriors, were the tops of the mountains, shining amid the golden shafts of the new morning against a background of royal blue. Everywhere in between them, below the height where Joseph stood, was a shimmering, sun-embroidered shawl of vapour wrapping the shoulders of those Pennine giants, like soft, clinging voil. It was a breath-taking panorama. The whole thing seemed alive: the great, wide sea of gold-tinged mist was slowly moving, gradually thinning, then shrinking, and now shredding gently apart into white puffs like fluffy cottonwool, until presently all the intervening valleys were basking in the splendor of a superb daybreak.

To Joseph it all seemed like a mighty parable connecting itself with his deep ponderings during the preceding night. It seemed to say, "When the sun rises the mists dissolve. So is it when the light of divine truth breaks upon a human mind from the written Word of God."

Joseph still was not (as he would have put it) "religious," but as he made his way down that mountain elbow and across the grassy valley toward yonder road, he was a different Joseph from the one who had climbed to that shepherd's halt the day before. Somehow, in one night, never to be forgotten, he had shed the chrysalis of juvenility and emerged to mental adulthood.

FIFTEEN
Any Port in a Storm

Making a wide circuit to avoid savage farm dogs, Joseph eventually reached the road. Judging by the sun, he took what must surely be the Manchester direction. A mile along the road he saw a cluster of houses at a place where the road broke into a letter Y. At the fork there were signposts: to the right Glossop, Hyde, Stockport: and to the left Sheffield.

In the window of a little grocery shop a card hung: "Teas, Light Refreshments." Being hungry and thirsty, Joseph decided to get a cup of tea before plodding on, if not too early for the shopkeeper. As he opened the door a bell went ding-a-ling which brought a bright little woman from the rear.

"Good mornin'. What can I do for you?"

"I would like a cup of hot tea, please, if you serve this early."

"We serves any time anybody wants it, son; but I don't remember bein' asked before at this hour o' day. Y'don't live round here, do yer? 'Ave y'been sleepin' out-o'-doors?"

"Well, I missed my way late yesterday, and had to pass the night on the hills."

"Y'did! 'Pon my word, lad, y'must be 'ungry!"

"Thank you, I am; but I have a little food left which a

farmer's wife gave me. If I could just get a hot cup of tea with it. . . ."

The brisk little woman eyed him rather uncertainly, then said, "A'right; just wait 'eer a minit while I gets that 'ot cup o' tea for yer."

"May I ask how much you charge?" stammered Joseph. "Is it more than twopence?"

Again she eyed him intently, and noticed he had reddened. "Son, we charge one penny for a cup o' tea, an' another penny for a buttered bun with it. But in your case it'll cost yer nuthin'. Wot would yer muther think o' me if I took yer last couple o' coppers when yer in such a predikiment?"

About five minutes later her head bobbed out and she called, "Come in 'eer, m'duck."

Rather shyly Joseph went. There was a neat room with a window looking on a well-tended vegetable garden. On one half the table was a folded white cloth, cup and saucer and spoon, a boiled egg in an egg-cup, a pot of tea, and three slices of buttered bread, also a dainty dish of marmalade!

"Oh, how very, very kind of you! You don't even know me!"

"Sit down, son. I likes the looks of yer. 'Ave a good breakfast: and there's plenty more if yer needs it."

Eagerly but politely Joseph sat down. How good it all tasted! But again he noticed she was concentratedly eyeing him.

"Excuse me lookin' sort o' steady at yer," she said. "Y'see, yer very like mi own son when he was your age. He was a dear lad, he was; but he's gone. A'll never get over it. He was killed in th'Boer War. Mind yer, it wasn't by a bullet. No; in Africa it was so blazin' 'ot in th'daytime, they sweat like meltin' butter: an' it was so icy cold at nights, they were stiff as brass statues; an' my poor, darlin' son, he got pumona, an' it finished 'im off."

With a sad, faraway look, she continued: "He used to love these 'eer 'ills, an' wander over 'em, like you. They'll never-no-more look the same to me. They're just like a picture-frame now round a blank piece o' cardboard where my laddie's 'andsome face used to be. Oh, son, these devilish wars, a'spillin' blood an' breakin' hearts an' wringin' tears! What blessed good d'they do? Cain keeps murderin' 'is brother; an' every time 'ee does, 'ee's a bit further from heaven, an' a bit neerer to hell. What's the good o' tellin' me mi son won a medal, when the devil's put 'im in 'is grave? Decoratin' a corpse dunna make it cum alive again. Oh, mi poor, poor boy! 'Ow I loved 'im!"

Joseph tried to say how sorry he was, and she came to his help.

"It does mi good t'hear yer, son. I thinks yer a gud lad, somehow. But, d'yer know, all the comfortin' words people speak are just about as good as puttin' a corn-plaister on a whoopin' cough. Y'see, laddie, mi boy's grave isn't really in Africa; it's right 'eer, in 'is muther's heart. It's funny, but when yer carries a grave inside yer, there's only one place y'can find comfort; an' that's in th'Bible."

"In the Bible?" responded Joseph with surprise—not surprise at the fact, but that he was meeting people here and there to whom it was so precious. Her words meant more to him after his night on the hills.

"Yes, son. Y'see, God's own Son was killed in a war—the 'oly war agin the traitor divil who causes all t'other wars. God saw 'is own Son bleedin' and dead, an' a corpse in a grave! So I sort o'knows He understands 'ow I feel about mi own son. An' besides that, He let 'is Son come back from t'other side o' the grave an' talk in 'is body again, to tell us that on t'other side o' the grave wounds are 'ealed an' tears dried, an' reunions makin' up for separations 'eer.'

"My own wonderful mother taught me to believe that," interjected Joseph.

"Bless 'er 'art; I'm glad she did. Yer may not realize it yet, son, but if th'grave ends everythin', then for most of us 'uman beings this upsettin' life 'eer is a mystery an' a mockery."

Ding-a-ling-a-ling. The shop bell rang. She slipped out of the living room to attend the customer. When she returned, Joseph rose to go. But she added, "A'm thinkin' yer should wash yer hands an' face afore yer go, son. The kitchen's next door, an' you'll find soap an' towel 'andy."

Joseph was more appreciative than he could put into

words. A few minutes later, as he was leaving, he said, "I never knew how many kind people there are until I got lost. I hope I shall be able to call again sometime and say another 'Thank you,' Mrs. . . ?"

"Armitage," she replied. "I'm sorry Mr. Armitage isn't 'ome. He's bin gone since seven this mornin', an' won't be back till about five."

So Joseph was on his way once more, feeling revived, except for rather sore toes and some stiffness in his knees. The stiffness gradually wore off, but not the toes!—and his boots were less comfortable after their soaking the day before. He forked right. Just there he saw several young fellows leaning on the stone wall near the signpost (which was a sort of chatting center). "Good morning," he said respectfully. "Could you tell me if this is the road to Manchester?"

"Manchester!" a couple of them gasped. "Hope yer no' tryin' to *walk* there! It's miles and miles away!"

"Perhaps I can get a lift," Joseph ventured; "but is this the way?"

"Yes, that's it alright," one of them replied. "But unless y'gets on wheels, by the time y'reach Manchester you'll have worn your feet off and be walkin' on two stumps"—at which the other fellows laughed.

"Thank you," Joseph responded, trying to laugh with them despite twinges in his toes.

However, Joseph had gone only three quarters of a mile along that road when he found yet another road sharply forking back slantwise through some other little town and signposted, HUDDERSFIELD. Suddenly he had a new thought. Why not Huddersfield instead of Manchester! Undoubtedly his worried mother would get the police looking for him, and they were sure to think Manchester the likely place.

Coming up the road toward the Huddersfield signpost was a four-wheel farm wagon full of early autumn produce, and drawn by two horses. Yes, it was veering toward the Huddersfield Road. Joseph ran round the corner, and as the wagon came slowly up the slight incline, he called up to the farmer, "Do you happen to be going to Huddersfield?"

"No, lad. Huddersfield's a good few miles further than I'm goin', but if yer likes to jump up, I'll take yer as far as I'm agoin', if this pair o' lazy old 'osses 'old out that long."

With ten self-conscious toes shouting "Hurrah!" Joseph was up in a trice beside the farmer.

"Mak' yersel' cumfortable, lad. Pull them two sacks from just behind, an' put 'em under yersel'. A've just bin awantin' somebody t'talk to. It gets sort o' lonely travelin' wi' nobody but 'osses."

So saying the hearty farmer turned on a tap of conversational verbosity which never stopped running until the cart wheels reached their destination. Never in his life, either before or after, did Joseph emit such a monotony of "Is that so?" and "Oh, I see," and "Oh, yes," and "Well, well!" When he and the farmer parted, still some miles from Huddersfield, Joseph's ears felt like two prisoners released from a long jail term.

Yet he owed more to it than he guessed. What he had surmised about the police was right. Only one day after he had been with Freddie and Tizzie Barton a policeman cycled round. They confirmed that Joseph had been there and had said he was making for Manchester. The police learned the same later from Mrs. Armitage, also from the youths at signpost corner. So it seemed certain that their quarry was now in the Manchester area, which they therefore searched extensively. It never entered their thinking that Joseph had taken the very opposite direction.

With sore toes and tired feet, Joseph found it a weary trudge to reach the outskirts of Huddersfield. The road became up and down. The ups were hard on the knees. The downs were hard on the toes. The day was now fast expiring. With a last flush of apology for disappearing so soon, the sun slid down behind a low barrier of thick cloud, causing an early dusk. The sky was already setting its evening lamps alight. To Joseph it seemed as though some peevish spirit-power kept putting Huddersfield a bit further away. His pace now was not as consistent, nor his gait as swingy. And since, as the old proverb has it, "troubles never come singly," there had to be the discomfort of intermittent showers from which there was scarcely a tree to offer shelter, and which left his clothes soaked. As he plodded on he finished the remainder of the sandwiches Tizzie had put up for him—by now rather stale, but sufficient to stave off hunger.

There is a waggish hyperbole round there that the year consists of "three months rain and nine months bad weather"! As the darkness came on, the cloud mass spread until it completely blacked out the starry lamps of the sky, and then, with no sympathy for a discouraged wanderer, began to drip a soaking drizzle everywhere.

At last, atop a rise, Joseph saw lights, and hoped they were Huddersfield. About forty minutes later he was in streets of houses and a few shops in some locality fringing the large Yorkshire city. But what should he do now? Wet and unkempt as he was, and a complete stranger, who would want to help him? He remembered his mother's advice: "If you are lost and need help, go to the police or to a Christian minister."

Under present circumstances the last thing he dare think of was going to the police. What about a minister? He might be miles from any (and in those days telephones were rare). However, an answer of sorts seemed to present itself a couple of streets further on. He heard singing from a smaller building next to a church. Seemingly, a meeting was in progress, for the building was lighted. Chiseled in the stonework over the entrance were the words, "Methodist Sunday School." Dare he peep in? At least it would be some help if he could only get temporary shelter there while thinking what to do.

As quietly as possible he pushed the door open slightly. Yes, it was a meeting, and there seemed to be about a hundred people present. Away at the front was a platform where, behind a table draped by a maroon cover, was a minister with graying hair. Joseph tiptoed in and, as inconspicuously as possible, sat at the nearer end of the last bench, just as the people sat again after singing. A couple of persons edged away to make room for him, looking him over rather suspiciously.

By now Joseph was too footsore, soaked and wearied to take in much of the preaching, though he was awake enough to realize that it was a well-expressed exposition given in a congenial manner. What with his wet clothes, now steaming in the warmth, and his tiring tramp, he was several times on the verge of slumber, but he tenaciously warded if off until the meeting closed.

Several then came to him with smiles of welcome and expressions of concern that he was so wet. One man said, "Good to see you, son. Anything we can do for you?" to which Joseph respectfully replied that he would like a word with the minister.

"Oh, that's easy enough. Let me take you to him. You'll like Mr. Hibbert. If you're wanting advice, he's your man."

"Glad to meet you," beamed Mr. Hibbert as he shook hands with Joseph. "But how wet you are! What can we do for you?"

"I wondered, sir, if you could give me some advice. My mother always said, if I was ever lost or in difficulty, to tell the police or see a minister."

"That sounds interesting. Step into this side room and sit down."

Joseph did so. "Are you an evangelical minister, sir?" he asked. "Do you believe the whole Bible is the Word of God?"

Mr. Hibbert jerked a curious glance at Joseph, and with a quizzical smile puckering his face asked, "What on earth makes you ask that?"

"My mother said that if I were in trouble I should go to some minister who preaches that the whole Bible is the Word of God."

"So your mother is a godly, Christian woman?"

"Yes, sir. She's the most wonderful mother in the world."

"What about your father?"

Joseph's face fell. "Sir, he's a drunkard. I don't like to say anything disrespectful; but he is cruel and hates me, and I think he tried. . . ."

"Have you run away from home?"

"Yes, sir."

"Where do you come from?"

"Sir, please, I'm not being deceitful, but I dare not tell you that—not yet. If my father found out where I am. . . ."

"I see."

"Can you help me, sir? I cannot go to the police because already they will be searching for me. Nor can I go back home. But my mother will be worried about me. I have no money; but if I could get somewhere . . . for just a short time, I would work hard if only to have a place to stay. And then I intend somehow to let my mother know I'm safe."

"Are you a Sunday school boy?"

"Yes, sir; both morning and afternoon; and I'm in the Boys' Brigade."

"What is your name?"

"Sir, I cannot be dishonest and give you a false name; but I'm afraid to tell you my real name, in case it should slip out and show where I am."

"I understand. You can trust me."

"Sir, my first name is Joseph."

"Very well, Joseph. Just wait here a moment or two."

Mr. Hibbert was gone several minutes. Then he came back accompanied by a middle-aged man with a firm but kindly face, and dark, well-groomed hair; dressed in a dark blue, pin-striped suit, and giving a total impression of being, perhaps, a prosperous businessman.

"Hello, Joseph," he began. "So you're in a tough predicament. So am I. My own predicament is: I like the looks of you, and I want to befriend you, but I don't know you, and you are a run-away; and how can I be sure you will be honest with me? Anyway, Joseph, I've come to say that Mrs. Ainsworth and I are willing to take the risk with you, if you. . . ."

Joseph intercepted him. Both Mr. Hibbert and Mr. Ainsworth saw the change which came over his face. Pale, and fighting back the tears, he stood and said, "Mr. Ainsworth, you are very kind. Thank you, sir. But I think now I ought not to trouble you. I don't want to be a risk to anybody. Perhaps, after all, I'd better go. . . ."

"You'll do nothing of the kind, young man!" exclaimed Mr. Ainsworth. "You'll let me finish what I began saying. It was this: Mrs. Ainsworth and I are willing to take the risk with you, if you are willing to take the risk with us!"

He and Joseph looked steadily into each other's eyes. It

was the beginning of a man-boy esteem which they both seemed to sense there and then.

"Joseph, my boy, the first thing we've got to do is, give you a hot bath, get your clothes dry, give you some supper, and chat about tomorrow. Come on; let's get cracking. Good night, Mr. Hibbert. Thanks for that fine word this evening."

As they strode out to the street Mr. Ainsworth explained: "I don't have the horse and trap with me. We live not so far from here—about twenty minutes' walk. Thank heaven, it's not raining. I hope you don't shiver in those damp clothes. I know Mrs. Ainsworth is going to mother you."

"Doesn't she know I'm coming?" Joseph asked.

"Oh, yes. She's gone on to get the bath and the bed ready. You'll have to wear one of my own nightshirts. You're not much less than I, so you won't get lost! When you're in bed you can have something warm and nourishing while your clothes are drying. You'll feel heaps better by morning."

After several streets they were in an open area with larger homes in their own grounds. Joseph was rather taken aback when he saw the Ainsworth dwelling. He had expected some small cottage, but it was a handsome double-fronted house, back from the road, and surrounded by well-kept lawns easily seen even in the vapory moonlight. One of the front rooms was lighted, and shed a rosy glow through its deep red curtain. The top half of the front door, also, emitted light through a varicolored mosaic of leaded glass.

Soon they were in the ample hall, with its oak staircase going up on the right, both hall and stairway being carpeted in turkey-red pattern. It was indeed a cheery entrance, and Mrs. Ainsworth was there to greet them. She was angular and rather sharp-featured, with searching but pleasant eyes and firm lips. She impressed Joseph as embodying the ideal head-mistress. Yet there was utterly no stiffness in her poise; and when she smiled there was a world of responsiveness in it.

"Come in, dear boy," she said, holding out both her hands to both of his. "This *is* a surprise! You may wonder whatever I mean, but we think you are an answer to prayer!"

Joseph gasped an intense, "Oh, thank you!" and gaped.

"Yes," she explained. "In our book of daily readings, today's text was, 'Inasmuch as ye did it to one of the least of these, ye did it unto Me'; and I prayed that if He wanted to send someone to me today needing shelter and food I might be ready. And here *you* are!"

In that moment another of Millie's counsels came floating back: "Joseph, if you put your hand in God's, He will lead you to the right people." He replied, "You are so kind, Mrs. Ainsworth; but I am ashamed to look like this. I've had to . . . I don't like to tell you . . . I've had to sleep outdoors the past two nights. . . ."

"Well, that may be very healthy, but it's not always so comfortable. Tonight we'll put the emphasis on comfort. The bath is ready. We'll dry your jacket and waistcoat and trousers, and wash your underclothes and stockings—and all will be ready for you by morning. There's a little bedroom for you. Daddy will show you which. Oh, before you go upstairs you must meet our daughter. I think she's rather shy about meeting a strange boy."

"Molly!" sang out Mr. Ainsworth. "Come and meet our guest."

Out came Molly from the living room into the hall. When Joseph saw her he could almost have reeled. (Many another boy had.) She was not merely attractive; she was uniquely beautiful, even stunning. Flowing, shiny dark hair, full eyebrows and long lashes, rich, deep-brown eyes, and charming round face—all evidently inherited from her good-looking father; finely regular features, firm mouth, full lips and bewitching smile—all equally clearly inherited in perfected form from her mother. To say the least, she was as startlingly beautiful as the most exquisite Spanish infanta who ever wore a coronet; almost as tall as Joseph; two years older than he; and, to his youthful eyes, nothing less than sensational!

As the saying goes, he was "rocked on his feet," but with

an Herculean effort he wrenched himself back to poise and sobriety, disguised his surprise, and politely said, "I'm pleased to meet you, miss."

She was as femininely developed in figure as she was extraordinarily attractive in face; and when she spoke it was in a round, contralto voice which could have set any young man's heart fluttering. Yet the moment she spoke, poor Joseph was inwardly flung down. She simply said, "You're rather wet, aren't you?" The contralto music of it could not conceal that she resented him and wished he had not come. Sensitive Joseph wished the same, and resolved not to stay longer than he could help.

It was there, in the Ainsworths' home, that Joseph first sat in a built-in bath. Cottages had no such modern luxury. It was a five-and-a-half feet long, by two-and-a-half feet wide, and one foot six inches deep—so the wondering Joseph roughly estimated! There were scented soaps! There were big, soft sponges. Hitherto his ablutions had been swills over a small zinc tub. Oh, the lovely feeling, the relaxing influence of that soapy sponging in that deep, hot water!

Joseph would fain have lain there an hour, but dreaded doing the wrong thing. So, after about ten or twelve minutes, he emerged from his liquid bliss and dried himself on the largest towel he had ever seen. Then, glowing and grateful, with the towel wrapped round him, he peeped out to the landing and quietly called, "I'm out, Mr. Ainsworth."

That kindly gentleman was waiting, and handed to Joseph a clean undervest, along with a brightly striped blue nightshirt. A few minutes later, Joseph was in a comfy bed overlaid by the prettiest eiderdown, and in such a daintily decorated bedroom, it seemed to him like one of the heavenly mansions.

Mr. Ainsworth's comment was, "Joseph, already you look a different laddie. By jabbers! I like the look of you even more, now! At breakfast tomorrow we want to mention one or two ideas which may help you for the days ahead. But Mrs. Ainsworth and I thought that tonight the best thing for you to have the hot bath, get into a warm bed, have a bite of supper, and then a good sleep. Mrs. Ainsworth will be upstairs in a minute with a cup of malted milk and something to nibble with it."

Minutes later, Mrs. Ainsworth was there, apologizing for intruding into a "young gentleman's bedroom"—her sharp features having lost their sharpness in that mothering smile. There was no mistaking those eyes now. An unusually kind heart was looking through them. She said, "I do hope you will like this. We think it's just about enough this late at night. We all want you to sleep well. By the way, I've brought you a fresh pair of stockings. I've been washing yours—and there are two potatoes in each!" (Northern counties folk used to refer colloquially to holes in stockings as "potatoes.") "Poor boy! How you must have tramped! I hope your feet are not sore. Are they?"

Joseph's reply was a sheepish look which admitted what she feared.

"Daddy, bring that flat, round tin of emollient from the cabinet in our bathroom—you know the one I mean: a yellow tin; I forget the name."

Daddy brought it.

"Rub it gently on. It works wonders. Good night, and God bless you."

"Yes, good night, and God bless you," echoed Mr. Ainsworth, as he gently shut the door behind him.

Then Joseph was alone. "Thank you, thank you, God," he said, "for bringing me here. Please guide me, and help me to obey You. And please, please, God, take care of my mother, and bless her."

Perhaps he would have prayed more, but the day's long traipse, the strain of anxiety, the church meeting, the interview, the strange, new experience, the hot bath and soothing supper-drink all now united in such an anaesthetic effect that he knew nothing more until seven o'clock the next morning.

SIXTEEN
The Big Eye-Opening

Joseph woke thoroughly refreshed, instantly realized where he was, jumped out of bed, heard the clock chime seven, thought to get dressed, then remembered he had no clothes. He opened his door a teeny bit to see if the Ainsworths were astir. At his door was a clothes-maiden on which were his underclothes, washed and dried, also his jacket, waistcoat, trousers, and a pair of slippers a size or so too large but usable. He pulled them in and dressed. Minutes later there was a gentle knock at the door, and Mr. Ainsworth's voice said, "Joseph, that same bathroom is all yours. No hurry. Breakfast at 8 o'clock downstairs."

At the hour Joseph was downstairs, buoyant but nervous. There was a wholesome breakfast of porridge and milk, eggs and bacon, toast and marmalade, all abdominally baptized in well-brewed tea, English fashion. Mr. and Mrs. Ainsworth kept up an easy conversation, agreeably impressed by Joseph's good manners and gift of discreet self-expression. Molly was silent. Whenever Joseph glanced at her she was looking away, yet the moment he turned to her parents he knew she was scrutinizing him.

Before they left the table Mr. Ainsworth brought his Bible. "Joseph, each day we have a brief reading from the

Book. Would you care to stay? Don't feel embarrassed. You need not stay if. . . ."

"Mr. Ainsworth, my mother does the same. I would like to stay. Thank you."

The passage was Matthew 26:1-13. Joseph had heard his mother preach on the woman in verse 7, and rather timidly said so—at which the Ainsworths gave a new look at him, and at each other. Then Mr. Ainsworth prayed a brief, practical prayer, after which they together repeated "the Lord's Prayer." A minute or two later that wildly beautiful brunette, Molly, kissed her parents good-bye, gave a curt "Excuse me" to Joseph, and was gone. Mrs. Ainsworth explained that Molly was away to the "technical college," having to leave early because it was nearly seven miles away.

At that point Joseph made a further remark which occasioned a questioning look between his two benefactors. "If it is not out of place to say so, sir, what handsome oak furniture this is!"

"Out of place!" echoed Mr. Ainsworth. "No, it's just the *right* place. You see, I made it all! Come into the parlour."

Joseph followed him. It was a spacious, choicely furnished room, every piece in egg-shell finished walnut, including a Bechstein piano.

"Every article is Ainsworth-made, except the piano which we stained and polished to match. Look through this small window at the side of the fireplace."

Away up the road Joseph saw a building on the side of which he read AINSWORTH FURNITURE.

"You see, I'm a furniture maker. I don't do upholstering, but all the solid wood pieces. We do only the good-quality stuff, and we're mighty proud of it."

"That explains a lot, sir," Joseph risked.

"Let's go back to the dining-room and chat a minute or two."

When they were seated by the fire Mr. Ainsworth continued: "We've been trying to think how best to help you. This is our suggestion at the moment. We'll have you at the works to do a few odd jobs and get into the way of things; and we'll pay you a weekly wage so you have some money of your own. For the next week, or until we find some clean lodgings, you are welcome under our roof. And, let me whisper, if Molly seems a bit reserved, don't misunderstand. She suffers from boys who make themselves fools because of her good looks. She abhors it. If ever Molly pays any attention to any young man, he'll have to be one she greatly respects. Actually, she's an affectionate girl at heart; and she's as good as she's beautiful."

By 9:15 they were at the furniture factory. Soon Mr. Ainsworth had to revise his thinking. During the morning two of the men to whom Joseph had been assigned reported, "That boy is too far ahead for elementary apprenticeship. He knows the different woods; he handles the tools like a practiced hand. He planes and buffs beautifully. He can even turn spindles."

During the noon meal Mr. Ainsworth asked him, "Wherever did you pick up your proficiency in woodwork, Joseph?"

Joseph told him how Frank Goodall had tutored him, though without saying his name.

"Ummm, that's interesting. How did you get on at school? You can be quite open with me. I'm only wanting to do the best for you."

"If it won't sound boastful, sir, I won a scholarship to the secondary school, but I had been there only a few weeks when I had to leave home."

"Ummm. I suppose you never had any office training, then?"

"Yes, sir; but not much. I did bookkeeping one full winter at night-school, and my sister Dorothy taught me more. She was the school's prize-winner."

"Well, well!"

Next day, at breakfast, Mr. Ainsworth said, "Joseph, we've done some rethinking. It's a pity to have you waste time just sorting and cleaning. You've skill enough for something further. With that bookkeeping you've picked up and your know-how in cabinet mâking, you may be just the right peg in the right hole at the right time. Our clerk who did the ordering and checking from the sawmills left us some weeks ago. He is not yet replaced, which makes it hard on Miss Mathers. So in the mornings we'll have you at those ledgers; and in the afternoons, if you have time left, you can be with Len Haydock in the bedroom furniture wing."

That was not the only rethinking Mr. Ainsworth did. In about four days Joseph began to know his way in and out the ledgers. Middle-aged Miss Mathers was tolerant and helpful. Certainly, Joseph's neat handwriting, after his predecessor's none-too-clear scrawl, was pleasing. At home, his alert gentility did not pass unobserved. He was quick to notice when anything needed passing to Mrs. Ainsworth or Molly, at the table. After meals he had a comical alacrity in clearing away the china and cutlery, and insisted on drying the dishes in the kitchen. Early in the second week Mr. Ainsworth had found lodgings, but they were not available until a week later. So Joseph's stay was extended. Molly had largely lost her dubiety, and was formally pleasant to him. Joseph never let his eyes linger on her.

One evening, about the end of his first week there, something happened which gave the Ainsworths yet another surprise. Molly was in the front room practicing her part in the next Sunday's choir piece. She had closed the door so as not to be heard by the runaway youth temporarily housed with them. Joseph had come down the wide oak stairway on his way through the hall to the living room. Passing the closed door he heard a rich, mellow, contralto voice and some strumming on the piano. He could not resist exclaiming to Mrs. Ainsworth in the kitchen, "What an exceptional voice your daughter has!"

"Thank you. She's practicing her part for Sunday's anthem. She really needs someone to accompany her on the piano. She's started piano lessons, but isn't beyond the simpler kind of playing yet."

Joseph hesitated. He had not presumed to touch the piano. But plucking up courage he ventured, "Do you think she would mind if I glanced at the music?"

"Do you play the piano?"

"Much too poorly, but if I could help. . . ."

Mrs. Ainsworth gently opened the door on Molly, and after a few whispered words brought the music. It was the usual church anthem style, and the organ accompaniment no problem. Joseph asked could he run it over, if only once, for Molly. After a few scales to loosen his fingers he played the accompaniment with precision. Pa Ainsworth broke from his reading and hurried into the parlor. The three Ainsworths could only look at each other and exclaim, "This *is* a pleasant discovery!" They persuaded him to play one or two of his pianoforte favourites—and were amazed.

From then onwards there was a marked change in Molly. She and Joseph enjoyed playing and singing together. Nor was that all. They found another point of mutual interest. Few people at that time in Lancashire cotton towns or Yorkshire woolen towns learned horseriding. That was an exclusive diversion of the gentry. The Ainsworths were not gentry by heredity but were well-to-do by business success and were "better class" people. To the stuck-up breed of aristocrats a man like Mr. Ainsworth, even though well-educated, was a parvenu. Anyway, Molly was learning horseriding—which she practiced in the two large fields between their house and the furniture manufactury. How could Joseph help asking at least to watch for a few minutes? The few minutes became a couple of hours.

When Molly returned home she could not suppress her excitement. "Daddy, he's a superb horseman! He knows all about horses from their manes to their hoofs. He brushed Sally down, and saddled and handled her like a professional. He's told me things I never knew before about horses and riding. I rode Sally and he rode Vic. We've had a great old time!"

"Where's Joseph now?"

"He sent me on home. He said he'd follow in a few minutes. He wanted to sponge the horses down and swill the stable floor."

It was an hour before Joseph came in, his face glowing after the outdoor exertions. "Those are two fine quarter-horses, sir," he said. "Molly is going to make a good rider. Have I time to clean myself up before tea?"

While he was away for his quick wash and brush-up Mr. Ainsworth said to his wife and daughter, "My dears, I think you're both thinking what *I'm* thinking. An unusual boy has come into our home. The more I watch him, the more I like him and trust him. But where has he learned such gentlemanly manners and clean habits and music and woodwork and bookkeeping and horseriding? It's time we had a heart-to-heart talk with him, and find out where he really comes from."

That evening, as they sat round the hearth, Mr. Ainsworth broached the matter. "Joseph, I wonder if you would trust us enough now to tell us who you are. We pledge not to betray you. Not one syllable shall leak out—not until you give us permission. You can trust us implicitly. We only want to help you in the best way open to us."

Joseph's head drooped. There was silence awhile. Then, rather pale, he replied, "Mr. and Mrs. Ainsworth, you have been so very kind to me. I will tell you everything. But, please, for my mother's sake, don't tell anyone else."

So he told them. The Ainsworths listened intently. Afterwards Pa said, "Well, well!" and Mrs. Ainsworth added, "You poor laddie!" while Molly sat silently, tears glistening in her deep eyes.

Joseph finalized with, "I asked God to guide me, but I didn't think He'd guide me to such kind people as you"—at which three pairs of Ainsworth ears perked up even more, and Pa said, "Maybe God had a bigger purpose than you think, in sending you here."

After a long pause Mr. Ainsworth reflected, "You're right, Joseph: for the time being it must not leak out where you are from. But I'm worried about that remarkable mother of yours. We ought somehow to let her know you're safe and sound. Ummm, D'you know, son, I believe we've hit the nail on the head. I know just what we can do."

"Oh, thank you, Mr. Ainsworth."

"Yes, that's it! Jim Gibson or Albert Ogden can do it easily. Look, Joseph, we have two salesmen who travel all over the north of England getting orders for us at furniture stores. If you'll write a letter to your mother we can get it mailed from any town we choose! As for folk around here, all they need know is that you are a young man with woodwork training, needing a job, and I employed you."

Before bedtime Joseph wrote his letter.

My very *dear mother,*

    Please try to forgive me for running away from home. I know you will be anxious about me, but you need not worry any more. You told me that if I put my hand in God's He would guide me; and He has. I have got a good job, and am staying with kind Christian people. Please try not to be angry, mother dear, but I dare not tell you yet where I am. You know why. There is a man who travels, and he will post this letter from some town or other; so do not think that the postmark on the envelope is the town where I am living.

    I miss you terribly. Do not let the police look for me any more. I am very well. I pray every night, and shall try hard to live as you have taught me. Give my fond love to Dorothy when you write to her, also to Mona. When you see Mr. Frank Goodall tell him I am sorry not to be coming in to see him. If you mention me to my father, say I am too far away for him or anybody to find me or even guess where I am.

    Dear mother, I love you more than ever. Please trust me, and do not worry. I shall write you again soon. Perhaps, before long I can think of a way to see you. I miss seeing Mr. and Mrs. Adair and Evelyn and Rickie. Please tell them a big THANK YOU for being so kind to me.

    With lots of love to the dearest mother in all the world,

                  Your loving son,
                  Joseph

What the letter meant to Millie no words could express. Joseph, too, was relieved to know that it would put her mind at rest. As for the Ainsworths, from the night Joseph told his story they treated him almost as one of the family, though they did not envisage housing him for more than another week or two. Confidentially, though, they were not unduly sorry when Mrs. Shepherd (the woman with whom a room had been booked) asked to have the time postponed just one further week because of roof repairs and some indoor painting. Joseph was sensitive and offered to go elsewhere meanwhile. That, the Ainsworths would not countenance; so Joseph lingered in their beautiful home.

More distinctly as the days passed they perceived that Joseph's gentlemanly complaisance was not a temporary artificiality; that he was an upright, gifted and unusually precocious young man. He was amenable and attentive, eager yet not unbecomingly forward, with definite ideas yet polite to listen. Molly lost her reserve and did not mind his hearing her sing all over the house. Their times at the piano she revelled in without disguise. Even when they were not practicing music she was drawn by his basically serious mind, and warmly responded in their conversations together.

But there were other influences at work. The Ainsworths were having an effect on Joseph. By the time he had been there nearly three weeks, the way they lived, spoke, behaved, prayed at the breakfast table, and reacted to daily exigencies, gave him a peculiar feeling that they had some secret which he did not know, and a quality of life with a kind of quiet joy in it. Once or twice it even irritated him a bit. Several times he felt sure that out of considerateness for himself they were not talking as freely to each other about spiritual topics as they would have done if he had not been there. Then there came an unforeseeable transpiring which changed the whole course of his life.

A chain of happenings led to it. When, at the end of his first week there, he had received his wage packet from the furniture works, his first concern was to buy a new Sunday suit and one suitable for work; also an extra pair of boots and new underwear. He knew, of course, that it would take several weeks' earnings to do all that, but he thought he might manage at once the new suit and boots. Mr. Ainsworth recommended a certain outfitter's shop. Joseph selected a ready-made gray suit, but found he was several shillings short. The tradesman said, "Take the suit, and bring the balance of payment next week." Joseph, however, preferred not. He bought new boots but had the suit set aside for him until next pay-day.

Mr. Ainsworth was disappointed. "Why did you not do as he offered?"

"My mother always taught me: Flee debt as you would a viper."

That reply secretly pleased the Ainsworths.

Later, on that Saturday evening, a parcel came for Joseph. It was the suit, with a note pinned to the wrapper: "Never mind the extra shillings. There is a reduction on this suit. Call with payment at convenience." Joseph rightly suspected that Mr. Ainsworth had a sly hand in this, but did not guess that the tailor was a leader in their Methodist church. Also, in his bedroom Joseph found two cardboard boxes. One contained new underwear and a note in Mrs. Ainsworth's handwriting: "To a dear boy, for next Christmas, but to be worn now." A smaller one contained three linen and three celluloid collars, after the fashion of the time, plus two colourful ties and two dinky bows, and a note from Molly: "With best wishes for your birthday, whenever it is."

Joseph's feelings were a turmoil of gratefulness and embarrassment. His cheeks burned. It was like living on charity; yet he knew that what the Ainsworths had done was no mere pity. His face was still red as he went downstairs and bashfully stammered, "Thank you." But Mrs. Ainsworth was sternly ahead of him: "Look here, young man, you'll have to get over that. If *we* were in *your* place and you were in ours, wouldn't you do just the same? While you're with us you're one of us. Do you understand?" She pretended to look severe, but broke down and gave him a kiss.

Evenings later, Joseph and Molly were at the piano a while. Then they went into the living-room just in time to hear daddy Ainsworth exclaim, as he glanced up from his reading, "Grand! Grand! That's grand!"

Molly whispered to Joseph, "I'll bet I can tell you what he's reading. It's one of Spurgeon's printed sermons."

"Spurgeon's sermons!" repeated Joseph. "Why my mother reads those, and sometimes quotes them at her women's meetings." He wanted to add, "Who on earth wants to read printed sermons?" but he refrained.

"Joseph, my boy, one of these days you'll have to read some of Spurgeon's sermons," said Mr. Ainsworth with happy animation. Then he pulled himself up. "Oh, I beg your pardon. Who am I, to be pushing Spurgeon on you? What young chap of your age wants to read printed sermons? Eh, but they're grand, Joseph. Other printed sermons are flat by comparison. Spurgeon's have atmosphere—yes, that's it, 'atmosphere,' as though you were actually seeing and hearing him. He's the greatest popular preacher of the Bible who ever lived, says I. Over seventeen hundred of his sermons are now printed! The Metropolitan Tabernacle in London where he preached holds five thousand people, and he packed it every week until he died—in 1892, I think. I've only one thing against him: he wasn't a Methodist! Joseph, lad, it's a grand thing to get converted early!"

"Converted!" The word came like an electric shock. That was what his mother was always preaching! Inwardly Joseph was resentful. This talk about having to get "converted" in order to be "saved" and "right with God" mystified and provoked him. Why must they keep harping on about it? He almost betrayed his unfriendly feelings, but respectfully hid them. At the same instant it darted into his mind that these three Ainsworths might have been "converted," and that perhaps this was the strange something which made them seem different. On an impulse, not of pleasure but of politeness merely, he jerked out, "Thank you, Mr. Ainsworth. My mother reads Spurgeon's sermons. I'm game to read one any time."

"Righto, lad. I'll put a volume of 'em in your room, and I'll mark one or two which might be more interesting to a brainy young chap like you."

Sure enough, by bedtime the book was on the chest of drawers in Joseph's room. He sat up in bed to read a page or two, thinking the dull stuff would prove a useful bedtime chloroform. The effect was the opposite. He was gripped, startled, disturbed. Under Spurgeon's dexterous elucidation of the Scripture Joseph saw, as never before, that whatever else the Bible is, or is not, it is the Book of salvation from sin. He saw, as never before, that whatever else human beings may, or may not need, their first and direst need is salvation from sin—from its guilt and stain and power in this present life, and from its damning consequences on the other side of the grave.

Sitting there in his nightgown he saw, as never before, that whatever else Jesus might be, He is the only but all-sufficient Saviour. He saw, as never before, that sin is not just crime—something done against one's fellowman, but monstrous rebellion against a holy God who absolutely must judge and punish it. He saw, as never before, that sin is not just *acts* of wrong, but an hereditary *condition* with an innate bias toward the wrong. He saw, as never before, that "religion" never saved anybody; that religion apart from salvation is merely putting fancy clothes over a rotting leprosy.

As a boy of tender years, Joseph doubtless would scarcely have worded it in the way it is here described, but it is substantially as he himself described it later. He saw, as never before, that all the members of Adam's fallen race are sinners in their very nature, unregenerate, spiritually dead, alienated from God through hereditary perversity. At that same time he saw, as never before, the wonderful love of God, yearning over the sin-cursed millions of Adam's posterity, the helpless victims of Satan's malicious duplicity, yet not now victims only, but rebels and prodigals and wilfully corrupt. Above all else, he now saw, as never before, the Lord Jesus as the eternal Son of God, born into our world, entering into blood relationship with mankind in order to be the race's substitutionary Sinbearer and Saviour.

Yes, in that sudden eye-opening he saw all that with bewildering newness; saw it in the way a boy in his mid 'teens would; saw it with a vividness which never wore off. Of course, he had been tutored from childhood in those great Bible truths by his exceptional mother, but they had lain in his mind like sleeping giants, unrealized as the tremendous and dynamic realities which they are. Now, they all sprang to life and overpowered him. The logic and force and coherence of them was compelling.

Where fine minds and clever brains have sometimes gone astray, he saw through to the real truth. Sir Arthur

Conan Doyle, progenitor of the famous Sherlock Holmes exploits, had said he could not believe in a God who demanded sacrifice before He could forgive. Young Joseph saw the fallacy there. The God whose holiness *demanded* atonement was the God whose infinite love *provided* it. Sin, in its essence, is insurrection against an utterly holy, righteous, faithful Creator. There simply must be reparation, or the universe becomes an inferno, and God ceases to be God. A leading evolutionary scientist had said, "I cannot believe in a God who demands blood." Joseph saw the utter casuistry of that. It is not that God demands blood, but that sin necessitates atonement if the universe is to be safe. But who could make the infinite propitiation required? Only God Himself; and (wonder of wonders) the God who *inflicts* the judgment on sin is the One who *endures* it in man's place!

Yet though all that now became flamingly alight it brought no comfort, but only torture. Not a wink of sleep was Joseph's that night. He remembered being with his mother when someone had asked, "Which is the greatest sin?" His mother had replied, "I should say it is that which breaks the greatest commandment." Then the questioner had further asked, "Which, then, is the greatest commandment?" and Millie had quoted the words of Jesus, "Thou shalt love the Lord thy God with all thy heart, and with all thy soul, and with all thy mind. This is the first and greatest commandment." Those words, Millie had said, mean at the very least that we are to put God first in everything. To his dismay, now, Joseph realized that instead of putting God first in his life, he had not even put Him last; he had left Him out altogether, as far as possible! He had chosen his own way, and had wanted God not to interfere! He knew that any pretense of religion on his part had been merely a cover-up of his guileful heart, and that he was an utter stranger to his very Maker.

He saw, now, why Jesus cried, "Woe!" to those religious hypocrites, the Pharisees, but held out welcoming arms to repentant, low-down "sinners." Joseph felt himself a bigger sinner than all the drunkards and other criminals in Strangeways Prison, because he had sinned against light and privilege which they had never known. He saw the corruption of his heart and the bigness of his guilt, and felt that if he were to die that night he would go to the lowest hell. In a word, he was "under conviction," or, as John Bunyan phrases it, "in the slough of despond."

The three Ainsworths saw the difference in him next morning at breakfast. He was pale, edgy, and without appetite, though still as polite and thoughtful. They sympathetically refrained from prying, thinking perhaps he was not well. In the office he was as concentrated as usual, but as soon as released he seemed glad to get home and be alone. When the Ainsworths and he went to church he was much different from the boy who had been there the former Sundays. He listened with strained attentiveness, and afterward seemed disappointed, as though Mr. Hibbert had not said something which Joseph had wanted him to say.

Another few days went by. Joseph was off his food. He looked unhappy. He apologized. The Ainsworths assured him they "understood"—and in truth they did, now, more than Joseph suspected; for twice they had heard him praying with troubled voice in his bedroom, and once it had sounded like crying. Several times during those days Joseph felt that the one who understood him best was Molly. Some of her comments made him marvel that she so accurately read his thoughts.

One day Molly and he were in the sitting-room, intending to look through some music. A bluebottle had gotten into the room and was buzzing round, every few seconds banging itself against the front window. "Have you ever thought what a baffling mystery a window pane must be to a fly, Joseph? The bluebottle sees right through to where it wants to go, but every time it tries to go it bangs against something it can't see, and wonders whatever is stopping it."

"No, I hadn't thought of it like that."

"Have you ever thought, it's sometimes like that with us human beings? We see certain truths very clearly, but when we try to act on them there seems an invisible barrier stopping us, and we wonder what on earth it is."

"Molly, you are a thought-reader. That's my problem just now."

"Yes, I know, and I'm so sorry for you, Joseph. You are wanting to ask me a question, and I think I know what it is."

"You do!"

"Isn't it this: you want to know whether I have been converted?"

"Molly, how did you know? That's just it. Have you?"

"Yes, I have."

"How did you get it, Molly?"

"Well, conversion isn't something you 'get'; it gets y*ou*."

"I see. But how do you make it get you?"

Molly smiled. "That's a comical way to put it, Joseph. You can't make it 'get' you. It just comes."

"Well, to me that sounds puzzling. If you can't *make* it come to you, can you tell me how it *does* come?"

"Yes, silly boy, I can. You're about as silly as *I* was. I knew well that I needed salvation, and I wanted the Lord Jesus as my Saviour, and I was willing to turn away from everything which I knew to be wrong. It all seemed so clear, yet every time I tried to experience it, I just couldn't. There was that invisible barrier."

"Well, I'm blest, Molly! That's me to the exact inch. But what was the barrier?"

"There were two things. One was my own pride. I'd been brought up in a Christian home, and always lived an 'upright' life—according to human standards. Why did *I* have to be 'saved' like those who had lived a low-down life in vulgar sin? God had to show me what sin really is. He had to show me how hard, cold, godless, selfish and sinful my *heart* was, and that I was just as desperately in need of forgiveness and cleansing as the worst criminal in jail. He had to show me that by nature I was spiritually dead and needed to be 'born again' into a new spiritual life—just as Jesus said to self-righteous Nicodemus."

"I've been going through all that, Molly."

"I know you have. Anyway, when I really saw what it cost God to save us, and how the Lord Jesus suffered in my place, that broke my pride once for all, and I came to God just as all other human sinners have to do."

"But what about that other difficulty?"

"I'll tell you. It was the very simplicity of how to become saved. I felt so grateful to Jesus, I was willing to do anything if only to get right with God and get peace in my heart. But that was where I kept going wrong. I wanted to *do* something to get saved. I just couldn't tumble to it that it was not something for me to *do,* but something that Jesus had already *done* on my behalf; and that all God now asked was, that I should believe on Jesus as my Saviour, and simply accept what He had done in my place."

"But, Molly, I *do* believe in Him, and yet that silly old window pane is stopping the bluebottle!"

"Yes, Joseph, and it is because you are thinking that believing is something that it isn't—just as *I* did. The faith that saves us is not merely *assenting* with the mind, it is *accepting* with the heart. And it isn't even accepting a set of truths; it's accepting a risen, living, personal Saviour into one's heart. There's nothing complicated about it. It's so simple that its very simplicity stumbles us in our anxiety."

"Oh, Molly, you are right at it now. But how, *how* does one accept Him?"

"Joseph, do you know that promise of Jesus in the last book of the Bible?—'Behold I stand at the door, and knock. If any man hear My voice and open the door, I will come in to him. . . .'"

"Yes, I've read or heard it a hundred times."

"Then why don't you act on it? Is it your pride which keeps you from doing so? Or is it that it seems too simple? too easy? too unemotional?

"It's not pride; not now. I know how deeply I'm a sinner and need to be saved."

"Then why don't you ask Him into your heart right now?"

"What! with you watching, Molly!"

"Oh, Joseph, you ought to have a witness. Let *me* be your witness. I've prayed so much for you to do it. Somehow, I feel this is the moment."

"But, Molly, *how* do I do it?"

"Kneel down, and simply ask Him to come in; and I'll kneel with you."

Joseph hesitated. "Is it truly and honestly as simple as that?"

"Try it."

They knelt together. "Now, Joseph, ask Him like this: 'Dear Lord Jesus, I open my heart and receive Thee as my Saviour.' Pray it audibly. I'll be your witness. Then believe that according to His promise He really comes in."

"But I can't see Him."

"No, but *He* can see and hear *you*—and He's waiting this minute. Believe His promise, and ask Him in."

"Molly, I will."

So they knelt down together in that sitting room, and Joseph simple-heartedly asked the Lord Jesus to come in. They lingered then in silence a moment, after which Molly suggested, "Now thank Him, inwardly and silently, for coming in as your Saviour. If a sneaky voice from somewhere says it's all make-believe, that's Satan's voice. He says that to all of us when we are accepting Jesus. Pay no attention. Keep your eye on the plain, unchanging promise of Jesus, and trust it."

They rose from their knees. "Have you really asked Him in?" Molly enquired.

"Yes."

"Then has He come in?"

"I think so. . . ."

"You *think!* Read the verse again."

Joseph read the verse again.

"Has He come in?" Molly asked again.

"I hope so. . . ."

"You *hope!* Read the text again."

Joseph did so. Then Molly asked, "Look here, Joseph: did Jesus clearly promise to come in if you asked Him? And have you asked Him? Then has He come in? Has He? Think, Joseph. Has He?"

Joseph thought. Then, like a sunrise, a look of discovery shone in his face, and he suddenly shouted, "*YES!* He's come in!"

"How do you know?" Molly persisted.

"Because He *PROMISED!*" sang Joseph.

"Oh, Joseph," she exclaimed with tears of joy, "that's it: you've got Him alright. So long as you kept saying 'I think' and 'I hope' I knew you were on sand; you were thinking it had to be some upsurge of feelings. But as soon as you say, 'Yes, He promised it,' your feet are on the solid rock of His promise. It's true, it's true, Joseph. He has come into your heart."

"Yes, yes, yes!" shouted Joseph. "I know it! Oh, how simple it is! How blind I was! Lord Jesus, you're mine!—my own Saviour! Oh, how wonderful! I'm saved! I'm *SAVED!* I know it!"

He simply did not know what to do or say to express his relief and joy. He knew that through simple appropriation of the Saviour's atoning death his sins were forgiven, his guilt blotted out, that he was covered before God in the imputed righteousness of the sinless Sinbearer, and that the risen Saviour had now come to live in his heart, bringing new spiritual life. His heart was bursting with the wonder of it. He wanted to run out and tell all the world what had happened.

"Oh, Molly, how can I ever thank you enough?"

Molly's eyes were still wet with tears—tears of joy at what had happened to Joseph, and of gratitude to God that He had used her to bring a soul to the Saviour.

At that point the two parent Ainsworths broke in, to see what the happy noise was. "Mr. and Mrs. Ainsworth, I've found Jesus as my Saviour!" Joseph beamed.

"Eh, laddie, that's the best news you could ever tell us!" responded Mr. Ainsworth.

"What an answer to our prayers!" Mrs. Ainsworth seconded.

"Thank you. Thank you. I don't know how to express my happiness or my thankfulness to you both, and to you . . . Molly, I am in your debt for ever."

"Son, we know now why God sent you to us. Didn't I tell you, perhaps He had a bigger purpose than you thought?"

"Yes, you did: and perhaps the first thing I should do now is to write and tell my mother. I know now: that is what she's prayed for, year after year."

They lingered and chatted about Joseph's new-found joy. Then Joseph slipped away upstairs to write the letter to his mother. When he was gone, Mr. and Mrs. Ainsworth looked at their dear, beautiful Molly. Tears were still glistening in those glowing, sympathetic eyes. Extraordinarily beautiful she certainly was in that moment, with that light of pure, inward gladness streaming out through her face. But there was another look there, too, which her parents had not seen before. Only dimly did they suspect what it was; but it was to become unmistakable as time went on. In Molly's deepest being there was awakening a noble, longing love for the runaway boy who had found shelter under their roof.

SEVENTEEN
Lakeside Rendezvous

The longer Joseph lingered with the Ainsworths the more genuine he found them. They, on their part, found Joseph the same. They were human, with the failings and limitations belonging thereto; but all four, now, were sincere Christians united by family and personal affection which made them a congenial quartet. Joseph's work at the furniture manufactory was conscientious. In the home he was willing, even eager, to help with household chores. He brought no little fun and teasing. His piano practicing and playing brought music which had not been there before. They loved it. He and Molly were just about as felicitously companionable to each other as two natures could be. More than once or twice Joseph suggested leaving them and going into paid lodgings, but each time they had some reason why it was not expedient at the moment. Molly, who had least wanted him to come, least wanted him to go.

With avidity now he studied his Bible, and devoured Spurgeon's sermons. Oh, the lively discussions which this occasioned at the meal table! How daddy Ainsworth revelled in it! Often Joseph and Molly studied and prayed together. Months slipped by. One day Mr. Ainsworth just could not help happily blurting out, "I always wanted a son, and God answered my prayer in the strangest way. Though you are not our son 'in the flesh,' Joseph, you are our son 'in the faith,' and we love you as one of our own."

Each month Joseph wrote his mother. He also tried to devise a way to see her; but various exigencies prevented it. Because of his father he still feared to divulge his whereabouts, but after some months he was able to give his mother an address in another town to which she could address any letter. She wrote such a letter of motherly heartache, it upset Joseph for days. It also told him that since his running away his father had never touched the drink, that he was now a sober, subdued man, though moody, and that for some mysterious reason he did not want Joseph home again.

So the second Christmas came and went with Joseph still at the Ainsworths'. So did the March, when Joseph passed his sixteenth birthday. He had let the Ainsworths into the full story of his life. What he told them about the Adairs was of particular interest inasmuch as the Adair Furniture House in Elmerton was one of Mr. Ainsworth's larger customers. Above all, they wanted to meet Joseph's extraordinary mother. Any such meeting with his mother, however, needed to wait until summer, when daylight was longer. It was too risky for Joseph to be seen in Elmerton, lest his father should be alerted. But a meeting-place somewhere near there needed to be found. The Ainsworths and he would have to go in their horse-drawn carriage, for the Huddersfield railway station was miles away from their home. Yes, it must be in summer.

Joseph kept thinking of the bench by Netherford lakeside where he had bandaged Evelyn's ankle. It was at the east end of the lake, near the Yorkshire road to Huddersfield. Also, there was a new roadway to that end of it, through a pretty new suburb called Hazelmere. If Mr. Adair would bring Joseph's mother in his carriage that way, they could drive to within a couple of hundred yards of the lake head. Joseph and the Ainsworths fixed on a day in late August. He wrote his mother. Her reply, as expected, was "Yes."

Thus, two years after his decamping, he was to see his mother again! But what a different Joseph! Two years make a big difference in any teenager, but it was more so with Joseph by reason of his abnormal experiences after becoming a fugitive, his having to fend for himself, his integration into the Ainsworth household, and, most of all, his decisive conversion. He was taller and fuller. No longer did he wear a lad's jacket and breeches or knee-high stockings, but adult suits with long trousers. Nor did he any longer wear the celluloid juvenile's collar, but a gentleman's neat linen collar and smart tie.

There were other maturings, too. With his fine mental ability and earnest study he acquired an unusually ample grasp on the main truths of the Bible, while his immersion in Spurgeon gave it all a systematized evangelistic form. Right from his conversion he knew he had to preach. Incredible as it may seem, ever since his wrecked child-conversion at the age of five, the "Hound of Heaven" (in poet Francis Thompson's phrase) had dogged his subconsciousness, giving the uncomfortable premonition that one day God would "get" him! But now the call to preach rang like a loud bell through his mind. He confided it to Mr. Ainsworth. That perceptive man had realized it already. "Joseph, you must leave the factory and get into training. My own part is a proud one: to cover the cost. It will be like putting my own son through college."

Joseph was enrolled at a college on the other side of Huddersfield. He and Molly used to travel to and from town together each day. Before he was seventeen he had matriculated.

While he was still sixteen Joseph preached his first sermon. It was on a weeknight and in the hall where, two years earlier, he had sneaked in as a weary fugitive. During the intervening time he had made so many friends in that church, the hall was about full with folk who wanted to hear—more so because they had been impressed by his facility of utterance in the occasional "testimony meetings."

Before the minister called on Joseph, Molly sang a solo, with Joseph playing for her. She sang, "I heard the voice of Jesus . . ." to the tune, *Vox Dilecti*, by John B. Dykes, which was then still new. The glow on that maidenly beautiful face and the tremor in her rich contralto voice gave the words new meaning, and as she sat down there could be heard whispered "amens" all over the room.

Joseph was so nervous, he could scarce hold himself steady. He wondered how he would manage to disguise his dyspepsia, dysphagia, and dysphonia; but the moment he actually stood at the desk he felt such release and verve, he could hardly believe it. His text was Revelation 3:20 (and Molly knew why): "Behold, I stand at the door, and knock. If any man hear My voice, and open the door, I will come in to him. . . ." Certainly, no one would have detected that the young preacher had even a wisp of nervousness as with obvious competence he handled his theme.

By way of introduction he regretted modern developments which depreciate the value of the individual—industrialization, mechanization, urbanization, over-population, along with the discovered immensity of the universe which made a human individual seem like a microscopic nonentity. But over against all modern collectivisms which lose the individual in the mass, the Bible puts its uniform emphasis on the unique value of each human being. Over against the sneer that our speck of a world could not be the object of God's special love, Joseph urged that God does not love this world for its physical size, but for its moral value. One God-conscious human mind, with a destiny beyond the grave, is of more value than all the material splendours of the Milky Way. The text highlights this, for it is addressed to each individual—"If any man"; and it is none less than God the Son, the risen Saviour, who seeks access to the heart.

Then Joseph pointed out (echoing his mother, Millie) that the text presents Him in three striking approaches: (1) standing, (2) knocking, (3) promising. Adeptly the young preacher expatiated on each, then closed by relating how Molly had led him to accept Jesus on the basis of that very text.

Despite inevitable touches of the novice, it was recognized that here was an exceptionally talented amateur. All were intrigued by his flexible vocabulary, skill, lucidity, and grip upon reality. Never had a half hour "run away in so few minutes." Many preachers must overcome handicaps: diminutive stature, feeble constitution, facial unattractiveness, weak or unmusical voice; but Joseph was already five-feet-ten, well-proportioned, with handsome face, keen bright eyes, firm but kindly lips, and a resonant baritone voice. Seldom is there such a blend of natural gifts and spiritual graces.

From then onwards Joseph Kennard could no more be hid than a beacon on a hilltop. Invitations came from all over the area. Soon he was in some pulpit almost every Sunday. He became known as "the boy preacher," though actually he soon looked more like a developed young man. People flocked to hear him. Many, especially younger people, were brought to the Saviour. Then came the request for a full week's evangelistic mission at a small Methodist church outside that locality, while he was on summer break from college. In all the higher senses the effort surpassed fondest expectations. Not only was the place packed night after night, but many were convinced and converted.

What was equally important, Joseph weathered it well. Although deeply in earnest he kept nervously at ease and well-poised. Through it all, his lovely, loyal lieutenant was Molly—just as full of good sense as of spiritual enthusiasm. They made an effective pair. Before Joseph's message each evening she sang some carefully chosen solo, her deep, rich voice being peculiarly suitable for sympathetic Gospel singing. In all the after-meetings she was the trustworthy counselor to female enquirers. She never pushed, but she was always ready to help. Pa and Ma Ainsworth were at most of the gatherings, praying for Joseph and Molly, and glorying in the young preacher's developing prowess. Their one regret was that he was not their own son, and their secret hope was that eventually he would become their son-in-law.

Through all those exciting months and unforgettable experiences and exacting hours of study, Molly was Joseph's unflagging *encourager.* It was she who bought him the best Cruden's Concordance, and Smith's Bible Dictionary, and Matthew Henry's Commentary, and other books. In the June when she was almost nineteen she both matriculated and obtained her diploma as a certified junior dayschool teacher. She continually helped Joseph in his studies from what she learned in her own. They became a closely knit pair. At times it was all poor Molly could do to prevent her deep love for him from spilling over into obviousness, but she fought it back rather than allow any such emotion to distract him from his high calling. How she loved him! Never did so beautiful a maiden have a purer love for any young man than Molly Ainsworth had for Joseph Kennard. How blind he was! Everybody else said, "What a girl!" And those who watched closest said, "How she adores him!"

Such was the Joseph who now went to meet his mother at Netherford Lake. At last the day came. It was kissed at dawnbreak by a rain-shower, after which it blushed into hours of rosy brightness. Mother Nature donned her prettiest adornments as though in honour of the historic occasion, and the song-thrushes saluted with their gladdest rhapsody. Although parts of the road were rather hilly, Mr. Ainsworth decided that since the weather was so pleasant in temperature and there was no need for any hurry they would manage with one horse. By 8 a.m. "Rip," the fine "standardbred" was harnessed in the shafts. Soon afterwards the four travellers were aboard, plus two collapsible chairs, cushions and rugs, for picnic use on the way—and, of course (in that region!) two large umbrellas in case the sky should change its complexion.

Mr. Ainsworth was wearing the pin-striped blue suit he had worn when he first met Joseph. Mrs. Ainsworth emerged in a two-piece suit of light gray, matched by a pale green blouse and white straw hat with a gossamer "fall" hanging from it and neatly tied under her chin. As for Molly, that paragon of brunette charm, her dark, flowing hair, with its natural sheen and waviness, looked so accentuatedly lovely on such a morning, a hat would have been an insufferable desecration. She simply had a bright yellow bandeau gently holding it above her forehead, and a matching fillet fastening it back behind her neck. As Joseph helped her into the carriage, guarding the skirt of her primrose dress from catching on the metal step, he could not help quietly exclaiming to her, "Molly, dear, you look stunningly beautiful!"

Soon they were jogging along the road on which, two

years earlier, a footsore Joseph had limped. Memories leapt out of their graves—which Joseph hurriedly buried again ere they sneaked through his lips into mention. What a day! What a scene! That was the "green and pleasant" England of yesterday, before the First World War. Only those who lived in it knew its soothing beauty and homey feel. Despite many social injustices, it was struggling with awakened conscience to extirpate such blemishes, until Kaiser Wilhelm soaked Europe in blood at the whim of Prussian ambition. It was of that England, green-swarded, homey, in the main godly, providentially prospered, and temperate in clime, that a famous pen wrote, "England, with all thy faults, I love thee still." Given fair weather, where was "green and pleasant" England's rival?

Even Rip, as he clippety-clopped along, seemed to be saying a horsy "Hello there!" to it all, by an occasional whinny as he cantered down a slope here and there. Soon they were rolling along ways which were strange to Joseph, though evidently known to Mr. Ainsworth, who told them of a large nursery where they could halt for refreshment and rest Rip awhile before the last lap of the journey. Rip seemed to know the place; and well he might, for he was born and grew up there. Joseph was not the only son who met his mother again that day!

After lunch they were on their way again with time to spare. An hour later they had their first glimpse of Netherford Lake. Joseph thrilled, yet at the same instant went inwardly limp with suppressed excitement. He had never before seen the lake from that angle. Encircled by verdant fields and graceful trees, with its placid water reflecting the azure of a perfect summer sky, it looked like a liquid sapphire in an emerald setting. Joseph was gratified to see and hear the admiration of the Ainsworths.

Rip seemed to divine by "horse-sense" that they were almost where they were going, for he shook his mane and pleasantly snorted at the lake. The carriage wheels rolled nearer and nearer until they were on the dirt track from the little brow of Hazelmere down to the lake head. No sign of Millie! But why be surprised? They were well ahead of time. Mr. Ainsworth braked the carriage, loosed Rip from the shafts, freed him from harness except halter, and gave him a long rope's length to graze. As Rip dawdled into his little grass heaven he gave not even a courtesy glance at his four passengers as they strolled through the gates to the pathway round the lake.

"This way," Joseph guided. "The wooden seat is round the bend."

Surely Netherford Lake had never looked more enchanting. The three new visitors agreed that it was exquisite as its glinting surface reflected overhanging boughs and fringing flowers and the nearer hills.

"There it is," Joseph indicated, with emotion difficult to handle. "That's the place!"

Yes, there it was: the bench where Joseph had bandaged Evelyn's ankle—an episode not divulged to the Ainsworths; and where he had wept his heart out on the night he ran away from home; and where, had he known it, real sweetheart-love for him had first awakened in Evelyn's young heart. What memories! He tried to hold them down and maintain his equanimity as he and the three Ainsworths now sat on the wooden seat beneath the willow, captivated by the scene.

After fifteen or twenty minutes they heard the creak of hinges away behind. Someone was coming through the gate. Joseph wanted to run round the bend and see if it was his mother, but thought he had better stay at the bench, the appointed meeting-place. Soon footsteps were heard. Joseph stood. Coming round the bend was Millie wearing her missionary uniform with the blue bonnet and smart bow as always. That was enough. Joseph ran forward, and the next instant they were in each other's arms. Joseph was now taller than Millie, but he leaned his head on her shoulder and wept tears of joy. Millie also wept with joy to see him so tall and well and handsome. Did ever such a brave little woman and her only son love each other more? The others stood and watched, deeply affected.

When Joseph looked up, whom should he see, now round the bend, but Mr. and Mrs. Adair—and, oh, superlative surprise, *Evelyn!* He shook hands warmly but respectfully with Mr. Adair, then with Mrs. Agnes who, however, turned it into a hug and a kiss. And now Evelyn: oh, what a dream! two years older, and two years lovelier, if that were possible! That soft, ample, wavy hair, no longer quite flaxen but still blonde, thrown back from her fine, open brow, and gathered behind by a pretty ribbon; those tender, clear, blue eyes which now fairly shone their girlish love into his; that dear, pure, playful yet thoughtful face; those velvet lips, and that smile—now two years more appealingly feminine! Joseph perceived instantly that she was no longer just a schoolgirl, yet neither was she a grown adult. She was rather taller, with a more womanly figure; slim, straight, supple, and queenly as ever. Round her neck was a thin gold chain which held on her bosom a small heart-shaped locket—that which Joseph had given her the evening he fled from home! It spoke worlds. Joseph's heart missed a beat!

They looked at each other—such a look. The others watched, especially Molly; though it was all in a matter of seconds. Plainly the two wanted to kiss each other. Evelyn's face flushed into added loveliness, and her look gave consent; but Joseph, suddenly becoming very proper, said, "It's so good of you to come, Evelyn"; and, taking her hand, he simply implanted a courtesy kiss on it.

"Bashful as ever, Joseph!" interjected Agnes, with a naughty smile.

After that came introductions. It was with keenest eagerness that the Ainsworths met Joseph's mother, that one and only Millie. She, on her part, could not thank them enough for their exceeding kindness to Joseph for so long. Mr. Ainsworth and Joash soon found much in common, and strolled by the lake together chatting about furniture both wholesale and retail. Both of them were prosperous and wealthy, but as always, of course, the furniture trade had never had such problems! They both wondered how soon the crash would come, and seemed to enjoy the matter immensely.

Millie and Agnes and Mrs. Ainsworth were three kindred spirits. None of them was of the fussy, frilly, showy type. Millie and Agnes had grown closer to each other than ever. They were more than ever one in the Police Court Mission work. They and Mrs. Ainsworth soon knew that they were all one, also, in the indissoluble bond that binds all true Christian hearts together.

As for Evelyn and Molly, they were immediately a mutual admiration pair. How could it have been otherwise? Without exaggeration, in face and figure they were two of the most perfectly formed young women eyes ever saw. It almost seemed as though Nature had incarnated two goddesses by mistake. To Evelyn, Molly was at once the most striking, gypsy-dark brunette she had ever met. To Molly, one glance at Evelyn explained all that Joseph had ever said. If anything, he had understated. Not only firm yet delicately proportioned features and rosy complexion and frank, open expression, but those limpid, steady blue eyes through which unmistakably a singularly pure soul looked out at you. . . !

"I'm so glad to meet you, Evelyn."

"Thank you, Molly. for coming all this way, and letting us meet *you*. Joseph has said so much about you in letters to his mother. We knew you must be extraordinary; but now that we see you, well, you are even nicer. . . ."

Two sincerer girls no one could ever find. Yet from that moment of meeting, each was the sorest of all problems to the other. As Evelyn saw the unaffected comradeship between Joseph and Molly, the evident understanding between them, their manifest fondness for each other, and the happiness with which they talked about things which they now had in common, especially their spiritual experience, she suddenly felt strangely far away from Joseph, and was quite sure he had now lost his heart to captivating Molly.

As for head-over-heels-in-love Molly, after seeing Evelyn her heart sank, sick at the thought that she had no chance against such a superb competitor. Within herself she said, "I know now why Joseph, although so friendly and appreciative, has not shown anything beyond that toward me." Poor Molly! The sword really pierced her heart; for she was old enough and developed enough to be painfully in love. Joseph, so she felt, was "the one and only" to whom she could give herself for life. There was no idolatry in it. It was the love of a noble, Christian heart. It was the kind of warm, affectionate, understanding, womanly love which brings heaven on earth to a man on whom it spends itself. This rendezvous at Netherford Lake to which she had so looked forward was proving itself a sharp-cutting surprise. It hurt. Inwardly, she resolved to take it bravely; and, just like the noble-hearted Molly that she was, she vowed never to commit the wrong of trying to steal Joseph away if he was really Evelyn's.

For Joseph and his mother it was a rapturous occasion. They could not be separated. There were so many things to be quickly talked over. Their gladness spilled over into the hearts of the Adairs and the Ainsworths. For Evelyn and Molly, too, it was "such a happy day"—outwardly. Time sped by. Millie chatted with the Ainsworths about Joseph's future. She was concerned lest he should be a burden to them. Did they have any suggestion?

"Mrs. Kennard," replied Mr. Ainsworth, "Joseph himself has something he wants to tell you."

"Mother, I've been trying to get to it. We think you'll be pleased. Perhaps it's your own prayers that are responsible for it. I'm studying to enter the Christian ministry. I'm too young to enter a theological college yet, but I'm at another college. Already I'm learning Greek and church history, and homiletics, and other subjects in preparation. Mother, I hope you are pleased."

Pleased! Millie's utter joy took liquid form in tears of gratitude. Pleased! On that agonizing night when she prayed him back from the edge of the grave, she had dedicated him to this very thing!

Joseph related how Molly had led him to the Saviour. Evelyn eyed her with guileless envy, at the same time no little mystified about this "conversion" matter.

Next, Joseph had to tell about the Ainsworths' generosity in paying for his college tuition, whereupon Millie struggled unsuccessfully to say a big enough "Thank you," and inwardly sang a *Laus Deo* that her precious Joseph had found a home with such delightful people.

Conversation galloped. So did the time.

With a knowing look at Joseph, Molly said, "What about some refreshment?" Joseph took her hand, and the two of them trotted round the bend, out through the gate, to the carriage. Soon they were back with the sandwiches, pastries, and cold drinks, which had been brought for the purpose.

It looked a jolly scene: the eight of them picnicking there, gaily chatting in that willow-shaded arbor by the scintillating lake. But the two amorous young *mesdemoiselles* were not as inwardly gleeful as they were outwardly glamorous. The longer they lingered, the more clearly Evelyn observed the rapport between Joseph and Molly; nor could she help deducing that Molly loved him very tenderly. On the other hand, Molly could not help noticing what a losing battle Joseph was having with his eyes. Time after time he would wrench them away from their worshipful surveying of Evelyn and pretend to be absorbed elsewhere, only to find them disobediently straying away to her again.

Among the five seniors Millie was the center-point. The big thought with the Ainsworths was the arranging for Millie to pay them a visit. It was decided that since Millie now knew their address she should write them whenever she could devise a way to come without arousing suspicion in Mr. Kennard's mind.

Too quickly the time wore away now to the point where departure was necessary if the Ainsworths and Joseph were to get home without hurry before dark. Joseph and Molly folded the chairs, gathered the cushions, tidied the willow arbor, and slowly led the little procession back round the bend, through the gate, to the carriages. Apparently the two horses had not even given a neighbourly neigh to each other. Rip seemed fast asleep standing up, and had to be slapped to a sense of responsibility again. Quickly Joseph harnessed him in the shafts. There were good-byes, not without tears, and a fond, final hug as Joseph and his mother parted again.

"Gee up, Rip!" The four-wheeler slowly rolled along the crunchy bridle path which had recently been widened into a carriage drive. As it reached the brow of the incline its four occupants looked back and waved parting farewells. Millie and the Adairs waved back before getting into their own conveyance. Then the Ainsworth carriage veered left and rolled away northeast along the Yorkshire road back to Huddersfield.

Molly was strangely quiet. Almost the only thing she said, was, "Isn't Evelyn beautiful! Such a pure soul! One could almost think she'd been born on the wrong planet!"

In the other quartette Evelyn, too was in lonely reverie. "Isn't Molly lovely! What a rich personality! How superior, yet how warm and kind and practical!"

Back home, Molly sighed to her mother, "What chance has a black raven against a bird of paradise? What chance has a dark pansy against an opening rosebud?" And her mother, after pausing, tried an equally poetic reply: "Molly, I still think some people prefer the copper beech to the silver birch."

Back in Elmerton, Evelyn mourned in wistful defeatism. "Mother, Joseph and Molly seem matched to each other like a hand and a glove, don't they?" And Agnes philosophically responded, "Evelyn, dear, many hands and gloves which fit each other never come together." But inwardly Agnes rather ruefully reflected, "Molly Ainsworth certainly is a girl in a thousand. How could Joseph help. . . ?" The question seemed to have only one answer.

So ended that unforgettable day of reunion at the memorial bench, round the bend, beside the softly murmuring water of Netherford Lake.

EIGHTEEN
Who Would Have Said?

Time never stands still; but since the twentieth century came in, time often seems to run like a man late for a railway train, portmanteau hastily packed to bursting-point. Such were Joseph's years up to the age of twenty. Having matriculated he studied for his B.A., with Greek as an included subject. He also kept on with his tuition in church history, theology, and hermeneutics. All that, plus Bible study, music, and continual preaching, was perhaps ridiculously too much, but it is amazing how much can be crammed in by a virile young man borne along by a dynamic urge.

For his B.A. classes Joseph had to attend Manchester University, which meant that now he was with the Ainsworths only weekends and Sundays. Again and again he apologized that even then he was often out preaching. They, however, had nothing but approval. Their conviction was that they were investing in the most gifted and promising young man they had ever known, and who, they fondly assumed, would one day marry their precious Molly.

Several times during those years his mother met him in Manchester; and three times she came over to the Ainsworths' when Mike was away on those strange, periodic absences. Millie soon saw what a gem Molly was. The two of them took to each other from the first. As Millie observed Molly's behaviour and heard her affectionate but always discreet references to Joseph she began to wonder if. . . ?

Mr. Ainsworth and Joseph decided that during the B.A. studies some other subjects should be suspended to allow more time for Bible study and preaching. All over the area, and beyond, Joseph was increasingly in demand. By general consent, there was not a young preacher anywhere to equal him in his remarkable gift of blending simple evangelism with deep Bible teaching for believers. The more he preached, the more he sensed his true vocation and the more proficient he became. Except in the formal Sabbath services, Molly usually sang, accompanied at the piano by Joseph—which in those days was a novelty enough to set a few cranky stick-in-the-muds averring that such prominence for a young female was a sad sign of latter-day libertinism!

One interesting development was, that in different areas whole groups of churches now planned *united* "After-Church Rallies," especially for younger people. In these, Joseph excelled. As one newspaper put it, "The signature of a Higher Power is on these joint outreaches to attract young men and women off the street." Joseph had started composing pithy choruses which caught on with the younger crowd. Molly was now two or three years more capable at the piano, and quite ably accompanied the congregational singing. It was a unique and telling partnership. How she loved her Joseph! Why, why did he not see it, and respond?

Then came a stunner: a letter from Harvey Street Independent Church in Elmerton, inviting him, or rather pleading with him, to hold a fortnight's evangelistic mission there. So Elmerton knew where he was! Did they know that he was the Joseph Kennard who had absconded years earlier? Had his spreading fame reached his father's ears?

Joseph and the Ainsworths did no little cogitating over it, at the same time praying for higher guidance. Molly's was the touchiest problem. How could she help reflecting perturbingly that the pure-souled enchantress, Evelyn, was at Elmerton? The fondest hope in Molly's heart was at stake.

Who Would Have Said?

How could she let Joseph go there? Oh, no! Yet dare she let her own self-interest hypocritically dissuade Joseph, if his going to Elmerton was of God's leading? Dear Molly was too genuine to indulge selfish wangling. Outwardly, at least, she was jubilant about his going. "Think what it could mean among your friends there. Even your father might . . . well, who knows, if we all pray enough?"

They all knew that at most Joseph could not go for more than ten days, and that it would have to be during the brief Michaelmas recess in late September or early October.

Molly's sorest moment came when Joseph asked, "Molly, would you come with me?"

She thanked him sincerely, but declined.

Joseph's face clouded. "Molly, how can I go without you? We're such a pair now. Nobody on earth can take your place, Molly."

At those last words Molly's heart leaped. Did he mean no one else could take her place in his heart?—or only in his work? Joseph put his arms around her and gave her a hug, though he did not kiss her. Mr. and Mrs. Ainsworth watched, approved, hoped.

Molly was silent for a long minute, after which, with a glance at her parents, she slowly replied, "Joseph, gladly as I would go with you, we think it unwise. You know how easily tongues are set wagging. For an unmarried young man and young woman to travel unaccompanied for a stay in another town might too easily cause criticism. It doesn't matter so much for me, Joseph; but we dare not take any such risk for *you,* right at the beginning of what is going to be a great life of public ministry."

Joseph looked pained. "Oh, those clacking tongues! Even around here there are some who 'talk' unless daddy and mummie Ainsworth accompany us each time."

That very mention of Molly's parents shot a brilliant new thought into his mind. The bright gleam in his eyes as he looked at Pa and Ma told them what it was. "Could you? Could you?" he asked. "Could *you* come, as well as Molly?"

The upshot was that all four of them went to Elmerton. Joseph was housed with the Adairs—for, of course, he could not stay at 12 Wragley Street. Mr. and Mrs. Ainsworth and Molly stayed with dear old uncle Ben, who was now just inside his seventies, but hale and hearty still. His attractive home was in part furnished with Ainsworth suites.

So, that October Joseph was back at Elmerton, with Molly at his side. To be staying with the Adairs and in such close daily company with Evelyn was to him "Paradise Regained." However, as the Adairs saw, everything was subordinated to the big business on which he had come for the King of Kings. He and Molly were "after souls." First thing after breakfast each day Molly came round, at which time she and Agnes went with Joseph into the lounge for prayer about the meetings. Evelyn thought it strange that her father, Joash, did not go with them, but assumed that it was because he had to get ready for going off to work. Later she learned the real reason.

Harvey Street Independent Church, Elmerton, had a good motive but an unhappy reason in inviting Joseph for his short campaign there. It had known better days, but seemed destined to see worse. After three decades of prosperity it had become a limping invalid. Owing to feeble ministries and two sizable secessions and neighbourhood deterioration, attendances had declined until it seemed on the way to a doddery demise. It seated over eight hundred, but if there were ninety there on a Sunday morning, and a hundred and twenty on a Sunday evening, that was about all. But it still had its faithful nucleus who loved the place and longed to see resuscitation. At present they had no minister.

The leaders kept hearing about this brilliant young preacher in Huddersfield and his magnetic drawing-power. Then, upon learning that he was no other than the son of Mrs. Millie Kennard, the Elmerton Police Court Missionary, known and respected all over the borough, they said, "What a draw it would be if we could get *him* here!" In fairness to them, however, they did not want him just as a "catch crowd." That was intended only as a means to a higher end, namely the winning of souls and the spiritual enlivening of the work at Harvey Street.

The added attraction of Miss Molly Ainsworth's coming

gave a further fillip to their hopes. Even so, the question was: could they allure the people in? Joseph had sent certain advance requests. There must be a good-quality piano; a "Welcome Social" the opening Saturday evening; and on the first Sunday, besides morning and evening service, an "After-Church Rally" at 8:00 p.m. Millie was put in charge of leaflet-distribution and other advertising outreaches. She and her willing women of the Wednesday afternoon meeting did a thorough job. Especially did Millie make sure that the after-church rally was prominently announced in all the local pulpits, for it was with this rally that the mission properly began—and it was to prove a fine bit of strategy.

On that first Sunday night there must have been over four hundred present, which seemed a lot to the Harvey Street few. Pat Flanagan, the Irish deacon, was so hilarious about it, he said, "I expected to find the place half empty, but instead I found it half full!—and even after that, two more came pouring in!" Joseph taught them a couple of new choruses which took on like a grass fire in a California drought. But the first major effect was Molly's singing, enhanced by Joseph's elegant piano accompaniment. That lovely face, the earnest concern, the rich, flowing, well-trained contralto voice singing forthright spiritual messages of choice quality—it was as winning and challenging as it was surprising. As somebody put it afterward, "That graceful young woman sang God into the building!"

By the time Joseph gave his message there was rivetted attention. Curiosity had given place to the realization that there was a "quality" about these two young innovators which sharply distinguished them from the plentiful ranters and rousers of the day. Joseph knew how to ring his pleasant voice round without noisy blast or guttural harshness. He knew already that truth has its greatest pull on thinking people when it is presented methodically in worthy language and apt similitudes. He was becoming a master at it. And from his mother he had learned the tactical value of a striking illustration. In fact, he was such a facsimile of Millie in style and method that one of her women said later, "Mrs. Kennard, you'll never be dead while that son of yours keeps preaching. He's you all over again."

Joseph's address was based on the words of 1 Samuel 3:7, "Now Samuel did not yet know the Lord." Although born of a devoutly godly mother and even brought up in the house of God at Shiloh, Samuel grew into his 'teens without knowing God by personal experience. Similarly, said Joseph, most who were then present with himself in Harvey Street church were "religious" by upbringing: but "religion" never saved anybody. Nay, very religious persons were often the most deluded because they trusted for salvation in their religiousness, not realizing that they were sinners needing a blood-bought pardon for their sins, and an inward cleansing from sin-stain, and an imparted new spiritual life which only Jesus, the risen Saviour, could give them. Joseph's own mother (he told them) was led to the Saviour by a scholarly cleric who was a devoted Church of England minister for years before he savingly knew the Lord Jesus! And Joseph himself (he added) had been brought up by the truest of Christian mothers, Mrs. Millie Kennard, yet had not become actually converted and saved until Miss Molly Ainsworth, their soloist, had shown him the simple, Scriptural way of receiving the Saviour.

Such was the main thrust of his talk, expanded and applied as best suited the type of people present. When the "invitation" was given no two persons prayed more earnestly than Millie and Agnes; and no two persons listened with a more puzzled look than Evelyn Adair and her father, Councilor Joash Adair. There was an encouraging outcome when nineteen persons, mostly young men and women, made their way into the "enquiry meeting."

Next day the gifted speaker and his soloist were grapevine top news. From one to another it was gossiped. In those days, before the dissipating influence of radio and television invaded and swamped people's homes, such a distinctive event was sufficiently exciting to bring many of those mill-town folk in. By Thursday night the building was full, and thereafter packed. It drew the very best out of Joseph and Molly. Perhaps Joseph tended to allow some fervidity in his preaching, which occasioned Molly's concern. She mentioned it to him. With a touch of impatient over-confidence he resented it, thereby hurting Molly. But half an hour later he humbly sought her forgiveness: "Molly, my faithful, loving friend. Forgive me. How can I thank you? Please pray with me, that I may keep low at Jesus' feet, and never forget how unworthy I am, and never strain after mere human effort in my preaching. Oh, Molly, how much I owe you!"

It was during those days, amid the crowds and bustle and need for quick action, that Molly showed what a blend of spiritual earnestness and level-headed command she was. She and Joseph's mother, Millie, were closely drawn to each other. The Harvey Street leaders insisted that she and Millie should hold a special rally for young women on the second Sunday afternoon. Molly had become a real favourite. The church was packed by young women of all ages. Molly had only a couple of suitable addresses in her little repertoire, but her talk on "A Modern Girl's Questions" was as persuasive as it was sympathetic. Chairman Millie afterward described it as "a gem of insight and wise counsel." Molly did not have the homespun wit or playful "asides" or impromptu flashes of racy phrase which made Millie the unrivaled platform personality around Elmerton, but there was a rhythmic fluency, a clear-headed directness, a modesty and educatedness, which made an irresistible appeal. At the end of the meeting over one hundred stayed for prayer and further counseling.

Even after that, young women continued milling round. They wanted "a word with Molly," a "handshake with Molly," a "Thank you" to Molly, a "question to ask Molly." Molly looked flushed and a little tired, but unruffled and easy in manner. Millie watched her, deeply impressed. Could it be, she wondered, that this talented, lovable girl, raven-dark and comely as Shulamith in Solomon's Song, was yet to be Joseph's wedded helpmeet—and not Evelyn?

Mrs. Agnes Adair watched, too, and wondered the same thing.

But there was one who watched with more intense concern than either of them. As the meeting ended and the chatty little groups dispersed until the church was empty, beautiful young Evelyn Adair sat in a rear pew, tears dripping down her cheeks, and a look of bewilderment in her eyes. Then she hastily rose and slipped away without waiting for her mother.

By the time that second Sunday came, the whole neighbourhood was astir. Big things had happened in scores of lives. But the peak surprise came in the last three meetings.

At the "After-Church-Rally" Joseph spoke on Nicodemus, the Pharisee who "came to Jesus by night" and to whom Jesus said, "Ye must be born again." Nicodemus was a remarkable man. He was a leading member of the Sanhedrin, the Jewish politico-religious parliament. He must therefore have been a very learned man, in Scripture, in mathematics, in astronomy, in civil and ecclesiastical law, and in languages—for every member was required to know several languages fluently. He must also have been a very *religious* man, a thoroughbred Jew, not only expert in sacred literature but belonging to the straitest of Jewish sects—the Pharisees. He must also have been a very *moral* man, for among the requirements of appointment to the Sanhedrin a man must be morally impeccable, physically handsome, well-to-do, and publicly trusted. He was also a middle-aged or perhaps an *elderly* man, for a member of that highest civil and ecclesiastical tribunal in the land had to be married and a parent with several children.

So, as Joseph pointed out, it was not to a drunkard or murderer or jail bird or guttersnipe or immoral man that Jesus said, "Ye must be born again" but to one of the most upright, educated, religious, mature men in the nation; a lawyer, a magistrate or "justice of the peace." Jesus was saying, in effect: "You know the alphabet of morality and religion down to x, y, z, but you do not know even the a, b, c, of *salvation*. Underneath all your religion and outward morality your heart is so alienated from God, your spirit so dead to Him, and your will so independent of Him, that all your self-merit in the eyes of men is as filthy rags to the holy eyes of God."

What then did Jesus mean when He said, "Ye must be *born again*"? Jesus pointed out that the Greek word translated as "again" means, literally, "from above." This is a new life "from above"—a new *spiritual* birth effected in us by God Himself. That is why Jesus added, "Except a man be born of the *Spirit*," i.e. the Spirit of God, "he cannot enter the kingdom of God." As members of a fallen race, not only are we human sinners "lost" by reason of guilt for myriad sins committed; we are by heredity spiritually *dead*, and need to be spiritually reborn. Salvation is not only a blood-bought cleansing from guilt, and reconciliation to God through atonement, it is a new *life*, an inward regeneration which makes us "alive to God." This new birth comes by our accepting the living Saviour into our hearts. He comes in by the Holy Spirit, who thereby effects in us the soul-winning new life.

Sitting in the tightly packed crowd that night was another well-meaning Pharisee. He was a very moral man, a well-informed man, a widely respected man, a well-known "religious" man, a family man, a prosperous man, a justice of the peace, a church deacon, a Sunday School Superintendent. His name was Joash Adair. It was as though the young preacher was aiming exclusively at *him*, exposing the fundamental fallacy of his thinking through the years, and the fundamental need of his being. He had assumed that being moral, religious, philanthropic, was all that God or man could ask. He suddenly saw it all as a gilded shrine built on a grave; a smart tuxedo suit dressing a spiritual corpse. He knew now that he was not right with God, that he was spiritually dead, that he needed this new birth, and that he therefore needed to receive the Lord Jesus into his heart by a definite act.

When, at the end of the message, the opportunity was given for all "seekers" to come along the aisles to the after-meeting, who should rise and unashamedly join the several others on their way but Councilor Joash Adair, J.P. He was such a well-known and highly respected figure in the public life of the community that when he was seen going to the enquiry room a whisper of surprise was heard throughout the congregation. What next!

That night, with a deep sense of need, and with the simplicity of a schoolboy, Joash Adair received the Lord Jesus as his Saviour. He understood now what his precious

Agnes had been trying to tell him for so long—ever since she herself had been "converted" in the Manchester Moody and Sankey campaign years earlier. Oh, there was singing in Pinecrest that night. But there was more to follow.

The next evening Joseph preached again on the words, "Ye must be born again." He began by relating a conversazione in which the speakers were three society ladies having afternoon tea together. Somebody said to them, "Oh, have you heard? Mr. So-and-so has suddenly become religious. He says he's been 'born again'!" The first lady exclaimed, "How strange! What a comic idea! Are you sure he's not going a bit peculiar in the head?" The second lady observed, "He must have been a very irreligious and wicked young man!" The third lady reacted, "He surely must be a very ignorant and uneducated person to think he required *that!*" All three ladies of fashion marvelled, little suspecting, in their imagined self-superiority, how spiritually dark their own minds were, and how inwardly dead to God they were. It was in a somewhat similar way that the superior Nicodemus had marvelled, which caused our Lord to reply, "*Marvel not* that I said unto thee, Ye must be born again."

There are three things, said Joseph, which mystify most people about the new birth. One: why do we need it? Two: what is it? Three: how does it come? Most people think they are sinners because they commit sins, whereas in reality it is the other way round, i.e. we continuously commit our sins of thought and word and deed because already, by heredity, we are born with a sin-prone *nature*. Man is body, soul, and spirit. By the body we have *world*-consciousness. By the soul (or mind) we have *self*-consciousness. By the spirit (the *pneuma*) we have *God*-consciousness. It is by the spirit that we are *capax Dei*, capable of God. When our first parents disobeyed God they divorced man's highest part, the "spirit," from its life-giving environment in God. Man became self-centered instead of, as originally, God-centered. That highest part, the "spirit" became defunct, or dead toward God. Sin is not merely something that we *do*, but something that we *are*, namely, alienated from God, morally perverted, and spiritually dead. One can be very religious, but spiritually dead. Religion cannot regenerate. Only the Spirit of God can do that. Sin is not only drunkenness, robbery, murder, outward demoralization: it is disobedience to God, living for self-will instead of God's will; avoiding or trying to evade God.

A certain father and mother (said Joseph) had an only child, a daughter. From her young years it became evident that she would be extraordinarily beautiful and gifted. Never did two parents love their offspring more, nor have higher hopes in a daughter. They lavished affection on her. In childhood they nurtured her, played with her, sat up whole nights if she had any illness, gave her always the best clothes, the best toys, the best home-life, the best education. They doted on her. When she was twenty-one, beautiful, talented, refined, they gave her an expensive coming-of-age party with her many friends there to celebrate the auspicious occasion. What a banquet it was! How charming she looked! How proud her loving parents were!

But, to their astonishment and grief, after the last guest had gone, that daughter came downstairs with her travel-bags packed and said, "I know this will hurt you, but I'm now of age and I'm leaving home. I've never loved you or even liked you. I do not want you any more. Never enquire where I am. I intend to live my own life and shall brook no interference from you. Good-bye for ever."

Some years later those parents learned where she was, and that she was a leading church worker, "very religious." Next they gleaned that she had been civically honoured for philanthropic work. Later they were informed that she had married an outstanding public man of high reputation. Such news comforted them, in that she was at least living a commendable life morally. But do you think that *any* such news could make up for her alienation and cold lovelessness toward themselves who had given her life and all the good things which had made her so privileged? How could *anything* compensate while she was dead in heart toward them? Similarly, that is the fearful estrangement of heart from God on the part of "religious" and "moral" and "decent" people who have never become "reconciled to God" through the atonement of Christ, never "born again" by the Holy Spirit into *new life* as redeemed children of God. That deadness to God, that living without God and living for self: *that* is the essence of sin.

Sitting in the crowd that night was one exceptionally beautiful daughter to whom all this came home with rapier edge. She was no committer of the vulgar, coarser sins. She shuddered at them. Her whole being revolted against the unclean. But she now saw the essence of sin and its religious disguise. She saw the ugly face behind its conceited masquerade. She saw now what the condition of being "lost" was; a being spiritually dead to God, inwardly alienated from Him, secretly rebellious against Him, self-centered, proud, outwardly pious but inwardly perverted. Her very sincerity made all this the more vivid and painful to her sensitive mind. She was now aching to know *how* this new birth happens. What brings it?

Even then she heard Joseph say, "Perhaps someone this very minute is asking: How does the new birth come? Well, Jesus gives the answer in the words following our text: 'And as Moses lifted up the serpent in the wilderness, even so must the Son of Man (our Lord Jesus Himself) be lifted up (on the Cross), that whosoever believeth on Him should not perish but have eternal life.' So it is by looking to Jesus on the Cross as our Saviour that you have this 'eternal life'; and if you have the *life*, you must have the *birth*. Don't waste time puzzling over the mystery of it. Receive the Saviour, and in Him the new life is yours."

In a flash that cultivated, beautiful young woman, Evelyn Adair, "saw" it! Any mystery about the new birth is only on *our* side, because we cannot understand how the Holy Spirit effects it in us. All that *we* have to do is, appropriate by simple faith what Jesus did for us on the Cross. The moment we really do that, we are saved, forgiven, cleansed from guilt before God, and the new life is ours! Oh, the never-to-be forgotten wonder of that hour when this soul-saving truth becomes luminous to one's mind! The moment of moments had come for Evelyn Adair. When the "invitation" was given after Joseph's message, she was one of the first to hurry anxiously along the aisle into the enquiry room. Molly was there to offer counsel. That night Evelyn met Molly in a new way—the two of them at the foot of the Cross. Joseph saw them a few minutes later, tears of joy streaming down their faces. He was beside himself with joy.

Yet there was even more to come: the most dramatic finale conceivable. Mike Kennard had kept hearing about the meetings, and was furious. His old truculence and exacerbation flared up again. But when he read in the news-paper about the public profession of conversion by Councilor Joash Adair he just gaped. He decided to be at the last meeting, Tuesday night, and spy from the back pew under the gallery.

That night Joseph preached on the words, "Behold, the Lamb of God that beareth away the sin of the world!" He illustrated our Lord's saving death as our substitutionary Sinbearer by reference to Leviticus, chapter 16, which tells about the annual "day of atonement" long ago in the nation Israel. Two goats were selected because a twofold truth needed to be objectified. One of the two goats was offered as a sin-offering to God. The other—the *azazel*, or "scape-goat," was *not* sacrificed. Aaron, the high priest, had to "lay both his hands upon the head of the live goat and confess over him all the iniquities of the children of Israel." Thus symbolically all the sins of the nation were transferred to the scapegoat, which was then driven away into the wilderness bearing away forever all the guilt of the people. Thus there was typified in advance our Lord's twofold substitution for us on the Cross: on the Godward side making propitiation for ever on our behalf; and on the manward side "bearing away" our damning guilt, to be remembered against us "no more for ever."

In the back pew Mike Kennard did no spying. To see that packed gathering, and Joseph whom he had driven from home now expounding there as that tall, handsome preacher with such eloquence and ringing voice first astonished him, then it floored him. He was listening to a young scholar, a pulpit genius. Soon even that was eclipsed by the message which the young prophet was proclaiming. Mike Kennard was gripped, shamed, melted, broken. All the heinous sins of his life rose up and pointed their condemning fingers at him. All in one intense, terrifying moment he

THE HIDDEN HAND

saw them in horrifying, countless, accusing array. Beads of
perspiration oozed from his brow and dripped down his
face. He trembled, as many another man has, on seeing his
hell-deserving sin and guilt in the light of God's holiness.
Then, as Joseph told how Aaron laid his hands on the
scapegoat, transferring the people's sins to it, to be borne
away forever; and how the Lord Jesus fulfilled the type,
enduring the penalty of the race's sin in our stead, bearing
away the deadly guilt of it that we might be free, Mike
emitted a loud, trembly groan which startled the people
under the rear gallery.

Most of the folk knew him, the mugwump, enigmatical
husband of the brave little champion, Mrs. Millie Kennard.
Her they admired. Him they despised. That night they got
the shock of their lives. At the end of this message, Joseph
announced the hymn:

> Not all the blood of beasts
>   On Jewish altars slain
> Could give the guilty conscience peace
>   Or wash away the stain.
>
> But Christ, the heavenly Lamb
>   Bears all our guilt away,
> A sacrifice of nobler name
>   And richer blood than they.

When they reached the third verse Joseph said, "Let me
call attention to this next verse; then, as we sing it, I want
all who are seeking salvation to make their way into the
enquiry room through either of the doors at the side of the
pulpit. Let me read the words first—

> My faith would lay her hand
>   On that dear head of Thine,
> With tears confessing, as I stand,
>   These countless sins of mine.

Before he was through quoting, Mike Kennard struggled
into the aisle and came staggering to the front, oblivious of

302

all the eyes staring at him. As he neared the side of the pulpit he looked up at Joseph, and with agony on his face, soaked with tears, he moaned, in his deep rumbling voice, "Joseph, my dear laddie, you'd better come down quick, and lead the blackest sinner on earth back to God."

The effect was electric—for a moment. Then the utter pathos of it melted all who had any tender sensitivity. Except among the young there were few dry eyes. There stood big Mike Kennard, haggard and shaking, looking up with such pitiful appeal at Joseph in the pulpit; and there stood Joseph, now gone rather pale, looking down at him with an expression of incredulity. Recovering himself, Joseph said, "Friends, this is a moment we shall never forget. I'm going at once with my father. I know this is an unusual good-bye procedure, but you all sympathetically understand. . . . You will finish singing the hymn while others are coming to the enquiry room. Then my dear mother will be in the pulpit, to close this eleven-day mission with a prayer of thanksgiving, and the benediction."

That was the night of nights for Mike Kennard. It was his first serious encounter with God, his first real shock at the corruptness of his own heart, and his first head-on collision with the devil who had blasted his life through the years. What he went through in one hour is knowable only to such natures as his. There are some people who seem to be constitutionally dramatic. They do things like actors on a stage, though not intending so. The lines of their character and disposition are drawn with the thick nib of an iron pen dipped in Indian ink. Such was Mike Kennard. There was a theatrical floridness about him. It was not put on. It just clung around him. On that crisis-night in Elmerton he was too shattered to be knowingly histrionic, yet even his conversion just had to be a *"striking conversion."*

Joseph and he knelt side by side at two chairs. Several who should have known better could not resist gathering round to watch and hear. For some time Mike knelt in a crumpled way, perspiring and occasionally shaking. He seemed to be staring at some ghastly spectre which no one but himself could see. Then his large head sagged, and he groaned, "Oh, God, oh, God, my sins! my sins! They're sinking me like lead to hell! Joseph, Joseph, tell me the Gospel quickly!"

"Father, you *know* the Gospel. You knew it and preached it before I was born. You can tell it to me better than I can tell it to you."

"No, no, Joseph. Don't you understand? I've known it for years without knowing it at all as you and your mother know it. I've known the outside facts, but not the inside experience. Don't you understand, Joseph?—I'm damned all the more because I've known it and yet *not* known it, through shoving it underground and going my own hell-bent way! Sins! sins! sins!—all through the years! Nothing but sins! They're coming like a black avalanche on me! Joseph, Joseph, what can I do? Tell me quick, son!"

"Father, you can do what Aaron did with the scapegoat. He knew that the first sacrifice had made atonement to God; and now he had to put his hands on the head of the scapegoat, and transfer all Israel's guilt to it, to be born away forever. Father, you know as well as I do that it was all a forepicture of what Jesus has done for you and me on the Cross. He has made full atonement for us, and now, by faith, we are to lay our hands on our great Substitute, and know that our ugly sin and guilt are borne away for ever. Father, by faith lay your hands there now. In one sense, God has already laid our sin and guilt on Jesus, but in another sense, by our own act, we have to identify ourselves with what Jesus did for us, making it ours by faith. Father, lay your hands now, by faith, on the great Sinbearer, and *believe* that your sins are borne away by Him!"

For a moment Mike was silent. He was breathing heavily. Then, with his eyes closed, yet as though inwardly looking intensely at something he stretched both hands forward, as if he were resting them on the scapegoat, and began confessing. On he went, from his early years up to manhood, confessing his misdoings. Joseph, realizing what was happening, cleared the room of all others. On and on Mike went, oblivious as to whether anyone else was there or not—for nearly twenty minutes. Then his words tapered off to a whisper. Then it was over. He knelt in silence. The trembling had ceased. A minute or so later he quietly looked up and round. Only Joseph was there. Then, with tears of joy streaming down his cheeks he sprang up. "Joseph! I'm saved! I'm *saved!* I'm *SAVED!*" The last "saved" was with a voice of thunder.

"Joseph, my long-suffering son, where's Millie?"

Millie, listening just outside, walked in. "I'm here, Mike."

Mike grabbed her in his arms and gave her a hug which almost crushed her ribs in. "Millie, I'm *saved!* Do you hear? I'm a saved man! I've come to Jesus at last, and He's saved me. I know it. I've got peace with God: the peace of sins forgiven and guilt gone forever! Jesus has borne it all away! Now I've got to *live* it all, as a new man. Millie, you've got a new husband!"

Millie looked carefully at him. If ever a wife knew her husband, Millie knew Mike. One careful, penetrating look told her the truth. This was no mere ebullition of the old Mike; it was reality. The prayer-wrestlings of years were suddenly answered—yes, answered through the son whom Mike had driven from home! Mike and Millie had never had such a hug since they were married.

Then Mike turned to Joseph. "Joseph, my ill-treated boy, how ashamed I am! What I've done, alas, can never be undone, and I shall never forgive myself. But *God* has forgiven me: will *you?*"

Joseph did not speak—not, at least, in words; but what he *did* spoke more powerfully. He came and embraced his father; and his father, for the first time ever, embraced his son. Few fathers have wept on a son's shoulder as Mike did that night.

Presently, wiping his eyes, he said, "Joseph, my dear, dear boy, this is not the prodigal son coming home to his father; it's the prodigal father coming home to his son!"

NINETEEN
Palms and Willows

The year 1910 put an unpleasant signature on the first decade of our twentieth century. It seems to have been a year of lurid crime. The famous Crippen murder and trial had stampeded the headlines and shocked the public. It was the more startling because both the crime and the arrest were by new scientific means. With surgical skill the torso of Dr. Crippen's actress-wife was rendered boneless and cleverly buried beneath the floor of the coal cellar. It was identified by new, scientific methods of "doctor detectives," specialists in morbid anatomy and pathology, who traced in the partial remains a fatal dose of the rare poison, hyoscine. When the fugitive Crippen and his paramour, Ethel Le Neve, fled under disguise and aliases to Rotterdam, and later embarked on the S.S. *Montrose* from Antwerp to Canada, the observant captain of that vessel became suspicious and contacted the police back in England by means of a new marvel, the "Marconigram," or wireless telegraphy.

There was widespread feeling that the Crippen trial marked a new era both in crime and in its detection. In 1910 only about one hundred vessels in the mercantile marine had radio. Within six months over six hundred were equipped with it; and, eighteen months later, radio was required by law on all ocean-going vessels.

There seemed to be, indeed, a curious mosaic of new crime patterns all over the newspapers. In one July edition alone, besides the Crippen monstrosity, there were twelve other spine-chilling crime captions.

The next year had much the same features. So far, science, evolution, Freudianism, psychology, the new rationalistic scholarship, higher education, had not found answers to the grim human problems of sin, guilt, hate, greed, lust, fear, sorrow, death. Another half-century and two world wars were going to write in blood and tears that man's moral problems can be met only by a spiritual remedy. The figment of a "war to end wars" would burst like a pricked balloon. It would be shouted from wrecked cities and battlefield graveyards that you cannot wash away human sin with the soldier's blood: it takes a Saviour's blood to do that.

A.D. 1912 came, bringing its staggering disaster, the wreck of the *Titanic*. That was the event on every tongue, both sides of the Atlantic. Yet although by comparison very small, there was another happening that year, which, at least to the citizens of Elmerton, would always mark 1912 as peculiarly memorable. It was what happened to Mike Kennard.

After that final meeting on the Tuesday night when Mike was converted, Joseph was fairly exhausted. Joash and Agnes shunted him upstairs as soon as they had given him a bedtime snack. Next morning they would not let him get up until they had served him breakfast in bed. It was Evelyn who brought it to him, carrying it on a pretty tray. Joseph was sensitive that his dream girl should see him in bed with his hair ruffled. Quickly he tried to pat it down, but desisted as he saw the roguish amusement on Evelyn's face.

How surpassing fair she looked! He still saw her as the twelve-year-old wood-sprite, innocent, unworldly, sylphlike, guileless as an incarnate cherub. Like Paganini and his peerless violin, she had then seemed to fill the very air with music. But he also saw her as she now was, standing there in college attire; pleated, navy-blue skirt, white blouse and neat costume jacket—a "student *teacher,*" if you please! She was now no mere *ingenue.* In face and figure she was a superb young woman with gentlewomanly bearing. She still had that tantalizingly magnetic expression of seriousness with a threat of breaking into laughter on little provocation. To Joseph it seemed like a thousand sunbeams all crowding to smile through one face, with now a gleam of coy cupidity. "Why is it I love her so?" he asked himself again. "It is because she is so beautiful? If so, I am not worthy of her. But no, there is something looks right through me from those tender blue eyes and says, 'Joseph, I'm the exact counterpart to your own nature. You need me for your own completion.'" Would he love her as much if she were not quite as beautiful? In those few seconds, while he looked at her as only love can look, there floated into his recollection the second verse of Charles Jeffreys' immortal ode to "Bonnie Mary of Argyle."

> *Though thy voice may lose its sweetness,*
> *And thine eye its brightness too,*
> *Though thy step may lack its fleetness,*
> *And thy hair its sunny hue;*
> *Still to me wilt thou be dearer*
> *Than all the world shall own;*
> I have loved thee for thy beauty,
> But not for that alone:
> *I have watched thy* heart, *dear Mary,*
> *And its goodness was the wile*
> *Which has made thee mine for ever,*
> *Bonnie Mary of Argyle.*

He succeeded in saying, rather dreamily, "Good morning, Evelyn," though *she* knew well enough it was not the dreaminess of drowsiness!

"Good morning, Joseph. I've been given the privilege of bringing breakfast *petit dejeuner,* if you please, because I'll have to be leaving for college in a few minutes, and won't be able to go to the railway station to see you off to Huddersfield again. I cycle to and from college twice a day."

"Do be careful about that ankle, Evelyn."

"I always am," she laughed. "That's my favourite ankle ever since you doctored it."

"It's been a high privilege to be at Pinecrest again these days, Evelyn. I wish we could have spent more time together; but the meetings. . . ."

"Yes, I know; but think what the meetings have meant to daddy and me! Life will never be the same again."

"Oh, Evelyn, how unspeakably grateful I am!"

"Joseph, eat your breakfast!"

"I will: but one word more, first. You're wearing again that little gold locket I gave you when I ran away. I've often reflected how presumptuous of me it was, to dash round and give it to you, with your photo inside, but I was only fourteen. Please forgive me."

"Forgive you! It's only sins that need forgiving; not loving deeds! I treasure it more each time I peep into it."

"Would you mind, Evelyn, if I, too, had a peep?"

Her pink cheeks blushed into roses. "Joseph, that *is* something that needs 'forgiving.' Let me think for a moment. . . ."

Unclasping the gold chain around her neck, she laid it and the heart shaped locket on the dressing-table. Then she said, "It's time I was away, Joseph. When I'm gone you can open the locket. Somehow, I think that one of the two faces in it should come out now, and a new one be put in: the face of the dearest girl I have ever met: Molly Ainsworth. I won't be jealous, Joseph. Who could ever be jealous of Molly? Anyway, if you want now to change the faces, please take the locket for that purpose. I shall thoroughly understand; and I think I could bear it better if you did it that way. . . . Bye, Joseph, I shall always . . . love you."

So saying, she hesitantly stepped to the bedside, held his face in both her hands, looked right into his eyes, as though taking a last, fond look, and slowly kissed his forehead. Before he could catch her hand she was gone.

What was breakfast compared with that locket! Quickly laying the tray down, he leapt out of bed to where the locket lay, and unsprung the clasp. Inside there were two faces, side by side. One was Evelyn (the photo Joseph himself had put there years earlier); the other was a picture of himself, eight years younger, evidently cut from a card which Evelyn must have asked for from his mother. Oh, delirious moment! So Evelyn *loved* him! Unbearable joy! He wanted to spring clean over the bed and all over the house. Evelyn, you've said it! Can you really mean it? Only a beautiful mind like yours could have done it in such an artistic way!

Joseph was too full for words—and for breakfast. Albeit, out of dutiful appreciation he forced himself to imbibe most of what Agnes had sent. Then he rose, washed and shaved, dressed, packed his travel bag, gave his hair a final grooming, and trotted downstairs with such vivacity that Joash and Agnes exclaimed, "Well! our tired preacher-boy looks fresh as a daisy!"

They sat and chatted about the meetings, especially the conversion of Joseph's father, until with undisguised reluctance Joash said, "I suppose we must be on our way to pick up Molly and her parents at uncle Ben's, then your mother at Wragley Street, and then get to the railway. You should be in Huddersfield by mid-afternoon. My! how we are going to miss you!"

"Yes, how we are going to miss you, our dearer-than-ever Joseph!" Agnes repeated, at the same time adding, with a smile through motherly tears, "Fancy! I now have to stretch up to kiss you, little boy! What a difference a few years make!"

"Yes, what a difference!" Joseph supplemented. "When I used to come here seven or eight years ago, there were horses and a landau, but now a limousine that carries all of us together!"

"Well, not quite," Joash reflected. "On second thought, since we can't all pack in for the one ride to the station, we'd better take you and your mother first; then James the chauffeur will come back for uncle Ben and the Ainsworths."

When they reached 12 Wragley Street, Millie was at the door waiting, and beaming with happiness at what had happened the night before. "Poor, dear Mike!" she said. "It was hard for him to go to work this morning. He wanted so much to accompany Joseph to the station. But it was too late to get leave of absence from work, and he's so anxious not to lose his job."

Naturally, Mike was the engrossing topic on the way to the railway.

Then "James, the chauffeur" swung round and went back for the Ainsworths.

While Joash and Agnes waited with Millie and Joseph on the station platform, Joash said, "I've often nurtured a secret thought, Joseph, that one day you'd become a partner in the Adair Furniture House. I can see now that I was wrong. Your calling isn't selling suites, it's saving souls. Nothing could ever repay you for what has happened in my own life this past week; but, if it doesn't sound absurd, when the time comes that you are ordained, I would like to buy a motor car for you . . . and . . . I suppose I should hopefully add . . . for your wife."

Inwardly he said, "I'm fairly sure it will be charming Molly."

Inwardly Millie thought otherwise. She knew what was in the locket—and in Joseph.

Uncle Ben and the Ainsworths now arrived. During the past ten days acquaintance had developed into hearty friendship. The Ainsworths knew the fine art of listening, especially to the reminiscent elderly—which continually blew new wind into uncle Ben's sails; for although he had not yet sailed into a placid dotage, he was well into his *anec*dotage.

The train now moved in. Soon the four travellers were aboard, after fond farewells. Joseph gave his mother a final kiss and whispered, "Mother, would you kindly give this little package to Evelyn? It has the locket inside, and a little note to her."

The guard blew his whistle and waved his flag. Slowly the train glided away from the station—until the tearful handkerchief-wavers on the platform, and the four farewellers craning from carriage windows could see each other no longer.

That night many folk in Elmerton felt a strange blank

without the meetings, especially the Adairs and uncle Ben, and, most of all, Evelyn.

Back at Huddersfield, during the following days it was not easy for Joseph to tear his mind away from the Elmerton excitements and bury his head in books, cramming for exams. Nor was it easy for his loyal Molly to settle down to hum-drum teaching again. Mr. and Mrs. Ainsworth noticed that Joseph seemed more and more "at home" with their dear Molly (at which they were pleased), yet never actually "in love" (at which they were sorry).

For the new-year holidays Millie came over from Elmerton to spend a few days with them—at Mike's happy insistence! Mike was a wonder. He was truly changed; just as affectionately husbandly and fatherly as formerly he had been the opposite. About once each month Joseph stayed the night at Wragley Street. His father seemed—so Joseph thought—like a ship which had plunged through terrible tempests, shaken, battered, broken, almost wrecked, but now resting at anchor in a sheltered harbor. Only once during those months did Joseph get round to the Adairs, on which occasion, alas, his queen of hearts was absent.

The following March Joseph became twenty-one, and in June secured his B.A. The Ainsworths made each event a royally celebrated occasion. Molly tried to hide her love, but only showed it more. Joseph applied to a theological college, but was informed he could not be accepted until one year later. Mr. Ainsworth's advice was that he should take B.D. studies at Huddersfield, which would later reduce time in the theological college.

Unfortunately for Molly, although in other ways Joseph was distinctly older than his years, there was one part which grew up slowly. From his mother and sisters he had learned such deep respect for girlhood and womanhood that during his late boyhood and early 'teen years he had been preserved from flirting about with girls and from listening to salacious sex talk among the boys. When Joseph was with girls his sex-difference awareness was comparatively unassertive until his later 'teens, by which time his mind was on higher things, especially after his conversion at the age of sixteen. He just thoroughly enjoyed being with Molly. He liked her beautiful face and mind. He liked her ways and winning smile. But sweetheart affection never crossed his mind.

Much less did he suspect that in Molly's heart a fire of love for himself was burning so intensely, she felt it would waste her away. Not until he was nineteen or twenty did he realize it, through his own now fully masculine love for Evelyn. Thenceforth he was painfully alive to the sensitive, delicate problem, and wondered what he should do. However, about that time, developments took a fateful turn in a new direction.

In the year 1912 Easter day fell on April 7th, which threw Whitsuntide in the week beginning May 26th. In the Lancashire and Yorkshire of those days, Whit Sunday was the time when boys and girls—many adults too—turned out in their new Sunday clothes. For one thing, that national church observance roughly coincided with the beginning of Summer. In earlier times, on Whit Sunday (commemorating Pentecost) all the girls and younger women dressed in white; hence the name, "Whit Sunday."

Until about the time of the Second World War, in many northern English towns, on one day during "Whit Week" all the local Sunday schools used to put on a united procession. Thousands of Sunday school scholars marched through the main streets, and thousands of watchers would line the footpaths. Each Sunday school had its own large (often costly) banner with brilliant ensign or picture on it, with high poles and long, golden cords or streamers; and each school was led by its own brass or silver band. Many of the girls were dressed in daintiest dresses and often carried artistic flower-baskets. At the end-point of the street procession, the different schools branched off to their respective "fields" where tea and cakes were provided, games were played, races were run, and prizes were given. It was the most gaily colorful day on the Sunday school calendar.

Always on the Saturday ending Whit Week, the church and Sunday school at which the Ainsworths and Joseph were members, near Huddersfield, held the "Annual Sunday School Picnic." The weather clerk often seemed to have a grudge against that stirring event, but in 1912 he was in his most cooperative mood. Day after day of golden sunshine and balmy breezes came dancing in like a troop of merry pierrots. What a picnic it was! In good old-fashioned style the children, teachers, and many parents went rumbling off in eight or nine red-white-and-blue wagonettes with decorated horses in the shafts. Those were the days! None of your petrol fumes, traffic crush, impatient speed and unpicturesque steel mechanism! In those days they really got a "kick" out of picnics—sometimes from one of the horses!

Laughing, shouting, giggling, waving streamers, off they went. Crack went the whips. "Gee up, Dobbin!" Round went the big cart-wheels. Get those gee-gees trotting! Over that hump-back in the road, down that slope, winding now among country lanes amid the Pennines! They were off again to Chadvale!

The last three-quarters of a mile being a stiffish incline, the horses and their gaudy chariots were left down at the turnoff. That three-quarter-mile upgrade used to seem fifty miles to those eager young rascals impatient to be at the picnic field. It was also an annoying hurdle to the rheumaticky legs of the older folk. Eventually, with puffings and pantings, all were happily herded into the picnic Shangri-La, a spacious field bounded by gray drystone walls amid flanking green hills sparsely dotted with trees and bush-clumps and bright with wild flowers—a delightful spot.

Then the field fun began. Everybody was in frolicsome mood, and the most unlikely were up to all sorts of capers. There were games of different sorts for different ages; three-legged and four-legged races causing the most comical spills and hilarious collisions. Some of the stiffest members of the church seemed to get well-oiled joints and sockets just for that one day in the year—though with even stiffer stiffness next morning! There were sack-races, egg-and-spoon races, and other competitions for younger and older.

On "Annual Picnic" day some magic stimulus ran in the bloodstream. Even grumpy old Mr. Frogarty, whose usual speed was that of a mole with gout, finished second in the three-legged race, with his right leg tied to the left leg of Sam Muggeridge, after which achievement, pulling panting Sam down with him, he sank to the ground dizzy, not through shortness of breath, but through covering the earth's surface at such speed!

The climax of the afternoon was always the tug-o'-war when, mysteriously enough, as often as not, the rope would snap in the middle, causing twenty or more persons on each side to tumble backwards over each other, some of them being of no little rotundity—who "ought to have known better"!

By the time buns and sandwiches and cakes were ready to be served, along with hot tea from the big tea-urns, young and old were hungry as winter-starved rabbits.

Oh, that "Annual Picnic"! It was the day on which, for the first time since winter, the ladies brought out their parasols, ostensibly to shield themselves from the solar rays, but with sly motive to outdo all others by garish colors, or to provide undercover protection for a fine old shady gossip. That was the day on which the young men brought out the wickets, bails, bats and ball for the first cricket game of the season. That was the day on which grouchy old Jeremy Toomey used to bless the world with his one and only annual smile from under his bushy whiskers—like a hidden sun popping its head out for a moment, then bashfully ducking back behind a physiognomical cloudbank for another year.

That was the day, too, when those rare ones who owned cameras brought them out and took another photograph; always of the same scene: the winding valley and the Chadvale viaduct in the distance, with its twelve mighty arches, hundreds of feet high, stretching north-south across the valley; and always the same camera-shy group of people in the foreground, rigid as a tableau. That was the day on which ex-captain Dogherty, formerly of the merchant marine, used to bring his long telescope, fix it on a swivel-top tripod, and charge one halfpenny for a slow-moving view along the valley to the Chadvale arches, afterward donating all the halfpennies to the foreign missionary society.

To describe all the peculiar notables at that social ensemble would take the art of a Dickens. To do justice to its world-shaking events would need the quill of a Shakespeare. To paint the early-summer glory of that picnic paradise, sequestered amid those ravines now recarpeted in freshest green, tapestried with those intermittent gorse thickets and leafy groves, would need the brush of a Mallord Turner or an Edwin Landseer.

Molly Ainsworth was there, of course, with the young women's class of which she was the teacher. So were her parents. So was Joseph Kennard, along with the young men's class of which he was a member.

Among the members of that young men's class was a curly-haired stripling named Alan Sutherland. He was a good sport and an adept at quick learning. There was scarcely a subject you could mention but he could say, "I know a bit about that." He knew a bit about music, a bit about sculpture, a bit about medicine, a bit about cotton-and-wool manufacturing, a bit about coal mining, a bit about the aristocracy, et cetera. Where he picked up all his "bits" was anybody's guess, but he had an exceptionally quick pick-up and a blotting-paper memory. His knowledge never went far in any given field, but he was an intriguing encyclopaedia of useful "bits." His pals laughingly chaffed him that if he lived in Russia the Tsar would acclaim him Professor Knowabitz.

Among other things, he "knew a bit" about photography, and had a brand new camera with him on the picnic. Like everybody else he lingered admiring the vista down along the valley, winding between steepish hills, its glistening stream flowing toward the high Chadvale viaduct with its mighty arches. It was a scene to tempt any camera; but Alan Sutherland got a new idea. Standing by ex-captain Dogherty, he asked, "Captain, would you mind if I photographed Chadvale arches through your telescope? It would give a closeup view nobody can ever get from the ground near to them. It would be as though one were photographing them near to, from mid-air!"

"If you think it will work, son, try it; but I'll have to charge you *two* halfpence for something special like that.

It's for the missionaries, so you can't grumble."

Alan Sutherland got the focus exact, fixed the telescope firmly, put the camera behind it, and adjusted the lens to what seemed perfect vision behind the camera eye. Then he clicked the little lever. Whether anything would come of it seemed doubtful; but Joseph happened to be standing near, and said, "Alan, that's one of Molly's favorite views. If the picture comes out really nice, will you let me have a copy for her?"

And so, with one thing after another, the fun-filled picnic hours scampered away until the one hundred and fifty or so picnickers made their way down to the wagonettes again in the late afternoon, and rolled away back to town. That night, after those hours amid the bracing mountain air, and the riotous rompings, many a little sleepy-head was off to dreamland almost before touching the pillow.

But now, away over the Pennines again to the Lancashire side, to 12 Wragley Street, Elmerton. What changes since the Kennards had settled there! By the year 1911, when Mike was converted, Dorothy had been away over eight years. She had completed her four years' training at Rochdale, done one year as staff nurse, and now, at the age of twenty-six, was a sister there. In well-known phrase, having "put her hand to the plough" she had never "looked back." There was not a more respected sister on any hospital ward than Dorothy Kennard.

As for Mona, she too had been away from Wragley Street now for over a year. She had married a young engineer whom she first met at the Choral Society. True to type, hers was a romantic, sentimental love-match, and the two young newly-weds were as lovey as two turtle-doves. Yet not only so: they were financially prosperous; for besides engineering wages there was income from a busy little millinery shop which Mona had opened in the new Elmerton outreach where she and her beloved lived.

So now Mike and Millie were alone, he being forty-nine, and Millie fifty-two. Mike was known all over the area for two reasons. First, he was the husband of the best-known and most respected little woman in the public life of Elmerton: police court missionary, salvager of fallen women, doughty champion of public morals, quick-witted denouncer of the brewers, well-thought-of by magistrates and law officers; favourite raconteur at young people's Sunday school parties, leader of the largest women's meeting in town, speaker at Christian Endeavour and Band of Hope rallies all over the area. How could the husband of such a woman be hidden?

Supplementing that, unfortunately, Mike was all too well-known by many because of his own unusualness. He would have been an observed personage anywhere. The commonest way of referring to him was, "He's a 'character,' and no mistake." Beer, bombast and buffoonery were always associated with him. As Bill Sykes, the lamplighter, put it, "He's a blinkin' riddle, that feller."

Millie often worried lest Mike's behaviour should adversely affect the work she was trying to do. People certainly considered him "a disgrace to her," but not in any way which reflected on Millie. If anything it rather worked the other way; for the women whom Millie sought to rescue could not say, "It's all very well for her to preach to the likes of us, but she knows nothing about it herself." No, they knew she had a drink problem with her own man.

The crowning notoriety came when Joseph ran away from home, and the enraged Mike dumped the young policeman and the next-door neighbour in the gutter. That was "town's talk" which made ears tingle!

But now, in a fittingly dramatic sequel, Mike Kennard, the bizarre enigma, gets converted through the preaching of his own long-lost boy. Mike Kennard's "got religion"! That was hot news locally. "Aye, he walked down the aisle in a packed church, and called up to the young preacher in the pulpit to come down and get him saved!" That shot an electric thrill through Elmerton gossip. Naturally, the prophets of scepticism saw it as a theatrical fake, or a "flash in the pan," or a "nine days wonder"; but they were wrong, and soon everybody knew it.

Mike Kennard was in truth a new man. He showed it and glowed it. Week after week, month after month, no drinking, no smoking, no cursing, no swagger, no silly brag; but a quiet, steady, humble, likeable Christian man! It could not have been more legible if he had gone round wearing a printed notice, THESE PREMISES UNDER NEW MANAGEMENT.

He started going to church with Millie. Some of the members were a bit leery of him, but soon were ashamed of their doubts. Moreover, however self-restrained he might be, such a man could not help being "felt" by the strong influence he emitted. He was much drawn to the midweek prayer meeting. It filled him with awed wonder that human sinners such as he could actually speak to GOD through the Saviour's Name. After some weeks he began to pray audibly in the meetings. Oh, that voice! That vibrancy! That vocabulary! That unpremeditated, river-like flow of language! The presiding minister might well be forgiven for a touch of envy at such natural gift and pervasive atmosphere. Not that Mike wanted to be heard: nay, that was the utter opposite of the new Mike. His praying was unusual. If ever a man knew the reality of a personal devil and the deadly grip of evil, Mike Kennard did: and if ever a man knew the reality of emancipation through the saving truth of the Gospel, *he* did. It all came out in his prayers.

Soon church groups were inviting him to "give his testimony." Everywhere he went, his large presence, dominating gifts, and earthquake spiritual experience made him a "big draw" as well as a prize trophy. Everywhere he gave a searching challenge. Everywhere it could be seen how genuine was his transformation. But one evening he said to Millie, "Millie dear, I'm thinking I won't give my testimony anywhere else—not for some time. It keeps calling attention to me, me, me. It could become a subtle temptation to pride. I want them to see *HIM* who did it all for me; but *I'm* getting in the way. I'm telling you this, Millie, only so you'll know why, if I say 'No.' "

Nothing could have revealed more plainly to Millie the spiritual progress he was making.

Most of all, at home with Millie and among close friends the difference in him was indubitable. It was as though a dark layer of evil had been clean lifted from his mind, and another Mike had emerged after being buried alive for

years. It was that truer Mike which Millie had always felt
was somewhere down inside him, if only she could get to it.
That was the inner Mike she had loved; and now it had
risen in victory. Where the demon had long gloated an angel
now sang!

One night soon after his conversion, as he and Millie sat
at their evening meal, he said, "Millie, I don't know which is
bigger: my thankfulness that I'm saved, or my shame at the
way I've treated you. I can never undo it, but I'll try to
make up in at least some degree." He fought hard to make
good his word.

For Millie it was almost like living with a new husband.
His tenderness, thoughtfulness, protectiveness, she could
scarcely believe. What days of happiness for her! Dorothy
used to come home for one full day each month, and always
for her holidays. Mona and her husband were often in, with
happy talkativeness. Joseph was now the Lord's, and was
preparing for the Christian ministry. They were days of
golden reapings after years of tearful sowings; days of full-
bloomed answers to persevering prayers.

There was just one thing which seemed to be worrying
Mike. From time to time he would refer to it with mysterious vagueness, as though wanting to disencumber his mind,
but prevented by some binding fear. Millie easily divined
that it concerned Joseph but decided not to show curiosity.
She knew now that he would not allow any known wrong to
continue in his life, and that he would not willingly keep from
her any serious matter which she ought to know. It was at
month ends that he seemed the more restless, which reminded her that until his conversion it was at month ends
that he used to go away on those strange excursions from
which he always returned with money.

Since his conversion those month-end disappearances
had ceased, but at the end of the next April he went away
again for two days only. Then, on the last Friday evening in
May, he said to Millie, "I'm wanting to get something off my
mind, Millie, but I don't know how to do it. You know it's to
do with Joseph, don't you? For twenty years, now, you and I
have kept our secret about him, but I'm wondering now
whether we ought to let it out. Oh, Millie, I wish I could tell

you all: but I'm under a sworn oath not to do so. You see, I've told you lies about Joseph. Or, no, not lies of my own; but lies which somebody else told me. Eventually I got the real truth from him, but I couldn't tell you, much less could I tell anybody else, for he threatened to shoot me if I did; and I know he means it."

He paused. Millie silently waited.

"Millie, it's not that I mind overmuch now being shot, but if the truth had to come out that way it would injure Joseph. I know I've done wrong, but what I did was done innocently at the time. It was this other man who was the villain. He tricked me into partnering with him in what he had done. I only wanted to help him in a sorry predicament. I didn't know at that time how he was lying to me. I should have gone to the police but I was scared after I had become an accessory and been paid for it. This man is very rich, Millie, and he's paid me every month to keep my mouth shut. He's been wild as a fiend at you, Millie, for giving Joseph such a good upbringing. He wanted him to be dragged up as an ugly, vicious young drunkard and criminal—out of spite to somebody; but you've gone and upset it all, and he can't do a thing about it now."

Again a pause.

Millie still listened without comment.

"And now, Millie, God has had mercy on me, and used that very lad to bring me back to Himself! Oh, Millie, why has God given me such a wonderful wife? such a nice, clean home? such good children? and . . . and Joseph? . . . and forgiven me and saved me?" He broke down, and wept tears of gratitude.

Millie said, "I understand, Mike; and we all love you more than ever, now."

"I'll never get over it Millie. But let me tell you my problem. As a Christian I've got to get this evil thing put right—about Joseph, I mean. Yet I don't know how to do it. You see, if the real truth comes out it will certainly hurt *you,* Millie. People will know, then, what we've hidden all these years. They'll think badly of you. They'll think worse than ever of *me,* because I'm now a professing Christian. It might even harm Joseph. He might be angry, and wish the truth about him had never been divulged—now that he is so widely known. Millie, the fact is, that what the hidden hand of the devil did, the hidden hand of God has overruled! Think of it: little Joseph now a handsome, gifted, educated young man going into the ministry!—and even despicable, conniving *me* converted and preaching the Gospel! Talk about God turning the tables on the devil!"

"Yes, Mike; it's almost too wonderful."

"Well, Millie, this is what I've decided to do. I'm going to see this man once more. I daren't tell you his name—not at the moment; I'm under oath and payment not to reveal it. In any case, he's somebody you've never even heard of. I'm going to see him, and tell him that unless he does a certain thing for Joseph, to compensate him, I shall make a clean breast of everything to the police; but if he agrees, then the compensation shall be given to Joseph, and I will tell the truth to Joseph privately, without disclosing the man's name. Then it will be up to Joseph himself to decide what he thinks best, and the matter could be finally cleared away."

"Yes, Mike, I'm following; but of course it's a bit mystifying that the man and what he did have to be kept so secret. However, I've every confidence now in my new Mike, and I know you'll only do what you are sure is right and wise."

"Millie, you know how much I love you now, don't you? Before my conversion I used alternately to hate you and to be thankful for you; hate you because your life was such a condemnation of my own; yet inwardly thank God for you because you were so patient and good to me. And Joseph, every time I looked at him I would get mad at him because of the way he had cursed my life; but yet I didn't want him to die because of the keep-silent money at the end of each month. Millie, I love Joseph now as much as any father on earth ever loved his son. God bless him!"

"I believe you do, Mike."

"Just one other word, Millie. If anything should ever happen to me, I've got written evidence, of sorts, to substantiate all I've said. It's hidden away, but I can't tell you where until after this weekend, because if I did, before seeing this man, I would be betraying my oath, and perhaps make things worse. I'll leave very early in the morning. He knows I'm coming. He'll meet me part way. By Sunday night I'll be back, and I'll have settled the thing one way or the other. Then I'll tell you everything, and I think you'll understand."

Next day Mike was up very early. Soon afterward he and Millie had breakfast together, also a short Scripture reading and prayer. Then, after a fond kiss, he strode off, apparently in the direction of the station.

The following morning (Sunday) as Millie was getting ready for church, the front door-knocker sounded. Tom Marland, one of the policemen from the central office, was at the door. Millie knew him well. He had a look on his face which betokened ill tidings. Albeit, Millie was not unduly alarmed, for occasionally she was called out in this way to see someone who was urgently calling for her.

"Mrs. Kennard," Tom began, "we've got upsetting news for you. . . . It's about your husband. . . . Something happened to him yesterday. . . ."

"Yes, Tom, go on. I'm listening."

"You'll need to hold yourself firmly, Mrs. Kennard. It's bad news. He had an accident. . . . In fact, it's worse than that. . . . He won't be coming home again. . . . He's been killed."

"Killed!" Millie could scarcely believe her ears. Her brain reeled. Mike killed! Oh, no! Surely there was some mistake!

She tried to sound calm, but her voice trembled. "Tom, are you sure it was Mike?"

"Yes, Mrs. Kennard. He evidently had an accident. He fell off Chadvale Viaduct. Do you know where that is? Yes, of course you do. It's on the Yorkshire side of the Pennines. It runs from the little town on the north side of the valley right over to the south side where the track joins the main railway line to Manchester. It's a favourite place for sight-seers, but it's risky. The narrow path along the side of the railway lines was never meant for the public; but every now and then somebody among those who walk across it gets dizzy with the height, loses balance, and falls over."

"Tom, am I really hearing you tell me that my husband

fell from the Chadvale arches into the valley below, and that he is dead?"

"I'm afraid that's it, Mrs. Kennard. I wish I were not the bearer of such bad news."

"Will you kindly come in for a minute, Tom? I'm feeling a bit faint, and I wouldn't like to be alone for the next minute or two."

Tom came in, and Millie sank into a chair. After a few minutes she said, "Tom, I'm going to make myself a cup of strong tea. Please be with me for a moment in the kitchen, just in case. . . ."

But Millie made the cup of tea for herself, and one for Tom, without mishap. After drinking it she said, "Thank you, so much, Tom, for trying to break the news slowly. May I now ask a favour? Please ask the chief to telephone Councilor and Mrs. Adair, to let them know. And perhaps he might ask them would they kindly come round here. I'll be in all morning."

In less than three-quarters of an hour Joash and Agnes were there. "Oh, Millie, what on earth has happened? Can it be true? You're not to be alone today. You're coming round to Pinecrest."

Later that day the police chief himself came round to tell Millie and the Adairs the full information he had on the matter. Mike's body had been found near the stream, underneath the fifth archway, fearfully disfigured through having fallen from such a height. Three young men out on a hike had found it, and had hurried to the nearby little town to notify the police. By the time the police reached the place, the body, so they judged, had been lying there for several hours. Just near the corpse was a bottle of whisky, strangely enough not broken, having fallen, presumably, on the upper side of the body. Mr. Kennard's clothes smelled strongly of whisky, as though he had been drinking and had spilled some. The body would not be brought to Elmerton until after the coroner's inquest.

Poor Millie! Satan's war chariot had come rumbling up when least expected, and would fain have crushed her beneath its cruel wheels. Joash and Agnes had seen Millie smile through many a reverse, and toss her golden hair back in pleasant defiance at many an opposition; but this time she was stunned, bewildered, broken.

"Oh, God, just when answers to prayer seem so clear, why this?—this seemingly mocking and useless heart-breaker?" Millie retired to the bedroom where she would spend the night. The floodgates of her grief gave way in sobs which she struggled unsuccessfully to quieten. Outside, Agnes and Joash heard, and wept with her. Just at the high pinnacle of victory, Satan's most prostrating reprisal. This seemed the supreme test. Could Millie survive even this enough to sing Hallelujah through her tears?

There was a further wound to be inflicted. According to the coroner's inquest there was no reason to think the death was suicide, for the deceased had been in excellent health and spirit when he left home, and was clearly expecting to be home again that Sunday evening. Neither was there the slightest evidence of murder, for the deceased appeared to have been quite alone. The local bank manager had attested that Mr. Mike Kennard, unaccompanied, had been into the branch office that Saturday morning just before the noon closing hour, and had changed a five-pound Bank of England note for five gold sovereigns, which five sovereigns had later been found on the person of the deceased. The local bank manager had also disclosed that the said Mike Kennard had often been in the bank before to change Bank of England notes, always about the end of the month. True, a bowler hat had been found in the stream about two furlongs away from the corpse, but it was soaked and badly out of shape, and wedged between stones, where it had probably been for some days. Inside, on the leather band, was the name JIM in capital letters. Where it was bought, or whose it was, or how long it had been in the stream, could not be determined, nor could it be in any way connected with the fatality.

Therefore, a verdict was brought in: *"Death through misadventure while under the influence of drink."*

What venom of the viper in that last phrase, "under the influence of drink"! How the enemies of the Gospel would now make sport of Mike's conversion! Evidently, behind the scenes he was still on the booze, and taking indulgent spells away from home! How derisively the Philistines would laugh at the way this vaunted new Samson had been tricked and mocked by that old Delilah, the bottle! How the prophets of scepticism would gloat that their vaticinations had come true! Apparently, Satan had played a master card.

Millie was still at Pinecrest when the coronor's verdict came through. Again the tears flowed, though Millie was now in calm self-control. There was a look of sad but quiet resignation in her face. From that time, however, as her friends began to notice, she looked older and did not have the same vivacity.

"Agnes," she persisted, "I do not believe that dear Mike was drunk at all when he was killed, despite the supposed evidence of it. Nor was it suicide. Oh, the exasperating mystery of it! The coroner's verdict seems to have shut the door against any other explanation; yet I believe there is one. Agnes, let's pray about it, now, and then every day. Satan has struck hard, but he can't fool God."

The two of them knelt together—as often before. This was the gist of Millie's pleading: "O God, amid the painful mystery of Thy permissive will, we pray for faith to accept Thy will and still to believe in Thy sovereign faithfulness. But if Mike's death was *not* through drink, we ask that for the honor of Thy Name, and for the sake of Christian witness in Elmerton, Thou wilt bring evidence of it to light."

Secretly Agnes thought it seemed too late, now, even for God to do that; but not for the world would she have discouraged Millie by hinting it.

Meanwhile two letters of grief and lovingly worded sympathy came from Joseph. He had been shocked beyond expression by the news, which he had first seen in the newspaper. When he had read that the dead man had been identified as Mr. Mike Kennard of Elmerton he had scarcely been able to believe his own eyes; but then the confirmation had come from Millie herself via the police network. His heart "overflowed with tender love and sympathy" for his "precious, precious mother."

Strangely enough (he told her) the very Monday he read

of the tragedy, he received a letter from Harvey Street Church in Elmerton, saying that all the people there were still praising God for the wonderful eleven-day campaign the preceding October, and were now sending him a unanimous invitation to come back as their minister for a period of two years, during which time they would impede him as little as possible in his studies for the ministry.

"Mother, do you think this is the hand of God?—such an invitation coming at such a moment? I am praying much about it. I could live with you at 12 Wragley Street. We would be together, even though under sadly changed circumstances. Does it not seem as though God Himself has graciously timed this invitation to match the hour of your sorrow and loneliness? Let us both pray over it, and make sure of being divinely guided."

At the end of Joseph's second letter were these words, "Does it not seem painfully ironic that father's death should have occurred on that Saturday, and at Chadvale Viaduct? On that very day I myself was within sight of Chadvale arches with our Sunday school picnic, admiring the view of the arches in the distance, probably about the same time (strange thought!) that the tragedy occurred."

What a strange mixture of contrarieties is the daily cup of human experience! On the same day, picnics and panics, singings and weepings, laughter and tears, cradles and coffins, victors and vanquished, wedding bells and funeral dirges, the palm and the willow! How true: the brighter the sun, the deeper the shadow!

Yes, Mike Kennard is truly converted; suddenly a dark hand strikes. Mike is dead! And Millie, brave little heroine of many an exploit, will never fully get over it, or be quite the same sturdy little champion again.

TWENTY
Far-reaching Choices

Mike Kennard's death precipitated major changes in at least three lives. In the case of Joseph it decided his acceptance of the Harvey Street pastorate in Elmerton, and his removal to live there with his bereaved mother.

It also occasioned a brave new venture by Dorothy, Joseph's sister. She resigned from Rochdale to open a private nursing home in Elmerton, to be near her mother. Her meagre savings were insufficient to start such a project, so she decided to risk a loan. However, uncle Ben pricked up his ears in philanthropic protest. He was outraged that goldilocks Dorothy should put her head in such a needless noose. Why should she not make him president and let *him* finance the venture? That is just what she and he agreed. Within ten weeks two double-fronted houses in Ashgrove Crescent were made into one, under Joseph's supervision, after which modern equipment was installed. From the outset it was a success.

Indirectly, too, Mike Kennard's death led to another decision which surprised everybody. Charming, cultured Molly Ainsworth offered herself for training to be a slum mission-worker! To many it was a sheer throwing away of romance and glamor for drab drudgery. In a worldly-wise sense, that indeed is what it was. Who among Molly's many secret adorers would not have eaten his hat to claim such a coveted prize? In Christian circles it was flabbergasting that Joseph and Molly, the preaching-and-singing pair, were separating—she for slum work, of all things! It was a shock to Molly's parents, though she had given hints beforehand.

There was one aspect of Joseph's removal to Elmerton which caused him uneasiness. What would be the attitude of the Elmerton people to the way his father had died? Would it reflect adversely on his son's ministry? His mother, too, seemed rather apprehensive. So were Joash and Agnes and Evelyn. But again came the unexpected.

On a Saturday, several weeks after Mike fell to his death, the Ainsworths and Joseph were finishing their evening meal when the doorbell rang, and Alan Sutherland was there—the boy who "knew a bit about everything." He had a nervy twitch which suggested inward agitation.

"What is it, Alan?" asked Joseph as they sat in the front room.

"Ugh, Joseph, I'm all dithery with shock. See, I can hardly keep still."

"Whatever is it? Can I help in any way?"

"No, no, Joseph, it's something to do with *you;* and by Jove it's ghastly. I haven't said a word to anyone else. You remember the Sunday school picnic, and how I took a photo of Chadvale arches through old Dogherty's telescope? Oh, stars above! how can I tell you? You see, I know a bit about photography, so I do my own developing and finishing. I left that film in the camera until I had used up the reel. I didn't develop it until last night. I never slept a wink afterward. I've been itching to get round here all day. You'll scarcely believe it, Joseph, but I unknowingly photographed someone who must be your father. And, Joseph, if it's your father, his death wasn't just an accident, and it wasn't a suicide: it was a *murder!*—and the telescope's brought it right close up! See, I'll show you."

He quickly pulled out an envelope containing the negative and two prints. Joseph looked at them. Even though Alan's word had prepared him, his eyes nearly jumped out at what he saw. It was indeed his father, but he had been pushed over the wall of the viaduct. His hat had come off and was in the air nearby. His body was just leaving the wall, with arms flung out wide, one hand evidently having knocked the bowler hat from the man who had pushed him over. The very look on his father's half-turned face could be seen; so could the arms and figure of the man who had thrust him over, but unfortunately one of Mike's outflung arms partly covered the murderer's face.

Joseph stared, aghast. Then he shouted, "Ma, Pa, Molly! Come here, quick!" And as they came in he said, "Look, this is how my father met his death! He was murdered . . . *murdered!*"

The three Ainsworths looked, or, rather, stared speechlessly.

Alan Sutherland was still jittery. "What shall we do, Joseph?"

"What shall we do, Alan? I'll tell you what we'll do: we'll thank God for bringing the truth out; and we'll get to the police office right away."

The Huddersfield, Manchester and Elmerton police wires were busy that night! The following Monday the newpapers carried headlines on the unprecedented photographic phenomenon which had inadvertently exposed a murder, thus negating the coroner's verdict.

The news of the photograph sped around Elmerton causing a quick reversal of feeling about Mike. Why was that bottle of whisky not broken after such a fall? Since it was not broken, how did Mike's jacket come to be soaked? Did that bowler hat with the name JIM inside have a connection, after all? Who was "that other man" in the telltale photograph? Could anyone recognize the partly covered face? Like bloodhounds wakened in the night and sniffing after a trail, the police were after "that other man."

All the more sympathy was generated for Mike as the press now made public Millie's testimony that for six years before his conversion he had not touched drink; also that his avowed purpose on leaving home was to bring into the open a crime committed years earlier by the man he was to meet. He had set out saying that as a Christian he must act according to conscience. Thus his name was largely cleared; and even though Millie's grief at his violent death was not assuaged she was comforted.

The hunted "other man" was never found; but as the weeks became months the excitement subsided, and by the time Joseph commenced his ministry the unsolved mystery had been buried in uneasy obscurity.

One of the most hurting moments of Joseph's life was his leaving the Ainsworths. He could never repay them for years of magnanimous kindness—which made it feel wrong that he should leave them without being able to give them something big and tangible in return. He had been over six years in their handsome home. They were deeply endeared to him, and he to them. They had taken the runaway boy in, feeding, clothing, caring for him, treating him as their own son. It was in their home that gifted, earnest Molly had led him to the Saviour; where daddy Ainsworth had been so truly fatherly, giving sagacious but never oppressive advice, showing untiring interest, and undemonstratively paying the bills for Joseph's higher education. It was there that mummie Ainsworth had washed and mended his clothes, laughed with him over table games, and never wearied in (as she put it) "domesticating" him. There had been an intertwining of hearts until it was as natural to kiss them "goodnight" or "good morning" as if they were his own kin. But now the painful parting had come; and this time he was not taking Molly, nor was he coming back to live there any more.

They had driven him the several miles to Huddersfield railway station. Now they were standing on the platform. The train had drawn in, and Joseph's three travel bags were in the eight-seater compartment. The four farewellers all had that same feeling of an aching inner emptiness.

Joseph embraced and kissed Mr. and Mrs. Ainsworth. He and they were weeping, but trying to look cheerful. The only one without tears was Molly. Joseph would long remember the expression on her face. He was blind no longer. Molly Ainsworth was compellingly beautiful. Never had she looked more so than in that emotional moment. There was a quiet radiance about her. He knew now how she loved him. He knew also that she had given him up to Evelyn. He knew what inward struggle there had been; that she had been alone, praying for grace and resignation and spiritual victory.

And now she stood there, so sad yet so pleasant, heaping good wishes on him for the days ahead. They looked into each other's eyes—a long look in which they remembered all they had meant to each other as partners in public ministry and in studies together at home. Then they were in each other's arms. Joseph hugged and kissed her, though not on her lips. Now there were tears in Molly's eyes too, but she was still very calm. Joseph knew with painful acuteness in that intense moment what a brave, noble, pure gem of a girl Molly Ainsworth was.

And now the whistle sounded. "Passengers all aboard, please." The train slowly glided away. Joseph leaned out of the window, waving and throwing kisses as the three Ainsworths became smaller and fainter, until they were lost to view. Then, with a feeling of sickly emptiness and fear, he sank down and sobbed, thankful that he was the only occupant of the compartment. He might have wept even more had he seen and felt the sorrow in the Ainsworth home that night.

As the train drew near Elmerton Joseph struggled to get his thoughts and feelings suitably controlled. On no account must he let the pain of leaving the Ainsworths seep through in suchwise that his mother might think he was not eager to be back in Elmerton. However, the moment he stepped out to the station platform, there was his precious mother with such a look of welcome; and there were Councilor and Mrs. Adair—and Evelyn. It was a welcome just as warm and reassuring as the Huddersfield parting had been heartwringing.

"Oh, Joseph, you've no idea how we've missed you, and been counting the days until we had you back," said Agnes. "And we've such a nice surprise for you, haven't we, Joash?"

"Yes, we have: that is, if Joseph likes it."

"You have me curious at once," responded Joseph.

"We've moved your mother from Wragley Street to a much nicer house next to Dorothy's new nursing home," continued Joash. "Uncle Ben and Agnes have been scheming again."

With a look which expressed such motherly friendship, Agnes explained: "You see, we just couldn't have your mother stay on alone at Wragley Street. Nor could she and you stay together there; it has no room for a minister's study. And since Dorothy was coming here, uncle Ben and I thought: Why not take the house next door as a nice new home for all three of you? Ashgrove Crescent is a delightful area, with a nice outlook on trees and flowers and Ashgrove Park."

Joseph looked questioningly at his mother.

"Yes, Joseph, I agreed; but it's much too kind of them. Uncle Ben is just as sly as he's generous. It was he who talked me into it: though to be frank, I did not need much persuasion. It will be wonderful for *you* there, Joseph, and even more so for me, to have you and Dorothy with me again."

Joseph had to appear thrilled about it, though secretly it seemed another sore break from a sentimentally precious yesterday. He accompanied them to the limousine, and the porter put the three travel bags into the "trunk." There was something askew in not going back to Wragley Street; but when they reached Ashgrove Crescent and he saw the new nursing home his presentiments soon changed. The whole facade of solid stone had been cleaned to its original brightness. The smaller, old-fashioned sash windows had been replaced by larger, modern-type frames having the upper part ornamented by leaded-glass patterns. There were pretty curtains at the windows. There was a front lawn of some twenty feet in width, separated from the road by a stone wall three feet high with a bright green iron railing running along the top of it. On the lawn, near the large wrought-iron entrance gate, was a newly painted signboard with the name of the nursing home in gold lettering.

Joash noted Joseph's look of pleasant surprise. "Don't you think my men have made an attractive job of it? You see, I still have a large interest in the Adair Building and Contracting firm, although Ted Matthews runs it now. Ted and I designed the whole reconstruction, making the two houses into one. Inside, you'd never know they'd ever been two. In fact, you'd scarcely suspect it outside either."

"You certainly wouldn't," Joseph concurred.

"And uncle Ben has furnished the whole interior—upstairs and down, in every room. He's adopted it as his pet avocation. He thinks your golden-haired sister is the best lass who ever donned a nurse's uniform. Mind you, he's cute. There's a card hung in each room: "Furnishing done by the ADAIR FURNISHING HOUSE." I'll bet, in the end, the old rascal gets far more back than he's given! He's always said, 'Those who give most get most.' "

Then Agnes interposed with, "But, Joseph, before you go in there, you must see your own new abode next door."

That, too, brought happy surprise. It had the same stone wall and grass lawn, and same kind of artistic iron gate as the nursing home. Agnes led the way into the hall. It was a spacious older type, but now all modernized. The hall and ample living room both had oak fittings, matching wallpaper, wall-to-wall carpeting and good-quality new oak furniture.

"They must have spent a mint of money on it," thought Joseph.

In the living room he observed several of the ornaments and pictures from Wragley Street, also Millie's rocking-chair, but apparently all the other furniture had been disposed of. That gave him another pang, for he had loved the Wragley Street furniture even though it was of the cheaper sort. Somehow that was *home*. Yet he had to admit that this, contemporary in style and superior in quality, was naturally more appealing.

There was a sitting room looking out over the front lawn to the park beyond the roadway. It was beautifully furnished in walnut—everything obviously new. Joseph was becoming worried. Who had paid for this expensive furniture? Or who was still to be paid? He was anxious to talk with his mother. He fairly gasped when he saw the piano there; not the tin-canny old crock from Wragley Street, but a new Bechstein in polished walnut, as befitted the decor. Under irresistible impulse he strummed a few chords. It was a glorious instrument.

"My! what a beauty! It's enough to make dear old Beethoven shout a *Te Deum Laudamus* from his grave!" Then delight turned to uneasiness. "But who bought this?—or who is still to be paid?"

Millie, who up to this point had silently watched Joseph's reactions, now spoke to allay his concern. "Joseph, you need have nothing but pleasure in it. The piano is all yours, bought and paid for. I tried to stop them. I told them how sensitive you would be; but they wouldn't listen. It's a present from Mr. and Mrs. Ainsworth and Molly."

"*A present from Mr. and Mrs. Ainsworth and Molly!*" In an instant Joseph was back at that Huddersfield parting. He saw those three dear faces again; and in that moment they seemed almost like angel faces. They had known that they were permanently losing him and had known how Molly loved him, yet in that hour of disappointed good-bye they had given this crowning expression to the love of their hearts for him. Could anyone charge Joseph with oversentimentalism as he sank into a chair and wept? "Mother, why is it that God has always given me such kind friends, when I know I don't deserve them? I loved the Ainsworths so much. Oh, Molly, Molly, what have I done?"

Turning to Agnes, he said, "I'm so sorry, Mrs. Adair. I should have covered my feelings better; but you always understand. Ever since I was twelve I've felt that you and my dear mother understand me better than anyone else."

"Perhaps we do," smiled Agnes: "more than you think!"

Upstairs was another pleasing discovery. There were three moderate-sized bedrooms, each tastefully furnished and carpeted: one for Millie, one for Dorothy, and one for Joseph; but Joseph's had a door leading to a further small room overlooking the rear garden, with a slantwise peep at the Pennines in the distance. This smaller room was newly papered and painted but left empty of furniture.

"This was my own idea," Joash explained. "These three bedrooms used to be *two* needlessly large ones, after the old-fashioned gentry style. One of them had madame's boudoir and coiffeur annex adjoining it. Ted Matthews and I managed to make three bedrooms out of the two, but we didn't want to interfere with this wall here. Then I thought: Why not leave this boudoir as a study for Joseph, and let the adjoining bedroom be *his* bedroom? So, if it meets with your reverence's approval, here is your 'den'!"

When Joash and Agnes had gone Millie gave Joseph her own welcome in her own motherly way. Then they sat and talked. Joseph confessed that he had a dull, empty ache at having left the Ainsworths, and a touch of sickly fear about the risky experiment of his accepting the *pro tem* pastorate at Harvey Street. He realized that a "special effort" such as his last year's evangelistic mission there, in which many from other churches had joined, was very different from the "ordinary" ministry in which the novelty of a new personality has worn off and the ministry must either flourish or wither in proportion to its inherent strength—or lack of it. Harvey Street was a downtown cause. Some thought its days were numbered. Had Joseph taken too big a risk for a young man not yet twenty-two?

Then they talked about the new nursing home and this agreeably furnished upper-class house in which they were now to live. It had all been kindly lifted out of Millie's hands by Joash and Agnes. The Harvey Street church had no manse for its minister but they had a "Manse Fund" containing money realized on the sale of the former manse, plus other contributions. Therefore, since they were not having to buy a manse for unmarried young Joseph, they were only too ready to pay a rent to uncle Ben instead. So Joseph need not think he was "living on charity."

Moreover, the nursing home would yield a financial return to uncle Ben if all went well. It had been in operation only a few weeks, but there were signs already that it would prosper. As for the furnishing throughout Millie's new home, it was all a present from Joash and Agnes. "Don't feel embarrassed about it, Joseph. They *insisted.* They said God had given them plenty money, but that no money could ever pay for what God had done for them through you and me. However, they said that if you, Joseph, feel too proud to accept it, you can pay them whatever you wish; only you must remember that because they are in the furniture business they get everything at factory price, and they will only accept what *they* have paid."

Joseph sat and pondered. "Mother, I think that with your income and mine we'll manage to pay them in installments, especially since, as you say, the rates on this house are included with those of the nursing home."

Millie added, "Joseph, the Adairs love you. Mind not to hurt their feelings. Think a bit longer over it and then casually chat it over with Mr. Adair. I think you'll be interested in his point of view. He has a different way of looking at things since his conversion. The other day, after he'd been on the magistrate's bench and we happened to meet coming out of court together, he said, 'Rather comical isn't it, Millie, that young Joseph Kennard is my spiritual father? It makes you my spiritual grandmother!'"

Joseph was appropriately tickled at the idea.

"So, Joseph, he feels a peculiar obligation to his spiritual father and grandmother! He's a fine man. I never knew a better. He's not the kind who makes a big flash and then dulls off. The more you know him, the more he 'grows on you.' He's the best alderman in the borough. They would make him next year's mayor if he would let them."

"Where's Dorothy?" Joseph enquired.

"She's in Manchester today. It had to be today or she would have been with us to welcome you. It has to do with some new equipment for the nursing home. She should be back in about an hour now."

"Is she well?"

"Yes, but you'll see a big difference. She's a business-like matron now. Her experience as hospital 'sister' has taught her how to supervise as well as how to serve. She has two nurses working for her and already needs a third. And the full-time cleaning woman (one of my own Wednesday-ites) looks after this house as well; so we've little housework problem."

"How is Evelyn?"

"You're going to see a difference there, too, Joseph. When you were here last year she was too modest to tell you about herself; but what a clever young lady she is! She finished her schooling in the June before she was eighteen, and won a first prize. Then she did one year as a 'student teacher,' at the same time studying for her full teacher's diploma. She became fully certificated and has now done two years of teaching. She had her twenty-first birthday some weeks ago."

"Fancy! Evelyn Adair, twenty-one!"

"Ah, but there's something else; and I have a feeling you and Molly are responsible for it. She's such a smooth-tempered girl; but just under the surface there's grit and a will of her own. It sounds unlike Evelyn, but as a teacher she's a thorough disciplinarian! I don't mean harsh or demanding: she could never be that, even if she tried. She has the knack of getting obedience through what you might call kind firmness; but she can be dominatingly queenly if necessary. Anyway, here's the special announcement: With her parents' approval she's making a temporary break from teaching. She wants at least one year's commercial training. So she's in the office at the Adair Furnishing House!"

"But where do Molly and I come in?"

"I'm getting to that, Joseph. You remember that Monday night when Evelyn accepted the Saviour. Well, her conversion may not have been of the flamboyant sort, but it was real. In her case there couldn't be the drastic contrast between pre-conversion and post-conversion behaviour such as there is in the conversion of very worldly persons or those who have lived in vicious degradation. Yet what a difference in Evelyn! How can I put it? In her case it isn't the difference between an ugly yesterday and a bright new daybreak; it's been the passing of a gentle Spring into a lovely Summer."

Joseph listened keenly, still waiting to hear where he and Molly came in.

"It seems as though the very moment she accepted the Saviour she yielded her whole life to Him, so that almost at once the first blossoms began to appear, and then the early fruits. All that Molly said to her I don't know, but Molly is her ideal. Evelyn is studying her Bible harder than she ever studied for her teacher's diploma. She asked my advice on good books for young Christians. She's been taking singing lessons for some months now. She can't forget Molly's singing for you. Her voice is very different from Molly's. It's soprano, of course. But, Joseph, you're going to be impressed. There's nothing fancy or quivery about her voice, but it's just about the purest tone; the very kind for singing the Gospel. You know what I mean: there are many brilliant voices that are excellent in operas and oratorios, but they are useless for singing a simple, spiritual message. The voice calls so much attention to itself and to the singer that it gets in the way, and the message can't get through. I don't want to exaggerate; but I have seldom heard a more *appealing* voice than Evelyn's."

"That's wonderful, mother. Tell me more."

"Well, perhaps there are two other matters which it might be good to mention. Here's one: Mr. and Mrs. Adair will not be able to attend Harvey Street, as they are members at Brandon Street Congregational Church. In fact, Joash has been Sunday school superintendent there now for about eighteen years, as well as being a leading office-bearer. But Evelyn has gone fairly often to Harvey Street, and sung there several times. She teaches a class for them, too. She wants to join their membership but is afraid they might think it's because *you* are coming."

"I see," Joseph mused.

"The other matter concerns Molly Ainsworth. Did you know yet, that Molly has been accepted for training in Manchester, to become a city missionary?"

"*What!* Molly Ainsworth . . . into slum work!" It visibly shook him. "Are you really sure about that, mother?"

"Yes, Joseph. When I was with you at Ainsworths' last time she opened her heart to me about it. She got me telling her about my own years of mission work. I asked her if she felt a real urge from God to such work, because the only thing that keeps one going on despite the shocks and disappointments in such work is a deep assurance of God's call, and the love of Jesus welling up in your heart."

"What did she say, mother?"

"She hesitated at first, but bit by bit she came round to it. She was struggling against a big disappointment, in fact the hardest-hurting disappointment of her life. As she had laid it before the Lord in deep sadness and much prayer she had gradually felt He was saying to her: Fill the painful blank in your life by giving yourself for others; by forgetting yourself in saving them. It had cost her many tears, but she had decided: 'Yes, Lord.' "

"Did she say what that big disappointment was?" Joseph asked, looking disturbed.

"Not in so many words, Joseph, but from observation I guessed fairly surely. When I asked her directly, she admitted it, and entrusted it to my discretion. Joseph, do *you* know what that awful disappointment is?"

"I think so, now, mother. Poor, dear Molly! I was so blind, for so long. Then, when I understood, I didn't know how to behave. Believe me, mother, never did I knowingly do anything to awaken such devoted love. I feel honored and humbled that such a girl should ever love me as Molly does. It cuts me to think that I have caused her such pain."

"You needn't answer me now, Joseph; but are you *sure* you don't love Molly? I am asking only for her sake. You don't need me to tell you that Molly is no ordinary girl. She is not only the most strikingly beautiful girl I ever saw, except perhaps for one other, but she is pure worth all through. Any man who claims Molly Ainsworth's love in wedlock is rich for life. I had been with her only a few days before I was under her spell. All the folk here in Elmerton simply 'fell' for her, as the saying is. I'm not pleading on her behalf. No, Molly would shrivel in sensitive shame if she were to hear what I'm going to ask you. Joseph, are you *sure* you don't love Molly? It surprises me that you could be so long with her and *not* fall in love with her. Look, I've said far more than I intended. It's not fair to have mentioned this when you are only just back home, and not yet even unpacked. But I had a reason for mentioning it right away which I'll tell you later."

"Mother, I wish you could see inside my heart. I feel stricken with guilt, yet it's a helpless guilt. Now that I know what Molly's going to do because of me I wish I'd never been there. Do I love her, mother? Yes, I should say so! I think there's nobody else in all the world like her. I love to be with her. I love her face and her ways. But why is it?— I've never once thought of loving her as a sweetheart. Why should such a peerless girl as Molly go and fall in love with a less-than-average fellow like me? And why is it that I don't love her in the same way she loves me? Mother, I can think of only one reason, though perhaps you won't believe it. I think it's because I lost my heart years ago to someone else—someone whom I daren't name, whom I probably can never have."

"I understand, son. That's enough to convince me. Forgive me that we got into this so soon after your arrival. We needn't mention it any more. But just while we're on this subject let me add a thought which it's always good to keep in mind. We mustn't think that *everything* which happens is directly caused by God. God is *never* the author of anything evil, nor must we think that God directly *sends* some of the troubles and disappointments which come to us on earth. There is God's *permissive* will as well as His predetermining will; and within the bounds of that permissive will human free-will is given wide scope. But God foreknows and anticipates all that is permitted. Whatever He permits He purposes to overrule for our good, if only we will rightly respond to Him. Often, to a truly yielded heart like Molly's, He brings the purest joy out of the severest permissions. Have no wrong regrets about her. She's weathered the crisis. She's going to find what all such find. She'll have a joy far richer than *you* could ever have given her. In her loneliness she'll find a companionship sweeter than any that *you* could have given her, in a love far richer than yours, Joseph. She'll know the embrace of two arms far stronger and far tenderer than yours—and in the most sacred sense, far more *thrilling* then mere human arms. And, in the end, two hands far more affectionate than yours will put a crown on dear Molly's brow such as *you* could never have put there. So don't mistakenly grieve over her. Pray for her, that all this may be increasingly real to her. In years to come, when *I've* slipped away, you'll have learned that what I'm saying is true. But now let's see to your unpacking. Then we'll get tea ready."

Joseph did not commence at Harvey Street until the third Sunday in October. It was an encouraging start. Not unexpectedly, attendances were unusually good; for many persons felt that inasmuch as it was his first Sunday there they could be present to welcome him instead of being at their own churches: especially since he had been such a blessing a year earlier. Monday evening there was an "Induction Social" with many present, and at which local ministers voiced fraternal welcome. In the schoolroom refreshments were served, convivially baptized in a river of well-brewed tea, at which interdenominational baptism there was informal hobnobbing punctuated by friendly handshakes, the whole being seasoned with exuberant good wishes for the new ministry.

But as early as the end of his first month there, Joseph realized something of the problem hanging round an undenominational church in a deteriorated locality. Harvey Street was a pleasant church, but the building needed both outside repair and inside renovation. Most of the members were persons of low income. About one-quarter of the names on the membership roll needed deleting. Sunday mornings saw the church only about a quarter occupied. Evening attendances were not more than three hundred. Yet the officebearers and members kept assuring Joseph that already the numbers were twice the average prior to his coming. The fact was, that Joseph's gifts as a preacher had begun to attract; but the building and neighbourhood were a hindrance.

Joseph was not the kind who could drag on with a quasi-Stoic "stick-to-it" endurance. He believed that somehow, with such a Gospel and such a Bible and such a Saviour, something commensurate should be happening all the time. Yet as the weeks became months at Harvey Street he had the feeling of "flogging a dead horse." Most of the members and many of the newcomers were congratulatory handshakers, encouraging back-slappers, and fulsome adulators, but at the same time were lazy "sermon tasters." Mixed in among them were the inner few who were spiritually alive enough to share Joseph's concern for a heavenly quickening and an ingathering of souls to the Saviour, but they seemed impotent.

Though Joseph did not then realize it, he was on the verge of a discovery which largely revolutionized his ministry. For one thing, as he cogitated and prayed over his problem, he was going to learn the difference between a preacher and a prophet. There are many preachers, but few prophets. A preacher can always "say something," but a prophet has "something to say." A preacher is often popular, but a prophet never—at least not with the "Vanity Fair" of this world. An artistic preacher casts a spell, but a prophet is weighed with a "burden." The professional preacher aims to please people, but the Lord's prophet burns to *save* them. The true prophet is not an habitual debunker, always looking round for something else to denounce. Such continuous castigators never run out of topics, but they eventually run out of public influence—or run out of town. Yet the "man sent from God" will indeed cry, "Repent," and will warn of the "wrath to come." Besides comforting those who "mourn in Zion" he will put his axe to the roots of rotten trees. He will be no mere man-pleaser. So far, much of Joseph's preaching had been an earnest but pleasant song. There was little thunder of the prophet, nor were there enough tears of the watcher for souls.

Closest to him were his mother and Evelyn Adair. Millie was his straightest counselor. Evelyn was his most cooperative encourager.

One day at the noon meal Millie and Joseph fell to chatting about these things, when Millie asked, "Have you ever studied Paul as the pattern preacher, Joseph? I did, years ago, and the effect has never worn off. In his first Corinthian epistle he says, 'Brethren, when I came to you, I came not with excellency of speech or of wisdom, declaring unto you the testimony of God. For I determined not to know anything among you save Jesus Christ, and Him crucified. And I was with you in weakness, and in fear, and in much trembling. And my speech and my preaching were not with persuasive words of man's wisdom, but in demonstration of the Spirit and of power.' "

"Do you see, Joseph?—first he got right on the *message:* the Christ of the Cross. Then he got right on the *method:* "not in persuasive words of man's wisdom, but in the demonstration of the Spirit." He put our Lord Jesus right at the *front* of the picture; then put himself right *out* of it; then trusted solely in the power of the Holy Spirit. Joseph, have you managed to get yourself out of sight yet? Many a man is prepared to preach the Cross but he insists on doing it his own way instead of the Holy Spirit's. So he preaches the powerful Gospel powerlessly. When the people go away saying, 'What a fine preacher!' instead of 'What a dear Saviour!' success is failure."

All unpredictably, the second arrow to pierce Joseph's smart armour was shot from the bow of Elmerton's fairest archer, Evelyn; and even Robin Hood could not have shot it straighter.

Joseph was more in love with her than ever. She was more in love with him than ever. Neither knew for sure what was in the other's mind. Joseph wanted to be with Evelyn all the time, but valiantly forced himself not to be with her more than infrequently lest people should talk. Evelyn wanted to be with Joseph all the time, but kept out of his way lest her motive should be misunderstood. It was one of those tantalizing situations which overtake idealistic young lovers with delicate sensibilities. To Joseph, Evelyn looked more adorable than ever. To Evelyn, Joseph looked more handsomely manly than ever. Whenever they were together they sensed that there was something unspeakably special between them; yet he for one reason and she for another dare not say it in words. Many masculine eyes were on Evelyn, and Joseph was scared lest anyone else should run away with her. Many feminine eyes were on Joseph, and Evelyn was scared lest he should fall prey to some fair maid whose parents fain coveted him for her.

After a Sunday evening service they were alone for a few minutes, feeling again so awkwardly happy to be with each other, when Evelyn said, "Joseph, I hope mine is not the tongue of the flatterer, but I consider you easily the best preacher I've ever heard. Your ringing voice, your flow of words, your varied vocabulary, your vivid imagination, your methodical presentation: it's all so mentally satisfying."

Joseph, recalling Millie's words about Paul, felt ten feet tall, and, in the same instant a squirming pygmy; a big success and a disaster; a fine preacher but not a true prophet.

Evelyn continued, "I really mean that, Joseph. You know

I do. Would you be offended if I asked a favor?"

"Of course, not, Evelyn. What can it be?"

"Would you preach the same kind of sermon you preached when you brought me to the Saviour, last year?"

"The same *kind* of sermon?" Joseph was inwardly jabbed. "Could you explain more clearly?"

"I'm not sure that I can. Perhaps it's something I *feel* without having sorted it out sufficiently to put into words. I wonder if *you* feel it, too, Joseph? I mean: your preaching now is not the same as when you were here for the mission a year ago. It is, and yet it isn't. Of course, you've studied such a lot, and your preaching is so intellectual—so book-ish. I suppose the fault is in myself—lagging behind."

"If there's any fault, Evelyn, it's not in you."

"How like you, Joseph! But I've thought of something which perhaps explains. When I go away now after hearing you, I find myself thinking of *you,* and how gifted you are. When I listened to you a year ago (please don't be hurt) I never saw you. You made me see JESUS—until I complete-ly lost sight of you, and you brought me to HIM. Oh, I can never thank you enough!"

The arrow was dead on target. Joseph limped home sore wounded. He went upstairs early, flung himself down at his bedside, and laid the gaping wound open to the great Heal-er. "Lord, you know how I deserve this wound. It hurts; but that is nothing compared with the way my proud selfism has wounded *You.* How could I have done it? What is this wound compared with those in Your hands and feet? Saviour, give me such a vision of Calvary that it will shame 'self' out of my preaching—for ever. Please heal this wound of mine, but leave the scar plainly there, always to remind me. . . ."

On into the hours of the night he prayed. Metaphorically, he took the hammer and drove the nails right through his wriggling, intellectual pride. It hurt. It always does. Self-love never dies easily. But before dawn the crucifixion was effected, and Joseph was pleading now that he might be a man "filled with the Spirit." When the sun rose, Joseph's physical tiredness was offset by a spiritual infusion from heaven; and after that night-time wrestle Joseph Kennard was truly in the Pauline succession.

TWENTY-ONE
Blow, Wind of Heaven!

Months went by. Joseph's night and day longing, now, was that there might break out at Harvey Street a real spiritual revival in which hundreds should be saved, and the whole locality affected. He was learning big lessons. After the earlier weeks with many transitory visitors, attendances dropped a little, but then came comforting indications that perhaps a steady work might develop. Over a period of perhaps five months there had been eighteen professions of conversion, which, however, seemed painfully slow after the outright evangelistic missions which Joseph had been used to holding. He knew that he could always attract newcomers by a certain kind of pleasing preaching, even though Harvey Street church was in a deteriorated neighbourhood; but what about the spreading crowds of godless outsiders all around the church's doors? It needed something more than gifted preaching to bring *them* in.

But that was just where an acute problem arose. The inner body of Harvey Street members were descendents of its socially classy days. They were charmed by Joseph's preaching qualities but they did not want to be churned into concern for the godless outside. They had succumbed to a paralyzing smugness and did not want to be disturbed. If

Joseph challenged them too directly they resented it; nor did they conceal the fact that they did not want the socially lower people of the immediate neighbourhood brought in. Joseph determined, however, that no social distinctions should blind him to the equal value of all human souls; and he aimed to draw the more local outsiders in, if possible.

Among other things he issued handbills all over the district announcing a special Sunday evening topic: WHY COME TO CHURCH? That may not sound an exciting title, but it happened to be a subject widely discussed in the press at the time. It led to a major change in Joseph's thinking.

He anticipated no difficulty in presenting Scriptural reasons why people should come to church; but he soon ran into problems. He could not find *any* reason stated in the New Testament why outsiders should come to church. True, there were good reasons given why Christian believers should come, such as Hebrews 10:25, "Not forsaking the assembling of ourselves together"; but where were reasons given why unbelievers should come?

He wrote in haste to a society in London for every available pamphlet on that subject. When a batch of twenty or more came, he heaved a sigh of relief; but soon his dilemma was worse than before. The pamphlets gave cogent reasons why *Christians* should come to church, but again not one why *unbelievers* should. That drove Joseph to examine the New Testament itself on the matter. Hour after hour he pored over its pages. It resulted in his surprising discovery of something which is so plain in the New Testament that it ought never *need* discovering. He marvelled afterwards that he could have been so blind to it.

The New Testament nowhere promises full churches. It nowhere tells us to build churches. The Apostles and early evangelists did not build churches, at least not in the brick-and-mortar sense. Doubtless they had to find convenient meeting-places, but any thought of brick and mortar was decidedly secondary. The church of the first days did not spend itself trying to get people inside buildings. It was all the while going out, going out, going out, with a saving message. Persecution only served to scatter the witnesses; it could not silence them. The Christianity of the first days loved the open air and the neighbourhood doorsteps. It was evangelistically outgoing and missionary. Its defense was attack!

Joseph grasped that the distinctive function of the Christian Church in this world is that of *witness-bearing*—to a glorious Saviour and great evangelical truths by which men and communities are saved. Therefore, as it was with the early church, so should it be today: there must be a going out to the people. The Church of the first days was far from being a newly opened store with a nice window display and the shopkeeper inside waiting for folk to come in and buy. It was a go-ahead firm of distributors with enthusiastic representatives bent on capturing the world's markets. Many of our churches today (mused Joseph) have the shop idea. They try to stock the window attractively, then hope for folk to come in and buy. Why wonder that so little business is done in some of them, or that the shopkeeper and his assistants doze into slumber?

As he thought the matter through, Joseph saw the *true* place of church buildings. The true Church was not buildings, though from Apostolic days onwards buildings were a necessary *strategy*. Christian forces needed such centerpoints for concerted operation. But a Christian church was never meant to be only "a place of *worship*." Worship and *witness:* Yes. Worship *only:* No. Much less was any local Christian church meant to be a covered-in nursery for the rearing of delicate hot-house plants, or a hospital for spiritual invalids. It should be a barracks for training soldiers in the fight against the world, the flesh, and the devil. Joseph saw the New Testament ideal: every Christian a soulwinner, and every local church a center of vital fellowship for evangelistic outreach. How right was John Wesley: the folk outside will not come in until the folk inside go out!

Another big lesson Joseph learned at that time was, that although God will use all a man's gifts and academic degrees He will not be dependent on any of them. If a scholarly Paul will lay his gifts and learning in prostrate surrender at the feet of Jesus, how mightily he can be used! But if Paul's gifts are *not* so yielded, God will bypass them and use an *un*scholarly fisherman Peter.

Still another thing which Joseph now saw more clearly was the difference between evangelism and revival. Evangelism is the constant obligation of the Church; but supernatural revival is the sovereign act of *God*. Therefore revival cannot be "worked up"; it must be "prayed down." How vital, then, is prayer! Certainly, prayer must be accompanied by willing work, for praying without working is disguised laziness; but on the other hand, so-called "Christian service" without prayer is an impertinence. Yes, if a church is to experience spiritual reviving there must be prayer, earnest and continual. Organizing can never be a substitute for interceding. There is a big difference between a church which is humanly galvanized and a church which is divinely energized. There must be a praying church if there is to be an answering God.

But again, Joseph reflected, if there is to be prevailing prayer, there must first be a putting things right among those who pray. There were wrong things at Harvey Street church: divisive cliques, jealousies, rivalries, long-persisting grudges or animosities between members, secret worldliness, cinema-going and theatre-going. Attendance at the Tuesday evening congregational prayer meeting was revealingly small. There seemed no concern about the thousands outside who knew practically nothing of the Gospel, and who were living godless, corrupt lives, "without God and without hope." How *could* there be an outpouring of "the Spirit from on high" until all these hindrances were cleared away?

Yet despite these things God seemed to be giving tokens of His readiness to bless. For some weeks Joseph had been conscious of new power in preaching. New vistas were shaping up in young Joseph's mind. There was another factor, too, which powerfully contributed to his reconstructed thinking. Evelyn had been reading a booklet by an American minister who told how spiritual revival came to *his* church. She was eager that Joseph should read it. Had he been a hundredfold busier he could never have said "No" to *her.* So he read it, perhaps more to please his longed-for Evelyn than from any other motive—for which he chastised himself afterward.

The American pastor described the downtown church where he ministered, the deteriorated locality, the diminished membership, the genial but lackadaisical attitude, his own efforts to draw people in by able preaching. It all seemed a very replica of Harvey Street, Elmerton. Joseph found himself asking, "However did you happen to find *this* pamphlet, Evelyn?"

The young American minister told how he became weary with blustering round in zealous inefficiency until at last he stopped short and rather desperately vowed that he would not enter his pulpit again until he knew by experience the promised enduement of the Holy Spirit. There were hours of intense praying in secret, of heart-searching, of struggling to the point of utter surrender, and of waiting, waiting, waiting. But the empowering envelopment came, and that young minister was never the same again. Nor was his church. He began to get the leaders and some of the understanding members low before God in similarly tenacious self-yielding and prayer for revival. By and by the whole band of believers was in the gracious grip of divine visitation, and scores of people were won for the Saviour.

Toward the end the pamphlet read: "The pulpit today needs broken men; not men with broken backbone, but with broken hearts over those who are unsaved; men who, through such brokenness and deliverance from egocentricity, have shed the last rag of professionalism. There can never be real spiritual power where the pulpit is a display-pedestal for ministerial ability. If there is to be a renewal of Pentecostal power among us, and a soul-saving work in any large way, we need *men who cannot be seen.*"

"Men who cannot be seen! Evelyn, that is a deep sword-thrust!"

In the margin of a page which told how the American pastor gathered an inner circle of likeminded members round him in a compact to wait on God for revival, Evelyn had written, "What about Harvey Street? We could at least begin with you and your mother and me. I'm sure the three would soon become thirty."

As, long ago, king Hezekiah spread Sennacherib's letter before God, so did young Joseph Kennard spread that pamphlet before Him. And, as heaven responded to royal Hezekiah, so was it with the inexperienced young minister who now "laid his all on the altar" in an irrevocable, lifelong, full surrender to Christ.

Singularly enough, when Joseph reached that full-surrender point—a surrender including all his feelings toward Evelyn, he found himself praying, as never before, with quiet ease, that God would give him the love of Evelyn's heart, and unite them in service for their Saviour-King. On that issue, however, the will of God and the scheming of Satan ran into head-on collision, as later events soon began to indicate!

Ten months or more had slipped away. Joseph had shepherded the Harvey Street flock through a Winter, a Spring, a Summer. The annual "Wakes Week" holidays were past. September was half through, with its rustling hints among the leaves that another Autumn was stealing in behind it. For weeks Joseph had been priming his people for what he now did. He had been opening up what the Scripture teaches about a deeper experience of Christ, of victory over sin, and infilling by the Holy Spirit. He had also sought to arouse concern about the godlessness, drunkenness, immorality, and crime in Elmerton, and the plight of the unsaved crowds all around the church's doors.

There was a new note of authority, urgency, compassion, in his preaching. It was truly Christ-centered and Bible-based. It was logical, eloquent, varied, lucid, direct—in a word, as "Kennard" as ever, but now it had new glow and grip; it was challenging, provocative, urgent, healthily disturbing. Most thanked God for it. Some winced. Others were not sure. But attendances kept up, and were steadily augmented.

One Sunday evening Joseph said, "Most of you will have sensed how burdened I am that a spiritual revival should come to us; that all of us who love the Saviour should come under its power, and that hundreds of souls should be brought to salvation. Perhaps some of us secretly think that this neighbourhood is too hardened in sin to be changed; and possibly some of you dislike my efforts to stimulate activity toward winning our Harvey Street area for Christ. Please try to be sympathetic. I myself am prone to the temptation to settle down and just go on in smooth unconcern about the thousands of unsaved all around us. But if the Bible is true, they are on the 'broad way' to an 'outer darkness' on the other side of the grave. I am now asking that all who share my concern will wait behind after this service, so that I may make certain suggestions. Feel no sensitiveness if you cannot or do not stay. Let the love of Jesus be in our hearts, and let no one be looking round to see who stays and who does not."

Nearly two hundred stayed; and this in brief is what Joseph said. "If the Bible is the Word of God, then on the other side the grave is a judgment day, a heaven, a hell. Human beings, apart from the Saviour, are unsaved and going to that judgment. God loves all of us, and through the Cross made atonement, that all might be saved. Harvey Street district is full of people who know nothing about this salvation. Must we not somehow tell them or be fearfully guilty? Our unconcern is a sure sign that we ourselves need spiritual reviving.

"What can we do? First, we must pray, and prayer for revival will be the uppermost pleading in our congregational prayer meetings from now onwards. Next, cottage prayer meetings are being arranged. See Miss Evelyn Adair for dates and homes. Next, beginning on this coming Thursday there will be a series of studies on methods of soul-winning. Next, we are organizing a visitation of every house and family throughout our area, with Gospel tracts, once each month. Mrs. Hattie Nicholson is in charge of that. Next, along with our Thursday studies we shall train members to go out in pairs to visit people's homes, seeking to win them for the Saviour. Next, we shall try to hold open-air Gospel meetings up and down the neighbourhood when weather permits. That is being organized by Mr. and Mrs. Bob Armitage. Finally we purpose to hold an all-night prayer meeting for revival. As many of you work long hours, the date of that meeting will be fixed as helpfully as possible, and will be announced next Lord's Day. There is nothing magic about an all-night prayer meeting, but it shows God we are in earnest, and it keeps us together long enough amid night-time quietness to get really low before God in unhurried intercession."

During succeeding weeks all this was gradually set in motion. The idea of all-night prayer meetings was considered fanatical by some. Others supported it. The first was on a Friday, beginning 10:30 p.m. About one hundred and twenty came. After an opening hymn and prayer, Joseph read out twelve Bible promises in which God pledges to answer united praying by His people, especially prayer in the name of Jesus. Then the meeting was thrown open for prayer. At intervals all present sang a hymn; then they went back to prayer. There were gaps when no one prayed audibly, so Joseph reminded them that during such there should be continuing *silent* prayer, with all hearts blended in one, unifying cry for God to send a spiritual outpouring. The meeting seemed earnest but not more than ordinary; and perhaps some wondered *why*, after all, an all-night of it.

At midnight refreshments were served. Then prayer was resumed. Again, prayers and silent intervals; then a much longer spell of voiceless interceding. About 2:00 a.m. a hush fell, but it was an intense hush in which they all felt a new concentratedness and an enveloping Presence. Now, also, whispered or murmured praying could be heard everywhere, even some low sobbing and an occasional groan.

It must have been about 2:45 when a clear feminine voice broke forth: "Mr. Kennard, may I say something to the meeting?" It was Mrs. Matthew Boyd, a member of the Mothers' Class. All present looked up and listened. Tears were streaming down Rachel Boyd's face as she began, "Friends, here we are, praying for the Lord to send revival, but how can it come when there are wrong things among us? It's over two years now since I spoke to Mrs. Stimson, the secretary of our class. She did something at which I took umbrage. I've paid her back by unkindness and saying hurtful things about her. How can I expect God to hear me until I put that right?"

Mrs. Stimson was in the company. Rachel spoke across the meeting, "Martha, I'm sorry. I've been all wrong. Even when they were crucifying Jesus He said, 'Father, forgive them . . .' and yet I've been unforgiving over a bit of a thing that isn't worth mentioning! I should have been loving and forgiving instead of touchy and nasty. I'm sorry, so sorry. I love you, Martha. Will you forgive me?"

Martha and her husband were some pews away. Martha came hurrying out into the aisle to where Rachel was. "Oh, Rachel, while I've been praying here the same thing has been convicting me. It's *I* who ought to be asking forgiveness of *you*." At once they were in tearful embrace, but the tears of contrition soon became tears of rejoicing that love had triumphed over mean spite.

What followed would be difficult to describe. People all over the gathering were breaking down in tears over the wrong things in their lives: their grudges, untruthfulness, prayerlessness, wrong motives and pious shams. The whole meeting became a confessional to the one great heavenly Priest and Saviour. Different ones were getting up and going to each other to ask forgiveness and to embrace in new affection. All kinds of animosities were rolled away. Joseph looked on in wonder, realizing that a heavenly breath had filled the place. Evelyn sat there thrilled and radiant, tears flowing down her face. The very heavens seemed opened, and the presence of the risen Lord swept upon them in a manner so overwhelming, they were all filled with joyful awe.

Eventually one of the deacons got up to speak: Mr. Theodore Manson, one of the most earnest of the office-bearers. His face was shining. "Friends," he said, "unless I'm much mistaken, revival has already begun. But there's been something on my mind for days now, that I'd like to share with you. In the eleventh chapter of John we're told how Jesus raised Lazarus from the grave. Some verses later it says that many poeple, after that, came to Bethany not just to see Jesus, but to see Lazarus whom Jesus had raised. Friends, we ought to pray that *another* Lazarus might get raised from the dead, here in Elmerton—some outstanding sinner everybody knows. If such a man got mightily converted, my! wouldn't folk come in to see Lazarus again!"

The idea caught on like a spark in dry timber: "Lord send us a Lazarus." Meanwhile about thirty members who had *not* been at the meeting got the surprise of their lives when members who *had* been at it called round with disarming humility to ask forgiveness for wrong things said or done; to clear up misunderstandings and end estrangements. Old sores were healed, and breaches repaired. The Spirit of God was moving. Those who had not been at that all-night prayer meeting now wished they *had* been.

The next Sunday, that nocturnal prayer meeting was all the talk. Both morning and evening Joseph preached on Lazarus—beginning each time by quoting deacon Manson's words, "Lord, send in a Lazarus."

The attendance at the Tuesday congregational prayer meeting was larger than hitherto. The urge to pray was stronger. The desire after spiritual victory and inwrought holiness was vocal. How the people now prayed for revival! How they pleaded that God would visit the neighbourhood and raise some Lazarus as a great sign! Many members asked for more prayer meetings. Soon, nearly every night there was a praying group in one room or another. Week after week they prayed that God would raise a Lazarus; that He would save the worst sinner in town.

God did! The man came, inexplicably (so it seemed) of his own accord! He was a dreadful character; a rough giant of a man, employed at the stone quarry on the south side of town. Everybody knew him. Nobody ever expected he would be any better. So far as the man himself could remember, he had never been to a religious service, except in jail. He was the terror of the neighbourhood, and did most extraordinary things out of sheer devilry. But after reading one of the Gospel tracts now being distributed he blundered in out of sheer curiosity. He had not the foggiest idea what he was coming in to see or to hear, but he came; and some of those who had prayed most importunately for a

Lazarus were scared when he appeared! They thought he was concocting some mischief, and almost forgot he might be the answer to prayer!

However, what he saw and heard he "liked" and said he would come again. And now some of the Christians were eager to pray with him, but they got no further than this, that he was willing to "sign the pledge"—not to drink any more. When they talked to him about being converted he seemed confused, and said, "No, no; not just now. One thing at a time." So he went out, and they thought they had lost him.

Two weeks went by. It began to seem unlikely that he would come again. But much prayer, now, was being prayed specifically for him. He came again!—to a Sunday evening service. He heard the love of God and the message of the Gospel clearly and earnestly presented. He also heard Joseph say, at the end, "If there are those here tonight who are seeking to get right with God, to find forgiveness and cleansing and eternal salvation, by receiving Jesus as Saviour, we invite them to come to the communion rail here as we sing a closing hymn."

The hymn was started, but it hardly got sung. The hearts of the folk in Harvey Street church nearly stood still as they saw the big, rough fellow in his working clothes (for he had no "Sunday best") walk down the aisle and fling himself on his knees at the communion-rail. That night he became truly converted; in a spiritual sense "raised from the dead." He was a saved man!

Next morning he told all his workmates what had happened. Then, men who before his conversion would never have dared to risk his anger began to persecute him cruelly. Yet he stood well, until one day, as they were blasting, his bar slipped and jammed his finger; and before he was aware, an oath escaped his lips. The men around him laughed derisively; but their laughter was only for a moment—he was evidently hurt. They released his finger and wanted to bandage it. But with tears dripping down his face, and with a broken voice, he said, "Nay, I've a bigger wound than this. We'll have that seen to first." And, surrounded by the men who had heard him swear, he prayed

THE HIDDEN HAND

with earnest simplicity that the dear Saviour who had saved
him would cleanse away the stain of his unintending sin.
Then he got up and said, "It's alright, mates. God has
forgiven me. Now we'll have this bandaged up."

The effect was beyond words. During the next few
weeks at least a dozen other men from the quarry started
coming to the meetings. The news of his conversion spread
around. People everywhere wanted to see this Lazarus
whom Jesus had raised to a new life. When it was announced that he would tell the story of his conversion, they
flocked from far and near. Whenever he publicly told what
God was doing for him, the church was packed—largely
from around the Harvey Street church!

But there were other Lazaruses! The younger folk of
Harvey Street had started open-air Gospel meetings up and
down the area. Occasionally Joseph was at them. One evening, as he was preaching at a corner near Harvey Street a
drunken man lunged inside the ring and threatened to floor
him. It was a tense test. The man was scarcely taller than
Joseph, but oh, his girth! As Pat Flanagan, the Irish deacon,
said afterwards, he was "a Sabbath day's journey round"!
Several in the open-air group knew him, and were the more
alarmed. He lived in Somerset Street. Formerly, during his
army career, he was champion boxer of his regiment: and
now, whenever he was going home tipsy, every door in
Somerset Street was locked!

He leaned heavily against Joseph, a ponderous fist raised
menacingly. "Shut up!—or I'll knock yer blasted head off!"
he bawled in his harsh, throaty voice. If ever Joseph
grasped that text, "*Watch* and pray," he did at that instant!
However, the blow never fell, but a big crowd gathered—
and heard the Gospel. Six weeks later that same man was
converted on that very spot; and a few weeks later again he
gave his testimony for Jesus! It was sensational. His transformation of character was marvelled at. When he gave his
story in the church the whole of Somerset Street came in!

Another Lazarus, though of a very different sort, was the
man with the wooden leg: Charlie Hacket the boot repairer,
lower down Harvey Street. He was no drunkard or gam-
bler, but he was Elmerton's most loquacious orator in

swear-words. He was as jolly and jocular as he was blasphemously profane, and as witty as he was wanton. In a way, too, he was popular, for he did a "reet gud job" (everybody said) in "mendin' boots and clogs." Nobody ever dreamed that "don't-care-a-damn" Charlie would ever get scared about his sins and get converted. But he did, one Sunday night in Harvey Street; and all his witty jocundity got converted along with him. It all became baptized in useful service for the Saviour. Many were the comical things he said in meetings, without realizing how comical they were. He became one of the unforgettable "characters" at Harvey Street.

Another Lazarus was Jock Yates. Harvey Street was three-quarters of a mile long. In it there were four saloons. Jock Yates owned one of them. He was as godless as the bleariest boozer whom he ever served with drink. One morning a big notice appeared in the saloon window: THIS SALOON PERMANENTLY CLOSED. THE OWNER HAS BEEN CONVERTED. GLORY BE TO GOD!

All these things could not happen without wide publicity. The Elmerton press reported them week after week. Everybody now knew young Joseph Kennard and "the revival at Harvey Street." The building grew too small. On Sunday evenings there had to be two services: one at 5:30 and the other at 7:15, both packed to the doors. While the second was in progress many who had been at the first stayed on in the school rooms with testimony and fellowship groups. There was now a spirit of humble and warmhearted cooperativeness animating the members. People were getting converted week after week, and new members were being received in. Workers were being trained for dealing with the many "enquirers." Millie was in charge of the women, with Evelyn as her unflagging lieutenant. They were wonderful days. They meant much work for Joseph, and were perhaps too exciting at times to be healthy for a young minister. But Millie kept a firm hand on him. He learned how to parcel the work out among willing helpers. He kept good hours, and let nothing interfere with his set times of waiting on God in prayer. He continued his morning "keep fit" exercises in Ashgrove Park, and maintained a healthy steadiness amid the effervescent enthusiasms of the thrilling spiritual upheaval.

The revival became the topic in all the other churches. Some of them were reaping benefits, for Joseph tried to divert his overplus to other churches where the ministers were truly evangelical. Some ministers of the "modern" type were superiorly amused. Two of them, hearing that another all-night prayer meeting was to be held, decided to attend together, "just for the joke of it," to see what this "revival nonsense" was.

As before, the meeting began at 10:30. The two clerical skeptics (not wearing their usual ministerial dress) sat in the last pew under the rear gallery in order to see better everything that happened. One was an Anglican, the other a Congregationalist. They had a merry time of concealed funmaking at some of the comical things they saw and heard.

First there was hearty hymn singing, then a brief opening prayer, followed by a short Scripture reading on which Joseph made pithy comments. After that came a ten-minute period for called-out prayer requests, and perhaps two or three spontaneous testimonies, or reports of what the Lord was doing in hearts and homes. As there was a little hesitancy Joseph asked, "Who's going to break the ice?" Still a momentary indecision, then the wooden-legged boot repairer, Charlie Hacket jumped up. "Pastor, *I'll* break the ice! I'll stick mi wooden leg through it!"—and bang went his wooden foot on the pew floor! It almost broke the wood as well as the ice! But after that there was a flow of eager testimonies about hearts healed and homes blessed. At 11:20 the meeting was turned over to praying.

The praying started slowly. It was earnest, but there was little exciting about it. The two skeptical clergymen glanced at each other in a way which said, "Pretty tame, so far."

Refreshments were served at midnight. Afterward prayer was resumed. Some who had prayed before prayed again. The burden was for revival in fuller, deeper measure; for souls to be set free from the bondage of sin; and for the whole of England to be shaken by a mighty visitation from heaven, like the great revival in Wales. And now they were praying for a deeper work of the Holy Spirit among themselves. The praying was livelier. It seemed as though everybody was being moved to pray. Sometimes two or three were praying at the same time, but no one seemed to mind, and there was not the slightest confusion.

Admittedly, as those Lancashire emotions were stirred, some amusing prayers trotted out. The two supercilious gentlemen of the cloth did not lack fodder for their amusement. One earnest sister prayed for the conversion of someone she had brought to church: "Lord, if one spark of saving truth has been deposited in her heart, blessed Lord, *water* that spark!"

A man who was praying that some obstinate unbeliever might be set free from Satan's power prayed, "Mighty Lord, give the devil such a knock-out blow that he'll remain unconscious for all eternity!"

Somebody prayed for an aged member who was weary with the weight of years, "Comfort and cheer 'im, Lord. He's got one foot in th' grave already, and t'other will be there soon!"

In those days almost as many women wore bonnets as those who wore hats. Some of the dear sisters who got carried away in prayer for the unsaved kept fingering their bonnets until by the time they sat down their bonnets were back to front!

Why deny it?—our two peeping parsons saw and heard enough to tickle their ulnar nerve. They exchanged looks of disdainful amusement from time to time. But were those night time perseverers in prayer the kind of people to regard lightly? Many of them were well educated and highly intelligent persons. Most of them, although very ordinary, working-class folk, were as level-headed as they were now spiritually in earnest. They knew what it was to have dealings with the Almighty. They had proved the effectuality of prayer in the name of Jesus. They were under no silly religious delusion. They knew what they believed, and *why*. They meant business, and believed God would answer their faith.

About 2:15 a.m., as in the first all-night prayer meeting,

an unmistakably supernatural hush fell upon them all. The vocal praying ceased. Everywhere was silence. No one needed to be told: in that hush was a Presence. Praying had given place to listening—listening to the footfall of Someone who invisibly filled the whole building. It was mysterious, subduing, awe-inspiring. It was overpoweringly *real*. Everybody was held in its invisible grip. The stillness could be *felt*. In those moments it was impossible to pray; one could only worship, wonder, adore—with prostrated heart. But, oh, it brought such a luminous awareness of the risen *JESUS*, such a sense of engulfing compassion, such an atmosphere of heavenly calm, of mind-elevating holiness and power. The *KING* was moving among His guests. His sceptre was touching this one and that one—healing, comforting, strengthening, revealing, reassuring.

And now, in that pervading Presence, prayer became the most vital of all realities. Doubts expired, and faith leapt heavenwards. Someone with a deep voice cried, "Glory!" Someone else was saying, "Jesus! Jesus!" All over the gathering there was a low murmur of worshiping, weeping, adoring, pleading. A man stood up, hands stretched toward heaven, and with tears raining down his cheeks began pleading for the salvation of his two wayward sons. A young woman was sobbing out poignant concern for her unconverted parents. Oh, it was prayer again now! And what praying! It seemed like storming heaven. Some who prayed were pleading so obliviously of all others present, it seemed as though they would pray themselves right into heaven! The whole building seemed alive with *GOD!*

In that back pew under the rear gallery there was no more peeping. Two stricken sinners sat there with their heads heavily in their hands. Presently one of them groaned, "Oh, God, forgive me!" A few minutes later the other wept, "Lord Jesus, forgive me, too." The two of them sank from the pew seat on to their knees and began struggling in prayer for forgiveness and cleansing from shameful failures in their lives, and for deliverance from professionalism, intellectual snobbery, prayerlessness, superficiality, egotism, pride, jealousy, carelessness about souls. Taken by melting surprise, they found themselves in a new way at the foot of the Cross. The Presence in that church was indeed their risen Lord, but the nail-scars were still in His hands and feet; and those wounds now shone with a piercing glory-light which exposed unbearably to those two men the ugliness of their self-centeredness and ministerial superciliousness.

Too soon, for some, gray dawn came and peered in through the church windows. Joseph announced that the meeting would soon be ending, but that any of those present could either leave or stay according as work or home duties required. A few tiptoed out. Most stayed until the concluding doxology.

Admittedly some of them looked a bit tired. Maybe, too, there was a touch of understandable reaction as they now wrenched themselves away to face the mundane humdrum of another working-class day. But offsettng any physical tiredness was an inner glow and gladness such as only vivid communion with God can bring. They went forth, a band of disciples with singing hearts. They had "met with God"! They had "seen the Lord"! Their cup was "running over"!

And from that back pew under the rear gallery two ministers slipped out to the chilly street never to be the same men again. That night was the greatest turning-point in their ministries. Soon afterwards two Elmerton congregations were asking, "What's happened to our minister?"

Yes, they were wonderful days. At times, for Joseph, they could have been almost as exhausting as they were exhilarating; but he was learning as never before the meaning of Isaiah's words, "They that wait upon the Lord shall renew their strength; they shall mount up with wings as eagles; they shall run and not be weary; they shall walk and not faint." Joseph and Millie—and Evelyn were seeing the desire of their hearts realized: heaven-sent revival had swept down on Harvey Street. The heavenly Wind was blowing. The valley of dry bones had "come alive"! The saints had taken down their harps from the willows. The songs of Zion were in all the streets!

TWENTY-TWO
Snake in the Grass

As history rolls on in the yearly cycle of human pathos there is no day but has its hour of pain, no song but has its note of haunting sadness, no garden but encloses some noxious weed, no rose of richest hue but has some thorn amid its leaves, no sky of clearest blue but holds the hidden vapour of some cloud, no hour of honest mirth but somewhere eyes are blinded by tears of pity, grief, or shame, no soul, however noble, but has some secret strife.

It is likewise true that there is never a genuine reality without some deceptive counterfeit; never a spiritual revival without its pretenders, cranks and adversaries; never a soul-saving work of God without some counter-move by the scheming prince of darkness. Why must such things be? why always a putrid fly in the apothecary's ointment? a traitorous Judas among loyal apostles? a bitter tear in every cup of merry pleasure? That is a mystery six thousand years old, and the solution still awaits a *novus ordo seclorum* in a promised "age to come."

How well-practiced is the arch-deceiver! How cleverly the dragon disguises as an angel of light! How craftily he picks out godly leaders as his objects of concerted attack! If only he can get one high-souled Job ("none like him on earth") to "curse God and die," or if only he can trip one royal David ("man after God's own heart") into the mire through a naked Bathsheba, he has won a damaging victory worth a thousand others.

So was it with young Joseph Kennard. You cannot have a soul-saving awakening such as transformed Harvey Street church and neighbourhood without provoking reprisal from the master-mind of evil. Joseph was leader, so he was the prime target. As, centuries ago, the king of Syria commanded his captains, "Fight neither with small nor great, save only with the king of Israel," so did the contriving Beelzebub train his ruiners on Joseph. He knew that any obvious, frontal attack of temptation upon a now truly consecrated young man like Joseph Kennard would be useless. There must be some subtle stratagem by which to entangle him and dishonour his character, break his spirit, and spoil his usefulness right at the beginning of his ministry.

Satan's crafty device was not by way of the usual "triangle," with two lovers both after one person of the other sex. It was a quadrangle. At one corner was Joseph Kennard. At another was Evelyn Adair. At the third was Adrian Raglan. At the fourth was Effie Crawley. Both Joseph and Adrian wanted Evelyn. Both Evelyn and Effie wanted Joseph. Adrian decided to frustrate Joseph. Effie decided to frustrate Evelyn.

Adrian Raglan was tall, straight as a flagpole, well-built, good-looking, the embodiment of young masculinity, vain as a peacock, and perkily proud as a groomed poodle. His versatility, volubility and volatility gave him a windy prominence in any company. In all the youth and social activities at Harvey Street he could be seen bobbing up and down like a cork on choppy waters—and with about as much weight of character. He would fain impress people as "a man's man," but inwardly he was a silly "lady's man," an inveterate worshiper at the shrine of feminine charms. He loved to be the social *bon vivant,* the jovial companion—especially to the girls. A pretty face, coy looks, roving eyes, kissy lips, appealing figure and legs, prostrated his philandering mind and knocked him off balance. Whatever brilliance there may have been inside his head was exceeded by the brilliance on top of it, where his well-oiled, scented black hair shone like polished ebony and was smooth enough for a fly to slip on. Whether such persons ever develop the capacity to look beyond mere "skin-deep" beauty to that inner charm of moral worth on which true love fastens is doubtful. Perhaps some do, but by then it is usually too late: wrong choices have been made. One of the things Millie had said to boy Joseph was, "beware of very beautiful women"; and for a time it had made him chary of his innocently immaculate Evelyn.

Perhaps we may concede that Adrian Raglan was about halfway to being "a man's man," for he certainly was already a *boy's* man. The younger boys thought he was *"it"*; and well they might, for he was their captain—handsome leader of their Boys' Brigade troop. Both the Boys' Brigade and Adrian Raglan were at Harvey Street before Joseph's advent there. That Adrian was the *wrong* leader, Joseph had soon sensed, but so far he had not been able to do anything about it.

Adrian was the pampered son of two better-class parents who were commendably "religious" but not spiritually minded. They had no real experience of soul-saving union with Christ. They and their son were very "proper" members at Harvey Street. They preferred religious decorum to unorthodox vitality. There was that about Joseph's preaching which captivated them, and they were truly glad to see the influx of many more people; but this "Hallelujah" and "Praise the Lord" business, this revival disturbance, this mixing-in of a lower, "mill class" type of people, this going into an enquiry room to get "saved" through the "blood," was objectionable double-Dutch to them.

As for Effie Crawley, she was of a different brood. There was nothing obtrusive about her, though she did have a way of worming herself in. She was rather tall and elegantly slim; always modestly dressed, usually in quieter shades. Her dark hair, although it did not have luster, was neatly stylish, somehow matching her even features and pale complexion. In a group she did not command particular notice, yet near at hand she had ample appeal. Her eyes were deep-set and contemplative. There was a lady-like reserve about her; a velvety softness; an almost mousy shyness, and a slight huskiness of voice which was strangely attractive in conjunction with her other distinctives.

She had started coming to Harvey Street about a month after Joseph settled there. Though a regular attender, she was not yet a member. She and Adrian Raglan were parallel in this: they each had an inordinate "crush" on someone of the opposite sex. Adrian wanted to be popular with all the young women, but beyond that he had eyes for none save Evelyn Adair. He eyed her gluttonously from head to feet. The sight of her ravished his sanguine mind. He determined to "get her." On the other hand, Effie Crawley had no concern whether she was a draw to other young men or not: her Delilah eyes were on one prey only: the handsome young Joseph Kennard. Adrian knew how Effie felt about Joseph; and *she* knew how *he* felt about Evelyn. This drew them together as sly consorts.

For long enough, now, Joseph and Evelyn had known for certain that they meant something very deeply dear to each other. They still avoided being together too often lest it should cause comment or hinder in any way the work at Harvey Street. Yet they could not help looking at each other in a way which unmistakably indicated tenderest thoughts. They both wanted to *speak* their love, but each had a disconcerting reason for dumbness. Joseph, on his part, was now convinced that his murdered father was not his *real* father. But he also knew that he was not born before his mother married Mike. Was he, then, the illegitimate child of his mother *after* her marriage to Mike? How could he think that of such a mother? When he had broached the subject she had hedged uncomfortably, and with a look of weary sadness had said, "Joseph, dear son, for your own sake, please don't try to corner me. You are my own precious son. God gave you to me. I promise you: one day you will understand." Since it could not be disclosed, Joseph suspected something ugly about his birth. How could *he* seek the hand of high-born princess Evelyn?

She, on her part, had the uncertainty caused by Molly

Ainsworth. Joseph had shown such fondness for her, his beautiful and devoted comrade who dearly loved him. And Molly was now in training for Christian work—surely to equip herself for lifelong link with Joseph. How dare she (Evelyn) try to come between them? She resolved to do nothing beyond showing warm esteem for him. Her problem was to prevent the yearning of her young heart from peeking out through those soft blue eyes which looked so longingly at him. Whether Evelyn's mother, the maternally astute Agnes, had some inkling of the excruciating stalemate is anyone's guess, but one morning Joseph received a letter.

> *Our dear Joseph,*
>
> *This comes with love from all at Pinecrest. I tried to call the other day, to say what I am now writing, but was prevented. We all seem so busy these days. Besides, you are so often out during afternoons. So I decided to send this note.*
>
> *You have no idea how we miss seeing you as we used to do. We thought (selfishly, I suppose) we would see you often when you came to live here, but it has turned out the other way. Of course you now have many more interests and are much busier (as well as older!), and who are we to expect special consideration when we do not even belong to your church (except Evelyn)?*
>
> *Anyway, lest you should think there is any change in us, we wanted you to know that you always have the same special place in our love and prayers. Please feel you can come round as often and informally as if you were our own son. My dear husband so enjoys talking with you about what is happening at Harvey Street these days; and of course no one else will ever mean to Evelyn what Joseph Kennard does (don't tell her I said that!).*
>
> *On the other hand, if your time is too full—well, we shall understand, and no offense will be taken. We only want to make sure you know that our*

friendship is always the same. Never hesitate to ask, if we can help in any way. You know how we all love your mother.

Meanwhile, this is an invitation for you to come over next Monday afternoon with your dear mother, and stay with us for the evening meal. We suggest Monday because we know that Tuesday and Thursday evenings are always booked, and you like to keep Saturday free in view of Sunday. Rickie, of course, is away at boarding school, but Evelyn can easily have time free from the office. Do not trouble to reply. Just let your mother telephone the "Yes." Our gardens are quite pretty just now.

Sincerely yours,
Agnes Lillian Adair

P.S. I cannot be deceitful, not even playfully. Your mother has already given me her secret "Yes." All we need is yours.

Joseph felt like putting that letter in a gold frame. He had prayed hard that under the pressure of his love for Evelyn he might not wrest things out of God's guiding hand. He had surrendered all his fond hopes to the will of God, and indeed was struggling to brace himself for the seemingly inevitable disappointment of *never* having Evelyn. The letter from Agnes seemed now to give a first hint that her parents, after all, might *not* frown on his union in marriage to her. Precious gleam of possibility! But what about that unpleasant mystery hanging over his own birth? Was he an illegitimate child? What would Evelyn's parents think if they got word of *that?*

The following Monday he and his mother went to Pinecrest. Nor was that all. From then onwards, under kindly pressure, he was there for short visits every few days. Besides those sacred hours of sitting or strolling with Evelyn in the gardens, there became evident again a strong attachment between Joseph and Evelyn's mother, Agnes. Nobody, except his own mother, seemed to understand him and his problems in the work of the church as did Agnes. There was a bond between them which made him feel that *she,* at least, would not be averse to his wooing Evelyn. It seemed noticeable at times how she contrived to leave him and Evelyn alone.

They say that love is blind. It is not truer that love is an added eye? It sees in its object of endearment what no other eyes do. Everybody else knew that Evelyn Adair was the most beautiful young woman in town, but Joseph was now discerning more than ever that the outward was the expression of an *inner* lovableness. He no longer thought of her as a nymph or a seraph. She was human, with the human limitations and constitutional imperfections which are innate in the best of us at present. But the more he was with her and probed her mind, the more he revered her as well as loved her. She could laugh. She could cry. She could express wisest sympathy, and she could express anger at hypocrisy or other evils; but never once did the watchful Joseph find the shadow of guile in her motives. Moreover, he and she were now so wonderfully one in the precious things of Christ! Indeed, in the deeper things of the Spirit, Joseph had an awareness that *she* was teaching *him.* Her prayer-life was apparently rich and constant. Her grasp of broad, simple, evangelical truth was remarkable, and her yieldedness now to the Lord Jesus was stamped on her whole behaviour. Joseph knew that Evelyn especially *liked* him. In fact, the more they were together now, the more persuaded he felt that she *loved* him, and was trying to show it without saying it. Dare he now tell her all his heart? Or ought he speak to her father first?

He observed that always when they were together she wore the locket. Dare he ask her if he was still inside it, hanging near her heart?

One day, when they were slowly walking side by side in "Little Eden," talking about doings at Harvey Street, Evelyn suddenly digressed on a happy impulse. "Joseph, look at that swing over there. Nobody ever uses it now. I'm sure it feels neglected. Do you remember when I was a girl of nine or ten, how you used to swing me on it? What about trying it again—if it will hold me now?"

"Are you sure it's strong enough still—for a grown-up young lady?"

"I'll risk it!"

"Let me wipe it over first, so that your dress does not get soiled."

"Thank you, Joseph. Now let me make sure I'm on properly. There! That's it. Now go ahead."

Joseph did, and as he watched her swing to and fro, painfully loving the very sight of her, she called out, with that characteristic look of lovely mischief in her sparkling eyes, "Oh, Joseph, isn't this just like those good old days when we romped up and down here!"

Each time she came swinging near to him, she held her head forward and gave him such a loving look as their faces almost touched. Inwardly Joseph was asking, "Oh, my Evelyn, what are you trying to tell me? Why am I so tongue-tied?"

After some moments he called, "Evelyn, I'm not too comfortable about the rope near that top, left-hand pulley. After being in the rain and weather all these summers and winters maybe it's not too safe. I wouldn't like another accident—like that ankle! Let me slow you down, now, and help you off."

Lower and slower she swung, until she came slowly enough toward him to get off. Exactly at the right moment she took her hands off the rope and quietly landed right in Joseph's arms, with their faces momentarily touching.

"Oh, Joseph, that was wonderful!" she whispered.

"Yes, so is this!" exclaimed Joseph, as he held her and she made not the slightest effort to break away.

"You are so naughty, Joseph!"

"Am I? May I ask you one question, Evelyn? Is my picture still in that locket—next to yours?"

"Yes."

"Shall I tell you when I first put *your* picture in that locket?"

"Please do."

"It was after that bicycle outing. Do you remember what you did as we sat by the stream together?"

"Yes, wicked young rogue that I was, I kissed you!"

"Would you mind, Evelyn, if I now paid you back?"

"Do you really feel in debt?"

She held up her face. They looked searchingly into each

other's eyes. What Joseph read in hers was deep, pure, womanly love. He gently kissed her cheek, slowly and fondly. His arms were still loosely round her shoulders, though not in an embrace. She did not move away, but her lovely face flushed now as she slowly said, "Forgive me, dear Joseph, if I'm wrong . . . but you can kiss my lips, too, if you wish."

A shock of ecstasy ran through Joseph's system. He knew what it had cost her to say that. From Evelyn Adair, whose lips had never been touched by any other boy's, he knew that it meant sheer love. "Oh, Evelyn, what can I say? I want . . . I long . . . I ache . . . but I . . . I daren't . . . not now. Please, please, don't be embarrassed. To think that you should trust me so is . . . is inexpressibly wonderful to me."

Inwardly he was saying, "I daren't until I have talked with her father."

Inwardly Evelyn was weeping, "It's because in reality he's given to Molly."

Slowly she drew away from him. Her peerless face was quite red now, though there was no look of shame in her steady eyes. "No, I'm not embarrassed," she replied. "I know you will keep it locked up in sacred confidence. I only thought that perhaps the moment had come when I should let you know how much I . . . I like you. No, I'm not sorry. I think you've given me the answer to something which has bothered me for months. We shall always be such happy friends, Joseph, shan't we? By the way, while we are here, do you remember that spot just over there where Rickie was so anxious to show how quickly he could get on the pony that he fell right over the other side of it?"—and with a pleasant toss of her shiny, wavy hair she turned the conversation away.,

But poor Joseph had crumpled up inside—and she knew it. The rest of the time at Pinecrest that day was misery. He was relieved when the time came to excuse himself, and he departed.

About 11 o'clock next morning Joseph heard the telephone ring downstairs. His mother answered it. She must have been there ten minutes. Then she came upstairs to tell

Joseph about it. A Mrs. McLean, wife of Councilor McLean, Stanley House, Chorley, had been in Elmerton visiting Miss Effie Crawley. She had learned that Miss Crawley attended Harvey Street Church, and she (Mrs. McLean) was now telephoning on Miss Crawley's behalf. She had found "poor Effie" distressed even to the point of being ill because of anonymous letters she was receiving; letters saying disparaging and obscene things about her, in the last of which the unknown maligner had threatened to inform others, including the Reverend Joseph Kennard. This had upset Miss Crawley so much that the visiting Mrs. McLean of Chorley felt she should telephone Mr. Kennard and put him on guard. Also, Miss Crawley wondered if she could have a brief interview sometime with Mr. Kennard about it. Miss Crawley herself would ring up later in the day.

Joseph and his mother were at once sorry for Effie. "When she 'phones," said Joseph, "tell her to be at my vestry at 7:15 next Thursday evening before the Bible School." Joseph often gave interviews on Thursdays from 7 o'clock until 7:45. His mother was always with him. If he interviewed women she was always in the adjoining room, with the door to the vestry slightly open. She considered that a wise precaution. So did he. Also, her advice was often needed as much as his.

Promptly at 7:15 Effie was there, looking troubled. Tallish, slim, prim, smartly but modestly dressed, polite and well-spoken, she certainly was gentlewomanly, even prepossessing. She confirmed what Mrs. McLean had said about the indecent, anonymous letters. Joseph expressed immediate sympathy. She said that her first impulse had been to inform the police, because the insinuations were so fearfully defamatory, but on second thought she had decided against that, in case the anonymous writer was a member of Harvey Street, and the exposure of that person should hurt the church's reputation. Also, she had thought it wise to come to Mr. Kennard first because he was her minister, and because he was mentioned in one or two of the letters, evidently by someone who knew him well. Again, she thought it just possible he might recognize the handwriting.

She had now received four, at intervals. One thing which deeply upset her was their raking up that she had been in prison—an episode which she had hoped was buried for ever.

"But you haven't been in prison?"

Tears glistened in her eyes. "Yes, I have. It was a very short term, and it was not my fault." She had been employed in a Customs and Excise office at Oldham. The clerkess next to her had stolen some coupons. When search was made she panicked and hid some of the coupons among Effie's papers, then testified later that she had seen Effie stealing them. So Effie was wrongly convicted and given a short prison sentence, to her unspeakable shame. Afterward, when it was too late, the other girl had confessed.

"Do you have the letters with you?"

"Yes."

"Do you want me to read them?"

"No, I don't; they are so unclean. Yet I suppose you ought to see the parts where you yourself are mentioned. In one place they speak about my feelings toward you, my dear minister. Please ignore or forgive that part. I cannot be hypocritical and deny the truth of just that one part, though little did I ever think it would come to light."

"I see. Well, perhaps you had better leave the letters with me, and we'll be in touch with you later."

She handed the four letters to him, at the same time remarking, "I'm not the only one, alas, who has received anonymous letters like these. Mr. Smethurst, the deacon, has one; so has Mr. Handsworth, the manager of Scribner and Wadsworth where I work in the office; so has Mrs. Tweedly of 32 Lauder Avenue where I now have rooms; and so has Mrs. Wilcox, my Sunday school teacher. They seem to have been sent just where they can damage me the most."

Back home that night Joseph read the letters. They made his hair stand on end. All four were along the same line. Effie Crawley had been in jail. She was now head over ears in love with the Reverend Joseph Kennard, but he was a pious deceiver. Although the public did not know it, he was the son of a prostitute. Did Evelyn Adair know this?

Effie Crawley herself (it was alleged) had lived in immoral relations with men. All this was going to be put round the town.

The perspiration dripped down Joseph's face. Sickly, he handed the letters to his mother. She went sickly too. For a minute there was deathly silence. Then the old fire of defiance was back in Millie's face. Joseph saw her stiffen as she said, "Joseph, my own dear boy, don't sink! Grip yourself. I've seen this sort of thing before. You see, Joseph, you simply cannot be God's champion without being the devil's target. You needn't be surprised except at the *form* of the attack. His purpose is first to *break* something in *you,* then to smash the revival at Harvey Street. But a million devils aren't as big as God. Satan isn't going to win. Let's commit it all to God. Then go to bed, Joseph. Read Psalm 3, and get a good sleep. First thing in the morning we'll collect all those other letters and see what a bit of detective work can do."

Next day she was on the job early. So far there were eight letters. She prayed with each recipient (except the manager of Messrs. Scribner and Wadsworth) and enlisted their cooperation against this underhand attack of Satan. They needed no assuring that the charges were false, and therefore for the Lord's honor swore not to breathe a word to anyone else.

Later, Joseph and Millie spread all eight letters and envelopes side by side. The script in each letter was the same—or attemptedly so: needlessly large and with variations in the way capital letters were written, which probably indicated disguise. The writing on the envelopes was smaller, different in style, and all the same. It suggested a female writer. Of the eight sheets containing the letters, four had the same watermark. One of the envelopes had the address written on a gummed economy label stuck over some other address. Carefully Joseph steamed it off and found underneath: "Mr. and Mrs. J. Hodge, 84 Holland Road, Elmerton."

Soon afterwards Millie called there. She was known to them by repute, as to many others. She said that in the course of her duties she was making enquiries concerning

Effie Crawley. Did they know her? Yes, they did. Was she upright? Yes, so far as they knew. How well did they know her? Only in a casually friendly way. They had met her at a Salvation Army meeting, after which she had visited them several times, though not recently. Did they have a grudge of any kind against Effie? None whatever (with evident surprise). Could they explain how this envelope got sent to Effie with a gummed label covering up their address? They "simply could not." Millie could see their surprise was genuine. Had they ever written to Effie? "No, we've never known where she lived, and in any case we've never had occasion to write." Had they ever written to her anonymously? Certainly not (they were aghast).

Millie was used to sizing people up. She knew the Hodges were being willingly frank, so she explained, "It's only this: somebody has written a letter or two without signing, and Effie wants to find out who it is. It's nothing more, so don't give it another thought."

However, Mrs. Hodge did give it "another thought," for she added as Millie was leaving, "Come to think of it, either Effie or anybody else could have picked up that envelope. I have a careless way of leaving them about. Still, that's not much help, because I'm always in when we have visitors. Only once Effie was here alone—just while I went round to the grocer's. I left her here reading. It's just possible she might have picked it up by mistake and then somebody else could have got it from her; but that doesn't sound likely, does it?"

Weeks went by. Then, interspersed over several days, the earlier recipients of the letters each received another, again anonymous. Each was handed on to Joseph with expressions of sympathy. The script in the letters and the caligraphy on the envelopes were pretty much as before. The contents were abusive and obscene, with new emphasis on Joseph's being a bastard who should be ashamed of paying attention to a pure young lady like Evelyn Adair.

As weeks became months without solution Joseph suffered mental torment. He began to *feel* what the letters asserted of him. He wondered what those thought who had received such despicable defamation of him and who knew

Effie Crawley's love for him. It was telling on him, and he showed it. It was telling on Millie, too, but she fought all the harder to hide it. Joseph marvelled at her, and took courage; but it was a prolonged inward crucifixion, his having to keep outwardly enthusiastic as leader in a wonderful spiritual revival, yet have this horrible thing on his mind all the while. He and Millie daily pleaded with God to intervene. From time to time, also, they re-examined the letters in search of clues, but it seemed futile.

There was worse to come. Beelzebub is merciless when he determines to grind a man down. For months Adrian Raglan had been "a thorn in the side" of Joseph. He was the most splendid idol of the Boys' Brigade and popular with most of the youth. He was so brawny and bonny, so manly and jolly. But he was an enemy of the revival, and a conceited rival of Joseph, whom he resolved to knock from his "parsonic pedestal." In surreptitious ways and by snide innuendos he sought to turn the boys and others away from Joseph. There are always some who will listen, though on the whole Raglan found his despicable objective harder than he had expected, for Joseph also was a boy's man; the younger folk loved his talks to them; and if there was one thing clearer than another to everybody it was Joseph's sincerity.

The driving cause in Raglan's hatred was Joseph's attractedness to Evelyn, and her apparent response. He continually sat near her and was all attention to her. He would accompany her out of church, offer to walk home with her, invite her to the Raglan home, or bring a posy of flowers for her. That was all done in the open. Little did he mind being seen making gentlemanly gestures to such an idolized "fair maid" as Evelyn Adair. He took great care that Joseph should see it all and become discouraged. Evelyn, on her part, never dreaming a young man could have such a shabby motive, showed pleasantness to him, thinking him a sincere, handsome young man, immaturely bombastic at times but quite congenial. She knew that many of the prim and pretty belles around her would have been dizzy with delight to have such a beau as Adrian Raglan pay them attention. In fact, he was such a gallant dandy of the *beau monde* as to attract notice anywhere.

Joseph poured it all out to Millie. She and he poured it all out to God. But if ever God seemed slow, it was during those painful months. Since that day on the swing Evelyn had been kindly as always, but there was a clear difference. She now seemed purposely aloof. Was she beginning to like Adrian Raglan, of all people? Could she not see through him? Why no solution to those awful letters? Effie Crawley semed to be bravely, quietly suffering. She seemed to find sanctuary in his presence, but was never forward. She was unobtrusively sympathetic. One day a telephone call came from Mrs. Tweedly of Lauder Avenue where Effie stayed, saying that anonymous letters were still coming, and breaking Effie's heart. "Poor Effie is away at work now and has no idea I'm 'phoning you. She is a darling girl, so clean and methodical and congenial in our boardinghouse here; so quiet and thoughtful; a favourite with us all. Do help her, if you can. Who can the foul fiend be who's sending these awful letters?"

"O God, please act!"

On the first Wednesday night each month there was the "Officebearers' Meeting," of which Joseph was *ex officio* chairman. Wednesday night also, each week, was when the Boys' Brigade met in the smaller Sunday school room. Between the church and the Sunday school building at its side was a stone-flagged passage or alley some twenty feet wide, leading out between the two buildings to the front gate and railings on Harvey Street. Adrian Raglan had decided that since things were moving so slowly he must speed them up. He chose the time and place carefully. It was a Wednesday night in that alley. The officebearers' meeting in the large church vestry was over. So was the Boys' Brigade rendezvous, a few minutes earlier. As Joseph came into the alley with the last two of his men, Adrian Raglan intercepted him: "Could I speak with you a moment?"

"Certainly," replied Joseph, bidding "good-night" to the two brethren. "What is it, Adrian?"—and as he spoke he noticed three uniformed boys standing under the light of the gas lamp which projected from the church wall at the street end of the alley.

Before speaking again, Raglan, catching hold of Joseph's coat at the top buttonhole, imperiously pulled him to the Sunday school wall. Then he said loudly, as Joseph tried to recover from his surprise, "Mr. parson, I think it's time you and I had a brotherly chat. I'd like to see what stuff you're really made of. It's alright spouting up there in that pulpit, but what are you like when you get a kick in the pants? It seems to me that fate has made you and me rivals for the same fair lady. She's a real pretty tart, isn't she? You're real gone on her, aren't you? Lovely face, lovely figure, lovely everything! Let me tell you: some of us can see right through you and your lousy revival. You're just as much taken with a nice pair of legs as anybody else. Let me make one thing plain. She's mine, not yours; and from tonight keep your eyes off her, or this is what you'll get"—and shoving Joseph to arm's length he swung a blow which sent Joseph staggering backwards across the alley and down against the wall of the church.

"Take that, Mr. parson. I know things about you that other folk are going to know soon enough. I know the dirty background you come from. You may think yourself a golden butterfly today, but you were a crawling worm yesterday, you son of a harlot!"

As Joseph opened his eyes and sat up, feeling at his bleeding lips, all in one glance he saw the grinning face of Raglan, the three uniformed boys—their eyes fairly goggling at seeing their revered young minister sent sprawling by their hefty hero, and a shadowy figure just beyond the corner of the building near the street.

Slowly Joseph got up, taking out his handkerchief to wipe the blood from his mouth. "Stay there a minute," he said to Raglan, though it was a bit difficult to say the words normally because of his already puffing lip. His mind was thinking fast and furiously. Stepping toward the three lads, he said, "Boys, you know our Lord Jesus said that if we were struck on one cheek we should turn the other. Well, that is true in every case except where it serves the purpose of

evil. Did captain Raglan ask you three boys to stay here and
watch him humiliate me?"

"Yes, sir."

"And did you see him strike me without my doing anything to cause him?"

"Yes, sir."

"Very well, I want your names."

"Yes, sir, Eric Jenkyns, Harold Booth, Percy Lees."

"Eric, what is your address?"

"Fifteen Reynolds Street, sir."

Joseph said the names over again, and Eric's address.
Then he took off his coat and his jacket and handed them to
Eric. Raglan watched, still grinning, and doubting whether
Joseph could say boo to a goose.

"Raglan, you're a bit taller and heavier than I; but let's
see what stuff *you're* made of. Put up your dukes! I always
give a man fair warning, though it's the last thing you
deserve."

So saying, Joseph started darting side to side in front of
Raglan. Rightly or wrongly, and unlike the usual steady
Joseph, he was blazing with anger, and his very intensity
put alacrity for the time being into his limbs. Sideways,
forward, backward, he pranced, watching Raglan's eyes
dancing about after him. He knew Raglan was puzzled
whether to be amused or wary. He also knew fighting
tactics about which Raglan (who now looked a bit clumsy)
was ignorant. He knew after only a few seconds of watching Raglan that he was too slow to land any heavy, well-
aimed blow on such a bobbing object. Raglan's fists were
up, but Joseph could see they were little problem. Out
came Joseph's long left, and dragged down Raglan's nose
and mouth, just to divert him. Up went Raglan's fists, to
cover, just as Joseph expected, leaving the lower face exposed. Out shot a lightning right which caught Raglan's jaw
and rocked his head. And now, all the silly twaddle in
Raglan's noddle came to his rescue too late. He flung out
fiercely and wildly, nowhere near Joseph's face. That was
his undoing. Like streaks of forked lightning, now, Joseph's
fists pelted him from all directions.

Literally, now, Raglan had his "back to the wall," and it

would not let him fall. Still came the rain of blows—eyes, ears, nose, lips, all got them—and Joseph seemed unable to stop, such was his rage, until, a battered freak, the handsome Raglan slid down the wall and lay huddled on the floor.

Joseph, panting, and trembling with anger, stood over him ready to swipe him if he tried to get up.

Raglan moved a bit.

"You're not getting up, Raglan, you dirty cur, until you say you're sorry for what you said about Evelyn Adair. If necessary, I'll keep you down there all night, unless you say you're sorry. In fact, if you don't, I'll thrash you until you do. You'd better say it at once."

Slowly Raglan groaned, "I'm . . . sorry." Then his head sank to the stone slabs again.

Turning to the three boys, Joseph said, "Eric, you can give me my coat and jacket now. And I think you'd better help captain Raglan home"—and in that instant he caught one more fleeting glance of that shadowy figure round the corner, as it now darted through the gate into the street and was gone. Who was it? All he could descry was, that it was a woman and (thanks to a yellow ray from the gas lamp as she reached the gate) that her dark dress or coat had a collar with white piping round it; and (oh, no!) it was about the same height and likeness as *Evelyn!*

Reaction now set in. Joseph went limp. He was exhausted and sick at heart. His feet were leaden weights as he now dragged them home. Millie saw there was something gravely wrong as he walked in with haggard face and swollen lip and blood on his face. He told her everything. Then, kneeling at her rocking-chair as he had often done in his childhood, Joseph, the man, wept in his mother's lap.

"Mother, why, why, why must men always compete and fight? Why did I have to fight tonight? Why did I learn boxing at Rostherne?—was it that God arranged it because He knew I'd need it? It's all so mysterious, so disheartening. Have I done the unchristian thing? And is this kind of thing the price of revival? And was that dark figure Evelyn? And who wrote those letters, and knows something about my birth that is so shameful? Mother, the fog seems to grow thicker—and now I seem to have lost Evelyn in it!"

"Son, sit up now, and let's bathe your face. Then we'll have some supper. You may not think so, but a good, warm nourishing something for your inner man is important just now."

Joseph's lip was swollen, but the cut was slight. "We won't put any ointment on it till we have eaten. Some gentle bathing in warm water will help. The swelling will subside by tomorrow maybe. While we're eating, there are some things I'd like to say."

"Mother, your sympathy is better than any ointment"— but even as he said so he observed that the flash of battle was in those bright eyes again. She seemed to be thinking fast.

As they sat at the table she began: "Joseph, I may not be a prophet, but I have a hunch that this may be 'the darkest hour before the dawn.' One little remark you've made sets me thinking. We may have a clue at last. Meanwhile we're learning new lessons in the 'holy war.' What is more, during these past few months, contrary to what you think, I've seen you developing spiritually more than ever before. Big lessons often charge heavy fees, but the earlier we learn, the sooner we profit."

"Heaven make me a quick learner, mother!"

"Joseph, I know how you love Evelyn. I've watched the two of you ever since you met when you were only thirteen and she swept you off your feet. You've never looked at any other, but you're afraid she can't ever be yours because of who she is and who you are. Well, you'd better accept this: the course of true love seldom runs smoothly. However, I think that at this unhappy moment a word of comfort may be wise. You're not the only one who can love. You may not have known it, but when you tore off your shirt sleeve and bound up Evelyn's ankle on that bench by Netherford Lake, the bandage bound more than her ankle. It bound her heart to yours. She's never looked at any other boy, though scores have idolized her. All the years you were away at Huddersfield she wore that locket. It was I who gave her your photo for it. Up at Pinecrest I've often seen her open it and look inside when she did not know I was watching.

There's not a finer, truer, purer girl on this earth than Evelyn Adair—and she loves you, Joseph. What is more, if you still keep torturing yourself that her parents frown on it, you're wrong. They feel honored. Why, Mrs. Adair herself loves you as much as Evelyn, only in a motherly way."

"Oh, mother, mother!"

"But now, back to grim business. Don't you begin to see the pattern of the enemy's attack? The two deepest delights of your life are your union with Christ and your love for Evelyn. If he can get at you through those, and tear you apart where you are most sensitive, and scandalize you through anonymous letters, and make you think God is mocking you, he's won. But I think he's met his match this time—I mean in Evelyn. Such purity as hers is better protection than a coat of mail. That lurking figure in the shadow wasn't Evelyn. I'd stake my life on that. Those two ideas—Evelyn and shadow, won't fit. That's why the shadowy figure may be our clue. But you must allow me a little time to think it through."

"Mother, you ought to belong to the Civil Investigation Department!"

"Joseph, cheer up. God is not mocking you; He's molding you. What seems to be the *breaking* of us often turns out to be the *making* of us. When the prodigal was leaving home his request was, 'Father, *give* me,' but when he came back disillusioned his prayer was, 'Father *make* me.' So long as we girate around the *'give* me' we're superficial, but when we get to 'Father, *make* me,' God can really do something with us. Joseph, God is tutoring you for ministry beyond Harvey Street, yes and beyond this land, and beyond the grave. Isn't that what he's trying to do with all of us? We all start out at birth with a human *nature,* and we all pass over at last with a human *character.* Nature is the raw material. Character is what we make of it. And in the making of character the decisive thing is not so much what happens to us, but how we *react.* It's not just the gales, but the set of the sails, which determines the way the ship goes. It takes big storms to make strong oaks. Put a cheerful courage on, Joseph. It's a privilege to go through the fire if we come out as pure gold! I think it's becoming clearer what God is trying to do just now."

Snake in the Grass

"What a preacher you are, mother!"

"Well, at the moment I have a very good listener. You see, Joseph, I've been listening carefully to some of your remarks lately. On the one hand there's the thrill of the revival, but on the other hand these filthy letters—and a suspense about Evelyn. You're puzzled. You're under strain. You've wondered if the reins have slipped out of God's hands. There seems neither sense nor reason in what is being permitted. Let me counsel you, son. Never expect events to be logical. History never moves in syllogisms. And don't envy people who never have trouble. However much money jingles in their pockets, they are life's spiritual paupers. They never know the 'higher education' of the spirit. The only people who really laugh are those who have wept; the others only cackle. Who can enjoy lovely Spring like those who have struggled through tough Winter? The only people who really enjoy joy are those who have had enough sorrow. Trouble is a great educator. A broken heart often sees more through a tear than a philosopher through a telescope. The only people who are of any use to understand and comfort the world's sufferers are those who themselves have suffered. None can mend broken hearts like those whose own have been broken at one time or another."

"Mother, you're not only the world's greatest preacher, you're the century's greatest philosopher! You remind me of Wordsworth's phrase about the 'still, sad music of humanity,' and Matthew Arnold's 'turbid ebb and flow of human misery.' Go on. I can take more of this sort just now. I don't feel half as much now like a torn animal licking its wounds."

"Joseph, let me add only one bit more. I know we're in big trouble just now, especially if those anonymous letters get gossiped round by the click-clackers before we unearth the writer. But let's still keep steady, and let's be fair to God. We mustn't let the favors of a lifetime be forgotten in the sorrow of one trial. No judgment of ours on God's dealings with us can be fair if it's based only on one isolated experience. And grasp this afresh, Joseph: God's highest purposes often wind to their loveliest fulfillments through strangest processes. Life's richest lessons are never

385

learned through text-books. The only way of learning them is living them. You never learn to swim just by doing the strokes on the kitchen floor; you must be in the water!"

"Mother, I wish all Elmerton were listening to this sermon."

"So do I, dear son. But I'm now at the conclusion—at last! My concern is, that although at the moment things look serious we shall not lose the sense of God's sovereignty or of His love-grip upon us. Let us bow to His will, but trust for His help. Try not to let the pressure of this trouble sicken you. There's still more to sing about than cry about. I have a firm presentiment now that there'll likely be a final thunderclap—yes, a final thunderclap, and that then the sun will break through full and clear again. Meanwhile, my own beloved boy, straighten your back and square your shoulders. If you want strong shoulders, don't run away from burdens. Many folk can't understand it, but weights can be wings, and burdens can be blessings, and trials can be triumphs. Weepings in the evening are often singings next morning. So, as Paul and Silas 'prayed and sang praises' in the dungeon at midnight, you and I will, in this predicament."

Even then Millie had to tack on a kind of addendum, for she was in fine preaching feckle and was much stirred. "In my heart of hearts, Joseph, I believe God has guided you to the one dear girl whom He chose to be your life-partner, and I am gladder than ever now that you never flirted about with those dollish girls who cheapen themselves 'two a penny.' From the moment God gave you to me, in your babyhood I knew you were meant for some special calling. Let this present trouble bring you even lower at the feet of Jesus. That's the only really safe place—especially for one whom God is using as He is using you. If this present trouble strikes one further, final blow at subtle pride, it will have been worth its weight in angels' wings! Amen!"

"You needn't have said 'amen' yet, mother. But, what do you think! Your sermon has made the audience hungry again! Could I have another slice of that well-buttered toast, and another cup of that hot, milky cocoa?"

TWENTY-THREE
Still Deeper Shadows

Next morning Joseph's mouth was still sore and his lip slightly swollen, but by evening, when he was due to speak at his Thursday evening Bible School, there was little noticeable disfigurement. He had slept soundly and taken the day restfully. Millie had been out most of the time, ostensibly visiting her women but (so Joseph suspected) exercising her detective instincts.

As they sat at their evening meal she was as pleasantly uncommunicative as she had been expansively sermonic the night before; but Joseph noticed a look in her eyes which seemed to say, "I'm on to something; at least I think so." His own mind was on the meeting which he had to address, so he did not press his mother to divulge anything which she might have uncovered.

The Bible school gathering was again exuberant. Revival joys were glowing through the whole work at Harvey Street. The keen appetite for Bible truth and the mutual affection among the members were delightful to see. Hundreds had flocked in. The jubilant singing nearly "lifted the roof off." Joseph felt unspeakable relief that so far, apparently, the ugly disparagements in those anonymous letters had not become known, and the work was not suffering; yet he felt a kind of helpless hypocrisy as he stood there before them all, beaming and rejoicing—thoroughly sincerely, while under the surface he was wretched with apprehensiveness. It was as though a haunting voice kept muttering inside him even as he preached, "If these trustful sheep of yours knew the slimy slander now being smeared over you by a hidden Judas. . . !"

As was often the case, now, even after the meeting was over the people lingered for informal fellowship; and from time to time little groups would break into some happy chorus. As usual, Evelyn had been present. Her parents, too, had come with her. But for the first time, instead of delighting Joseph, their presence disturbed him. There could be no doubt about it: they were listening and watching him with a strange, even strained attentiveness. He had not needed to glance more than casually to see that they did not join in any of the singing. They were observing but not enjoying. Agnes looked pale, worried. Evelyn looked ill. Joseph was alarmed. *Something* was wrong. Had they learned of the awful, anonymous defamations? Was this going to be the "thunderclap" his mother had intuitively prognosticated?

Following the meeting, Joseph was in his vestry as usual for brief chats with one and another. Presently Evelyn came in. She was so pale and her posture so listless that Joseph quietly exclaimed, "Evelyn, Evelyn, are you not feeling well?"

As she replied her voice was so weak, all the strength seemed to have gone out of her; but she was quite calm and looked at him with steady, sad eyes. "I've come to return this," she said, as she laid the little gold locket on his desk. "I have felt for some time now that I could not honorably wear it; but after the way you treated Adrian Raglan last night, and the remarks you made, Joseph, I could keep it no longer."

She turned to go, but saw such a look of horror on his face, she simply had to hesitate a moment. He seemed to be catching his breath as he sank into his chair, looking at her with anguished surprise. Inwardly he heard his mother's voice, now like the distant tolling of a knell—"A final thunderclap . . . thunderclap . . . thunderclap." It had come!

He steadied himself and said, "Evelyn, excuse my confusion. This has knocked me sick. There is some awful misunderstanding. . . ."

"I am sorrier than I can say, Joseph, to have upset you so; but there is no answering an eye witness, is there? I shall always treasure the memories of so many happier days with you, and shall continue to pray for you."

So saying, she slipped away, leaving Joseph dazed in weary dejection. He kept hearing Evelyn's words, "There is no answering an eye witness." So she *was* that lurking, shadowy figure last night! Yet if so, how could she have so wrong a misunderstanding of it? Heartsick, he picked up the locket, unclasped the spring, and looked inside. His own face was there. Evelyn's was gone.

How many minutes he sat there, head sagged, eyes closed, too dreary for tears, he did not know; but when he eventually looked up, there was his mother, Millie. She said, "Joseph, it's that final thunderclap. Brave it, my precious boy. This is the most jagged-edged test of all. I know how it hurts; but still trust God, and don't give Satan the laugh. Tell me what Evelyn said; and don't be too occupied with your own wound to remember hers. I've been watching her. You saw how ill she looked. It wasn't mere anger or peevishness. It was *grief*. The enemy's slash has hurt her as painfully as your wounds hurt you."

Joseph told her exactly what Evelyn had said.

"Well, Joseph, for your comfort, Evelyn was *not* the figure in the shadow last night. I went over to Pinecrest this morning, just as though I wanted a little chat with Mrs. Adair about Police Court Mission matters; and without saying a word to make her suspect anything I gleaned that Evelyn was at home the whole evening. Another thing is certain: when she left for the office this morning she knew nothing whatever about you and Raglan last night, or she would have told her mother. No, Joseph, Evelyn was not that shadowy figure last night; but I begin to think we may soon know who was—and whose is the hidden hand behind those letters. But there's something we must do right away. Deacon Smethurst is outside with his motor car. He'll take us round to Pinecrest. You'll stay in the car while I have a word with the Adairs."

While they were driving through the dark roads out to Pinecrest, deacon Smethurst kept assuring Joseph that he and the others who were known to have received the anonymous letters were keeping their lips tightly sealed. They would cut their tongues out rather than help the devil's dirty work. Such faithful friendship certainly was comforting, and Joseph thanked him accordingly. Soon they were at Pinecrest, and Millie made her call.

"Why, it's you, Millie! What brings you round at this time of night?"

"Agnes," replied Millie as they kissed, "I rather think you guess why."

Agnes's silence gave the answer.

"Would you mind, Agnes, if Joash and Evelyn sat with us, too?"

"Indeed not, Millie. See, here comes Joash. Let me call Evelyn."

All four of them looked strained.

Millie began: "You know why I've come. It's because of what happened tonight. I mean Evelyn's giving the locket back to Joseph. It's fairly broken him. You see, it came as an almost unbearable blow on top of a fearful trial that he's been enduring for months now. I'm going to take you all fully into my confidence about it, but first let me get one thing clear. Evelyn, you told Joseph that what happened last night between him and young Raglan had finally led you to return the locket. Since you were not on the spot, what do you think happened between them?"

"Oh, Mrs. Kennard, I would rather not tell you, because I know it would upset you as well. Please, for Joseph's sake, let it go."

"No, Evelyn, it is for Joseph's sake you must tell me. You see, I *know* what happened last night, but I think that *you* are being cleverly deceived. Please tell me frankly."

Evelyn did. "About eleven o'clock this morning I was telephoned at the office by a woman who said she was the mother of one of the three Boys' Brigade boys who witnessed the fight last night. She said that the three boys had come home dumb-struck at what they had seen. In fact, it wasn't really a fight at all; it was a vicious attack on captain Raglan by Mr. Kennard. The boys were walking a little ahead of captain Raglan in the passage-way between the church and the Sunday school building when Mr. Kennard intercepted Adrian, and said, 'Raglan, it's time you and I had a talk about Evelyn Adair.' . . . Oh, Mrs. Kennard, I can't go on."

"Evelyn, you must. Don't spare either me or Joseph. It's more important than you think."

"Well, Mrs. Kennard, the three boys reported that Joseph had warned Adrian to stop paying attention to me, after which he said such rude things about me that Adrian had to stop him; but Joseph pushed him away, and seized a long, thick bar of wood which was lying there, with which he struck Adrian right across the face. Before Adrian could recover, Joseph struck him again and again, like a madman, all over the head and neck until Adrian fell down, with Joseph shouting at him, 'Let that teach you! Leave Evelyn Adair to me!' This woman who telephoned me said that the three boys had needed to help Adrian home, and that today he was in bed, all bandaged up."

"Thank you, Evelyn. I think you know how much I love your mother and you; but I want to make you thoroughly ashamed of yourself, if I can. Don't you think that story sounds faked? You have known my precious Joseph now since he was thirteen. Until he was driven away he was with you more than with anyone else except myself. And now, more recently, month in month out you have seen him again in public and in private. You have heard his preaching and seen his dedication. In all these years did you ever see Joseph show temper? Has he ever been wrongly forward to you, Evelyn? Have you ever seen him with anything but self-control? Did you get that woman's name? Have you confirmed what she said? No? And yet have you put that against all the solid worth you have found Joseph to be? Oh, Evelyn, if you had seen him sob with his head in my lap last night! I know he was telling me the truth. It was not Joseph who intercepted Raglan; it was the other way round—as two of the deacons who were with Joseph can testify. It was

Raglan who had decided to humiliate Joseph and break up the revival. And Raglan had those three laddies there to watch. But things didn't turn out as expected, for Raglan didn't know that my Joseph is a trained boxer. It was Raglan who said the smutty things about you, Evelyn. How do I know? Well, you see, when Raglan suddenly struck Joseph down, and Joseph saw the three boys watching, he knew in a flash that Raglan had staged it. So he quickly took the names of the three boys as witnesses. Then he thrashed Raglan. And, Evelyn, the thing that infuriated him was the way Raglan had spoken of *you*. Can you understand his heartbreak when you returned that locket tonight?"

Evelyn, now, was weeping. Agnes was listening open-mouthed. Joash looked angry on behalf of Joseph.

Millie spoke again. "Joash and Agnes, we have known and trusted each other so long, now. Will you be frank with me? Have you received any anonymous letter about Joseph?"

"Yes, we have. It came a few weeks ago."

"You have not mentioned it to anyone?"

"Not to a soul, Millie."

"Agnes, why did you not tell *me?*"

"Oh, Millie, how could I? We knew how it would hurt you, as it had shocked Joash and me. We thought it best to say not a word: but I will admit, something in it did disturb us a bit."

"Did you destroy the letter?"

"No."

"Could I see it, please, Agnes?"

"It will upset you, Millie."

"No, not at this stage, Agnes."

"Very well, I'll get it."

Agnes brought it from her desk, and handed it to Millie. It was the same large writing in the letter, and the same smaller kind on the envelope. It was a deadly missive.

> *Dear Councilor and Mrs. Adair,*
>   *If there is anything from which I shrink it is the writing of an anonymous letter—something I have never done in my life before. But what I have to say*

> *here is so ugly that I simply dare not sign my name, lest I should become involved in something which pains me more than words can say. It is only out of sincere concern for yourselves that I write; and if you doubt what I say, you can easily investigate and verify it for yourselves.*
>
> *It concerns the Reverend Joseph Kennard. I wonder if you know what hypocrisy is wrapped up in his pious profession? Did you happen to know that Mr. Mike Kennard was not his real father, and that Mrs. Kennard is not his real mother? I have it on enough warrant that he is a bastard of the worst kind—of a prostitute and probably born with venereal disease. To see your pure, beautiful daughter allowing such a pariah to pay attentions to her deeply disturbs me, especially when I think of her father's prominent and highly respected position in Elmerton. I can do no other than at least write and inform you.*
>
> *With true concern,*
> *A Well-wisher*

Millie read it slowly, sick at heart, but doing her best to hide any shock. Then she held up the sheet of paper in front of the gaslight which projected from the wall near the fireplace. "Ah, yes; it's the same watermark," she muttered just enough for them to hear. "Agnes, may I take this letter?"

"You certainly may, Millie. So far as we are concerned, we are glad to be rid of it. Of course, but strictly between ourselves, we had wondered for some time whether Mike was his real father, but we knew you were his real mother. Naturally we were curious to know just what the facts of his birth were, because we have loved you and him so much. But we just hadn't the heart to touch on something which might be painfully sensitive. We didn't know whether you had been married prior to marrying Mike Kennard. We didn't think you had, from different remarks you have made; but we left the matter there. Millie, dear, do you think we could *ever* doubt you after these years of such open-hearted friendship? And every syllable of what you have said about poor, dear Joseph is true."

"Joash and Agnes, you must not fail Joseph and me at this point," responded Millie, now looking deeply dejected. I think it would kill poor Joseph, strong though he is. Let me explain. Five other persons have received one or more of these anonymous letters, each letter more or less the same. All those persons, except one, are members at Harvey Street, and they have all kept their lips sealed for the sake of the Lord's work. The allegations in the letters are libelous enough to put the writer in prison. Joash, we can see it now: this is nothing less than a plot of Satan to kill the revival, to smirch Joseph's character, to hit at the police court mission work, to tear apart the friendship between you and us, to bring shame on Harvey Street church, and to ruin Joseph's powerful influence right at the beginning of his ministry. Never did the enemy of souls devise a cleverer 'all in one' policy—if only he can pull it off!"

"What can we do about it, Millie?"

"We must all be on our knees about it. A spiritual foe can be defeated only by a spiritual weapon. I think that at last God may be giving us clues. You see, Evelyn, besides those three lads who saw what happened last night Joseph caught a split-second glimpse of a shadowy figure round the corner of the church, keeping away from the light of the lamp. He couldn't see who it was, except that it seemed to be a young woman about your own height and build, dressed in a dark coat or costume. She darted out through the gate to the street and was gone before he could even guess who she was; but she was not quite quick enough to cover at least one little detail; and she may be our lead to the hidden hand which wrote those defaming letters. Her dress or coat was a dark one with white piping around the collar."

"Can we make you a hot drink, Millie?"

"No, thank you, Agnes. Mr. Smethurst has waited out there too long already. What time is it? Dear me! I see it's well after ten o'clock! I must run. Could I ask one more favour? Would you mind not going to bed until I have telephoned you about a certain matter?"

As they stood under the front door porch Millie added,

"Agnes, there's one thing I can't put off saying, before I go. It cuts so deep and hurts so much. It's about Joseph's birth. Yes, Joseph is my son; and no mother ever had greater cause to thank God for a gem of a son. Mike was not his real father. That part of those letters is true. But Joseph's birth was honourable and pure, and I'll tell you more about that one of these days. In fact, you may smile when I tell you that when he was two years old his photo was in a magazine as the prizewinner in a 'Competition for Healthy Babies' fed on Farrow's Patent Baby Food! The doctor's printed tribute was, that he had never examined 'a healthier little chap' in his life! Did you hear that, Evelyn?"

Then Millie was gone. The Adairs heard the car drive away down Woodland Bypath toward Clifton Boulevard. Then they sat downstairs, waiting, thinking, wondering, and silently praying.

Eleven o'clock. . . . Five minutes past. . . . Ten past (that was late in those days). . . . Quarter past . . . almost twenty past, then the telephone rang. Joash and Agnes both rose to answer it. Agnes was there first. Millie was at the other end.

"Agnes, this is Millie. Sorry to keep you up so late. We have a message for Evelyn. Will you tell her: we have seen each of those three mothers whose boys saw what happened last night. Not one of those mothers telephoned Evelyn today. They did not even know Evelyn or that she worked in her father's office. The person who telephoned Evelyn was someone else *pretending* to be one of those mothers; and what was told to Evelyn was a fandangle of lies. Also, please tell Evelyn that the three boys did not tell any such story as that which the voice told Evelyn. And one thing more: those three boys and Joseph will be round to see Evelyn at the office about 4:30 tomorrow afternoon. Please keep praying, Agnes, that the snake in the grass may soon be dragged into the open. I won't keep you longer. Good-night, and God bless you."

TWENTY-FOUR
Miracle at Midnight

It was a weary yet encouraged Millie and Joseph who returned home late that Thursday night. They had settled it that the "mother" who telephoned was a fake, and they had proved to Evelyn that the story was false. Their bedtime snack was a talkative time. At last they were picking up a trail. It was a young woman of Evelyn's build who had lurked in the shadow; a woman who had telephoned Evelyn; one who presumably knew Adrian Raglan and had been intendedly present at the fight. All seemed to point to some young woman who knew certain members of Harvey Street church fairly well.

But which young woman? and what the motive? and who told her Mike was not Joseph's father? "I know it's late," said Millie, "but let's have another look at those letters."

There were now twelve, including the three written to Effie herself. The one written to the Adairs was now compared with the others. All were similar, but one feature now seemed worth noting more carefully. Eight were written on sheets of paper all bearing the same watermark. They were not torn from a writing-pad but were separate sheets, commercial size, rather suggesting having come from some office. The smaller writing on the envelopes surely was a feminine hand. Could the writer, then, be a clerkess in an office? Which young woman had been particularly friendly with Adrian Raglan?

Millie and Joseph looked curiously at each other. They were both thinking the same—Effie Crawley. She was a clerk at Scribner and Wadsworth's; just the kind of person who fit the parts, even to being the same build as Evelyn. Yet how could it be Effie, since three of the letters were written *to* her, and defamed *her*? Again, how could *she* have written those which denigrated Joseph, when she had such tender regard for him?

Millie kept looking at the first letter sent to Effie, like a cat watching a bird. Presently she jumped up and went to the telephone. Joseph heard her give the operator the police office number. "Hello, is that police headquarters? . . . Yes, George, this is Mrs. Kennard. You were quick to recognize my voice. . . . Thank you. . . . I'm sorry to ring up so late—were you having a sly snooze? . . . Listen, George, I'm wondering could you help me with a bit of information? If you can't, don't worry; it can wait till morning. Do you have anything on a Miss Effie Crawley? She served a short sentence in Strangeways, probably two or three years ago. . . . I see. That's kind of you. We'll wait."

Turning to Joseph she said, "I just thought we might get clear on one point right away. Constable Farley isn't sure he can get to the right files at the moment. But he'll let us know. Meanwhile, tired laddie, you be off to bed."

Joseph, however, preferred to wait. Nor was it long before the bell rang. "We've spotted her, Mrs. Kennard. She's a tricky one. She's had four sentences: one for libel, two for grand larceny, and one for forgery. Before her last sentence she was a domestic with a woman doctor in Oldham. That doctor's a widow with an only son, and she charged that Crawley put bits of broken glass in the son's porridge. So Effie's dangerous. Keep her away from your porridge! That doctor diagnosed her as a schizophrenic with two distinct personalities: one a quiet-spoken, respectful young woman, the other lewd with tendencies to violence. She not only forged the doctor's signature, she imitated her handwriting and even impersonated her voice on the telephone. Not so pretty, Mrs. Kennard!"

"No, George, it isn't pretty. Anyway, thank you. We'll be careful."

Millie and Joseph stared blankly at each other. So the maligner *was* the pensive, ladylike Effie Crawley!

"I think we need do no more tonight, Joseph. We're both tired. Let's get a good night's sleep. We've some important snooping to do tomorrow. Even now we don't have the evidence that Effie *did* write those letters. Perhaps we're getting a clue to the motive. It's jealous love for *you*. But why did she send letters disparaging herself *to* herself? Was there some sly reason? Why! of course! That was her means of first contact with *you;* of interviewing you and arousing your sympathy, and opening the way for further appointments! Good-night, my dear boy. Don't forget Psalm 3, verses 5 and 6!"

Next morning they were later rising. Joseph had to forego his pre-breakfast sprint in the little park. It was 8:30 before they sat at breakfast. They planned the order in which they would visit places where they hoped to gain information. The clock ticked round to 9:20. They decided to leave at 9:45. Millie had cleared the table and washed the dishes. She must quickly tidy the dining-room. Joseph must shave; and he was at the foot of the stairs on his way up for that purpose when the doorbell rang. Millie hastened to see who it was. Joseph lingered on the off-chance that it might be someone for himself.

Who should be there but Evelyn, with the glow of an early morning walk tinting her soft complexion! Did ever fair morning bring fairer caller? There she stood in a smart, two-piece gray suit, with pastel blue blouse, and wavy-brimmed felt hat to match. Oh, that dear face! Those blue eyes, so sad the night before, were glistening again, and her kind face was lit by a smile which was more beautiful to young Joseph than a Mediterranean sunrise.

"Good morning, Mrs. Kennard. Am I too early?"

"Too early! Come in, dear. This is a pleasant surprise!"

Entering, she saw Joseph at the foot of the stairs. "Good morning, Joseph"—rather quietly.

To him she was almost like some radiant visitor from a celestial realm. His immediate impulse was to exclaim, "How wonderful to see you!" but just as quickly he remembered the returned locket, and, inside him, shining sunrise became weeping sunset. With a self-suppression which was plainly artificial he courteously said, "Good morning, Evelyn." Then, chagrined that he was not yet shaved, he glanced upstairs and began apologetically to excuse himself.

But more quickly than he could turn, Evelyn stepped forward and put her hand on his arm. "Please, Joseph, don't mind about not having shaved. Please stay. It's you I came to see, as well as your mother. I've scarcely slept all night for thinking of you and praying for you. I had to come first thing this morning to tell you how sorry I am that I ever listened to anything against you. It was said to me with such seeming sincerity and truthfulness, I was momentarily deceived as well as too upset to think normally. Joseph, I'll never, never doubt you again. I don't mind your mother hearing. I came to ask what I don't deserve—your forgiveness."

Joseph was on the first step of the red-carpeted stairway. Her hand was still on his arm. Oh, the pleading in that dear, upturned face which searched his own! Why could he not think of some sublimely noble reply? Why did he stumble over his words?

"Evelyn," he found himself saying, "there is nothing to forgive. You did what you thought right. In any case, I am not worthy that such a pure heart as yours should even *ask* my forgiveness. Does a worm pardon an angel for fluttering its wings?"

It sounded too poetic for such a moment; but Evelyn tried to think it meant "Yes."

Then Millie spoke: "Evelyn, have you walked all the way over from Pinecrest?"

"No, not quite that far; but I've walked most of the way from Scribner and Wadsworth's."

"Scribner and Wadsworth's!"

"Yes, that was the other reason why I came over. . . ."

"But, Evelyn, why do we keep you standing here? Come

into the sitting-room; or maybe it's warmer in the dining room. Don't worry about that shave, Joseph. A few whiskers are no disgrace to any man."

Evelyn needed no prompting. Right away she began to tell them. During the night she had wept at having so hurt Joseph. She realized now that there had been a deception. She not only longed for Joseph's forgiveness, but also to help in some practical way towards vindicating him, especially after what Mrs. Kennard had said about a Satanic plot. She had been up during the night, praying that God would guide her, in her helplessness, to find the writer of those evil letters. Then she had sat up in bed putting different pieces of the mystery together. And now she knew who the writer was!

"But, Evelyn, how on earth could you. . . ?"

"All I know is this," she continued. "As I pondered certain things I knew instinctively who the writer was, and I went to see her this morning on her way to work."

"You've been to see her! But how could you be so positive?"

"Well, as I sat in bed last night I remembered what you said about that dusky figure who darted out through the gate: a female figure in a dark dress with white piping round the collar. I had seen that collar somewhere. Yes, I remembered. It had been in church several times, and always on the same person: a person about my own height and build. I knew because one Sunday evening I complimented her on it, and said how well it went with her deep blue outfit. Next, I remembered that the voice which came to me over the telephone had a slight huskiness, just like the voice of that same young woman. Then I recalled one or two things Adrian Raglan had said when he walked me home. He said that this young woman was crazy about you, Joseph, and had determined to get you. Then Adrian tried to turn me against you by saying that this same young woman knew some ugly things about your father, and about your being an illegitimate child. It all tied together. Somehow I knew her. I saw her in my mind like a beautiful statue, but as I looked it slowly turned into a witch, and a hand from heaven pointed accusingly to her: a witch with an evil face and a collar with white piping round it. I knew her: it was Effie Crawley."

Millie and Joseph fairly gasped. "And you went to see her this morning!"

"Yes, Joseph. Please try to believe I am sincere. I don't wish to sound like a martyr; but I felt that since I had so deeply hurt you I must act to defend you. I just had to do it, whatever the risk, before I could honorably ask your forgiveness."

Joseph's voice was strangely faint: "Thank you, Evelyn."

Evelyn resumed. "Scribner and Wadsworth's opens at 7 a.m., the engineering sheds, but the office not until 9 o'clock. I waited down the road the way she would come. She was surprised to see me. I said, 'Effie, may I talk to you on the way to work? You may wonder why I'm asking you, but do you love our Lord Jesus as your Saviour?' She looked hard at me, and said she did. Then I asked her, 'Do you love Him for being so wounded for us on the Cross, to save us?' She looked very curiously at me, but nodded Yes. So I said, 'Effie, forgive my asking once more: Do you love Him *very* much for being so wounded?' She hesitated but again said Yes. So next I asked, 'Effie, if you so love Him why do you keep driving more nails through His hands? Every time you do, His heart quivers with new pain, and He calls: Effie, why do you do this to Me when I love you and suffered to save you?' She stopped and asked me, 'Whatever do you mean?' So I said, 'Effie, every time you send one of those evil, anonymous letters you not only tear an innocent human heart, you drive another cruel nail into the heart of Jesus. Don't deny it, Effie. You were seen on Wednesday night when Adrian Raglan waylaid the pastor. Adrian told me you knew ugly things about Mr. Kennard's babyhood and that you would not hesitate to spread them. Effie, there's enough libel in those letters to put you in prison a long time; and yet those letters are about friends who love you and want to help you. Yes, Effie, we still love you and want to help you. . . .' By that time we were at the office door."

"Oh, Evelyn, what a risk you took! What did she say?"

"She didn't say another word, but she went into the office weeping."

Evelyn looked relieved as she finished. Loosely encircling her neck and falling over the front of her blouse was a gold chain with a pendant watch hanging from it—wrist watches had not yet become common. Joseph noticed it the more because it hung where the lover's locket used to be. She glanced at it and said, "Well, I must be going, or our office will think I'm lost. Daddy said if I rang from here one of the men would come with the car. May I use your telephone?"

Perhaps she wondered why Joseph and his mother seemed short of comment. They were both thinking, "Evelyn has got there with one step instead of our twenty!" While she waited for the car they told her the process by which they, also, had reached the same conclusion.

"But don't forget," Evelyn assured them, self-deprecatingly, "had it not been for your clue of the white piping round the collar, and your ferreting out that it was not one of those mothers who telephoned me, I could never have guessed who the writer was."

The car was now at the gate. As she left them it seemed to Joseph that she invisibly pulled heaven away with her. Rather wearily he said, "Oh, mother, what a girl!"

"Yes," Millie agreed. "Didn't I tell you that in gentle Evelyn the deceiver had met his match?"

As Joseph and his mother conferred on the new turn of events they sanguinely decided none-the-less that they should pursue their own investigations; for what if Evelyn had now put herself in danger? Were Effie Crawley's tears genuine? or was she play acting? Did not the police office say she was sneaky? Was she not a split personality with criminal urges and tendencies to violence? Would she later deny having written the letters, and devise revenge against Evelyn! So they set off on their round of enquiry.

First they called on Mrs. Tweedly where Effie had lodging. They thanked her for telephoning about Effie, only to learn she had *never* telephoned; it must have been Effie impersonating her, to say complimentary things about herself. "We had to get rid of her. Articles went missing from different rooms. Unfortunately, *all* our boarders came under suspicion. At last a trap was laid, and the pilferer was Effie Crawley."

Next through the police and postal authorities they found that the Mrs. Councilor MacLean of Chorley who had first telephoned Joseph about Effie was nonexistent.

Then, during the noon break when they thought Effie would be away from the office, they called at Scribner and Wadsworth's. The police chief had rung through and asked the manager, Mr. Handsworth, to wait in for them. The notepaper used there had the same watermark as that which Effie had used. However, Effie would be back no more. That morning she had been "sacked" at a moment's notice, for thefts and a forgery. They were "preferring charges" against her.

Further searching seemed needless; so Joseph and his mother returned home. However, Millie thought she might as well ring through to the Customs and Excise Office in Oldham, where Effie purportedly had formerly worked. They had never known such an employee.

So there it was: the indications now amounted to certainty that the anonymous libeler was Effie Crawley. Where was she now? She no longer stayed with Mrs. Tweedly. Earlier that day, when charged with embezzlement at Scribner and Wadsworth's, and the manager had rung for the police, she had grabbed her coat and dashed out of the building. The police were now after her. Where had she run? Where would she hide?

It was superfluous now for Joseph to take the three boys to testify in Evelyn's office, but inasmuch as the arrangement had been made they were picked up at St. Thomas' school. Their ride in the Adair limousine was a grandiose thrill. It awed them, the way it whizzed them along the roads. They were fulsome in their eulogies of "Mister Kennard." Captain Raglan had told them to watch him "bash the parson," but he got "bashed" himself. "Mister Kennard" went at him like a "spring-heeled Jack."

When the three boys were gone, Millie and Joseph reported their findings during the day. They and Evelyn all felt the same commingling of anger and pity: anger at such evil, and pity for its perpetrator. Equally, too, they were relieved that at last the ugly affair was getting cleared away before those anonymous letters had been thrown to the beasts in the arena of public scandal.

About ten-thirty next morning Millie telephoned the police headquarters. Had they found Effie Crawley?

"No, Mrs. Kennard. She's probably miles away by now. A young woman fitting her description was seen on the railway platform late yesterday, boarding the train for Manchester. There's a big crowd o'folk there. To find a slick customer like Crawley—it's like looking for a grain of salt on Blackpool sands. Or she may have gone on to Liverpool—and that's worse. We'd be glad to call the hunt off, only Scribner and Wadsworth are pressing theft and forgery charges. In several months she's fleeced 'em of over three hundred pounds! That means she's plenty cash on her. She can easily slip out of sight like a sly little fox in a covert—easily, with that much money. Probably we'll never hear of her again now until the next time she's in trouble with the law."

Millie repeated this to Joseph. They were both vaguely sorry. It seemed an untidy finish to a messy episode. It was at best a Pyrrhic victory. They could not now get a written confession. Still, they could at least inform those who had received the letters that the culprit had been found: Effie Crawley, a jail bird with a bad record, and that the malicious vilifications were now demonstrated falsehoods.

"Maybe we should ring up the Adairs, and let them know that Effie has not been found."

At Pinecrest it was Agnes who answered. Millie said, "We thought that maybe we should let you know: I enquired at police headquarters a few minutes ago. They have not found Effie Crawley. They think she may be miles away by now; but they're going to keep looking."

"Millie, they needn't search any further. She's here, at Pinecrest."

"Agnes, you can't really mean. . . !"

"Yes, Millie, she's here, poor girl! She rang the bell late last night. When Joash opened the door she staggered into the hall and said, 'Please, oh, please let me see Evelyn;

please!' Evelyn had gone to bed, but she donned her robe and came downstairs. When Effie saw her she dropped at her feet and held her, and sobbed and shook and sobbed and trembled. Millie, it was heart-rending to see. She just couldn't stop, and we couldn't speak. We could only stand there and let her sob it out. It was awful to watch. It was as though a reservoir had burst its sluice gates and the water was gushing out till there was no more left. We thought at one point that she would go into a convulsion, but no, she sobbed on again until gradually her sobs became whimpers and she sank flat at Evelyn's feet."

Millie listened, wordless.

"When she looked up, Millie, oh! I never in my life saw such a change in a face! It was as though her sobbing had flooded some awful evil out of her being. We helped her to the sofa, and, what do you think?—she limply sank down and went right off to sleep! She must have slept over half an hour while the three of us sat round, wondering what to do. Then she began to twitch and tremble; and indistinctively she kept saying, 'Oh, no!—they're after me again! Those evil beasts! Evelyn! Evelyn!' So Evelyn said, 'It's alright, Effie. I'm here. You're quite safe. No one can harm you now.' Then Effie slowly opened her eyes and looked round at us as though the light was too strong. When she saw Evelyn again she said, 'Oh, Evelyn, I'm so weary—and you are so strong.'"

"What an experience!" interjected Millie.

"Yes, but there's more. We gave her supper and a warm drink. She grew calmer. In fact, she became very still, and then said, 'How can I thank you? How I envy you!—such a home of love and purity! Do you know, ever since I was a little girl there's been so much filth shoveled on top of me that the part which wanted to be good has been like a little child buried alive. It's never had a chance to see anything clean and lovely. Since I was a child I've never seen anything really beautiful until this morning. Did you wonder why I stared at you, Evelyn? As I stared into your pure face and kind eyes, and saw those tears trickling down your cheeks, and heard you say you still *loved* me—oh, Evelyn, the buried something inside me caught a glimpse of you. It

struggled up and started calling you, 'Please help me! I can
see you! I like you; I love you; I want you. Please, please,
Evelyn, help! Help me to get out of this grave and climb up
over all this filth that's on top of me!' I made up my mind
there and then to confess in the office what I had done, but
before I had a chance I was charged, and they rang for the
police. I could think of only one thing: run! But that something underneath has been calling out all day, 'Evelyn! Evelyn!'—and I had to come or I would have killed myself."

Agnes paused. "Are you still there, Millie?"

"I was never more here in my life. Is there more?"

"Yes, there's the best of all. She'd nowhere to go, but she
offered to walk round until morning if she could come back
and talk with Evelyn. We could see she sincerely meant it,
but of course we couldn't hear of it. We left her talking with
Evelyn in the living-room. Joash and I went off to bed,
though only to lie awake and be on hand if needed. Effie
confessed to having written all the anonymous letters. That
part about Joseph's having been born illegitimately she got
from Mike—not directly but through the barman at the
saloon where Mike used to drink. She poured out her
whole wretched life-story to Evelyn. Oh, Millie, what an
upbringing she's had, or, rather, what a down-dragging! Her
parents were drunks. From her young years they taught
her to be like a young animal to men. They taught her
thieving and every vice. She broke the law, and was
hounded by the police. She was caught, and placed in a
reformatory. It was there that she was given commercial
office-training. Other things she picked up by her own
mental quickness. I won't tell you more, Millie; but how
that poor girl has suffered!"

Agnes sounded a bit weepy herself.

"What I want to come to is this: they talked and wept
together on into the early hours of the morning. Then they
knelt and prayed together, and Evelyn had the joy of bringing her to Jesus. I know, Millie, you are bound to listen a bit
skeptically. In your kind of work you have to watch cau-
tiously—and we Adairs are such novices; but if I know
anything at all, Effie Crawley is truly converted!"

"No, I'm not skeptical, Agnes. I'm lost for words."

"Well, to conclude. Effie then dozed off, resting on the sofa, and Evelyn slept in a chair. We had an early breakfast. Effie had a bath, and tidied herself up, and looks much brighter, but still weary. A little while ago she wrote a full confession about the letters. Joash and I have signed as witnesses. It's written on an affidavit form from the Magistrates' Office, and Joash has appended a magistrate's note about its voluntariness. Effie insists on giving herself up to the police and serving sentence. She is able to give a good part of the stolen money back. A few minutes ago we telephoned Mr. Handsworth of Scribner and Wadsworth's at his home, and asked if he would now drop the charges. He said, No, he was responsible to his superiors; the law must take its course. He doesn't believe characters like Effie Crawley *ever* change. They're better in prison. Effie says that in prison she can help some of the other young women there. If only people knew, she says, most of the girls and women who end in the gutter or on the gallows have a crushed angel buried somewhere inside them."

"Well, Agnes, it's a long time since I heard a story like that. These wretched anonymous letters have certainly had an unexpected outcome. We've got to help Effie now."

"Yes, and that's just where we need your guidance, Millie. What's the next step? Can you help us?"

"Maybe I can. First let me tell Joseph about the new development. He'll be knocked over with delight. In half an hour or so, I'll be in touch with you again."

It scarcely took that long before Millie was through to Pinecrest again. "I've been in touch with headquarters, and the assistant chief says that if I, as police court missionary, will assume responsibility for the wanted female, he won't interfere—particularly so because the arrest warrant is not yet actually written, and Effie is voluntarily giving herself up. He agrees that she can stay either with me here or with you, seeing that Joash is a magistrate. On Monday I'll get a word with the town clerk, and see if we can keep Effie out of court."

Monday soon came. Millie was the town clerk's first visitor. That elderly and portly official knew Millie well enough to call her by her first name. "What can I do for you, Millie? Is it another prosecution you want waived?"

"It's an extra-special one this time. If we can save her from coming up in court, I think she'll never appear there again." Whereupon she told him the Effie story—except the anonymous letters.

"That's good enough for me, young lady, if Scribner and Wadsworth will drop the charges. Let me have a word with them. Kindly wait here."

He was away only a few minutes. "Millie, they're still on the 'phone, and they agree to cancel the prosecution if they can recover two-thirds of the stolen money."

"Please tell them that not only two-thirds, but the whole of it will be returned, with little delay."

Soon afterwards Millie was singing to Agnes, "Yes, the prosecution is quashed. The town clerk was sympathetic. I put four considerations before him. First, Effie had voluntarily given herself up and could return most of the money. Second, we believe Effie is now truly changed. Third, I had been in touch, on Sunday, with Carol Manson of the rescue mission in Oldham (he remembered her) and she was only too willing to take Effie under her wing. Four, I had also telephoned that lady doctor in Oldham who knew Effie, and she said she would take special interest in Effie. So, that's that, Agnes. Effie is free!"

"Isn't that heartening, Millie! D'you know: it's exciting to me that you and we are 'pulling something off' together."

"By the way, Agnes, that medical woman in Oldham sounds the right sort. She seems to be a true Christian, and eager to help. From time to time she renders professional service at Carol's rescue mission—always free. But she was telling me that poor Effie is an epileptic; not the serious kind called *grand mal,* but a milder form, *petit mal,* probably brought on by brain hemorrhage due to the way she was treated in infancy, or by early traumatic experiences. And, like many such epileptics, she is definitely above average in intelligence. Anyway, so far as indictment here is concerned, the case is closed."

But in another sense the "case" was not closed. Millie and Agnes accompanied Effie to Oldham and saw her housed with Carol. She and Carol became life-long friends.

Over a year later Carol wrote that Effie had become her most effective co-worker, adding, "We always find that those who help the down-and-outs most are those who now live top-level but once were very low. Effie combines the two."

Nor is that all. Apparently, Effie gradually shed her liability to fits. She took late training in Manchester for slum mission-work. Sometimes, at weekends, she assisted Miss Molly Ainsworth, who by then had been working in the Ancoats area for about two years.

That mention again of dear Molly Ainsworth calls for an accompanying comment here, lest it should be overlooked later. Her name became almost a byword among the poorer women around there. She did not have the fire or force of a Millie Kennard, but she had distinguishing gifts as a speaker, singer, pianist, adviser. Let it be added with fond esteem: such were her tender-hearted ministry and winsome influence, she was known all over the area as "the angel in blue." Dear Molly!

TWENTY-FIVE
Hail, Smiling Morn!

Before leaving for Oldham, Effie was with the Adairs ten days; the sunniest days of her unhappy life. The impression made upon her never wore off. She had seen something in Evelyn and the Adair home which left an unending afterglow. Never for years afterward did Evelyn have a birthday without a letter of fond gratitude from Effie.

As for Adrian Raglan, neither he nor his parents were ever seen at Harvey Street again. Adrian did not even resign as captain of the Boys' Brigade. He just disappeared with his nose rather swollen, while his parents resigned with *their* noses indignantly upturned.

The anonymous letters, which Millie and Joseph had studied like baffled hieroglyphics decipherers, were duly cremated without funeral rites, and great was the blaze thereof. But there was one letter which eluded that cremation; and before it, too, was deservedly devoured by the flames it provoked an exciting sequel to the episode of the anonymous letters—the very opposite of what they had intended!

Weeks elapsed after Effie Crawley had moved to Oldham. Greatly relieved in mind, Joseph was conducting the work at Harvey Street with his former vibrancy. The people noticed. They were pleased that he had recovered (as they thought) from his "winter tiredness" or his "not feeling too well for a spell." Not more than a handful knew about the anonymous letters, and even they now knew that the letters were confessedly falsehoods.

Christmas came and went. New Year's Day brought Anno Domini 1914. Joseph would soon be twenty-three. The Harvey Street folk said there had never been such Christmas and New Year gatherings, so full of spiritual rejoicings. The revival fervour kept burning on amid Winter chill. The people kept flocking in. The enquiry room was continually busy. The auxiliaries were thriving. Finances had never been so good. Young men and women were beginning to offer themselves for full-time Christian service on overseas mission fields or in the home country. The revival was no mere emotional froth. It was not only a time of songs and wings, but of changed *lives*. The people were *living* their Christianity. They were bearing each other's burdens, sharing each other's problems, caring for each other's well-being, and supplementing each other's "joy in the Lord." In a spiritual sense, Joseph's cup of rejoicing was full to the brim.

Yet at the same time there was a hunger and painful ache in his heart. He wanted Evelyn, and wondered why, although she now seemed more necessary than ever, she appeared more unreachable. Intermittently he and his mother were round at Pinecrest, but for the very reason that he so hankered after being there he purposely did *not* go too often or stay too long. The frustration seemed to sap his strength and leave him weary through sadness. The months of suspense and worry through those anonymous letters had so flung him back on God, in many an hour of wrestling prayer, that he was spiritually mellower. Also, during those times he had felt surer that God meant Evelyn for him: yet for a very real reason he kept thinking now that somehow he must be mistaken.

Evelyn was always genial. She had been forgiven for momentarily doubting him. For his sake she had risked herself with Effie Crawley. Since then she had seemed politely pleased at his visiting Pinecrest. She was unaffectedly natural, conversational, sometimes even playful, in his presence. That, however, was the very feature which disturbed him. She was too much at ease in his presence to be in love. He longed to see that flush of coy shyness which lets the secret out where there is sweetheart love; but it was not there. She was so attentive, so interested in everything he said, so animatedly willing to chat whether in lighter or more serious vein. But now he could never get near her, mind to mind; and she never let their eyes meet as before. At church she was his best-loved worker: in Sunday school, choir, and most of all in the personal work along with Millie. Yet with diplomatic deftness she contrived that they should never be alone together.

The most sickening recoil came one day when they were chatting together at Pinecrest. Evelyn always enjoyed reminiscences of their younger years, when she and Rickie and Joseph had played together. The conversation turned to some escapade or another of those departed days, and Evelyn said, "We've always been such good friends, haven't we? And we always shall be." Then, seeing Agnes beckoning, she said, "I think it's time for afternoon tea, Joseph."

"That finally settles it," he thought. "She thinks of it now as no more than friendship. Why has she changed? Or is it that *I* have stupidly imagined what wasn't there? At any rate, I've got to accept the present reality. I'm a friend, but no more." He tried to say to himself, "Joseph, be brave," but he was too love-sick to hear his own voice. As he walked home his head seemed to have grown too heavy for his poor neck to hold upright any longer.

Had he only known it, there was the very same hunger, pain, ache, in Evelyn, who with good reason thought he had committed himself to Molly. She was trying to be natural, pleasant, friendly, but no more than that, for *his* sake! There seems to be a naughty streak in providence which so manipulates circumstances that those who love each other most become the biggest puzzle to each other!

That evening Joseph sat for a time with his mother in the dining room, ostensibly reading a book, while she sat with a writing-pad on her knee, answering a few letters. She noticed now and then that he was not making much headway with his reading. Then, quite abruptly, he said, "Mother, you know how I love Evelyn. Well, I know now that she is not for me; so I've let her go. I only wanted you to know, so that any change in my attitude won't perplex you. Please pray that God will give me grace to take the disappointment as a Christian should. It's hard, mother. You know that I've always told you everything. Evelyn has made it quite clear. I cannot have her; so the sooner I try to forget, the better. But though I can't have her, I have the best little mother in the world, haven't I?"

He was trying to appear jauntily happy, but he had the expression of a crumpled autumn leaf.

"Why do you think Evelyn does not love you?"

Joseph gave his reasons, finalizing with, "When she returned the locket she left my photo in but had taken her own out. Her explanation was that she was returning it because of the Adrian Raglan affair, but even after learning that she had been misinformed she didn't ask for the locket back, nor has she ever mentioned it since."

"Joseph, if Evelyn Adair doesn't love you, I'll eat my bonnet strings. I won't say any more for now, but I'm just as puzzled as you are."

Many a person today, judging Joseph by bolder modern ways of doing, would think him needlessly bashful or timid. Why had he not openly pressed his love upon Evelyn long before now? Anyone who thinks that way, however, is out of touch with the social mores of those days. For a young woman to marry into a lower social level was "marrying *down*," and carried a stigma with it. In a way, too, it cast reflection on her parents that she had not "done better." The Adairs were rich. Joseph had nothing but his character—and his "calling" which was not a lucrative one. By now (so he reasoned) Evelyn *must* have reflected on this. Was it one reason for her recently changed attitude? But even if she were willing to link up with him, would her parents agree when it came to the actual decision? Perhaps mother Agnes might be inclined favourably, but what about Councilor-father Joash? To ask, and to receive "No," was not a comforting thought!

Next Wednesday afternoon, after her women's meeting,

Millie sat chatting with Agnes, as was usual. "Agnes, if there's one thing I've always avoided, it's meddling in matrimonial or love affairs, but I'm going to risk asking you a question about Evelyn. I think you've sensed for some time that Joseph loves Evelyn. In fact, since he was thirteen there's been only one girl in the world for him. For years he's had girls galore round him, but he's had eyes for none but Evelyn. Well, Agnes, my laddie is nearly eating his heart out these days, wondering why Evelyn has changed. I've seen him sit there forlornly holding that locket which Evelyn returned. And now he's reached the decision that anything special between them is over. He talked to me about it a night or two ago. Evelyn had gradually made it clear, so he said, that on her part there was nothing more than friendship; so he was praying for grace to accept what he should have known was inevitable. He said he was determined now to turn his mind away from hoping for anything more than friendship with her. Agnes, do you think Evelyn *does* love Joseph? I'm asking only in order to get at the real truth, for *his* sake, though he would be upset if he knew I were asking you."

"Yes, Millie, Evelyn loves Joseph. At first she was girlishly secretive. Afterwards she became quite open about it. I've seen *her* fondling that locket, too. Since she returned it to him, however, she hasn't mentioned it once. After Joseph came back to live in Elmerton, Joash and I rather wondered why he didn't spill his heart out quite frankly to Evelyn, seeing he was twenty-one."

"Perhaps I can explain that Agnes. You know how sensitive he is about matters of love and courtship and marriage. He has a keen sense as to what is honorable and proper. He's always had a stabbing fear that his love for Evelyn could never be more than a longing—like a man admiring an exquisite statue from outside the railings round it, entranced by its beauty but aware of its inaccessibility. You see, Agnes, you Adairs are rich; we Kennards are poor. You live in a big house and grounds; we've had to live in Wragley Street until recently. Evelyn's father is an honorable Councilor; Joseph's father—well, you know. He wouldn't have dared to seek Evelyn's hand without first seeing you and Joash. Soon after he came back to live here he said to me, 'Mother, how dare I expect a princess to look at a peasant! Besides, her parents will expect her to marry some well-to-do young chap on their own level.' And now, Agnes, these anonymous letters come, smirching him as a son of harlotry! Although they've been exposed as false, he's sure that they have affected Evelyn's thoughts of him."

"Millie, are you really sure that those are Joseph's only reasons for not telling his love to Evelyn?"

"Yes, Agnes. No son and his mother were ever closer than Joseph and I. From his very childhood he was driven to me by his father's hatred and by the illnesses through which I nursed him. As he grew older and stronger he was 'all boy,' caught up in sports and a fight or two, but he never grew away from me. He had his faults, but even they—forgive me—were nice ones! There are 'spots' even on the sun, Agnes! I can't recall his ever once deceiving me. He always seemed to mix well at school, yet—how can I put it?—he seemed to grow up with an inner loneliness, a furtive dread of his father, and a feeling of being in some way where he shouldn't be. So I used to be all the fonder with him; and he's stayed so close to me, he's almost *too* boyish at times. But it's lovely, Agnes, and I'm glad he's like that. He doesn't hide anything that I ought to know; and I'm sure he's being frank with me about Evelyn."

Agnes still looked strangely unconvinced. "Millie, let me ask you once again: Are you *sure* that those are Joseph's only reasons for not opening his heart to Evelyn?"

"Yes, Agnes."

"Well then, Millie, I'm as puzzled as you are. Evelyn still loves Joseph, but there's one big reason why she won't say so any more. Evidently *we* know something about Joseph which you don't. It's something which, apparently, he has *not* told you."

"Well, you have me guessing, Agnes. I'm blest if I know what it can be."

"I was on the point of blurting it out, Millie, but I'm glad that I didn't for the moment. I wouldn't like Evelyn to think that I had taken it out of her hands and was trying to be a match-maker for her. It's something which Joseph and Evelyn themselves must settle. You see, dear Millie, I'm not sure, after all, whether Joseph *does* love Evelyn as much as you think. Ask him if there's something he *hasn't* told you."

Millie did so, that same evening. She not only asked, she probed; but it was like probing a ray of morning light— utter transparency. Joseph wondered whatever his mother was trying to get at.

This was telephonically communicated by Millie to Agnes next morning; whereupon those two scheming matrons put their naughty heads together in a sly little plot. In modern psychoanalytical phraseology, they decided that some potent "catharsis" was necessary to bring the frustrating hidden complex into full exposure!

This was it: Joseph's birthday was the following week. Agnes was to ask Evelyn to call round with a little present for Joseph on her way home from work that evening, and Millie was to persuade her to stay for "high tea" and a piece of birthday cake. Millie would plan it that matron Dorothy had to leave the table early for her duties in the nursing home, or else Dorothy would not be present at all. Millie was somehow to arrange for Joseph and Evelyn to be alone, and that Joseph should then ask Evelyn for the little photo back again.

Time seemed to turn the handle of the days round unusually slowly, but at last Joseph's twenty-third birthday arrived. The postman brought a sheaf of birthday cards which were set out on the mantelpiece and the sideboard in the dining-room. There were cards from his mother and two sisters, from the Adairs, Frank Goodall of the Mechanics' Institute, Ben Revell, his former Sunday school teacher, from various members of Harvey Street church, and (most lingered over) from the Ainsworths in Huddersfield, and from dear Molly, now in Manchester.

Millie prevailed on Joseph to take the day off, or at least part of it, as a birthday break, and get out into the fresh air. By midday the sky had cleared; the March air was nippy, and the roads were clear of snow again; so Joseph swung away on his bicycle out to the edge of the Pennines, and climbed up part of the way to Cragston Pike. He was back home about 4 p.m., looking ruddy and refreshed. Already the table was set, with dainty, laced-edged cloth, pretty china and the silver which graced their mealtimes only on special occasions; and already the ice-topped birthday cake was in the center, with a serviette over it. A cheery fire crackled in the grate. The room was bright and cozy. Spider Millie had weaved her web. Soon the pretty fly would be in it! All looked delightful; but was it quite fair? Did cunning Millie and Agnes have no twinges of conscience? They were too honorable and too wise to "force the issue," nor would they knowingly have been unkind enough to "corner" Joseph and Evelyn. Still, it was naughty to risk even what they did.

About 5:15 p.m. the door bell rang. Pretending surprise, Millie "wondered who it could be." It was Evelyn! At the sound of her voice Joseph was up from his chair—for to him it *was* a surprise. He heard his mother say, "Come in, dear," then add in a low voice, "your mother whispered through the telephone that you were coming; but I haven't told Joseph, so that it could be a nice surprise. *Your* coming will be the best of all birthday presents."

"Thank you, so much, Mrs. Kennard, but I think I had better just give him my birthday good wishes and then be away home. They'll be waiting for me. See, this is why I came round: it's a book for Joseph with our birthday greetings written in it."

Meanwhile Joseph, still looking fresh from his outing, had come into the hall.

"Hello, Joseph. Happy birthday! and many happy returns of the day!"

"Thank you, Evelyn. How kind of you to bring this book round! From something your mother said, I have a sly suspicion which it is. I'll read it with all the more pleasure because your names are written in it. Thank you, also, for that choice birthday card which you all sent."

"Evelyn, I won't press you to stay if you'd rather not," said Millie; "but when your mother whispered that you were coming with this book I couldn't help saying how we would love you to stay with us for Joseph's birthday tea, if you cared; and your mother said she would be pleased for you to stay."

There was a flicker of indecision in Evelyn's face, so Millie at once came to her rescue. "Evelyn, perhaps I said the wrong thing. You won't hurt our feelings, not in the least, if you don't stay. You have things to do. Please don't think another second about it: but it's so good to see you. It was just selfishness on my part to want you to stay."

And now it was Evelyn to Millie's rescue. "But, Mrs. Kennard, it was far too kind of you to give me such an honor. I would love to stay. May I just 'phone home to tell them?"

Joseph hasted to take her coat and hat, handling them with such reverence, they might have been the "ark of the covenant." From her wavy hair to her feet he surveyed her face and form as she stood at the telephone—no, not with that horrible, smoochy, sexy relish with which many a youth looks at girls nowadays, but with the purest love that ever a clean young man felt towards the purest young woman who ever inspired it.

As the three of them sat at the table, Joseph gave a look at his mother which said (and she knew it), "Mother, you rascal, I know now why you set the table for three! You knew that Dorothy would *not* be coming, and you wangled that Evelyn *would!*" But there was no condemnation in his look. His artful mother had brought him the dearest of all birthday presents—and the most painful.

It was a convivially happy time. No one would have guessed from outward appearances that underneath those simple birthday pleasantries the love of two young hearts lay tortured on a rack of cruel misunderstanding. Millie was thinking, "What a couple of engaging conversationalists they are!" Joseph was marvelling that Evelyn could be so ripplingly pleasant in the triangular interchange of chatting and listening without ever letting those dancing eyes once really look at him. Evelyn was inwardly praying, "Lord, help me to cover up my sadness, and to be birthday-happy without going one step further than is wise."

Eventually the stream of conversation came to a temporary stop at the birthday cake. As Joseph cut it into appropriate portions Millie and Evelyn watched with a concern as concentrated as if he had been carving up an empire.

After that, through the cleft cake, the stream of conversation purled merrily on again until Millie said, "Well, I think I'm going to bustle you two into the sitting-room while I clear the table here."

It was just what they both wanted—and dreaded.

Evelyn immediately protested, "Oh, no, Mrs. Kennard, I want to stay and help you . . . please!"

"No, Evelyn, not this time. Any other day, Yes; but not on his birthday. He can have me any day, but he has you only on occasions. Besides, I think he wants to play something for you on the piano. . . . Joseph, I think you ought to go and stir the fire in the sitting room."

Joseph went.

Evelyn stayed, and Millie quickly whispered, "Yes, do go, Evelyn, dear girl. Don't think I'm interfering, but I've told him to ask you for something, and he won't if I'm there. It's a very small something, Evelyn, which you can easily give him if you will. Please say Yes, if you can; for I know he would treasure it so much; and *you* won't miss it."

So Evelyn went.

As she entered the sitting-room Joseph was hanging the fire-tongs on the back of the coal-scuttle after building up the fire. He did not play the piano, however, as Millie had suggested. Instead, even before showing Evelyn to a chair, he came a step or two forward and looked at her in such a way that she simply had to look right at him in return.

"Evelyn," he asked, trying to look pleasantly amused, "would you tell me quite frankly: Did you know in advance that my mother would be asking you to stay with us for tea?"

"No, Joseph, it was an unexpected pleasure."

"How interesting!" he muttered audibly. "D'you know, I suspect there's been a little scheming by our two mothers! *My* mother set the table for *three* although she knew Dorothy was not coming. And *your* mother sent you round ostensibly just to leave the book, knowing you would be asked to stay, yet she didn't forewarn you. *My* mother told me to ask you for something, and I have a clue that *your* mother knew about that, too. I think they have slyly planned that you and I should be alone just now. The dear rascals!"

"Yes, the sly rascals!" she agreed, laughing. "That's if they really did it in collusion."

"I think they did, Evelyn. My mother gave herself away again a few minutes ago. Just before she adroitly maneuvered us into this room she whispered the old proverb to me: 'Faint heart never won fair lady'!"

"That certainly does sound suspicious!"

"Evelyn, I've told you this only so that you may know it is none of *my* doing. So please don't feel awkward. You and I know each other so well, now; we can be thoroughly natural in each other's presence. As you remarked some days ago at Pinecrest, we shall always be good friends after those happy times when we were youngsters. We'll have some piano in a few minutes. I've taken such a liking to Grieg's *Peer Gynt* Suite; and there's something I want *you* to play for my mother."

"I shall enjoy that."

"But there's one other thing, first, Evelyn. It's something I'm almost too nervous to mention. Yet since we *are* alone—perhaps for the last time, please let me try. I know now why our mothers have planned this little trap. It's all been done in kindness, largely for my sake. If I try to wriggle out of it *my* mother will think me a coward."

There was a look (was it of loneliness?) which then came into Joseph's eyes, and which Evelyn had noticed once or twice before during recent weeks. Or was it a look of weary sadness? How eagerly would she have flung her arms around him!

"Evelyn, it's something so small, in a way, but it means much to me. It's the locket. I wanted to ask if you would care to have it again, just as a reminder of happy times together. Or, if not, would you give me that little photo of yourself which used to be in it?"

"Joseph, you need not have felt any sensitiveness. I was proud to have the locket, and I've wept that I so wronged you at the time I returned it to you."

"Will you let me give it to you again?"

"That is more than kind of you, Joseph. However, I think that *you* ought to keep it. I don't think it rightly belongs to me. But I will gladly give you the little photo of myself if you want it; though I would prefer you not to put it into the locket."

She was watching him closely. There was no mistaking his honest perplexity.

"But why not in the locket, Evelyn?"

"Because someone else belongs there."

"Someone else! Oh, Evelyn, what can you mean? No one else will *ever* go there. It's either you or no one."

She was watching him intently now. She saw perplexity become pain.

"Evelyn, in all honesty I had nothing to do with our being here alone, and I certainly never intended to get into this: but why do you speak about 'someone else'? And why have you so changed toward me? A few months ago over at Pinecrest I thought I was in Paradise with you, for you said I might . . . I might even . . . kiss your lips; and I nearly went delirious with joy. The whole of my being said Yes, and I wanted to smother you with kisses. Then I suddenly realized I had never said a word to your father about my love for you, so I mastered my burning desire, and drew back."

And now it was Evelyn whose eyes shone with intense surprise. "Joseph, was that the *only* reason you drew back?"

"Yes, Evelyn; and was I wrong? I loved you too dearly (and still do) ever to presume in any way."

"Joseph, let me ask you one more question: Do you love Molly Ainsworth?"

It was as though Joseph had been thunderstruck. "Molly Ainsworth! Oh, Evelyn, Evelyn, why do you ask that? Of course I love Molly. How could it be otherwise? She's one of the loveliest characters I ever knew. It was she who led me to the Saviour. It was she who taught me the first steps in the Christian life. It was she who studied with me, and bought me books, and sang at my meetings. . . . To me, there's no one quite like Molly Ainsworth. . . ."

Joseph was not looking right into Evelyn's eyes. "Evelyn, don't *you* love Molly, too? Remember: it was she who knelt with *you* as well, and led you to Christ. Did you ever know a purer heart or a dearer girl?"

It was in that instant, looking full into Evelyn's searching eyes, that he realized the true meaning of her question and his own innocent but stupid obtuseness. "Evelyn! how could I be so slow? And how could you ever have misunderstood? Are you asking if I love Molly as a *sweetheart*—in the way I . . . oh, Evelyn . . . in the way I love *you?* Then the answer is No. I've had girls, girls, girls round me ever since I went to St. Aiden's; more so at Huddersfield; and most of all since I entered the ministry. They're as plentiful as clover in a meadow, and many of them just as fragrant; but while I've liked many and respected all, I've loved only one. Of all those other girls Molly Ainsworth, to me, is the noblest and best. She's the truest and dearest I ever knew—except for one other; and I've been in love with that other, that one-and-only other, since I was thirteen. Evelyn, don't you even yet know who that other is? Surely, surely you do. Forgive me; I'm flinging off all silly reticence. Evelyn, I'm twenty-three today. For ten years, now, I've loved, ached, prayed, and longed for you—but somehow always thinking it must be a loving you without ever having you, because of our different social levels. But never forget this one thing, Evelyn: even if I never have you, I have loved you with utter honesty; and tonight my heart has been laid bare before you about Molly."

Evelyn looked more than uneasy. She seemed alarmed. Indeed she *was* alarmed. She saw the intensity in Joseph's frank, open, handsome face. Every native instinct within her rose up and cried, "Evelyn Adair, *traitor!* You gave that locket back to this prince of a man because you cruelly misjudged him; and when his honesty was vindicated you promised you would never doubt him again. But you *have.* You, who love him, have hurt him most. It is your hands which have driven the hurting nails through his honest heart, because, once again, you have taken another's word instead of his!"

She had gone pale. She was near to tears. Joseph saw it and felt immediately guilty. With his head down in shame he now quietly said, "Evelyn, poor, dear Evelyn, what have I done! How cruel I am! Forgive me, if you can. It really does look, after all, as though you were deliberately cornered—though heaven knows it was none of my doing. I had vowed never again to speak of my love to you; and I now vow that after this I never will again. Try never to feel awkward in my presence. Never, *never* will I embarrass you. In any case, I may not be much longer in Elmerton. I withdraw my request for you to take back the locket, though I still would like that dear photo of you. I can at least secretly sing with Tennyson,

> *'Tis better to have loved and lost*
> *Than never to have loved at all.*

"Please, let's say nothing of this to our two mothers—except that I asked for that photo, and you are giving it to me. I know that what I've said frankly to you tonight you will keep locked up in sacred confidence. Don't let it deter you from continuing to help in the work at Harvey Street. I'm not ashamed of what I have confessed to you: but from now it will be firmly put away from my mind—for ever."

Evelyn was too upset for disguise, though in fact disguise was now the last thing she wanted. Her fingers seemed trembly as she tried to open her dainty, beaded handbag. From it she slowly drew an envelope containing a letter, and, without comment, handed it to him.

He knew the handwriting on that envelope, and quickly took out the letter. It was that same, large script as the other anonymous letters from Effie Crawley.

> *Dear Miss Adair,*
>   *This letter is bound to cause you pain, but it is written from a sense of duty, for your good. I am sorry it must be anonymous, but do not doubt the truthfulness of it. Your parents have already received a letter from me about the Reverend Joseph Kennard and his background, so I will say no more about that. But I must inform you, for your own good and to clear my own conscience, about the hypocrisy of his attentions to you.*

> *I do not know whether he has actually professed love for you, but I do know that you seem to be falling prey to his charms. So I think you ought to know that he is already engaged to Miss Molly Ainsworth of Huddersfield. I know her, and she has told me about her love for him. I have it on good authority that they are engaged even though not yet publicly announced. It is to be kept secret until she completes her city-mission training in Manchester.*
>
> *It hurts me to tell you this, but then he has no right to mislead an upright, Christian young woman like you when other young men far worthier would gladly claim your hand.*
>
> > *Sincerely yours,*
> > *A Concerned Friend*

Joseph ran his eyes through it. As he did so, Evelyn saw the changes on his expressive face—from surprise to anger, from anger to pain. "So this is it, Evelyn!—and you never told me!—and it might never have come out if our mothers had not trapped us! What depth of Satanic guile can human beings sink to in such cruel inventions of lies!"

Evelyn stood there, helpless, frozen.

Joseph went to the sitting room door and called, "Mother, could you come for a moment?"

Millie came, and Joseph handed the letter to her.

As she read it Evelyn saw the fire of indignation in those bright eyes.

"The young demon!" exclaimed Millie.

"No, mother, not a demon any more," Joseph corrected her, "but certainly she was demon-possessed when she wrote that letter."

Tears were trickling down Evelyn's face. She looked forlornly at Joseph and his mother. It was only too evident how disappointed in her Millie was.

At last she found words. "Mrs. Kennard, I know what you are thinking, and how disappointed in me you are. You are wondering why I ever paid heed to *this* letter when all the others had been proved to be wickedly false. But there's something you don't know. On the night when Effie

Crawley and I stayed up together she told me the whole story of her wretched life, and confessed to writing all the anonymous letters. If ever anyone was broken by remorse and repentance, she was. Afterward she knelt with me, and while we prayed she opened her heart to Jesus. I shall never forget it. I know she was sincere—just as you yourselves found later. But one letter—the one she had written to me—still bothered me, so I asked her about it and she said that the part about Joseph and Molly was the one thing which was true."

"You amaze me, Evelyn," interposed Millie.

"I knew you would be surprised, Mrs. Kennard; but Effie really meant it. Let me try to explain. When Joseph and Molly came to Elmerton in 1911, Effie went to some of the meetings. At first she couldn't make much of the preaching, but she became infatuated with Joseph. She went to the enquiry room one night, mainly out of curiosity, and to get nearer to Joseph. Instead, she met Molly and thought she was the saintliest young woman she had ever met—only she still had a notion that 'religion' was a hoax. Here's the strange thing: Effie has an uncle near Huddersfield, and he works at Mr. Ainsworth's furniture factory. So Effie got the idea of going to Huddersfield on the pretense of wanting 'religious help' from Molly, and of seeing that uncle at the same time. Her chief purpose, of course, was to see Joseph again, but in that she was foiled because by that time Joseph was away studying in Manchester. However, she *did* find out how deeply Molly loved him. Strangest of all, that uncle at the furniture factory told Effie how everybody was 'smitten' with Joseph, especially Mr. and Mrs. Ainsworth, and that on one occasion he overheard Mr. Ainsworth say to someone in the office vestibule, 'Yes, we think the world of Joseph. In fact, I've wished he were my own son; but I'm glad now that he isn't, because we hope to see him marrying our daughter soon. There's a secret understanding between them, but we're saying nothing in public about it yet.'"

Evelyn paused and Millie interjected, "Evelyn, why ever did you not let us see that letter? From my own contacts with Molly I could have refuted it at once. It is quite true that Molly loved Joseph—she still does. She tried to hide it, but in the end she couldn't, and Joseph began to see it. Molly herself told me how Joseph eventually had to tell her about *you,* Evelyn. Molly is something like you Evelyn. She had never looked at any other boy. In her bitter disappointment that Joseph could not be hers she flung herself on God and asked Him to show her what to do. As a result, she decided that the way of victory was to forget herself in full-time service helping others. So she went into training for city-mission work."

By now Evelyn was a picture of grief. "Oh, Mrs. Kennard, what can I do? I *wanted* to show you the letter, but mother and I were so sure Effie was sincere in what she said, we were afraid to hurt *you* with it. Mother said, 'Evelyn, be brave. Now that you know about Joseph and Molly and that *you* can never have Joseph, ask for grace to live with your disappointment, and don't ever again be more than pleasantly friendly with Joseph.'"

Then, looking with pitying appeal to Joseph, she said, "Oh, Joseph, how can you bear the sight of me? Once before I was deceived into misjudging you, and afterwards I vowed with tears I would never doubt you again. But I *did!* Can you ever forgive me? Yes, Joseph, I *love* you. My mother knows it. My father knows it. Rickie knows it. Uncle Ben knows it. Your own mother knows it. Others know it—and *God* knows it. From the day you bandaged my ankle at Netherford Lake you have been my one and only sweetheart-love. I've always been yours. I still am—if you still want me."

They looked into each other's eyes—oblivious now of Millie's presence. The next moment they were locked in each other's arms. Through their tears of sudden rapture each thought the other looked more beautiful than ever. Lifting her beautiful, tear-bedewed face to his, Evelyn said softly, "I'll say it now, dear Joseph: You can kiss my lips, too, if you wish—and you needn't ask daddy first!"

How long those lips were pressed together in that first, heavenly kiss of reciprocated love, Millie did not know. For a moment or two she watched—and wept. Then she stole away back to the living-room, to ring the news through to Agnes.

When she returned to the sitting-room they were still in each other's arms; so she said, "Joseph, Evelyn, you are being watched! You'd better not use up all your kisses now, or you'll be bankrupt by tomorrow. Save a few for a rainy day."

Is there anything more touching than the radiance which glistens in the eyes and on the faces of two lovers who love with a pure love like that of Joseph and Evelyn's? The dark clouds of misunderstanding at last were gone! The sun had broken through, full and clear! At last they were each other's, and *knew* it!

Millie gently piloted them over to the piano. "Don't you think a little music would go well with this new-found joy of yours?"

"Yes, mother, it would; but not until we've both given *you* a hug and a kiss." Whereupon Millie, attacked on both flanks, yielded to pressure under a bombardment of affection from two grateful young hearts.

"My dear little mother," Joseph said with a twinkle in his eye, "you and Evelyn's mother tricked us very neatly into your little trap tonight, didn't you?"

"Tut-tut, both of you. Let me tell you: the only one who got trapped tonight was the devil. I could wish it had trapped his tail off, only that wouldn't be much use in Elmerton—there are too many saloons here which 'retail spirits!'"

Switching at once from that touch of sombre humour, they remembered that Joseph was to play from Edvard Grieg's *Peer Gynt* series. "Indeed I will," he said; "and my three favourites in it all fit this happy occasion—'Morning,' and then 'Anitra's Dance,' and then 'Solveig's Song.'"

He flexed his fingers in a few scales, then turned to Grieg's choice pastorale, "Morning." But after the first two or three bars he stopped and sat silently on the piano stool. Then, looking round at his mother and Evelyn, he said, "Please try not to think me over-sentimental, but somehow on this *so*-happy night I just can't play this piano. It was given to me by Molly and her parents. Let's just be silent for a moment and pray a prayer for Molly. . . ."

In any case, time had run away quickly, and Millie had a suggestion which was as thrilling as it was simple. "Joseph, I know it's a fair distance from here to Pinecrest, but we have a clear, moonlit night. Don't you think it would be enjoyable if you walked Evelyn home?"

As the two of them went out together through the front garden gate, Millie "happened" to peep through the sitting-room curtains and saw them for the first time arm-in-arm. "Yes," she mused to herself, "arm-in-arm at last; and I think they're heart-in-heart for ever."

What they talked about on that walk home, and how many times they stopped for an embrace or a kiss or both, is a secret forever locked up with them; but the happily comical abnormality was, that after Joseph had walked Evelyn home, Evelyn brought Joseph back again to *his* home— in her daddy's car!

While Joseph was gone, Millie thanked God once more that His gracious plan for Joseph had come into clear focus again. That night a song of her childhood came stealing back into her mind and sang there, off and on, for many a day.

> *Hail, smiling morn,*
>   *the eastern heavens sweeping!*
> *Hail, day new-born!*
>   *Farewell, sad night of weeping!*
> *The early lark is upward winging,*
> *The mavis on the bough is singing,*
> *The flow'rs from slumber are awaking,*
> *New rays of golden hope are breaking;*
> *Hail, smiling morn*
>   *of love and joy and song!*

TWENTY-SIX
Netherford Lake Again

Joseph surely won heaven's approbation during the months following his twenty-third birthday, for the way he manfully controlled his emotions. It is not easy for a man in public prominence to maintain normal poise, gravity and concentration on administrative leadership while experiencing such ecstasy as that of Joseph during those days. He and his darling Evelyn were so deeply in love after such frustrations, their hearts seemed unable to contain.

The enriching revival continued at Harvey Street. The sanctuary was crowded, and, as always, such numerical expanding and spiritual abounding brought not only new joys but new problems, new pressures, and much more work. Through it all young Joseph kept level-headed as well as enthusiastic. As before-mentioned, his mother, Millie (now fifty-four) was his watchful, wise and faithful monitor. Her own thirty years in full-time Christian work and in dealing with human nature were a continuous help to him. Some of her impromptu sermons and sayings to him behind the scenes he would never forget. "Joseph," she exhorted him on one occasion, "let this be your threefold character: intensely spiritual, but perfectly natural, and thoroughly practical."

His *song d'amor* to Evelyn was the continual melody in his heart, accompanied by a continual *Laus Deo* for the tidal wave of blessing on his ministry of the Word. He knew that Evelyn was God's gift to him, and that their love for each other must be on the altar of glad yieldedness to the Divine will. He knew also that no Christian ministry can have the power of God moving through it unless there is regular prayer and study of God's written Word. The office-bearers were unitedly behind him, so he had no worry there. They provided him with two paid assistants for hospital and membership visitation, which much eased his burden. They insisted that he take sufficient time out for recreation. He kept up his daily exercise, had the good sense to get plenty fresh air, and kept physically fit.

Evelyn was his unsparingly loyal adjutant. She was leading soprano in the choir, teacher of a young women's class, pianist at the Thursday Bible School, additional visitor when required; and now, also, Joseph's fondest, fairest, *frankest* critic. Blest is the minister who has such a critic; and wise is he who heeds!

Joseph and Evelyn's touchiest problem was to prevent their love from spilling over into unwise obviousness. When referring to her in public or among members, Joseph's ever-present liability was to speak of her as "my darling Evelyn" or "my precious one" or in some other such affectionate phrase; but by constant watchfulness he succeeded in reserving those sweetheart endearments for private use.

Spring stole in late that year, which made its arrival the more welcome. May was well in before the days were warm enough as well as long enough to bring out the cricket players or tempt people to picnic among the hills. One pleasantly warm morning Joseph cycled over to Pinecrest immediately after breakfast. Agnes greeted him. "You're bright and early. We hear fine reports about Thursday's meeting. . . . Yes, I know: you want Evelyn. She's just gone into 'Little Eden' for something, I think. Was she expecting you?"

It was the sunny morning which had tempted Joseph over, in connection with which he had a happy proposition to press upon Evelyn.

He strolled out through the gardens to the outgarth behind. There the Pennines stood in full view away east, with the morning sun now risen just high enough to set on each summit a coronet of gold. Nature, that greatest of all artists, with the sky as her canvas, was busying her brush among slowly dispersing white clouds, making glittering palaces on the edge of spreading lakes and fleecy mountains.

It was a captivating scene. Joseph let his gaze slowly travel from the Pennine slopes back over the intervening sweep of undulating grassland with its chaparrals of furze and other stubby evergreens, back to "Little Eden" and the flower gardens at Pinecrest. The ash trees and silver birches were re-leafing. The herbacious borders were dressing up in their Spring colours. The daffodils and tulips were posing gracefully like models in an exquisite beauty contest, surrounded by other blooms, all with their faces upturned to the smile of the sun, and their lips pouted to the kiss of the dewy breeze. A silver-throated thrush warbled in a tree-top. An exuberating lark was soaring and singing. Gangs of blackbirds were sputtering in neighbouring trees. The shrill voice of the robin could be heard among the early blossoms. Bees went buzzing by, already rich with the spoil of plundered beauty. The fragrant dampness of the dawn still lingered. The morning rays had kindled a sunbeam in every dewdrop. Mosses, laurels, blossoms, flowers, were throwing perfume on the breeze. It was the Easter-to-Whitsuntide "rustle of Spring," in which all who are "tuned in" can hear the wings of the resurrection angel turning winter's graveyard into a world of resuscitated loveliness.

Joseph stood there, inwardly responding to it all, and reflecting that the landscape which, amid its bleak, winter wrappings had looked ghostly gaunt, now smiled in renewed youth, when suddenly *there she was*—the one who gave a crowning finish to it all: Evelyn! He had not noticed her as she slyly flitted toward him, dodging between the gorse copses and round the moss-bordered paths until she stood in the rustic archway now festooned with dangling creepers at the edge of the garden where Joseph was. But now he saw her. What a setting for the fairest jewel he had ever seen!

He hurried a few steps toward her, then stopped, struck again by her beauty against that sylvan background. As he saw her in that rustic archway, to *his* eyes her cheeks were two pink roses. Her lips were shaped for innocent laughter. Her brow was noble and open. Her silky, fair hair falling wavily over her shoulders was surely made to caress. The little, winged god of sweetheart-love stood tip-toe on the horizon of her limpid, blue eyes, and shot golden arrows at him. Spring morning never kissed a face of purer beauty. For a few seconds he stood. In a mental flash-back he saw her momentarily again as he had first seen her there, years earlier, a dream of girlish charm, with soft, sunny curls peeping out under a dinky little floral bonnet. Girlish charm had now developed into womanly glory. Joseph could scarcely believe she was his.

What a despot love is! Well has it been said that he is the only despot against whose tyranny men and nations never rebel. His yoke is a twining of tender arms, and the crack of his whip a guileless kiss. He is a regal anarchist who flings bombshells of innocent mirth into the palace of the heart, and often stirs otherwise obedient emotions into open rebellion against calm logic!

"Why do you hesitate, Joseph, darling?"

"I'll tell you why, my Evelyn. I would not like anyone else to say this to you, but *I* will: To me you are intoxicating. Why should you be mine? In having you I am of all men the richest."

They embraced and kissed amid the floral creepers of the archway. Then Evelyn found a dry garden-seat where they sat and talked.

"Evelyn," Joseph began, "in the words of Solomon's Song, 'the winter is past . . . the flowers appear on the earth, and the time of the singing of the birds is come.' And the time for picnics has come, too! You remember your birthday wishbone when you were thirteen, and the cycle outing when you sprained your ankle. Don't you think it's time we did it again?—not the sprain but the picnic! What about next Tuesday, if the day is good and you could be excused from the office? I can arrange accordingly if I have your 'Yes.' "

Never did a little fish nibble more willingly on a hook.

So Tuesday came, with armfuls of balmy, sunny hours. With well-oiled "bikes" off they went, about 10:30 in the morning. They went the same route as years before: round by the Haystack Inn, then along Old Oak Road, and eventually over Moorlands Road into the lower hills. They pedaled to the same pace where, once before, they had dismounted because of protesting leg muscles. Now they were on that higher ground again, dodging the same old dents and lumps, laughing again at the same old jerks and jolts. They found the same grassy bank by the stream where they had picnicked a decade earlier, and the same shadowy little covert from passers-by on the stony road. The birds were nesting in the trees, with always two or three darting to and from the now leafy boughs. The brook still babbled musically by, here and there gurgling round or splashing over the impeding stones, and glistening in the morning sunshine. Away up there to the east was Cragston Pike, with its turreted tower still on lonely sentry duty, but seeming to look down with a "Glad to see you again. I still remember when you slept on my spiral staircase through the stormy night."

They reclined and chatted about all the strange happenings since they had last sat there as young boy and girl; of the cruel misunderstandings which had hurt them so much, and of the sovereign kindness which had brought such sunshine after such dark clouds. They paddled again in the stream, then sat on the bank, dangling their feet in the water.

"Joseph, how wonderful that after such frustrations we should really belong to each other!"

"Yes, Evelyn. If I may be poetic, on the looms of heaven God weaves the tapestry of the rainbow from the dark storm-clouds!"

"I like the poetry, Joseph; but I like the reality even better!"

"Yes, so do I."

There they sat, their arms—and their hearts—interlocked, and their feet in the stream. It was serenely thrilling. Yet there seemed to be a suggestion of impatience in Joseph's manner which Evelyn noticed now and then.

After a while he said, "What about moving on now, love, past the quarry and up to Netherford Lake? I'd like us to have leisurely time there. But if *you* would sooner we stayed and had our picnic lunch here, as before, that's perfectly alright with me. Whether here or there, my picnic heaven is just being with you. I only thought how good it would be to sit on that lakeside bench again, with some vivid memories—and you."

The idea appealed to Evelyn, so they travelled on, partly riding and partly walking until they passed the wide mouth of the old quarry on to the steep and stony rise immediately leading up to the lake. They recalled their grim yet comic struggle there years earlier to lower Evelyn down it after she had sprained her ankle. Evidently others had suffered slips and falls there; for now, through somebody's kindness, there were rough steps made up it. As before, Joseph carried his own bike up first, then went down and brought Evelyn's. Once inside the big iron gate they walked along with their bikes and propped them up where they could easily see them from the wooden bench further on. To their relief, there was no one else up there.

They were glad to sit and get their breath back after the climb. Joseph seemed much inclined to be meditative, but Evelyn was inclined to be hungry.

"My dear 'silent partner,' are you too wrapped up in thought to feel pangs of hunger?"

Joseph laughed. "What a rascal memory can be at times! Fancy, my letting it run away with me from *now* and from *you!* Yes, come to think of it, I'm hungry, even ravenous."

The sandwiches, in fact everything except the mineral drinks, had been prepared by Evelyn, but had been carried in Joseph's larger saddlebag. The very thought that those hands had prepared it all made Joseph feel he was committing sacrilege in eating it! However, at that moment hunger proved stronger than reverence!

Only those who have been in love as those two were can know what it meant to them to sit in that willow-shaded nook by the water's edge. Their love had shed away its first anxieties and had become a satisfying rest in each other. It was no mere amorous sentimentalism which set them luxuriously confiding that they had been "made for each other."

Having tidied up after their picnic meal they strolled arm-in-arm round the lake. What a view from up there!— the higher hills to the east, and the winding valleys to the west, their deep floors all covered again with new carpets of soft green tacked down by a myriad daisies, buttercups, dandelions and bluebells, and the brook a winding line of coruscating silver. Had it ever looked more appealing? And, gently lapping at their feet, the shimmering water of the lake surrounded by rhododendron bushes coming into bloom, intermixed with copious other bushes, plants, flowers, trees, all now in their most colourful Springtime gaiety; the Pennine slopes looking peacefully down on it all; the turquoise blue of the sky (not *too* common in Lancashire!) reflected in the lake! Evelyn had to keep a firm hand on Joseph lest it should provoke a further spasm of poetry!—though she, just as much as he, revelled in the aesthetic enjoyment of it all.

Yet still there seemed that touch of impatience about Joseph.

"Is there something on your mind, dear?"

"Well, yes, there is, love, but it's something very pleasant. Shall we stroll back to that memorial bench again now?—and I'll tell you what it is."

So they sat again on that same wooden bench in the shaded willow arbor by the lake, and there (as Evelyn expressed it afterward) Joseph preached the tenderest sermon she had ever heard.

"Evelyn, dearest heart, this wooden bench by the lake means more to me than perhaps you know. This is where I bandaged your sprained ankle on our first picnic as boy and girl, and where—as you afterward told me—love for me suddenly awakened in your heart. Later, when I fled from home as a boy of fourteen, after dashing round to give you the locket I had to decide quickly where to run; and in my desperate plight I vaguely decided to try for Cragston Pike before nightfall. My face was swollen and my mouth hadn't

stopped bleeding. My nose wouldn't breathe properly. I had
no money but two pennies, no food and no overcoat. I came
up just the way by which we came today. When I got to the
grassy bank by the brook where you and I had picnicked
together not long before, I sank down and cried. I was
tiring and frightened, and I thought I would never see you
again. Then I got up and struggled on again to here. My
shins were bruised and one knee had started to bleed a bit.
By the time I reached this bench I was exhausted through
the running and tramping and climbing and nervous tension—and dusk was closing in. I just couldn't stagger any
further. I collapsed at this bench and sobbed my heart out.
Looking back now, Evelyn, I can clearly see that *God* met
me at this bench. Even at the time I *thought* He had,
though I was only fourteen; but now in retrospect I *know*
He did. In my boyish way I told Him that if He would look
after me and bring me back to my mother and you, I would
try my best to be good and please Him."

"You never told me this before, Joseph."

"No, Evelyn, and I'm not sure I would be telling you now
but for a very special reason. However (if I'm not boring
you) let me remind you: it was at this bench, when I came
back two years later, that you and my mother and your
parents met me and the Ainsworths. Evelyn, can you imagine what *that* day meant to me?"

Joseph paused. Evelyn sympathetically waited.

"Evelyn, dearest sweetheart, I thought that this wooden
bench by the lake should be the place where I ask you the
most sacred question that any man can ask a pure woman. . . . Evelyn, dear treasure, will you be my wife?"

As he asked he slowly drew from his pocket a little jewel-
case. One glance and Evelyn knew what it was. The two
seconds he took to open it seemed an hour. But there it
was, at last, in its soft, silk cushion—the engagement ring!

A little nervously Joseph explained: "I hope you will like
it, Evelyn. It took four of us to select it—your father, your
mother, my mother and myself. I think it should fit your
finger, because about ten days ago your mother was mea-
suring when she started reminiscing about rings and had
you unsuspectingly trying some of them on! Of course, the

fit can easily be adjusted; and if you would prefer some other style of ring I shall not be hurt, so long as you have said your 'Yes' to me. We can go and choose another one instead—just the two of us."

He took the ring out. It was gold, bejeweled alternately with three diamonds and two sapphires.

Evelyn looked and looked, held it, and fingered it tenderly. Then, as it became blurred by her tears of joy, she said, "Oh, Joseph, how beautiful it is! How good God is to me! And how I love you! It will be my life-long treasure, all the more so because it is so needless."

"So needless, Evelyn?"

"Yes, in a way, dearest, because you have already put our engagement ring round my heart, a ring that is lovelier and more sacredly binding than any you could ever put on my finger. But this one, worn on my finger, will be the beautiful outward symbol of that ring around my heart."

They paused, both admiring it.

"Joseph, is anybody watching?" They glanced quickly round the lake.

"Yes, dear—*God*. But let's stand behind the bench in the shade of the arbor."

So there they stood, in the soft shade of that willow nook behind that lakeside bench, as she held out her hand and he gently slid the ring upon her finger, then reverently held it and kissed it.

"Oh, Joseph," she whispered, as they lingered there in each other's arms. "If there can be bliss like this on earth, what must heaven be?"

"Evelyn, don't you think we're there already—in heart?"

They were young and very human, healthily sanguine, with the same physical desires as others who have passionately loved, but theirs was a pure-hearted rapture which transcends and controls the merely physical, and which, after wedlock, sublimates it into the most sacredly thrilling communion two human hearts can know. In these present days, thousands of our young men and women who marry never know the exquisite bliss which Joseph and Evelyn knew. They blast their own paradise by premarital self-indulgence which is deceptively called "love" but which in reality is impure lust. The curse of God be on those who have taught our boys and girls that love is such animal gratification! They have dragged that purest of all words, "love," down to the gutter. They have degraded womanhood and debased the minds of our young men, and mocked ten million hearts with cruel delusion, and broken homes asunder without number. In the end promiscuity cheats our youth of the very thing which it promises to bring, that is, satisfaction and fulfillment; for mixing bodies sexually with mere paramours soon becomes not only unsatisfying but even repulsive, leaving in the end only the bitter dregs of remorse or coarse-mindedness. Whereas those who marry for true, pure love, and not merely for physical attraction, find that the physical endearments of the marital union become even sweeter as the years slip away. One of the desperate needs of the present hour is a rediscovery of virtue; for it is virtue, not lust, which carries the keys of happiness.

Joseph Kennard was human indeed, with the common human limits, liabilities and infirmities. He could be angry, impatient, out-of-sorts. He could think and say and do the wrong thing, like all the rest of us. But why should all those be detailed here? Rightly are they taken for granted. But in all truthfulness, it was the higher qualities which had the ascendency in Joseph, and which are the more germane to our story. Must a story be smutty or an expose of ugliness in order to be "human"? Many writers today, of a sort, seem to think so. Blind fools! Perverted thinkers! If in reality human life were what they keep telling us, the globe on which we live would be a revolving pigsty! There is more good than evil on earth, or the race would soon be self-exterminated, but the evil runs away with the publicity, thanks to the ignoble order of muck-rakers. That which, in part, makes the story of Joseph and Evelyn outstanding is the triumph of the higher over the lower, of the spiritual over the sensual, of pure love over dark antagonism. Admittedly, Joseph may have started with the advantage of a nature hereditarily refined, but that could easily have been coarsened under wrong influences. It came under *right* influences: a godly-wise mother, the Sunday school, the

Bible, Christian teaching, uplifting friendships, and culminatingly his conversion to Christ.

Joseph Kennard was a beautiful young man. That very expression, a "beautiful young man," could sound almost effeminate to some ears today. So much more the pity! There can indeed be "a beautiful man," all the more manly because *gentle*manly. Of course, the sexy young females of our day who think they are now "liberated" by a permissive society which increasingly enslaves them to the vulgar do not talk any more about a "beautiful young man." They prefer a fellow with freak irregularities of face, hair, clothes, habits; a pop-yelling, raucus, ranting "mod" with a mass of hair like a floormop or a superannuated scrubbing-brush. As the Old Book says, "Verily, they have their reward"—in what later miseries!

More than once or twice, as Joseph thought about his unsullied Evelyn, he recalled words of his mother's during his later school days. "Education is not meant just to polish you on the outside, but to make you a gentleman in *character.* True gentlemanliness is good manners outside with good motives inside. What's the good of covering a room with fancy wall-paper if the plaster under it is full of dirty holes and cracks?"

Well, that was Joseph Kennard: tall, well-built, finely sculptured features; firm yet mild in disposition; inclined to be over-sensitive, easily shocked by human wickedness, often discouraged by sin-proneness of heart, but constantly winning through union with the living Saviour.

With a simple change of gender, much the same was true of Evelyn. What we have reported of her in this story is not knowingly overdrawn or overtinted anywhere. She was as vulnerably human as the rest of us, and doubtless, if some photographer of *hearts* could have given us a photograph of her inner being, we would have found the usual battlefield of the upward-pulling versus the downward-tending. But (forgive the too quick change of metaphor) the fair flower grew up amid Christian influences—especially that of mother Agnes, and then came to full bloom of beauty through an early union with that heavenly Saviour-King who beautifies all that He touches.

In that leafy shelter by the lake, there they stood, with love-locked hearts. At last the engagement ring was on Evelyn's finger! They rode home at sunset with sunrise in their hearts. Some days later an envelope was handed to Evelyn in which she found the first of Joseph's poems to her.

> Sweet earthly joy: pure, human love;
> Thrice sacred 'tis when heav'n above
> Approves with favoring smile the tie
> That draws two hearts so gently nigh:
> 'Tis human joy, touched with divine,
> One sparkling drop of heavenly wine
> Which overflowed the brimful cup
> The angels, overjoyed, did sup:
> For, in their effervescent mirth,
> They spilled a blissful drop on earth,
> Just one delicious taste of heaven,
> What joy to human hearts it's given!—
> The grapes of pure, celestial bliss
> Compressed into a human kiss!

TWENTY-SEVEN
The Loudest Thunderclap

From various references to her in the local press, and her frequent appearings in the police court, and her large women's work in the town, Joseph's mother, Millie, had become one of the best-known personalities in Elmerton. Her most effective contribution was her Wednesday afternoon women's meeting, still held in the main hall of the Mechanics' Institute.

Every so often Joseph addressed that meeting; and the women always said, "His preaching is just like his mother's." On such occasions, while Millie and Agnes were chatting after the meeting, he always slipped in for a chat with his loyal friend, Frank Goodall, the woodwork man there. That is what happened the Wednesday after his engagement to Evelyn.

The usually calm Frank was curiously jumpy. "Joseph, I'm glad you've come in. My! you look in fine fettle. But, laddie, I'm in a hotty-motty about you. I'm blest if I even know whether to tell you. If what I'm thinking is true, it could cause no end of a bust-up!"

"You've got me guessing, Frank. Out with it, before the two ladies are here."

Frank certainly did seem nervously taut.

"To begin with: it's about Evelyn's father. I suppose you know he's been superintendent at Brandon Street Sunday school for twenty years now. Well, they're presenting an inscribed plaque to him as a mark of appreciation, and they came to me to get it made. I'm doing the wood background, and Finches up the road are doing the metal part—an inscribed silver shield; and then I'll affix the silver shield to the walnut back."

"Yes, Frank, I knew about that."

"Aye, but there's something I never knew till now. I always thought Councilor Adair's first name was 'Joash.' That's how it always appears in public. I never knew until they brought me this inscription: he has two names, 'Joseph Ashley.' Did you know that?"

"I'm not sure that I did. It never occurred to me to ask. It's taken for granted everywhere that his name is 'Joash.' "

"I know it; but his full name is Joseph Ashley Adair."

"That's interesting."

"Joseph, it's more than interesting: it's startling. Good heavens! I hope I'm not meddling with something I should keep mute about! You see, after the way your father spoke to me about you once or twice when he was tipsy, I knew he was not your real father. In a maudlin way he fumbled it out that he wasn't, and that *your* real name wasn't just 'Joseph.' I couldn't make out distinctly, but he seemed to say that your name was 'Joseph Ashton,' or 'Joseph Apsley,' or 'Joseph Asher'; and he said something about people getting a shock if they knew who you really were."

"Are you suggesting that I might be Joseph Ashley Kennard?—sounds rather nice doesn't it?"

"Oh, there's more than that. After your father got . . . well, after he was changed, he used to call here sometimes for your mother. So I thought I'd tell him what I've just told you. He seemed surprised, and said, 'What a fool drink makes of a man!' I agreed with that, and said I was glad he was now sober. He replied, 'Frank, I'm not only sober; I'm *saved*. I'm a new man!'—and, Joseph, he *was!*"

"You're right, Frank. He *was* a new man."

"But it was what he said afterward that hit me. He said, 'Frank, you're a true friend of Joseph's aren't you? and I believe you're a clean, trustworthy man. I'm going to risk saying something to you that I've said to only one other; but please, for Joseph's sake, don't let it out just yet. After what Joseph and Millie have said about you, I think I can trust you, and I'm beginning to think that maybe one or two like yourself should know. I'm speaking thoughtfully, and I'll tell you definitely: I'm *not* Joseph's real father. I used to hate him, but now, God knows, I love him, and I wish I really *were* his father. I'd be proud. He's not an illegitimate child, though. He's the son of a well-to-do family, and he's related to an affluent man whom you know. I intend to make it public, now that I'm a converted man; but I can't honorably do so until one matter has been put straight. Then I'll "out with it" whatever it costs me. I've got written evidence to prove it all; evidence which I've got secretly hidden. But for now, Frank, keep your lips tight, and put a prayer up for me.' "

If Joseph had felt any nonchalance at first, those last remarks had blown it to the breezes. "Frank, that certainly *is* a bit startling. Go on."

"Well, as you know, your father—poor chap—was . . . was murdered. I pondered now and then what he'd said about you, but I said to myself, 'All that's buried in his grave, now.' Then, lo and behold, this plaque comes! How could I help connecting it? Joseph, you're not going to like me for what I've done, but I did it with a good intention. I confessed it to your mother last week. I thought, 'If my pal, Joseph, ought to be coming into some money, I'm going to turn a few stones over. Every now and then your mother and I chat a few minutes. Just in a casual way I asked her about her work before she came to Elmerton; what part of Manchester it was, and whether it was successful, and which church she went to, and why she came to Elmerton. She was glad to tell me."

Again Frank halted and looked uncertain.

"You know that old proverb about helping a lame dog over a stile; well, that's what I meant to be doing for you; but I'm wishing now that I'd listened to that other proverb which says, 'Let sleeping dogs lie'—for I seem to have stirred up a hornets' nest, as they say. I once said before,

I'd never stick my silly nose in other folks's affairs, but I've gone and done it again! I went sneaking off to Manchester. I saw the mission where your mother worked, and the house where you lived, and the 'Church of England' where she often attended. Round there they all remembered your mother, and asked how she was getting on. I wanted to find out about *you;* and bit by bit I *did.* I got it mainly from an old lady over ninety—a spinster. When your father and mother went to live there, they had the two girls, but not you. That was in 1890. It was not until two years later that *you* appeared. Everybody was quite pleased, but the funny thing was that you were already a baby of about one year old! There was a bit of talk about it, but the explanation given was that you had been with some relative meanwhile owing to baby sickness and your mother's hands being full with the mission work. The talk soon died down."

"Frank, what on earth are you going to say next?"

"It'll surprise you, Joseph. I'd done all I could for one day; but I went to Manchester again on my next free afternoon. This time I went to the Registrar of Births, Marriages and Deaths, but he sent me over to the Anglican church where your mother had attended. He said that the clergy at that church had their own safe, and kept their own records. The curate there was a nice chap. He told me they didn't have the information at hand for so far back, but that if I would call again in about two hours he might be able to tell me what I wanted to know. Two hours later I was back, and sure enough he had what I wanted to know. Joseph, you were christened on Sunday, May 29, 1892, but the certificate says you were born March 18, 1891. Why did they not get you christened for a year and three months? That's the strangest thing, especially among Church of England people. The curate himself said it was a bit 'abnormal,' and it led him to mention another peculiar thing: *the father was not present* at the christening!"

"Frank, I'm getting afraid of what you're going to say next."

"So am I, Joseph. The certificate said that 'Kennard' was not your real name, but was given as your *legal* name; and that the real parents are unknown."

"Oh, Frank, what have you uncovered?"

"I don't know; but your mother had not been married before she became Mrs. Kennard. She was a single young woman, working as a city-mission deaconess right to the time she married Michael Kennard. So it began to look as though she was not your real mother."

Joseph went pale.

"I knew it would upset you, Joseph. I began to wish I hadn't started poking round. It seemed to me that the upright thing was to mention it to your mother; and that's what I did—last Wednesday. She was sort of quietly upset when I told her, but she looked steadily at me and said, 'Frank, I know how much you think of Joseph, so I won't chide you for what you've done. You meant well; but I'm sorry you did it without telling me. You might possibly have injured Joseph so cruelly, you would never have forgiven yourself. Yes, Frank, I'm his mother. There *was* something unusual in the way God gave him to me; but leave *me* to tell him about that at the appropriate time. You know how much I love him. Meanwhile, leave the matter alone, Frank, for Joseph's sake, or you just could hurt him badly.' "

"My dear Frank," interposed Joseph, "I don't know whatever to say. There's *some* mystery about me, but it's exasperatingly elusive. My mother is a very wise woman. Perhaps her advice is best: let the matter drop. One thing I know for sure: my dear little mother would never deceive or harm me. I'm glad you were so open with her."

"Thank you, Joseph, for not being angry. It was all done on the spur, in the hope of clearing up something which has puzzled us. I jolly well wish we *could* drop the thing there; but whether you'll want to do so when I tell you something else, I don't know. You see, Joseph, I hadn't the heart to say more to your mother; she looked so sad. But there are two or three things more. First, the old dame in Manchester says your mother is *not* your real mother. Along with that is what your father said on that day when he was tipsy, about your name being Joseph Asher or Apsley or something like it. And added to that is this, that he said something about your having a rich uncle, a Mr. Addie or Adder or something. Joseph, to me it's mighty like 'Adair.' "

"Wait, Frank, your imagination is running away with you. I never thought my steady old friend, Frank Goodall, could get his feet off *terra firma* like this."

"I think I'm still on *terra firma,* Joseph boy. I've told you what your father said after he became a changed man—I mean your being related to an affluent man whom I know. What I didn't tell you was this: he said that this affluent man lives in Elmerton! Think, Joseph: it wasn't your *drunken* father who said that, but your father after he became upright and honest."

"But, Frank, we're no further, really. We've no real facts. Don't you think we're on boggy ground?"

"I'll tell you what I really *do* think—and I haven't breathed this to another soul. I believe that this affluent man in Elmerton is old Mr. Benjamin Adair, and that you are probably related to him. It couldn't very well be the other Adairs—I mean Councilor and Mrs. *Joash* Adair, for when you were born they were not yet married. He's one of the richest men in town; and it sounded to me as though your real name might turn out to be Joseph *Adair!*"

Joseph was about to interrupt him, incredulously, but Frank motioned him to wait just a moment more.

"I'm trying to let this thing drop, Joseph, but I'm blest if I can. Your father told me as sanely and plainly as ever a man spoke that he had papers or evidence of some sort hidden somewhere. The only possible place I can think of is 12 Wragley Street. Where else is there he could hope for papers to be found if anything happened to him? I think you should have another talk with that champion little mother of yours; and if I were you, I'd pry into every nick and corner of 12 Wragley Street. It's up to you now, Joseph. I've got it off my chest. I swear to you: not one syllable of it will escape my lips to any other human being. So don't be *too* hard on me."

Often the very effort to forget a matter is that which emphasizes it in the mind. Joseph tried to forget what Frank Goodall had said, but in trying to tread it down he stirred it up. It would not be silenced, and soon it spoke out—to Millie.

She took it calmly. "I understand your feelings, Joseph. I would feel the same if I were in your place. But I also think that if you were in *my* place, you would say to me what I'm going to say to you. I'm sorry you've been made to doubt that I'm your mother. But if you do really doubt it, then I make you a promise. When you and Evelyn are married, I'll have a chat with you, and I'll clear up for you once for all what seems to you to be some mystery hanging over it. Meanwhile, dear son, my motherly recommendation is: Leave it for the present. There's so much, just now, to keep your heart singing."

"Mother, I think I trust you even more since you cleared up the misunderstanding between Evelyn and me. However, if you won't be cross, there's one thing I *would* like to do, because if I don't do it now, I never will; and once it's done, it will put my mind at rest on *that* score. It has to do with those papers which my father said he left hidden. There's only one place they could be, and that's 12 Wragley Street. I'd like very much to have one careful look round there. Then, if we find nothing, we'll consider the matter dead and buried."

"Very well, son, you shall. I know Mrs. Crawford well—the woman who lives there now. She'll be cooperative. But is it worth your time? As you know, after your father's death I told the police what he had said about some hidden evidence, and they ransacked the place from top to bottom. They went round tapping walls and looking under floorboards. They took two or three of the stairs up. They even looked under the stone flags in the backyard. Then, some days later, as I told you, there was a strange man came round and showed me a note which said he represented some detective agency in Manchester. He, too, combed the house, but found nothing. He seemed angry, and kept pumping me with questions of a sort that made me think he knew more about your father than he was letting on."

Joseph's hopes, therefore, had dragging feet as he and his mother went round to Mrs. Crawford's the next afternoon. Although she had not been apprised in advance, and Millie offered to come on a later day if more convenient, the elderly Mrs. Crawford insisted they should come in.

Without pretense she felt honored to have a visit from the much-talked-of young preacher and his well-known mother. "Mr. Kennard," she said, "I'm a pernickity old thing. I don't like a cat's whisker out of place or a paw-mark on the floor, so you'll find the house clean and tidy. There's not a corner I haven't looked in with a magnifying glass and scraped out with a meat-skewer. Just you look round for them secret whatever-they-are while your mother and I chat a bit; but I'll bet you'll find nothing."

Joseph preferred, however, that they should accompany him. They began upstairs. There was no trap-door through the ceiling anywhere, so there could be no papers hidden between ceiling and roof. Mrs. Crawford did not mind the floor lineoleum being eased up while Joseph sounded the floor-boards and lifted two loose planks up. In fact, she seemed rather to enjoy possibly being part of some exciting mystery. One of the two bedrooms was not in use. It was not furnished; so it was a simple matter to go over it inch by inch. It was such an *obvious* house in every part as to make investigation almost too easy. Millie herself could guarantee that there was nothing hidden under the wooden stairs from the kitchen to the bedrooms, for she had seen right under them when the police were searching. So from bedroom and stairs they came to the kitchen. There could be nothing underneath the kitchen floor because it was concrete. There were no fixed-in drawers, nor was there any place underneath the kitchen sink where papers could be hidden.

So they were soon back to the front room downstairs, the living-room. Almost inch by inch Joseph sounded the walls for any hollow place, but the bricking was everywhere as solid as the paper and plaster were unbroken. Carefully he examined the floor-boards and everywhere round the iron-work and outer woodwork of the fireplace and mantelpiece. That left only the built-in cupboard and drawers in the alcove between the chimney breast and the front wall of the house where the window was. That might have seemed a likely place for something to be hidden, except that it was too easy and too obvious and had already been thoroughly examined by the police. So Joseph's investigation seemed to have ended as negatively as that of the police and the strange detective man. Why bother to open that cupboard and those drawers underneath it? Don't waste further time. Mrs. Crawford's obliging smile said, "There now, didn't I tell you?"

A discouraged Joseph hesitated. Then that streak of awkward obstinacy in him said, "You'll not be really satisfied until you've looked over the very last inch for yourself." The cupboard reached right to the ceiling. Underneath it was a space used as a shelf. Then, underneath that, were the drawers. The whole was one, built-in unit.

"If you won't think me annoyingly obstinate, Mrs. Crawford, I think, after all, I *will* just take a look for myself."

He stood on a chair, opened the cupboard doors, reached up and felt along the back sides of every shelf. There simply could be nothing hidden there. The woodwork and the plaster had never been disturbed. So he climbed down and tackled the drawers. There were four: two top drawers as a parallel pair, and one larger drawer underneath them—as long as both the parallel drawers together; then another similarly longer drawer underneath that. The bottom one was deeper, as it was intended for keeping heavy blankets and the like. Politely asking Mrs. Crawford's permission, he pulled out the two top drawers and examined carefully behind; then pulled the heavier articles from the longer drawer beneath; and finally lifted out the blankets and other contents of the deeper drawer at the bottom. He had to kneel low to look in. Carefully he felt round the plaster and the woodwork of the middle drawer, and then did the same round the deeper aperture where the bottom drawer belonged, sweeping his hand slowly over the wooden platform on which the bottom drawer rested. All the success he had was to jagg one of his fingers on the sharp head of a metal screw which was sticking up a bit. So he slid the drawers back in again, and, as his finger was bleeding a little, he got his mother to put the blankets back in again.

So the search was over. Millie and Joseph sat for a few minutes with Mrs. Crawford before leaving.

"Joseph, your finger is still bleeding," observed Millie.

"Hadn't you better keep your hankie round it?"

It was as he was wrapping his handkerchief round the little cut that a thought suddenly hit him which changed everything. "Yes, mother," he said, starting up; "my finger's bleeding! But why? What's that screw doing down there on that drawer platform? They never screw those down. They use wire nails! And why should it be a whole board of walnut? They use only cheapest wood for that! Let me have that drawer out again!"

Out came the blankets again—much more quickly! Out came the drawer again! Joseph was on hands and knees again, peering intensely into the recess. "Yes, mother, it's as I suspected! There's a small screw in each corner—and two along the edges! The walnut board is screwed down! I need a small screwdriver—a screwdriver, please."

"A screwdriver! A screwdriver!" echoed Millie, suddenly jolted. "Why, Joseph, what a thing! When the police gave me the contents of Mike's pockets, there were four gold sovereigns, a handkerchief, a penknife, a pencil, and a small screwdriver with two little keys attached to it by a string!"

"Where are they, mother?"—his voice was tremulous.

"Why, they're at home somewhere . . . in the tool box, I would suppose."

"Is there a small screwdriver here, Mrs. Crawford?"— but that dear lady was already in the kitchen, to fetch her little assortment of tools.

Yes, there was a screwdriver, but it was too big. They needed one short enough to stand upright in the recess, and with the metal lip thin enough to fit the screw-head groove. Would Tom and Tilda next door have one? Joseph hurried out, sprang over the low dividing wall, and knocked urgently on the Hibberts' front door. Tom was at work, but Tilda was in. She was delighted to see Joseph again and wanted to chat. "Yes . . . yes . . . yes," he replied in quick succession to this and that and the other question, trying to look composed and pleasant. . . . "But have you a screwdriver—a very small one?" Oh, why did she dawdle like a crocodile with rheumatism? Yes, they had one, but it was too large. No, wait a minute, there was a smaller one. Would that one do? Yes, it would. "Oh, thank you, thank you"—and Joseph was back again in number 12 with the speed of greased lightning.

In no time he was at work. The screws fit tightly but came out easily. The walnut board was wedged perfectly but was lifted up with little effort. It had evidently been cut to exact measurement. Joseph's eyes fairly stared. He could scarce believe what he saw. There, underneath the walnut platform, was an oblong metal box, about eighteen inches by nine, and some three inches deep! At each side of it were tight-fitting bricks, to prevent any tapping on the wood platform from giving a hollow sound. Joseph lifted the metal box out, handed it to Millie, made sure there was nothing else of interest in the aperture, then screwed the walnut board in place again.

There were two locks tightly fastening the lid of the box—one at the right end, the other at the left. So now: the keys! Where are the keys? Mrs. Crawford did not detain her visitors one precious minute. She wished them "good luck" with the keys, and said she would take the screwdriver back at once to Tilda, next door.

Never did legs seem so slow or a mile so long! And when they got back to Ashgrove Crescent, where was that old tool box? It was seldom if ever used now, because the maintenance man from the nursing home next door looked after all the minor household repairs. It seemed to be lost. Then Millie thought it might be in the outdoor shed by the wall of the back garden. Joseph hurried there. At that moment it looked to him like the "Black Hole of Calcutta." Only the gardener and the maintenance man ever used it, and apparently the height of their ambition was to preserve its chaotic disorder. The work-bench was piled up with fondly treasured junk. The floor was so littered with all sorts of things, there was hardly room to step one way or the other. The rough, wooden drawers were crammed with tools, boxes of nails, screws, hinges, knobs, and what not? The shelves were a disorderly aggregation of paint cans, brushes in jars of turpentine, wooden mouldings, lats, rods, sticks, string, saws, short planks, bags of garden manure, a bag or two of cement, not to mention all the other ingredients of that untidy man's paradise. No blame to the Kennards! Most of that back-shed jungle was there before they came. Joseph had several times thought of trying to bring civilization to it. With a groan he now wished that he had done so.

Find that old tool box there! Joseph thought he might as well have been digging for emeralds or diving there for pearls. But it *was* there! Naturally, it had to be right underneath everything else, but it was *there!* He recognized it from olden days in Manchester and afterwards at Wragley Street. With some struggle he extricated it from its imprisonment, and as he strode back to the house with it he clutched it so tightly, he might have been carrying gold of Ophir.

It was a clumsy monster, much too big and heavy. It was in rough sections meant to give it some orderliness, but the contents had spilled over the dividers into a general jumble. In the main division there were two or three sets of pincers, a small saw, a gimlet, a cork-screw, a larger and a lesser screwdriver, an axe, a metal file, a set-square, and other such. Yes, and there, recognized at once by Millie, was the small, all-metal screwdriver from Mike's pocket! "Yes, that's it! That's it!"

But the string was gone which had held the two small keys. No, there *was* a bit of string mixed in with all the other things! Keys! Keys! where are you? The bottom layer of the box was about an inch deep in nails—thick nails, thin nails, long nails, short nails, wire nails, flat-head nails, other nails, screws of all sizes, old curtain-rings, staples, tacks, U-shaped fasteners, wall-hooks, chair-castors, drugget-pins, old gas-jet burners, washers, etc. It took about ten minutes of sorting and sifting to pick out small keys which might be the right ones. But none of them would fit Mike's box. However, at last two were found which seemed to match each other, and looked newer than the rest.

"Mother, these must be the two!"

It was an intense moment as Joseph tried the first key on the first lock. It did not fit. He tried it in the other, and it *did!* One lock was unfastened. He put the other key in the first lock, and it worked! Millie and he were almost afraid to open it. "Open it, Joseph."

Joseph opened it. What a surprise! Of all things they never would have expected!—a baby boy's woolly hat with blue ribbons! a baby's knitted coatee! a pretty shawl, and a pair of little woollen shoes! What in the name of creation could it mean? But even that was eclipsed by the next discovery. Wrapped in the soft shawl was a small, white handbag. They opened it. Inside they found a lady's hand-kerchief, a little, gilt-edged notebook, a key ring with four keys on it, a purse with nothing in it, a pencil, a comb, and a small, round mirror. Written in the front of the notebook, in a handwriting which both Millie and Joseph knew well, was the owner's name. They saw it, and looked at each other aghast. Then each of them sank into a chair—dazed. The name was *Agnes Adair!*

"Oh, mother, what have we found?"

Millie was deathly pale.

"See, mother, at the bottom of the box there's a long envelope, with a letter or something in it."

Millie did not speak. The moment she had dreaded for years had come. Was Joseph going to find that his real mother, after all, was a harlot?—or what? How on earth have those articles belonging to Agnes Adair got in there? "O God, give both of us calmness and sanity and trust in Thy faithfulness!"

Tensed up, now, Joseph opened the flap of the unsealed envelope and drew out a large, folded sheet of paper. Carefully he unfolded it and spread it flat. The writing on it he recognized at once. It was his father Mike's. Like Mike himself, it was different from all others. How characteristic of him it was!—elaborate, almost copperplate, with grandiose capitals and sweeping loops. It was dated November 20th, 1911.

TO WHOM IT MAY CONCERN

I, Michael Andrew Kennard, formerly of Everey Street, Manchester, but now residing at 12 Wragley Street, Elmerton, Lancashire, having recently become truly converted by the saving grace of God, do hereby make this exposure of a wicked kidnapping, and at the same time confess my own unintended but guilty complicity in it.

On March 31st, 1892, Jacques Inman Malvern, formerly of Knutsford, but then of Manchester, met me by appointment secretly and told me that he was in awful trouble, and that unless I would help him he would commit suicide. He brought with him, in a bundle, a baby boy of one year old, and said he had wronged a pure girl who had given birth to his child. If it should become known to his father, it would mean being disinherited and disowned. They had kept it secret from the girl's parents as long as possible, but were unable to do so any longer. It would cause heartbreak and scandal if discovered. He knew what a good Christian wife I had, working among women, and said he was sure she could easily find a decent home for the baby.

He pleaded so hard for himself and for the pure girl he had wronged and for her parents and for the baby, I could see he was desperate, and I was sorry for him. But not wanting any part in such a matter, I still said, No. He kept pleading, and said he would give me five gold sovereigns every two months if only I took the baby. In my foolish worship of Mammon I was allured by the gold sovereigns and said, Yes. But I warned him that if he defaulted in paying me I would expose him. We shook hands on it, and he fled, leaving the baby there with me. He said that the reason he came to me was, that we had been such good friends; but I had only known him because I used to manage his gambling bets for him.

I carried the child home and told my wife that a bosom friend of mine, a most honorable gentleman, in a moment of weakness had got a young woman of high birth into this awful trouble, and that he was almost dying with broken-hearted repentance; and that for the noble girl's sake, far more than his own, he simply must find a home for the baby, at least for the time being. My wife wanted no part in the matter, and felt sorrier for the baby than anyone else. She

*could not leave the baby in the street gutter, but did
not know of anyone who could take him. I assured
her that we should be keeping him only for the time
being. On that understanding my wife took him in.
From that point onwards my wife knows the story of
how he was brought up in our home.*

*Afterwards, Jacques Malvern began to change his
story. He said it was not his child at all. He had said
so only in order to make me think him desperate
and to get my sympathy. It was another man who
had done the wrong, and he (Jacques Malvern) was
befriending him. He wanted to stop paying me the
five sovereigns every two months. But I held him to
it. Then, later, he said he had better tell me the real
truth, and have done with it: the baby was the child
of a prostitute, so why should he keep paying me to
keep a thing like that secret? I warned him that I
had the baby's clothes and a woman's handbag with
the name, "Agnes Adair," in it, and that if he defaulted I would at once go to the police. It was not
until seven years later (1899) that I learned who the
baby really was: the son of Mr. and Mrs. Joseph
Ashley Adair of Elmerton, Lancashire. He told me
then because I charged him with having been lying
all the time, and said I was going to the police,
whatever it cost me. Even yet I have not got out of
him how the baby came into his possession, though I
have my suspicions.*

*To this let me add: about one year after he brought
the baby to me, and when it looked, after all, as
though we would have to keep the baby in our home, I
compelled him, under threat, to sign a confession
that it was he who brought the child. That signed
and sealed confession is attached hereto. The signing witnesses did not read the confession, but they
witnessed to the signing of it at Messrs. Fowler and
Rankin's of Manchester. At the same time I bound
myself never to divulge its contents for any reason.*

*For whatever guilt is mine in all this I now un-
feignedly repent and confess my sin: though I can*

say in all honesty that I was tricked into it from the beginning. It is my earnest purpose now to do all in my power to make whatever amends can be made, in whatever way is most compensating to that dear boy who so strangely became my legal son: Joseph Ashley Adair (junior) alias Joseph Kennard, and publicly known as my son.

Michael Andrew Kennard,
November 20th, 1911

Joseph tried to read it to his mother, but had to give up. They read it together in silence. Then they both sat, looking vacantly at nothing—like two overcome travellers in a hot desert, too limp even to speak to each other. Eventually Joseph broke the silence. "Mother, I think you had better read the letter here which is addressed to *you.*"

So Millie read it, while Joseph watched and waited. Then she handed it to him, and he, too, read it through. It read as follows.

My precious, long-suffering Millie,

How can I unburden my wicked but repentant heart? However hard it is for you to believe it, through all the years I have loved you; loved you as the finest, dearest woman I ever knew; loved you even when I was behaving worst to you, and inwardly cursing myself for it. In one way, I hope this letter will not need to come to you. I would rather say it to you, after I have put one big thing right in connection with Joseph. But I am writing it in case anything unexpected happens before I can do what I have in mind.

If you have read my confession you will understand better, perhaps, my cruelty to Joseph. It seemed as though, through my confounded weakness, he was thrust into my life to be a continual condemnation in my conscience, and to keep me on edge lest what I had done should get known to the police. First he was supposed to be the son of a high-ranking lady; then of somebody else; then the real truth seemed to be that he was the son of a no-good and a harlot; and every time I looked at him I detested him. When he was very ill I wanted him to die, and yet I didn't because I was getting a sneaking love for him, and also I knew that if he died I would lose those five gold sovereigns every two months. It was eight years before I dragged out the real truth, that he was the son of Joash and Agnes Adair; and soon after that you gave me the awful shock of saying you were going to Elmerton as a police court missionary. Can you understand, now, why I flared into a rage when you told me?

The reason I got the truth about Joseph was, that I had the name, Agnes Adair, in the handbag. Malvern, the man who gave the baby to me, was furious when he knew I had that handbag. He never meant me to have it, but it was wrapped in the baby's shawl. Then he said that this Agnes Adair was just a go-between from the mother of the child to himself. But I knew he was lying. Why were the initials, A.A. on the shawl? And why was the address in Pendleton, Manchester, at the front of the little notebook?

When my deceiver saw that I had got to the real truth, he gave me supposed proofs that this Joash Adair was the biggest hypocrite and scoundrel on earth, and that he had many enemies, and that one of them whom he had formerly tricked into jail had stolen the baby from him and left it on a doorstep. Can you understand, now, why I did not want Joseph or any of you to go to the Adairs? But after a couple more years I knew I had again been deceived.

It has been twenty years of inward torture to me— all for those damnable gold sovereigns! At times it drove me to drink. Sometimes it had me almost demented. You know now why I had such a lot of confessing to weep out on the night I was converted.

But now I know the whole truth about Joseph's identity. He is Joseph Ashley Adair, named after his father. The only thing I still don't know is how Malvern got hold of little Joseph. But I intend to find out *this weekend, and also to claim a compensation of ten thousand pounds for Joseph. If my deceiver, who is rich, will not agree and also confess to his crime, I shall consider myself free from my sworn oath and shall divulge it all. In any case I shall make it all known to Mr. and Mrs. Adair, and to Joseph himself, even if it is never made public.*

My dearest Millie, how can I thank God for you?—for the way you have put up with me through all these years? But God knows I love you truly and deeply; and by His help, in the days to come, I intend to show you more successfully what I've always wanted you to know.

> *Your unworthy but repentant and loving husband,*
> *Mike*

Well, there they lay on the table—the little woolly hat and coatee, the tiny shoes and the knitted shawl, the handbag, the confession and the letter. To Joseph and Millie they had just about turned the world upside down. As the two of them sat there, they felt the earth itself must have gulped with astonishment and missed a heart beat. Mike Kennard had spoken from his very grave! As blinded Samson, long ago, slew more Philistines at his death than in his life, so had murdered Mike put more right in his death than he ever did in his chequered life.

Millie slowly sank into her rocking-chair.

Joseph spoke. "Mother, you look so sad. Are you thinking you've lost me now that I know who my real parents are? Let me tell you something, right from my heart to yours. I've known for years who my real mother is. She's *you*, the bravest woman I know; the 'dearest little mother on earth.' I'm grateful to know, at last, that I had such a fine man and such a lovely woman as my father and mother; but if you can believe it, I'm even more grateful that God overruled an evil hand and gave *you* to me as my mother. What seems to take me *from* you brings me even closer *to* you."

As he spoke, he went and knelt at her lap.

"Mother, I worship God more easily at your knee than in

the loftiest cathedral. I've seen more heavenly light and love streaming on me through your face than I ever saw through beautiful church windows. I've learned more truth and wisdom at your knee than I ever learned from a pulpit. In my childhood your lap was the first altar on which I gave my little heart to God. At your knees my infant mind learned to pray. At your knees I've wept and sung. Here I've brought my childish prattle and my growing-up problems. This, to me, is earth's most hallowed spot, and I would not be ashamed for the whole world to see me kneeling here now. Nothing, *nothing* can ever un-mother you to me. An evil hand took me away from the mother of my body, but a higher Hand gave you to be the mother of my mind. Oh, what a mother you have been! How I thank God for you! And how I love you!"

"Thank you, Joseph. That puts a new rainbow in my cloudy skies."

"Mother, let me try to make that rainbow even brighter. Did you think I was slipping away from you when I put the ring on Evelyn's finger? You are mistaken. I don't love anyone on earth more than I love you—simply because I *can't.* The highest thing I can think of saying is, that I love you as much as I love Evelyn, only that the two loves, of course, are different in kind; there can be no rivalry. Those two loves will go singing in my heart to its last beat—not as two separate songs, but as a duet—the sweetest duet a human heart ever heard. What can I say more? Already I feel the surging of new feelings toward Mr. and Mrs. Adair, and I begin to understand why there has seemed such a kinship of disposition between us. I know now why Mrs. Adair has looked at me in a way that made me feel a bit sensitive sometimes. She has seen in me something of a replica of what her little Joseph would be. What a surprise she is going to get! Yes, I shall feel toward her, now, strange new feelings of closeness. But even that can *never* un-mother *you* to me—my dearest little mother in the world.' "

Joseph stood and gently lifted Millie from the rocking-chair. He held her in his arms and reverently kissed her, again and again.

Weatherbeaten Millie found herself once again "singing Hallelujah through her tears." After all, Joseph was still truly hers. If those papers on the table had brought the biggest surprise of his life to *him,* they had also evoked the most convincingly worded expression of his love for *her.* She knew that behind his elegant way of putting things there was sincerity transparent as June's clearest morning. Brushing the tears from her face and her heart she said, "Yes, Joseph, you are right. You are still mine. *God* gave you to me as surely as He *ever* gave a son to a mother. But, Joseph, aren't you hungry? It's past teatime. You clear away all those nails and other things, and I'll have something ready in a jiffy. After that, you should be off to Pinecrest to let them know. What a shock of joy for Agnes! I know now why she never actually said that their son 'died,' but always that he was 'taken away' from them!"

Still in a state of strange new wonder, Joseph cleared away the nails plus all the untidy odds and ends and carried the cumbersome old toolbox back to the usual lodging place among its higgledy-piggledy neighbours which cluttered up the backyard shed. Meanwhile Millie had the kettle whistling; and soon the two of them were at their hurried replenishment. As they were finished, Joseph said, "How slow of me, mother! I should have said it right away: I'm not going over to Pinecrest alone. You are coming with me."

"No, son, not this time. Besides, while you are away I've something to do. I must ring up police headquarters. You see, we've found your father's murderer now, Joseph."

"Mother!"

"Yes, I think we have. Look at your father's writing again. See how those big capital letters stand out in the name Jacques Inman Malvern. What was the 'name' they found in that bowler hat near your father's body after he was murdered? It was JIM. But those three letters are not a name, Joseph; they are the initials of the murderer— J.I.M. I think it's time the police had a word with that bank manager near Chadvale arches. However, leave that to me. Off you go on your bike! It's a delightful evening. Don't forget to take those dinky baby clothes and the handbag and the confession; but leave Mike's letter here with me."

The Loudest Thunderclap

It was not exactly palpitation, but never before had Joseph gone over to Pinecrest with such unusual excitement of heart. He cycled as slowly as his racing thoughts would allow him, not wanting to be at the Adairs' before they were up from their evening meal. Arriving there, he passed through the front gate and peered across the lawn at the large window of the dining-room. As it faced west he could see, in the glow of the westering sun, that there was no one in the room. The meal was over. He rang the bell. Minnie, the maid, opened the door. "Hello, Minnie." Joash, Agnes, and Evelyn, sipping after-dinner tea in the parlour, heard his voice; and before you could say "Jack Robinson" Evelyn was in the hall to meet him.

"How wonderful to see you, love!—the more so because so unexpected! Have you had your evening meal?"

Joash and Agnes gave him their usual beaming welcome, and in a matter of minutes Joseph was sitting with them in that spacious, tastefully furnished lounge looking out over "Little Eden" to the Pennines away on the eastern skyline. Naturally, they were curious about the metal box with locks on the front of it, but were too polite to mention it—more so because Joseph looked uneasy as he sat with it on his knee and softly drummed his fingers on it. They could sense, also, that there was something he wanted to tell them without any need for their asking. Nor had they long to wait.

After some of the usual social pleasantries Joseph said, fidgeting with the box, "In a way, Mrs. Adair, this is not just a courting visit to see Evelyn, nor a social call on Mr. Adair and you. It's kind of pastoral call; a very earnest one, as though you were two members of my own flock. In fact, it's so outstandingly important that before I get into it I would like you to ask Minnie to clear the tray and cups."

At that, the Adair curiosity was the more stimulated, for the request was so unusual. They chuckled, and Joash teased, "That's the first time I ever knew a parson have the cups of tea removed!"

Joseph was too serious to make any quip in return. He remained silent until Minnie had gone out of the room and closed the door, by which time the Adairs knew that he must have something exceptionally important on his mind.

"Mrs. Adair, did you once have a son before Rickie was born?"

Joash and Agnes exchanged a surprise glance as she replied, "Why, yes . . . we did."

"Was his name, Joseph, like mine?"

"Yes, and you've often reminded us of him."

"If he were still alive, would he be about the same age as myself?"

"Why, yes . . . he would; but Joseph. . . ."

"When did he die?—and please, Mr. Adair, don't be angry at my asking. If you knew all that's in my heart you would be the opposite of angry."

"I'm not one bit angry, Joseph, nor is Mrs. Adair; but naturally we're taken by surprise that you've sprung these questions on us. We know you too well to think you would ask us without some good reason. So don't hesitate. You see, Joseph, dear boy, it's a subject we keep off, both in public and in private. When we lost him, it nearly finished us off—didn't it Agnes? However, we don't mind being frank with *you,* Joseph. You're the one exception. You'll soon be in the Adair family, we hope."

"Mr. Adair, I'm the luckiest young chap in Elmerton. Fancy! a nobody like me with a jewel like Evelyn, and being in the Adair family!—but let me go on, though I'm almost too nervous. Did your little Joseph really *die?*"

"Oh, Joseph, please don't touch on that. Whatever can be on your mind?"

"Dear Mrs. Adair, I think I know why it's so painful for you. So let me ask you, instead: Was he born on March 18th, 1891?"

In a split second, Joash and Agnes passed from curious interest to intenseness. "How did you discover that, Joseph? Have you been hunting in the Registrar's Office? Yes, that was the day of his birth."

"No, I would never be so rude as to go rooting at the Registry Office. I esteem you far too much to do any such thing. Let me explain. We've found the papers my poor father left hidden. You will be as surprised as my mother and I were when I tell you that he mentions *you,* and your long-lost baby. That's why I've brought this box over to show you."

Joseph opened the box, and tenderly took out the little woollen hat with the blue ribbons, the pretty woollen coatee, the little shoes, the shawl, and the small, white handbag. "Mrs. Adair, have you ever seen these before?"

Agnes jumped up excitedly, quickly examined them, and gave a wild cry, "Oh, my baby Joseph! My darling baby! My darling, darling baby!—and, sobbing, she sank back into her chair as Joash hastened to her side and put his arm round her shoulder.

"Yes, yes!" cried Agnes. "These are his baby clothes! Joseph, Joseph, where did you get them? Tell me quickly: is my little Joseph still alive? For years we've thought him dead, but never knew for sure. Oh, Joseph, hurry! hurry! What is it you have to tell us?"

Joash and Agnes and Evelyn were intense. Agnes was white.

"Yes, I'm hurrying—and praying fast, too," responded Joseph. "See, here is the answer to your question, in this written confession by my father."

Joash and Agnes and Evelyn bent over it. When they came to the name, 'Jacques Inman Malvern' of Knutsford, Joash and Agnes gasped. They could not read quickly enough. By the time they reached the identification of their son as the handsome, gifted young minister standing before them that moment, their feelings were simply inexpressible and uncontrollable. The agonized questionings of twenty-two years were suddenly answered—in an almost unbelievably amazing way! Their long-lost, precious little Joseph was alive! He was found! Yes, alive, and found, and standing there that moment *before them*—the dear Joseph Kennard whom they had loved from the very first day he had started coming round their home!

"Oh, Joseph! Joseph! I can't believe it! I can't believe it! It's too wonderful to be true! But it *is* true. I know it. You are my own, my very own Joseph!"—and she flung her arms around him in a rapture of motherly emotion no pen could describe.

Joash, too, stood there unable to hide his agitation of surprise and joy. "I'll tell you one way you can make sure, Agnes, if you have any doubt left. Look at his right arm."

"His right arm," Agnes repeated excitedly. "Yes! I'm almost too afraid to look! I'm sure you're my son, Joseph; but to settle it beyond all possible doubt: if you really are the same little Joseph, you have a naevus on your right arm—a birthmark, a 'mother-spot' as they call them. Maybe it's grown fainter now. At the time, they said it might be an after-effect from a frightening experience I had, not long before my baby's birth. I was attacked and hurt by a bantam cock. Afterward, when they saw the birthmark on my little son's arm, they imagined it was the same shape as that fierce little creature. I know it sounds silly, but it *did* look a bit that way!"

"Well, there's one thing about it that isn't silly," said Joseph. "It's still there!" Taking off his jacket and rolling up his shirt sleeve, he bared his arm. There it was, between wrist and elbow: the darkish brown birthmark!—and even yet not altogether unlike the shape Agnes had mentioned!

"Joseph! Joseph! our long-lost little Joseph! It is too wonderful! My heart feels as though it will burst with joy." Agnes hugged him again, and so did Joash, forgetting his usual staidness in this amazing discovery and new joy!

Indeed they were now *weeping* with joy—all except Evelyn. She had gone pale. At a glance Joseph saw there was something wrong. She slowly backed toward a chair, steadied herself a second, then sank down as though she was about to faint. Those pure, blue eyes had a look in them which Joseph had never seen before, nor had Agnes, nor had Joash. It was more than a look of intensity; it was a *stare* with agony in it—not at anyone or anything in the room, but at a stark reality. She was trembling now. "Joseph," she faltered, "I must give you . . . I must give you . . . the engagement ring back . . . Oh, Joseph! . . ."

In a flash it dawned on him what she meant. He slowly broke away from Agnes. The room began to swim round. He staggered to the sofa, and heard himself saying in a distant sort of way, "Oh, God! No! Why did I have to discover all this? Why did I listen to Frank Goodall? My gladdest discovery has become my blackest grief! Evelyn is my *sister!* We are sister and brother . . . we can never . . . never . . . be man and wife!" Then everything went dark, and he knew no more.

TWENTY-EIGHT
Agnes Tells Her Story

Neither Joseph nor Evelyn could be described as the swooning sort. They were decidedly the opposite. But the revelation of Joseph's identity by Mike's confession had plunged a sword into the deepest, tenderest and most sacred passion of which any human being is capable. It had dashed to pieces the dearest hopes of their hearts, and mocked their most confidential secrets. Anyone normally capable of empathy can realize to some degree the emotional extremes which choked them as they now looked helplessly at each other, suddenly aware that they were brother and sister; that neither legally nor Scripturally could they ever be married; and that they must go through life with the excruciating embarrassment of having expressed sweetheart love to each other, even though that love had been chaste almost to the point of purism. The discovery which, under other circumstances, would have made a long-lost brother and his sister uniquely happy was a traumatic irony which knocked Joseph and Evelyn deadly sick.

It was the more sickeningly devastating to Joseph after all he had suffered mentally since he fled from home; his alternating hopes and fears concerning Evelyn; then the open showing of their love for each other; then Evelyn's mysteriously changed attitude and the months of torturing misunderstanding; the anonymous letters; Evelyn's returning of the locket; then the glorious breakthrough which had unshackled their love from its dreary chains of frustration; then (oh, sweet bliss!) the engagement ring; then the stabbing fear that after all he would prove to be a son of harlotry; then the bewildering joy of discovery that he was none other than the long-lost son of his dearly loved Adairs; and now, all in a second, the crash from that dizzy height to this abyss of hopeless grief! Is it surprising that after such poignant, long-drawn-out emotional alternations Joseph should momentarily black out?

Although he lost hold of himself for only two or three minutes, it seemed much longer to him. It was not a faint in the usual sense. There was no shivering cold of a swoon. On the contrary, perspiration dripped down his face. Although he was too full-blooded for proneness to faints, the shock had momentarily stunned him. He heard Agnes's voice, "My poor, dear Joseph! It's all been too much for you. See, Joash has brought the smelling-salts. Put this handkerchief to your nose, and gently inhale. Yes, that's it. Joash, please tell Minnie quickly to make a cup of strong tea— immediately; that's if you think you could drink it, Joseph. Let me wipe your face. . . . That's better."

Slowly Joseph lifted up his sagged head. He was still a bit blurred. "Thank you. Yes, please, a very strong . . . cup of tea . . . would be helpful. I'm so . . . ashamed. Where's . . . Evelyn . . . my poor, poor Evelyn? Oh, God . . . please help her—and me!"

"Evelyn's here, Joseph; and she's not 'poor, poor' Evelyn. She's smiling at you. Oh, if only I could have told you quickly enough before you flopped down here! But it was impossible. Dear boy, you're going to marry Evelyn. She knows something which you don't. I had to get it out to her all in one breathless minute after you collapsed. I'll explain later; but listen to this right away: You and Evelyn are *not* blood relatives. There's nothing to stop you and your lovely Evelyn from going to the marriage altar! And the sooner you get there, the better!"

"But how? . . . What? . . ."

"Never mind the 'hows' and the 'whats' just now. You'll soon have the answers. Ah, here's the cup of tea—and one for Evelyn. Let me fix the cushion behind you."

Joseph was feeling more like himself again. The trembles had subsided; though he was still limp. Joash had opened the side panels of the window, and the cool evening air now began drifting in. "How refreshing is that fragrance wafted in from the garden! . . . Mmmmm, this cup of tea is working magic. . . . I think I'm alright now. . . . Evelyn, you were much braver than I—as always . . . weren't you?"

"Let me tell you, Joseph: it is Evelyn who is *needing* to be braver than you, just now. Poor, dear girl! Wait till you hear my story! But I won't start until you are completely yourself again."

"Mrs. Adair—I mean, dear, newfound mother and (with a glance at Joash) my dear, newfound father, if there's anything will give new strength to my feet, and new wings to my mind, it's to learn that my 'pearl of great price,' my Evelyn, can still be my wife."

And so began Agnes's story.

She said: "When Joash and I were children, we grew up at Rostherne. Yes, in the Rostherne you love so much, Joseph. My dear Joash—your real father—was born and reared in that very house where you used to stay with your grandparents. With all the other Rostherne children we went to the only school round there. I'm always glad we were brought up there, and not in a town or city. To Joash and me it seems only yesterday that we were merry children gamboling in those verdant meadows, or skipping in those peaceful old lanes, or frisking among the cornstacks at harvest-time.

"I can't say just when it began, but your father and I were drawn to each other while we were still at school. By the time he was twelve and I was eleven, well, I don't know whether one could call it love or not at that early age, but to me there was no boy like him, and to him there was no girl like me; and we both knew how we felt toward each other. Joash left school at the age of thirteen and was put to work in housebuilding on the Lord Egerton estate.

"But a while before that, while Joseph was still at school, there was a boy who used to come over from outside Rostherne, from somewhere nearer to Knutsford, and he wanted to have me for *his* girl. He was the son of a rich merchant. He went to a private school somewhere but used to come and play with us children at Rostherne. He made us all envious because he would ride over on a bicycle—and only people with money had bicycles like his. Or sometimes he would gallop over on his own pony. He was always dressed in full suits, and I suppose he was a very good-looking boy. He was about as tall as Joash, and perhaps a bit stouter. His name was *Jacques Malvern.*

"As I say, he wanted me to be his girl, but that didn't suit Joash one bit. Nor did I myself like that other boy; though *he* thought that because he was good-looking and had a rich father he could lure me away from Joash. He kept boasting, too, that he was the best fighter among the boys; and the other boys were afraid of him. So he used to pick quarrels with Joash and then say, 'I'll fight you for Agnes Robson.' But my Joash knew he didn't need to fight him in order to keep me, so he would evade fighting. Then this Jacques Malvern would sneer at Joash, with the other boys and girls listening. 'He won't fight for his girl. He's a coward. He's afraid to fight me.' In that way Joash would be goaded to fight.

"At first Joash didn't do so well, for he had no heart to be fighting; but as Malvern kept waylaying him it got Joash's temper up, and once or twice Joash really pelted him. However, Malvern was a nasty, dirty fighter; and because he was heavier than Joash, whenever Joash's fists were too quick for him he would try to trip Joash up, then roll down on top of him, tearing with his fingernails at Joash, as though trying to scratch his eyes out. Sometimes Joash's face was marked for days.

"Well, one day he was there again when we came out of school—just before Joash left school altogether. I said to Joash, 'Oh, I'm so sorry: this is all because of me. I hate him, Joash. What can I do? If he starts fighting you again, I shall start hitting him myself.' I saw such a fierce look come into Joash's eyes. He said, 'I'll finish it this time, or I'll eat my cap.' Malvern sneeringly challenged him again, but this time he got the surprise of his life. Oooh, how Joash went at him! He made his nose bleed and gave him one smack so hard it knocked him over; but as Malvern was getting up he quickly ducked and caught Joash's leg, and pulled him to the ground, and started clawing his eyes again. I couldn't stand to see any more of it, so I jumped in between them and we all rolled in the road together. I managed to hold Jacques Malvern's hands away from Joash's eyes, and although he tried to throw me off, he couldn't. Then he got his hands free and started scratching *me*. He glared at me like a tiger, and I screamed. It got Joash free for a second, and he gave Malvern such a kick, it hurt him badly, and he had to stop clawing me. Joash shouted at him, 'You dirty rotter! You can't beat me, so you fight a girl!' Then, all the other boys started shouting, 'Dirty rotter! Dirty rotter!'

"That was the last of the actual fights, but not of the enmity. When Malvern got up he stared at me, and said, 'I'll get you yet. I've got plenty money. He's got nothing. You're my girl, not his. I'll never let you marry *him*. If you do, I'll get my revenge.' He was so mad, he didn't know what bad enough to say—and he wasn't quite fifteen years old at that time!

"Joash's face was bleeding from the scratches, and there was a torn place just under his right eye which left a mark even after it had healed—perhaps you have noticed it. At times it seems to get a bit redder and show more. We didn't see Malvern much after that. But one day a bricklayer working with Joash on the Lord Egerton estate brought a message from Malvern, 'I haven't forgotten. I'll get even yet.'

"Joash and I were always shy with each other—which, I suppose, was because we knew how we felt toward each other. Then came an awful blow: our family moved from Rostherne to Rochdale in Lancashire. Joash and I thought we might never see each other again. Joash was only fourteen, and I was thirteen; but the night before the removal we met secretly and kissed each other, and I cried on his shoulder. Joash said we must pray to God to bring us together again somehow—though neither of us could think of a way to help God do it! Meanwhile, Joash had a clever plan. We were going to write secret letters to each other every three months—and we did, until we got caught. Joash never looked at any other girl; and I never looked at any other boy.

"Then, what do you think?—our family went back to Cheshire, to live in Knutsford, and I became a servant-girl in one of the big houses near Rostherne. My parents guessed why, but they didn't seem to mind. So Joash and I were together again; and in 1890 we got married at the dear old Rostherne church. It was a wonderful wedding; the nicest in the world's history up to that time. There were only two things that marred it. Joash had to wear an eye bandage because that scar under his right eye had become inflamed again somehow. The other thing was, that when we walked out of the church, whom did I notice lurking among the folks but Jacques Malvern. I didn't tell Joash; and he's never known it till this minute.

"Oh, we were so happy; and we took such a big risk! We left Rostherne and went to live in a northwestern area of Manchester because there was a lot of house-building going on there, and that was Joseph's line. He had saved up forty pounds, and I had fifteen. To a country boy and girl that amount seemed a small fortune, but to start up in business it was practically nothing. Joseph bought a small holding, and fairly quickly 'got in' with contractors; and in three years he was making a good living for us. He had his own small brick-and-timber yard, his own equipment, and was employing four other men. Of course, he worked hard, and the contractors liked his work; but besides that, providentially we had 'hit the boom' just at the right time—and, of course, he had a good little bookkeeper called Agnes!

"We had rented a nice little house near a pretty park. Howburn Park it was called, because of the little hill, or 'how' near it, and the stream, or 'burn,' running through it. Today you'd never know it had been there. The little hill is covered with houses; and what they've done with the stream, I don't know. There's a railway track runs there now! But, never mind those details; what I want to tell you is, that it was there, in that house, in the second year of our married life, our first baby came—a bonny little baby boy. Oh, how we loved him! And how proud of him we were! People used to stop us when we had him out in his pram, and say, 'My! what a lovely baby!'

"I had a favourite walk for wheeling out our little Joseph in his pram. It was along an avenue with trimmed elm trees on each side and flower gardens belonging to the high-class houses around there. Then I would turn left to Howburn Park and sit a while. On sunny days there were sometimes five or six of us, all wheeling our prams round, and we used to have good old chinwags in Howburn Park, as young married mothers do. One day, when little Joseph was one year old—that was in 1892, I put him in his pram and went my usual walk to the park. It was a bright Spring afternoon, but the air was nippy, so I wrapped Joseph up warmly. There was only one other woman at the park. I knew her quite well. Hers was a baby girl.

"Inside the big park gates she had turned right, and I had turned left; so when we saw each other, she was sitting over on that side, and I on this side, with a couple of flower beds between us. She called a greeting, and said something which I didn't catch. She beckoned me over, so I tied my pram to the bench where I had sat, and strolled over to her. I wasn't with her more than six or seven minutes, and I was where I could keep an eye on my own pram; but when I came back and looked inside it, to my horror it was empty!—little Joseph was gone! I was frantic and screamed for help but there was no one there except that other woman. We ran out to the road, looking this way and that, but it was a quiet road and there was not a soul in sight. The other woman ran home with her baby and then hurried round to tell Joash what had happened. He got in touch with the police . . . and I suppose . . . they did what they could.

"Little Joseph was never seen or heard of again. Our grief was almost unbearable. We felt it would have been easier if we had seen him die and knew for certain that he was dead. To think that he might be alive somewhere, perhaps suffering in some evil or cruel house nearly drove us demented. Eventually the police said they had reason to think he was dead. There were two other cases of baby-snatching about that time. One of the kidnappers had been caught—and was a semi-imbecile. Both the babies had been killed and buried—both baby boys.

"We stayed there another two years, all the time paying sleuths and investigators. At last they said, 'One thing is certain: he's nowhere in this area. And it's unlikely that anybody from a distance would know anything about Howburn Park. It's some local fiend who's done it. The little fellow's been done for, sure enough, and secretly buried, like those other two!' So, trying to believe that Joseph must be dead, we felt it would be a relief to get away from that place of bitter memory. Uncle Ben had been trying to get us to Elmerton; and early in 1894 we came.

"Because we didn't like the modernistic preaching at the Anglican church in our area of Elmerton, we started going to Brandon Street Congregational Church—a struggling little place then, but the people were warmhearted. The Sunday school was very small, and they seized on Joash to become teacher of a young men's class. Only three months later, because of a terrible accident to someone, he was asked to act as superintendent *pro tem*—and the *'pro tem'* has now lasted twenty years!

"From the first February Sunday we went to Brandon Street we became close friends of Richard and Donna Harwood. The four of us were always together. Richard was a tall, strapping American; one of the most handsome and charming men we ever knew. He represented a manufacturing firm in San Diego, California, and had been in England four years. Donna was a dear little Yorkshire girl. They fell in love, and were married at Brandon Street. Richard became a teacher in the little Sunday school, and, soon afterwards, the superintendent. What happy times we had with them! They were the truest, jolliest, dearest friends. It soon seemed as though we had known them all their lives; though it had been only a few months. In the July of that year a fearful thing happened. They went on an outing by railway train to Altrincham. On the way back, the train was in a collision. Several people were killed. One of them was our beloved Richard Harwood; and one of the badly injured was Donna.

"A special messenger was sent to us from the hospital in Manchester urgently requesting us to visit Donna. We went. She was dying, and knew it. 'Oh, Joash and Agnes,' she said, 'in the short time we've known you, we've loved you so dearly. Richard has no relatives in England, and my own parents are dead, and I've no sisters or brothers but one, and he's away in Australia. What about my poor, little darling baby?—my little Evelyn? Joash and Agnes, I've no one but you. Will you please take my little treasure as yours?—with all the love and gratitude of my heart?' We said we would. Two days later she was gone; and dear little baby Evelyn came to live with us, a sweet mite of one year and some months. The following year another little son was born to us, and we called him 'Richard'—after your father, Evelyn.

"Evelyn, dear child, it is a strange, strange providence that on the very day when our long-lost Joseph turns out to be the Joseph Kennard who has been on and off our doorstep for years, we are having to tell you who *your* dear parents really are. Evelyn, we can honestly say that if they gave you *life*, we have given you *love*. Even they could not have cherished and treasured you more than we have. You know how we love you, don't you? So far as motherly affection goes, you might just as well have come from my own body. You are really mine—ours, Evelyn. There never was a lovelier baby girl, either in looks or disposition. You were God's gift to us, even though it was the hand of tragedy which brought you. In our home and to our hearts you have been continual sunshine. Never has a day ticked away but we have thanked God for you. Never have I said my nightly prayer without asking God to help me fulfill my covenant with dear Donna. And now, to think that through the overruling of God's hidden hand you are going to be the wife of our own dear Joseph! . . . [The tears were flowing down Agnes's face] . . . Come here, Evelyn. Let me kiss you again—my sweet, precious girl! [They held each other and wept together.]

"Well, that's my story—I mean *our* story, Joseph. But please just let me make an appeal to you and Evelyn. You both may ask: Why did not Mrs. Kennard tell Joseph sooner that she was not his mother who gave him birth? and why is it that *I* have not told the story about Evelyn until now? Would *you* have done so if you had been in our position? I don't think so. Joseph, your wonderful mother Kennard was so afraid it would be confirmed that you were the child of evil parents, she dreaded its ever becoming known that she was not your real mother. It was for *your* sake she wanted to keep the secret, least of all ever suspecting that you would turn out to be the son of her dearest friend—myself! Only recently, when Frank Goodall started prying, her fear was lest anything might be dragged to light which would hurt you and your ministry before you were married to Evelyn. And in *your* case, Evelyn, when once Joash and I had made sure that you did not remember our dear Dick and Donna, we said: Why should we trouble her trustful young mind by telling her about the tragedy which took away her parents? We prayed that nothing might ever be said which could cause you to suspect anything or to doubt our fond love for you. Mrs. Kennard and I talked it over, and decided for *your* sakes, not ours, that since our two big secrets had been successfully kept until now, we should wait until after your wedlock before telling you. After wedlock you would have each other, which could *counteract* what we had to disclose to you. In any case, Joseph, you *are* the son of Mrs. Kennard *legally*. And you, Evelyn, *are* our daughter *legally*.

"Oh, there's just one other thing occurs to me. Do you remember, Joseph, one summer when you were staying at Rostherne, two men came round to see your grandparents? Yes? One was uncle Ben. The other was . . . your real father, my dear husband. Do you remember how he kept looking at you? Shall I tell you what he said when he came back home? He said, 'Agnes, what do you think? When we called on the Kershaw couple, they had a boy from Manchester staying with them; their grandson. When I saw him, I fairly blinked. Agnes, it was like looking at a young boy edition of *you*. He had just your shape of features, the same colour of eyes, and the same expression. It was remarkable. Uncle Ben noticed it too. But the still more surprising thing was that his name is Joseph, and he's twelve—just the age our own little Joseph would have been if he had lived. There was, in fact, a flicker of wonder in our minds, but it was immediately quenched; for how could he be *our* little Joseph since he's the son of the Kershaw daughter and her husband?' Yes, that's what Joash said. And now we know who that little boy really was! And that boy knows who his real parents are! Joseph, my own dear, long-lost boy, let me give you another hug and kiss! I've a lot of leeway to make up!"

Such was Agnes's story, with Joash assisting by occasional promptings and amplifying insertions. By now, all four of them were thinking the same thing. Was there ever a more strangely tangled skein of human lives than that which was represented by themselves—those four human beings in that parlor, and Millie over there at Ashgrove Crescent? Was there ever a more dramatic pathos than the way in which the tangled strands were eventually being sorted out and wrought into a clearly patterned tapestry?

After some silence, intense with memories and wonderings, Joseph asked, "Did it not occur to you that Jacques Malvern might have stolen me out of that pram?"

"No, Joseph, in the first shock of it *nothing* occurred to us. But in any case it could not have been Jacques, because at that time he was in Llandudno, Wales. To his credit, we will say that he wrote us at once from Llandudno, the day after the kidnapping, saying he had just that minute seen it reported in the local Llandudno newspaper and was writing at once to express his great sorrow, along with the hope that our child would soon be found unharmed."

By now night was enwrapping the earth, and the stream of air through the open window had become chilly. Joash had lighted the chandelier, remarking as he did so, "Joseph, what was the first thing God did when He started to make this messed-up earth nice again? He said, 'Let there be light.' It seems to me He's been saying again, 'Let there be light' on some other messed-up affairs. There's been a lot of darkness, by jingo! That kidnapping was a dastardly, dark affair. That bringing of my little son to Mike Kennard by that scoundrel, Jacques Malvern, is another deadly dark mystery. How did *he* get hold of you, when he was in Llandudno at the time? That's another dark enigma. Mike Kennard's years and years of deceiving your mother—that's another dark chapter. And that man, apparently Jacques Malvern, who used to give Mike the five gold sovereigns: where is he nowadays? That's another dark bit. And then Mike Kennard's murder: ugh! that's a very dark episode. But God has said, 'Let there be light,' and it's surely begun to break on our minds today! Think of it: Mike Kennard gets converted through that stolen baby! That kidnapped child grows up and leads his own real father—myself, to the Savior! And through that long-lost son our darling Evelyn is converted! Through that stolen baby all three of us have become *SAVED!*—and hundreds of others, too! Yes, God has said, 'Let there be light'; and the light's going to shine now until it brings the last bit of all this darkness skulking out of its hiding place!"

"I'll say 'Amen' to that!" exclaimed Joseph.

Then Mr. Adair added, with a happy excitement unusual in his steady disposition, "But it's Evelyn I'm thinking most about just now. This day, which is a day of *glad* discovery for you and me, Joseph, may seem a day of *sad* discovery for Evelyn. But no, Evelyn, try not to think of it that way. Try to be happy with us. Now that you *know* at last what we haven't felt able to tell you before, we love you more than ever. God has given us two sons: Joseph and Richard; and He knew how much I wanted a daughter, so He sent *you* to us; only in doing so He made a lovely mistake and sent an angel!—the dearest, sweetest daughter He could have picked for us anywhere. Heaven knows how mighty proud of her we are!"

So saying, the honorable councilor gathered her in his arms and fondly kissed her.

What a study in faces as Joseph and Evelyn slowly walked over the lawn to kiss good-night at the gate! Agnes, indoors, was still fondly holding the baby's woollies and that white handbag, her eyes glistening and her face beaming.

Joash was standing with his hands clasped behind his back, looking at nothing in particular, but thinking profoundly, with a look of "Well, well, who would have thought it? Amazing!" Joseph's face was bright with smiles, but a discerning eye could have detected weariness hiding beneath. He had weathered another ordeal of contending emotional opposites. Evelyn's beautiful face was pale and sad but struggling to smile.

Gloaming had gone and night had come as the two lovers stood at the gate; but it was night at its best. It was as though an angel had spilled an extra basket of stars across the dark bosom of the expanse. The moon was full and clear. A pleasantly chilly, fresh breeze from the hills wandered over Kenyon's Meadows to Woodland Bypath and stole around Pinecrest slyly kissing the flowers as they slept. The pines and ash and silver birches, with their slightly swaying boughs, looked almost like animated figures bending to and fro in silent worship to the silver queen of the deep sky. There seemed to be a mystic eloquence about it. Yet night, even at its best, is still night. Mystery lurks in its shadows. The breeze which laughs as it plays in the sunshine becomes a whimper as it wanders through the night. Even when night sings there is a sigh in it. The more silent it is, the more wistful and haunting it seems.

It all seemed to be in melancholy sympathy with Joseph and Evelyn as they stood there in the moonlight on that night of bewildering discovery.

Joseph, sensitive as ever, needed no telepathy or extrasensory perception to tell him that something had given way inside Evelyn. They stood there silently. They looked, with such strange new feelings now, into each other's eyes. They held their faces soothingly close to each other; but they still remained silent. They were both thinking vividly. Yes, what a reversal!—the Joseph who for years had thought of himself as the lower-breed commoner reaching after an inaccessible queen now found himself the well-born, and his queen an orphan! Evelyn must have known the thought was there, for she cringed in his arms.

And now Evelyn spoke. "Joseph, this has been a day of wonderful discovery for you, but can you enter into what it means for your mother Kennard and for me? I shall always think of you now as the man with two mothers. Mother Agnes gave you your *nature,* but mother Millie built you your *character.* Be careful: don't hurt your mother Kennard. She has no husband. Don't make another empty space in the heart of the bravest woman I ever knew."

"Evelyn, if you only knew how I love her. . . ."

"Joseph, do you realize you have an orphan in your arms? Can you enter into how I shall feel when I go back into the house? Please pray for me. There's an awful loneliness creeping over me. I know I shouldn't let it, but somehow I can't stop it. . . . Do you love me as much now that you know I'm not an Adair, but an orphan?"

His first answer was to hold her tightly and press his lips to hers. Then he said, "Did you love *me* when you thought I was the son of a whore, Evelyn? You did. Can I forget that? Listen, Evelyn, purest treasure of my heart, and let me say it with such utter meaning that it will sing in your heart for a lifetime: More than ever, you are my dear, dear queen; and more than ever my heart is at your feet. Never did I love you as I now do, after learning the strange tragedy hidden away back in both our lives. More than ever I can see the hand of God bringing us together. Evelyn, fairest of the fair to me, I love you utterly. More than ever you are God's answer to the aching need of my being for a love like yours. Now that we both know who we are, we mean more than ever to each other. Until now I have loved you as Evelyn *Adair;* but now I love you even better, if that were possible, just as Evelyn, *Evelyn, EVELYN, MY EVELYN!*"

She laid her head on his bosom and quietly wept—shaking a little now and then—and still wept. After that, lifting her lips to his, and with her lovely face serenely silvered in the moonlight, she whispered, "Good-night, my own dear Joseph. I'm glad you love me now just as Evelyn. It makes us both the same. You see, ever since I kissed you on that bicycle picnic when you bandaged my ankle, that's the way I have loved you—just as *you;* just as Joseph; my very own *JOSEPH.* Good-night, my darling Joseph. Kiss mother Kennard for me."

When Joseph got back home, Millie was in her favourite meditating place, the rocking-chair, slowly rocking to and fro, her Bible on her lap.

"You look pensive, mother."

"Yes, I'm trying to blend a singing hope with a weeping memory. Between a stormy yesterday and a tomorrow of golden promise I'm pondering how best to use today."

"How like you that sounds!"

"Come and sit down, Joseph. We'll have a snack together in a few minutes—it's getting on for bedtime; but tell me first what happened at the Adairs."

Concisely as possible, Joseph told her. When Millie heard Agnes's story about the fights in Rostherne, the kidnapped baby, the railway disaster, the death of Evelyn's parents, and the disclosure that Evelyn was not really the daughter of Mr. and Mrs. Adair, her eyes opened wide with amazement.

"I never heard the like of it! Talk about truth being stranger than fiction! What a day this has been! What an opening of graves and unlocking of secrets! I'm glad the ghost in your past has turned out to be such a friendly one; but I'm sorry for Evelyn. More than you guess, Joseph, she's suddenly in mourning, twenty years after the funeral. Today has bereaved her sorely. Although the Adairs think the world of her, the fearful surprise tonight will have cut like a razor edge into her sensitive nature. She'll need a shoulder to weep on. Have yours ready. Tell her something to jolt her mind into an opposite direction. Give her a counteracting shock of joy."

"What do you mean, mother?"

"You know well enough what I mean. Get married. Never mind the etiquette of a long courtship. Bring the wedding forward. Don't ask her if she will. Tell her you simply can't wait. Give her a final warning—not a day longer than four weeks to wear her wedding dress."

"Oh, mother, you are the wisest, scheming rascal who ever lived! What a dull-brained clodhopper I am! I won't lose a minute"—and springing up he hurried to the telephone in the hall.

Millie heard, without any eavesdropping: "Yes, lovey, it's Joseph. I'm glad you hadn't gone to bed. I forgot to mention something before I left you. . . . No, not that: something much more important. You know how I told you that I now love you just as 'Evelyn.' Well, if you hadn't been weeping, sweetheart, I wanted to add that I shan't tolerate you just as 'Evelyn' any longer. It's got to be 'Evelyn *Kennard.*' Mother and I have just had a 'counsel of war,' and we're serving an ultimatum on you. We've brought the wedding forward. You've just four weeks to get your trousseau ready and your wedding-dress on! . . . No, I won't hear of any compromise either from you or the Adairs. My mother will know how to deal with mother Agnes! And I know how to deal with *you*. I shan't wait, Evelyn. Just four weeks! So get busy, precious bride-to-be!"

When he returned to Millie she said, "Bravo! That'll set Evelyn singing in her sleep. And now, Joseph, from the happy to the ugly. I think we've identified your father's murderer tonight, and I feel pretty sure he was your kidnapper. When you had gone over to Pinecrest I started thinking about those gold sovereigns which your father used to bring home at month-ends. Then I recalled what had been said by the manager of that branch bank at Chadvale—how he gave five gold sovereigns to Mike in exchange for a Bank of England note, and said he had often done so before. If true, where had Mike got the Bank of England note from? On both scores, was anyone likelier than a banker? I remembered then how anxious that Chadvale bankmanager was to stess that Mike was alone, and just as anxious to impress us that he had afterward seen Mike with another man—which means that the banker was no longer in the bank, for he said the two were heading in the direction of Chadvale arches (which he could not have seen from the bank).

"Anyway, I thought that although there might be nothing in it, we might make an enquiry. I rang the police chief at his home, and told him about Jacques Inman Malvern, and the three initials making JIM as in the bowler hat. I asked would it be worthwhile to see if those initials and the five gold sovereigns matched up at all.

"Well, he acted quickly. He gave instructions for the head office to enquire at once. They got through to the local constabulary at Chadvale, and they in turn contacted the manager. His name is Charlesworth; but he's been there only about a year. They asked him for the name of the preceding manager. It was Jacques Malvern! When they asked the new manager where Jacques Malvern now was he replied, 'We've no idea. He often used to stay in Knutsford. His father was a rich man there, and left Jacques well off. Jacques didn't really need to work at all. He wasted a good deal—we think through gambling. A couple of years ago he tansferred most of what he had to Switzerland. Soon after that he embezzled over three hundred pounds from the bank here and absconded with it. There's been a search for him ever since, but so far there's not a trace of him. Why a man of his means should steal and run we can't fathom.' "

Millie's rocking-chair was still now, as she said, "Joseph, I think we've found the hidden hand behind twenty-five years of evil and torture and murder!"

TWENTY-NINE
The Bells Are Ringing

"Will wonders never cease?" "What on earth next!" "Talk about miracles still happening!" Such was the reaction everywhere when the revelation became noised abroad up and down Elmerton about Joseph and the Adairs. It was headline news. "The Reverend Joseph Kennard turns out to be the long-lost son of Councilor and Mrs. Joash Adair!" "Our well-known Mrs. Millie Kennard is not his real mother, but took him in as a baby, little dreaming he had been kidnapped!" "Beautiful Evelyn Adair, in reality the daughter of Mr. and Mrs. Richard Harwood, victims of the 1894 train wreck!" "The kidnapping of baby Joseph Adair exposed after twenty years!" "The murderer of Mike Kennard discovered—Jacques Inman Malvern, local bankmanager at Chadvale, and owner of the bowler hat with the initials J.I.M.! Mike Kennard's murderer probably the long-unknown kidnapper! Murderer is bankmanager who robs bank, and absconds!" It was a "field day" for the local press, and high-grade lubrication for the wheels of gossip. And every reference to it ended with, "The wedding day is Saturday, July 18th!"

But something else happened before the wedding—on the Sunday afternoon preceding it. Brandon Street Sunday

School was packed full to witness it. An artistically inscribed silver shield on a polished walnut mount was to be presented by the church's minister to Councilor Joash Adair in grateful recognition of twenty years as Superintendent of Brandon Street Congregational Church Sunday School. The minister was chairman for the special occasion, and the church's officebearers ringed the platform. Joseph, too, was on the platform as a local minister, and son of the Superintendent. There must have been over six hundred scholars, teachers, parents, members, visitors, tightly packed in for the occasion. Ordinary classes were suspended. Millie and Agnes were there, in the audience, near the front. Evelyn sat next to them.

Various tributes were paid to Councilor Adair by the secretary and selected co-workers, all leading up to the presentation. The minister then said, "You are all expecting me, as minister of the church, to make this presentation. No, there are other hands far more significant than mine at a moment like this," whereupon four scholars—two little boys and two little girls—came to the platform. Then, each holding one corner of the plaque, they lifted it up to Mr. Adair.

It was a picturesque but touching moment. The fingers of the four little scholars had twanged the heartstrings of the beloved Superintendent. Joash was a man inwardly as strong as he was tender, but it took him all his time to handle his emotions as he thanked one and all for that "undeservedly gracious expression of esteem and loyalty."

Then he said, "You have been kind enough to suspend classes so as to attend this open gathering and presentation; but I wonder how many of you happen to have noticed the passage of Scripture set by the syllabus for our senior classes today? Strangely wonderful providences have been working themselves out lately in my own life and in the lives of several others, as you all know. Is it just by chance that the Scripture passage for today is Genesis, chapters 45 and 46? They complete the narrative about Jacob and his twelve sons. You all know how Jacob had a young son who was specially dear to him. One day the other sons brought home what seemed to be clear evidence that the boy had been slain by a wild beast; and for twenty years Jacob thought his beloved *Joseph* was dead. Then there came a dire famine, and the sons of Jacob had to go down into Egypt to buy food. There they eventually found, to their utter astonishment, that the greatest dignitary in mighty Egypt, next to the king himself, was that brother of theirs whom they had wickedly sold into slavery all those years before! When they reported this back home to Jacob, for a while he would not believe them, but at last they took back to him some tangible evidence which convinced him, and he exclaimed, as the last verse of chapter 45 says, 'It is enough: *Joseph, my son, is yet alive!* I will go and see him before I die.'

"Friends, over twenty years ago my dear wife and I had our first-born child; a baby boy. We called his name, 'Joseph.' One year later an evil hand stole him from his baby carriage; and for more than twenty years we have had to think that our little Joseph was dead, at the hands of a human 'wild beast.' But now, after all those twenty years, to our sheer astonishment we were given, only a few days ago, the indubitable evidences that our dear son was 'yet alive,' and not only so, but that he was actually talking to us in our own sitting-room! You know to whom I refer: a fine, gifted, young man who has already endeared himself to people all over this town and area; a young minister of the Gospel who has already brought hundreds of souls to the Saviour and has set the songs of Zion ringing in the hearts of as many others.

"Did you ever hear anything like it? He has, so to speak, come back to us from the grave. He has brought his own father—myself—to know the Saviour as I never did before! He also brought his 'legal' father, Mr. Mike Kennard, to the Saviour! Also he led our beloved daughter, Evelyn, to know that same dear Saviour! Was anything ever so wonderful? Even that is not all. During all those twenty years God gave us in our home the dearest treasure of a daughter who ever breathed: our lovely Evelyn. And to give it all a golden coronation, that same Joseph and Evelyn are to become man and wife next Saturday!

"Friends, I am not usually a man to display my emotions;

but was there ever a moment like this? Along with this gracious presentation of yours today, *GOD* has made a presentation so wonderful that words break down. . . . My heart is too full to say more; but I want all of you to rejoice with me in my song of gratitude to God: 'JOSEPH, MY SON, IS YET ALIVE!' Yes, 'JOSEPH, MY SON, IS YET ALIVE!' "

Turning sideways on the platform he said in trembling syllables, "Joseph, my long-lost boy, where are you? Come here, my son; and let us exalt the Lord together in the presence of His people!" Joseph stepped forward; and there, on that platform, father and son embraced each other, weeping. Instinctively the audience quietly stood— and watched—and wondered—and wept. Except among the very young there were no dry eyes in the building.

Yes, the wedding bells rang at last for our dear Joseph and his Evelyn! Saturday came, and with it a smiling sky. The marriage ceremony was at 10:30 a.m., by which time not only was the church packed to capacity, but both sides of Harvey Street near the church were thronged. Never had there been a wedding with such a background of life-drama and human pathos, nor ever a union of two young persons more widely admired.

As for Evelyn and her train, it was an "all white" wedding. She chose to wear the carefully kept dress her mother, Agnes, had worn at her own wedding twenty-four years earlier in Rostherne, only now it was expertly adapted to its beautiful new wearer.

As for the groom and his consorts, it was tailcoats, striped trousers, and patent leather shoes.

Not a few notable personages were present, including several councilors and local ministers. Many of Millie's women were there. The Elmerton Watch Committee, which had brought Millie to Elmerton fourteen years earlier, was amply represented. Some members of that energetic committee had now removed to the better land, but others of them, whom we met earlier, were still active and watch-doggy as ever. Stocky Mrs. Dingwell was there with healthily persisting proclivity for "putting two and two together"—only her problem now was, that in the wedding service "two" became "one"! Mrs. Tuttle, the talker, was on hand, with undiminished loquacity. Widow Musgrave was there, looking fourteen years older, but still wearing a brown felt hat with a stiff brim, and her now-graying hair in a tight bun at the back of her neck to hold the rear hat-brim up. Llewellyn Lewis was there, too, with a wedding-day panegyric on Lloyd-George. Hugh Bingham slipped in with unabated dueling ability, though his former antagonist, Bella Tinkler, no longer tinkled on earth. Mr. Alexander Pomeroy, the now-aged chairman, was brought into the church in a wheelchair. Last, but not least, Effie Crawley, the converted writer of the anonymous letters, had come over from Oldham to join in the congratulations.

The wedding party included Councilor and Mrs. Joash Adair, Mr. Richard Adair, the younger brother of the bride-groom, Mrs. Millie Kennard, Matron Dorothy Kennard, sister of the bridegroom, Mr. and Mrs. Ambrose Barnton (nee Kennard), Mr. Frank Goodall, Mr. and Mrs. Ainsworth of Huddersfield, and their daughter, Miss Molly Ainsworth; also officebearers of Harvey Street Independent Church, and other close friends.

The service was conducted by the Reverend Mortimer Hibbert, formerly of Huddersfield; the minister to whom Joseph had gone when he reached the outskirts of that city as a footsore, fugitive laddie on a wet night years earlier. Two of the local ministers also participated.

It was a reverent, moving, solemnly joyful ceremony. Beyond that there was nothing but what one may see at other such elegant weddings. There was nothing spectacular or supernormal; nothing exceptional other than Evelyn, and the fact that the bridegroom had composed his own wedding hymn.

There never could have been a bride anywhere to surpass Evelyn. She was the embodiment of radiant purity. It lit her face and shone through her eyes. Those shy but beaming, blue eyes; that healthy, rose-pink complexion; that demure look and sunrise smile, so happily friendly yet so truly queenly! Let no one be jealous of her. It was not of her own doing. She was made that way, and was too modest ever to exploit it. Judging from her modest behaviour, she might have been the plainest Jane in the kingdom.

As for Joseph's wedding hymn, he put it to 10. 10. 10. 10. meter, so that it could be sung to a well-known tune. This is what it said:

> *Oh, lovely bond, uniting heart to heart!*
> *Oh, solemn vow, that only death shall part!*
> *Statute divine, enriching love and life,*
> *Blending as one the husband and the wife.*
>
> *Oh, holy troth, with sanctions all divine!*
> *Blest by our Lord in Cana's wedding sign;* ·
> *Symbol of Christ and of His mystic bride,*
> *Even His Church for which He bled and died.*
>
> *These hearts united, bind to Thee above;*
> *Live in their living; love in all their love;*
> *Till life's horizons melt in fairer sphere,*
> *And Heaven perfects all that earth made dear.*

There was a silence in which one could almost hear hearts beating as Joseph slowly placed the ring on Evelyn's finger, and as the minister thereupon said, "I now pronounce them man and wife." Joseph momentarily embraced Evelyn, though only with a polite formality such as was becoming in that hour of public witness. As he did so, Evelyn whispered, "We're one at last, Joseph!" And Joseph whispered back, "Yes, one—for ever!"

As they afterwards came out from the signing in the vestry and walked down the aisle arm-in-arm, one could hear the subdued exclamation everywhere, "What a couple!" Between the foyer and the outer gates was a happy tumult of well-wishers, some of whom became covered with confetti almost as much as the bridal pair. Into the street the shower of confetti continued, until the Adair limousine looked embarrassed by such lavish affection toward it. Our grateful bridal pair had neither heart nor mind to hurry. They knew how genuine was the esteem and love of the dear flock at Harvey Street, many of whom lived in poor homes with few material possessions or physical comforts to adorn their days on earth, and few changes to break the grinding monotony of the mills. It was another of those occasions beyond analysis, when laughter and tears, like bridegroom and bride, become one.

Before Joseph and Evelyn reached the car they had weathered a rain of daring kisses from heaven knows where. But at last, with car windows open and hands waving grateful appreciation, they slowly moved away.

By noon the wedding party and an inner circle of guests were sitting at the marriage feast in Elmerton's best hotel. To record here all the flamboyant felicitations, sagacious admonitions, and remarkable prophecies expressed in long speeches and short telegrams would run away with half a printer's ream. They were enough to last the happy pair for at least a thousand years. We must leave them to the pen of the recording angel and the office files of heaven.

At two o'clock the bridal pair left the happy guests for an hour, to prepare for the train journey to Llandudno, Wales, where they were to spend a brief honeymoon of one week. What the guests never knew was, that after Joseph and Evelyn had changed for travel, James, the Adair chauffeur, ran them in the car away out of Elmerton, up Rosewood Lane, to Hazelmere, over the rise and down by the more easily accessible entrance to Netherford Lake.

Leaving James and the car for a few moments on the widened bridle path, they went, hand-in-hand, along the margin of the lake, and round the bend to the wooden bench inside the willow-covered alcove. What a shrine of hallowing memories that wooden seat by the lake had now become! Yes, it was where Joseph had bandaged Evelyn's ankle, and where love for him had first awakened in her young heart. It was the place where, later, Joseph had sobbed out his heart in appeal to God when fleeing from home as a boy of fourteen. It was the spot where, also, there had been the reunion with his mother and Evelyn after his years in Huddersfield. And it was the place where, just recently, he had put the engagement ring on Evelyn's finger.

There, once again, they now sat—*married!* their minds a maze of memories and wonderment. It was not yet

3 o'clock. The sun was still high but slightly over toward the west, away from the Pennines. The lake again was a picture of serenity. Although late in the season for rhododendrons, many of the bushes fringing the lake were still ablush with crimson and gold. The flowering plants and shrubs around the water were all in their most colorful hues. The sun was throwing velvet flames across the surface of the tranquil mere.

Netherford! Had it ever looked more satisfying?

The languid zephyr from the west could do no more than persuade little riplets to come lapping at the edge of the lake where Joseph and Evelyn sat.

Were ever two young hearts more blissfully and innocently and completely one in each other's love?

"Joseph, dear," Evelyn quietly reflected, "it looks as though all Nature is in wedding-dress today; as though the sky were the bridegroom and the flower-bestrewed earth the bride."

"Yes, my treasure, they're married today in symbolic harmony with the wedlock of your heart and mine."

"I could not help a silent chuckle, Joseph. When we were coming out, after the wedding service, I heard one of the women say to the others, 'It's over, now'; and another woman laughed back, 'Nay, it's only just begun!' "

Joseph smiled, too, and added, "There are always the two aspects, aren't there? I think we're both relieved that in one sense 'it's over now,' and that we're husband and wife at last. But how precious a thought it is, that in the other sense it's 'only just begun'! Lovey, I'm not just speaking in the thrill of wedding-day sentimentalism; no, Evelyn, I'm thinking with deep gratitude: I believe God brought us together, despite some hidden hand of evil which tried to frustrate it; and now we're going to be sweethearts for ever. When we both said in the marriage ceremony, 'Till death us do part,' I could not help inwardly saying, 'But even the grave is only a temporary separation to those who are united as you and I are—in Christ. Heaven, at last, will erase all earthly imperfections and give us afresh to each other in perfect love without a shadow. Yes, my dear, dear, dear love, we'll be sweethearts now right on to the end of the years—and then beyond. Let's kneel down at this bench, and thank God who watched over us through so many strange happenings until He brought us here as husband and wife."

So there they knelt and yielded their future, their love, their all, to the heavenly Father, and to that dear Saviour who, to all who really know and possess Him, is "heaven begun below." Then, in the quiet of that willow covert, they stood, enfolded in each other's arms for a long, long kiss.

It was Saturday—and Summer. Several other people were around the lake. A couple of them saw Joseph and Evelyn kneeling in prayer at the memorial bench, and blinked their eyes incredulously. But what did it matter? The thing which mattered was the wedding-day covenant which was made there.

Afterward, when they were in each other's arms, Evelyn suddenly whispered, "Joseph . . . we're being watched!"

But he drew her closer to himself and said, "Yes, of course we are, dear; not just on earth, but *in heaven!*"

The week's honeymoon at Llandudno was a week of fond wonder and pure bliss; a "holy of holies" into which we will not intrude. What they talked about as they walked round the Great Orme and planned for the future we will leave locked up where it belongs.

Quite out of keeping with the happiness of such a honeymoon, yet not in any way spoiling it, there was one discovery which they then made that ought to be mentioned here because of its significant contribution to the full story of Joseph and Evelyn. It added one more pointer toward the solution of the mystery surrounding Joseph's abduction from his baby carriage twenty-two years earlier. It also linked on to something which they suddenly discovered later, after they had been married more than twenty years and had been travelling for some time in America.

One morning of that honeymoon week Joseph said, "Dearest, if you don't mind, I would like to make one or two enquiries today, beginning at the Town Clerk's Office." Joseph was remembering the letter which purportedly had been posted by Jacques Inman Malvern from Llandudno the day after the kidnapping, in which he said he had just read of it in the Llandudno local press. By the end of that day they had found that in 1891 there was no Llandudno daily paper, nor was the kidnapping reported in the Manchester Guardian, nor in any Chester paper. So Malvern could *not* have seen any such report in the newspaper, as he said he had. Then how did he know of the kidnapping if he was at that time away in Llandudno? That was something else which had to be left unsolved for the time being. But the answer came unexpectedly, years later.

More than that we will not add about that delectable week. But as the two of them were in the railway train, rolling back to Manchester and then Elmerton, Joseph said, "Darling, after the agony of those anonymous letters, then the providential trap laid for us by our two mothers, then our sudden discovery that we had both been loving each other all the time, and then the thrill of being able to let our love leap into expression like a freed bird, I wrote a little sonnet about love. It isn't exactly either Italian or Elizabethan in form, and maybe it's a bit too vivid; but it expressed my intense feelings at the time.

LOVE
What a whirlwind in a sigh!
What an earthquake in a cry!
What a cloudburst in a sob!
What a landslide in a throb!
What a river in a tear!
What an ocean in a mere!
What an aeon in an hour!
What a Sharon in a flower!
What a sunrise in a smile!
What utopia in one mile!
What a world in one bright eye!
What a fever in "Good-bye"!
What a hell in one seared bliss!
What a heav'n in one sweet kiss!

"Joseph, I do declare, you are love's poet laureate! One of these days you'll blossom into a modern troubadour and become famous!"

"Thank you, Evelyn; but if *you* put the laurel on my brow, that's fame enough for me! However, after this never-to-be-forgotten honeymoon, I have a couple more lines to add. They complete the poetic quatrain idea of the little sonnet which I have just read, and they add my heart's finishing touch:

> *What a joy—almost divine!*
> *What a rapture in "You're mine!"*

"Oh, Joseph!"
"Oh, Evelyn!"
They sat there, with their arms tenderly round each other, watching the fields and hamlets and lanes and hills filing behind as the train jigga-jig-jigged along the rails. And they journeyed on together, getting more and more in love for thirty-eight years—until they reached the first junction for heaven.

THIRTY
Swiftly Fly the Years

Dear reader, I was glad, as no doubt you yourself were, that the preceding chapter rang the wedding bells and gave us a snapshot of honeymoon happiness in Llandudno, Wales. Having brought you to that point, I can now lay down my pen; but where I leave off another must take over if you are to get the completed story. Let me explain.

Most melodramatic love stories, whether fictional or factual, end with the hero and heroine married at last. Everything leads to *that*. I suppose it is understandable that the story should end there if it is only or mainly for the reader's entertainment. Yet from a practical standpoint it is a bad fault.

In all true love of men and women for each other the wedding day is not the climax, but only a climacteric. Where love is deep and noble its finest chapters are written *after* marriage, not before it. The premarital intrigues of scheming enemies, and the exploits or sufferings of the hero and heroine on their way to the marriage altar, run away with all the interest. The post-wedding years of day-to-day life together do not have the same histrionic excitement (thank heaven!), and therefore they are usually left unrecorded.

That, I agree again, is understandable, and it will continue to be the fashion. But it none-the-less a bad weakness. It always leaves one asking, "Yes, but how did the two of them get on together after the mystery and excitement *before* their wedlock gave place to normal life *after* it?" What happens *after* the wedding is no mere addendum to its dramatic precursors. On the contrary, all pre-wedding developments are only the prologue to the real life story of true lovers.

Well, we must accept it that we cannot alter the apparently necessary fault. But in the case of Joseph and Evelyn we simply must break out of line, if only to give at least a pleasant synopsis of their thirty-eight years together. To do that is not only desirable, it is delightfully *incumbent* on us, if we are to be fully faithful to our story; for all of that which preceded their union at the marriage altar reaches its coronation in the continuing significance of their life and ministry together afterwards.

However, the telling of that, even though very briefly, needs a pen other than mine. I have asked Evelyn herself to write it for you. At the time of my asking her she was sixty-two years old. As she and I walked and talked together in her quiet, little garden, I could not help but observe that the years had exercised their kindliest artistry upon her. There was the same feminine tallness, the same straightness without any suggestion of stiffness, the same suggestion of queenliness without a fleck of haughtiness. Her light, wavy hair was still wavy, only now it was rather silvery. Her complexion was as pinky fresh as ever, and her skin smooth, with few lines on it. Her eyes were rich blue, as ever, but I noticed that a far-away look was in them, especially as we spoke of Joseph; and she had to put glasses on when reading or writing. Also, owing to a rather bad road accident a couple of years earlier (a drunken driver being the cause), she was using a walking stick.

Most of all, I could not help sensing the rich mellowness of her character. Her face still had that charming peculiarity of looking deeply thoughtful but ever ready to break into girlish merriment at the slightest provocation. Her face

now had a beauty which only years can give to those who
walk in heart communion with the heavenly Shepherd; and
I found myself wondering once again, which is the lovelier,
the fresh beauty of the Spring, or the golden loveliness of
Autumn and harvest. As I walked with dear Evelyn, the
still-lovely but now-elderly Evelyn of our story, and listened
to the seasoned kindliness coming to me through her soft,
sympathetic voice, I began to agree with the writer of the
following lines.

> *Yes, Spring has charm. Arrayed in unspoilt green,*
> *Bedecked with blossoms—like a fairy queen;*
> *Her magic wand gray Winter's spell transforms*
> *To laughing loveliness in sprightliest forms,*
> *And wakes the merry songsters in the trees,*
> *And scents with dew-kissed petals every breeze:*
> *Yes, Spring has charm. Yet none the less I hold*
> *That lovelier still is Autumn's mellowed gold:*
> *Tho' not with livelier, yet with kindlier eyes*
> *She smiles upon us from soft-dappled skies:*
> *Her deeper crimson and her wistful brown*
> *With russet hues weave Nature's richest crown;*
> *Her laden boughs and glorious, waving corn—*
> *It was for these that Spring was ever born!*
>
> *Yes, youth has charm. Who doubts it or denies?*
> *Unfurrowed brow, undimmed and questing eyes;*
> *Lithe figure, supple limb and graceful poise,*
> *And brave horizons bright with promised joys,*
> *And merry heart, all filled with gleeful play,*
> *And life, and love, and laughter, all so gay!*
> *Yes, youth has charm. Yet none the less I hold*
> *That fairer haloes cling around the old:*
> *The mellowed lustre of the long-lived wise*
> *Beams out from kindlier if less lively eyes;*
> *The ripened fruit, and gold of harvest field,*
> *And softer hues which weathered seasons yield,*
> *And milder charms which now the brow enring—*
> *It was for THESE that youth awaked in Spring!*

Perhaps, before I hand over to Evelyn, there are two aspects which I should mention. The first has to do with the principal figures in our story.

During the December of the year in which Joseph and Evelyn were married, good-natured old uncle Ben said his last good-bye to the Adair Furniture House which he had established. He was greatly missed. As one of the store employees put it, "Even the polished mahogany seemed to lose some of its shine when the cheery old man no longer came round."

Our strong, gentlemanly Councilor Joash Adair died early 1940, several months after the Second World War began, when he was seventy-three years old. He was commensurately mourned as one of the finest and most respected public men Elmerton ever had.

And how can I write it without moist eyes?—our dear, always-gracious Agnes Adair was one of the casualties in a German air raid two or three years later. The bomb which so violently took her also destroyed Pinecrest and "Little Eden" and the flower gardens, with all the hallowing memories which had clustered around that beloved homestead. Oh, the callousness of "man's inhumanity to man"!

Rickie, the second son of the Adairs, and brother to Joseph, was still alive and well at the time of my handing this over to Evelyn. He was a much-respected citizen, happily married, and the father of three grown children. The Adair furnishing establishment, however, was no more—another casualty of German destruction.

Joseph's golden-haired sister, Dorothy, who meant so much to him, and who grew up to own her own large nursing home, not too surprisingly became the precious prey, eventually, of a local doctor. So far as I know there are no children to the marriage.

In the case of Joseph's sister, Mona, and her husband, there are no less than seven children—all now grownups, of course.

But perhaps the happiest item in this brief round up pertains to Molly Ainsworth—with whom all of us, I should think, fell in love, and for whom we felt keen sympathy. How she loved Joseph! How she must have wept in secret that he could not be hers! How noble was the victory of her resignedness and unselfishness! She told herself that she would never marry any other; but I am glad to report that she was wrong. Near Fairfield, Manchester, there was an outstanding, well-to-do Christian gentleman, known far and wide in Christian circles for meetings which he organized and led in the city each week, and particularly for conventions which he used to arrange, known as "Deeper Spiritual Life" conventions. He was also one of the directors at the head of the city-mission work. Everywhere his name was known and greatly esteemed. At the age of forty he was still unmarried, and people used to wonder why such a handsome, well-to-do man remained in lonely bachelordom. It was because he had not yet seen Molly Ainsworth. From the moment he saw her he was all hers, and somehow he got his gentle fingers on lonely Molly's heartstrings. So she was married after all—when she was thirty-seven; and it was a true love match, with a real "happy ever after."

Finally, I must make parting reference to Millie, that is, Mrs. Mike Kennard, than whom never did any story contain a healthier character or doughtier little combatant in the war against wrong. Never once did she bow to the flatteries of the sycophant or cringe before the threatenings of the traducer. Never once, amid disappointment, opposition, perplexity, did she let her banner drag on the ground. What a mother for a boy like Joseph! What a son for a mother like Millie!

Evelyn will be telling you about the extended travels which she and Joseph undertook, but, lest it might be omitted, let me mention here that after they were married they lived for a few years with Millie at Ashgrove Crescent; and in later years, whenever they were back in Elmerton, that is where they stayed—though of course they were continually round at Pinecrest. A deep attachment developed between Millie, who was not the real mother of Joseph, and Evelyn, who was not the real daughter of the Adairs. In some ways, the most tender love story in the Bible is that between a mother-in-law (Naomi) and her daughter-in-law (Ruth). Millie and Evelyn became a modern version of it. Millie's tact and Evelyn's unobtrusiveness were a perfect match. Every preacher needs critics. Millie and Evelyn were Joseph's—his sincerest and severest! Millie used to say to Evelyn, "Now we'll start. I'll do the stabbing and you do the bandaging." So Joseph, oft-wounded, oft-mended, learned his lessons!

Later, when Joseph and Evelyn were permanently away, Millie had a nicely furnished room in the nursing home next door (and the house where she and Joseph had lived became a new part of the nursing home). But she kept her rocking-chair and one other from Wragley Street. Once, when Joseph was visiting her, he said, "Mother, you seem fonder and fonder of that old rocking-chair."

"Maybe I am," she replied. "I've reached the time when actions creak louder than words."

Joseph was sitting in the old chair opposite to the rocker. "Mother, why on earth don't you get rid of *this* old chair!"

She replied, "Joseph, you don't understand. That isn't just a chair; it's a companion. Stain it, polish it, cushion it, do anything you like, but don't take it away. It's been with me now twenty-eight years—all the time in Manchester, all the years in Wragley Street, and again the years here. If *you'd* been sat on as much as that chair has, you might not look half as pleasant. Fat people, thin people, tall people, short people, good people, bad people, old people, young people, laughing people, crying people; they've all been interviewed sitting in that chair. I can see them all—just the ones I want, at whatever time best suits my mood, including you and Evelyn during your absences. When I look at that chair I don't see just a chair; I see those who've sat in it through all the years. That chair is a 'garden of memories.' It's my little Westminster Abbey."

So the chair stayed. So did the rocker. So did our champion, Millie, until she was sixty-five. She kept in the "firing line" of the battle right to the end, or rather, to the time of her translation. During the Winter of 1924, she took a bad dose of the "Flu." She seemed to get over it, but it left her with bronchial trouble and a weakening cough. She was given all the loving attention and expert care that Dorothy and her doctor-husband could provide, but she had come to the one battle which she would not win—at least, not physically.

She called Dorothy to her room one evening, and amid her coughs she said, "Dorothy, my dear daughter, so good to me through all the years, let me hold you and kiss you. Never will you know all you have meant to me. I don't want to alarm you. No, I only want to spare you any such alarm by telling you in advance that I think my time has come to cross over. I may be wrong, but I have a feeling. . . . Well, anyway, just in case. . . . I want you to say my loving good-bye to Mona and her dear Ambrose, if they're not round again before I'm away. And I have a special word for our precious Joseph and his Evelyn. . . ."

Her premonition was right. During the night she pressed the little button which brought the night-nurse, who in turn sent for Dorothy and her husband. Millie was conscious right to the end. There was just a short struggle; then with her hand in Dorothy's she breathed herself away into invisible arms waiting just beyond. Joseph's "best little mother in all the world" had gone.

Millie Kennard had the biggest funeral ever seen in Elmerton up to that time. Aldermen, councilors, lawyers, doctors, ministers, chief of police, members from all the churches and religious organizations, and at least three hundred of her own women, and many others gathered to it.

The minister who officiated said, "Today the whole of Elmerton weeps at this grave, and at the same time gives praise to God for one of the most remarkable women who ever lived here. Her influence for good has been felt all over this area. Hundreds of women have been befriended by her, and lifted to life on a higher level. Hundreds have been saved from drink and immorality and prison. Hundreds have come to know, through her, the one and only true Saviour of human beings and human society. It is fully befitting that in Elmerton today a signal of townwide honour should be given to this noble woman who has meant so much to so many. It is a signal of honor and mourning accorded to very few: the flag above our Town Hall hangs at half-mast, and Elmerton thereby bows its head in mourning."

As the body was committed to the ground, someone among the women in the crowd started the well-known Sankey hymn,

> *There's a land that is fairer than day,*
> *And by faith we can see it afar,*
> *For the Savior waits over the way*
> *To prepare us a dwelling-place there.*

To most of the gathered hundreds the hymn was familiar. They needed no one to tell them the words; and they sang all three verses, with the chorus each time—

> *In the sweet by-and-by,*
> *We shall meet on that beautiful shore;*
> *In the sweet by-and-by,*
> *We shall meet on that beautiful shore.*

It was too moving for any restraint of tears. Oh, the sore void that Millie's passing left in many hearts! And, as the crowd dispersed, perhaps the saddest weeper of all was our dear Mrs. Agnes Adair.

The other aspect which I am thinking it well to mention before handing over to Evelyn is, that the year 1914, when she and Joseph were married, was the fateful year in which the First World War broke out. Never will those of us who lived in England at that time forget the five awful words which we saw on the placard boards outside news agents' shops on August 4th, that year: BRITAIN DECLARES WAR ON GERMANY.

That monster war was waged on a scale utterly surpassing anything ever before it in military history. For the first time, whole "nations in arms" fought each other. Not merely thousands or even tens of thousands, but *millions* were ranged in colossal antagonism. Altogether that global conflict saw the employment of no less than fifty millions of armed men. It not only transformed and multiplied conventional weapons, but brought weapons far more deadly, devastating and diabolical than any ever used before: airships, airplanes, bombs, submarines, torpedoes, underwater mines, hand-grenades, poison gas, artificial fog, tanks, liquid fire. It cost not only 50,000 million pounds (or 250,000 million dollars); there were thirty million casualties, and no less than eight million deaths. In France alone 21,000 factories, 630,000 homes, and 1,659 townships were wholly destroyed!

To refer to such a gigantic disaster here in a mere couple of paragraphs may seem at a glance to be a preposterous disproportion, but in reality it is not so at all. In our narrative of Joseph and Evelyn we are concerned with accompanying world events only so far as they affect what we are relating. Far more preposterous would be our trying to add to what the able pens of outstanding historians, statesmen and others have already written about that First World War. I simply mention here (to save any need for Evelyn's doing so) one or two things which "belong" to the Lancashire of our two dear newlyweds.

The first acute difficulty in Britain was to build up a big enough army. At the beginning of the war there was a highly trained force of regulars and the "Territorials"; but the whole of them numbered less than 750,000. These now began to be called into action. Soon all Lancashire was excitedly astir with hurried mobilization. There were the "King's Own Royal Regiment" at Lancaster, the "Lancashire Fusiliers" at Bury, the "King's Regiment" at Liverpool, the "South Lancashire Regiment" at Warrington, the "East Lancashire Regiment" at Preston, the "Ninth Battalion Manchester Regiment" at Ashton-under-Lyne, not to mention others.

Joseph and Evelyn, in the first flush of wedded happiness, were scarcely back a fortnight before the black pall of the war fell over Europe. Indeed, although time's chroniclers never gave it even a passing nod of acknowledgment, that Llandudno honeymoon of Joseph and Evelyn Kennard symbolized the farewell bowing-out of an England which is no more; which lived and loved, laughed and wept, and sang and sighed, on the other side of that dividing war. Many a wistful heart still wishes that Father Time could turn the clock hands back. But I must desist, before sentiment runs away with me. Let me now hand over to Evelyn.

LOOKING BACK OVER THE YEARS

Yes, this is Evelyn Harwood Kennard writing, and I am grateful for the privilege. Little did I ever expect to be writing a closing chapter to the story of Joseph and myself. When I was asked to write it, I shrank from doing so, for it involves unavoidable reference to myself. It also stirs up within me such affecting memories that to write about them is far from easy. It is for Joseph's sake alone that I have yielded to the kind request, encouraged by the thought that his remarkable life story (so well covered in its early part by the foregoing pages) might be of profit to some reader.

I have gone through the preceding chapters—with what tender emotion you will sympathetically understand. Let me bear my witness that the leading characters in the story have not been overdrawn; though of course the references to myself are far too generous, and I must put them through the sieve of my own better knowledge of myself. Otherwise the narrative is true to the facts, both the outward and the inward.

So now I will begin, keeping a tight rein on my emotions, and guarding against the ever-present temptation to over-eulogize my unspeakably dear Joseph.

As you already know, only ten days or so after our little honeymoon ended, the thundercloud of the First World War broke with its deluge of suffering upon Europe, and indeed over all five continents.

The day Britain declared war on Germany we happened to be in Ashton-under-Lyne, about six miles from Manchester. I recall Joseph's coming into the house the next day, with the newspaper in his hand, and then exploding, "Oh, why has it to be?—war and bloodshed just to satisfy Kaiser Wilhelm's grabbing pride! The Germans have been preparing for this ever since the Boer War. It was the Germans who taught the Boers trench warfare. Why has England been deaf all these years to the warnings of Lord Roberts?

Ever since Bismarck's 'blood and iron' policy, war has been the chief industry of Prussia. And now war—with Germany armed to the teeth, and Britain brandishing a rusty old sword that wouldn't cut a mouse's tail off!"

A few evenings later, as we were walking back from a meeting, we passed the railway station there and saw a large crowd of people. Several hundred soldiers of the Ninth Battalion Manchester Regiment came marching to the station to entrain for France. The crowd cheered and cheered. "Them fellers'll soon teach the Germans a thing or two!" somebody shouted. "Let 'em 'ave it, lads!" somebody else sang out, and everybody else shouted "Hurrah!" to it. We heard a laddie ask his father "Daddy, who are all these people that are cheering?" His father's laconic reply had a smack of grim irony in it: "Those who are not going, son."

The roadway at the side of the station dips down deeply, and a great iron bridge goes over it. As the train slowly moved out from the station and over the bridge, many of the soldiers were leaning out of the carriage windows, waving and calling to the people in the street below. One of them with a loud voice shouted, "We'll soon finish the war!" Not one of them ever came back.

Soon the whole pattern of life was changed. Everywhere the hoardings carried urgent and stirring placards appealing to able-bodied young men to enlist in defense of the motherland. As the months passed by, the enormity and brutality of the German atrocities in Belgium—especially to women and children and prisoners, Germany's callous breaches of international law, in defiance of human conscience itself, the submarine sinkings of merchant vessels and passenger liners, especially the sinking of the gigantic Cunard liner, the *Lusitania,* in May 1915, with a loss of twelve hundred civilian lives: all these things were shocking the world and enraging Britain. Lord Kitchener, Britain's Minister of War at that time, was inspiring such confidence, such a sense of duty and righteous indignation, that literally millions of volunteers came freely forward to form the "New Armies."

Conscription did not come until 1916, by which time it was more than apparent that only by an agonizing total effort of the whole nation could that biggest of all wars be won. Civilians had to submit to more and more control by the State. All the great industries were governmentally supervised. More and more the supply and distribution of food had to be regulated, until even the amount that each citizen was allowed to eat was rationed.

More or less as in other churches, the life and work of our Harvey Street church in Elmerton suffered. Soon scores of our young men were away in the fighting forces. Many of our young women were gone, also, as nurses, munitions workers, or in other forms of national service. There was a corresponding disorganization and diminution. Then the tears began to flow. All over the town, as well as all over the nation, casualties began mounting. Some of our finest Harvey Street boys would never come back. Others were invalided home—minus an arm or a leg, or in other ways disfigured or maimed for life. Oh, the heartbreak of those days! Even to remember them still hurts after all the intervening years.

Joseph read and thought much about the causes of the war. One day, late in 1915, when fortunes were pretty black for the Allies, we were sitting at our evening meal when he began thinking aloud. "Evelyn, the awful guilt for this war lies squarely on the shoulders of Germany. The huge increases in the German navy during recent years; the ambition to become the super-power in Europe; the confessed purpose to split the British Empire by controlling the Middle East; the greed to annex extra-European territory; the speeches of the German Kaiser and of professors in German universities, glorifying Germany and exalting war; the itching of the German War Office for a chance to display the irresistible might of the German war-machine; the collusion of Germany with Austria in declaring war on Serbia; the sudden, unprovoked declaration of war on France again, and the treacherous violation of Belgium's neutrality; and the shocking barbarities all calculatedly set in motion! Ugh! Evelyn, we're not just fighting a war; we're fighting a *beast!*—the cruel, evil, greedy beast of Prussian militarism!—and I'm going to enlist in our British army to help fight it."

I must have turned pale, and he must have seen it, for at once he said, "Forgive me, sweetheart. I did not mean to be so cruelly sudden. I'm sorry if it sounded drastic, for I've been slowly thinking and praying about it for days. I don't want to act rashly, yet neither do I want to be a shirker. Evelyn, dear, what do *you* think?"

Inwardly torn, I did not reply. How I loved him! He was watching me carefully, and he correctly read my thoughts. "Evelyn," he said, "you are torn between loyalty to your country and your care for me. You don't want to let your country down, but you don't want to lose *me*. Lovey, I'm torn in just the same way. I love my country, but I love you even more. But now it's my very love for *you* which seems to tell me I should go. While other men are away fighting for homeland and loved ones can I stay here? Harder than facing a bayonet, Evelyn, would be my having to leave *you*. Yet ought I not offer?"

Words cannot describe my feelings. How could I part with him? What if he were killed? Would even winning the war be worth *that?* How could I live without him? But if I refused to let him fight for his country and loved ones when millions of others were doing it, how could I live with the memory of my selfishness?

(What I feared is happening: I am spending too much time on details and feelings. From now onwards let me try to summarize things.) Joseph went to the recruiting office, but was turned away because he was a Christian minister exercising wide influence in the area, and such were needed to boost morale at home just as much as others were needed to fight "at the front." But some months later, as the outlook seemed to grow blacker for the Allies, he offered again. When they found that he had two diplomas for First Aid they drafted him into the R.A.M.C. ("Royal Army Medical Corps").

He said farewell at the church, recommending his weeping flock not to wait for his return but to call some other under-shepherd to care for them. He left home in April, 1916, to report in Manchester. His father and two mothers and I went to the railway with him. No pen could tell our inward void and apprehensiveness as the train pulled him away from us, waving his good-bye and throwing kisses to us from the carriage window.

He was away over two years. They were the bleakest of my life. But I had conquered my selfishness (I hope), and filled all that time helping with various forms of war-work. My Joseph was invalided home in June of 1918. We met him at the railway. What a shock! How changed he was! He was in the blue woollen suiting which all invalided soldiers wore. He was emaciated. His lips were pale. His eyes were too bright, with an expression of haggard tiredness. To save us from worrying he had not told us in his letters what had happened.

During all of 1915 and on into 1916, parts of the western front looked like military deadlock. The opposing miles of trenches with their lines of barbed wire in front of them stretched all the way from the Belgian coast to the Alps. Sometimes those opposing lines had a "no man's land" of several hundred yards between them, and at other times only sixty to eight yards. Indeed, in some places they remained in the same position for four years. At times, parts were flooded. Filling that long, long line of trenches, hundreds of thousands of soldiers on opposing sides faced each other, or, rather, lived more or less underground in "dugouts," amid conditions of fearful hardship, most of all in winter when the trenches got full of water and sludge. Fighting was incessant. Night-raids, bombings, air-battles, artillery duels, bayonet charges, all took place continually along that far-extended "front."

R.A.M.C. work was often mortally risky. After gory encounters in "no man's land" certain picked R.A.M.C. men had to crawl out under cover of night to drag in wounded men who might be lying there. In one such operation the blast from a bursting shell flung Joseph back on to the barbed wire, with his chest and both legs punctured by shrapnel. In both arms he was fairly badly torn by the twisted barbs before being pulled into the British trench again. An artillery duel began, and for four days, in that condition, he stood in mud and water above his waist. He could not remember his being taken to the hospital afterward. All he knew was, that weeks later he was in some medical unit somewhere "behind the lines" recovering from operations to extract shrapnel, and from severe pneumonia. Then he was invalided home.

That was the Joseph who came back to us in June, 1918. Can you imagine my rush of contrary emotions?—my gratitude to God that he was alive and back home, my shock at the suffering written so plainly on his face, and my alarm at his physical condition. We could see at once that he was still a sick man. In an instant we were in each other's arms; but even his embrace was limp.

Well, certainly no beloved invalid ever had a more pampered convalescence. For the first several days his recovery seemed likely to be a slow, even doubtful process. He could not get the horrors of the battlefields out of his mind. At night he could not sleep peacefully. He would suddenly start up in bed, the perspiration oozing down his face, then hold his head in his hands and pray for the fellows back there in the grim struggle. Also, he had recurrent pain from places where the shrapnel had pierced him; and he limped on one leg.

However, after some ten days the restoration set in quite remarkably. Several factors all combined: good food augmented with strengthening tonics; the genial June and July weather; the early loveliness of the summer; the quiet walks in and around the park; the kind greetings of hundreds whom he kept meeting who were *so* glad to see their "dear pastor" home again; and the news that the vast, new Allied offensive was so cracking the enemy that the war might soon be over (thank God, it soon was).

Naturally, I want to tell in detail how affectionate Joseph was to his dear mother, Millie, and myself during his convalescence, but I am resisting that temptation. It was wonderful to have him back, and then, after the first anxious fortnight, see the mending process giving us back the handsome Joseph we had known before.

One day, toward the end of July, he said, "According to my medical check-up yesterday, I ought to be ready to return to France in two or three weeks." My heart sank; so did his mother's. "I dread to go back," he said; "yet I dread even more not being *able* to go back. That's where love and duty both point, whatever the cost." But there was no going back. When he went for his next check-up he was informed that for a time he would be sent on medical service to a military hospital in the south of England. He must wait until sent for. But before he was sent for, the war was over!

By the time August was halfway through, he really looked like our own Joseph again. He was deriving much pleasure and physical benefit from cycling. Yet it took me by surprise when he said, "Evelyn, dear, what about a cycle outing to Netherford Lake again?" We picked a fine day, and off we went again, just the same way we had gone both times before—first as young boy and girl when he bandaged my sprained ankle; then, years later, when he put the engagement ring on my finger. We sat again on the grassy bank by the stream. We paddled; then sat on the bank with our feet dangling in the water—more in love, now, than ever.

Joseph had such a way of saying things, my memory could never let them die. As we sat there, his arm round me, he reflected, "Treasure, since we last sat here we've lived ten years in four birthdays. Father Time has made us four years older in age, but tyrant War has made us ten years older in experience. War crams twice as much into a year as peace spreads over a decade. In peace we learn slowly and constructively: in war the ugliest realities are clubbed into our heads in concentrated agony. It disturbs the clock. It distorts reason. It opens human eyes in the wrong way. Evil knocks down in a year what goodwill slowly built in a century. Angels weep, and demons mock, and humans groan. Evil seems omnipotent, and virtue paralyzed, and heroism helpless. Already this vast war makes those innocent pre-war days seem ten years ago."

I agreed.

His arm drew me closer as he added, "Thank heaven war does not age *love!* Doesn't our love grow younger as it gets older? And if that sounds too paradoxical, listen to what the musical chatter of this stream is saying. It's saying, 'I, too, keep growing older, along with these hills all round me, but, unlike them, the older I grow the fresher I am. The earth of these dear old hills gets older year after year, but *I* am new with bubbling fresh water every new minute. I was here when you sat on that grassy bank four years ago, and I'm still here, only I'm not the water that flowed merrily by you then. I'm the same stream, but fresh, fresh, fresh, from hidden springs all the time.' "

"That's a beautiful thought," I said.

"Yes, darling Evelyn; and isn't it true of our love?"

How long we sat and thought and loved I did not notice. A lot of heaven can be compressed into a few exquisite moments. Eventually our amorous philosophy spell was interrupted by pleasant hunger pangs, so we opened our little commissariat and lunched there by the stream. Could even Adam and Eve ever have been happier in each other's love amid the fair bowers of their paradise than my Joseph and I were as we sat there that day?

Afterward we made our way on past the old quarry, up to the mesa where Netherford Lake lay glistening in the sunshine. Soon we were sitting again on that willow-shaded bench which by now had become to Joseph and me a memorial of outstanding experiences both poignant and precious. As we sat in that favourite place, with the peaceful lake before us and that much-loved scene all round us, Joseph opened his heart concerning his plans for the future.

"I used to dream of one day being an evangelist on a big scale, holding city-wide campaigns. But even if I had the gifts and drive necessary for that, I know now that God is not leading me in that direction. After the war is over, if I'm spared, I would like to spend about ten years up and down Britain holding meetings in churches to open up the Scripture teaching on the deeper Christian life. I know that's not the kind of ministry which hits the headlines, but what does that matter so long as one keeps in the will of God? I believe it could bring many hundreds into rich blessing."

That is just what eventuated after Joseph was discharged from the army. The elderly minister who had most acceptably filled in for the time being at Harvey Street was anxious now to retire. Under urgent pressure we went back there, but on the understanding that it was not permanent. Our intended six months there, though, extended into two and a half years. Even then we left only by deliberately tearing ourselves away. We had grown so to love those dear people, and they were so manifestly sincere in their affection, it was hard to leave them. They saturated our departure in a flood of expressive grief.

Thereafter, for ten years, we were up and down the land in one town or city after another. What years they were! The ten or twelve years following that First World War were a period of peculiar opportunity. The mind of the nation was on the other side of the grave. Hundreds upon hundreds of thousands of sons, fathers, brothers, sweethearts, had laid down their lives and gone beyond the grave, leaving a nation of bereaved hearts behind them. The nation became grave-conscious, eternity-conscious, sin-conscious, God-conscious.

That post-war decade, as evangelists of the time all testified, was the most fruitful in all their experience. If only our Protestant pulpits as a whole had rung true to the Bible, what a nation-wide awakening there might have been! But like a deadly miasma the rationalistic, so-called "higher criticism" was spreading through our theological colleges and among our pulpits. The process had set in by which the faith of our British people in the divine inerrancy of the Bible was gradually broken down.

Joseph's method was to go to a church or group of churches for two or three weeks. The first week or so would be spent in opening up to Christian believers the deeper teachings of the Scriptures in relation to the Christian life. Then there would be two or three days, perhaps, on the importance of soulwinning, when those who had come into new blessing would be urged to go out, now, and bring in the unsaved. The remaining days would be all-out evangelism. It worked wonderfully well. Everywhere the blessing of God was on the ministry. Christians came into new experience of union with Christ, and hundreds of others were led into the joy of salvation.

Financially, they were lean and difficult days for the churches. The whole country was war-impoverished. But Joseph and I were no burden anywhere. Dear old uncle Ben had remembered us very generously on his way out to heaven. Whether such freedom from monetary problem was good for us spiritually I am not sure; but it certainly was a boon at that time.

Joseph became more and more widely appreciated. The inevitable happened: invitations farther afield. We had three wonderful years in Australia and New Zealand, followed by over two years round South Africa. We visited conferences and Christian centers in India, Egypt, Syria, Palestine, Jamaica, Trinidad, and other lands, everywhere preaching—or, as Joseph preferred to call it, "opening up the Word." Eventually a whole new chapter began when we accepted long-standing invitations to Canada and U.S.A. But at this point let me quickly tell you about our two little princesses.

In the fifth year of our wedlock God sent us a darling little daughter. Joseph wanted her named Evelyn, but I gradually won his agreement that she be named after his two mothers, Mildred Agnes. Two years later another wee daughter arrived, and at Joseph's insistence we called her Evelyn Donna—after my own Yorkshire mother. We wanted a little son, also, but he never came.

Although away from home so often, we never had the problem which overseas missionaries frequently have through long separation from their children. For the first few years after our little ones came I accompanied Joseph only intermittently. When school years came they were suitably linked up in Elmerton. Joseph had ample breaks between his bookings, for further study and preparation, when we all had precious home life together. When we were both away, we knew how well looked-after they were with mother Millie and matron Dorothy. And later, after losing our unspeakably dear, dear mother Millie, and we had made our home at Pinecrest again, we knew how smothered with love they were there, whenever we were away.

By the time we started going overseas they were aged thirteen and eleven. In between trips we were longer at home, and sometimes I stayed while Joseph was gone. We determined that nothing should occasion any parental neglect of those two young hearts. Always our summers and the summer holidays were spent with all four of us together.

Again and again Joseph and I felt that God was far too kind to us. Mildred and Donna both came to know the Saviour in their young years. Both of them were in every way a joy to us. During part of our Canadian and American tours they travelled with us (when they were twenty-one and nineteen) and simply revelled in it all. And, after what happened to Joseph and me when *we* were only in our teens, can I call them naughty for falling in love when *they* were "much too young"? Singularly (or ought I say "guidedly"?) they each married an overseas missionary. Mildred (a trained nurse) married a Harvey Street young man who qualified as a doctor; and together they went as medical missionaries to India. Donna after medical graduation, married a young minister, a fine, handsome young stalwart, in feature and stature much akin to Joseph, and they are now in Malaysia. How we missed them! How I still do! But how grateful we were that both of them were in full-time ambassadorial service for the heavenly King! As it happens, both are due for a furlough sometime next year; and I can scarcely wait to see my own precious "bairns" again.

Somebody has said that it is the "human details," not mere outlines, which make life stories entertaining. So, you will enter into my regret at having to review our thirty-eight years of wedlock so skimpily. But there are two or three things which I simply must tell rather more amply before I bid you farewell. The first of them pertains to our Canadian and American itineraries.

Over on the western side of the Atlantic, especially in U.S.A., how different we found public ministry from that in Britain! We wondered whether Joseph's type of ministry would "take," and were rather apprehensive at first. The kind of hymns sung and the way of leading services were different from our British forms. But oh, what eager response to the Word! If I may be pardoned for just one reference to my own part: I always sang some carefully selected solo in Joseph's meetings, accompanied by Joseph at the piano. In U.S.A. Joseph's playing and my singing seemed to be an unusual attraction! I think it was because we were using solos they had never heard before and which were attractively different in their way of expressing the truth.

All our nervousness was soon dissipated as we saw the earnest crowding-in to hear the Word. Joseph's ringing voice, varied vocabulary, deep but lucid and well-illustrated expositions "caught on" everywhere. Never can I forget our series in Toronto, Hamilton, Montreal, Winnipeg, Calgary, Edmonton, Vancouver; then down in the States—Philadelphia, New York, Buffalo, Harrisburg, Boston, Chicago, Portland, San Francisco, Los Angeles, San Diego, and eventually right over to Florida.

In San Diego, for the first time I met members of my own dear father's Harwood family—my father's younger brother, Mr. Adrian Harwood, and his wife, now in their mid-sixties. He showed us photographs of my father (his brother Richard) as a boy and youth. Joseph and I were quite taken aback by their likeness to myself. "Now I know where you get your extraordinary good looks from!" Joseph teased me. The Harwoods were well-to-do people living in the La Jolla area, in a Spanish-type house with a glorious seaward view. Can you share my feelings? It was strangely *exciting* to be for the first time in my life with my own family flesh and blood, and there was a *felt* kinship as well as physical likeness. If my daddy was as nice as uncle Adrian I can well understand why Ma and Pa Adair so took to him.

But now from the happy to the grim. It happened in Philadelphia. Throughout our North American tours we practiced the same procedure as in the old country; the first week devoted to Bible teaching on the deeper Christian life, then an evangelistic follow-up and climax. Some of those series are everlastingly unforgettable, not merely for crowded attendances and exuberant blessing among believers, but because of remarkable conversions. The aroused Christians brought in all manner of persons, from rich relatives and outstanding professional men down to those from slummy surroundings.

One night, near the end of our Philadelphia series, Joseph preached a powerful message on three coordinated texts, one of which was Matthew 12:31, "All manner of sin and blasphemy shall be forgiven unto men." Afterward, when the invitation was given, among those who came into the ante-room (some fifteen in all) were three down-and-outs from some slum area: two men and a woman. Joseph and I spoke to them just as earnestly as if they had been princes from a palace—which seemed to surprise them. We asked them if we had made God's way of salvation through the Lord Jesus plain enough to them. "Yes." Did they now realize their need of receiving Him, the living Saviour, into their hearts? "Yes." Will you do that now in simple faith upon His promise to come in? "Yes." That is what they then did as we knelt in prayer with them.

On the cards which they signed their names were: William Dillon, Edward Palmer, and Lilian Johnson. We felt pity and concern for William Dillon, the oldest, who gave his age as 69. He was not only unkempt and haggard; plainly he was ill and had to be helped to walk. His nose was continually running. His eyes were bloodshot. He could not stop shivering or trembling. We urged him to get home quickly, get something warm, and go to bed. "Tomorrow morning we'll have a doctor round to see you," we told him—and we arranged so.

Two nights later we reached our final meeting. There was a crowded building, and a climax of effusive but sincere rejoicing. I thought we would never get away from those dear folk who surrounded us afterward, saying, with that generous warmth so characteristic of Americans, that they would not let us escape unless we promised to come again soon. But Lilian Johnson pressed through them to us with an urgent message. Bill Dillon who had been converted three nights earlier along with herself and Ed Palmer, was dying, and he was calling out "something pitiful" for Reverend Kennard. Would we please . . . *please go?*

Although the hour was getting late, how could we say No? The place was a fair distance away but one of the deacons immediately insisted on taking us there in his car, and then back to our hotel. So we went, accompanied by the said Lil Johnson and Ed Palmer. Just where the abode was I do not know. I recall our eventually passing Walnut

Street and Cherry Street and (I think) Arch Street, then going a roundabout of corners until we entered a short, dingy street without any light but what streaked out through torn old window curtains here and there. We pulled up at a dilapidated tenement, groped single file through the front door, then slowly picked our way up two flights of unlighted, creaky wooden stairs, in a badly smelly atmosphere, to a door which Lil Johnson opened into a hovel where Bill Dillon lay, evidently dying, on a dirty-looking bed, with torn blanket and sheets over him. There was an electric light but it had been shaded for the sake of the dying man.

Bill Dillon seemed startled to see us. With what bit of strength he had he seemed strangely excited. He did not wait even for a first word from us. In jerky sentences, with abrupt stops and starts as he caught his breath, he began, "Mister . . . Joseph . . . Kennard . . . I know who you . . . really are. Your real name . . . is Joseph Ashley . . . Adair. I'm the man who . . . stole you . . . out of your pram . . . over forty years ago. I couldn't . . . die . . . without telling you."

It was about the last thing in the world we had ever expected to hear; and it came so abruptly, under such sickening circumstances, we could only gasp. He saw our astonishment, but did not wait until we could comment—as though he was afraid his last breath might come before he could get out what he wanted to say.

"I'm the man who . . . who murdered . . . your . . . your pretended father . . . Mike . . . Kennard . . . I . . . yes . . . I did it."

Joseph now interrupted him. "But how could that be? Wasn't it Jacques Malvern who did that?"

"Yes . . . yes . . . *I'm* Jacques Malvern. . . . Dillon isn't my real name."

Again we gasped. Then Joseph asked, "But if you are Jacques Malvern, how could *you* have snatched me from my pram in Howburn Park when you were in Llandudno, and wrote a letter from there to Mrs. Adair?"

"No, no . . . I wasn't in Llandudno. I . . . I wrote that letter in Manchester and . . . and paid the guard on that train to North Wales to mail it . . . at Llandudno."

Joseph and I just stared again, hardly believing our ears. The mysterious riddle of over forty years was being solved for us at last, without our asking. And now the dying man was weaker but steadier. In a low, husky voice he slowly explained.

"When your father opened his builder's yard in northwest Manchester I was cashier in a bank near there. I knew your mother used to take you to Howburn Park. I watched without her knowing. I was full of hate because she married Joash instead of me. I planned my revenge and kept waiting for a time when my bank hours would be early enough or late enough to do what I wanted. The chance happened to come that day in Howburn Park. I got you. When your mother and that other woman went running out of the park I was still there behind the bushes with you, and I quickly took you out by the opposite gate, got to where I had left my horse and trap, and covered you up, and made away with you. You know what happened after that . . . I mean with Mike Kennard.

"My life has been a hell on earth, and it all began with my hatred of Joash Adair when we were boys at Rostherne. I hated him because the girl I wanted loved him instead of me. When she married him I hated her too. I so gave way to my hate, it mastered me until it was like a mad demon I couldn't shake off. I had to do what it told me. And yet the more I hated them the more I hated my own hate that I couldn't shake off. Then I hated Mike Kennard and wished him in hell; and the more I wished him there, the more I found myself there. In the end I murdered him, and at the same time murdered the last bit of decency and peace inside myself.

"When my bowler hat was found by the police near Chadvale arches I felt sure that the initials J.I.M. would give me away sooner or later. I transferred all my money to Switzerland. Later, when that photograph of the murder was in the newspapers, I knew the truth would get out. I got my money transferred to America. At the last minute I found I had not left enough for my getting here, so I stole from the bank, and fled. My wife had left me years before that, with our son. I never saw them again. I kept seeing Mike Kennard's eyes looking with stark horror at me as he fell over that parapet at Chadvale. I tried to forget it in gambling, and to drown my misery in drinking. Gambling filched all my money away, and drinking took my health away. I became a wreck, in the gutter. When I saw your name advertised I knew who you were. I knew my days were few, but I got out of bed to come and hear you. And, if you can believe it, I think God . . . I think merciful God . . . God spoke to my sinful, weary, weary heart through those texts you preached about. . . ."

At that point he could scarcely see or speak for tears; but although in evident pain, he was calmer, and struggled to speak again. "Joseph, tell people that hate is a boomerang which always swings back on the thrower. Tell them that revenge which seems sweet as nectar beforehand is bitter as gall afterward. Tell them that evil never pays except in misery. Tell them that gambling and drinking are poison fangs of a viper which bite the burning fever of hell into the veins. But the worse thing of all is hate . . . pride and hate.

"Joseph, last night I had a dream. I never believed in dreams till this one. I saw Mike Kennard calling to me from the other side of the grave. I couldn't see his body clearly, but his face was all shining, and he kept calling, "Jacques, I've forgiven you . . . and God is offering you forgiveness, too, because His Son, Jesus, shed His blood to save sinners like you and me. . . .

"Joseph, what was that first text you quoted, about 'all manner of sin being forgiven?' "

Joseph quoted it to him again.

Then Malvern went silent awhile.

After that he asked, in a husky whisper, "Will you say that other text again . . . about the blood . . . cleansing?"

Joseph quoted the First Epistle of John, chapter one, verse seven, "The blood of Jesus Christ, God's Son, cleanseth us from all sin. . . ."

Malvern's eyes were closed now. His strength was ebbing. He was breathing with difficulty. His voice was only a whisper. Joseph bent over him to listen. Malvern kept whispering, "The blood cleanses . . . cleanses. . . ." Then, with a final effort, he said huskily, but just enough for us all to hear, "I've ruined my life . . . I'm sorry . . . sorry, Joseph . . . forgive . . . Jesus has me . . . just in time . . . He sent you . . . just in time. . . ." Then he sank back—dead.

It was a grim end to a rich series of meetings. The shock of it, suddenly contrasting with the soaring climactic gathering in the church, left our feelings overwrought, and both of us experienced a sickly weariness. However, a light supper had some restorative effect, and Joseph said, "We must write home early tomorrow and let mother Agnes know that it *was* Jacques Malvern who stole me from my pram forty-one years ago. How she and pa Joash will open their eyes when we tell them about tonight!"

After some silence, he added, "Evelyn, dear companion of the years, what a story our life is making! Talk about the 'hidden hand' in things! Think of it: tonight the hidden hand behind fifty years of hate, evil, pain, and dark mystery has been exposed—the hidden hand of Satan through a human dupe. Yet also, as clear as Cragston Pike tower on a sunny morning, we see *another* hidden Hand overruling the hidden hand of evil, and in sovereign, gracious irony turning Satan's trickery back upon himself. Through the stolen baby and the wonderful little other-mother God gave him, all the main actors in the life-drama get brought to the Saviour! The little baby grows up, gets converted and becomes a Christian minister. Then, through him, Mike Kennard and Joash Adair, and you, dear Evelyn, and even Jacques Malvern the Judas, are all brought back to God and are eternally saved! One day I'd like to write the story of it all, and entitle it, THE HIDDEN HAND."

THIRTY-ONE
How Can We Say Good-Bye?

Dear reader, do I need to apologize? This is Evelyn Kennard writing again. I feel rather sensitive about intruding thus further. In some ways I would have preferred to end my grateful review at the death bed conversion of Jacques Malvern, already described, even though a grim scene with which to close.

However, I have been kindly entreated to unbind a further sheaf of memories, right to the time of my beloved's passing. So I will link up where I left off, that is, with Joseph saying he would like to write the drama-like story of our life under the title: THE HIDDEN HAND. Little did he think that the story *would* be written, but by someone else's pen.

Several years later the colossal horror of the Second World War engulfed us all. In our case providence was singularly kind. From the April until late July we were in Britain. Our darling daughters were then aged twenty and eighteen. The elder had completed one year of nursing training, and the younger finished her schooling that June. They had both eagerly coveted to see America, so we brought them over for two months. They revelled in it. Before their return sailing date Britain was again at war with Germany; so we cancelled their ocean passage for the time being. Later they were not allowed transport. Mildred linked up with a hospital in Los Angeles to continue nursing training. Donna, whose urge was to become a missionary doctor, enrolled in preparation for that in a college at Santa Barbara, a hundred miles north of Los Angeles.

The reason why southern California was chosen is a happy one. We were near our Harwood relatives. Also, my aunt Nancy Harwood (Mrs. Floyd Stevens) lived in a "luxury flat" just north of Los Angeles, which she wanted our girls to adopt as their "home away from home" as long as they were in America. She and they became quickly fond of each other. Until recently she and her husband had lived in Montecito, adjoining Santa Barbara. She was now widowed, hence her moving south to be nearer her relatives. Our two daughters seemed to break comfortingly into her loneliness.

That was not all. Although she had left Montecito she had not sold their pretty house in Picacho Lane there, in case she and another sister might wish to live there later. Against our sincere protestation she adamantly insisted that Joseph and I make it our home "until further notice."

How fortunate we were! Santa Barbara at that time was about the nearest thing on earth to the Garden of Eden. Picacho Lane, Montecito, was sheer beauty. The name, "Picacho," pronounced *pee-kah-cho,* refers to the sharp-pointed mountain peak to which the lane points. Juan Romero says, *"Si, el mas alto picacho de la Sierra"* ("Yes, the most high point of the Sierra"). Our view of the mighty mountains and of the Pacific Ocean stretching away eastward and southward was almost breath-taking at times—especially early morning and sunset. All around us were orange trees, lemon trees, avocados, and a continual extravaganza of succulent plants and gorgeous flowers. Geraniums and other such, which grow only by cultivation elsewhere, were in wild profusion around us there. We gradually got used to it but never ceased to marvel at it.

The Spanish-type buildings, the elegant homes of the rich, the florid glory of their lavish gardens, the winding lanes, the orange and lemon and avocado groves in the valleys between Montecito and Summerland, and our walks among the mountains or along the ocean beach—all were an aesthetic delight such as we had never known before. Sometimes we would carry lunch with us and walk, with happy dilatoriness, all the way from Butterfly Lane on Channel Drive, Montecito, along the winding beach to Summerland, and then on to Carpinteria. It was the one break in our busy thirty-eight years when we really "took time out." Of course, even then we were away on Bible ministry recurrently for a month or two at a time. But toward the end of the war, such ministry was less for a while; so we had homelife again for weeks on end, with our dear Mildred and Donna coming whenever they were free. Happy, happy days! How sweet their memory still! As we tramped the hills or the shore Joseph would say to me, "Sweetheart, isn't it lovely to be courting again? But I love you thirty years more now than when we started. And isn't this an incomparable place? There's only one spot on earth which attracts me more—you know where: that bench by Netherford Lake.

The one deep shadow on it was our bereavement through daddy Joash's death, and, later, that of dear mummie Agnes's awful end on earth. I will not dwell on those war years, so awful in Britain. Thank God, they are gone—though what a residue of bereavement, bewilderment, sorrow and brokenness they have left in their wake! At the time, Joseph and I felt a kind of helpless guilt that we were escaping while others were suffering so much.

As soon as permitted after the war, Mildred and Donna were back in England, to link up with overseas missionary societies—and with their sweethearts. They stayed with their aunt Dorothy, in her quarters at the nursing home. Joseph and I resumed in full our Bible-teaching itineraries, but felt we ought to return to Britain after two more years. If anything, those last two years in U.S.A. were the best of all; so full as to be exhausting at times, but crowded with imperishable memories of great meetings, bringing blessing to untold numbers, and hundreds of others into life-changing union with our Lord.

So, at length, we returned to our native England, little anticipating that my Joseph's translation to heavenly service was so near at hand. We both knew the spot where we wanted to make our home, even though we expected to be away from it for considerable spells. It was up at Hazelmere, near Netherford Lake. There were several well-built and pretty little homes dotting the rise on that side of the lake, two of which were for sale. The second of them was just ideal, with a dream of a garden at the rear, looking right across the mead to the lake—to that bend where the memorial bench was.

But before I end my retrospective resume, do you not think I ought to say something, however briefly, about my Joseph as a preacher?—and (may I?) about our married life together?

Of course you will be amused and charge me with amorous prejudice when I say that my Joseph was the best preacher I ever heard. I will not linger over his natural gifts of appearance, voice, vocabulary, flowing eloquence, aptitude of phrase, and extraordinary facility of illustration. All those would have been as mere spray on a wave apart from the *substance* of his message. I have a jealously grateful persuasion that much of what he taught still comes today through the ministry of those hundreds of theological students whom he addressed from time to time.

To Joseph the life-and-death issue of Christianity was the divine inspiration and authority of the Bible. Strangely enough, that was settled in his mind even before his conversion!—ever since that second night out on the hills after he ran away from home! If the Bible is authentically the written Word of God, then we have certainty—about God, origins, man, morals, the race's future, and human destiny beyond the grave: but if the Bible is anything *less* than that, we do *not* have certainty, which means that the whole superstructure of Christian theology and of our social ethics becomes tottery.

To him the most dangerous foes of the Christian faith were those who destroy faith in the Bible. I remember his saying to a great crowd in London away back in the twenties, "If the higher critical, or so-called 'new theology' or 'modernist' ideas of the Bible ever capture the British pulpit, in forty years from now our sanctuaries will be largely deserted." He lived long enough to see that very thing happening, alas.

Some of Joseph's forecasts are proving remarkably (and regrettably) true. He said, "If the break from the Bible continues, the moral downgrade will become a landslide in the next half-century. Crime and violence, rebellions of youth, the vulgarizing of womanhood, and sexual rotten-ness will threaten the very foundations of society. Not one in a million people will see the deepest cause. If the Bible is not the Word of God, there is no real moral authority anywhere. Everything becomes merely relative. What is right? What is wrong? Who knows? Who cares? If the path of philosophy pioneered by Kant and Hegel is pursued to its logical conclusion, it will end in *illogical* chaos. Existential-ists and rationalist theologians will reach a point where, for all practical purposes, God is ruled out—as a dead concept. Young folk will go to inane and demoralizing excesses. They will need pity as much as censure, for having been 'educat-ed' in a moral and philosophical vacuum."

Of course, I am altogether prejudiced; but I used to love the way he kept in sympathetic touch with human struggle, pathos and emotion. One exposition along that line I vividly remember because of its unusually powerful effect at the time. Joseph's text was the pathetic outgush of Jacob, in Genesis 42:36, "All these things are against me!" The three propositions were: (1) The mercies of a lifetime may be forgotten in the trial of a moment; (2) A judgment of God's dealings with us based on one isolated experience is seldom right; (3) The most gracious purposes of God often wind to their fulfillment through strangest processes.

He was keenly grieved that fine minds like Conan Doyle, author of the famous Sherlock Holmes stories, should be turned away from the Christian faith through such misconceptions as that the God of the Bible demands blood before He will forgive. I remember with what feeling Joseph commented: "Those oft-quoted words of Hebrews 9:22, 'Without the shedding of blood there is no remission,' are not an independent statement uttering a fundamental law of the universe. They should in all fairness be taken along with the preceding word that it was under 'the *law*' (i.e. the law of Moses) that this necessary purging by blood obtained. It was fundamental to the Mosaic economy, but it is not fundamental in God! The fundamental truth of the universe is not that God demands blood, but that sin necessitates atonement. What, then, can be such an atonement? Who can make it? The wonder of the Gospel is, that the very God whose holiness and righteous law *demand* atonement is the God whose suffering love on our behalf *provides* it!

But, dear reader, I am detaining you too long. Let me hasten to a finish. It was as my darling *husband,* of course, that Joseph was most precious to *me.* If I may dare say so, with one trustful touch of frankness, our love for each other was so deep and sacred to us that all the physical aspects of wedlock grew sweeter as the years passed by. Our kisses meant more after thirty years of married sharing, I verily believe, than when he put the engagement ring on my finger.

I have seen him wearied, frustrated, discouraged, angered; for we had our meed of problems, oppositions, trials, as well as all the happier accompaniments which I have preferred to mention; but my Joseph never let them have the slightest corrosive effect upon his love. We loved each other more, and learned from each other more, and leaned on each other more, as we grew older and (I trust) mellower. Not so long before he slipped away to heaven he said to me as I walked into our sitting-room, "Treasure, even more now than when I used to meet you at Pinecrest in our youthful years, I thrill when you enter the room."

I cannot put into words my pity for those many young men and women today, growing up in our so-called "permissive society," to whom sex is little more than animalism, who never know the bliss of an undefiled masculine-feminine love, of going to the marriage altar pure, and of a subsequent heaven-on-earth partnership such as that of Joseph and myself. Easier divorce and broken homes are not the answer to present-day matrimonial miseries; the only true answer is a return to Christian ideals. I would say to all young people: If you would know true married bliss and satisfying fulfillment of love, let the Christian standards of wedlock be your guide.

Never once through all our years together did Joseph

omit handing to me a pleasant little poem on our wedding anniversary. This was the last one:—

> *I've a dear little wife*
> *As my partner in life;*
> *Each birthday increases her worth;*
> *And the longer she's mine*
> *Sure the more I incline*
> *To name her the best wife on earth.*
>
> *In my garden of flowers*
> *She's the queen of the bowers,*
> *The loveliest rose of the plot;*
> *She's my "alpha star" bright*
> *When I tread thro' the night,*
> *And what that is good is she not?*
>
> *How the years wing away!*
> *Thirty-seven today*
> *Since wedded together were we;*
> *But I'd have her to know,*
> *As the older we grow,*
> *Still dearer she's growing to me.*

That brings me to the last and hardest part to tell. I mean his passing "yonder." When the Harvey Street folk knew we were back in Britain they sent a unanimous invitation for Joseph to return as their minister. He considered it a "trustful risk" on their part, for his earlier ministry among them amid those exciting revival days was now over thirty years ago, and he himself was as much older. It was anything but an attractive proposition. The Harvey Street church building had been destroyed in an air raid. The congregation had been depleted and then scattered. Those who still cohered as "Harvey Street" church were having to meet on Sundays in a Secondary School hall. Finances were crippled. Facilities were hamperingly restricted. Joseph could see there would be dismal problems, yet he felt the urge to help them in some way, even if he were with them for only a year, to help during that difficult period of reconstruction.

It took us some time to settle in and furnish at Hazelmere, so we did not commence our ministry with them until that March. After the abundance and wealth and crowds in U.S.A., how different it was to be back with comparatively small companies, and in such disadvantageous circumstances! Also, we missed the balmy climate of Santa Barbara, though I must say that Spring, which came in early that year, displayed that charm which is peculiar to it in England.

I could see that the work was a test to Joseph. He put all he had into it. Post-war conditions were altogether against it. Penury, paralysis, weariness, disillusionment were everywhere. After the *First* World War there had been a nation-wide responsiveness to the Gospel; but after the *Second* World War it was the opposite. There was skepticism and spiritual apathy on every hand. It seemed as though another twenty-five years of faith-destroying modernistic preaching from our British pulpits had largely incapacitated our people to make an intelligent response to God.

However, by about September things began to take on a new look, at least in our own little corner. Attendances swelled to such proportion that the school room (which seated not more than four hundred) was much too small. A new church building became imperative. We got prayer-meetings and district visitation going. The younger people began to show new enthusiasm. During the last week of October Joseph held a week's special evangelistic meetings, and had scouts all over the district to bring people in. That week there were over thirty conversions. It seemed to give a fillip to the whole work. Joseph was a bit tired but very encouraged. Things were "on the move" again.

Then the blow fell.

Near the end of November there came a blast of bitterly cold, wet weather. After a Thursday night meeting Joseph was implored to visit a man who was critically ill. He went, though the hour was late and the address some distance on the farther side of town from Hazelmere. He had gone into town by bus, as car petrol was still rationed. He missed the last bus back in the Hazelmere direction and had to struggle back for five miles in bitterly cold wind and driving sleet. His umbrella was blown inside out and torn beyond further use. A sudden squall swept his hat away. The sleety rain soaked through his coat and trousers, so that when at last he reached home, bareheaded and soaked to the skin, he was chilled to the bone, empty, and exhausted.

It brought on a heavy cold in his head, accompanied by irritation and congestion of the lungs. Soon afterward he became feverish. Then coughing and chest pains followed. He developed acute difficulty in breathing, by which time the doctor was getting worried about him—the more so as Joseph began spitting blood. My poor Joseph had pneumonia.

He struggled with it for about eight days, when it reached its frightening crisis. To all appearances he would have survived the pneumonia, only right on top of the crisis he had a sudden heart-attack. There were all the terrifying pains of angina pectoris, followed by a coronary thrombosis. My darling was indeed in deep trouble. Again and again it seemed as if he might be dying.

The doctor was coming in two or three times a day now, evidently alarmed. One afternoon, on coming out of the bedroom, he said, "Mrs. Kennard, I think you must prepare yourself for bad news. So far as I can see, your husband does not have even a fighting chance now. There's such a collapse of the heart, it's beyond further rallying power. . . . I wouldn't be surprised . . . please try to be brave . . . if he were gone before tomorrow morning."

Oh, the desolating shock in those words! Oh, the frantic heart-cry to God, "Please, please, *No!*" Surely I was not hearing the doctor correctly! Vaguely, fondly, naively, I had thought my incomparable Joseph the one exception—that *he* would never die!—but he might be "gone before tomorrow morning"! How could I live without *him?* How could I bear *that* void? Dazed and sick at heart, I sank into a chair.

I managed to hold back my tears until the doctor was gone. Then the floodgates of my grief gave way. I tried to muffle my lips lest Joseph might hear, but he must have heard, for he called me. In my inward strickenness I cried to God for grace to bear this, my supreme trial, bravely and resignedly. I remembered that word in Joseph's sermon, "The mercies of a lifetime can be forgotten in the agony of one trial."

Wiping my eyes, and trying to look cheerful, I went into

the bedroom. Joseph was quiet and, for the time being, free from pain, having been given medication.

"Darling Evelyn," he said, "you needn't try to hide anything from me. I know what the doctor told you. He's right: I'm going; but not quite as soon as he thinks."

Unable to find words without sobbing, I knelt at the bedside and quietly wept, with his arms around my shoulder.

Presently he said, so soothingly, "Look up, sweetheart. I want to talk with you. I know it's harder for you than for me; but let's both be brave. We're Christians. This isn't a terminus; it's only a junction. Let's make the most of these days together."

It was then that he told me something he had considerately withheld from me for thirty-eight years. The reason he had not been sent back to France after being invalided home during the First World War was, that the pneumonia and rheumatic fever which had laid him low had damaged his heart. The army doctor had said, "While you are young, and so long as you keep in good general health, it may never bother you; but if you should ever be in critical sickness or under excessive stress, it could suddenly finish you off, like an ambushed beast springing on you."

Dear reader, can you believe me?—those last few weeks with my Joseph were the richest I ever spent on earth. Four times it seemed as if he were certainly dying, but each time, as he struggled, he said, "No, darling, not yet. Whatever the doctor says, I'm going to see the new year in with you."

Our fellowship together was on the very borderland of heaven. Often during those days, as Joseph lay with his eyes closed and his lips slightly moving, I could see that he was in some new, deep closeness of communion with our Lord. Then he would call me to his side, and hold my hand, and tell me all about it. It was as though he was trying to take me with him, in thought, hand-in-hand along that borderline.

"Evelyn, I have always said that there are three things made perfectly clear in the New Testament concerning Christians when they depart from this earthly life. First, they are *"with Christ,"* which is the most ineffable of all consummations. Second, they are with Christ *consciously;* there is no passing into some so-called 'soul sleep.' Third, they are with Christ *locally.* Heaven is not just a condition; it is a place, the 'Father's house,' the heart's true home; and it is not far from here. I've had all that confirmed to me, now, Evelyn. I'm not just imagining. I've seen Jesus. I've had a glimpse of that heaven. He's preparing us . . . me . . . all this is part of His plan. . . .

"I've been talking to Him about *you,* darling Evelyn. You'll be alright when I'm away. The parting is not for long. Loved ones in heaven are tender links between here and there. The thought of them is meant to break wrong over-absorption with things of earth—where we don't stay for long. I understand our Lord's words now—'in the resurrection they neither marry nor are given in marriage.' In heaven there are felicities and expressions of love which sublimely outclass the merely physical here on earth; but heart-unions made on earth, in Christ, go on unbroken there.

"You see, precious Evelyn, in that exquisite life yonder we do not lose our identity. I shall always be I. You will always be you. Dear mother Millie will always be that same *person:* so will mother Agnes and father Joash. Heaven does not obliterate our personal identity; it *sublimates* it; it fulfills and utterly satisfies it. That includes our wedded love, Evelyn. Heaven will not end it, but *crown* it! I know it, Evelyn, I *see* it.

"Our dear ones already there are waiting for us. They see us, and know us, and pray for us. Yes, they are praying for us. We do not believe in so-called 'prayers for the dead.' God's written Word nowhere gives us any warrant on earth to pray for the departed. But that in nowise affects the fact that *they* (our departed Christian loved ones) pray for *us.* We do not believe that the New Testament gives any warrant whatever for any set of men in any ecclesiastical system to look upon themselves as a separate priest *class.* But just as definitely the New Testament does teach that *all* born-again Christian believers are priests of God in Christ, having "access to God" continually through the

Name of Jesus. Does the believer's priesthood end at the grave? No! on the other side the grave the translated believer's priesthood enters upon its highest exercise. What is our Lord Jesus Himself doing yonder? As Hebrews 7:25 says, "He ever liveth to make *intercession*" for us. Even so, our departed Christian loved ones are in that heavenly ministry of intercession. They are continually praying for us.

"But how can they do so unless they see us and know what is happening on earth? The bliss of heaven does not depend on their having a thick cloak thrown between them and us. The bliss of heaven is that of larger light, not of deeper ignorance!

"But does it not spoil their bliss in heaven when they see the troubles which come to us on earth? Well, does it spoil heaven for *Jesus?* Yet do we not want *Him* to see all that happens to us on earth, and to help us amid it? Our departed Christian loved ones now see us in a different way. They do not see our earthly troubles *isolatedly* as we down here do, wondering why they have been permitted and what is going to happen next. No, from heaven they see them in the context of the plan that God is working out for us. They see, as Romans 8:28 says, that 'all things working together for good to them that love God, who are the called according to His purpose.'

"Evelyn darling, dearer to me than ever, now, as we reach this point of temporary parting, you are mine and I am yours for ever. Whatever heaven may yet prove to be, and wherever it is, while I have conscious being I shall love and pray and long for you *there*, as I have loved and prayed for you *here*."

Dear reader, if I were to record all the other things which Joseph said during those days on heaven's borderline, it would absorb pages. I must cease. We had loved each other before, but in those last days together we experienced heights and depths of love surpassing all before. We knew now, beyond power of words to express, that our love was not merely physical. Does it sound unpardonably crude even to mention that word, "sex," here? Well, let me use it if only because of the way many people seem to think in these days—days of such carnal, moral deterioration. Joseph and I were loving mind-to-mind, heart-to-heart, spirit-to-spirit. Any thought of the merely sensuous was utterly out of keeping; yet we knew a soul-thrill of love which was almost heaven. It was the love of a masculine heart and mind for a feminine heart and mind, and of a feminine heart and mind for a masculine, in which each found perfect counterpart and joy. I loved the body he had lived in; but I knew now with fresh-opened eyes that I loved *him*—God's wonderful, wonderful answer to my heart.

On December 28th, he had the worst heart attack of all. I braced myself for the parting as I held him gently in my arms; but he whispered, "Not yet. I'll enter the new year with you."

December 31st came. He asked me to hand him a book of daily readings. Turning to one of its pages, he said, "Sweetheart, when I've slipped away I want you to learn this by heart." It read:—

> *E'en for the dead*
> *I will not bind my soul to grief;*
> *Death cannot long divide:*
> *For is it not as though the rose*
> *which climbed my garden wall*
> *Now blossoms on the other side?*
> *Death doth hide,*
> *But not divide:*
> *Thou art but on*
> *Death's other side.*
> *Thou art with Christ, and He with me;*
> *In Christ united still are we.*

Through that night he seemed to sleep fairly comfortably, but he was now very weak. I rose early without disturbing him. About 9:15 I tiptoed in with some light breakfast. He was awake. His eyes were unusually bright, and his pale face wreathed with such a kind smile—oh, such a smile! "Happy new year, sweetheart mine!" he greeted me. "Didn't I tell you I would enter the new year with you? Please let it *be* a happy year. Remember who is with you every day of it! His love never fails. His power never wanes. His wisdom never errs. His care never changes. His presence never leaves you. He will never let you down, and never let you go. His love-grip is as mighty as it is tender. And, don't forget: *I'll* be watching and praying too."

We had our breakfast together, then our daily reading and morning prayer. As he was half-lying, half-sitting, in bed, we gently rested in each other's arms.

During his illness I had never been away from him for more than a few minutes at a time; but about 11 o'clock, as I was in the kitchen just a moment or two, I heard him call, "Evelyn, Evelyn." At once I was with him.

"Evelyn darling, it's hurting so badly again. Will you help me to say my favourite hymn just once again?" I did. We slowly went through the four short verses together, pausing as he had trouble in breathing. It was Charles Wesley's—

> *O Thou who camest from above*
> *The pure, celestial fire to impart,*
> *Kindle a flame of sacred love*
> *On the mean altar of my heart.*
>
> *There let it for Thy glory burn*
> *With inextinguishable blaze;*
> *And, trembling, to its source return*
> *In humble love and fervent praise.*
>
> *Jesus, confirm my heart's desire*
> *To think and speak and work for Thee;*
> *Still let me guard the holy fire,*
> *And still stir up Thy gift in me.*

When we came to the last verse he pressed my hand, indicating that he wanted to say that verse alone. Slowly he got it out—

> *Ready for all Thy perfect will*
> *My acts of faith and love repeat,*
> *Till* death *Thine endless mercies seals,*
> *And makes the sacrifice* COMPLETE.

When he got to that last word—"complete" he *shouted* it, with a gleam of triumph in his eyes. Then he gave a look—oh, such a look at me, and thrust his hand out as though feeling for me. Quickly I held his hand. He drew mine to his lips, and kissed it. Then, with a deep sigh, he lay back—and was gone. I gathered that dear, dear face into my arms, and kissed it with my tenderest kiss of farewell. Then, with my arms stretched across his body, I knelt at the bedside, and wept and worshiped, and prayed and—yes, I praised. As I looked for the last time at that noble, beautiful face, now placidly serene in death, I thanked God through my flowing tears for such a gem of a husband, and for the wedded happiness of those thirty-eight years. . . .

And that, dear reader, is where Evelyn's pen left off. There are indications that she intended to add something further, but we cannot be sure. The fact is, that in the August, about fifteen months after the May when I asked her to write her memories for us, she, too, passed over—only three and a half years after that New Year's Day on which Joseph had triumphantly departed.

The cause of her so soon following him is a regrettable one. The car accident, already mentioned, had inflicted more internal injury than was at first suspected. As long as she could, she kept on with her teaching the Young Women's Class among the Harvey Street people. Once or twice she preached for them, and several times sang solos there—for her voice had lost little of its rich timbre. But for about two months prior to her demise she could not go into town or walk much.

Minnie, who had been maid in the Adair home at Pine-crest from the age of seventeen, and had married later, but was now a widow, and several years younger than Evelyn, had come to be her companion after Joseph's passing. They had many memories to share, and were a real comfort to each other. Minnie looked after Evelyn with tender loyalty.

Toward the end, Evelyn was not able to move around much. In between meals she enjoyed sitting in the pretty garden behind their cottage, with her Bible and another book or two—and her memories.

After the noonday meal one sunny day in August when all nature seemed to be singing with summer joy, Minnie helped Evelyn to the well-cushioned wicker chair which had been carried to the garden. She left Evelyn sitting there. The Pennine hills smiled over from near by. Old Cragston Pike tower said another silent "Hello there!" The meadow between Evelyn's garden and the fringe of Netherford Lake was bestrewn with daisies and buttercups, and the water glistened beyond. Evelyn's heart sang back to it all.

After washing the dishes and tidying the dining-room, Minnie indulged in her usual "forty winks." That afternoon she must have taken fifty, for, when she wakened, the clock announced that it was already time for their afternoon cup of tea. Glancing through the window into the garden she noticed that Evelyn had altered the direction slightly in which the chair was facing. Soon she had the tea made, and with pretty cup and saucer, and a few dainty cookies, she quietly carried the tray out to Evelyn.

But our dear Evelyn would need no more afternoon cups of tea. She, too, had fallen asleep, but not to waken again. She had sunk back into the comfortable cushions, and, except that her head was hanging unusually heavily to one side, Minnie would scarcely have detected what had happened. The dear, beautiful face was there, eyes closed, and the now-fragile body was reclining there, but Evelyn herself had silently gone.

Before sinking into her wicker chair for the last time she had managed to move it slightly, so that it faced in her favourite direction. She had sat there, looking down over the mead, to the scintillating water of Netherford Lake, her gaze on the memorial bench in the willow alcove round the bend, and just seeable from her garden. Her Bible was beside her, in the chair. On her lap was a book of poems, still open at the page over which her hand lay. Minnie was thoughtful enough not to close it without noting the page. It contained the following verses. The author's name was not given, but I have seen them elsewhere attributed to the late Arthur T. Pierson.

> *Back of all that foes have plotted,*
>   *Back of all that saints have planned,*
> *Back of schemes by men or demons,*
>   *Moves a higher, hidden Hand.*
>
> *Warp and woof are Heaven's making,*
>   *All the pattern good and wise;*
> *Tho' on earth's side oft perplexing,*
>   *Clear and right to heavenly eyes.*
>
> *All earth's agents act with freedom,*
>   *Choosing, whether love or hate,*
> *Faith in God, or bold defiance;*
>   *None are shackled slaves of fate.*
>
> *Yet the Hand that guides is hidden,*
>   *Moving secret and unseen,*
> *Firmly guiding life's great drama,*
>   *Every act and shifting scene.*
>
> *Even human wrath, unknowing,*
>   *Serves that all-controlling Will;*
> *Man proposes; God disposes;*
>   *All things His design fulfill.*
>
> *To that goal of all the ages,*
>   *All of history's windings tend;*
> *And despite all foes or factions,*
>   *God proves Victor in the end.*
>
> *Mysteries which hurt and baffle,*
>   *Past our power to understand,*
> *In the end are turned to blessing*
>   *By that Sovereign* HIDDEN HAND.

Had Evelyn been given some premonition that the time of her departure had come? That is easily thinkable, for she lived so continually close in heart to our dear Lord that she could have heard His whisper. We cannot know for certain. But she sat there, taking a last, long look over the mead and the water at that memorial bench around which there now clustered such hallowing memories: the bench where her polite, stripling Joseph had bandaged her ankle, and where love for him had suddenly come to life in her girlish heart; where Joseph had sobbed his poor heart out on the night he ran away from home; where, later, she and her parents and mother Millie had met Joseph again, along with the Ainsworths and Molly, after his years in Huddersfield; and where, years later, young man Joseph had plighted his love to her, putting the engagement ring on her finger; and where, on their wedding-day they had knelt together, yielding themselves to God for all the years ahead; and where, after Joseph's war-time absence they had once again knelt as young husband and wife to ask guidance for the future.

Yes, it was as she sat there in her wicker chair, taking that last, wistful look across the mead and the water, at that willow-shaded bench of such tender meaning, that she silently slipped away with her precious memories into the land of tearless reunion and never-ending fulfillments.

POSTSCRIPT

Dear reader, will you think me unduly sentimental if I drop a parting word in your ear about my own visits to that memorial bench by the quiet lakeside? It is still there, and, to me, is deeply affecting; not only hallowed by clinging memories, but fragrantly haunted by mystic presences.

Once a year, usually in September, I visit relatives in that area; and in the afternoons I go for meditative walks. As though an invisible magnet were drawing my heart, I find myself leaving the town outskirts of Rosewood Lane, then winding along for a couple of miles northeast until I reach the rise and picturesque grove where Hazelmere is situated.

I linger by the pretty cottage where dear Evelyn spent her last few years on earth. I peep over the wooden fence at the rear, into the garden where she tended the flowers and hoed the borders and trimmed the bushes; and where she later sat with her wistful memories and tender hopes. I see again, in imagination, that radiant face, that sunrise smile, and that graceful form moving to and fro. Some of Evelyn's own plantings are still there, and every Spring they break out again in new flowers—like resurrected memories assuming tangible beauty.

After lingering there a few moments I wander slowly down the now-widened bridle path to the big iron gates which open on the walk round Netherford Lake. My heart always seems to beat a bit faster as I approach the bend round which is the bench in that little willow alcove.

I know it sounds silly, but for some impelling reason I always tip-toe the last two or three yards to the bench, before quietly sitting there. The lake seems to know me now, and laps a pleasant welcome at my feet.

There, in pensive solitude, I sit and remember. It is serene and captivating as ever. The September sun dips early beyond the lake and those Lancashire towns down there. Between the clouds the dipping sun shoots fingers of gold and crimson across the lake. I watch and am reminded of Millie's sagacious little aphorisms, such as, "It takes clouds to make a lovely sunset," and "Clouds are only dark until the sun shines on them," and "A life without trouble is sunny, but it's a sunny desert." Yes, it was at this bench that Millie and young Joseph were reunited—weeping tears of joy—after his runaway absence from home. Millie, where are you now?

I still sit there. A suggestion of the first Autumn amber is in the trees. The later Summer flowers still bloom and nod in the breeze like a fringe of lace round the lake. Memory becomes sensitive. Yesterday comes running back and says, "I'm still alive!" Voices that were stilled speak again. I hear Joseph's sonorous baritone and Evelyn's musical laughter—or was it just the louder lapping of the water at the lake edge? Vanished forms walk back from the misty shadows. Yes, I am seeing tall, handsome Joseph again, and his graceful "queen of hearts"—or was it just the silhouette of these near-by trees against the fast-setting sun? Faces now absent, which once smiled on us, are suddenly here again. Yes, I see them: Joseph and Evelyn, only the features now have an unearthly radiance—or was it just some mirrored reflection in the rippling lake?

Oh, but I am sure now. Was not that the rustle of Evelyn's dress, or the footfall of Joseph on the leaves of the willow arbor? Scarcely dare I look round, for I sense they are standing behind the bench, in each other's arms. I cannot help hearing Evelyn say, "Joseph, someone is watching us!" and Joseph replying, "Yes, darling, it's *God.*" I hear them moving—or was it only the whispering boughs?